A Careless Feast

Also by Mara Rostov

EROICA
NIGHT HUNT

A
Careless
Feast

MARA ROSTOV

G. P. PUTNAM'S SONS
New York

G. P. PUTNAM'S SONS
Publishers Since 1838
200 Madison Avenue
New York, NY 10016

LIBRARY OF CONGRESS CATALOGING IN PUBLICATION DATA

Rostov, Mara.
A careless feast.

I. Title.
PS3568.08493C3   1985   813'.54   84-24929
ISBN 0-399-13068-3

PRINTED IN THE UNITED STATES OF AMERICA
1   2   3   4   5   6   7   8   9   10

For Jay,
Friend Lover Husband

When the careless feast of love is past
And I am alone again at last,
I see by dusk of dawning day
The shattered shapes of human clay.

——M.R.

I

Ursula's Viennese grandfather, Melchior Augustus Enerde, failed to enter the twentieth century when it finally arrived in 1914 because of a birthmark on the nape of his seventeen-year-old bride's neck. Although she had been his ward for eight years when the marriage took place, her own modesty and the general conservative dress of young girls of patrician Viennese families kept the mark well hidden below high sailor collars and the stand-up lace bibs popular at the time. Even on their wedding night as the girl lay in exhausted sleep, Enerde, a man in his middle forties and wildly in love, was awake and happily unaware of the mark. He rose from the nuptial bed to fetch a lamp so that he could finally see his young wife who had so shyly some hours before hidden her beauty under the veils of gown, coverlet, and darkness. Thus he had twice possessed her without seeing her. He was accustomed to viewing the women he took to bed in full light and stone naked, though occasionally some piquant little tart might feign a charming modesty before the abandonment to various exotically erotic positions which he found at once both titillating and unseemly.

But the girl whose gown he now removed with such loving caution and freshening desire, he knew was as innocent as a rare snowflower growing on some inaccessible mountain peak. For ten years she had been his to nurture, creating with Svengalic intent the bride of his fantasies, a girl truly pure and modest on whom he could sate his inclination toward delicate voyeurism. *After all*, he thought as he gazed with burgeoning joy at the perfect breasts, peach-colored, ripe and round, under the same fruit-hued light cast by the lamp now beside the bed, *it does no harm to look*. And look he did. His eyes, long jaded to the women who played any game he paid for, burned with a new luster in the presence of the girl's sleeping nakedness. He considered tasting the dropletlike navel and running his tongue over the pale skin of her belly to the triangle of gold floss, and spreading once more the rich young thighs, and perhaps . . . perhaps she would not even awaken, not at the mere brushing of his tongue. Then as he positioned himself to follow his desire, she turned from lying on her back, one arm resting above her head on the pillows in a rich billowing of her own gold hair, to lying on her side, the arm above barely missing Melchior as it fell heavily in advance of the turning body. The position was equally lovely to him. One knee was partially thrust forward, forbidding him his taste, but the other leg showed the back of the knee—mysteriously fascinating to Melchior. With her breasts hidden from him, the full curve of her pale buttocks was

[9]

so exquisitely revealed to him that he could have wept with joy. And she was exclusively and permanently his. "Amalia, Amalia, Amalia," he whispered. "Mine, all mine, mine alone!"

This could not have been more true: Amalia was the child of his stepbrother, Günther, who died in the local flu epidemic in the dark sick February of '04, which also swept away Melchior's father, Augustus, and his sickly second wife, a bachelor uncle, and Amalia's titian-haired mother, Dorothea. Certainly they were now alone, the last survivors of a clan whose snobbery was a legend and a proverb in the city. If it had not been the birthmark which he was shortly to see and which made him deny the times, Enerde would have tended to ignore the new century anyway, as he would naturally have snubbed any nouveau riche upstart intent upon invading the rarefied territory of the aristocractic class. At forty-six, he was clearly one of those men who believed in the permanence of things: his family (related to the ancient Wittelsbachs of Bavaria, of whom Franz Josef's Empress Elizabeth was the most famously tragic) would always be the confidant of emperors; his vast textile concern would belong to the Enerde clan intact for perpetuity; and people who amounted to little (those many who worked for a daily wage) would remain, as ever, simple, respectful, and basically satisfied with their lot. He was a man unconcerned with what the rest of the world was up to, or as he put it to a friend at his hunting club, "what it did to itself." He frequently quoted the old saw that things were as they were meant to be. And who would refute a circle? Enerde continued to enjoy the weather at the several family retreats and the peace at the Vienna mansion with its ten-acre garden (more park than garden) enclosed on all sides by high walls, studded on top with pieces of broken glass, which effectively shut out the charming, picturesque, seedy Viennese suburb which had been forest when the great house was built. The baroque mansion in its eclectic style was a parody of a half-dozen castles the builder, Enerde's great-grandfather, had seen on a trip through Germany and France, where he had gone to find a third wife, the first two—local girls—both dying in their first pregnancies with their infants still inside them. Their deaths started a rumor that Enerde women would never be a match for their men. This rumor Enerde intended to scotch with his marriage to the magnificent Amalia, whose strong young body would bring him the children for whom he hungered. Here was the new blood the line needed. He had deeply admired his stepbrother's exquisite burgundy-haired wife and had vivid and disquieting dreams about her. She shone in the Vienna mansion like a fiery moon, deeply mysterious and sensuous. Her death was a greater blow to him than even his father's had been. But instead of leaving for a trip around the world (which his doctor recommended), he stayed on in the great house in Vienna and took an active interest in the rearing of the orphaned Amalia.

The house, made of stone, marble, brick, wood, and various other materials that struck that earlier Enerde's fancy, was considered lofty by some and ugly by most. Ornamented with pillars and pediments, swags and scallops, medallions and plaques, it reared its profound presence over the surrounding neighborhood like a gaudily dressed duchess too fat to walk. On the first level, marble terraces surrounded the house on three sides, with steps leading to separate well-planned formal gardens. The back was intentionally uninteresting, with several doors for servants and tradespeople. The interior was a mass of magnificent confusion caused chiefly by an octagonal main drawing room with a vaulting frescoed ceiling dominated by mythical monsters subdued by mythical men. It was this room that produced a pretentious dome. Such a room might fit a Belvedere palace or the opulent dwelling of a prince of Spain or France, but in the Enerde house it created structural difficulties which the architect had not been able to solve. As a result, the four niches (crowded with various Muses) in the great eight-sided room became convexing bulges in both the formal and informal dining rooms, a picture gallery, and a reception hall. Fortunately, a whole wing, library, music room, smaller sitting rooms, conservatory, situated to the far right of the hub off both sides of a second gallery, was less formal, less formidable than the near-grotesque octagonal design. The house seemed to have been planned by two estranged architects who agreed only on the entry hall and the great curved stairway which led to a landing cantilevered over the foyer before splitting off in opposing directions to proceed to a second floor comprising several separate wings of bedchambers and suites whose heavily draped windows and walls assured the ultimate in privacy. The third floor, whose stairway was considerably less pretentious, comprised wings of simple square rooms designed to house an enormous domestic staff. The fourth level of the great house was used for storage at the time of Melchior's marriage.

It was in the great master suite of the second floor that Enerde lay with his bride, feeling the profound pleasure of knowing that the beautiful sleeping girl was his alone, that she had loved him since childhood, when her sea-blue eyes gazed upon him with vast and depthless adoration. He sighed in memory of his waiting, of his rushes into the night to seek relief from the desire he had for the growing child. When he felt for the first time her budded breasts and suddenly rounded hips through a summer middy blouse and pleated blue skirt as she sat on his lap and kissed him after a picnic in the alpine house in Italy, he wanted to cry in pain, but instead laughed casually, called her a sweet child, and told her to run tell the boatman to get the canoe ready. When she had scampered away, he quickly relieved himself of the heavy burden between his legs, catching the semen in a dinner napkin, which he stuffed among the others in the basket. With shaking knees he followed her to the lake. "And still only thirteen," he had groaned in agony. Now all that was behind him. At last his patience and his suffering had been rewarded. All things come to him who knows how to wait, he intoned silently as he stroked the long slender back and leaned forward to kiss the elegant neck, smoothing aside the hair that flowed over her skin. In the half-light he dreamily covered the curved bone at her neck with his mouth and contoured the rise with his tongue. Perhaps a minute passed in this luxurious delight, unexpectedly heightened by the pronounced shape of the curve of the bone. Then, as if his own tongue were sending him a new message obliterating the one in his blood which roared down his body to his groin to fill and tighten the organ to bursting, he began to sense not with the hot blood now but with some thin filaments in his brain which even seemed to speak to him beyond the tongue which in its paradoxical urgency still fluttered around the girl's nape, putting taste away and making

[11]

some crackling electric announcement, "I have seen this before." Slowly he pulled away from the sleeping girl and brought the lamp within reach to glow on the warm wet nape where a pale berry mole covered the exact raised bone that had also in the exact same way covered his father's neck, a mark not only identical in shape and texture but casting back the same rose-opal color as well.

He discovered soon after his marriage that Vienna's own motto, which he had intoned with mock seriousness at his friends' unfortunate and sometimes ludicrous romantic entanglements, "It is always too late. Tsk, tsk. Don't you see, old chap, it is always too late," ironically fit his situation. The wedding night resulted in a pregnancy. But he could not know that at the time of his discovery of the birthmark. That night he crept silently, carrying his lamp in front of him like a lamenting scholar who hated a truth that had just been revealed to him, to his dressing room, where he cast himself on the couch and wept. Then he cursed in loud whispers to alleviate his rage at his father, knowing at the same time that his father, fornicating with his stepson's wife, would no more consider the act unhealthy than would a maggot despair of the cadaver upon which it fed. That was the Vienna of his time—the golden-surfaced city within which blind worms ate the heart as clearly as ripened fruit, seeded with another season's lice, teemed and squirmed with vermin within the pulpy rotting flesh that was its harvest.

Before he even thought of possessing her again, he told himself a thousand lies: the birthmark was a coincidence—remote—but a coincidence nonetheless. Didn't the most extraordinary coincidence sometimes happen? . . . There was no blood route back through the stepbrother that he knew of . . . but it was possible (wasn't it?) that there was one he did *not* know of. Hadn't he himself made love to the wives of acquaintances met casually (and even sometimes not so casually) at the thermal and mineral spas so generously sprinkled all over middle Europe where the ladies went to take the waters? He thought feverishly of a summer week at the Grand Hotel at Karlovy Vary, carefully planned to the last detail, even to the shade of sheets (lavender) that the particular lady liked to lie on as she moaned exquisitely into his ear before the moment of crisis when her bite once actually broke his skin. Couldn't Dorothea . . . with some distant Enerde cousin . . . ? The nape was a common place for a mole. Hadn't he read that somewhere?

Every answer demanded another question, and another, and another. In the end the whole fabrication of interlocking deceptions fell in a heap around him like an unraveling mesh net of which he was left holding only a single delicate and irrefutable part, the catch—the truth: *his* father had also been his wife's father. This is how he first worded it, unable yet to say, "I have lain with my blood sister." And when he was able to say that, he was able to minimize it. "But only half! Only half! We had different mothers. And didn't the old holy ones in the Old Testament marry their half-sisters? Abraham and Sarah . . . weren't they thus related? And if it was right for them . . . who could cry out against this union?"

He could . . . and did, weeping with despair, less finally at the moral transgression than at the old rumor that Enerde women died young, that some fatal gene carried by the men caused some gross and incomprehensible reaction at birth which left the mothers unable to labor, which in fact stopped that labor, stopped it cold somewhere in some advanced stage of the birth process which even denied the women the relief of a Cesarean, and which left them dying in the prime of youthful health. He shuddered at the denials of the medical profession, at the scoffing, tisking, chortling that accompanied such negations. "Nonsense. No such thing. If there were, we'd know about it." He felt himself grow cold: sixty years ago they didn't even know about germs. And forty-six years ago, not one of the three physicians attending his mother (his father's second cousin) could give a reason why her labor stopped, and although they could grasp him by the head and pull him from her before he suffocated in the birth canal, they could not stop her from dying.

And then there were the old horror stories of interfamily births: imbeciles, slobbering half-wits who could live for sixty years without developing more than an infant's brain, blind children, deaf children, children without spleens, without stomachs, without anuses.

For weeks he pondered these terrors as he lay wretchedly awake in brotherly innocence beside his sleeping bride.

Amalia, unaware of how often men felt inclined to copulate, saw nothing extraordinary about his abstinence. She had loved him always and for her that love needed no more physical performances than the sweet kisses she had long been used to. Having not yet been awakened to the possibilities of more electrifying pleasures, she longed for nothing more than to lie beside him secure in the knowledge that she would (as her old nurse had assured her on her wedding day) know whenever he wished to "fill her with his love." The nurse's description of the act of love was somewhat meager, as Melchior soon discovered, but his gentleness, his care, his immense love for the girl and most of all the patience of his age, his years of careful nurturing, made the first night, if not high passion for her, at least an unfrightening although rather curious experience. And best of all, she had said to him that she was glad he liked it all so much, and didn't he say that because of what they did she would one day become a mother? Didn't he? He did.

As the days passed and Enerde found himself each night staring into the wakeful darkness of his insomnia, he traveled through lower layers of his memory, into deeper regions of his being like Dante descending, except that it was his own soul he sought and with which he had to come face to face to ask the ultimate question: *Had he not always suspected something?* There was the color of her hair, darkly blond like his own. Didn't he remember the whisperings of servants, or at least know of them, those careless voices that invariably harbor subtle possibilities and wretched truths. Not that any such voice threw suspicion on his father, but only that she did not have a single characteristic of the dead stepbrother who supposedly was her father.

Then the doctors confirmed that she was pregant and horror after horror climbed out of the black pits that were his nights and stood around him in the dark, panting and salivating like hungry beasts with bloody jowls and fiery eyes. He returned to the church which he had always considered a rather dull joke. He gave generously, prayed, and confessed everything

[13]

except the truth. For penance he decided not to make love to her again. Certainly God would reward such a sacrifice and give him a healthy child and a well wife.

Meanwhile, the rest of the world was apparently doing what it was meant to do, mainly blowing itself to bits. Melchior failed even to acknowledge the Great War. He left his newspapers unread, ignored his mail, and refused to let anyone speak of anything unpleasant in the house. Any servant who was anything but cheerful was dismissed at once. Amalia thrived. Again and again as she drifted into sleep she would murmur to Melchoir how happy she was.

After a pleasant and uncomplicated pregnancy ending in a long and painful birth, she was delivered of a healthy baby girl and died twenty minutes later.

2

As he clung to the body of his dead wife, Melchior shrieked and swore at the doctors. They were still in the Dark Ages. They were ignorant fools. They practiced witchcraft. They had *let* his wife die. They deserved to be shot. In fact he would have them all shot. All but one left in a rage, muttering about madness and muddleheadedness. The remaining doctor, Enerde's own personal physician, Berthold Frichter, a young man with a fetish for neatness and a taste for aristocratic comforts, whose father, grandfather, and great-grandfather had been physicians to the Enerde family for a total of a hundred years, took himself out of the raving widower's sight to avoid any accidental injury to himself lest the grieving husband should have a gun handy. In his favorite Enerde chair, warming a healthy portion of his favorite twenty-year-old Enerde brandy, Berthold Frichter licked his black hairline mustache with his quick pink tongue and contemplated a famous eighteenth-century nude hanging under a peach-toned light on the wall in front of him. Lying on her stomach on a red sofa of disarrayed velvet pillows, the blond flesh of the girl's buttocks and spread thighs offered an erotic and abandoned position to the fretting viewer.

"What a lot of fuss," grumbled Frichter, listening to Enerde's wailing beyond the wall, "when the world is full of women just dying to drop their drawers for him." He let Melchior rave and curse until he wore himself out, then he gave him a heavy sedative and moved into a suite in the house to wait for the new father to wake up and acknowledge his daughter.

Enerde awakened weeping, wandering about the house while Frichter explained that no one could have saved Amalia, that her kind of internal bleeding was always fatal. Finally Enerde let the doctor place the child in his arms. Enerde gazed at the tiny face, the miniature hands smaller than his thumbnail, and whispered hoarsely, "Mine. Mine alone."

"Until some prince comes along," laughed the doctor.

Enerde glowered at him and the doctor cleared his throat and set about fussing with his pocket watch. "I know a good wet nurse," he said after a moment. "A regular milk machine. Could feed three this size . . ."

"What's the matter with her size?" Enerde demanded.

"Why, nothing. She's a good size. Seven pounds. She's an ideal size . . ."

"Is there anything wrong with her?" Enerde's brows lowered darkly.

"Wrong? Wrong? Certainly not. She's a healthy baby."

"I mean is she normal? Does she have all her faculties? No lies now."

"As far as anyone can tell at birth, of course. Her reactions are excellent. Healthy pair of lungs. Of course she's normal. Why shouldn't she be?"

Enerde gave no reply and the doctor also fell silent. He knew the old rumor. All Vienna knew it—not that nasty little one about Dorothea Von Gostling possibly having borne some other man's child than her husband's, but that older one, that there was something—no one knew what—*wrong* with the Enerde girls. He thought "girls" because like everyone else he could not remember any of them as women, because so few of them ever seemed to get far enough along in adult femalehood to be called women. There was never much pity attached to the Enerde clan's tragedies since there seemed to be enough of them born into the world to keep their wealth intact and growing so that whatever pity they might have garnered from a soft heart was counterbalanced simultaneously by an envious one.

Melchior named his daughter after her dead mother in a sad attempt at minimizing death. There was nothing he would not do for the child, and in her early years he never spent a night away from home. He never did make love to a woman again and even said to himself, not just thought it quietly, but actually said it aloud one morning to his hand-carved beveled-glass shaving mirror, "I do not want it. I do not even miss it." And that was a truth, as though his glands had died with the first Amalia, or before, on the very night that his tongue told him about the mole and he knew that he was doomed. It was as if he had become impotent, a man still young, still healthy, still virile, letting his organs teach him through the knowing cell and the doomed blood how not to want love, at least not the blind, surging, thrusting, pitiless, blood-pounding passionate love that had brought him to this ruin. So he gave it up as he gave up hunting, as though the ejaculation of that weapon, too, was but a reminder of the damage he had done with his once-living, rioting organ. He began to age more quickly. He stopped his daily exercise regimen, ignored his diet. He no longer shaved the tip of his chin or trimmed his beard, so that in a little while the hair grew bushy and long and gray.

The war worsened. While other men stared with incredulous, horrified eyes at the casualty lists, Enerde discussed his child's weight, temperature, pulse, with her nurse, who gave him a daily report: what she had eaten, how long she had slept. The child talked and walked approximately when she was supposed to, and Enerde was elated. She was normal. Normal! In

[15]

time she joined her father at his daily tea and cakes in the garden. Thus while the rest of Europe's aristocrats who had once rattled their sabers and thumped their drums, fairly itching for a "good old-fashioned war to pep things up," as some called it in its early stages before it turned out not to be old-fashioned at all, but a horror of steady, ceaseless, monotonous, meaningless massacre bereft of the glorious inspiration of banner-flowing, sword-gleaming cavalry charges, Melchior Enerde sat in his wall-enclosed garden and watched his child, which, because she had cost him so dearly, he loved with a love more akin to pain than pleasure. He worried about ordinary things happening to her, scraped knees, measles, a cat scratch; and he worried about things that were not ordinary, that is, everything else: lightning striking, paralysis and plagues, devouring dogs. He worried about the central marble stairs, so he had them richly carpeted. He worried about the windows, so he had them barred. He worried about gas fires, so he installed electricity. The fish ponds in the garden were stretched over with nets. Angular furniture was replaced with rounded pieces. The nurse slept in the child's room. Servants were ever present when she played with her toys. She was, in fact, never alone. When she cried, she was picked up. She was never in a darkened room. She was never cold. There was nothing Enerde would not give her. She lived in a whole suite of rooms filled with playhouses, dolls, and a hundred other toys ordered from Europe's most famous toy houses. Her wardrobe was princely, the tiny dresses and undergarments ordered from Paris, Geneva, Brussels. She was the only child known to have a sable cape and hat before she was five.

Among the servants, there was only one who knew of Enerde's worries over his child's normalcy. Aloysius Rätzel was one of the legends that clung to the Enerde family with dear and enduring tenacity: a doorstep foundling, a parlormaid's afternoon pleasure, an aristocrat's abandoned love child (no one knew); he was taken in as an infant and raised within the great family as a companion for Melchior, born the same year. Playmate as a child, batman in the army, gunbearer at royal hunts, valet and confidant to a careless young sensualist, and head houseman for a middle-aged groom and child bride, he loved Enerde with a constant, selfless affection that knew no asperity and expected no recognition. He was to serve Enerde for seventy-five years before a final act of self-denial relieved him forever of his duties. It was said by some that in their twenties, young Enerde had saved Rätzel's life; others said the reverse was true. The legend was acceptable either way. Rätzel had the kind of sad face that is sometimes seen on smile-painted clowns; no amount of upturned mouth paint, or smiles for that matter either, could keep from it that expression of gravity, a remote suggestion of mourning. It was not a soured sadness, nor mopishness, but an inborn melancholic cast of his features already present from childhood, if not birth, that in another age would have passed for romantic world-weariness. The features lied. He was cheerful and genial but without any of the irritating heartiness or annoying jollity that sometimes flaws a cheerful nature. He was a tall man, equal in height to Enerde, who towered above his friends and employees by half a head, but unlike Melchior he did not pander to a military stance, as though his very origin, the position he was given as a child and which he kept through those seventy-five years of variable and willing servitude, had decreed he should walk less tall, or at least less proud than the man he served. He never married, and if there were women in his life, no one knew of them. He was never ill and no one remembered a time when he was gone—even for a day—from within an hour of Melchior's reach.

Enerde made few decisions without mulling them over out loud with his lifelong companion, but one he kept to himself for some years was his intention to rear the first Amalia to be his wife. However, what no one knew, not even Melchior, was that Rätzel had long divined a nearer relationship between Enerde and his Amalia than either of them knew. He saw that it was not merely that the color of their hair was the same; it had the identical texture, the same thick abundance, the same weight. In their voices he heard that similarity of tone in the sounding of certain vowels that identifies siblings, that catch at the end of laughter that marked a genetic relationship. Others thought Amalia was imitating her beloved stepuncle. Rätzel knew better. Nor did he look far to find the girl's father: old Augustus sitting with his stepdaughter-in-law and her child in the garden at teatime always seemed to reflect a special glow, an almost smug sated expression which was actually the satisfying of a sweet tooth. He loved cake of any kind, as did Amalia, to whom he fed it while the child sat on his knee. Rätzel had long seen the identical expression on their faces whenever they let something sweet melt on their tongues and linger in their mouths.

After the flu epidemic carried away most of the family and Rätzel saw Melchior's intention to marry his stepniece, he tried quietly to discourage the man.

"But this comes as a bad surprise, Rätzel, I thought you liked my little beauty. You know the women I've spent my time with. They bore me. They are jaded, fickle, not to speak of ill-tempered when they can't have their way. Amalia's young freshness makes me feel like a boy of eighteen. I feel as though I am beginning my life again and not many men get that opportunity."

Rätzel thought carefully. At all costs he meant not to cast a shadow on Augustus. "It's her age."

"Ah, but that's just it; her age suits me very well. I love her age as I love her eyes."

"But a difference of twenty-nine years . . . You will surely predecease her and she will be a long time a widow."

"Look at me, Rätzel. Do I not look younger than my age?"

"Yes."

"Then let me tell you: I *am* younger than my age. I see fifty years ahead of us. No. It is a perfect alliance. Mutual love. Mutual trust. And, Rätzel, her purity is like a drug for me. No morphia gives me such euphoria, such a sense of the rightness of things. No, you'll not change my mind with clever arguments. I mean to marry her. She must be mine. She *will* be mine."

Rätzel knew Enerde was disappointed that he did not welcome the marriage enthusiastically. It was the only faint shadow cast upon the event, and because it was still there at the time of the wedding there occurred between the two men a thin division, the merest crack in their long stone-solid relationship. Yet when Amalia died, it was Rätzel who was able to take the dead girl out of the man's arms, and in that moment as Enerde relinquished his burden there passed between the men's eyes a look of such raw grief and despairing regret that the very look—had it been a sound—would have howled down the walls of the room. "You knew," said Melchior's eyes through the continuing ululation of sorrow. "Yes," answered the other's eyes, "I knew." They never spoke of it, but like Enerde, Rätzel watched the growing motherless child as a scientist watches a culture which will prove forever a long-disputed theory.

The Enerde household staff was made up mostly of men: cooks, house-cleaners, gardeners, coachmen (later chauffeurs); and a few women: nurses, chambermaids, seamstresses—all of whom Rätzel hired. The war invaded the house only to spirit away some of the male employees, but when that was over they returned to their old positions not much the worse for the experiences except for the head gardener, a dark-haired man who returned with a permanent look of astonishment and rage on his face, as if he were helplessly watching someone set fire to a shrine. He was called simply "Graz" after the city of his birth. He came back hesitantly to stand, with that constant anger on his face, cap in hand, before Rätzel and explain in a flat voice that he would like his job back but since he was now deaf he would understand a refusal. Rätzel assured him in writing that the flowers would never know about his disability and he was welcome to communicate with the other groundsmen in whatever way he could devise. Graz nodded his dark head vigorously and said that he was learning lipreading. They exchanged a few comments on the tragic times and the fall of the great and powerful and how even with the death of the young wife, the Enerde house had been lucky not to have suffered a great loss in other fortunes. Rätzel carefully wrote one last important note for the gardener. "Do not mention in any way anything negative or unpleasant. He wishes this to be an isle of contentment for the child." The gardener nodded and stuffed the note in his pocket.

This attempt to keep all unpleasantness from touching the child worried Rätzel; not that he wished the child at this early age to experience a greater reality of the vagaries of life, but he knew that all this appearance of serenity had an effect on Enerde that resulted in his chronic unwillingness to look at the real changes in the world around him. He continued to behave in the new century as if he were still living in the previous one. At age fifty, he still held his belief in the permanence of things, although his friend the emperor was dead and his heir in exile; the work at the Enerde textile mills was frequently disrupted by malcontent daily-wagers who complained con-tinually about their lot; and the Enerde forests, held in perpetuity by imperial decree, were vandalized, poached, and beset by squatters. Enerde, in a meeting with his alarmed executive employees, only waved a soothing hand. "Gentlemen, gentlemen, it's only temporary. Only temporary. A passing disturbance. A little touch of the *Föhn*. After the blow, things will return to normal. Now, we go on with our policies as before. All employees of long standing will receive assistance if there are interruptions in pro-duction; that is, if work is halted for reasons beyond their control. Tell them to be patient. We intend to care for them as long as feasible. Everything within reason, of course." He would hear no more gloomy reports and predictions, but stretched his arms back for the waiting overcoat held by his valet behind him, donned his top hat and gloves and clamped his cane under his arm. His chauffeur drove him home. It was Amalia's sixth birthday and Enerde wanted to be there when she opened her presents. That was the year he decided she was ready for her first jewels. She opened one beautifully wrapped package after another and looked at the gifts of exquisite porcelain and mechanical playthings—music boxes, dancing Harlequins, puppets—without taking any of them out of their boxes. Occasionally her small hands lingered over a ribbon in a doll's hair, a sash or a feathered hat, but then she turned to the next unopened package and seemed more interested in the actual removal of the wrapping than the treasure inside. When all the presents were opened, Enerde called her to him. "I have something very special for you this year. A wonderful surprise." He took a slender silk box from his pocket and as she sat on his lap, he opened it, watching her large gray eyes as she took the necklace of rubies from its velvet bed. The nurse and French governess, straightening out the gifts and wrappings and ribbons on the floor, made astonished exclamations over the beauty of the necklace but Amalia only smiled faintly and returned it to its box and said she wanted her cake now. Everyone laughed; and later, after the cakes, after the puddings and candies, after Amalia was asleep and the necklace was back in the safe, Enerde, enjoying a final cigar on the balcony before retiring to his study, commented to Rätzel that he thought the birthday had been a great success. Rätzel agreed. "She's perfect, isn't she?" said Melchior.

"Perfect," said Rätzel into the moon-mysteried, windless night.

Many of Melchior's contemporaries may have shaken their heads at his failure to come to terms with changing events, but his lawyers did not: there was a side to Enerde's thinking that was years ahead of his countrymen. Even before the war he had invested heavily in forests on the western American continent in both the state of Washington and the virgin wilderness of British Columbia. His advisers in the Enerde banks in Switzerland, where his family had been making new money and storing much of the old for generations, recommended investing some of it in textile mills in Massachusetts. If there was to be a war in Europe, reasoned the bankers, America would certainly not be a part of it, except perhaps to prosper from it. Melchior followed their advice, buying into textile mills and securing large tracts of forests through a legal firm in New York. By 1914 he could afford not to pay much attention to the war in his own backyard. He had other yards to play in. By the time the war was over and the economy or what was left of the empire lay in ruins, he alone could keep his mills running with American and Swiss money until the country began to revive a little and the appearance of prosperity returned to Austria. There were bananas on the tables again and furs in the store windows.

During those years, Enerde continued to give his daughter annual "wonderful surprises" on her birthday: jewels of sapphires, opals, emeralds; and when she was sixteen, a three-strand necklace of pearls of such perfection in color and shape that even Rätzel, who was unmoved by precious baubles, was impressed. He watched the presentation as he did every year, with Enerde sitting in his great chair (in the formal dining room by then) while Amalia opened one package after another in the same tranquil, polite, grave passivity with which she lived her life. It was not that she was meek, but there seemed to be nothing that could excite her, nothing that could make her laugh or cry, be sad or joyful, in fact, call up any kind of enthusiasm or spontaneity. It seemed to Rätzel that something in her had not been born, something critical that animated human emotion. Perhaps some gland had failed its function. He once believed that the onset of puberty would bring the missing elixir or venom or collection of secret nameless cells or whatever the missing component was that could make her at least smile at several hundred thousand schillings' worth of pearls, rather than just brush her fingertips over them without even removing them from their silken box. Her father cajoled her into putting them on, himself removing them from the box and placing them around her neck, lovingly fastening the diamond clip at the nape.

Rätzel knew that Enerde anxiously waited for his child to show some sign of vitality, of that missing spark of vigorous life they both remembered in the long-dead Dorothea.

It was not that she was unhealthy or even physically weak. At sixteen she was taller than average and if not statuesque as her mother and grand-mother had been, at least comely and well-formed, with a long tiny waist and fine high breasts. Her birthday gifts at sixteen would have made normal girls dance with joy, the women said to each other later, the same nurse and governess who had been present at all of the annual parties—parties that bore no more resemblance to a birthday celebration than a wake might have. In fact there was something of the aftermath of death about Amalia's parties: the solemn accepting of the presents by the girl might have been seen as the collecting of an inheritance after the reading of a will, except that the gifts were all new, the packages exquisitely wrapped in brocade and velvet cloth. There were pastel dresses from Paris with matching cloche hats, soft leather shoes from Italy, gloves and handkerchiefs from Switz-erland, fans and scarves from Spain, furs from Finland. As with the dolls, Amalia did not remove the elegant items from their containers, but only touched a fold of silk here, a flowerlet of embroidery there, and moved on with no interest to the next richly wrapped gift. It was not that she showed actual indifference or even a hint of boredom; she was simply not interested in clothes any more than she had been in dolls. In fact, she was not interested in anything. Of all her studies, she did well only in French, speaking the language with an exquisite accent in a voice as soft as sifted ashes. "Why French?" Melchior, who did not like the language particularly, wanted to know from the governess. It was an insulting question to ask of a French-woman. But the governess was not fool enough to show umbrage and risk an exceptionally well-paying job, although it was without challenge. She told Enerde that some children simply had a gift for languages and this usually made them fond of the subject.

Enerde was not fooled by the woman's answer: he was used to listening to employees tell him what he wanted to hear. He mulled the problem over with the one person he could always trust to give him an independent opinion.

"Do you think she should get away from the house more?" asked Enerde of Rätzel some days after the sixteenth birthday party.

"More? She doesn't get away at all. She has no desire to. She knows no more of Vienna than she does of London. Her world ends at the garden wall. Graz says she sits in the lilac arbor for hours without moving. He thinks she doesn't even smell the flowers. Sometimes she sits in the garden house looking at nothing, or at least that nothing that exists at the end of that vacant stare with which she seems to watch the world pass in front of her, though I'm not sure she's actually watching even that. Yes, she should get away from the house, and more; but I don't know what more you can do for her. It's obvious that there is nothing more you can give her. You tried having young people her own age here. You surely remember that. She hid from them; no, not hid, nothing that emphatic. She simply went up to bed while they sat around down below and waited like paid mourners for the funeral to begin."

"What have I done wrong, Rätzel?"

"Nothing."

"The doctors say she's completely normal. In excellent health. All the female functions are developing on time . . . normal. Normal. Normal! Completely normal!" He paused, and then in an already grieving voice, "I could send her away to school, force her to make friends, but I can't bear to part with her. She is all I have. There must be some other way."

It was the nurse who finally suggested that Amalia be taken on drives through the town in the hope that the girl might find the trips interesting. The woman, hopelessly bored ever since Amalia no longer needed a nurse, hoped she herself would accompany the girl on these sojourns. Enerde listened to her suggestion and after a week of mulling over the idea decided it could do his daughter no harm. There were already stories circulating about the princess that could not laugh, lifted from an old fairy tale and applied with a certain gross and ribald levity to the dovelike Amalia. And indeed, Enerde *would* have given a fortune to anyone who could awaken his lethargic child and enliven her with at least some of the spirit of her demonstrative and loving mother and at least a little of the fire and mystery of her grandmother.

The drives began on the pretext that they were educational. Each day in the middle of the afternoon, the governess and Amalia would sit in the back seat of one of Enerde's handsome touring cars, a lap robe across their knees, while the chauffeur drove in a leisurely fashion about the city, the governess pointing out various old buildings and landmarks for their history. They walked through the gardens of Belvedere and Schönbrunn, the liveried driver strolling a respectful distance behind them as the governess detailed the lines of succession of the royal families, and told old and amusing anecdotes about them, as though any minute a coach full of Hapsburgs or Hohenzollerns might sail past waving handkerchiefs at them. Later they would stop at one of the fashionable hotels and have tea in the salon or garden. No one ever knew if Amalia enjoyed the excursions; she appeared to look at the elaborate architecture much the way she might look at one of her dolls still in its coffinlike box. One imagined that she might even touch it once or twice casually, lightly, with delicate fingertips. The governess told Enerde that the trips were hugely successful and that she wished he had thought of them before. They took longer and longer walks, the governess carrying the lace-ruffled parasol to keep the sun from their faces and chattering in French to the docile Amalia, who may or may not have been listening. After a time the woman would motion to the driver, who would turn off whatever path they were on and bring up the car. So passed Amalia's sixteenth summer.

It was on a day in September when the honey smell of summertime still lingered in the air and the leaves of the chestnut trees had only begun to gather in the gutters that they happened to be having tea at one of the old royal resorts across the river. "It was quite near here that the empress used to ride her horse. Perhaps even as near as that path by those trees," said the governess, pointing in the direction of a little wood. There was a gentle murmur of voices on the veranda, for it was one of those selected places where genteel young girls were taken by mothers or governesses so that the world of society might be kept aware of their existence until they were old enough to be brought formally into it through some elaborate ball before they were married off to the most suitable suitor, or, as some wag not of that class said, "the highest bidder."

Amalia's existence was, of course, well known since her birth; and the other girls who on this day smiled so sweetly at one another and lifted their cups so elegantly as they spoke in voices as soft as certain bird sounds, hated her thoroughly. Not only was she by far the wealthiest, but she possessed a deceptive fragility about her person that was highly prized among the robust young women who seemed unable to achieve the pallor, the other-worldliness of the silent Amalia. But Amalia seemed to be no more interested in them than she was in anyone else who entered the fringe of vision around the dead circumference of her world. The girls wore white voile or lace or silk dresses with pastel sashes and carried gloves and diminutive purses that held handkerchiefs. Generally they knew each other and they talked softly across the tables about nothing. No one ever laughed. A few gentlemen frequented the place, sipped aperitifs, and pretended to read.

The governess had just placed her cup back on its saucer when someone spoke into their little circle in flawless French.

"No, madam. Please forgive my presumptuousness, but not there. In a grove not far from here. She loved to race her mount. My father used to say that seeing the empress ride was one of the supreme pleasures of life."

The governess turned to the table behind her with the intention of staring disapprovingly at the stranger and rebuking him for his rudeness. But once turned, she did not speak for a moment at all; then she tilted her head slightly and touched her hair with a faintly fluttering hand. "I beg your pardon?" she said, the statement carrying that quality of question that does not actually ask.

"I said that the empress raced her horse in a grove there to the north." The man who spoke, as he raised a graceful hand toward the direction, had eyes the color of wet leaves and hair of the blackness and sheen that looks permanently pomaded but which in fact is not. But his matching mustache was.

"Are you sure?" asked the woman.

"Quite. My father often spoke of seeing her ride. He said that she was the most beautiful woman in all Europe."

During this exchange the governess seemed almost to have forgotten Amalia. "How is it," she asked, "that you speak French?"

"My first language—from the crib until eight, we spoke nothing else. It is, therefore, most loved."

"Then you are French?"

"No," said the man, producing a card from his vest pocket, "although I have spent many happy hours in the divine Paris." The governess took the card and read the name—Count Pavel Stephanovitch Bronevsky—not knowing that merely having accepted the minute scrap of paper would shortly cost her her position in the Enerde house. For as she took in the name, glancing for a moment back at the face of the handsome man, Amalia reached across the table and plucked the card from her hand.

3

For the merest moment the governess considered snatching the card back, for there passed through her mind one of those foreshadowings of calamity that people sometimes experience, not an actual knowledge, but more a sense that the universe had paused for the millionth of a second and in that time everything had altered, shifted in such a way that all subsequent events were forever beyond human control, that nothing one did could have changed the march of those events to an orderly and uncontrollable disaster. The governess was later to reconsider that fragment of time and even believe that it had lasted for some minutes while she contemplated taking back the card from Amalia and returning it to the man with some polite comment that this was not the customary way in which a girl of Amalia's breeding should meet any gentleman, however refined. She even tearfully said as much to an enraged Melchior some days later when he questioned her as to how his daughter should come to meet a penniless Russian dandy who had the presumption to request the privilege of calling on him.

Before Enerde talked to the governess he had Bronevsky hurriedly and superficially investigated. His card told no lies, but then neither did it speak the volume of truths uncovered by Melchior's man. When Melchior first received the letter from Bronevsky in which the Russian carefully spoke of the joy he experienced when Amalia accepted his card, he went into a mindless rage. Amalia take a card from a stranger? Amalia, who had to be begged to accept Europe's most famous pearls, take a card from some insignificant foreigner? Impossible! He demanded and received within hours some current facts about the man. Bronevsky was thirty-two years old, honestly titled through a father of the same name; he had exchanged Russia for Paris during the Revolution; he ultimately left France for Geneva, where he lived for six months before coming to Vienna to take up a rootless residence in a small, discreet hotel which catered to deposed or banished nobility who still had resources. However, Bronevsky's resources had run out weeks before. "How does he live?" Melchior demanded. Recently all his debts had been paid by the owner of a shipping firm, A. Mundt, an Austrian well known to Enerde. "Why?" asked Melchior. Unknown. "Does he have other family in Vienna?" Unknown. "Is his mother living?" Unknown. "Unknown? Too much is unknown!" Melchior rushed home to question the governess, who, of course, knew nothing at all.

"But it was all completely innocent, perfectly proper, just a chance meeting. . . ."

"Chance! Chance! Chance!" shouted Enerde. "Nothing is by chance in this maggot-eaten town. Design! Everything is by design! Design and damnation!"

"But he had no way of knowing where we would have tea."

"He had every way of knowing. That place is a showcase for foolish women to advertise their children. But my daughter! My Amalia! How could you be so stupid as to take my child to that auction block?"

The governess had no answer for Melchior although she continued to give a half-dozen that she should not have: the place was fashionable; it was part of the old royal estate; other young girls went there; all were chaperoned; all was decorous and proper; only true gentlemen visited the place. The last was too much for Enerde. He summarily dismissed the governess, giving her twenty-four hours to be packed and out of the house.

Then he sat in his half-darkened study with the portrait of the first Amalia smiling down on him and brooded. *He must not be hasty. Perhaps the child took the card merely so that the man would stop annoying them.* He did not believe this. *But there were other possibilities. After all, she had not said anything about the card. Perhaps she had thrown it away.* He did not believe this either. He was only praying that anything but the truth would be true. What he believed was his own fear, as he had believed it when the first Amalia carried her baby. He felt a sense of dread, as if someone had already entered his house and was even at this moment plotting some monstrosity against his child. He rushed out of his study and hurried to her rooms. She was seated by a window overlooking the garden, a closed book in her lap, her hands lying across it, inert and slack like the slender bodies of white boneless fish. Enerde was both depressed and heartened by the sight; depressed because he had seen her sit in this lethargic and unliving way a thousand times and always her stillness, her passiveness saddened him; heartened because the fact that she had not changed might mean that she had forgotten all about the upstart Russian and his accursed card. "How are you feeling, my love?" He spoke gently as always; and although he wanted to ask about the card, he could not bring himself to do so: if she had thrown it away, he did not want to remind her of it; if she had not, he did not want to draw undue importance in any way to the incident of her taking it.

"I am well, Father." He smiled and kissed her hair.

"Good, good." He stood for a moment before the window and stared unseeing at the chestnut trees below. "Would you like to go for a drive . . . with me?"

"If you like, Father."

It was late in the day and he did not want to go for a drive. "Perhaps we could take a little trip. The house in Yugoslavia is very lovely at this time of year."

"Yes, Father, if you like."

"Good, then I'll make some arrangements to be away for a few weeks. I need a little vacation, and it would do you good, too."

She did not reply, so after a few moments he kissed her hair again and left the room to contemplate the meaning of her willingness to leave the city: if she were thinking about the Russian she would not want to leave. On the other hand, perhaps she thinks it might be a good place to bring up the fact that she wants to see him again. Halfway down the stairs he struck his forehead with the heel of his hand. "How absurd I'm being. Nothing has changed. She is exactly the same. The Russian is the furthest thing from her mind. She has not even mentioned him. She has forgotten him entirely." Still, he felt a nameless anxiety that would not sleep, a premonition of danger, but danger of an unusual sort, an apprehension of shame, of gross and unendurable ruin, of something squatting in the dark leering at him, something with a lascivious, salacious, evil grin on its face. In that moment, Enerde was like a man who sensed his own doom, not where his actual life was concerned, nor even Amalia's life, but where the *control* over his life was at stake and his control over hers. He thought briefly of the old adage: It is always too late. But then he cursed himself for being a fool. No, it was not too late: He was in control; he would fight this Russian wolf who was sniffing at his door. He planned a course of action without taking Bronevsky into consideration at all. A trip to Yugoslavia would bring him into long daily contact with his daughter, and he would soon find out if she remembered the card.

Enerde hurriedly arranged to leave Vienna, moving with such uncharacteristic haste that his executives looked at each other in wonder and with a certain alarm. He was like a man fleeing a city in which the first few cases of plague had just been discovered, not knowing that the germ he feared was already upon him—or at least upon his beloved child.

What had caught Amalia's attention in the tearoom and what the hapless governess had missed entirely was the way Pavel Stephanovitch did not look at the girl. Any woman with even a small amount of experience with the actions and reactions of a rake (especially one wearing lavender gloves) would have recognized that the total ignoring of the lovely Amalia was a serious and premeditated method of conquest—perhaps the oldest known. But of course, Amalia knew nothing of rakes: the men orbiting her world— her father, Rätzel, Graz, other gardeners, housemen, chauffeurs—were at all times aware of her presence, so completely did Enerde organize his house around his daughter.

As for the governess, her knowledge of rakes was acquired from nineteenth-century novels in which the scions of aristocratic families "took advantage" of innocent chambermaids making up the beds in elaborate country houses where the rich went to hunt and play when they tired of city life. What she saw in Pavel Stephanovitch Bronevsky was a distinguished gentleman elegantly clothed with the garments and language of the very upper classes at their very best behavior. Bronevsky spoke with exactly the correct balance of authority and detachment and the properly prepared aloof face, so that when the woman turned toward him, all her resolve to admonish him melted away under his expression of reserve and dignity. And if the cut of his coat hadn't further served to flummox her, his extraordinary good looks did, although a certain veiled contempt rested in his handsome face, since he was of that long aristocratic line who intimately understood that they are a class both revered and despised and that almost all outsiders would happily sell their own souls to belong to it. Any *insider* would have recognized Bronevsky's expression, certainly any Russian insider who had ever seen the calm, poised, waiting face of a wolf.

Amalia, looking up from her tearoom sweet, saw only that the man was totally different from those who peopled her world. He seemed, in fact, to be a creature from quite another world. The dark emerald in his eyes captivated her as no stone jewel ever had, although he did not direct his gaze at her. It soon became painfully obvious to Amalia that he did not even see her. Unused to such curious treatment, she examined the man at some length as she waited with growing consternation for him to turn his eyes upon her. Bronevsky was dressed in a silver-gray suit with a white velvet vest. There was about him an air of patient waiting which no sixteen-year-old could have understood. His lavender gloves lay crossed on the brim of his upended gray top hat resting beside a half-empty aperitif glass. A young girl would not have seen that the drink was being carefully nursed or that the silk hat and attending gloves resting precisely where they were and as they were amounted to a form of presentation. A world-wise woman used to the "cures" at the various spas would have smiled into her sleeve at such unsubtlety; but then, Bronevsky, in all fairness, would have behaved much differently with a woman of a different wisdom. In Amalia's world, men wore sturdy dark suits or servants' uniforms, and most of these men were inclined to a thickness through the waist and thighs and tended to walk heavily. But the Russian was as slender as a fencing master and held himself with the same athletic bravura and boldness. If such a thing as love at first sight is possible, then it happened to Amalia; for it was, indeed, that first sight of him that took her breath away. Added to this visual assault to her awakening senses was the melodious murmur of his voice speaking the only language, if not the only thing, that had ever interested her. With her eyes and ears thus overcome by such beauty, she was not even aware of his scent, a toilet water that finally brought a blush to the governess's cheeks. Almost any man (beyond the age of eighteen) would have roared with derision.

Amalia took the card from the governess's hand for the simple female reason that she did not want another woman to have it. What happened after that was something the governess did not mention to Melchior on the day he questioned and dismissed her. Bronevsky, upon seeing the girl seize his card, finally turned to her and with the eloquence of the born courtier

[26]

that he was, rose, took her hand in his two beautifully manicured ones, bowed low, and kissed her pale fingers. Then, straightening up slowly, he sought the clouded gray center of her eyes with his brilliant green gaze. The lingering connection between their eyes and his capacity to project a wonderful softness completely mesmerized Amalia. After Bronevsky released her hand and left without a word, the girl sat a long moment holding the kissed fingers to her mouth. When she looked up at the governess, her eyes were filled with tears. "He's beautiful," she whispered.

The governess, herself tight-throated by the romantic exchange between the couple, could only smile and murmur, "Dear, dear child."

"When will I see him again?"

"Oh, my dear, your father will have to arrange that."

"When?"

"Well, that's hard to say, but I'm sure he can arrange anything. And for you, little dove, I'm sure he will."

"Should I ask him?"

The governess thought quickly. "No, no. I'm sure he'll want it to be a surprise. You know how he loves to give you surprises."

"Yes, but when?"

"Be patient, my sweet. If I see things correctly, that beautiful gentleman and your father will make you a splendid surprise. But you must be patient, and don't let on that you know. Things will happen in their own time. Of that I'm sure. Just wait. It will happen. You'll see."

Father and daughter, accompanied by a large retinue of servants, arrived at their retreat in the Julian Alps on a mild autumn day. Each evening after settling in, the two sat on the terrace and watched mute swans glide over the ice-green water. In the mornings they breakfasted in a yellow-tiled garden room ornamented with white trellised arches interwoven with tropical vines. Before lunch, they walked along the lake on paths which ran through upland meadows that had belonged to the Enerde clan for over a century. They talked always of minor matters. That is, Melchior talked and Amalia agreed. Would she like to see Geneva? Rome? Perhaps even London? Amalia thought that they would all be nice. Melchior smiled. Of course, they *could* go to the house in Bavaria. She agreed again. He felt elated: hadn't she always enjoyed the carousel of all white horses? Yes, she had.

As one idyllic day melded into the next, Enerde began to feel secure again. He had fled the plague and won. In another week or two, he would explain to her that the governess who had been called "home" to France at the death of a near relative was unable to return because of other commitments. He thought it best not to tell her the truth, lest its telling should bring the tearoom incident back into the foreground.

In late October when the rains were suddenly cold and the trees dropped red leaves, they returned to Vienna with Melchior in high spirits. He was looking forward to the holidays, to buying the gifts he was planning for Amalia. He wanted to make her a gift of something unusual, something that would raise her perception of who she was. He had come to believe that perhaps he had kept her too much to himself. In a flash, it came to him that he would give her a party. "A ball," he said aloud, ignoring completely the past failures of parties arranged for the shy girl. "Yes, a great ball! A splendid ball! A magnificent gown . . . and . . . and for her wonderful surprise—a diamond tiara. Yes, yes. A diamond tiara. A crown for my princess. And all shown off at a splendid ball. Yes, that is the answer." The house had not seen a ball since . . . since Dorothea. For no logical reason he could think of, the long-dead woman was of late frequently on his mind. On some nights she seemed to hover near him in the dark as he tried to sleep, her musical laughter low and close as voices in a dream. If he sensed omens in such visitations, he dismissed them quickly, fired as he was by the glow of his own plans and the certainty that Amalia had forgotten the Russian. And even if something—something—like the man's calling card might nudge the memory back upon her, a bright, blazing ball would certainly char away a mere scrap of paper in a hurry. But the Russian was really of no importance: there was no way he could make his presence known to her again. What really mattered now was bringing her out of her cocoonlike slumber and making her drink the wine of awareness. He thought in those terms, particularly whenever he saw her with her eyes fixed on nothing particular, not even the vacant space in front of her, so that she would not have seen anything passing into it either. At times, he got the disquieting notion that in her own docile, gentle way, she was waiting for something, or someone, actually biding her time through the long, rain-filled hours in patient and unsullen listening as though she knew someone would come to her. The helpless fury he felt when he saw her inert folded hands and nearby the ever-present abandoned book of French verse, would throw him into a kind of fever which invariably made him rush to check on the plans for the pending party. "Well, Rätzel, how's it going?" Used to his old friend's melancholy face, Enerde did not see the deeper, darker concern in his eyes of late.

"All progresses well. No one's declined to attend as yet."

"No reason they should."

"No, but it makes perhaps too many."

"Nonsense. It's time the world saw her."

"Still, it's a large group, and with her natural timidity . . ."

"This will bring her completely out of it. Certainly you've seen the beginnings of change in her. You saw how she was at the last fitting, quite jolly. Color in her cheeks. And her appetite is better. I know this is just the thing."

Rätzel nodded and moved on to other subjects: the positioning of the orchestra, the ordering of more flowers from Italy, the decision to give music boxes as favors to the ladies. Rätzel waited a moment longer as Enerde, in his high good spirits, talked on of a trip for himself and his daughter in the spring. "When it's warmer; I'll take her then. A glorious holiday: Berlin, Paris, London, even New York if the mood strikes us. She's ready for it. I feel it. You'll see. This ball will show her the possibilities there are for . . . for pleasure, for enjoying life more. I'm sorry now I didn't think of it before."

"She may not have been ready for it before."

"Then you agree she's ready for it now?"

[28]

These curious circular discussions always ended in Rätzel's discomfort. He did not wish to make his friend doubt, knowing as he did how much pain Enerde suffered in doubting his child's normalcy; at the same time, he felt an uneasy apprehension for the shy girl and privately wished that the party were postponed until her eighteenth birthday. Still, he nodded to his friend's question, knowing that the plans had already gone too far for them to turn back now. But the thing that so cheered Enerde was exactly what disturbed Rätzel: the girl's interest in the coming celebration. Knowing her shyness and her past indifference toward any kind of social gathering, he could not imagine the reason for her sudden interest, her "jolliness" as Melchior had called her new behavior, which Rätzel would not have described in quite the same way. What he saw in the previous week was a girl who appeared not to be jolly or even excited over the coming event, but rather to be balancing on the edge of hysteria. The two women working on the dress chided her gently with soft laughter and pulpy words, speaking through the pins sticking from their mouths, "to stand still." But what the women and Melchior saw in Amalia's trembling—youthful anticipation—appeared to Rätzel to be a form of desperation. She seemed to him to wish to say something, but held back out of some deeply private reason of her own. In her usually placid gray eyes he saw a fluttering of distraction, a beating of nervous wings that folded into stillness after a few moments as quickly as they had become turbulent. He wondered if he shouldn't talk to the girl and draw her out the next time he found her alone. Perhaps there was some way he could settle whatever fears she had; yet, fear was not precisely what he saw in the dark quivering centers of her eyes. Nor could he name what he did see. If, indeed, it was desperation, it was of a peculiar sort, for it did not seem to make her unhappy. Melchior was right in that respect; the girl showed moments of gaiety, but they were abrupt, brief, and to Rätzel, frantic. However, the days were suddenly filled with countless details and the opportunity to sound out Amalia was lost to Rätzel in the bustle and commotion of the final preparation for the ball.

The celebration took place a few days before Christmas, the heady odor of hothouse flowers permeating the galleries and sitting rooms with a somewhat unnatural aura, considering the time of year. Rätzel, walking through the halls on the morning of the party, wished now that he had persisted in his plan to decorate the rooms only with fir in keeping with the Christmas holidays. But Melchior wanted rather to avoid the holiday's intrusion on the ball; it was after all his daughter who was to be the center of everything, he pointedly retorted to Rätzel's suggestion. All else seemed to be in perfect order. Dancing was to be limited to the large reception hall after the guests passed through the octagonal room which had been suitably arranged for the company's formal meeting with Amalia and Melchior. Father and daughter, with Rätzel playing the role of an arriving guest, had gone through the motions of a rehearsal for this event the preceding evening. As Rätzel took the girl's delicately outstretched hand and kissed it, he again had the notion that she was wavering under the inability to bring forth some desperate words. He raised his eyebrows in a questioning gaze, but in that very moment her decision to speak seemed to fail her, and even as Rätzel watched, the agitated center in her eyes closed and the bland gray cloud returned to them. He quickly made a charming remark on her gown and told her that she was an expert at welcoming guests and that this was no mean talent, and on and on, ending with an ancient joke about the empress who drank out of her finger bowl. But it was Melchior who laughed. Amalia smiled nervously.

Now, with the great day finally at hand, Rätzel's uneasiness over the girl's silent agitation increased. Twice he asked the women attending to Amalia's dressing as to her state of mind.

"Splendid," said one of them. "She is tremendously excited. Her eyes are absolutely afire with anticipation. And she looks more beautiful than we've ever seen her. Her cheeks are red as apples. It's all wonderful. Absolutely wonderful." Rätzel nodded and turned away, worried about the "fire" in the girl's eyes. He had seen that fire and wished he understood it. For the rest of the afternoon he wandered from room to room checking details, giving last-minute instructions to the servants. For a time he strolled about the elaborate garden, free now of all fallen leaves and autumn's last debris. The twilight sky drooped with rain clouds. Under a stand of naked white birches he stopped and for a time looked back at the house, musing over the old sorrow of the first Amalia's death. "Damn it, it's a mistake!" he heard himself say harshly, and returned quickly to the mansion, feeling in his very bones that something was wrong, that both he and Melchior had overlooked something, something that was upsetting the girl. Yet he could not deny that Amalia, even in her state of distraction, was feverishly awaiting this celebration.

Minutes before the first guest arrived, Melchior and Amalia descended the great staircase, the girl's hand resting on her father's outstretched arm. Below, in the foyer, the lined-up servants clapped and smiled, the women murmuring over the exquisite evening dress of white tulle embroidered with opalescent beads. Rätzel handed the royal-blue box that contained the tiara to Enerde as they entered the brilliant octagonal drawing room. He saw Melchior smile broadly and give him just a shade of a wink as if to say, "You see now that it's already a success. She's perfectly composed." And it was true: Rätzel saw that the girl was calm. He began to feel more at ease as he watched Melchior take the diamond crown and place it on the girl's beautifully coiffed head, beautiful even if the hairstyle did look somewhat like a fashion from the turn of the century. "And that, my dearest love, completes the picture." At that moment the first of the guests was announced, and Rätzel moved to one of the side doorways from which he could watch the procession of richly dressed people brought into the domed room.

Within minutes Rätzel saw that something was amiss, for although Amalia held out her hand to each guest exactly as they had rehearsed, she seemed to be totally indifferent to the person presented to her, giving each face no more than a hurried glance, so that before she even withdrew her captive hand she was already looking at the next person about to be presented. "Say a few words, my dear, to each person," whispered Melchior, not yet alarmed at the speed with which the girl abandoned each face as it came before her. Rätzel, looking for all the world like a guard of royalty as he moved closer to this clustering up of the visitors, saw at once that she was looking for someone. "Slower, dearest," whispered Melchior into her hair.

"Much slower. Tell each person that you are happy at meeting him. As we rehearsed, my love. As we rehearsed."

But Amalia seemed not to hear him. She continued to give her hand to whatever gentleman wished to kiss it, and she did not acknowledge the mild greetings of the women at all. Twice, Melchior pressed her shoulder gently as he brought his arm around her, making some comment to the persons before them that his lovely daughter was indeed the pride of his life. An effusion of compliments poured forth from all. But Rätzel, watching with bad foreboding, saw that curiosity followed by confusion dominated the expressions of the guests. Fortunately the orchestra began playing and trays of champagne were being circulated. The main rooms filled up quickly as the hosts received the last trickle of announced guests. Then there occurred a pause when no one new was brought into the room. Amalia leaned toward the archway as though to look around its curve, her eyes still searching, dodging people who passed in her line of vision. Her father, by now perplexed, took the girl's hand in order to lead her to the large reception hall. "Come, my dear."

"But, Father, where is he?" she cried, holding back.

"Where is who, my love?"

"The man. The man. My wonderful surprise."

Melchior blanched. "But, my love, you are wearing your surprise."

"What surprise?"

"The tiara, my angel."

Amalia, breathing heavily until now, didn't breathe at all for a moment; then with a sharp release of her breath she cried, "The tiara?"

"Yes, the tiara," said Melchior, looking nervously away from the girl for an instant. They were not quite alone. Several couples seemed to be waiting about, their smiles uncertain.

"I don't want a tiara," cried Amalia, tearing the jeweled crown from her hair. "I don't want a tiara. I want . . . I want . . . " She began gasping, tears streaming down her face. "I want . . . I want him."

There was no doubt in Rätzel's mind as to whom Amalia was referring, and he knew there was no doubt in Melchior's either, although he heard Enerde ask in a surprised voice, "Who, my love?"

"Him. Him. Him," cried the girl, her face contorted with disappointment, her hands mauling the diamond crown distractedly as though she were pulling at a mere handkerchief. The guests still in the room pretended to be engaged with each other's presence, although Rätzel knew it was all sham. Their glittering glances and extravagantly casual conversation offended him more than the girl's deplorable outburst. Without a word to Enerde, Rätzel took the tiara from Amalia, and grasping her hand firmly, drew her out of the room, away from the party, which he knew could and would go on pleasantly and decorously without the girl's presence. Enerde would see to that. And certainly no one would make any indecorous comment, at least not within their host's hearing. He knew, too, that later this lewd town would speculate on the girl's words. But that hardly mattered now: the future was clear. Rätzel, leading the weeping girl to one of the small private sitting rooms in the informal wing of the house, saw that the Russian suitor whom Melchior hated without ever having met was already an undeniable, intimate part of their lives.

4

Melchior Enerde sent his detectives across Europe in search of information on Bronevsky, particularly information that would discredit him in the eyes of a young girl, not merely make her doubt, for she surely had not the experience of doubting someone's veracity or motive and certainly not this suitor's, since she had yet to actually meet him; and clearly with her innocence and naiveté once she did meet him—should such a travesty take place—she would believe whatever he told her. No, something else was needed, something ugly that would be revolting to her. Enerde hoped the Russian drank heavily, had disgusting personal habits, kept a mistress. But the detectives discovered that Bronevsky only kept a horse which he rode daily and well. He was also an expert with the foil and the pistol and he had the added audacity to ski proficiently. His manners were refined and urbane. The detectives could find neither mistresses nor illegitimate children. When the first reports came back to Enerde, he was enraged at the man's impeccable credentials: Bronevsky was educated in Paris and Berlin. He learned both these cities' languages before he spoke Russian. He excelled in his studies in his student days, but never formally used his education. "You mean he never worked a day in his life," roared Melchior at the detective.

"As far as we can ascertain, no. But he did remain with his aged, exiled father in Paris until the old man died."

"So what does that prove?"

The detective shrugged. "He must have had opportunities to marry well. The man has an extraordinary . . . brilliant appearance."

"Extraordinary? Brilliant? You mean he loves his mirror."

"Perhaps, but I've not met him, only watched from a distance. In public he's aloof and withdrawn."

"You mean arrogant."

"I couldn't say, sir."

"Well, I could, and I don't have to meet him to know that, or watch him from a distance, either. I see the whole rotten scheme. He means to have my daughter. My daughter! The bastard."

"*That* he's not, sir. His title is inherited quite legitimately."

"That's no value! What good is a Russian title? What good is a Russian?"

"He's just been taken on for quite an important position by Mundt Shipping. Mundt apparently sees something in him."

"So I've heard. That stinks too. Mundt has no principles. Why has he

[32]

been supporting a bankrupt Russian? I'd like to have the answer to that. It's not like Mundt to do something for nothing. What does he get from the Russian?"

"From our inquiries, we know Bronevsky has been taken into the firm as some sort of consultant. His duties are a bit vague in that area, although they say he has a keen business sense."

"If he had a keen business sense, he wouldn't be broke. Bah. It's all humbug. Mundt's always been jealous of me. They all are. It wouldn't surprise me if Mundt put the Russian up to this. Wouldn't surprise me at all."

But, of course, this *would* have surprised Enerde. He did not believe Mundt or any other businessman would go through an elaborate scheme of this nature merely to create discomfort for one of their own kind. That would smack too much of an expensive practical joke, and Melchior knew that these men whom he understood only too well would enter into a joke only if it did not cost them anything or if they could benefit from it. Mundt, he reasoned, must be gaining something from his treatment of Bronevsky: feting him around town, introducing him to his own family and friends, presenting him for membership in his club; all this had to be paid for. But with what and why? Melchior did not believe Mundt's own words for a single minute. "Yes, yes, he's a man of vast business acumen. Wouldn't have thought it, but he's just what we need. Put everyone on their toes. Marvelous mind."

Enerde had searched Mundt's face sharply, looking for a reason for the lie. But the bulging jowls and mean merry eyes gave away nothing. Enerde knew that Mundt's business was solid, although like himself, the man had no sons to inherit it. Was he buying a husband for one of his four fat daughters? No, even though the girls were not much to look at, he wouldn't buy a powerless, penniless Russian. Still, one or another of the Mundt daughters was sometimes seen in Bronevsky's company. This rather amused Melchior. But when Amalia discovered it through two chattering servant women one winter morning soon after the party, she fell into a paroxysm of hysterical weeping that brought the doctors running and turned Enerde into a desperate man. He decided on an interview with the Russian.

"Summon him," said Rätzel when Melchior wondered aloud what might be the best way to meet the Russian.

"No, no. I want to watch him first and I don't intend to give away my position."

"He knows your position."

"How could he?"

"How could he *not* after the party?"

"Have you heard anything?"

"I don't have to hear it. I know it's out there; the fact is, your daughter wants the Russian and everyone knows it." He hesitated and sighed. "Summon him."

The two men finally met at an exclusive hunting lodge where the Russian was the guest of another blueblood also distantly related to the old Hapsburgs and a brother officer of Melchior's in a long-forgotten war. The carefully contrived meeting fooled no one, least of all Bronevsky, who played his role with meticulous attention to detail: he never forgot for an instant that the meeting was supposed to be coincidental and that his past had been carefully investigated. And now that he knew he had won, knew that his long search and his patient pursuit were about to be rewarded, he felt he could afford to be humble. He divined that this particular father, from what he had gleaned of the family's history, would deny his daughter nothing. Still, he had ensured even that certainty with the appearance of acceptance by Enerde's class—men like Mundt. Upon arriving in Vienna he had waited for months at the various hotel tearooms where mothers and governesses were known to take the wealthy daughters of the upper-class merchants whose generations of old money made them, in their view of things, almost aristocrats. Not in Bronevsky's view; he knew them for the smug, cliquish, bigoted burghers they were. No group worked more diligently at keeping the lower classes in their place or more vigorously at cultivating the friendship of the titled idle. But he needed them; they would lead him to a nobler match. It was in just such a beferned public parlor that he first heard of the fantastically wealthy Amalia Enerde. Not that he heard anything kind about her or for that matter unkind; it was the tight tone of the woman talking that caught his ear and jarred his imagination. "She's a mild-looking little thing and not at all brilliant, but with that money she could get a prince . . . and probably will, some chinless wonder, no doubt. My son, a splendid boy as you know, couldn't even get an introduction." The tense skin around the woman's mouth told the eavesdropping Bronevsky that if the lady wasn't tasting bile she had at least bitten into sour grapes. He located the Enerde mansion one bright summer morning and waited five more weeks before he saw the girl leave it for her first outing with the French governess. Stalking them was ridiculously easy and making the contact amusing although unchallenging. But by then he needed a base to work from and a sponsor who would sweeten the air around the father. He met Mundt at the riding park where both their horses were stabled. Buying the horse had put Bronevsky further in debt, but he needed the setting, the aura of primitive heat that appeals to certain sensual men. His careful shopping had rewarded him with the shipbuilder. Bronevsky was not so obvious as to admire Mundt's horse: he offered to buy it, knowing that Mundt would turn him down, but knowing, too, that the man would be curious as to exactly what the offered price might be. They talked around the edge of the subject as they watched grooms work on the animals late one afternoon. "I might consider it if the price appealed to me," said Mundt, tapping his crop against his boot.

"The price," said Bronevsky, after a long hesitation, "should not be reckoned in money. A man's favorite mount is a value beyond that kind of exchange."

"True. True," said Mundt earnestly, trying to hide his curiosity by stifling a yawn. They dropped the subject.

A week went by before Bronevsky returned to ride his horse, during which time he heard each day from one of the grooms, to whom he passed a comfortable sum of borrowed money, that Mundt was coming oftener to the stable and that twice he'd asked after Bronevsky's riding hours. When they met again, Mundt asked him if he had purchased another horse. Bronevsky told him not yet, but that there was another animal he was considering. "Frankly, I'd like to make an exchange, but the fellow doesn't deserve my price. He's not up to appreciating it, no matter how fine his animal."

"You want to exchange horses?"

"No. No. I'd not sell my mount. I've an heirloom in mind, but it's not something just anyone deserves. It's quite unique, you see, and should belong only to an extraordinary man whose scruples would never permit him to show it to a lady." Bronevsky sighed as he pretended to ignore Mundt's glittering gaze. "There are not many such men about. One has to be particularly careful in these times of moral degeneration."

The shipmaker nodded. "A painting, you say?"

"No, not a painting."

Again there was a languid pause. "Perhaps I can help you out. I understand you only recently arrived in Austria, but my family's been here forever, and I assure you I know everyone. I'd be willing to help you see it's properly placed. I, myself, know a little of the sculptor's art—having studied it once as a youth. . . ."

"It's not precisely a sculpture," said Bronevsky, frowning pensively, "but your training might still serve, if you'd like to take a look at it and if you're sure it's no trouble. . . ."

"Trouble? Nonsense, my boy, I'd be delighted to help." He clapped Bronevsky on the back.

"Well, if you're sure it's not an inconvenience . . ."

They agreed to meet at Bronevsky's lodgings the next day at eleven. At present the item, said Bronevsky to Mundt's concern for its safety, was judiciously stored in a bank vault.

On the following morning when they met, Mundt, fairly exuding a prurient anticipation, was all eagerness to get on to the business of aiding his "new young friend." But Bronevsky stalled, ordered tea, paced the floor in butter-yellow boots. "You realize that there was a time when such rooms as I have here would have been barely adequate for my valet."

"Yes, yes. I can well imagine."

"If I had been older when my country passed through its great crisis; if in fact I had been in Moscow rather than Paris, even as young as I was, you can guess I would have fought to the death to free my country from those criminals." Bronevsky smacked his fist into his open hand.

"My dear boy, I'm sure you would have. You strike me as a man of fierce determination and responsibility. I knew it when I first clapped eyes on you. 'There,' I said, 'goes a man of heroic will,' and I thought then, 'All he needs is a little opportunity.' "

Bronevsky, standing in the middle of his genteelly shabby sitting room, knew that his guest had already absorbed the situation. It was time to bait the hook. From a polished wooden box on the table he brought forth a second box covered in red enamel and gold scrollwork. This he held gingerly for a moment in both hands, as if it needed defusing. "You understand," he began, "that I do not part with this casually. It must only become the possession of a gentleman."

"Of course, of course," said Mundt, rising rapidly. Bronevsky held the box in one hand and raised the lid: inside, a large cobalt-blue egg sat in a

[35]

white mink bed. He touched a discreet hinge and the shell opened at mid-point to reveal not a bouquet of jade and quartz roses with warbling bird or a royal carmine carriage whose wheels revolved, but a naked nymph about to be possessed by a satyr whose impressive organ hovering between the spread pearl thighs of the reclining girl was a ruby red.

Mundt took the jeweled egg from Bronevsky with quivering hands. "There's a spring at the bottom," said Bronevsky mildly. "You can barely feel it with your finger. It turns a key that sets the thing in motion." He watched Mundt's eyes as the key clicked into place.

Enerde's detectives had no difficulty in discovering that an arrangement of some kind had been made between Mundt and Bronevsky, and this they reported to their employer. "What good is this?" shouted Enerde, throwing the folder down on the table. "I could have got this from common rumor. Why? That's the question. You've found out nothing. He's never worked in his life. He's lived off some hoarded foreign currency and a few family trinkets. When he ran through those, he got hired by an established legitimate firm. . . . Why?"

The detectives didn't know. The meeting at the hunting lodge began with some awkward introductions, awkward because Enerde twice asked the Russian to repeat his name, as though he had never heard it before. Bronevsky went through the charade soberly and with quiet dignity, refusing to acknowledge in any way Enerde's unveiled contempt for him. "What precisely brings you to Vienna?" was Melchior's first question after the insulting introduction.

"It was my father's last advice."

"Your father advised you to visit Vienna?"

"My father advised me to settle in Vienna."

"Really? And why did he advise that?"

"He believed Vienna to be the most cultured, the most modern, and yet the most classical of all Europe's cities."

"Did he?" The acid in Melchior's tone was neutralized by the oil in Bronevsky's.

"Yes. Further, he was convinced that Austria held the last great stronghold of an independent aristocratic society." There was a delicious silence after this statement, as though the several men listening to Bronevsky were actually tasting this flattery as they might swirl about in their mouths a delectable brandy.

"You know something of our history, do you?" asked Melchior.

Fed the right question, much to Enerde's too-late regret, Bronevsky launched into a discussion of Austrian leaders dating back to 976 with the first Babenbergs. Bronevsky, of course, knew of the vulgarly excessive esteem with which the aristocracy viewed itself. "Unlike other aristocratic societies—say, those of France and Germany—Austria has never demeaned its standards, never fused with lower elements. In short, it has never fallen from grace, regardless of the external vicissitudes wreaked upon it, which, by the way, have diluted less noble societies, like, say, those of the French and the Germans. One feels that if the aristocracy is to survive anywhere, it will survive here, and . . ."

[36]

"Yes, yes. Well, that's a known fact. Hardly something new." Melchior hesitated from picking up another subject for fear the Russian would continue to make a good impression. Melchior knew he was losing ground and this made him hate the Russian even more. The old sense of disaster swept back over him like a garish light suddenly focused on him. He ended the meeting abruptly when he thought he detected a smirk about the Russian's mouth and a victorious gleam in his eye, although the man never ceased being respectful and pleasantly confident. Melchior raced home only to sit in the oncoming dark and feel tears on his cheeks. From the beginning he knew he was doomed: taking Amalia away, giving the party, hiring the detectives—all had been useless and he knew in his soul even as he took those measures that they were useless, that all was lost. He had only deluded himself. When Rätzel found him sitting in his unlighted study, he looked up at his friend with red eyes. "What shall I do, Rätzel?" he whispered. "What shall I do?"

Rätzel spoke kindly, although the words were harsh. "You have already decided. Asking is past." And then even his tone turned harsh. "But since you intend to take the man in, to give him to her for a husband, you must intend also to give him a decent chance. Not only for her sake and his, but also for yours."

"I will be a laughingstock."

"Not if it's successful. And that success depends a great deal upon you."

On the day of the marriage, Bronevsky had a messenger deliver a package directly to the shipping magnate A. Mundt, with an unsigned note, "As per our agreement."

From the beginning, Pavel Stephanovitch Bronevsky resolved not only to be a good husband to the gentle Amalia, but also to become an acceptable son-in-law to her father. It was in his mind that he would work diligently and happily at whatever tasks Enerde set before him. He told himself earnestly that once taken into the family and, therefore, the firm, he would not at all object to starting in a relatively low position—not too low, of course. Once established, he would prove himself hardworking, resolute, creative. At age thirty-two, he knew how fantastically his luck had changed. Behind him lay ten years of hideous genteel squalor; at least that is how he viewed the anxious pretense to wealth, the false face, the insubstantial answers to the questions of curious commoners whose very queries told him they already knew his circumstances. For years he had been selling off family heirlooms and sundry antiques from a once richly furnished house in Paris—now also lost. He had used his last valuable trinket to secure not so much an introduction into Viennese society as to leave a good impression in the mind of the man whose daughter he intended to marry. It was not until the marriage arrangements were made, in the presence of no fewer than three of Enerde's lawyers, that Bronevsky realized they (the lawyers and Enerde) believed he truly was in the employ of A. Mundt Shipping.

"Due to the extreme youth of Miss Enerde, our client will not permit the marriage unless it is agreed that she will continue to live at her father's residence." A waiting pause had filled the room, as if the three lawyers and Enerde expected a protest. Bronevsky heard the controlled silence and hesitated for a long moment, finally releasing his breath and moving into a slow nod. "Yes, I'll agree to that," he said with measured calm as though he were conceding an important condition. For a fleeting instant he wanted to roar with laughter. Of course they would live in the mansion. Where did they expect him to live? And then like a tiny hook in his brain, a strange desire pulled at him; he actually wished he did have a position with A. Mundt. However, since his arrangement with the shipping magnate was of quite a different sort and one that would end on the day of the marriage, he could not very well correct Enerde's false impression. Bronevsky realized that he would have to think up some acceptable lie for the reason of his leaving the shipping business into which he had only so recently immersed himself. It was clear to him that Enerde believed he was earning a living and would continue to do so and, therefore, be able to support his bride in an establishment of their own—hence the condition that she live at home. He marveled at this discovery, but more than that he marveled at his own unawareness of the fact that he was working from a position of power, a position of options: in short, he could have made some demands of his own. But because he wanted more than anything to have his future father-in-law accept him—even like him—he made no demands at all and agreed to everything.

On the day of the wedding, he moved his two trunks into the Enerde mansion, still stunned at his extraordinary good luck at finally being freed from the specter of pauperism. He saw his life as finally beginning, saw his future spread out before him as a scene in a dream in which he walked upon a golden road leading straight to the crown of a peak where a pearled palace waited, all the doors opening for him untouched as he neared them. Gone was the agonizing fear of poverty, the sordid pretensions and deceptions, gone the dark nights in which he was alone with the haunting awareness that his own life was fading away before his very eyes, actually getting thinner and thinner until it was only a sort of mist through which he saw his own transparent body drifting down a street littered with fallen beggars.

More than anything, Bronevsky hated the position of professional exile. Only too well did he know the pitiful picture Russian nobility presented to the other aristocracies: the smug, complacent English; the ironical French; and worse of all, the mocking Germans with their Olympian arrogance. He had lived in the pale of all their scorn, heard himself lament his lost homeland in the presence of their polite, false sympathy. Yet how could he fault *their* want of concern when he himself had always resented his country's cultural backwardness, its stolid bovine peasants, its fat priests, its outhouses. And his image of himself, which he knew was also the foreigner's image of the Russian aristocracy in exile—the rootless, aimless, superficial man mentally arrested in the previous century—was an image he wanted desperately to change. And as much as he loathed men like A. Mundt, he knew he had to join them to become effective, and this he had temporarily done. From that position he had achieved his goal: entrance into the Enerde family. Yes, he would be a good husband: considerate, attentive, loving, even faithful. And he would be a good son-in-law, do whatever Enerde expected of him. He was less sure of these duties than he was of the ones he was to perform as a husband. But he would learn, and what he dreamed of now was of a day in the future when Enerde would look at him with pride as he introduced him to his most intimate friends. Never in his life had he so longed for camaraderie with another man, for friendship, for trust, for familial love.

On his private balcony, he looked over the garden park, over the candling chestnut trees, the long beds of brilliant begonias bordering paths that led to a half-dozen different fountains. He had been married an hour. In the suite adjoining his, the bride was dressing for the wedding breakfast. Below, the guests were collecting in the drawing room. The open air expanded with the boudoir scent of lilacs; scarlet birds sang sweetly in the trees; God was in the blue of the morning sky. All the omens were kind, beneficent. He returned to his sitting room just as the clock over the mantel chimed eleven. It was a seventeenth-century clock from which a naked cherub, blowing a little trumpet, popped out of the works and marked the quarter time, followed ultimately by the skeleton Death with his scythe to hack away the hours. Bronevsky smiled at its charm, straightened the white flower in his lapel, and went to breakfast.

It had been agreed at the meeting with the lawyers that there would be no immediate honeymoon trip. Enerde gave the girl's extreme shyness and fragility as the reason that she should remain in a familiar and comforting environment at the time of her marriage, since that event was already change enough for anyone with a sensitive, high-strung nature. Bronevsky couldn't agree more. He was, therefore, surprised when, upon agreeing with his future father-in-law on this matter, he saw a whiplash of white-hot anger pass over the man's face. For a few seconds he thought Enerde had mis-understood him, so he hurriedly tried to reinforce his answer: "Familiar surroundings and the company of those she loves most will make the change more acceptable . . . more agreeable . . . more—"

Enerde stopped him with a wave of his hand and turned to one of the lawyers. "Yes, yes. Well, let's proceed now that that's decided. Brückner," he continued, peering under his fiercely overhanging eyebrows at the youngest of the lawyers, "what was that other point you felt should be made?"

Brückner, a sandy-haired, sandy-skinned man, a thirty-year-old who looked forty, picked up one of the documents and while gazing at it through wire-rimmed glasses, spoke to Enerde without looking at Bronevsky at all. "The hiring and dismissing of servants, sir. This matter shall remain entirely in Mr. Rätzel's capable hands, and, of course, yours, sir, should the occasion and condition demand it." Bronevsky nodded politely, although no one spoke to him. And in this way was everything decided. There was no mention of money.

There was another matter of some importance that was brought to Bronevsky's attention before the marriage, although not by the lawyers. It was Berthold Frichter, who paid him a visit at his lodgings a week before the wedding. The doctor, all friendly and rather too full of good cheer, did not seem to have anything particular to talk about at first, at least not anything particular that Bronevsky could make out. The man accepted a brandy and smoked his cigar as if he were an old friend and quite used to Bronevsky's faded quarters. First he talked casually of some Enerde history. "My father was their family physician for forty years. Knew them all. Your fiancée's grandmother, Enerde's own mother . . . died in childbirth, you know." Bronevsky nodded, wondering why the physician had come. The doctor hurried on, warming his drink with his fat hands in a slow distracting way that made Bronevsky uncomfortable. "I was there . . . at the time of Amalia's mother's death. Terrible. Terrible. A most beautiful young girl. Seventeen. He fears over that."

"Over that?"

"Well, yes. Don't you see that he might fear that? His mother died in childbirth; his wife died in childbirth. He's naturally concerned about his daughter."

"Certainly only a coincidence," said Bronevsky, looking over his brandy glass at the suddenly serious doctor.

"Not entirely . . . at least not when you count in the others."

"The others?"

"There have never been any middle-aged Enerde women, none of them have ever reached thirty."

"To what do you attribute . . . ?"

"A certain weakness in the genes was my father's opinion."

"And yours?"

"Not that at all. No scientific evidence to back it up. I'm inclined to think those young brides were just a bit too young, and perhaps the men a bit too, well, how can I put this?" He took a long swallow of his drink and put the glass down as though he were trying to balance an egg on its end. "Can I be direct with you?"

Bronevsky was taken aback by the doctor's suddenly intimate tone, his air of confidentiality. "By all means."

"Enerde fears for the girl's delicacy. She has never known any roughness, any suddenness, anything uncouth or . . ."

"Good God, sir," said Bronevsky, leaning forward in his chair. "What do you take me for? Some coarse fellow from the Steppes? I am a gentleman. I am deeply aware of my fiancée's inexperience. Does her father think I am not capable of gentleness, tenderness? Is that why you came? Does he think I mean to force her in some vulgar way, subject her to . . . to brutishness . . . to . . . ?"

"No, no. We . . . he knows you are a gentleman. Never any doubt about that, which is why I can plainly talk to you of this particular little detail." He pulled at his cigar, examined the end of it, and proceeded to relight it. "I thought it advisable to perforate the hymenal membrane surgically . . . " He sucked the cigar again, coughed lightly, and spoke through a blue cloud of smoke. "Much better that way, no discomfort, no strain, none of the mess that sometimes occurs the first time. You can understand the value in performing this procedure through a medical method."

Bronevsky put on his bland mask which he had used for years to hide behind and leaned back in his chair. "Yes," he said, careful to avoid any interpretive inflection. "I can understand it."

"Well, that's all fine then. You obviously see the need for control."

Bronevsky nodded slowly, his expression unchanged. *In another time I would have shot this bastard for that word.*

The doctor chatted on, becoming jovial again. "You're a lucky man to become allied with such a family. The empress was a cousin, you know. Somewhat distant but still a cousin." He stood up, squashing out his cigar amid the cigarette ends in the ashtray. "Never tried those," he said, eyeing the cigarettes with a certain suspicion. "Can't have much of a kick in them. Not like a good cigar." He laughed. "Well, to everybody his own pleasures, I say. Especially when there's no harm in it to others, eh, my boy?"

Bronevsky's controlled face entered into the laughter as the doctor gave him a wink. "Quite right," he responded with that blandness that had served him now these long years and even more so these last few months. He watched the doctor descend the stairs and wave to him from the landing. For a time, Bronevsky sat in his half-darkened rooms and smoked steadily, staring through the stale cloud at the chair where the doctor with his disgusting smug tone had told him how to behave on his wedding night. *Control! How dare he!* But Bronevsky sighed and let his anger sink back into a part of his heart where he kept such things under careful containment. He knew exactly how such men dared: they had the money to dare, the power. They ruled the world with their money. He was a beggar beside them, and they knew it and this let them say anything and do anything without any more concern for how it touched others than the sea does beating against the naked land. Again he wished he had made a different agreement with Mundt for the egg. He could have asked for a real position with the firm instead of a sum of money and the lie that he was a member of A. Mundt Shipping. Why didn't he think of that when he had Mundt wetting his pants for the egg? That fat fool would have promised him anything. Why did he fail to look at other possibilities? Even as he thought of his own narrow view of the road ahead of him, a voice in his soul said: *Go! Leave Vienna! Take what's left of Mundt's money and get on a train. Never mind where; just go. Go now!*

But he did not go, although he was to remember this exact moment for years as one remembers and fixes inwardly forever the absolute instant when the wrong road was taken.

During the first days of his marriage, Bronevsky saw little of his father-in-law. He and Amalia seemed to have the enormous house to themselves, with the servants seeing to all their needs. Rätzel made contact with him at least once each day to ask if there were anything particular they might want. Amalia, radiant with the glow of good health and contentment, said they needed nothing at all. "Dear, dear Rätzel," she said, "how could we

[41]

want anything more? It's all so perfect." Bronevsky smiled at her youthful exuberance. He was fond of the girl and saw her adoration of him as the best singular piece of good luck that had ever come his way. With his learned patience, he bore up well under her effusive and constant pledges of eternal love. She was, however, a passive lover and expected him to take every initiative even to undressing her and carrying her naked from the couch to the bed, where she lay literally inert while he proceeded to caress her. He noted only a slight change in her breathing as he brought her to crisis. He knew she reached the pinnacle when he felt under his deft fingers the swelling labia, the rising clitoris, the richly wet vagina. He was astonished that she showed no other reaction, but lay inert with closed eyes, only her breath becoming perceptibly louder. He had known women to scream, weep, beg to be taken under his caress. Even when he finally used his mouth and sucked the tightened glands and reached with his tongue into the orifice, she showed no greater reaction. She never touched him except to kiss his mouth or bring her arms around his neck, and even this latter he had sometimes to do for her, actually picking up each arm and placing it over his shoulder. At times he wearied to the point of anger, but was careful to conceal these feelings. He tried to teach her, taking her hand and placing it on his genitals. She withdrew, not hurriedly, not even slowly: she simply withdrew her hand and returned her arms to her side or to the pillow on which her head rested. He tried to talk to her of the joys women could bestow upon men, but she seemed not to comprehend. "Oh, sweetest, dearest beloved, let's not speak of others. Let's speak of us. We are so perfect in our love. I wish for nothing more."

He despaired and lusted for the chambermaids who were neither pretty nor young. He imagined them trying to entice him. He imagined them lying in wait for him in empty rooms. He longed to have one surprise him in his bath, enter his room while he was dressing, and roughly press herself against him. He began to imagine that they wore no undergarments, that when they leaned over the sill to air out the eiderdowns they were actually attempting to allure him. He arranged for little opportunities for the maids to find him in his apartment, but each time they mumbled apologies and rushed away. The fancies for these women began to fade. He searched elsewhere. He wondered how he could arrange to use one of Enerde's big touring cars and go off by himself. However, he did not dwell on that plan long, since Amalia had dissolved into a river of tears when he suggested to her at the end of the second week that he would like to exercise his horse. He quickly consoled her with assurances that he could send a messenger to the stables to have one of the grooms take the animal out. After that he only suggested outings that would involve both of them: drives into the country, some musical evening at one of the opera houses, even a picnic in the woods about the city. But Amalia declined, always sweetly, always lovingly, always definitely. "My most precious darling, we'll have a picnic in the garden, under the birch trees, our own little woods with only the birds and flowers to join us." She rang for a servant and made her request for a picnic in a breathless, hurried way that quite charmed Bronevsky. But she would not leave the estate.

From the beginning he slept in her suite entirely, since she told him she was unable to remain alone. "I've never been alone. I wouldn't know how." She laughed lightly. "How beautiful you are when you look perplexed." She placed her fingers between his eyebrows to rub out the frown. He began to wait until she was asleep curled up against him like a silk-threaded cocoon on a branch, then, gently untwining her from him, he crept to his own rooms to sink into a chair and smoke cigarette after cigarette until the first hint of dawn turned the windows a dull purple and he returned to her bed. If he saw Enerde at all, the man only nodded to him curtly, said a word or two of greeting, and hurried on. Bronevsky wondered why he did not dine with them. He decided finally that Enerde was merely giving them the necessary privacy for the first weeks of marriage. But by the end of the third week, when Rätzel asked him one morning if there was anything particular he desired, Bronevsky spoke out quickly, for his bride was momentarily out of the room. "Yes. I want to start . . . I want to begin my position." He saw a question rise in Rätzel's face, but the older man said nothing. "I would like," continued Bronevsky, "to speak with my father-in-law."

Rätzel nodded. "Of course."

The meeting did not take place for another week; each day Rätzel informed Bronevsky that Enerde had pressing problems at one of the factories and would try to make time for him the next afternoon, but the next afternoon a similar answer would meet Bronevsky's query. On the eighth day, Bronevsky rose early, dressed quietly, and went in search of Rätzel. He found him drinking coffee with the cook in one of the pantries. "I wish a car today. I intend to speak to my wife's father."

The cook picked up his cup and vanished through a swinging door, but Rätzel continued to gaze at Bronevsky in a musing, contemplative manner that quickly angered the younger man. "Why do you stare at me? Get me a car."

"The chauffeur will take you wherever you wish," said Rätzel, rising.

"Good. I wish to be driven to my father-in-law's office."

"That's easily arranged, but Mr. Enerde is not at his office, he—"

"Then I shall be driven to wherever he is. I *will* talk to him *today*."

"If you will come with me, please . . ."

"With *you*? I don't understand this house. What is your position in this house? My wife says you are a friend of the family's. What is going on here? We never see anyone except the servants." Bronevsky hurried after Rätzel, who was striding from room to room.

"There *is* no one except the servants. Wait in here, please." They had stopped at the library door, a room of locked glass cases which Bronevsky had wandered into several times when he managed to free himself of his wife. Unfortunately, he had no key that would allow him to reach the books, and usually she was quick to find him. Standing in the room now in the early morning, he considered quite sanely breaking all the glass.

"Whatever you tell him, make sure it is accurate." Rätzel spoke from the doorway.

At Rätzel's voice Bronevsky turned sharply. "Accurate?"

"Tell him the truth," said Rätzel, meeting his eyes. "No matter what. Tell him the truth." And then he was gone.

[43]

A few minutes later Enerde strode in and closed the door behind him. Bronevsky was still standing staring at the locked cabinets as his father-in-law walked to a desk and sat behind it. He did not invite Bronevsky to sit. "Rätzel tells me you wish to drive somewhere."

"No. That is, I had wished it, but since you are here, there's no need. What I wish is to start my position with the firm."

"Why do you need to discuss this with me?"

Bronevsky could hear a remote hum inside his head and recognized the beginnings of a migraine. "Well . . . it's *your* firm."

"My firm?"

"Yes. I wish a position in your . . . in the firm."

Enerde jerked his head back as though something were swinging toward him. "It was my understanding that you were employed with Mundt Shipping."

"I let that go."

Melchior stroked his beard for a long moment, and it was this motion that convinced Bronevsky later that Enerde already knew the truth, but at that confrontation at that raw moment he did not know, could not know, what harm his lie would do him. "Why did you do that?"

Bronevsky looked at the question and half-laughed. "Why . . . " He could not bring himself to say: *because I am married to your daughter, because I expect you to treat me like a son-in-law and take me into the firm, and because I never worked for Mundt . . . that was all a fraud and a lie so that I would appear acceptable in your eyes instead of contemptible and worthless.* "I let that go because I preferred a position with . . . with Enerde Textiles."

Melchior took his watch out of his vest pocket and began slowly to wind it. "That is commendable, but at the moment, there is no position open." He pocketed his watch and rose.

"But I want to work," Bronevsky heard himself say in too high a voice, too plaintive a tone.

"Also commendable, but you should not burn your old bridge until the new one is built. But then, you are young and perhaps bridges are not so important. You shouldn't have much trouble finding a new position."

"But I need money. I need my own—"

"Well, if that's all, it's easily settled. I'll call my bank and arrange an allowance for you."

For perhaps a minute after he heard Enerde's footsteps vanish from the marble foyer floor, Bronevsky stared with blank horror at the door through which Melchior had left. Then with a cry, the cry of an animal with a paw crushed in a trap, he lunged toward the nearest of the glass cases and smashed his fists into the doors. Unmindful of his bleeding hands, he thrust them though a second set of the beveled glass doors. Before he could repeat the action, someone stopped him; a powerful grip held his wrists until his fists opened, the crisscross of cuts dripping brightly on the oriental carpet. Looking up through brimming eyes, Bronevsky made out Rätzel's sad-dog face. "You should have told him the truth. It's no good now."

6

In the days before Amalia's marriage, Melchior could console himself with only one abiding fact, which he held hidden and waiting in his deepest consciousness and of which he was absolutely positive: Bronevsky was not related to him. And it was perhaps this single comfort that gave him the courage to endure and control his hatred of the Russian. "She would have to marry sometime," Rätzel said to him on the eve of the wedding, "and I don't find Bronevsky malicious or base."

"Bah. I have only bought her another trinket. Isn't that what everyone is saying?"

"If you give him half a chance, he might surprise you."

"He won't surprise me!"

"At least he showed enough character to get himself hired into some sort of situation. The man's not afraid of work."

"I still don't believe that. He's a dandy. A fop. Men like that don't understand work. Tell me what he can do that he could not have been doing in the last ten years. Can you see him doing a day's honest work now? A consultant! Mundt's lying. I'm sure of it, but I don't know why. That doesn't mean I won't find out. Somewhere up ahead the truth will scratch at the door like a hungry dog."

Rätzel, too, believed that Mundt was lying. But what did that matter? What if Bronevsky and Mundt did make some arrangement between them? Mundt would not have involved himself in it for nothing, so Bronevsky must have had to pay him, and if not with money, then possibly some favor. That was their affair. The only thing that counted now was to make the best of the situation here—in the family. Bronevsky did not strike Rätzel as a stupid man. If he was good to the girl and showed himself to be a man of honor and decency, things would work out, and it was clear that the young man wanted things to work. In time Melchior would soften and if not actually come to love the Russian, which Rätzel knew would probably not happen, at least he could come to accept him. And after a grandchild or two . . . He sighed, knowing that in that direction lay both hope and horror.

Since Enerde had made sure there would be no immediate wedding trip, Rätzel saw to it that the two young people had a maximum of privacy during the first weeks of their marriage. He had no trouble convincing Enerde to allow them to dine alone for a time. Melchior spent most of his days at one or another of his factories snarling at his executives and his evenings at his club playing cards with what appeared to his fellow players to be a furious elaborate concentration on the game. Rätzel knew he was only trying to escape his own rage. For he alone understood how Melchior viewed the Russian: he had done him double damage—not only had the man robbed him of his child, he had also made him look foolish in the eyes of men whom he had always considered fools. It was already known that Bronevsky brought nothing to the great house except his fancy wardrobe, a pair of dueling pistols, and the cost of keeping his hungry horse. It was true that there was malicious talk of Enerde buying his child another mechanical toy, and the prevailing stories making the rounds in particularly vulgar language asked if the servants would be needed (as they were years before) to wind up the most recent acquisition or if Amalia could manage it alone.

Rätzel believed that it was up to Bronevsky to prove himself an honorable man at heart, and he believed the Russian would do this, could do this by exemplary behavior. When Bronevsky first spoke of wishing to speak to his father-in-law and made the slip about wanting to work, Rätzel knew at once there was no position at Mundt Shipping. He told Enerde only that the man wanted to speak with him, but Melchior quickly divined that something was amiss. He put Bronevsky off until he discovered—not from Mundt, but from one of Mundt's men who needed a rather large private loan—the crux of the agreement between Mundt and the Russian. That crux did not actually mention the lewd little egg: the Mundt employee said the object was a rare work of art for which the shipping magnate had been searching. The story did not surprise Enerde, who never believed the initial lie to begin with. Bronevsky, however, could still have saved himself had he known Enerde only a little better. Melchior was one of those men who practiced entrapment to determine a man's character. He frequently tested employees to see if they were telling the truth simply by asking them certain dangerous (to the employee) questions to which Enerde already knew the dangerous answers. His employees were soon wise to the device, so told the truth no matter how embarrassing or damning.

Bronevsky had failed the test.

When Rätzel told Melchior of the Russian's collision with the bookcase doors, Enerde laughed. "So, the peacock's feathers are finally ruffled. And will it survive?"

Rätzel, who each evening met with Enerde in his study before Melchior retired for the night, put down his brandy glass. "If you think to find any sweet revenge in the man's discovery that he is caught in a golden cage, remember who comes and goes in that cage with him."

"You suggest he would dare to hurt my daughter?" Melchior asked harshly.

"No. He would do her no harm. But if *he* is miserable, do not count on *her* being happy."

"He won't stay miserable long. He will come to wear his idleness like a comfortable old coat. Especially now that I fill the pockets."

"And will this make him virtuous?" asked Rätzel, looking hard at his friend.

"Virtuous? What a word for him, Rätzel. Was ever a liar virtuous? Does a right-minded man worm his way into the pure heart of a young girl through deceit and trickery? No, no, do not speak of virtue. He is a fraud and a cheat."

"And will your treatment make him better? Will cruelty cure him of it?"

"No more. I'll discuss it no more. He has made his bed . . ." Melchior, horrified at the adage he was about to use, turned from Rätzel's piercing eyes and left the room.

Within a month of her wedding, Amalia was pregnant, and the house took on a new aura, a certain density, a feeling of coming darkness that made people leave the lights on in unused rooms. Rätzel saw in Enerde's anxious eyes the old haunting dread of easy death arriving suddenly, striding in an unerringly direct line into his daughter's room, plucking up her life as he might some diaphanous garment covering her breasts and vanishing with it, leaving behind the lifeless clay meant for the grave. He seethed, swore, then rearranged his face and visited his child, gently asking after her health.

"Oh, Father, dearest Father. I am wonderful. I feel glorious."

Enerde noticed that she looked glorious, but still he was afraid. The first Amalia had felt glorious and when the time came she had died in minutes, looking into his face with a perplexed expression as though she were about to ask him something, something simple, something easy to answer. But before she could speak, she died, her eyes still open, her expression still asking, but the question dead on her lips.

Then, in her second month, Amalia began to suffer severe nausea, vomiting her breakfast in the morning and her dinner in the evening. She complained continually that the food was badly prepared, that it let off an unpleasant odor, that it was too hot, too bland, too acidic. The cook varied the meals constantly, prepared them with extraordinary care to their taste, their scent. He bought only the freshest vegetables and fruits, the finest meats. He made each dish a work of art, giving attention not merely to its taste but also to its color, its form on the platter or serving dish, its appearance under the dining-room chandelier. By then, Enerde was taking his dinner with the couple, generally ignoring Bronevsky, but chatting with Amalia or at least at her. Halfway through the meals she would begin to complain about the meats or one of the sauces and then with a sudden clapping of her hand to her mouth, she would rush from the room. Enerde quickly hurried after her, while Bronevsky stayed and finished the wine left in the carafe. Since he would not see either father or daughter again during the evening, he took to repairing to his own quarters with a bottle of brandy.

The doctors told Enerde that the vomiting would end during the fourth or fifth month. The cook complained to Rätzel that he was at his wits' end. "She has the maid bring her tea and cakes at least four times a day. Why doesn't that make her sick?"

"It probably does. Don't worry about it; another few weeks, she'll eat everything you put in front of her. Her mother was the same way. Only she never complained."

But Amalia continued to be sick morning and night through her seventh month. To her request for cakes, she added puddings, candies, jellies, jams, syrups. And because she seemed to be vomiting as much as she was eating, the doctors let her eat whatever she wanted. "The system knows itself," intoned Frichter. "I've never paid much attention to all those wild-eyed dietitians who harp on what to eat. I say, 'The system knows itself.' Let it decide what it needs." Amalia's sick mornings and evenings finally stopped and she was ravenous for everything—including the teas with cakes and puddings.

In the seventeenth winter of her life, she bore identical twin boys and lived. In Melchior's jubilance, he almost forgave Bronevsky for being a fraud, for being Russian, for being Bronevsky. The black-haired infants became Enerde's consuming delight. He spent hours with them, hurrying to the nursery morning and evening to watch the nurses bathe them or talk to the woman who breast-fed them, making sure she had no illness that might be passed on to the children. The wet nurse soon learned that a sneeze on her part had the grandfather running to the doctor for consultation. Each week she was subjected to a physical examination by Frichter, who told her that it was all purely routine and considering the amount of money she was receiving for her services, she should be rejoicing rather than complaining.

Enerde marveled at the perfection of the babies, at the black silk of their hair, the emerald green of their irises.

They were christened Paul and Günther, the grandfather and father each picking a name. Amalia was quickly well again, her cheeks rosy, her voice no longer petulant and complaining. Ten months and one week after the birth of the twins, she bore a third son, flaxen-haired and brown-eyed, whom Amalia named Melchior. Enerde was delighted with his namesake, but a little anxious for his daughter; he talked privately to Frichter. Yes, it was somewhat soon, said the doctor, but Amalia was surprisingly healthy for all her seeming fragility and she had suffered no nausea with the second pregnancy. Still Enerde pressed the doctor to warn Bronevsky that there should be no more children for at least two years. The doctor found Bronevsky in his private sitting room playing solitaire and warming a snifter of brandy against his forehead. It was eleven in the morning.

"Well, well, well," began the doctor. "A celebration is certainly in order. Three sons! By God, that's wonderful. Yes, I will join you in a little libation." Bronevsky had held the glass up to him in a wordless gesture as old as civilization. The doctor continued to gush after he was seated and sipping the brandy. "Our little mother is doing just fine. Just fine. And you know, of course, how the grandfather feels. Wonderful! Wonderful! I shiver when I think back on the day his wife died. He thought his life was over. Said as much. He was inconsolable. We were afraid he might do himself in. It was his daughter that saved him. I put that sweet babe into his arms myself and watched the light of life come back into his eyes. You can't imagine what she meant to him." The doctor made the motion of brushing a tear from his eye. "You see, he had no one else . . . only that dear babe. And here she's given him *three* sons."

"Grandsons," said Bronevsky softly.

"Yes, yes, of course. Grandsons. And don't think that *that* grandfather doesn't appreciate . . ." The doctor didn't seem to know quite where to go from there. He took a long gulp of brandy and more or less pulled himself out of the hole. "Appreciative. That's what he is. Appreciative. Deeply, *deeply* appreciative." The doctor looked away from his glass just long enough to see the smile on Bronevsky's face and realize at the next instant that it was not a smile at all. He had seen such grins on the faces of men who were sick of living, men incapable of feeling joy, knowing it was forever beyond them and yet who were bereft of the courage to end their miserable lives. The hanging one-sided smile lasted only briefly, the man's extraordinary stone-chiseled mouth returning to its perfect shape in a few seconds. The doctor blundered on. "Well, as I was saying: three sons! Not many men are so lucky as to get, haha, I should say beget, haha, three sons, I say, that's rather good don't you think?" Bronevsky did not answer. "Well, well. Three sons," Frichter continued. "Seems like enough to me. They'll be a handful, those three. Just imagine. Three!" The doctor nudged Bronevsky with his elbow. "Time to give the little mother a rest, eh?"

Bronevsky smiled and raised his glass before he drank. The doctor left feeling he had carried out his assignment. He assured Enerde that the Russian understood him perfectly. "He'll behave himself. He is, after all, a gentleman."

Five days short of eleven months later, Amalia gave birth to a fourth son: this time the parturition was dreadful, and through Amalia's screams, Enerde prayed to God to save his daughter and begged the devil to drag his son-in-law to hell. He stormed Bronevsky's quarters himself, in the middle of the night, and accused the Russian of trying to kill his wife with his lust. Rätzel ran in and pulled Enerde out as Bronevsky stood quietly in front of the cold hearth in his dressing gown and looked after the retreating figures as he might watch some mildly interesting street scene which in no way involved him. Amalia named the boy Boris.

The fifth son was born a whole year later, after another difficult birth. The doctors and Rätzel kept Enerde and Bronevsky apart, but the next day two of the physicians confronted the new father and told him that there were to be no more babies. He agreed with them completely, earnestly, his face taking on an expression of profound sincerity, at once troubled and questioning. "Gentlemen," he began hesitantly, "I'm in a quandary. Since the birth of our third child I suggested to my wife that we wait . . . for a time." He shook his head and sighed. "What am I to do? She is . . . insistent. I can hardly deny her the rights of the marriage bed. I advise you to talk to *her*." He continued to appear troubled as the two men passed a look between them and left.

"He's lying," screamed Enerde when the doctors reported back to him. "Amalia! Amalia insistent!" Even though Enerde did not believe his son-in-law, he insisted the doctors tell her that another pregnancy might endanger her life. Amalia, they told Melchior later, listened to them politely and said, "I think I shall call him Alexander. It's one of dear Pavel's names, you know."

The following year, a sixth child, shriveled and blue, was born dead. This time Amalia was ill and bedridden for several months. Enerde threatened to kill Bronevsky if he coupled with Amalia again, calling him a beast, a swine, a wolf, a murderer. Bronevsky, his eyes cold, smiled at the old man surrounded and literally held down by the three attending doctors. "I am only earning my salary," he said softly, laughing as Enerde struggled to free himself from the grasp of the physicians who, still a little dazed at seeing Melchior disarmed by Graz and Rätzel, darted oblique glances at each other and at the weapon which Rätzel still held in his hand. The rumor that greatly amused Vienna society later was that it was Amalia herself who was disarmed of the meat cleaver.

On a cold February morning a year later, Amalia bore her last child, a girl. When Enerde saw her, he momentarily forgot Bronevsky, for the baby's features within days of its birth took on a cast which was astonishingly familiar to him: the plane of her forehead, the set of her eyes, the whole structure of her face was clearly her great-grandmother's. Enerde had long hoped for a girl, another earlier Amalia, but it was apparent that the child, even in infancy, was the blood image of the mystifying Dorothea. Melchior wanted to name her after the dead woman, and his daughter consented; but the birth certificate read Ursula Amalia Dorothea Elizabeth Paula, which annoyed the grandfather, since he wanted her to have his choice as her first name, but he said nothing, knowing that once Amalia thought on a given name, there was no changing her mind.

The birth of seven children in five years led to a scandalous story involving Bronevsky's sexual appetite. It was sincerely believed by many that he had fathered a dozen illegitimate children during this same period, since it was in the long waiting months of Amalia's pregnancies that Bronevsky began to spend his nights in the various clubs and cabarets in the city. There were jokes about a whole population of Bronevskys growing up to Russify Vienna and that if Amalia was unsuccessful with the butcher-block weapon, someone else should attempt to cut off the source of the pregnancies.

There was no humor, however, in the Enerde doctors' views that additional births for Amalia would endanger her life. To Melchior's half-mad rage, there were several miscarriages but no more babies. The facts were that within months after the birth of the last child, Amalia was already carrying the disease that was to terminate every subsequent conception in the first few months of its doomed life and kill her five years later on her birthday.

There were other rumors around the time of the birth of the last child: Bronevsky, it was believed, had the legendary Turkish passion, but this was a fiction: young boys bored him. In fact, all children bored him. An only child himself, he was astonished at the brood of infants, crawlers, and tottering little people that filled the children's wing with shrill cries and sudden laugher. He rarely visited the extensive nursery. When he did, he found himself in the way of bustling nurses who delighted in placing a child on his lap. Usually this resulted in some unpleasant wetness on his trousers or saliva drool on his vest or coat sleeve. After a while he did not sit anymore, but stood briefly, explaining that he had pressing business matters to attend to and had only dropped in for a brief "hello." The nurses nodded pleasantly and if Enerde was there, which he usually was, the grandfather smiled congenially and told him by all means to tend to whatever matters needed his attention.

Enerde already knew about these matters: his lawyers annually paid off gambling debts for his son-in-law; and occasionally women who claimed they were friends of his asked for various kinds of aid. Enerde paid. His lawyers objected to this giving away of money to women of "doubtful class." But Enerde refused to heed their advice; above all he knew he could not let Amalia hear the rumors about her husband. Once he would gleefully have told her himself, but now, sickly as she was, he could not bear the sight of her sad little face tightening up into tears and turning away to the wall. Although Enerde avoided his son-in-law whenever he could, he was cordial to the man when they met at dinner. But these meetings too became less frequent as Bronevsky spent more and more evenings in the town. Enerde paid all the man's expenses without flinching and additionally gave him a large allowance. Bronevsky usually rose late, had lunch with his wife in her suite, then went riding. He would return in the late afternoon, visit his wife briefly, and if he did not stay for dinner, he changed into evening clothes and drove into the city to one or another of the all-night haunts where he was well known for his wit and generosity. Occasionally one of Enerde's lawyers would make a pointed statement about Bronevsky's tailor or restaurant bill, but Melchior always silenced him with a single motion of his open hand. He even bought his son-in-law a fine new mare when his old horse became lame. In no way did the grandfather discourage Bronevsky's forming a routinely pleasurable life for himself away from the estate.

Rätzel alone understood Melchior's new attitude toward the Russian. "No matter how you isolate him, he is still their father."

"I don't isolate him at all. He can see his children whenever he wants."

"You know that he does not want to see them."

"Is that my fault?"

"What you are doing will come back to haunt you one day."

"No. Never!"

"Then one day it will haunt them."

"Not likely. He finds the children noisy, messy, and his findings show in his face. From their infancy, they will remember that he did not wish to be with them, that he excluded them from his life."

"And will that make them happy?"

"Ah, but, Rätzel: Amalia and I do not exclude them."

"For certain you do not."

The men fell silent then, for the thing they could not discuss was Amalia's strange indifference to her children. It was true she did not actually exclude them from her life, but the hours she spent in the nursery were like the hours of old, of her growing up when she sat in a chair by the window and stared into dreamless space, her eyes bereft of light, dead to life. Whenever Enerde placed the infant girl into her arms, she let the child rest like a bundle of clothing on her lap so that one of the nurses always sat next to her lest the baby, not at all inactive, drop to the floor. Rätzel, watching, knew from the beginning that Amalia did not want to hold her babies. She seemed to have no aversion to spending time with them as long as she did not have to touch them.

"When she feels better, all that will change," said Melchior. "I'm confident of that; you'll see."

Rätzel had no such confidence. It seemed to him that the children were not Amalia's at all, but rather that they had come through her from some other woman, some wild woman from the jungle, for they bore no trace of Amalia's gentle beauty, none of her softness, not the dove eyes or fine ash hair, not the dainty elegant mouth or small voice. Frichter had commented several times on their curious genetic jumble. "Peculiar brood, only one brown eye in the whole bunch. And from the looks of it, he'll be the only blond." He was speaking of Melchior's namesake, whom everyone referred to as the "second child," since the twins from the beginning were viewed as one. "The black hair on those three I know belongs to the father, but where did that red hair come from?" Ursula's and Alexander's hair was not actually red; it was more the color of burgundy wine. Later someone was to describe it as "dark fire," for it had a particularly disconcerting gleam that made strangers stare. All the children's coloring had an unsettling effect on people who saw them for the first time. Five of them had the dark-leaf irises of their father; all of them had the sharply arching, outward-sweeping eyebrows that the eye followed, so that there was in their faces a remote suggestion of another race. "Tartars," Bronevsky once laughed when he was quite drunk. "All Tartars." Enerde had been furious at his words, but even Ursula, for all her great-grandmother's expression, carried that curious foreign cast to the eyes that had come from Bronevsky's own face and which had blinded forever the gentle Amalia the moment she saw him. The children's mouths were broad, their sullen lower lips a kind of defiance to the well-defined peaks of the upper ones sweeping long-winged to the corners. In profile, their identical foreheads and chins and noses had the straight-cut clarity of the artist's marble and came unerringly from their Russian father. Only in Alexander and Ursula was it slightly marred by a softness, a blurring of the hard edges, a difference in size rather than shape.

Rätzel, who always joined the governesses (and later the tutors) and chauffeur who took the children to the zoo or other outings about the city, was quick to see strangers motion to one another as the children entered into their immediate range of vision or passed through a crowd, heedless of the stares that followed them. Graz once commented to Rätzel that the children were marked with the mystery of the rain forest. Rätzel wrote back on his pad, "Don't you mean the taiga?"

"No," said Graz flatly. "These are tropical growths. What an abundance of hair—black, red, gold. The greenest eyes I've ever seen. Startling. Something peering out of the . . . the . . ." He shrugged. "Just kids, just good-looking kids."

But Rätzel knew why Graz shrugged away his thought. He had had the same thought: there was a harsh quality in the children's faces, a look of brooding intensity that with the upward sweep of the outer corners of their eyes gave them an expression at once secret, insolent, aloof. One of the children's first tutors, a woman with an astonishing overbite and a missing chin, who was hired to teach them an early appreciation of music and the basics of structural German, left a description of them for which Rätzel was always grateful. "Why, they're not mean children at all. Who says so? Oh, those funny looks? Don't let that fool you." She was speaking to a new arrival on the tutorial staff. "That's just energy." And then, as if she liked her thought: "Yes, that's what they are, energetically beautiful."

Rätzel, watching them as they developed, saw that there was a certain truth in the lady's description: like all children, they were wonderfully energetic, but in the Bronevsky brood, this force seemed profoundly heightened by their extraordinary coloring, in the same way that red flames look more dangerous than blue fires. At rest, their perfect, chiseled profiles had the detached cruelty of stone.

During the early years a succession of governesses passed through the Enerde mansion in astonishing numbers, many of them English. Enerde reasoned that the children should have a clear knowledge of that language, since much of their future inheritance was located in areas where English was the prevailing tongue. The nursery, he decided, was the only true language university. Rätzel hired all but one of these accomplished women, even the Russian-speaking governess who, at Amalia's insistence, was installed as a balance to the English ladies. She further demanded that the children's father have a word in the selection of this woman. Enerde knew that telling his daughter about the clause in the marriage settlement which clearly gave Bronevsky no such authority was futile: Amalia would only have wept without end until he gave in to her. "Anyway," Rätzel said, "why *not* let him find the right woman? He knows the language."

Enerde grumbled and concurred, but with the stipulation that the woman must speak excellent German also. He did not want the children to absorb any "peculiar habits," such as a foreign accent in their own language. Rätzel always believed afterward that Bronevsky might have had an ally if he had not behaved so impulsively. The first woman interviewed was somewhat young and pretty and Bronevsky smiled at her warmly and spoke to her with such obvious delight in his own tongue that the glow in his eyes was not lost on Amalia, who waited quietly through the discussion of duties, then announced that the woman would not do, that her tone was wrong. Rätzel, who was of course present, knew precisely what she meant. The young woman smiled back at Bronevsky exactly the way he smiled at her, and when they spoke in Russian, the sibilant words sounded to Amalia much too intimate, although they carried no more intimacy than the children's ages. The applicant, not knowing that Bronevsky was not the real power in the hiring, tried too hard to impress the wrong person. When the woman was out of the room and on her way out of the house, Bronevsky exploded into a rage. "She is perfect," he shouted. "How dare you dismiss her." Rätzel's stare bought his voice down to seething softness. "All right. All right. But I do think she is right. Her tone is perfect. What do you mean, her tone is wrong?" He directed the question to his wife, who did not answer him. "She has a lovely tone. She is an altogether lovely person. We may not even be able to find such a lovely person again."

At the time of this interview, Amalia knew of her husband's long absences from the estate, although everyone gave perfectly good lies for his absence: he was working with Enerde at one of the plants; he was supervising the opening of a new factory; he was investigating problems at one of the forest holdings; he was visiting sick employees. "You know," said Rätzel to Enerde one evening, "he could be doing all of these things. Even now you might yet save him."

"No. Never! Why should I save him? It is his fault that Amalia is unwell. Let him eat out his own guts and see how it feels."

[53]

Rätzel knew that arguing was pointless, but he also knew that Amalia would not believe the excuses forever, or worse, she would hear the truth from some careless servant.

But it was Bronevsky himself who gave the game away. After a violent quarrel with one of his mistresses, he came home three days too early from a supposed forest inspection. Amalia, delighted at having him with her, innocently commented on his work. She was so glad that dear Pavel was such a help to the firm by helping dear Papa to see to the trees.

"See to the trees? See to the trees?" exploded Bronevsky. "What trees?" Had he not been drunk, he might have seen that it was to his benefit to play the role created for him.

"The forests . . . Papa's forests . . ."

"Is that what they tell you? That I am hard at work with the firm? Hoho. Let me tell you, my dear stupid little wife: I have never set foot on any of the firm's properties except this accursed house . . . this . . . this fortress of torture. Oh, do not mistake me, I wanted to do honorable work, but he denied me my rights. I am only here as a . . . a . . ." He meant to say "whore," but instead began to weep, and Amalia, stunned at this news, slowly pieced together the fabric of a different illusion: he left the estate to get away from *her!* She began to worry that he might meet another woman more desirable. From this false position, she tried briefly to be seductive, a gift she did not possess. She came to his suite one night naked, standing in an awkward, adolescent position under an unflattering light that exaggerated her sagging belly and stretch-scarred hanging breasts. Her pathetically prominent rib and hip bones hollowed shadows on her body, giving her the appearance of a skeleton.

Repulsed, Bronevsky groaned and turned away, but not soon enough. Amalia, seeing the expression on his face before he could hide it, gave up on life.

The second applicant for the Russian-language position came a few weeks after the first. She was a woman of perhaps thirty-eight or -nine who looked like a weather-worn icon. She arrived with a suitcase. Rätzel understood at once that the woman had no place else to go and that she had come prepared to take any work available. Her name was Luba and her dark face with its small mouth, straight thin nose, and mournful eyes was already set for disappointment and defeat. Rätzel formed the impression from her fine posture and old, elegant fur hat that she had suffered some bizarre comedown in the world. Bronevsky looked at her surreptitiously through a few inches of open door as she sat straight-backed on the edge of a chair, her hands wearing black mended gloves, resting on a worn handbag. "Ridiculous," he whispered to Rätzel. "She looks like a scrubwoman."

Rätzel pushed open the door, virtually forcing Bronevsky in ahead of him. "Madam . . . ?" he said to the lady, who rose with profound dignity to face him.

"Luba Nikilaevna Kazlova." Rätzel was taken by her tender voice as she answered Bronevsky's questions, which seemed to him abrupt and curiously rude, although he did not know the language. After several exchanges between the two, Bronevsky turned to leave. The woman nodded slowly and with a hesitant beginning said to Rätzel, "Perhaps . . . perhaps I could help in the kitchen, then." Rätzel caught Bronevsky's eye and saw him shake his head briefly as he left the room.

Rätzel held in his hands the woman's references. Trained as a nurse, but having become governess for five years to three little girls, now removed to Germany, where she did not wish to go, the Moscow-born Luba had, in Rätzel's eyes, all the qualifications necessary for the position. She spoke German and French as well and it was clear to him that Enerde would accept her. He spoke to her casually of the children as they visited the nursery, which Amalia was at that moment also visiting, seated in her chair near the window, a shawl over her thinning shoulders. The six-year-old twins, accustomed to their mother's silent attendance, were whispering in a corner over a large coloring book on which both were working, their thick black hair touching as they knelt forward over opposite sides of the same square page. Blond-headed Melchior, red-faced with weeping, was being comforted by a large-bosomed English nurse who at the same time scolded in a low voice a pouting Boris standing feet apart, hands clutched behind his back like a dour miniature professor scowling at the weather. The four-year-old Alexander, at once aware of the stranger, abandoned his toy soldier and ran to Rätzel, hanging on to his leg and looking over the new arrival with hostile interest. Another nurse came in from one of the bedrooms attached to the large central playroom. "Well, she's finally sleeping. I've never known a child who so abhors going to sleep. What a fight with that will." She clapped her hands lightly. "Teatime, everyone. Let's put away our things now and we'll have some delicious milk and bread with butter." None of the children seemed to hear her. The woman made a hopeless upward flap with her arms and rolled her eyes.

Rätzel glanced toward Amalia at the far side of the room. "What is it this time?" he asked softly, out of Amalia's range.

"Chocolates! A whole box of chocolates. They're all stuffed with it, even the baby. We can't stop her. We've tried asking her not to give them sweets, but she just goes right on doing it as if she doesn't even hear us, and it's gotten to be a constant thing. Every day a half-hour before their afternoon snack, she brings pounds of sweets."

Rätzel nodded. "When I get the opportunity I'll talk to her. For the moment we have some good news. This is Luba, Madam Kazlova, here for the Russian assignment." He saw the Russian woman catch his eye briefly.

"I thought . . . the gentleman said that I . . . Wasn't that gentleman their father?"

"Yes." Rätzel waited a moment, recognizing one of those silences in which thoughts are quickly and clearly rearranged. "And if you'll come this way, we'll have you meet their mother." Rätzel put his hand on Alexander's head and stroked it lightly. "See to your soldiers, and go to the table. I want to talk to all of you."

Alexander obediently returned to his army of little lead men and its acompanying blue-wheeled cannons, shelving them in ready formation on one of the child-height cabinets that ringed the room.

Amalia acknowledged the introduction with a faint nod of her head before

[55]

she returned her attention to space. A few minutes later, Rätzel introduced Luba Kazlova to the five little boys standing by then around a low central table where they usually gathered for special meals. At the time there were three other women employed in the children's wing: the large-bodied English nurse and two Austrian governesses, one who also spoke English and one whose first language was French. They greeted the new woman graciously, but Rätzel knew from past experience that they would soon enlighten her on the hopelessness of her tasks: "The children," they would tell her, "are little monsters, virtually untrainable and certainly a little mad."

A short time later when Rätzel showed Madam Kazlova to her room in the employees' hall, the woman asked gently, "May I be permitted to know the mother's illness?"

Rätzel appreciated the wording and the even, inflectionless tone of the question; but still more, he liked the tender concern on the woman's face, the knowledge in the eyes that she had walked into a tragedy in progress.

7

Luba Kazlova's question could not be answered, although Rätzel tried. "The doctors think she suffers a kind of anemia that is difficult to correct."

"Poor lady."

"Yes."

Madam Kazlova seemed to want to ask something else, but she hesitated for such a long time, Rätzel finally decided to help her out. "If there are any problems, please feel free to discuss them with me."

"Well . . . the father . . . the children's father said I wouldn't do at all. I wouldn't like to be the cause of any bad feeling."

"Madam, do not worry on that point. He will soon understand that you are meant for this house."

She nodded slowly. "They are quite unusual-looking children."

"Yes," said Rätzel, noting her expression of careful attention to the children. She had about her a subtle aura of waiting, a sense of serene patience, as though she had lived centuries and knew that there was no comfort in knowing the future and only madness in trying to hurry it.

She was the only Russian-born governess the children were ever to have, and from her they not only learned their father's language but also received the first true expressions of deep maternal concern they were to experience as small children. Through the whole "time of the governesses," as Rätzel later referred to those early years, Luba Kazlova alone embraced the youngsters in that warm tender loving that is all comfort, all peace, all safety for children and which some women, whether mothers or not (and some men), are able to project. The children, of course, fastened to her spirit quickly as they might gravitate toward a delicious aroma or seek out some urgent food that could gratify a particular hunger. Nobody quite understood what it was that Luba had: she was not beautiful or very clever; she rarely laughed and she had no fascinating stories to tell about her past or her travels. In fact, she did not speak of her past at all. Years later Ursula was to realize that this woman somehow figured in her first memory. As in a dream she saw herself in her grandfather's lap. He was holding her close, tighter than usual, and there was some great noise, a disturbance, a sound of drums which terrified her. Her grandfather was talking softly, but still holding her tightly. Then someone else came close, someone her grandfather spoke to gently: "See that she sleeps." The person was a woman with the pleasant scent of oranges clinging to her garments, and who held her as tightly as her grandfather and who whispered to her in the same soft way in a language she already knew was vastly different from her grandfather's and which she must have heard before.

"That was Luba," Günther was to tell her when they were all trying to glean their first memory from the chaff of countless other early impressions. "And the commotion that frightened you," Günther went on, "was the arrival of the paperhanger who took over the country, or at least the clanging of bells and beating of drums that signaled his arrival. Grandfather and Rätzel were horribly upset, but a lot of the servants went down to the boulevard and cheered and one of the drivers got drunk and smashed Grandfather's favorite car into a tree."

Other governesses, English, Austrian, Swiss, German, came, stayed a few months or a year, and left gratefully, although their salaries were far above generous. To these governesses who had quit in anger (or thought out loud that they were considering it), he handed a generous termination sum. This was always a surprise to the women, but Enerde had the conviction that once employees voiced a desire to leave, it was best to let them go at once lest they infect the others with their dissatisfaction or neutralize their own with theft. Rätzel's concern took quite a different direction after one of the German governesses, a tall handsome lady from Berlin, beat four-year-old Boris' wet bare bottom with the back of a wooden bath brush when she discovered him manipulating in dreamy reverie his stiff pink penis in the evening tub. His screams terrified the twins, who ran to Rätzel for help. The woman was dismissed at once, without severance pay and with the dubious consolation, when she demanded termination money normally given governesses, that she was lucky to be let off without the same treatment applied to *her* bare bottom, suitably wetted and held firmly over the rim of the blue-tiled tub. In her hasty departure, she left a locked trunk which everyone assumed she would send for and which was finally relegated to one of the storerooms in the second cellar, where it remained forgotten and still locked, gathering years of patient dust until a ten-year-old Ursula, no stranger to the workings of simple (and some not-so-simple) locks, discovered it, opened it within seconds, and wondered why a lady would need an assortment of sausage-shaped leather things with thongs attached, several articles of hairy clothes—mostly breeches with patches of bristles

[57]

("Goat, I think," sniffed Günther, to whom Ursula showed her find) sewn into the crotch, several pairs of long black gloves and a collection of straps, cords, and harnesses.

The only other governess that ever hit any of the children was an exasperated French lady named Mademoiselle Lalique, who tried to cure the five-year-old Melchior's fear of the dark by locking him into a lightless linen closet, where he whimpered in terror for an hour until the twins found and freed him. Mademoiselle Lalique, catching the children in the process of liberating their brother, cuffed Paul, the only one within immediate reach (they were all running), about the ears. The racing Günther, seeing his twin fall as he looked back over his shoulder, turned abruptly and with head down charged the woman with the full force of his speeding body. She was ill-prepared for the violence of the boy's anger as his head caught her squarely in the lower belly, sending her backward into the open doorway to the linen room, where she sprawled spread-eagle among the hampers and baskets used to collect the soiled linen. Mademoiselle Lalique was not dismissed, since knowledge of the incident never reached Rätzel. However, she quit a few days later, saying only that the Austrian climate was injurious to her health. Thus they came and went, these ladies hired to civilize the children and prepare them for "the time of the tutors."

Luba Kazlova arrived when Ursula was two. By then a dozen women had already come to the household, stayed for a time, and left in anger or relief, and once, in the case of a Miss MacBride, in sadness, for she liked the children and they apparently were charmed by her lilting English and fresh-faced youth and vitality. But so was Pavel Stephanovitch Bronevsky. She left early one morning, weeping softly, her usually springy walk subdued and halting, her voice sadly protesting to Rätzel that she had not opened her door to the children's father for anything except his insistence that they discuss her manner of teaching. The whole thing was a dreadful mistake and not her fault at all. She could not very well turn him out of her room, even though it was late at night, since she did not want him to think that she thought he had some evil intentions in visiting her, and by the time she realized his intent was vile, it was too late. She was afraid to scream for fear someone would blame her for his being there. He was naked and mounted on her by the time the door opened and the light switch was turned on by someone Miss MacBride could not see from her position.

Rätzel told her he was grieved to see her go, gave her twice the amount she had coming (along with an excellent letter of reference), and had her driven to the train station clutching a ticket that would take her all the way home to Scotland. The woman who reported seeing Bronevsky enter Miss MacBride's room was threatened with instant dismissal if she told anyone else about the incident. "I had no intention of divulging this scandalous behavior of that Scottish person to anyone except yourself, sir," she said to Rätzel, who wondered what the informer was doing up at one in the morning. He did not ask. The woman's name was Agnes Schneider and Enerde had hired her himself some months before as a favor to a business acquaintance who was sending his child away to school in Switzerland and still had six months of the woman's contract to pay for. "She's not much to look at. A little on the sour side, too, but she's a good teacher."

"I'll take her, but I never give a contract. They come and go when *I* want them to. But I'll finish this one out for you, and if she's as good as you say, I'll keep her on."

Agnes Schneider was plainly ugly and knew it. Born of a German father and an English mother—stable groom and cook's helper—to a titled house in East Anglia, Agnes was sent away to school by her sacrificing parents in the belief that an education would give their daughter a sure passport to a grander life than their own. Agnes' poor face betrayed them all. From childhood her lashless eyes stared angrily from their fleshy sockets, and her chin protruded, witch fashion, nearly as far as her perpetually damp nose (she suffered from pollen allergies). After a brief adolescence of chubbiness, she turned into a woman of sharp angles. Overly tall and graceless, she tended to lurch when she walked fast, which she did frequently out of nervousness and a justifiable anxiety over her hounding fears that she was unlovable. What she did possess on the positive side of the ledger of her looks was beautiful hair, a thick wild-honey-colored mane which, however, she drew back into a tight unbecoming twisted bun at the back of her head as if to throw dirt into the face of the Fates who had given her so little else. She also had beautiful hands, although she seemed unaware of their pale elegant grace and perfect half-mooned nails.

Rätzel soon saw that Agnes Schneider and Bronevsky were forming a curious alliance which at first had the makings of a scandal but which ultimately settled down into a shabby little secret that everyone knew and everyone kept: Agnes Schneider had fallen in love wih Pavel Bronevsky. The whole thing might have been a small, vulgar joke, since Rätzel knew that Bronevsky disliked homely women. But the immensity of the governess's love for the fatally handsome Russian was of epic proportions: she would have killed for him.

Agnes Schneider first saw Bronevsky on the very day that she entered the house. She was walking beside Rätzel through the main foyer toward the great central staircase. "I shall require a good deal of time with the children. Exposure to the language to be learned is everything. One doesn't simply give it an hour here and an hour there and expect the language to remain in the memory. It must be used."

Rätzel assured her there would be plenty of time. "Although you realize, of course, that there are six other women and one man on the teaching staff at the moment. But you will find that the children are remarkably intelligent; all of them have a formidable gift for languages. Their mother speaks to them only in French and their father in both Russian *and* French. The little girl seems to make some sort of game of the different languages and is the most gifted of them all."

At that moment hard footfalls sounded from the top of the marble stairs (long freed of the protective carpeting once installed for the second Amalia). It was early evening and Bronevsky was just embarking on one of his forays into the city. He was in excellent humor, having discovered that his father-in-law had that very afternoon replenished his bank account and paid off his most recent debts accumulated over the previous three months. Bronevsky's face, handsome in repose, became endowed with breathtaking beauty when he was joyous. The white of his fine teeth against the coal-black mustache, the green fire of his eyes under the high-arched eyebrows, the velvet-textured skin which gave back a light all of its own, the rich head of hair, the elegant grace of his step, the slender hips sheathed in silver-gray, winking from inside his swinging great cape as he bounded down the stairs, were the colors and motions of a royal figure in a romantic historical novel. Miss Schneider stopped at the foot of the stairs as she saw Bronevsky come toward her and quite literally could not believe her eyes. Rätzel, who had commenced up the stairs, turned to look back when he realized the woman was no longer beside him. He saw at once the stunned look of marvel on her face and knew he was gazing into the raw unsheltered opening of a woman's soul. He returned to the foot of the stairs at the same moment as the children's father arrived in front of Agnes, who seemed to have turned into a pillar, if not of salt, then certainly of a substance in equal danger of early disintegration. He introduced them. Bronevsky, in his high marvelous humor at the sudden windfall of new funds, bowed as he took Agnes Schneider's hand and kissed it, holding onto it for the slightest moment longer than was necessary. He said he was delighted to meet her, enchanted, charmed. He turned and with a dramatic toss of his cape strode out the front door. Rätzel tore his eyes away from the governess's face for he knew he was staring into a wound no man had a right to see. A few moments later, Miss Schneider followed him up the stairs to the staff's hall in silence. He introduced her to the others, knowing that even as the woman acknowledged meeting her associates, she was still in shock, still caught— as an animal is caught in one blind snap of the hunter's trap, the hair-trigger springs still whirring furiously after the single scream of the doomed creature has long ended.

It was clear to Rätzel from the beginning that Miss Schneider would be quite different from all the other governesses who had come to the Enerde house. In the first few days of her tenure in the mansion, Agnes did not see Bronevsky again. When she had her equilibrium back, she immersed herself in her work, organizing and reorganizing the classrooms, scheduling in careful graphs the times not only she, but all the other teachers were to have the children. She was a natural organizer and quickly saw that the disciplines had to be put into order. She was hired to teach the children Latin and English and this she set about doing with dogged persistence and the patience of iron. She made no overtures of friendship to the children or other employees. She had the servants clean up the classroom and place everything in what she called "its proper place." The damage was slight. One of Günther's cultures was thrown out as "disgusting fungus" and a star chart of Paul's was lost in the shuffling and removal of books and papers from the study tables to the shelves along the walls. A strange drawing of Ursula's tacked to the wall was labeled "grotesque" by the new governess and burned with old lessons ("outdated"). Two of the other teachers quit within a week. The others complained to Rätzel en masse. He told them that he would talk to Miss Schneider and clarify her position to her. But he failed to do so for a few days for want of time, and by then the children let her know in clear terms exactly how many of their hours she was going to receive. They refused to see her at all. She rushed to Enerde himself, claiming that the other teachers were unduly influencing the children against her. In the end Rätzel met with the staff, and set hours were more or less decided on for each person, with the provision that special trips or unusual projects could be arranged on agreement with the others. Miss Schneider did not believe in outings and this caused immediate dissension. The war in the classroom finally began in earnest.

Agnes, not knowing Bronevsky's position in the house, drew some false conclusions and waited in the foyer one evening in order to apprise him of her view that there were bad influences at work on the children. But when she finally saw him, he had just had an unpleasant scene with his wife, whose constant weeping by then totally repulsed him, and he was in a vicious humor. Miss Schneider, after begging him for a few moments of his "valuable time," began to speak her complaint rapidly, discovering to her dismay that she was stuttering, not normally one of her afflictions. Reduced finally to an embarrassing silence, she could only stare into the beautiful face helplessly, and what she saw there drew her to the very edge of fainting: for the merest moment she saw in his eyes a revulsion, a cruel twist of the mouth, an inward draw of the nostrils, a infinitesimal pulling away of his head. But then he was suddenly speaking to her in a warm, soft voice. Yes, he understood her problem. He would see what he could do. At the moment he had an important appointment, but in the morning he would set things in order. She could come to him at any time with any problem. He was always glad to help. He pressed her damp hand and left.

Agnes Schneider soon discovered that he was helpless in matters involving the children and as time passed she came to believe that like herself, he was misunderstood by everyone and that the world in general conspired against him as it did her. And because he was always courteous and sympathetic toward her, she came to believe that he felt the same affinity for her that she felt for him. They commiserated with each other in maudlin set phrases: "Life is unfair," "The powerful are unjust," "We sensitive ones are always doomed to serve the vulgar," and on and on. Their absurd, cloying sympathies irritated Rätzel and this kept him on guard for any plot against the Russian governess whom everyone else liked in a passive pleasant way that needed no overt demonstration. But unfortunately for Agnes Schneider, Bronevsky's proffered sympathies were to her a growing sign of his affection for her. For the first time in the thirty-six years of her life she felt physical desire for a man and was stunned by it. At first his nearness only confused her and she was reduced to a vague feeling of uneasiness, a slight shaking of her knees, a rush of blood to her extremities, and finally a remote dizziness as though she might faint if she did not quickly sit down. Early one morning, she found his white silk scarf lying on the stairs. She took it to her room and behind her locked door kissed it until she discovered herself weeping. She intended to return it, but put it off, telling herself as the days passed that she would give it up the next day. At night she spread it over her pillow and breathed in his scent. One night she wrapped it around her bare breasts and dreamed that she was lying in his arms. She awakened with hot tears on her face. She tied it tightly around her waist and waited to sleep, to dream. But it was uncomfortable and kept her from sleeping. She carefully straightened it out on the bed and knelt naked down in front of it, staring at the shimmering silk fringes, at the slightly shadowed center that she knew had curved around the back of his beautiful neck. Slowly she took it up and wrapped it around her bare hips, bringing the ends down over the flossed mound, pulling them over her vulva and around to the back, where she could, by tightening her buttock muscles, hold the scarf to her without using her hands. She was astonished at the quivering effect this had on her thighs. This use of the scarf became a ritual each night as she lay in her bed. She soon discovered that her vagina would quickly produce a rich thick liquid when she brought the scarf over the vulva. A slight discharge at first alarmed her, but she discovered that it had a curiously pleasing scent and as she sniffed the tips of her fingers the entire lower part of her body from her waist to her knees seemed to rise and fall as if it were breathing of its own accord. The first time she parted her legs and slowly trailed the scarf across the open lips, she screamed when some violent implosion inside the saturated vulva sent her into a frenzy of gasping and shuddering.

During the days she was subdued and calm, her patience with the children deserving of the begrudging compliments made by other members of the staff. She became helpful to the other teachers, offered to assist Rätzel in caring for the house accounts. He pleasantly declined the offer, and there remained between them an unacknowledged lesion, a small but continuous unspoken sense of distrust. Agnes Schneider soon learned that the man she loved spent most of his nights in the arms of other women. In the early evening, she would conceal herself behind one of the inlaid oriental screens in one of the formal rooms off the foyer and wait for his footsteps on the marble stairs. She would listen to him leave the house, speak a few words to his chauffeur, and drive away. Sometimes as she lay in her increasingly bitter bed, she waited all night just to hear his footsteps on the marble stairs.

When he did not drive into the city, she spied on him. She discovered that his balcony faced a section of the garden where she could conceal herself behind the rhododendrons and watch the light in his rooms. One night, dressed in a rich velour robe, he walked out of his room, glass in one hand, bottle in the other, and stood in front of the stone balustrade of his balcony, his strong calves, socked and gartered, clearly visible to Agnes Schneider, who was holding her breath amid the shrubbery. The robe's belt hung loose at the sides and in the stir of the night air the garment's open front moved faintly. The man wore nothing else, but the ledge of the balustrade concealed exactly that space between the man's black pubic hair and upper thigh from the eyes in the rhododendrons. He filled his glass and upended the bottle to his mouth, draining the last of the liquor before he dropped the empty bottle into a flowerbed below. He held the glass up to the stars as if toasting some snickering god before he drained that, too, and returned to his rooms. Agnes crept across the lawn and searched in the flowerbed until she found the bottle. She licked the rim with her tongue, emitting little sharp cries as she knelt on the moist earth.

Even in this state of anxious eroticism, she managed to maintain a stern discipline in the classroom and a certain leadership over all the teachers save Luba. She had already discovered that Bronevsky hated the Russian woman, and this added to Agnes' loathing of her. She was reasonably civil to everyone else, but she did what she could to discredit Luba: "That Russian person," she complained to Rätzel one afternoon, "is constantly disrupting the children's schedule."

Rätzel, without looking up from a household ledger on his desk in a small sunny study he had occupied for over thirty years, said, "That Russian person's name is Madam Kazlova."

"That may be, but I insist that she not invade my study hours."

"Miss Schneider," began Rätzel, looking up at the fast-breathing woman, "the children are learning both languages, Russian *and* English, and the knowledge of one does not cancel out the knowledge of the other. From what we already know about these particular children, there is even a good chance they will learn German at the same time. And it must be no secret to you by now that they are well into a fair understanding of French, since it is the only tongue in which their mother speaks to them. I do not object to your arranging certain hours for the study of English, but I do not want any hours so cemented down that there is no longer any flexibility to them and—"

"Perhaps I should take this problem to the children's grandfather. It seems to me that he feels their knowledge of English is much more important than you seem to think. Perhaps once the priorities have been sorted out, there won't be any problems with scheduling."

Rätzel placed his pencil on the ledger and leaned back in his chair, gazing at the woman for a long moment. "Miss Schneider—"

"I do not believe that there is anything we have to discuss, Mr. Rätzel. You recall, of course, that it was Mr. Enerde who contracted me personally for this position, and he assured me at the time that he wished the children to learn English above all else."

Rätzel shrugged. "You are quite right. See him, by all means. I could very easily be wrong on the priorities."

Miss Schneider's excessive graciousness when she thanked Rätzel for his "time and attention to this most important matter" made him smile a little, yet his impulse to warn her not to disturb the grandfather just now was powerful enough that he actually started to speak, but her expression so dismissed him that he knew any suggestion of his would be misunderstood. He let her go with her taste of victory clearly showing in the set of her mouth.

Miss Schneider found Enerde seated in the white latticed gazebo in the garden with Ursula on his lap whispering something into his lowered ear. The boys were seated around a tea table on which the used dishes had been pushed to one side, leaving a free space for a large book from which Luba Kazlova was reading: " 'As the wolf started back toward the forest, he said: "Good night to you, my poor friend, you are welcome to your dainties— and your chains. As for me, I prefer my freedom to your fat." ' "

The children watched her dreamily, their faces resting on the heels of their hands, their eyelids partially lowered in an expression of cat contentment, of cozy, easy pleasure. The twins spoke simultaneously. "Read another."

Madam Kazlova smiled. "In a moment, but first the application." She turned her face to Alexander. "Alexy?"

[63]

"Better skinny freedom than fat slavery." He giggled, giving the answer already familiar to all of them, since Madam had begun to reread the old fables for the second time in a month.

"I think Alexander would prefer fat freedom," said Enerde, stroking Ursula's hair as she leaned her head against his beard.

"So would we all, sir," said Madam Kazlova, turning the page.

Into this soft hour of relaxed reading on a warming day near winter's end strode Miss Schneider, bearing her stiff complaint on her square shoulders like one of those large upright beetles capable of carrying something twice its size on its back. The boys looked up as she stopped in the archway of the gazebo, her expression heavy with disapproval and exasperation. The twins nudged each other faintly, a mere brushing together of their sweatered shoulders, their faces taking on the bland mask so natural to Bronevsky and which Enerde had finally learned was a feature of their father's as genetically reproduced in his grandchildren as the color and texture of their hair. He found their capacity for draining their faces of all feeling both fascinating and disconcerting. And they all had it; even Ursula at three could turn her emotionally stormy face into perfect calm within seconds whenever conditions called for it.

"I'm afraid it's time for English lessons," Miss Schneider announced heartily.

The conditions were right: the children's faces folded into stillness like the final movement in the momentary fluttering wings of sleeping birds. Madam Kazlova, who was just reading the beginning of the next tale, stopped in mid-sentence and closed the book.

"Join us, Miss Schneider," said Enerde, motioning to the last of the chairs, earlier pushed somewhat outside the circle of the table.

"I'm afraid I'm much too busy, sir. There's so much to be done. The children should be at lessons."

"I insist," said Enerde blandly. It was the very mildness of his tone, a little *too* bland, a little *too* soft, that made Miss Schneider, after taking one look at the grandfather's face, quickly take the offered chair. Luba Kazlova reopened the book and continued to read in her melodious German as the grandfather and the children repositioned their bodies into relaxation and their faces into expressions of pleasurable listening. Miss Schneider, seated wall-straight on the edge of her chair, seethed with rage, for she had taken personal offense at being told to wait, believing incorrectly that the grandfather's intent was to humiliate her by showing his preference for the Russian governess. So convinced was Agnes Schneider that people disliked her, that they injured her for the mere pleasure of assuaging their own innate appetite for cruelty against her, that it never entered her head that Enerde did not wish to be interrupted during his hours with the childen. *Anyone* intruding upon these tender times would have been told to wait, for the hours were sacred and inviolable to the old man. It was a weakness on his part not to make it brusquely clear that these times were not to be interrupted for any reason. Had he said something to that effect, Miss Schneider might not have taken his words and actions as a personal rebuff and seen Luba Kazlova as the cause of it, thus adding jealousy to her hatred. At the end of another fifteen minutes of listening to Luba read, Enerde fed his foible further by praising Madam Kazlova's ability to keep the children's attention.

[64]

"It's Aesop, sir, not me," she said in genuine modesty.

The grandfather demurred and told the boys to go with Miss Schneider for their English lessons; then, taking Ursula with him, he repaired to his study unaware of the damage he had done. But the children knew it, saw it, since they were much closer to the raw edge of life among the governesses, who were ferocious in their jealousy of one another, each believing herself to be the most indispensable to the family, the most important influence on the children. Except for Madam Kazlova, they fought over the children's time like tigers, each trying to take the greatest credit for teaching them to read, to work with numbers, to play the piano, to learn history, to sing, to draw. They gave Rätzel whole stacks of the children's work with the urgent request that they reach the grandfather's eyes at the earliest possible moment. Besides workbooks of grammar exercises in four different languages, there were pages filled with rows of mathematical problems; drawings of bowls of fruit, vases of flowers, and a dozen or more of a chair, under which the teacher had written "perspective" lest there be some question about the reason for drawing this solitary and rather ugly object; penmanship—rows of war wire briefly coming into existence on the page between two infinities; nature-study reports from the garden: "The Life of the Water Spider," "Garden Plants That Heal," and so on. Rätzel carefully filed them in large individual folders in his office. When the women later asked about the grandfather's reaction, Rätzel told them to see Enerde himself. But the governesses did not do this: Enerde was much too formidable. The only woman who did not fear the grandfather was Luba Kazlova, nor did she present Rätzel with any proud results of the children's lessons. She continued to read to them from Aesop; adding other legends— old river myths from the Rhine, the Danube, the Don; moving subtly to *The Song of Roland* (which made Alexander cry); on to Dumas's Musketeers and imprisoned Count—whose damp, rat-rioting cell made them shiver; on to Sir Walter Scott—quickly abandoned when Madam saw the children yawn—thus making room for Dickens, whom she quite preferred to read anyway and who immediately enthralled the children's imaginations with his grotesques.

"The time of the tutors" began when Ursula was past four and her twin brothers nine. After a particularly unpleasant squabble between two of the governesses, Miss Schneider and a Miss Vogal (an Austrian lady), over a difference in opinions as to organizing the classroom, and not, as Rätzel at first thought, a difference in the method of teaching English, he suggested to Enerde that they start hiring men for the children's further education. With the abrupt and violent departure of Miss Vogal, who, as she went out the door, threw a book at the Englishwoman, there were only two governesses left: Luba Kazlova and Agnes Schneider. The latter had vanquished all the others; it was the Russian woman alone that she could not inspire to anger or reduce to frustration. Luba refused absolutely to fight. She simply conceded every point before it became an issue. In this way she survived.

With only two governesses left, a number of tutors entered the house, some living for a time on the premises while others arrived early, stayed through four meals, and left after dark. Rätzel always carefully screened the tutors, with Enerde occasionally sitting in on the interviews. The absolute qualifications each tutor had to possess were the ability to speak and read at least two languages and to compose a convincing document (notarized) that they were neither drunkards nor Bolsheviks. Both men knew that the economic and political times were hideous: throughout that decade the terror of both national and private bankruptcy was haunting every country around the world. Underneath this surface fear and attached to it like leeches on the belly of a sick beast was the dread of Communist uprisings. In England, shrill cries for social reforms merely increased the convulsions of a dying empire; the successively demoralized governments of France looked on in paralytic fear as Germany twitched off its dried outer skin and quickened into ferocious new life, its mad-eyed head poised, quivering and waiting; new Russia practiced old purgings and pogroms, made more acceptable to the exhausted onlooking peasants as famine carried away their energy and numbed their will; further east, Japan invaded China with atrocious vehemence. It was said that there was hunger in America.

Since the end of the Great War, a nasty joke, first circulated among foreign diplomats, made its way into public places to the effect that Austria was the decapitated head of a whore the rest of whose body had been fed to jackals. Allusions to the sexual organs—"Who got the purse?"—had the diplomats howling with laughter for years. The question had a number of uproariously obscene answers. But a much more interesting question was pondered concerning the severed head, for it was said that it kept winking its eye brazenly and making pulpy, slushy sounds with its wet pursed mouth as though it was unaware of its missing body.

Because of the unsettled times and vast unemployment, Rätzel interviewed an unusual variety of tutors, some who turned out not to be tutors at all but hungry, out-of-work professional people and failed businessmen. Only two of these were hired, one for only a brief period of time—a lawyer who was hired because he spoke English—but after three months Rätzel discovered that he spent one night each week with a Nazi-party group and was in the process of becoming a member. Rätzel, in one of the most uncustomary acts of his life, dismissed the man with a lie: "We need a woman because of the girl. Anyway, with your talents you should get something better."

"I'm in line for something better," said the man, nodding his head.

The parting was so amicable as to border on the grotesque. The other non-tutor hired was a lens maker by the name of Wolsky who had lost his small shop several years earlier and who had been living a perilous existence washing windows. Rätzel was moved by the irony of his situation and the extraordinary angst in the man's owl eyes magnified in size and intensity through the quarter-inch-thick lenses sitting on his nervous nose. He hired him because he spoke Polish and Russian along with German and because of his astonishing credentials: born in Warsaw and formally trained as an eye surgeon, he had begun to lose his own sight in his thirties because of a rare retinal disease. Knowing that there was no possiblity of cure and that the condition could only worsen, he apprenticed himself to a lens maker, whose trade he learned rapidly. In time he immigrated to Vienna and set up his own shop, only to discover that he was not a businessman. When Rätzel interviewed him he had been washing windows for three years. Besides Rätzel, the only people in the Enerde house who liked him were

[66]

the children. "Describe the stars to me," he would say to them at night when he took them out to one of the upper balconies to watch the constellations appear in the early-evening sky. "Tell me what you find inside the flower," he said one day after giving each of them a rose to dissect.

Miss Schneider complained directly to Enerde. "The twins are cutting up *worms* for that man and the others are watching! That poor little girl!"

"It's called dissection. And I understand from that poor little girl that she gets to help her brothers the next time."

A newly dead pigeon brought in by one of the gatekeeper's dogs, an extra fish provided by the cook, and one day a bull's eye which Wolsky purchased himself at the butcher's all became part of the biweekly anatomy lessons. Wolsky convinced Rätzel that the children needed a microscope and a telescope. The instruments arrived and were set up by Wolsky as the children helped excitedly. But when they looked into the microscope at a drop of water, they were reduced to openmouthed silence.

The twins claimed the two instruments most of the time. Melchior was shy of the microscope and rejected the telescope altogether. Boris finally preferred to read; Alexander lost interest after the initial novelty wore away; and Ursula, by then the twins' shadow, alone shared with them the cell and the star.

Wolsky and Madam Kazlova at first regarded each other with suspicion, but in time they became friends and for the children the Russian lessons doubled in both quantity and quality. The couple took the children to museums and memorials, churches and cemeteries, palaces and parks and gardens and frequently the zoo. Rätzel always attended these outings. He spent more and more time with the children, since they only rarely saw their parents: their father seemed to live only at night, using up the daylight hours for sleep; their mother, deeply ill with a wasting disease, no longer left her bed. Their grandfather, troubled and confused by the government which he finally decided simply to ignore, spent his spare hours with his daughter. What they talked about or if they talked at all, Rätzel did not know. But from the expression on Enerde's face as he walked the halls through the long nights, Rätzel knew that Death was waiting quietly inside the house, perhaps in one of the vacant rooms rocking silently in an old chair to the beat of Amalia's heart.

The fourth decade of the century was about to end, and it seemed to Rätzel that the whole world was entering a twilight, rolling inexorably toward a time of darkness. Sitting alone late one afternoon in the garden, he saw the glass shards on the top of the wall catch the final moments of the failing sun. They exploded into an instant of blinding, crackling light and then went out, the uneven edges of black glass silhouetted against a blood-red sky like a ragged putrefying jaw.

Rätzel shook himself out of this grim fantasy and returned to the house, which seemed to him lately always to have a bad smell. In the upper gallery he stopped one of Amalia's nurses. "How is she tonight?"

The woman shook her head. "She won't take any medication. Her father's with her now. He seems to be the only one that doesn't upset her. It's a chore just keeping her clean now that she has so little control over the bladder. And bedsores! Oh, my, her poor feet. I tell you, Mr. Rätzel, to hear her scream . . . it breaks my heart." Rätzel nodded and wanted to walk on, but the woman continued insistently. "Death marches around this house just waiting to get his foot in the door. I swear sometimes at night I hear him tramp, tramp, tramp past the main gate just as sure as—"

"Stop. There are children in this house. Such . . . such fancies would terrify them."

"Oh, I wouldn't say such things to the children, the poor little loves . . . motherless." She began to weep.

Rätzel hurried away. Everyone except the children knew that Amalia was dying. Enerde had stopped the children's visits to the sickroom; for some reason, a puzzle to everyone, the sight of the children sent her into hours of silent weeping. Enerde himself wandered the house at night like a ghost, frequently coming to Rätzel's room to ask the same question. "There's still a chance. She's young. The human system can work miracles. We've heard of such miracles." And then the pause and finally the explosive, hopeless, impossible, unbearable question: "My God, Rätzel, why doesn't she want to live?" And then the dry weeping of a man who was caught on the cutting edge of despair.

During the long days of Amalia's dying, Rätzel saw that a semblance of order and normalcy was maintained. All lessons continued. All meals were served on time. Amalia had been moved to a large room with arched windows that faced the afternoon sun. A nurse or doctor was always with her. The children's father, who had retreated into an alcoholic haze from the trouble that now afflicted the house, one dreary overcast day staggered drunkenly into his wife's room. The nurses ran for Rätzel. But when he got there he found the man slumped beside her bed retching. Under the frail light the head on the pillow with its thinning hair and sallow skin stretched taut over the fleshless ones looked like a skull. The sickroom was close and rank with the smell of disinfectants. Rätzel knew he would not have to warn Bronevsky not to make any more drunken visits as he led him, still gagging, from Amalia's room.

In the middle of the night on her twenty-seventh birthday, Amalia died. No one was with her. The doctor, after listening to her heart and taking her pulse, had gone downstairs to tell Enerde that both were strong. One of the nurses entering the room twenty minutes later to sit by her bed for the night smelled the relaxed bowel and discovered that Amalia's eyes were open and that she was dead.

* * *

After she was five, Ursula's greatest fear was that her grandfather would become sick and die. She knew that this had happened to her mother. Somewhere in the dancing light of memory she could see her mother's face when there was no sickness in it, when the gray of her eyes was like dove's wings and her lips pink, her mouth sweet-smelling. Rising into her child's mind were her mother's hands, pale, fluttering, drifting toward her breast, floating upward to her throat as though she were caressing some fabric draped there. Her mother was still walking then, or at least sitting in a chair by the window in the central room of the nursery. Then the chair was empty more and more, and her grandfather told her that her mother was tired, that she was resting. After some more time passed, it seemed that her mother was always resting. Then someone said she was sick and the very word "sick" took on a new dimension. Before, when people were sick, they threw up. Melchior was always getting sick. If one of the teachers spoke loudly to him or frowned at him, he was sick. If Boris made him cry or Alexander teased him, he was sick. She asked her grandfather who it was that made her mother sick. Her grandfather didn't seem to understand her question, but when she asked Rätzel he told her that the sickness inside of her mother was different from Melchior's kind. Her mother couldn't throw up her sickness. Ursula pressed him for details. Rätzel told her that some things could not be explained: sometimes a sickness started in people and nobody knew why it took such a long time to leave. He told her the doctors were helping as much as they could to hurry the sickness out of her, but sometimes all they could do was wait just as she was waiting. Ursula looked at the empty chair where her mother used to sit and went in search of the twins, but it was Boris she found first, sitting in a wicker chair in the solarium, reading. He asked her why she was crying. She told him what Rätzel had said.

"He's wrong," announced Boris. "Things get sick because the parts wear out."

Ursula stopped crying. "What parts?"

"All the parts can wear out. The insides of Graz's ears wore out until he can't hear anymore. Rätzel walks funny because his knees are wearing out. Don't you remember that old gateman that we used to have? He wore out all over at the same time and died."

"Died?"

"That's when everything wears out all at once and they put you in a hole in the ground. That's what they did with the gateman. That's what they do with everybody when all the parts wear out all at once. The new gateman told me. He said sooner or later it happens to everyone and then they put you in a box in a big hole in the ground and cover it up with dirt and worms get into the cracks and eat you. It happens to everybody."

With a wild cry, Ursula lunged at her brother, her fists pounding him furiously. "No," she screamed. "No. No. No." She sank her teeth into his hand as he raised it to shield himself from this unexpected attack. One of the gardeners heard his scream and rushed in to pull the two apart.

By the time Rätzel and the twins arrived on the scene, the gardener had let go of Boris, who cowered in his chair holding his slightly bleeding hand out for all to see, but the man still held onto Ursula, her arms flailing futilely just out of reach of her brother. Rätzel called one of the nurses to see to Boris' bitten hand, then turned to Ursula. "What happened here?"

Still watching her brother, she shook her head without stopping. Günther sat quickly beside her on the settee and held her face still with both hands. "What did he say?"

Ursula breathed long heaving breaths. "He said . . . he said . . . he said . . ."

Günther stroked her cheeks gently. "Ursula, now stop. Just stop a minute. What did he say?"

"He said everybody is going to be put in boxes in the ground and worms will eat them. Everybody!" She looked into Rätzel's close face. "It's not true! It's not true!" She looked hard from Rätzel to Günther and back. But Rätzel's eyes did not say it was not true, and Günther looked away.

"Ursula, you have seen dead things before," said Rätzel quietly. "Sometimes there is a dead bird or two in the garden. You've seen rabbits and fish and chickens. You have watched the taking apart of things that were no longer alive." He spoke on softly, further reminding her of the anatomy lessons, of the creatures she had seen which no longer had life in them. "You have just not thought about them as being dead."

"But not people," she whispered to Rätzel. "Not Mother or Grandfather or . . . or . . ."

"That's not something you have to worry about now. Your mother and your grandfather are very much alive." Rätzel quickly broke up the discussion and walked across the room, motioning to Günther to follow. "Take her upstairs. Convince her she must not bite people. She listens to you. I'll talk to Boris . . ."

"But it's true," said Günther, his face sober, reflective.

"What?"

"They put people in the ground and worms eat them."

Rätzel studied Günther's eyes for a long moment, as though the boy had asked him a question which he was obligated to answer. "Yes, it's true, but I'm not sure she understands that a dead person does not feel anything." He hesitated and looked back across the room at Ursula's bent head. He placed his hand on Günther's shoulder. "You understand that, don't you? That dead people do not feel anything?"

"I think so."

"Well, then, it's all right, isn't it? It's not so bad if one can't feel it. It doesn't matter then, you see." He looked intensely into Günther's eyes. "Now, take your sister upstairs and get her mind on something else. Remember to convince her that she is not to bite."

In the early morning after their mother's death, the children were brought once more to the sickroom. The grandfather, gasping great sobs and clutching his daughter's hand, knelt beside the bed while each of the children was brought close to the face on the pillow. Someone (Ursula never knew who) lifted her up to kiss the dead woman's mouth. Always after that, whenever she smelled camphor oil, the taste of those icy lips would return to her on a ripple of uncontrollable nausea. On both sides of the bed, thick ivory candles burned on alabaster stands, the smell of wax commingling with the sickly-sweet odor of musk doused on the bed linen in the futile attempt to overpower the odor of disinfectants. Ursula saw Alexander gag and turn away from the bed. The twins stood in deadly silence immediately behind her. Boris was weeping quietly, as Melchior, on his knees, clung to the bedspread hiccuping wet spongy sobs. She looked to her grandfather and saw, between the downward sweep of his white mustache and his beard, the black hole of his mouth pulled to one side, revealing an arc of long yellowed teeth. A little stab of fear pricked her heart for she recalled in that moment the strange story of the worms that ate people. She looked back at her mother, who was now smaller than she had ever seen her and whose face seemed to have flattened out on the pillow so that even the pillow did not seem dented, but simply held in its dead center a headless face fringed with a few wisps of hair that someone had combed out into an ashy halo. It was Luba Kazlova who entered the room sometime after the children were brought to it and took them away.

The funeral, considered old-fashioned even by the old people of the time, was decorous, proper, and appalling. It was not Pavel Bronevsky's drunkenness that astonished the mourners; they generously attributed his stumbling to grief, since he was also wailing loudly before the service, and he passed out halfway through the Mass and had to be carried home. It was the children's silence that set the people to giving each other oblique glances and little nudges. After a long ceremony in a cold church, the children, leading the procession of mourners, followed the coffin to its grave in the city's huge central cemetery while a dozen musicians played a dirge. Rätzel stood next to Enerde and held him firmly by the elbow as the priest intoned his final prayer over the casket. Ursula stood between the twins. She did not have to turn to know that Luba was behind her. The Russian governess had not left them now for three days, sleeping on the sofa in the central room in the nursery, leaving the children's bedroom doors ajar and her own light lit through the night so that their rooms were never totally dark. During the day she continued to read to them, old Russian folklore ballads consisting of betrothal songs, harvest songs, and funeral songs that spoke eloquently of God.

At the funeral, Ursula, unable to take her eyes away from the grave into which her mother's coffin was finally lowered, saw some of the soil slide away from the excavated pile beside it and drop into the hole. Ursula stepped quickly forward to see if it had dropped on the blanket of pink roses covering her mother's casket. It had. "No," she said in a voice louder than the priest's. The twins sprang simultaneously and grabbed at her as she stood on the edge of the grave, but it was Rätzel who, letting go of Enerde, pulled all three children back from the crumbling ledge of dirt that would have slid them on top of their mother's coffin. In a curiously comical flailing of legs and arms, a noiseless tussle took place on the soft pile of unstable earth before Rätzel pulled all three children away from the grave, moving them in a single sweeping motion to the waiting arms of Luba and Wolsky. The priest cleared his throat, looked up at the clouds of summer, and hurriedly ended the prayer. The mourners began to move from the site, spreading slowly outward like thick dark syrup. Ursula felt someone take her hand, but she snatched it away. "No! No! No!" she cried, and began to run back down the center of the seemingly endless avenue of trees along which the white monuments, turned gray under the cloud cover, appeared to her to make a solid, continuous wall. She knew now what was under them: people lying in boxes. People being eaten by worms. She heard the muffled munching and crunching of the worm teeth as they ate and ate and ate. Then someone grabbed her around the middle from behind and she went sprawling on the gravel. When she turned her head angrily, Günther's red-rimmed eyes met hers. "Why don't you just cry like everybody else," he said hoarsely.

"No!" she screamed. "No! No! No! No! No! No!"

Ursula's first dream of the funeral came two nights later, the events rolling out in front of her much as they had on the day of the actual interment, except that the musician's instruments made no sound, although they were beating on them as before. She was back behind the coffin again watching the players lined up on both sides of the jiggling horses pulling the wagon, on which the nest of caskets (there were three, one within the other holding the eighty-pound corpse), completely covered with its rose blanket, looked somewhat larger than before. The dream ended just before the wagon reached its destination. The next night the dream returned: the musicians beat on their soundless drums with curious animation and the coffin, still larger than the night before, was being moved faster by the horses. For several nights the dream came back to her, always with subtle changes rearranging reality. The change that most alarmed her was the ever-increasing speed of the wagon. She began to stay awake as long as possible, staying in the twins' room until Günther in exasperation told her she had to go to sleep. Reluctantly she returned to her own bed and lay in the darkness trying to hang onto consciousness. When she slept, she entered the dream running, for the horses were trotting fast by then, the musicians taking giant steps behind their huge still drums, whose sides breathed in and out in great silent swells. Her brothers and all the people following were also moving at much greater speed. In subsequent dreams she found herself running faster and faster yet falling behind the procession. Each night she entered the race with terror in her heart, since she alone could not keep up with the wagon. No matter how fast she ran, she lost ground, the distance between herself and the marching mourners became greater and greater, until the final dream, when she lost sight of the cortege altogether and she raced furiously down the long avenue alone until she reached the open grave. Exhausted and gasping, she knelt beside the opening and peered over the edge. At the bottom of the hole stretched out on top of her mother's coffin lay her grandfather.

Her screams brought her brothers running, and when Enerde heard the details of the nightmare from the twins the next day he came out of his own paralytic mourning with a jolt. He tore down the shrouds draping his daughter's portraits, threw out the black wreaths, and returned to his routine of visiting with the children, having tea in the garden, and taking long walks outside the wall. He took Ursula with him, and the two became a familiar sight—the tall white-bearded man listening attentively to the clearly adoring little girl as the two walked daily on the wooded paths in a large park not far from the mansion.

At this same time Ursula believed that her mother's death caused her grandfather to stop his daily habit of leaving for "the office" for a few hours each morning after breakfast. But the facts were that coinciding with Amalia Marie's death was the German confiscation of the Enerde Textile Mills. Two years earlier, when Austria was drawn into its fatal alliance with Germany, the factories were more or less left alone, but some months after the war began they were placed into the forced production of military uniforms and parachutes.

Enerde was enraged that anyone could touch what was his. Having lived serenely through the shimmering summer before Sarajevo, through the autumn of the Old House with its falling shadows and dying echoes of empire and kingdom, he believed himself secure in his wealth. He was thus unprepared for the takeover of the mills and had his lawyers protest vehemently to a puppet government which besides being indifferent was also powerless. But his continued complaints were duly noted as dangerous by the Germans; therefore they allowed him to keep his office—but not his power—since his presence at the plants pacified many of the loyal skilled employees who might have become belligerent and troublesome under a more iron rule. They saw him somewhat like a defanged lion who had nothing left to attack with except the sheer weight of his shoulders, themselves bony and covered with only scant-haired, shriveled skin. But during the second year of the war the Germans suddenly locked the old man out and seized the plants for the *good of the state,* a phrase that made no sense to anyone except the conquering Russians five years later, who noted that the Enerde family had continued to receive a percentage of the profits of the business from the Germans, and therefore claimed the factories as German external assets, in short, booty—a concept the Russians understood clearly but which left the Americans, also conquerors, but unused to medieval war plundering, in gentlemanly bafflement.

During the war, Enerde, who continued to believe that the confiscation of his property by the Germans was only another symptom of his country's temporary madness, retreated further back into the nineteenth century, where life had been more orderly, more controllable, less real. Certainly no one could take a dark little dwarf like Hitler seriously for long. Good sense was bound to return soon, and men who had welcomed the vulgar little upstart would be embarrassed at their lapse of clearheadedness and throw him back into whatever gutter he came from. Enerde put more locks on his gates and ignored the war.

Unfortunately, it did not entirely ignore *him:* many of the younger servants were absorbed by the army or war work. Bronevsky lost his valet as well as his horse groom. Good tutors became rarer. They also became older. Most of the men interviewed were past sixty: a Monsieur Doubois, a kind fool, prone to excessive sentimentality, came to teach mathematics, French, and, unintentionally, an early prejudice against the whole nation of France. His maudlin attempts at justifying the Pétain government were met with contempt by the other teachers and this filtered down over the children like poisoned air. He did win the kids back slightly with his proficiency at the foils, which all of them took to with great seriousness, although a Herr Herring, also past sixty, claimed fencing was passé and the children should become proficient in the use of the pistol. Herring only won over Alexander, the others preferring the bow and arrow, which a Herr Müller claimed was the only honorable weapon of the hunter. His romantic views of the American Indian touched and tainted the children for life as Rousseau's sterile Noble Savage never did. A Herr Süss, short and very fat, a scholar of the ancient Classical World, extolled the wise sayings of Greece, not the least of which was "moderation in all things," even as he reached for yet another cream-drowned torte. This modest irony was not lost on the children, who rather liked him anyway for having committed to memory the entire *Iliad*. Herr Süss, in a wine-warmed moment, tried to form a friendlier friendship with Miss Schneider, who was horribly insulted when she realized he was slyly insinuating sex. Luba Kazlova continued to read to the children, reaching out in every direction and pulling in the quaint Quixote, the insatiable Faust, the cynical Raskolnikov, and one bright afternoon a whaler name Ahab. Miss Schneider admonished her to stay away from Virgil and Shakespeare: "They are my property," she hissed at the Russian woman through her teeth as they passed each other at the entrance of the classroom. This room formed the terminal of one of the long upstairs wings and was from the beginning designed as a classroom. Virtually soundproof and removed from the rest of the activities of the house, it became an island of both peace and war in the children's lives. Alone in it they were at peace. But with the jealous teachers ruling it, it was more often a battleground.

Wolsky, whose life was vanishing into total darkness, was carefully protected by the children, who became his eyes. Ursula and the twins were particularly fond of him and continued to describe the world to him in detail. To the outrage of Miss Schneider, all the children spent a whole day blindfolded as Wolsky taught them to use their other senses. "*Now* where are we?" he asked as they all inched their way around the ten-acre park surrounding the house. "In the vegetable gardens," said Günther. "I can smell the onions."

Miss Schneider complained to Rätzel. "They'll break their bones stumbling around out there. And when are they going to return to real lessons?"

Rätzel rarely allowed himself the caustic comment. He told the woman gently that the children would return to "more formal" lessons when the current informal lesson was completed. She stormed away twice that day, for that evening, the children, still blindfolded, silently ate their dinner with slow, careful movements as Wolsky talked them through the ordeal. "Don't make any sudden motions. Feel what you touch. Decide what it is before you use it. Notice how differently—how much deeper—things taste when you cannot see them. Be careful of the soup; it is very hot." Rätzel and Enerde watched and with their glances ordered the other teachers to remain silent.

Whenever the family traveled, the teachers in residence went along, hugging their briefcases to their chests on the train or private cars that took them to Yugoslavia, Italy, Germany, Switzerland. It was in Switzerland in 1943 on the last night of one of these holidays that Luba Kazlova and Wolsky abruptly departed.

For years Ursula remembered the minutest detail of that parting. Some hours after everyone went to bed, she was awakened by the weeping Luba, who bent over her and kissed her. Always a light sleeper, Ursula felt the

[74]

tears at once. She sat up and saw the twins standing silhouetted in the doorway to her room. "I must leave you now," said Luba. "No, don't turn on the light." Ursula got out of bed and saw by the hall light that Luba was dressed in her gray traveling suit.

"Where are you going?"

Luba did not answer. "Away," said Günther. "She can't come home with us right now." They watched her walk away from them, carrying a wicker suitcase. From the balcony at the end of the hall the three children looked down from the second floor of the house to the driveway, where Wolsky, his upturned face white under his dark hat, looked blindly toward them as Luba joined him. Rätzel, who was holding the door to a car open, spoke a few words. Both teachers waved to the children and hurriedly entered the car. Rätzel stood for a moment in front of the house after the car had gone and looked out over the silent Swiss night. Ursula, stunned by this strange event, ran down the stairs to meet Rätzel, just entering the foyer. "Where are they going?" she asked.

"They cannot come home with us," said Rätzel.

"But where are they going?" Ursula was not used to evasive answers. Rätzel himself had taught all of them that directness was a virtue.

"If all goes well, to England or Canada. Or perhaps they will stay here. But there is some uncertainty about that."

"But why don't they come home with us?"

"They are foreigners and our government would have found out about them sooner or later and not let them stay with us. Now, go back to bed. We leave early in the morning." He walked her back up the stairs, waiting a moment when he saw the twins, as if to say something more to them. But in the end he only wished them a good sleep.

When the children were alone, Ursula started to cry. "I don't want them to go away."

Günther led her back to her room. "I know, but it can't be helped. They could get in trouble if they come back with us. Rätzel says we only came on this trip so we could leave them here. They are illegal."

Ursula stopped crying. "What does that mean?"

"I'm not sure," said Günther, "except that they are illegal in our country . . . and Germany too . . . and other places."

Ursula returned to her bed and waited for sleep. But it seemed to her that there were people wandering about the house, people tiptoeing and pausing, people whispering and becoming silent. Several times she saw a sliver of light shine under her door as if someone were walking past with a lamp. She fell into uneasy sleep and awakened abruptly when someone entered her room. For a moment she believed it was Luba. She was not gone! It was all a bad mistake. Luba had come back to see if she were warm. But then she heard that it was Rätzel, for he had a limp that she recognized and in the dark the odor of his pipe tobacco seemed stronger. She knew he had come to see if she were covered. In the past five years it was Luba who had come each night to her room to pull the kicked-off eiderdown back over her head, tucking it gently at the sides and then kissing her on the forehead or hair, the scent of oranges clinging to her blouse. For years after Luba was lost to her, Ursula remembered her as warmth and comfort, as a vibrant voice that never tired of reading wonderful stories, and always as the fragrance of oranges, which both of them loved. "You see, Little Bear," Luba said once as she carefully peeled an orange for the two of them, "the packaging is quite extraordinary: there is a strong external cover, then a thin protective one on the inside, and the pieces themselves are separately wrapped. And in bite sizes! What a miracle is an orange!"

The departure of Luba and Wolsky saddened everyone except Miss Schneider and the children's father, who held an odd little celebration in Pavel's rooms after the family returned from Switzerland. "I commend you, dear lady. How did you manage?" He poured them both a glass of champagne.

"I simply wrote an anonymous letter to someone in the government who I thought should know that there were two Jews in this house. Those two never fooled me. I can always tell a Jew by that passivity they affect. Disgusting people, so humble on the surface, so corrupt within. No, they didn't fool me. It's too bad the government's inquiry warned the old man. But don't worry; Switzerland won't keep them either. Another letter took care of that."

9

It was two years after her mother's death that Ursula first discovered she could draw. For some months she had been covering wrapping paper and carton lids with her large scrawls of animals copied from a book left open and abandoned by one of her bored brothers. Across a pastry-box lid vaulted a Cretan bull; an arc of ruined stone Delian lions glared darkly through the print of a city newspaper; a centaur, fierce-eyed, rearing, fought off an enemy lost at the edge of a piece of butcher's wrap. Around each central figure she had sketched repeatedly its eye or head or hoof, reinforcing the animal's energy. Having run out of paper, she filled Melchior's penmanship workbook with her drawings, ignoring the lines and margins with cavalier abandon. Melchior complained to the grandfather. "Not only this! She does it on everything. She put that dumb winged horse all over my big kite and she even made fishes on the lid of Paul's telescope box."

The old man studied the notebook with its fiery-eyed crouching panthers and plunging eagles. "Bring me the fishes," he said without looking up from the exercise book. Melchior brought the telescope lid as Ursula, told by an anxious Alexander that their grandfather had ordered her to the library, stood at a distance watching the old man's startled face. Finally he looked at her. "Where did you see these kinds of fish?"

"I don't know," she said, shooting Melchior a murderous glance.

"Did you see these in a book, too?"

"I don't know."

"Of course you know. Think." He turned the lid toward her. "Come here."

The fish were not quite fish: they had the fat bodies of dolphins and big smiling lips. Some were in the act of turning; some sat on their tails; others stood on their heads; one leaned back rakishly on his fins.

"Now, Ursula, think back. Did you see the fish in a book . . . like the other animals?" His voice was gentle.

Ursula shook her head. "No. I don't remember pictures of fish."

"But you have seen plenty of fish."

"Oh, yes. The cook gets them from a man who brings them to the back gate."

"But those are dead."

Ursula could see that Melchior was waiting for her grandfather to scold her. Of all her brothers, she liked him least. He was always crying about something, sniffling and hiccuping and running to tell when any of them gave him even the slightest shove. He didn't deserve to have her grandfather's name. He was nothing like her grandfather . . . except for his brown eyes. She wished *she* had her grandfather's brown eyes.

"Ursula?" The grandfather turned her face toward him. "These are not the dead fish the cook buys. Certainly not this one here making himself comfortable. What is he leaning against?"

"He's just leaning."

"He looks like he's about to light a cigar."

Ursula studied the fish. "He's just had dinner."

The grandfather examined the lid again. "So he has. Yes, that's obvious, now that I look at him closely. Yes, he's had quite a good dinner and he's pleased with himself." He laughed. "Ursula, how long have you been drawing these animals?"

"I don't know."

"Do your brothers draw animals?"

"I don't know."

"Well I *want* you to know. I want you to know that they do not draw animals. Melchior here does not draw animals. Do you, Melchior?"

Melchior shook his head with such smug satisfaction that Ursula wanted to sock him.

"You may go, Melchior," said the grandfather. "And close the door after you."

Ursula watched her brother drift toward the door reluctantly, hanging back until the grandfather urged him out sharply.

"Now, Ursula," began her grandfather, spreading the drawings on the table. "You may not use any of the workbooks for this kind of thing, and probably you should not use cartons or lids or anything that we need to store things in." He hesitated and leaned back in his chair. "You haven't started decorating the walls anywhere, have you?" Ursula shook her head. "And *did* you draw a flying horse all over Melchior's kite?"

Ursula nodded. "But it didn't hurt it. It still flies."

Enerde turned the pages of the handwriting book slowly. "Well, if Mr.

[77]

Spinoza thinks nature abhors a vacuum, it's clear that you feel equally offended by it. I can see that no blank space is going to be safe from you." He paused at a stag's head. "Ursula, do you know why your brothers do not draw animals into their workbooks, or anywhere else for the matter?"

"No."

"Because they do not know how. They have some gifts of their own, but they do not have this one." The old man smiled and pulled her close to him, stroking her hair, kissing it loudly. He was laughing.

The first large drawing tablet her grandfather bought her, Ursula filled at the zoo, her flying hand summing up the animals in trenchant strokes: the languor of the lions, the rhinoceros' flat-footed durability; but it was the monkeys' sad-faced humanity that she caught with striking and disquieting accuracy, covering over half the pages of the pad with their huddled, stoop-shouldered forms, their small sorrowful eyes staring from beneath the ridge of forehead bone with sullen, defeated resentment.

"No, I don't think they hurt," said Enerde to her question, as he sat on a bench beside her, his gloved hands resting on a silver-headed cane positioned squarely between his spread knees. "It's just the way their facial bones come together." He studied a drawing of two rhesus monkeys squatting on a ledge of rock. "If you look at pictures of their bones you'll understand everything about the animals' expressions. I'll give you some bone books." That afternoon on the way home from the zoo, he bought her a new tablet.

A few days later Enerde unlocked all the library cabinets and let the children loose among his books. Ursula was stunned at the greatly expanded size of her world and rushed from one volume to the next in a delirium of delight, abandoning a book of exotic birds for one of exotic fish to a third of quite ordinary snakes, rare enough for her narrow world. Paul and Günther attacked the anatomy books while Boris and Alexander lay sprawled on the floor with a whole set of volumes about machines—airplanes, automobiles, trains—between them. Melchior turned slowly in the center of the library and looked anxiously at the gaping cabinets.

Agnes Schneider first heard about the opening of the library from one of the tutors who was just returning to the classroom from belowstairs. He was smoking a cigarette and it was clear to the governess that the man had just eaten. According to the schedule of lessons and teaching assignments, which she as senior member of the staff now carefully arranged and supervised, the man was supposed to be instructing the children in ancient history and other sundry mythologies at that hour of the morning. The instructor, the last of the young ones, was a student at the university and did not live in the mansion. For some vague reason the army had rejected him when he tried to enlist, and this made him surly and embittered.

"Why are you not at your post?" Miss Schneider asked him, stopping him at the top of the stairs.

The young man had a lean sharp face, softened only by large unhealthy-looking lips which he chewed habitually. "The grandfather collected the little cannibals before I could get at them this morning." He had a bray like a donkey and thought himself witty.

"What do you mean, collected them?"

"He came up to the classroom and got them."

"What for?"

"He told them they were going to spend the morning in the library."

"What for?"

"I don't know and I don't care."

"You're a disgrace. If you don't care for the position, why don't you quit?"

"I like the pay and I eat every meal." He laughed his jackass laugh, blowing smoke at her through his liverish lips.

She drew back, waving her hands back and forth in the air in front of her face. "See that the missed lesson is made up, and do not smoke in the classroom. Don't tell me you don't, because I can smell it after you've used the room." She dismissed him with a last wave of her hand and hurried away with the intention of telling Rätzel of the young tutor's bad habits, vulgarity, and general indifference toward his job. But she would see about the children first. The grandfather's interrupting the schedule made a mockery of all her efforts. Now that she was the senior member on the staff and Rätzel had come to accept her organizational ability and even complimented her on the scheduling arrangement, she could bring him around to backing her up when she saw the need for various corrections. The library indeed! If people kept to their hours and organized their lives, the world would run much more smoothly. Now she was forced to wear her shoes out in this monstrosity of a house trying to discover what the old man wanted with the children. What business did he have spiriting them off to the library? What this house needed was a strong woman to run it. How could men run a house? The cook was a particularly vulgar person of low birth who told unsavory stories of his war days. Cooking rats, indeed! And when she objected to these obscenely described tales, Rätzel had the gall to tell her that the cook was originally hired because anyone who knew how to make a good rat stew was bound to be a master at cooking anything else. These low types always stuck up for each other. If the children's father, the real master of the house, as his aristocratic mien clearly indicated, could only take over his true position and not be forced to live in the false one he now so unhappily had to endure, all their troubles would be over. And as for instructors, one good teacher was all that was needed. One good teacher with a clear understanding of organization and a commitment to the values of hard work, perseverance, determination, and diligence was what was called for.

Miss Schneider lurched to a stop at the open library door and clapped her hands to her mouth as if to hold back a cry. Ursula, hearing the loud gasp, looked up just in time to see her grandfather motion the woman to silence with the raising of a single forefinger into the air in front of him. He was seated in a deep wing chair. At his feet, the twins crouched over an immense anatomy book where the huge figures of a naked man and woman stood out sharply in rich pink paint against the white page, their sexual organs shaded in a somewhat deeper tone of the same color so that the nipples and penis, scrotum and labia made a more ponderous statement than the rest of the body, particularly the two faces, which were doll-bland and imbecilely asmile with tiny teeth.

Ursula, lying on the floor in a corner, her arms sphinx-fashion cradling a book of mythical beasts, surveyed the room: Boris sat on one of the window seats, a dark leather volume resting on his crossed knee, his free foot tapping the air to some silent rhythm. In the companion wingback to the one in which their grandfather sat, the bookless Melchior huddled peevishly, his arms wrapped like a straitjacket about his chest, his face pale and agitated. Alexander pulled book after book from a cabinet, glanced at each title page, and returned it with an exasperated shrug. It was obvious to Ursula that he was going to be hard to please. She watched her grandfather motion to Miss Schneider to enter the room. The woman quickly regained her poise, her large smile overcompensating for the earlier reaction of outrage. "What a nice special treat," she said. "What lucky children you are to get this rare visit to such a wonderful library."

Only the two Melchiors looked up at the governess. "You're quite right," said Enerde, clearing his throat comfortably. "Too rare. Too rare. In the future the library will no longer be locked. Every cabinet will be open to the children." He rose. "See that they spend some time here each day, though from the looks of things, that won't take much urging."

"Are you sure they are ready for this, sir?" Miss Schneider was still smiling as she spoke.

Enerde looked at her in puzzlement. "Ready for what?"

"Why . . . *this*"—she motioned, her arms encompassing the entire room into the gesture.

"This?"

"All these books."

"I don't take your meaning."

"I mean, sir, that young children should not be given too free rein with . . . with an *entire* library." Her voice was vibrantly earnest, her smile all but faded.

"Nonsense. That's what a library is for. And I like your word for it: 'free rein.' Yes, that's very good, 'free rein.' "

"But, sir, if you let them read anything they want, they will lose interest in their formal lessons."

Ursula watched her grandfather's face become sober. "Nonsense. You see to it that the lessons are kept interesting and you'll not lose them."

"But, sir . . . the staff can't compete with some of these books; many of them are full of . . . of pictures. Why, they'll stop reading altogether. They'll stop being *readers*; they'll only be lookers. It's a mistake, sir."

By then it was clear to Ursula that all of her brothers were listening to the delicate argument taking place above their heads. The twins were looking away from Miss Schneider toward the windows, their expressions dreamy, bland, so bland in fact as to express minds that were vacant of any concern on the matter and totally disinterested. Ursula knew better. The twins were devouring every word.

The quiet argument in the library suddenly took on a new tone. "Mistake? What is a mistake?" Enerde's voice hardened, thickened, though it did not rise in volume.

"Oh, I mean no offense, sir. I only mean that some of the books are too—too mature for children."

"Nonsense. If they find them interesting, they are ready for them. If not, they will ignore them."

"Oh, I quite agree. Absolutely, sir, absolutely. But couldn't they find them a little . . . *too* interesting?" Miss Schneider tilted her head to one side as she spoke, her smile sincere, earnest, confidential.

Enerde glanced down at the children. Even Melchior had a book in his lap by then, over which his blond bowed head seemed frozen. Alexander appeared deeply engrossed in a combat diagram ("The Battle of Shiloh: American Civil War") in a book of war maps. The others were, as before, to all appearances lost in the volumes open in front of them. Ursula no longer watched her brothers, and the many-headed monster on the page in front of her faded as her eyes gazed at some midpoint between herself and the page as she listened to her grandfather's voice drop even lower, become even thicker. "Too interesting? Can a book be too interesting?"

"What I mean to say, sir, though I seem to be saying it badly, is that some of the books are not meant for children; they are—how can I put it?—they are too *adult* for children." She dropped her voice to a whisper. "Note, sir, the book the twins are . . . examining, for example. Would you not call it a . . . rather gross book?"

Enerde answered without looking down at the two boys. "No, madam, I would call that an anatomy book. Are you implying that my library is not morally sound?"

Miss Schneider babbled furiously that she did not mean that at all, not at *all,* and hastily retreated to her room to weep over the unfairness of things: she had been promoted to being in charge of all the other tutors and now her authority was being undermined by the grandfather's interference. The library was full of lascivious books that would corrupt the children, making them coarse and depraved. And worst of all, nobody paid any attention to her opinion. She was giving every hour of her life to making these children normal, and now their own grandfather was destroying all her work. Perhaps she should leave this dreadful place. But even as she looked about her room through swimming eyes, even as she thought of packing, as she saw herself placing garment upon garment into her trunk, she knew she could not leave the house of her love.

The children had long hoped Miss Schneider would leave. In their eyes she had caused the departure of every tutor they had ever liked. They did not give her credit for getting rid of the ones they did not like, although she did this also. In Ursula's mind Miss Schneider was somehow responsible for the loss of Luba and Wolsky, although she had no facts upon which to base her belief.

From the time of the opening of the library a subtle change took place between Miss Schneider and the children: unknown to themselves they began to assault her weaknesses. For reasons unclear to them, she was fanatic about secrets: "Vice is nourished by secrecy," she pronounced from her private pulpit. Vice was fairly abstract to them, although they had some undefined idea of what she meant. They discovered early that her mania manifested itself in a number of physical ways: she sifted through their private belongings, their clothing, their books, for any evidence of concealed wickedness. They dubbed her "Miss Schnabel," a cruel double play since not only did she stick her beak into their secrets but her suffering wet nose was long and nib-sharp as well. The children soon learned that the surest and quickest way to drive their snoopy governess into shrieking lunacy was to answer her prying questions with the smug implication that they could not betray a secret. But after the incident in the library, their strategy took the form of action.

One profoundly clear memory that Ursula nurtured with care over the years was the expression on Miss Schneider's face after demanding of Günther that he reveal what he had in his trouser pocket. When he refused adamantly, she pulled his hand forcibly from the pocket and plunged her own into it, not knowing that Günther had removed the bottom of the pocket and had for some time been disturbing his somewhat well-developed and not at all juiceless root. After the lady rushed from the room, Paul asked, "Did it do it?" Günther, who was barely thirteen at the time and not wishing to be disbelieved, nodded proudly and showed them. Ursula, who had seen her brothers urinate with far greater convenience than herself, had long ago been told by Günther that she was not supposed to have "one of these." Some time passed before she understood that her brother had not urinated into the governess's grasping hand.

But it was a snake that finally freed the children from Miss Schneider's snooping. There was in the Enerde mansion an enormous room on the fourth floor, sheltered under the mansard roof, its finely leaded windows staring out from under deeply hooded gables. A lovely circular stairway at one side of a raised stage at the far end of the room led to the flattened roof crowned by the garland of intricate baroque wrought-iron fencing. This top floor had once stored a collection of antique arms which Enerde's father donated to the National Museum when his son was born, turning the space into a playroom complete with puppet stage and fine handmade toys. When Enerde was fourteen he and Rätzel more or less abandoned it. For fifty years no child laughed in it. Neither of the Amalias liked the large, silent room with its vaguely slanted walls and shadowy corners. But after the birth of the twins, Enerde modernized the area, installing a bath, repapering the curved walls and alcoves, and introducing an elaborate toy train set which encircled an extensive village, each car and tree and policeman directing traffic modeled to his desired scale. The children loved the room, and for a number of years two maids and a supervising governess gave it a biweekly cleaning.

Some months after the scene in the library, an employee from the Enerde Textile Mills forest division caught a handsome Aesculapian reptile in one of the firm's wooded holdings and presented it to the children one fine sunny Saturday. They took it to the fourth floor at once, where Miss Schneider was supervising the cleaning with the two upstairs maids. All three women shrieked as Günther, the snake curled around his neck, fell writhing to the floor among them, aping a colorful death as the other children argued heatedly over who would get their brother's possessions. The women ran screaming from the room. That afternoon at dinner, Paul announced that the snake preferred to run loose in the room and that anyone going to the fourth floor should be mindful of where she stepped. From that moment on the playroom belonged exclusively to the children.

Actually the snake did poorly, paled, and died soon after its arrival, but the kids continued to tell the governess anecdotes about the snake's charms and on a given morning celebrated the birth of twenty-five baby Aesculapians, all beautifully bronze-colored and marvelously active, and also loose in the room.

Miss Schneider complained directly to the grandfather, who reproved her mildly for her fears and told her it was healthy for children to be interested in such things. "Why," he remembered, "as a boy I had a snake or two myself. They make fine pets. Not at all the slimy things most people think they are."

"But they crawl up one's legs and try to enter the body," wept Miss Schneider.

"Nonsense. That's an absurd myth. Leave the children's snakes alone and they won't give you any trouble." The statement's ambiguity only came to Miss Schneider later as she lay in her bed, the door to her room sealed with a towel pinched under it, her mind feverish with its visions of vipers slithering along the hall outside.

The governess's only hope that she could yet control the children lay in getting rid of all the other teachers: she believed she would then be indispensable to the family, failing to consider Death's last laugh on that outrageously tenuous presumption. But if Miss Schneider thought of death at all, it was the grandfather's demise for which she waited. She believed that if she alone were the children's teacher when their grandfather finally died, Pavel Bronevsky would turn to her for help. Did he not already open his heart to her about his long-suffering trial in this house where his natural abilities were thwarted and abused? Did he not trust her with his innermost thoughts, his longings to break free of this languid existence and yet give his life some great meaning? She grasped at the most meager evidence of affection from him: a casual smile gave her hopeless hope and sent her into an orgy of dreaming that he was secretly in love with her. Her delusions knew few limits: other women did not have her beautiful soul, her sensitive nature, her loyalty. She believed that if he knew her—really came to know the depth of her love for him—he would be moved by her kindness, her devotion, her passion. She created opportunities to have their paths cross, making the encounters appear accidental, spontaneous, casual. Every few months she wrote him formal notes (delivered under his door) inviting him to visit the classroom to hear the children at their lessons. When he did finally visit one day, to her, as well as the children's great surprise, she was quickly reduced to repetitious babbling. "Up, up children. Rise quickly. Up. Your dear father is honoring us with his presence. How excellent, how truly excellent of you to honor us, sir. We all know how busy you are, don't we, children? Yes. Yes. We do, indeed. Up, up, children. Günther, Ursula, up. Up, up!"

As the minutes passed, the children became much more astonished at their teacher's behavior than at their father's appearance in the classroom. They were used to visits from Rätzel; and even their grandfather occasionally wandered in and sat in a chair by the window, browsing through some of their workbooks. But neither of these visitors ever surprised anyone and the children went on with their work, sometimes even growing unaware of the guest among them. But never in all the days at their lessons had any of their teachers' nature turned abruptly into one they no longer recognized. Not only was Miss Schneider's transformation bizarre, it had a quality of madness to it, only the children would not have called it that. They first saw her behavior as marvelously strange: the twitching shoulders, the fluttering hands, the near-hysterical voice, all were as unforgettable as a giant bird flapping about the room might have been. By the time of their father's third visit, they knew what to expect and her hysteria was only funny to them and easily imitated and caricatured. Alexander would prance about behind her back, rolling his eyes heavenward and taking quick mincing tiptoe steps in little circles as the others tried to stifle their laughter, usually unsuccessfully. Bronevsky's visits did not begin until after Wolsky and Luba Kazlova had made their escape in Switzerland. Miss Schneider had by then vanquished most of the other tutors, wearing them down by endless revamping of schedules which gave them the early morning between six and nine, which everyone hated except the children, or the hours immediately after midday dinner, at which time the children's lethargy and sullenness was matched only by their indifference to the subject taught. One particular tutor, the last woman hired, a middle-aged Italian lady named Alfreda Scotti from Geneva, gifted in the art of painting with watercolors, but employed to continue the French lessons and account for the history of the world, left because Miss Schneider discovered that these difficult hours were ideal for Miss Scotti. She loved the morning light, teaching the children the use of their watercolor sets and forgetting all about the Dark Ages. The children absorbed her love for Turner and Constable with their seas and heaths and listened to the woman talk of "streams of light" and "the color of God" in her rich throaty French. Discovering her mistake, Miss Schneider rescheduled Alfreda's hour, giving her only the weekends in which to teach. For a time Miss Scotti spent the other days in creating subtle little pictures of areas of the garden and surreptitiously trading off an occasional Sunday afternoon for a few early hours during the week with one of the men who particularly hated mornings. But Miss Schneider frequently arranged outings for the children's weekends, leaving Alfreda with nothing to do. This confusion of hours and uncertainty of her position on the staff got to her before she got to Columbus' discovery of America, and she gave notice to Rätzel without giving him a reason for her resignation. On the morning she left, she gave Rätzel some drawings of Ursula's. "I would not ignore these if I were you."

Rätzel looked at the pictures and felt himself color: Graz's astonished expression, bizarrely exaggerated, stared back at him. Only Miss Scotti's fine mustache, which lay like a faint shadow along her clearly delineated upper lip, and narrow-set intense eyes dominated another sheet. Rätzel's own sad countenance stared back at him forlornly. He looked up from the drawings at the waiting woman. "What do you suggest?"

"If we were not at war, I would say a good school in Paris or Florence. There is also a man in Berlin that I know of, but in these times, these places will soon be doomed." She smiled. "Don't let it die. And by the way, there are more of these, but the girl has hidden them. They are all of Miss Schneider and they are stunning. I'm not sure if the cruelty in them is intended."

[84]

Rätzel smiled faintly. "Would you like yours?"

"I have mine." She drew a tablet from her train case and took two loose sheets out of it, placing two caricatures on Rätzel's desk: Luba's long face, clouded with her dark sorrow, stared back from one sheet. On the other, Alfreda's countenance, her eyes caught in a moment of narrowing, gazed at the world with amused skepticism and irony. It was not a particularly flattering portrayal, and yet it carried an appeal far more powerful than beauty.

"She does them from memory," began Miss Scotti, "but I've watched her draw directly from models—mostly her brothers—all caricatures. Boris was insulted. The others only laughed. Caricaturing is her true gift, although she draws well generally. The one of her mother she does over and over. I rescued this one from the trash bin."

Rätzel picked up the sheet with Luba's sad face on it. "That's not her mother."

"Not her mother?"

"No. A former teacher. A lady who was like a mother to her . . . to all the children."

"Well, whoever she was, she certainly left a mark on that child." She picked up the drawings. "I'm sorry to leave you, but I know when it's time to move on. Perhaps you'll find someone who can stay a long time. This continuous arrival and departure of people can't be very good for the children."

Rätzel nodded. "Good teachers are very hard to find now. If you could give me a reason for your resignation, it might help."

Rätzel had a good idea why Alfreda Scotti was leaving, but he did not wish to dismiss Miss Schneider until he had hard evidence that the woman was causing the other teachers to leave. "If there is something you would like to say about your position here, some complaint . . . rather . . . some protest, it would help me toward solving the tutor problem. I don't have anything definite from anyone. No one gives any particular reason, you see, except that they wish to try something else. Miss Scotti, anything that you say will be kept confidential. I understand that you may not wish to make any accusations, but for the good of the children any recommendation or suggestion you would care to make would help."

Miss Scotti laughed. "Well, I'm afraid that would amount to the same thing. No, there is no particular reason, except perhaps that I don't have enough to do, and the fact is, I want to go home before the war ends. I don't think Austria will be a very good place to be when this war is finally over."

The woman's brown eyes deepened perceptibly and she lowered her voice. "I could take the girl with me. Geneva will be safe. I have relatives who have a house there. She would be in good hands. At nine, she is old enough to be away from home. Believe me, I would take good care of her."

Rätzel searched the woman's face. He liked her hard practical view of the world, her clear sense of self-possession, her unwillingness to leave blame behind for her own departure. "No. But thank you very much. Her grandfather couldn't bear it."

The woman shrugged, shook Rätzel's hand for the second time, and left.

Rätzel felt in his heart that Miss Schneider was somehow at fault for many of the classroom problems, yet his emotions were mixed about letting her go: she was an exceptionally good organizer. Also, she never missed a lesson of her own in the schedule and she frequently took over the duties of others. She did not coddle the children, but then, neither did she abuse them. She was not as imaginative or innovative as some of the other tutors, or as humorous, and certainly not as handsome. He summed her up in that most devastating of all impressions for either man or woman—she was sexless. And for this terrible judgment he felt a certain guilt, a disquieting equivocation which forced on him a tolerance that bore no relationship to the teacher problem. He told himself that *he* had not hired her, that teachers were hard to find, that she would mellow as time passed, knowing that none of these were valid reasons for keeping her on. At times, after other teachers left abruptly, he decided to take the matter to Enerde, bolstering his determination with the memory of Luba and Wolsky. Yet he would suddenly find himself reconsidering: he had no proof, no facts at all that Miss Schneider had revealed Luba's and Wolsky's identities to the authorities, only a premonition. Thus something always held him back. He would see her wretchedly unhappy face and relent, hear her fast angry footfalls on the stairs and reconsider, sense her profound despair and become indecisive.

The children told him nothing, not about Miss Schneider or any of the other teachers. Not that he believed they were conspiratorially quiet; they were simply so constituted that they kept a good deal of information to themselves, or perhaps they had lived with the bickering among the teachers and the sudden departures for so long that they now considered the conditions quite normal and acceptable.

With the departure of Miss Scotti, only four tutors besides Miss Schneider remained: the university student, a writing master, a mathematician, and a music teacher. This last man, an elderly concert pianist, was carefully nurturing the twins' gift for playing the piano. "The others are hopeless. Forget about them," he said to Rätzel excitedly. "But these two. Ah, these two. Give me these two for ten years and we shall have such concerts . . ."

"Teach all of them," said Rätzel. "Teach all of them at least the rudiments of the instrument."

"Not all of them have ears."

"Teach them anyway. Grow ears for them."

The piano teacher let his shoulders sag hopelessly and for another few months tried to teach all the children the mysteries of music before he was found dead in his bed one morning, the victim of a diseased heart.

The writing master was a man named Kogel who enjoyed eating more than anything else and was shaped like a pear, as though his intake of five meals a day hated to leave him. He was hired to teach the children the technique of writing clearly in German. "The subject is not important," he stressed repeatedly, slicing the air in front of him with a cutting motion of his stubby hands, his wattled cheeks shaking loosely. "It's all in the manner of presentation. Did you state the argument cleverly?" He ended every lesson with a motto as useless to him as it was hilarious to the children: "Strive for lucidity." They liked him anyway, mainly because he could fix things. Forcibly retired from one of the local schools soon after the Germans arrived in '38, he had been able to find work only as a handyman until he answered Rätzel's advertisement for a mathematics teacher and settled for the writing job when another man more qualified showed up the same day for the same job. This second man was an old employee from one of the Enerde mills, where he had worked as a bookkeeper. His hatred of the Germans verged on the pathological, for he was one of those fascinating anomalies of human nature—the permanently angry but patient man. Fierce-eyed with a thin hairless face and a comically shaped bald head, he convinced Kogel shortly before the end of the war to join him in a conspiracy against "the invaders," as he called the Germans. They left the mansion late one night with the intention of blowing up something. The device, carefully put together by the bookkeeper and Kogel, who had by then fixed all the chairs in the house and tightened every door and window hinge, worked perfectly—twenty minutes too early. No one ever knew how the book-keeper managed to get enough explosives to blow two men and one small rowboat into thousands of pieces in the middle of the Danube near one of its charming old bridges soon to be blown up by more successful demolition experts. Rätzel and Enerde waited for the police or the military to show up. When no one came, it was clear to them that no one knew where the two dead men had lived, let alone what they were up to.

Miss Schneider, who was still scheming at emptying the house of its various instructors, felt wonderfully elated at the abrupt departure of Kogel and the bookkeeper. She had not actually desired their deaths, but since "that was their fate," as she told the children, "it was meant to be." The twins groaned at this rounded logic and hung Ursula's caricatures of the two men on the wall in the playroom, where a row of other teachers's faces gazed down from amplified and extended, augmented and inflated like-nesses.

It was Alexander who got rid of the braying university student, or at least who set a process into motion which caused the grandfather to threaten to shoot the man. At age twelve, Alexander decided to become a boxer. For a few days he danced around the others taking playful jabs at the twins, who shrugged him off, poking his gloved fist near Melchior's startled face and Boris' cold shoulder. Melchior ran and hid, whereas Boris told him that his aggressive tendencies were the signs of a difficult oncoming puberty, thus embarrassing Alexander into leaving him alone. For a time he jumped rope, shadowboxed, and imitated the attitudes and postures in a book of famous pugilists. Ursula drew him as he "worked out," but when he saw the drawing, the unflattering jutting chin, the lank hair hanging over the eyes, the inflated chest, the overlong arms ending in gloves larger than his head, he took an unplayful jab at her cheek. Coming out of her stagger, she swung her heavy wood-backed drawing tablet against the side of his head and knocked him cold. Günther and Paul bent over their brother and quickly saw that he was not dead; "eight, nine, ten," said Günther as Alexander opened his eyes. "Now, you knew better than that, didn't you, little brother?"

Alexander slunk off dazed, but a week later he asked the university student to help him train. The man agreed.

The first warning that something was wrong came when Alexander, crying and swearing, ran from the old nursery (now a sort of makeshift gymnasium) and locked himself in his room. Rätzel opened the door with a passkey and talked to the boy alone. No, the man had not hit him. No, he had not shoved him. "What, then?" asked Rätzel. A few minutes later an angry Rätzel came out of Alexander's room and went to find Enerde, saying nothing to the children waiting in the gallery. By the time the grandfather had his gun loaded the university student was gone. All Ursula could make of all the commotion was that the student had failed to come out of a clinch. Boris told her that the man had a "serious physical disorientation." Dissatisfied with this answer, she asked the twins. But they put her off, telling her they would let her know when they knew more themselves.

Miss Schneider never knew what caused the man to leave without his belongings, although she asked everyone. "Now, then, Ursula, we are both women, so you can tell me anything," she began early the next morning when she found the girl alone in the wintry garden sketching the naked trees. Ursula did not answer. She hated to be talked to while she was working.

"Was Alexander injured? He looks all right to me. What did he say? Did anyone see that awful, coarse person hit Alexander? Why was your grandfather so upset? Come on, now, you can tell me anything. We women have to stick together."

Ursula had done a dozen drawings of the governess. She was easy to caricature: a hook of nose reaching for a jut of chin, the two separated by a slash of mouth and looked over by a small flattening, lashless circle—only four lines—and Miss Schneider's profile roared out of the tablet like a flying witch. "Your nose is dripping," said Ursula. "You better go inside."

"Oh, you nasty child. You mean, thankless child. The whole lot of you are as vicious as wolves. You'll be sorry one day for your heartlessness. You'll remember that I offered you friendship and you threw it in the mud." She rushed away and almost slipped on some black ice on a path some distance from the trees Ursula was drawing, her body teetering crazily until she regained her balance. "Oh, oh, oh, my ankle," she cried, clinging desperately to the hand held out to her.

The hand was gloved and appeared from under a cape and belonged to Ursula's father, who was just then coming home from a night in town. For some time now, the family knew that he did not use the front door if he arrived home after daylight. On some mornings the children caught glimpses of him from the upper stair landing as he weaved his way through the garden to one of the back doors. Miss Schneider fell against his chest with a motion that might have passed for fainting. She was weeping.

"Poor, dear lady, let me help you. Here, I'll carry you." He swung her up into his arms. "We'll have to see to that ankle. Can't have you walking on a sprained ankle. And a very nice ankle it is, I must say." Miss Schneider leaned her head againt Bronevsky's neck and whimpered. "There, there," he said. "We can't have such a splendid ankle damaged any further." He hiccuped loudly and staggered a bit under his burden but seemed then to collect himself and proceed further along the path, breathing heavily, stumbling forward into the white puffs of his own breath. Slowly one arm began to fail him as it inched down his side, causing the tall woman's hips and legs to slide downward across his body until her feet dragged on the ground. He staggered under the awkward uneven pull of her weight, since she still had both her arms wound about his neck. "Dear lady, I'm afraid I can't . . . seem to . . ."

"Oh, please don't let me go," she cried. "Please take me inside. I can't walk. Please. Oh, please, please."

"I'm frightfully sorry. I can't seem to get my breath. I'll send someone out to . . ." He ended in a profound hiccup.

"Oh, no, no. Please. Please try."

He staggered on another dozen steps, dragging her along the path, his hands flailing the air like a tightrope walker losing his balance. Abruptly he stopped. "I'm sorry, but I'm finished," he whispered hoarsely, his breath coming in gasps. "It's the cold, you see; and I haven't slept all night. And I'm afraid I'm not at my best. Actually, I'm rather ill."

"I don't care. I don't care. I love you. Don't let me go. I love you. I love you! I adore you! Adore you! Take me. Please. I beg of you." She slid down the front of his body and grasped him about the thighs with both arms. "Love me. Love me. I beg you on my knees to love me. Give me this. I beg of you. Give me your love and I'll be your slave forever. Your slave. Your slave!" She thrust her face into his crotch.

Ursula, watching from behind a winter-struck hedge, saw her father grimace, his lips pulled back so that she could see his clenched teeth. He mumbled something under his breath as he struggled to pull away from the woman, pushing down on her head with his hand and stepping out of her encircling arms with a high, awkward hop. Once free, he bolted, the cloak which Miss Schneider grasped in her hands ripping from his shoulders as he ran, the button flying into the air like a leaping bug. Miss Schneider fell forward onto the cloak, her whole body shuddering with short cries that came from her wide-open mouth. Ursula saw her father running in a wavering line around a curve in the garden walk. Twice he plunged headlong into the hedge, each time shaking himself loose and running again in a slow-motion, lethargic gait that a pantomimist might use to mimic a drunk. Then he was gone as the path turned toward the house.

Ursula looked back at the prostrate governess, and just as she decided she should go for help, Agnes Schneider rose to her knees, picked up the cloak, and gently brushed it off. Folding it carefully before she got to her feet, she glanced anxiously around the barren garden, then rose and hurried away in the opposite direction, clutching the cloak against her chest as one might carry a rare treasure from a burning house.

IO

"Would you ever be someone's slave?" Ursula wanted to know of Günther later that day in the library.

But it was Boris who answered her. "Certainly not! What an absurd question."

"I didn't ask *you*," she retorted, throwing him an icy glance.

"What do you mean by slave?" asked Günther, putting down his book.

"I'm not sure." She had images of people in chains rowing longboats, and shackled black men standing on auction blocks, Eliza with her baby running across a half-frozen river, hopping from one chunk of ice to the next as men with howling dogs closed in on her, but she knew this was not what Miss Schneider meant by slave.

"Well, there are different kinds of slavery. Give me some idea of what you mean and maybe I can answer you."

"I don't know what I mean," she said, looking down at her book to estimate how many pages remained to the end of a section. "Schnabel told Father that she wanted to be his slave." Ursula looked up just in time to see the twins give each other one of those quick glances that was like a shouted word of warning. Boris ringed the neck of his blue turtleneck sweater with a bent forefinger, cleared his throat, and stuck his nose back into his book. How curious all this was, thought Ursula—these strange glances and shiftings about.

"When?" asked Günther.

"When what?"

"When did Miss Schneider say this?"

"This morning in the garden. Father was just coming home along that path by the hedge and she fell on him."

"She fell on him?"

"She slipped and fell on him. She said her ankle was broken and he tried to carry her but couldn't. Anyway, her ankle wasn't broken because she walked perfectly fine after he couldn't carry her, so she just made it up." Ursula became aware of the large silence in the library. The twins were watching her closely and she knew that Boris only pretended to read. "She said a lot of nonsense about love, but I think he was pretty disgusted over the whole thing." She hesitated. "Why do you suppose she lied about her ankle being broken?"

No one answered her, and it was in that charged silence, in the expressions on her brothers' faces, that a mystery began to unravel for her: there was something peculiar going on between her father and Miss Schneider. The woman's babbling in the classroom, the way she lurked about in the foyer whenever their father went out at night, and now this new business about love and being a slave—all these things were in some way tied together. "What is she doing?" Then, even before her words were fully out, it came to her what Miss Schneider wanted. "Oh! She wants to take Mother's place." Ursula saw at once from the twins' dropped eyelids and Boris' even more obvious pretense at reading that the truth was jumping about in the room like an angry ape.

"Ursula," began Paul, "it's better that we don't talk about it; we don't really know what it's all about. And it's not a good idea for Melchior and Alexander to hear any of it just in case it's not . . ."

"They know," said Boris, "and it's true."

"You told them?" asked Günther.

"Why not? Schneider's abnormal behavior around our father is not exactly a secret."

"Abnormal?"

"I assure you I could chart a perfect pattern of obsessional behavior where she is concerned."

"Don't bother," said Günther. "You've probably done enough damage already."

"It's not damage at all. People ought always to face the truth."

"Whose truth?" asked Paul blandly.

Boris drew himself up with irritated disdain. "You know what I mean. There's only one truth. In any circumstance, there's always one set of facts that is more . . . more real than any other set. And I believe that people ought to face those facts head-on."

"Why? Why should Melchior face those facts, as you put it, even if they are true?" Paul's voice was still calm, still gravely gentle—a stone wrapped in cold silk.

"Because facing the truth makes one strong."

"Batshit," said Günther. "He doesn't have to know anything about it. It makes no difference whether it's true or not. You don't have to muck things up with a lot of your theories. Thinking about Miss Schneider lusting after Father isn't going to make Melchior strong. He's going to worry about it and feel bad. Why can't you just shut up. Not everything has to be said."

"It doesn't hurt him to know the truth."

"Don't be an ass! Of course it hurts him. How did it come up, anyway?"

"I don't recall." Boris put on a miffed air and returned to his book.

"Well, recall!" said Günther, rising. "Just how stupid were you?"

"I only answered his question."

"What question?"

Ursula closed her book, feeling a sudden uneasiness as Günther stood over Melchior, his face set in suspicious anger.

"Well, it appears that last night Melchior saw Miss Schneider following Father—at least as far as the gate. So, today he asked me if she was trying to bring Father something he had forgotten, and he couldn't see why she just didn't call out to him. She couldn't, of course, as you well know."

"Get on with it."

"I just told him the truth."

"The truth?"

"That Miss Schneider wanted to be one of Father's women, that she had a physical obsession for him." The smug tone of Boris' voice caught Ursula off guard and it was that rather than the actual statement that made her draw in her breath.

"And did that information make him strong?" asked Günther.

"Well, he *always* cries, but when he thinks about it, he'll be glad he knows the truth. Anyway, he'll console himself with prayer. He sneaks off to church, doesn't he? So why can't he understand Miss Schneider sneaking off after Father?"

"You think that's the same thing, do you?" asked Paul.

"Of course it's the same thing. He's obsessed with the Church. It's a weakness like any other."

"I suppose you told him that, too?"

"I had to. I believe knowing it will help him to neutralize all this incessant churchgoing."

"What business is it of yours if he wants to go to church?" Günther sat on the edge of the reading table and stared angrily at his younger brother.

"All fixations are unhealthy and should be neutralized as early as possible."

Boris' superior tone, his certainty of his judgments, his smug face, his foot tapping the empty air, all drove Ursula into a fury. She would think about Father and Miss Schneider later. At the moment she wanted to pound Boris' head with the nearest heavy object. "I don't know what you mean by an obsession, but I think he goes to church because he's afraid of the dark," she said, seeing at that same moment the twins turning toward her, their faces carrying a look of wonder, their mouths shaped into an odd identical half-smile.

"How ridiculous!" said Boris.

"No," intoned the twins simultaneously. Günther continued. "Not ridiculous at all. No, no, not at all. Ursula, what a fine thought!"

"I see no connection," said Boris, readjusting himself in his chair. "None whatsoever."

"Boris, there's more than one kind of dark," said Günther.

"Spare me an explanation, please. Metaphysical discussions are a complete bore. I'll bet I could cure him of his phobia in a week, given the chance. All the answers to human problems lie in analysis. Freud is the true God of the modern age."

"How amazing," said Günther after a moment, shaking his head as though in admiration. "Do you realize, Paul and my dear sister, that our brother here is at fourteen already a hopeless nincompoop, an old fogy with a petrified brain, beyond help? Too bad." He laughed briefly. "So it's to be joy through Freud, is it?"

"Not a bad motto," said Boris, unruffled. "I tell you now that I intend someday to be the greatest psychoanalyst in the history of the world."

"In the meantime, where did you leave Melchior?" asked Paul.

Boris shrugged. "I have no idea where he went. One can't stay with a patient twenty-four hours a day."

Ursula and the twins left the estate by an old forgotten gate unrecognizable as such from the outside and hidden behind a choked rose arbor, its massive canes naked now except for a few of last year's dried, malformed blooms. The children had already quietly searched the house for Melchior, but found only Alexander asleep on a couch on the top floor.

The church they raced to was a poor one, old and small, with crumbling external stucco the color of urine, and a worn threshold older than the present church and originally built for one of its ancestors. The smell of incense, musky and mysterious, tickled Ursula's nostrils, bringing into memory her mother's funeral with its chanting priests swinging their smoking canisters in short arcs over the people's heads. She did not actually dislike the smell, but she distrusted it; there was a gamy essence to it that made her wonder what the priests burned. They found Melchior prostrate at the feet of a suntanned Christ nailed to His cross in a dim corner to the right of the apse behind three staggered semicircles of candle ends which flickered petulantly and dripped wax onto wrought-iron holders, forming oozing stalagmites and dull puddles. In the late afternoon the church was empty except for the boy stretched out before the cross.

Melchior rose to his knees when the twins spoke to him, but he refused to come away with them.

"No," he said quietly but firmly. "I am praying for Father and I am not finished."

"Just exactly what did Boris tell you?" asked Gunther.

Melchior dropped his chin to his chest. "He told me where Father goes . . . at night . . . and why he doesn't come home until morning."

Günther squatted down beside his brother. "How long do you intend to pray?"

"I don't know. He's . . . he's full of sin."

"Couldn't you pray for him at home?" asked Ursula.

"It isn't the same. This is the house of God. He hears better here. It's made for that."

Ursula looked toward the shabby cloths covering the altar and realized they were sheets. All the high windows were boarded up since the two major bomb attacks a year and a half before had blown out the stained glass. And although services were still held on Sundays, the pews were missing from the nave, and even the primitively wood-carved stations of the cross were gone now. Only this painted-doll figure of Christ with His sad eyes and curiously half-smiling mouth remained. And, of course, the stubby bits of candles which she had seen old women come and light the other time she had been in the church to get Melchior. The crisis that time had been beyond her comprehension. It occurred the year before and all she knew of it was that her brother had opened a door and seen something that sent him into a fit of weeping. The twins had tried to console him then, too, but he broke away from them and an hour later she went with them to the small yellow church to bring him home. She had come to realize rather early in her life that problems were not to be taken to her grandfather or even Rätzel, that they—the six of them—were to work things out among themselves. "Maybe," she said to the twins, "we could help with the rest of the praying that needs to be done and then we can all go home."

She saw Günther smile before he could turn away, but to her surprise he said, "Why not? Right, Paul?"

"Right."

Melchior frowned deeply. "Will you do that?" He looked hard at each of them. "Will you pray for Father?"

Günther glanced away toward the figure of Christ. "Sure, why not?" Paul nodded.

"Is there something particular that we're supposed to say?" asked Ursula, looking over her shoulders at the gray windows in the church.

Melchior sighed. "Ask God to give Father strength to resist sin. Ask Him to give Father courage to turn away from evil and march onto the path of righteousness. Ask Him to give Father the grace to make him contrite and feel true repentance, the humility to kneel before heaven and beg for forgiveness. . . ." Melchior continued with the prayer instructions, his voice getting stronger, deeper, weightier. Ursula saw the twins give each other one of their motionless glances, a look that seemed to be formed only by a darkening of their irises until they appeared almost paralyzed. Abruptly Melchior stopped talking, bowed his head over his steepled hands, and whispered his words so fast and so softly they made only a steady sibilant hum. She followed the twins' example and knelt before the cross, but somehow Melchior's instructions sank out of sight in some deep place in her mind as she noticed that Christ's toes were missing. She wondered if one could walk without toes, and after flexing her own, she decided against it. No, Christ would stumble and fall on those feet. Toes were needed to push off with or root one to the ground. The wounds made by the nail could heal, the bones could mend, but toes were essential. Toes were truly magnificent. So were fingers. Even more magnificent. Christ's fingers were all there although somewhat curled because of nails driven through the palms. Ursula looked at her own steepled hands and Melchior's instructions came back to her. She glanced surreptitiously at the twins and knew at once that they were not praying either. They were merely waiting for enough time to pass. Melchior would quit after a while and they would all walk together out of the dingy little church, through the small stone-tumbled cemetery, down a narrow back street to the secret gate in the wall and on to the informal dining room to have late tea wih Rätzel and Grandfather. She looked up at the figure on the cross: He was fading into the darkening church. Only the candles now gave off any real light, although it seemed to her that they looked like drops of honey. She knew that Melchior must have brought and lit them, since Rätzel said the churches were out of candles. Silently she said the Lord's Prayer, the only real prayer she remembered from the first five years of her life. Her mother's funeral was Ursula's last formal confrontation with the church, since Enerde had not taken the children to Mass since their mother died, saying only that he had changed his mind about "all that." Apparently young Melchior alone missed the litany and the mystery, the kneeling and rising, the indefinable comfort.

Ursula suddenly remembered her father saying that morning in the garden that he was ill. Just as she was wondering if there was a prayer that would make him well soon, Melchior slowly stood up, crossed himself again, and they all went home to tea.

Years later, the children were to think back on the time of the war as the *"island years."* The physically insular quality of the times created by the isolation of the estate with its glass-crowned high walls and bolted iron gates was obvious enough, but it was quite another isolation that protected the children from the intimate facts of the war that raged ferociously across the world outside their little Eden. They were permitted no radio, and the newspaper purchased daily by Enerde's chauffeur was taken directly to the old man's study. Rätzel cautioned the teaching staff and the servants to make no reference to the war. In fact, instant dismissal was assured for anyone who discussed anything of a political nature in the presence of the children.

However, the war frequently entered the house through the kitchen, where shortages were more obvious than elsewhere in the mansion. The children had a vague notion of rationing, but experienced it only in the scarcity of sugar, chocolate, and soap. Honey became the sweetener for everything and the white hives in a far corner of the garden kept them in good supply. Ursula enjoyed watching Graz with his strange netted head-gear remove the honey from the hives, the bees attacking him in a furious dark cloud that terrified Melchior, who hid his eyes behind his hands while the others futilely cheered the deaf gardener on. He always gave them each a piece of the comb to lick clean and years later Ursula was to remember with a sudden quickening of her heart a glimpse she had of Paul turning away from his comb to lick a droplet of honey from the corner of Günther's mouth.

Although gasoline was scarce, Enerde seemed always to have enough to take *two* touring cars when he took the children on excursions to one of his country houses in the lake region or to Salzburg for the festival or Innsbruck for skiing. One of the supreme moments of pleasure that the old man held close in his memory occurred at a ski resort where he sat late one afternoon waiting for the children to come in. When they did, directly from the slopes, tearing off caps and scarves and laughing, their usually pale skin turned a rose-opal, a whole room of people fell silent and watched them pass. He was profoundly aware of the children's astonishing beauty created from some dark magic of the genes never to be explained, and yet, its effect on strangers always excited him. When people asked about them, he would smile broadly and announce with great force, "Oh, yes, they're mine, all mine."

Pavel Bronevsky never went on these trips; he continued habituating Vienna's cabarets and private gaming clubs, where he was immensely popular and envied. Each day now he rose at noon, breakfasted on his balcony or in his sitting room (depending on the weather), read the latest gentlemen's magazine, and discussed the previous night's events with his remaining valet, who made the appropriate sounds at the appropriate times and laughed hugely when laughter was called for. The valet was a trim little man with a hairline mustache and the face of an intelligent fox.

Sometimes Bronevsky took out his guns and carefully cleaned and oiled them whether they needed it or not. At four his chauffeur drove him to the stable where he kept his beloved mare. He rode for exactly an hour. Upon returning to the mansion, he rested for an hour after the valet gave him his daily massage. Then he got up, dressed, and began the whole process over again. If he experienced any of the dark side of pleasure, no one knew it; for he was one of those men whose accounts of his exploits verged on the fantastical: no woman ever disappointed him; no game was a complete loss; no hour of his nights was wasted in useless pursuit. He was urbane, witty, but for all his intimacy with his friends, he remained aloof. One had the impression that there was a side to Bronevsky that sought the dark of the moon, that drifted in lonely splendor in deepest space. It manifested itself in a curious vanishing of his presence in a full room of pleasure seekers. His emerald eyes would darken and his whole expression would direct itself to a point a few inches or a few light-years in front of his face until he seemed paralyzed beyond all awakening. This distance gave him the reputation of being a deep, serious thinker. To Viennese society he was known as the White Wolf. He knew of the sobriquet and was greatly pleased by it. He also knew that during those vanishing moments when his friends believed him to be at the core of some mighty thought, he was thinking of nothing at all. For years his mind had begun to drift away from him, touching little shores the way a castaway boat meandered without aim or will amid reedy backwaters.

He rarely saw his children and almost never thought of them. Sometimes days passed before he discovered they had gone to Yugoslavia or Italy or Switzerland on holiday. He had no shortage of money and the wine cabinets were always open to him. He was forbidden only one thing: no friend of his was ever welcome at the Enerde mansion. And had he brought someone home with him, he was quite certain the person would be physically restrained from entering the house.

On their trips abroad the children frequently came face to face with the war: a convoy of troop trucks on the highway, a mile-long line of flatcars carrying tanks, a swiftly passing newspaper headline on a kiosk as their train carried them south or west let them know the war was in vigorous health. Thinking to protect their grandfather from something he could not bear to talk about, the children did not speak to him about the war. In his turn, Enerde did the same for them. Thus life went on with a sort of imbecilic normality, sometimes desperate and demented, as when most of the male staff except Graz and a few old men were called into the army and everyone—the men themselves as well as the family—pretended they were going on holiday and would soon be back. None of them ever returned. In time only old people and the deaf gardener and the children and their father and Miss Schneider lived in the house. But Enerde continued with the illusion that all was well with the world. He spent more time with the children, creating a limbo-land of garden gatherings where even cloudy days were bright with his cheerful presence, where friendly dogs thumped their tails and pompous pigeons strutted on viridescent lawns; it was a time of perpetual afternoon with honey cakes and strawberries and tea. The children equaled his pretense with charming adventures. On their last trip

[96]

abroad they stayed on the shore of an emerald lake afloat with snowy swans. The house, a white-stoned villa, was half-hidden from the road by curtains of citrus-bright and plum-purple bougainvillea imported from Brazil as a domesticated ornamental shrub which, however, escaped captivity and cultivation, rioted and went wild, covering half the roof tiles of the main house and draping every balcony. Grandfather Enerde called it a South American takeover—showy but not worth worrying about. And there was a boatman, dour, splenetic, and Italian, a misplaced, displeased gondolier named Iago, spiritual cousin to Miss Schneider (also packed off to the Lake), who considered six sly half-grown Austrian children descending on him as a singular curse from the Angel of Vengeance sent to punish him for some remote sin he no longer even remembered. One morning upon rising, he found one of the boats adrift some hundred meters from the still-locked boathouse. In it a sheep grazed serenly on a solid mat of turf covering the craft's entire floor, as though having grown there the whole season. He reported the matter to the grandfather, who wanted to know if the animal was harmed. "No." Was the boat damaged? "No." After a pause he asked if anyone was injured. Miss Schneider reported that all the children were in deep slumber. After breakfast that warm spring day, the grandfather recommended that all the boys help the boatman thoroughly clean the boats and aid a stray animal's return to a hillside pasture some distance away where others of its kind grazed languidly in the sun. Straight-faced and serious, the boys showed a strong eagerness in assisting the miffed Iago, who cursed steadily under his breath in a language they all understood.

Ursula, who watched the operation with her grandfather from one of the balconies, thought the sheep looked splendid and not at all out of place in his little pasture in the lake. And she said so.

The old man shifted in his white wicker chair. "It is not the nature of sheep to ride about in boats." He stroked Ursula's sun-browned arms, which she had thrust around his neck from behind. "But it is the nature of boys to invent pranks."

"Not girls?"

"Not girls."

"But I helped."

"I know."

"Shouldn't I help now?"

"You should keep an old man company."

"You're not old, Grandfather."

"Eh? Not old? What is old if I am not old?"

She kissed the back of his neck, inhaling deeply his scent of clove and lemon which he took in his tea. "The pyramids are old."

"I am older than the pyramids." He spoke slowly as he pulled her into his lap.

"Then, Grandfather, you will live forever."

He shook his head. "I have already done that, but I need a little extension, just until you are old enough . . . safe."

That his grandchildren might be in real physical danger only came to Enerde when Budapest fell to the Russians in the last months of the war and the Danube valley lay open to siege like soft, spread thighs. Rumor of

Red Army rancor and rapacity paralyzed Vienna with terror. By then all hope of the Americans capturing the city had vanished, and the grandfather, with horrifying visions of the Romanovs lying in their own fatal blood in a cellar in the Urals stuck fast in his mind (he was that far from the present), forged documents identifying the children as his, replacing the Bronevsky name with his own.

On a given morning with the overcast sky smelling of gunpowder, and distant shelling rattling the windows, Enerde called the children to the library and cautiously explained the documents to them. "You should know," he began in a soft voice, "that this is nothing but a minor precaution just in case anyone asks questions. You all know the history of the Russian Revolution and the . . . the stupid treatment of the upper classes by the Bolsheviks." He paused, knowing as he watched the children's faces that his odd use of the word "stupid" was not lost on them. But how could he speak the horrors that his mind pictured for him? He continued pleasantly. "We wouldn't want these soldiers to make any absurd connection between those families and you . . . us. You are Austrian through and through." Again he paused, sensing beneath the children's gravity an aura of aloofness, a detachment at once polite and secretive. He wondered if they felt his fear. With excessive casualness he went on. "If asked, stress also that in no way are you German. You are Austrian to the very heart." He smiled at the ring of waiting faces.

"Who would question us, Grandfather?" asked Günther.

"Well, my boy, probably no one. I don't think these Russians are particularly interested in Vienna; it's Berlin they want. It's not really our war, you see. We've been dragged into it by cowardly men who didn't have a shred of honor in them. Contemptible, vile men who betrayed a thousand years of noble heritage and who should have been . . . been . . ." The tight rising rage in his own voice stopped him, and he breathed deeply to calm his heart. "Still . . . someone might ask . . . some soldiers perhaps. It wouldn't do to tell them anything about our family. Best to stay out of their way altogether." He caught the children glancing at each other furtively. *Stay out of their way!* Good God, what was he saying to them? How stupid he was being. He should have taken them away long ago, but how could he have known it would come to this? The Russians in Vienna! It was unthinkable. Why had he not left them in Switzerland on the last visit? Vienna's centuries-old motto loomed into his mind: *It is always too late.* And now, what could be done? When the shelling finally stops and the conquerors come, where could he hide them? In the cellar? That's what others were doing, hiding their children and women and silver in the cellars. And that's exactly where a Russian would look first—the filthy swine! And running out of the city now was also stupid. Also already too late. They would be shot on the road. No, the best thing was to meld into the crowds, become as inconspicuous as possible.

The children waited quietly in this long lull, glancing occasionally at the trembling windows. Enerde touched Ursula's cheek and turned her face toward him. "Are you afraid, Little Bear?"

She shook her head. "No, Grandfather."

He smiled. "No, of course not. Now, listen to me. I have arranged to have your hair cut." With a shaking hand he lifted the stream of red hair off her shoulder.

"I can cut it myself, Grandfather."

"This is not an ordinary haircut, Ursula, it must be cut very short, until it looks like Alexander's. And you will wear some of his clothes. You must not wear a dress again until I tell you to."

"You want me to look like a boy, Grandfather?"

He looked away from her to his grandsons. "Yes. It is very important that people—soldiers in particular—believe she is a boy. These are all sensible precautions. We shall, of course, attempt to stay indoors until this passes. This army is on its way to Germany and they will not waste much time here. Still, if we should be forced to leave the house, we must stay together. Families have been separated during times like these and spent years looking for one another. This must not happen to us. Keep your identity cards with you at all times, and only show them when absolutely necessary. If we should be forced to leave the house, do so naturally. If you are on the street and are stopped by soldiers, German or Russian, do not try to run. Tell them you are on your way home. Be as casual as you can. You have one advantage with the Russians: you know their language, but they do not know this, so you must not speak it. It is enough that you understand it. Always keep something back." He was close to weeping. How could he have known the Americans would let the Russians take Vienna? Why had he not even considered that? The roads to Switzerland were closed now. Where else could he have taken them? The retreat in Yugoslavia was overrun with partisans. The house in the Italian Alps where the family had been during the two main allied bomb attacks on the city in the autumn of '43 was in the hands of a bunch of fanatic Germans and being shot to bits by the Americans.

"Should we bolt the doors and windows now, Grandfather?"

The old man stared at Günther blankly. "Bolt the doors? Yes. Yes, you boys do that. We still have a few hours, I'm sure. But do it now, anyway. Yes, that's the idea. Before it's too late."

Ursula's hair was cut off by Ewald Berghoch, the cook whom Enerde's guards had found living in one of the Company forests after the Great War. In the band of homeless men whom he led, he was famous for his rat stew and his ability to box. Now in his forties, Berghoch usually had a cigarette sticking from his blunt pug face. He was an expert in dealing on the black market, and with the Enerde money available to him, the family lacked little in the way of good food and he himself was never without cigarettes. Rätzel once asked him how he could taste food beneath that immense intake of tobacco.

"I can't," he answered. "A great cook doesn't have to taste his dishes. He knows. And I am a great cook." He was not fat, although his compact body gave the impression of considerable weight and immense strength. He still rode a bicycle to one of the local markets before dawn each morning. By the time most of the gardeners were absorbed by the army, he personally cared for the kitchen garden, enlisting the children's help for an hour each day with Rätzel's approval. The children adored him. Not only was he a superb cook, teaching the youngsters the enjoyment of subtle tastes, but

[99]

he also bandaged their scraped knees expertly, refereed their quarrels with wisdom, and taught them (without their knowing it) that malice drinks its own poison. Like Rätzel, he disagreed with Enerde's treatment of Bronevsky, but said nothing. Of all the employees ever retained by the family, only Miss Schneider disliked him. It was a sign of his humanity that he understood her reasons and pitied her.

He always addressed the children in the third person, not for reasons of formality which that form implied, but because he had used it with them when they were babies. Rätzel sometimes joined in this game; thus the children saw the whole thing as sport and continued to play it willingly.

"Does Ursula know that her hair grows almost two centimeters a month?" asked Berghoch.

Ursula shook her head under the rapidly moving clippers which Waldi (as the children called him) used to give shape to the boyish cut. On the floor around the chair lay swaths of her thick red hair like fallen birds.

"Then she *should* know and not be concerned about this haircut."

"She's not concerned."

"Then why does she make a shelf of the lower lip?"

"Is everyone going to be shot, Waldi?"

The clippers stopped. "Who speaks such stupidity?"

"Miss Schneider says we shall all be shot and killed or worse and that we should take poison."

Berghoch removed the towel from Ursula's shoulders and brushed the loose hair from her neck. "Ursula will not be shot or killed or worse. Our kind does not die so easily. In fact, I have decided against it. Ursula and Berghoch refuse to go." He stepped back and motioned her to rise. "Yes, that's good. Ursula is a very pretty boy; only for a while she will be Ulrich. Alexander's clothes fit well. Two sets of twins in the house. That's good luck." He rumpled her hair lovingly. "Poison tastes terrible. Miss Schneider won't like it. Very bad for the stomach. Believe it. A cook knows these things."

Explosions, round and drum-hollow, rolled over the city in a series of muffled echoes. The house shuddered. "It's nothing to worry about. We are away from the center, and the Russians are still south of the city. If the shelling gets close we shall wait in the cellar until it stops. We have a few turnips put aside there. But there's time enough for that. Now, go join the other boys."

"Grandfather says we have only a few hours."

"Just an expression. We have several days. A cook always knows when things are ripe. Now, go. If I know boys, they are on the roof watching the fires."

Passing the library, Ursula saw her grandfather at his desk reading a newspaper, the front page turned toward her, its headline shouting: "VIENNA'S HOUR HAS COME." She hurried on.

On the second floor's gallery she came upon the two old housemaids who had been with the family forever. They were seated on a bench weeping, dressed in black from head to foot. Ursula thought they looked like spiders.

The cook, the governess, Graz, and these two women both in their sixties were all that remained of the once large domestic staff. When they saw Ursula, the women wailed louder. "What will become of us, Master Alexander? We're too old for Siberia."

Ursula shook her head and mumbled that she did not know. Was that what her grandfather meant about getting separated? Miss Schneider had told them about people being exiled to Siberia, and later they had all examined the area carefully on the globe.

"Not much of a prison if people aren't actually locked up," said Paul. Günther agreed. Melchior wondered if there were churches in Siberia. Boris suggested that the skiing was probably excellent. Alexander shouted that he would escape. And Ursula announced quietly that she would not go and no one could make her.

She hurried on down the dim hall: the electricity had gone off the previous night. Ursula did not even glance down the hall that led to her father's quarters. She had not seen him for several days. She reached the roof by the spiral stairway leading from the playroom to a cupola centered on a wide expanse of flat roof edged by the wrought-iron railing. The wind blew sharply and the sky was a huge bruise of smoke-purple clouds.

"You're wrong," Melchior was saying, "that fire is at the cemetery."

"*You're* wrong. There's nothing to burn at the cemetery. That's the Quellenstrasse tenements burning," said Alexander.

"You're both wrong. They are destroying Belvedere and Schwarzenberg Palace." Boris' usual tone of superior finality brought Günther into the argument.

"Really? Belvedere? Schwarzenberg Palace? Great military objectives, no doubt! Certainly no need to go after the radio and power stations or the train depots or even the barricaded enemy when one can shoot pretty empty palaces."

"And what about the zoo?" added Paul with mock seriousness. "Must shoot up the zoo. What with all those dangerous caged animals. The giraffes might get loose, and who knows what devilment they could think up against Russian tanks." He turned away from Boris with disgust. "No," he continued quietly, "those fires are factories being burned. The question is, who is burning them? The departing Germans or the arriving Russians?" He stopped when he saw Ursula. The others turned also and looked at her. None of them spoke until Alexander hit the railing with both fists.

"I'd like to kill every Russian . . . and . . . and every German, too. I'd like to blow them up . . . blow them into little bits."

Ursula's neck was cold and when she ran her hand over it, it felt bristly and strange. She knelt down behind the railing next to Alexander. "Waldi says they won't be here for a few days."

"What if we do get separated?" said Melchior. "There are people down on the street leaving the city. What if we have to leave and we get lost?"

"We won't get lost. Don't be stupid. Anyway, we're not leaving. We'll stay in the cellar until it's over. Now, quit crying." Günther leaned against the railing as he spoke. "But we could do something that would always make us know each other . . . just in case. I mean, if we were separated for years, we should have some kind of pact, something that we could say or do that only we knew about. We should have a code."

"What kind of code?" asked Paul.

"I don't know exactly, just some kind of code that only we would understand."

"That's not a bad idea. Just in case," said Paul. "Let's go down and figure out something."

Alexander was reluctant to leave the roof. "One of us should stay as a lookout."

None of them said anything. Ursula, watching her youngest brother's angry face, knew that three days before, Alexander had stopped two German soldiers on the street and offered to help them fight the Russians. He was twelve years old. The men laughed, patted his rosy cheek, and told him to wait for the next war.

"Listen, Alexander," said Paul, "we'll know when they get close. Anyway, it's going to rain; we can come back up later."

"Maybe you could throw rocks at them," said Boris with an unnecessary added laugh.

"Shut up, Boris," said Günther. But it was too late. Alexander sprang forward, butting his head into Boris' midsection, knocking them both down. They cuffed each other furiously as the twins pulled them apart.

"You're both crazy. This is no time to fight. Not on the roof, anyway." Paul held the squirming Alexander. "Don't be a dope, Alexy."

"He started it."

"*You* started it when you talked to the soldiers. I could tell Grandfather about that, you know," said Boris.

Ursula, who always feared her brothers' quarrels, crouched against the railing and watched them with anguish and fascination, knowing at once what Boris' threat would bring. She saw Günther's arm raised for a brief moment against the darkening sky, saw it fall in a clean arc without haste, slapping Boris fully across the mouth.

The fight was over, and as usual Melchior was the only one crying.

An hour later, seated on the floor of the playroom around a single burning candle, the children considered the impossibilities of a code. "It won't work," said Günther. "None of these words or phrases we've come up with will work. And the reason is that *nothing* we *say* will work. We couldn't wander from stranger to stranger years from now saying '*The deed is all, and not the Glory,*' or any of these other things we've listed. And if we *were* separated for years, we *would* be strangers: we wouldn't recognize each other. No, it's got to be something we can see."

"We could make some mark on the flesh," said Paul. "Nothing vulgar, of course." They knew about circumcision and shuddered at it, although Waldi had told them it was a hygienic practice and not at all "pointless" (Günther and Paul's favorite word at the time the matter came up).

"In some primitive societies," began Boris loftily, "people cut their fingers and let their blood mingle to show that they are blood brothers. . . ."

"That's stupid, we're already . . ." grumbled Alexander.

Boris waved an objecting hand. "I was thinking of a scar."

They fell silent.

"It doesn't sound very Christian to me," said Melchior finally.

[102]

"Why does everything have to be Christian? Anyway, it isn't *un*christian. What's *un*christian about it?" Boris wanted to know.

"I don't know for sure. It just seems pagan to me."

"Melchior, everything seems pagan to you unless some priest blesses it," rejoined Alexander, exasperation edging his voice.

"A tattoo would work," said Ursula, "if we knew how to do it."

"Too late for that," said Paul, "but it's a good idea. No, I think it's going to have to be a scar of some kind."

"It can't be at the end of the finger," mused Günther. "Any little cut would just heal up and not even leave a scar. But I know that some animals are frequently notched on the ear for identification. And they say it doesn't hurt while it's being done."

"Who says so, the animals?" asked Paul, raising his eyebrows. They all laughed, a laughter much brighter, much longer than the small joke deserved.

They finally settled on an incision on the right earlobe. A half-hour later the collected blood filled a glass vial. "We shouldn't just throw it out," said Günther, swirling the tube slowly.

And because they liked ceremony and the times were bizarrely dangerous and they were a little crazy with repressed terror of the war that suddenly seemed to surround them locked in their citadel, they decided to heat the blood over the fireplace embers and pour it onto the Austrian soil.

"That should do it," said Günther, holding the glass tube with a pair of tongs. "Boiled blood."

It was raining when they carried the container to the garden, where they immediately fell into a disagreement. The Enerde gardens had the usual company of posturing Greeks. "We'll pour it at the feet of Athena because she was the most brilliant," said Boris in a voice meant to shut out any discussion.

"No, no, she's carrying a sword. You might as well spill it in front of Ares. They are really two of a kind," said Melchior petulantly.

An argument developed on the inherent differences between the War and Wisdom deities. Günther ended it by pointing out that the goddess's head was damaged on one side.

"Apollo, then," insisted Boris.

"No," said Günther. "His eleventh finger is missing." They all giggled, not because of the god's missing penis, but because of the way it was lost: the year before, he had taken a misdirected soccer ball in the groin, and the cracked, already jocularly mishandled lower digit had snapped off with a thunk.

Günther examined the blood closely, blinking against the rain. "Well, hurry up and decide before it coagulates completely, if it hasn't already."

"The only one that has nothing wrong with him is Hermes; even his little wings are still on his feet," said Ursula.

There were a few minutes of further dispute as each argued for his favorite god. Only Melchior remained silent: Christianity had no representatives among the rhododendrons and lilacs and chestnut trees, richly candling, pungent and lovely in the rain. In the end, because Hermes was undamaged, resting as he was under a linden tree, his seated form suggesting a tranquillity among the frozen tensions of the other Olympians, the messenger of the gods received the blood, in a chunk by then, which had to be scraped out of the tube with a twig. The children stood around it and watched the rain dissolve it slowly and carry it into the earth.

Years later, Ursula would feel the small notch in her right earlobe with astonished disbelief, not at the scar and not because they feared at the time that they might be imprisoned, but because they had been able to sharpen a straight razor and each take his place before their grandfather's long-retired shaving mirror and cut into his own flesh.

II

The lunatic pretense that there was no war, or at least that it had nothing to do with him, came much closer to home for Enerde a few days later when the siege of the city began in earnest with several sharp explosions nearer than the southern districts. Anxious, nervous tradesmen who still came to the gate to bring fish and milk reported fighting in the city. The children, who were spending all of their free time on the roof, that morning saw with hypnotized horror the outward-rushing mass of debris held together only by curls of flame and ballooning balls of lead-gray smoke that rose into the sky in massive clusters above the nearby Danube. Ursula dropped to the tiled roof and in turning her head away from the explosion saw the leaded cupola windows fragment into solid masses of cracks. She drew her knees to her face, but almost at once someone began pulling her toward the cupola. Afterward when she was to think back on those few seconds when they all left the roof and raced down the spiral stairs, it was not the explosion that was to spring into her memory but instead the windows of the cupola: the thick splendidly shattered centuries-old glass windows wrinkled instantly into a thousand minute lines from which not a single sliver fell to the roof.

The children were still running when they reached the foot of the main stairway, where the cook collided with them, catching the flying Ursula in his arms. "Here, here. Nothing to get excited about. The Germans are only blowing up the bridges on the river. We've been expecting it. It's all right. It's all right." He led them into the dining room, where their grandfather stood silhouetted against a red sky which filled the great Gothic east window. Slowly the old man pulled the massive draperies closed. In one corner, half-hidden in the dim room, huddled Miss Schneider and the two maids.

Ursula saw her grandfather motion to Rätzel. "Get him. Everyone, sit down," said Enerde, lowering himself into the high-backed chair at the head of the table. Ursula saw that he moved in a strange slow way she had not seen before.

"They broke the cupola window, Grandfather," said Melchior.

"Yes? Well, that's to be expected, isn't it?"

Ursula sat at her place to the right of the old man. He patted her hand. A few minutes later Bronevsky and Rätzel entered the room. The children started to rise, but Enerde motioned to them with a fluttering, downward hand.

Ursula was stunned at her father's appearance: his face was the yellow of old plates marked with stains and his hands shook. He stared at them all through watery eyes. He wore a maroon silk dressing gown over his trousers. A scarf hurriedly tied concealed his neck. "So, I'm to be allowed in for the finale, am I?" He snorted a single laugh and pulled a cigarette case from his pocket.

"Sit down and be quiet," said Enerde through his teeth, his words spread out evenly with perceptible pauses between them.

"Well, it's no difference to me. Let them come. I'm ready. One hell is as good as another." He stopped across the table from Ursula, stared at her, then at Alexander beside her, a frown forming between his arched eyebrows. Slowly he lit a cigarette and exhaled deeply. "That won't save her," he laughed. "Remember, old man, that you deal with new Russians. Not polite ones. Thugs! Ha, ha. Now you'll see that there's a difference."

Ursula jumped as her grandfather shouted, "Be quiet!" She had never heard him shout before; when he was angry about anything, he always spoke more softly than usual and much more slowly.

Her father continued. "You think they won't find the cracks in this house? They'll find them, even the little ones. And they'll stuff them . . . and make you watch."

"If you speak once more, I'll throw you out of this house for good." Enerde spoke softly again, but Ursula saw that he was trembling. She glanced at her brothers' bent heads and cast her eyes down too. It was always this way when her father was near; none of them seemed to be able to look at him. Over the years since her mother's death, Ursula had come to believe that her father must once have done something terrible to receive such hatred from her grandfather. There were times when she looked at her father secretly, trying to discover what he was to her, this tall, slim man dressed in elegant suits and ruffled shirts. At holiday times, when the whole family ate in the formal dining room, the occasions always stiff and uncomfortable and sad, Ursula would surreptitiously watch her father's face. He seemed always to be waiting for something. Eating little, he drank glass after glass of wine and tapped the table with manicured nails; sometimes, that thin tapping was the only sound in the room. He never looked at any of them and he always left before dessert. Then their grandfather would become talkative and ask after their studies and make little jokes.

Except for a single time, Ursula could not remember having been totally alone with her father. And that one time occurred in the middle of the night the year before. She awakened to laughter outside her room. On opening the door, she saw her father lurch along the hall, clutching the curved balustrade of the cantilevered gallery, the shadow of his hunched form and dragging cape projecting a molelike animal on the two-story wall beyond him.

"Eh? Who . . . ?" he hiccuped loudly.

Ursula took a step back into her doorway. Her father stopped. In the amber wall light she saw at once that his face was beautiful, his eyes glistening darkly, his skin glowing a warm apricot with a few soft shadows flattering the features which his habits had been coarsening for years. He leaned against the balustrade and blinked rapidly, as though clearing some film which covered his eyes. Abruptly he smiled, his teeth bright below the black mustache. "Ah, one of my cubs." He hiccuped again. "Are you one of my cubs?"

Ursula, unable to move, remained silent. Her father stepped toward her just as Miss Schneider came from the stairs to the staff's hall, her face angry, grimacing. "What are you doing up, you wicked girl? Get to bed!"

"Oh, come on, let me talk to her. . . ." But Miss Schneider shoved Ursula's door closed, and for a brief time the girl stood in the darkness behind the door and listened to the governess urge the man to go to his rooms. "Here, lean on me. You need sleep, sir. You'll be fine in the morning, you'll see."

Ursula heard a dragging sound and then the woman's whispering faded away. When she opened the door a minute later, the gallery was empty.

"If the fighting comes to our street," her grandfather continued, "the women and children will stay in the back cellar. We've made it comfortable and there are enough provisions for several days and, of course, the door to it is well concealed. Still, this is only a precaution. Essentially there is no reason for the Russians to be in this part of the city; on the other hand, these soldiers are not entirely predictable. This is not a normal war for Austria since we are not in control of our own country. You should all know that a few days ago the Russians issued a statement that they wish only to destroy those forces which began this war, not nations; therefore, if they see themselves as liberators of Austria, we shall have no troubles. We are, after all, Austrians."

Bronevsky laughed.

Ursula watched her grandfather's face. His expression did not change. "Rätzel and Waldi and I shall remain here abovestairs and wait out the siege of the city. We are far from the center of things so we are well out of it. Graz will stay as lookout on the roof to keep us informed of what is happening. There is no need for fear; everything is under control."

There was a moment of complete silence. "And what about me?" At her father's words, Ursula looked quickly at her grandfather. His face was calm, remotely speculative.

"I advise you to stay with friends. Though I do not believe the Russians will bother us, you would be difficult to explain in this house should it come to that." He turned away from Bronevsky and spoke directly to the children. "You'll have to stay off the roof from now on, at least until all this is over. Now, we'll just go on about our business. Dinner will be at the usual time. Everything normal." He paused and looked questioningly at Rätzel. "Was there anything else?" Rätzel shook his head. "Good, then go now, keep busy, and stay calm."

As the children left the room, their father suddenly rose from his chair near the wall. "One moment!" he said loudly, gulping air, sputtering so that his tongue jabbed about in his mouth with furious and choking uselessness.

Ursula never heard the rest of what her father had intended to say, although she knew that for a short time the other four men remained in the dining room with her father, who had begun to shout incoherently in a thin high voice. She did not see him again until after the city fell a week later. Through much of those seven days, she and her brothers watched the war from their playroom windows, where they could see fires burning through the night to the south and east. Sirens rose and fell, one upon the other around the clock, each dying cry obliterated by the vigor of the next rising scream. Rumors entered the house through the tradesmen met by Rätzel or the cook at the gate, usually both, for they were anxious for any news about the fate of the city.

The milkman, a rosy-cheeked cherub of a man, short and bald with clacking dentures, was bitterly direct. "There is house-to-house fighting in all the southern and eastern districts. Bombing has destroyed the inner city: Saint Stephen's is burned; the Opera House is gutted; the Burg Theater is rubble. The banks have closed up shop. There are no more stores open since day before yesterday, Saturday. Good luck. God save us. But it is probably already too late."

"Maybe you should stay put for a while," said Derghoch.

Ursula and Alexander, hidden in the rhododendron garden near the gate, saw the milkman shrug. "They won't stop giving milk. I might as well deliver it as see it go sour. But I tell you both, if the Russians steal my cows, I'll kill them."

"I don't think the Russians will take your cows, but the Germans may want your horse."

"My horse? Impossible! My horse is a thousand years old. He's blind. He knows the route from pure heart. If he had to take one step off his usual road, he'd drop dead."

"*And* the cart . . . they'll want that, too."

"What for, for Gods sake?"

"For hauling. You think they'll leave Vienna empty-handed?" The cook shook his head. "You know the stories about their plundering and looting. The Russians are expected to do plenty of that and I'm sure they're doing it, but it's the departing Germans I'd keep an eye out for. In a few days the roads west will be choked with their retreat. Only they'll be out of gas. A horse and cart will be worth gold."

"But the American armies are overrunning Germany. How far west can the Germans retreat before they are on another front?"

"If they're smart they'll hide their loot where they can return to it someday when this mess is over, and in the meantime, make themselves inconspicuous, dump the uniform, or even surrender to the Americans," said Rätzel.

The milkman looked off down the empty, tree-lined street as though soldiers might be hiding behind the trunks. "You think any of them will come through here?"

"It wouldn't surprise me," answered Rätzel, "although most of them, of course, will stay with their units and they'll move on main highways like Heiligenstader Strasse, but it's the stragglers that I worry about. They're the ones that think the war owes them something and they'll take it from whomever they can."

"Rätzel's right," said the cook. "They're not choosy; they will as easy steal from their own. Believe me, I know soldiers and these are seasoned thugs. They know it's over for them. They'll cut off your hand for a two-schilling ring."

"Well, I don't know. At least I can talk to the Germans. They're more like us. The Russians I don't know. The wife is scared sick of them. There are so many rumors. You know, people come to the creamery and they talk. One hears everything. It's the molesting that terrifies her. The stories of that are the worst. Everyone seems to know someone that it has already happened to. She stays in the cellar all day now. She screams at the least noise. Everywhere I go now, people sit in their cellars most of the time. Me, I can't stand the cellar. Close places drive me crazy. Man wasn't meant to live in the ground like a rodent. It's not a human thing to do. I'd rather take my chances out in the open. Anyway, I have to take care of the business. How can I do that if I'm burrowed into a hole like a common rat?"

"You're right. Absolutely right," said the cook brusquely. "Business as usual. That's what we have here. Everything normal. Well, perhaps not as normal as we'd like it, but the appearance of normal, that's what we've aimed at. No one to the cellar unless it's absolutely necessary. Lessons as usual; although Rätzel's had to talk to the instructress twice about frightening the children. *She's* a little crazy about the molesting business, too."

"One would think" said Rätzel, "that the army would be too busy for that sort of nonsense."

"It's a time-honored custom . . . for the conquerors," said the milkman.

"How does it apply to liberators?" asked the cook. The three men laughed briefly, then fell into uneasy silence. "Well, I have to move on. I'll deliver as long as it's possible. If I don't show up, know that I'm dead." He clucked to the horse.

Ursula heard the cart wheels creak and missed Waldi's parting words to the tradesman. She turned to Alexander. "The milkman's right. I'm *not* going into the cellar."

"You'll have to if Grandfather says so."

"No."

"Ursula! All the women have to."

"No! I'm staying with Grandfather."

"He won't let you."

"He will."

As it turned out, none of the children were in the cellar when the war finally reached their street. It arrived in the late afternoon, two days after the capture of the Parliament Building when the Russians announced that Vienna was liberated and the citizens could bury their dead. No one in the Enerde household knew later if the gate was left open through some momentary carelessness due to the deep relief felt at the cessation of the shooting or if the soldier managed to climb the twelve-foot wall, somehow avoid the glass shards, and drop unseen into the garden. The children saw later where he discarded the remains of a pear in the orchard near the well house before he made his way to the back doors. In the kitchen he surprised Rätzel, who was seated on a bench with his trouser legs rolled up rubbing grease on his arthritic knees. "Get out of my kitchen," said Rätzel without rising.

The man grunted, turned his back to Rätzel, and with the muzzle of his gun barrel knocked the lid off a pot of vegetable soup simmering on the stove. Sniffing the dish, he picked up a loaf of potato bread on a cutting board and dipped it into the soup. He ate rapidly with loud, slurping noises, his gun held loosely under his arm. Finished, he stuffed the remaining bread into his pockets and turned to Rätzel, who had not stopped rubbing his knees. "Where do you keep your money?"

Rätzel laughed. "Don't be ridiculous. The Russians just made our money worthless. Take the food and go."

"Then something else if the money's no good."

"There's nothing."

"Don't fool with me, old man, this is a rich house. Maybe I'll just stay until something can be found."

"The Russians may find you first."

"You'll make sure they don't. Any house with a German soldier in it is . . . *pouff.*" He made a slashing motion in the air with his hand.

Rätzel wiped his fingers on his handkerchief spread in his lap and rolled down his trouser legs. "All right, what do you think you can carry with you?"

The soldier hesitated, picked his teeth with his thumbnail. "Maybe that's not such a good idea." He looked around and belched. "Maybe I'll just stay here for a while. Get me some other clothes."

"You can't stay here and endanger this whole family. There are children. Go now. It will be dark soon; you can still catch up with your unit. The war is already to the west of the city. It is over for us. In a few days it will be over for you, too."

"You make my point exactly. Why go on? Why take a bullet in the last minute? No. I stay. In a house this big there must be a thousand hiding places. Now, get me some clothes."

"No. You can't stay here."

"Get me some clothes or I shoot the first person that comes through that door." He motioned with his gun.

Rätzel rose slowly. "You wouldn't shoot a child."

"The first one that comes through that door."

Rätzel knew that the cook was momentarily in the vegetable garden and the children upstairs in the classroom. At five they would come down, a little light-headed with hunger, crash through the swinging door, and pester the cook until he gave them each a slice of buttered bread. Berghoch would pretend to be angry. It was an old, fond charade. He contemplated the soldier's coarse, bearded face. In uniform, the man had no singular identity. The eyes peered out from the square overhanging helmet with the fierce cruelty of a hawk. "What did you do before the war?"

"I'm regular army. Quit stalling."

"Then for the sake of all that's decent, quit this house." He began casually to tidy up the work counter, wiping off the cutting board with a cloth he picked up with studied casualness. "There is an honor to your profession. Your leaders hold you up as the country's best men . . . loyal, courageous, honorable. . . ."

"The army's finished. It's every man for himself. . . ." He stopped, turned his head at some scuffling sound.

Rätzel knew that it was the children coming down the stairs. He picked up the bread knife, stepped in front of the soldier, and plunged the blade into the man's chest with both hands. The soldier leaned forward and seemed to sigh, his mouth wide open; then he raised up on his tiptoes, clutching the gun. The weapon rose with him so that the end of the barrel rested directly against Rätzel's midsection. He fired only once.

It seemed to Ursula that the muffled explosion shook the house as none of the bombs or artillery shells had ever been able to do. At the bottom of the stairs, they all stopped. "Where was it?" she asked, looking to Alexander.

"It shook the stairs. It had to come from below the stairs. The kitchen or the storage pantries, the little dining room, somewhere in back," said Alexander with a certain hesitant wonder.

"Maybe one of those soups finally blew up," said Günther. It was a joke pertaining to the cook's more mysterious recent dishes.

"No, it was a gunshot," said Alexander, heading toward the back of the house. Ursula went with him. The others looked after them but did not move immediately.

Rätzel was still alive when Ursula knelt beside him and screamed at the dead German soldier lying across him to get off. She tore at the uniformed arm, pulling the body slightly to one side so that the great wound in Rätzel's midsection bubbled up the shredded intestines. Rätzel uttered a single sound and when Ursula looked into his face she saw that he was forming the silent words of their old children's game: "She is not to cry."

Around midnight on the day Rätzel was killed, Graz loaded the dead German soldier into a wheelbarrow and pushed him to a street some distance from the house, where he left the body propped in a seated position against a lamppole, his helmet on his head, his rifle resting in his lap. He appeared to be asleep or drunk, having slid down in front of the pole like a comic character in a film. Early the following morning, with the boys helping, Graz made Rätzel's coffin, fashioning it out of dismantled benches he took from a long-roofless summerhouse in a remote part of the garden where puppet shows were performed when Rätzel and the grandfather were small boys. Ursula watched listlessly. The box was shaped like a human body, broad at the shoulders and steadily narrowing as it reached the feet. It looked like a long brown leaf. She remembered her mother's triple coffin. Did it make a difference what one was buried in? Years ago Günther finally admitted to her that the flesh was eaten by worms no matter how many coffins one was buried in. And then the worms died, too. What ate them? Günther wasn't sure at the time. Perhaps something smaller. But in the end only the bones were left. She wanted to know for how long. He wasn't sure of that either.

Before noon, the family buried Rätzel under the floor of the summer-house, all of them standing silently around the opening in the floor as Graz and the cook packed down the earth solidly over the coffin. Above them, where a roof had once sheltered shouting and partying youngsters in another century, chestnut trees, candling white blossoms, blazed in the warm morning air. The sky was glassy clear, still and deep. Lilacs in abundant purple clusters exuded an intimate oversweet bedroom scent as of soap through the latticed arches. Birds sang. The war had moved westward. During the night, a brief wind-driven rain cleaned the city of the layers of blue-black smoke which had covered it since the beginning of April. Occasionally a rapping sound, not much louder than light hammering, came to them from the direction of the Vienna woods.

"He was more than a brother to me all my life." The grieving children watched the gardener replace the floor bricks as their grandfather spoke. "If the time should ever come when he has to be moved, you will see that a proper job is done."

Ursula saw the old man look at the twins. They both nodded. "He's not to become a public body, dumped with a bunch of others." The boys nodded again. Tears ran on the old man's cheeks and Ursula could feel her eyes fill. She had sworn not to cry again, but her grandfather's face wrenched her heart.

It was the milkman who had told them that morning about the public bodies as he stood beside the sheet-wrapped form of Rätzel in the freshly scrubbed kitchen, the children silent, the grandfather looking down upon the dead man with stricken, unbelieving eyes. "You'd best bury him on your own ground. It's what others are doing. One hears everything. They say there's twenty thousand dead. Whole families trapped in their cellars under their bombed and burned houses. There's fear of pestilence. And there are no more empty coffins in the city and no way of transporting the filled ones to the cemeteries. There are hundreds of mass burials, mostly for the unidentified and for those who have no means. They're uncoffined. All put in together. But when people can manage at all . . . well, there are fresh graves everywhere. Between the trees lining the avenues, on the palace grounds, in the parks, in private gardens—wherever the ground can be dug up. They don't look very deep to me, and they are only mounded with a few broken bricks and wired crosses. Sometimes there is a helmet on the cross, but that soon disappears. Souvenir hunters! The devils. Even the crosses vanish. During the night. People violating the curfew . . . prowling the ruins for firewood or anything that will burn. There's no services, no gas, no electricity, no telephone, no trains, no streetcars, no police. Only the Russian military. You have to have a reason for being in the street. They question everyone, and they press everyone that's able into cleaning the streets of debris and garbage and the dead. You have to be able to prove where you live. A piece of paper with an address is not enough; you have to have a key. They are shooting looters. Not their own, you can be sure. The Germans left trucks filled with loot stranded in the streets. Out of gas, just as Berghoch said. The Russians are filling the tanks and driving the stuff away. Gone for good, you can bet. But the worst is water: there is none. The pipes are busted and the storage tanks damaged in many districts.

[111]

Wherever there is still a working faucet, thousands fight each other to use it; the weak are crushed. You are lucky to have a well." He sighed. "Thank God, the fires are finally out, but danger of new ones is great. There are pockets of gas. Crews are trying to fix the leaks. But it's dangerous. Now and again a weakened building collapses without warning, raising a cloud of powdered plaster like a big smoke ball. I tell you, it sends people running. The Russians raise their guns if anyone balks at doing the work."

"They have not bothered you?" Enerde asked.

"They told me to see to my cows. They have some sympathy for dumb animals. And they left me my horse. I explained he was blind and of no use for any other job." The men hesitated. "Which reminds me . . . has he returned?"

Ursula heard the milkman lower his voice and saw him turn his face from her and her brothers, directing his words solely at her grandfather, who shook his head. She wondered why people still referred to her father only as "he" or "him," why they did not call him by name. It was absurdly obvious whom they were talking about.

"He's lost that fancy mare of his. I didn't see it myself, but one of those old grooms told it to the wife. The riding stable caught fire. He had been staying there with the horses. We all knew it. The groom said the place exploded with flames, all at once, and the animals were trapped. Three got out—on fire. Truly, *on fire!* His mare was one of them. He ran after it, screaming to it to stop. But the animals' manes and tails were actually in flames and they shrieked horribly. No one had a gun to shoot them. They ran headlong into that stone wall that encloses the park at the end of the street there. They died where they fell, but not right away."

Ursula listened with growing revulsion. She saw Alexander turn away and Melchior grow pale. The others listened with downcast faces.

"When was this?" asked the grandfather in a flat voice.

"Last Wednesday, I think, or Thursday. I've lost my sense for time. One day last week."

"And him?"

"It's said he screamed like a madman. He tried to keep the people from the animals, but they shoved him aside and fell on the poor beasts with their carving knives and cleavers, and the animals still alive. Think on it, alive! They said the horses' screams could be heard the whole length of the park. In an hour there were only bare bones." He sighed again and gestured vaguely with his big hands. "Well, at least it was a little meat for somebody. But I can sympathize. A horse is a horse, even if it's only used for trotting in circles in the park."

"Where did he go?"

The milkman shrugged and shook his head. "Poor Rätzel. What a waste, and after it's finally over. I talked to him about this very thing. He said it was the stragglers that one had to look out for." He looked away. "Well, we did it to ourselves. We accepted the Germans. No. Worse! We welcomed them."

"Not everyone," said the cook.

"Most did."

"The times were bad."

"It wasn't just that. Many agreed with that mad swine. And I know of some who relished being part of an empire again. That it was someone else's empire didn't bother them at all. It was all shameful . . . obscene. Bah. It's all a rotten business. What can we expect now? Russians! And they'll never leave. We're stuck with them."

"No, no. The Americans won't allow that." Enerde shook his head rapidly. They were no longer making any attempt at speaking away from the children.

"The Americans could have been here long before the Russians if they had wanted to be here. The radio says Patton is *running* across Germany. No, no. They've given us to the Russians. The Americans promised us to the Russians. For punishment. You cannot imagine how ignorant they are: they steal lightbulbs thinking they can be made to work anywhere. They think the light lives inside the bulb; they tap them and peer into them and wait for the light to come on. And telephones! They just cut away the wires and walk about holding the instrument to their ears, waiting for a voice to talk to them. It would be comical if they didn't get so enraged when the apparatus fails them. That big blacksmith from the railyards is dead because he couldn't get a water faucet that some soldiers ripped out of a washbasin to produce water. The smithy laughed when they explained to him what it was they wanted that little metal gadget to do. They kicked him senseless, and then they shot him in the head. That is the breed of barbarian that is in control of Vienna. And in a few days all Austria will fall to the swine. It's all hopeless. It's been hopeless for years, but we are wonderful fools, we Austrians. We know when a situation is hopeless, but we say: 'So what? That's not so serious. We're still alive. There's still the opera and the theater and an occasional sausage with our beer to smack our lips over. And . . . our memories! Don't forget our beloved memories. Don't take everything so hard. Don't be so German!' "

When Agnes Schneider heard about the death of the horse, she wept loudly, and passionately begged Enerde to send someone out to search for Bronevsky. "He knows his way here," said Enerde, annoyed at the woman's persistence. "If he doesn't, there are houses all over town that will open their back doors to him."

The governess retreated. She had hoped to take over the supervision of the house after the death of Rätzel, but Enerde turned down her offer, telling her to stay with the job for which she was hired, particularly since there were no other teachers at the moment. To no one's surprise (except Miss Schneider's), the cook took over the business of the house. Ursula's brothers, who had been helping the gardener for two years, were assigned various additional duties in the kitchen to lighten Berghoch's load. "And teach them how to cook," said Enerde, lumbering out of the kitchen.

Ursula followed the old man to his study. "What shall *I* do, Grandfather?"

Enerde sat down heavily and put his hand on her shoulder, his eyes dark with sorrow. "Be a little girl again."

Bronevsky returned a week after the city settled nervously into its uneasy subjugation. He burst into the small dining room during the evening meal, his eyes bloodshot in rage, his clothes filthy and ragged, flailing his poorly bandaged fists at Enerde. He smelled of burned cloth and rancid grease. "That's right. Don't think of me!" he shouted. "It's all right if I starve while you stuff yourselves!" He glared at the table and snatched a piece of bread from a plate, wolfing it down in unchewed bites.

"You stink," said Enerde evenly. "Go clean yourself. Berghoch will bring you some food."

To Ursula's consternation, her father began to weep noisily, a piece of the unchewed bread falling from his open mouth. "No one knows what I've been through. I've suffered horribly." He took another bite of bread, chewing it this time. "I've been in agony. My life hung by a thread, a thin thread. And you were all safe here. I see that now." His eyes roved over the children's embarrassed faces. "See my hands? Burned to the bones." He stretched his bandaged hands over the table between Ursula and Alexander. "I may still lose them. Have to have them cut off. If there's infection, it's the surgeon's knife for sure." Tears ran off his face to his open collar.

"You're making a spectacle of yourself," said Enerde quietly. "It must be obvious even to the youngest of these children that there is nothing wrong with your hands."

"Liar," shouted Bronevsky. "The flesh is burned away, hanging in rotting shreds! I'll show you." He began to pluck lamely at the soiled bandages, and might even have been forced to produce the evidence for his words, had young Melchior, pale and groping for his napkin, not vomited his earlier lunch and his half-eaten dinner—a concoction of potatoes, string beans, and beets—over a wide area of the table, splattering the twins extensively. The boys jumped up, knocking over their chairs, and in the ensuing confusion and exclamations of disgust over the sour smell and the furious wiping from their faces and hands of the colored slime (brightly dominated by the beets), the children's father hastily retreated from the dining room. Ursula, the only one watching him, saw that he opened the heavy double doors easily with his bandaged hands.

The mess was cleaned up quickly and the weeping Melchior, comforted by his grandfather, was led away to lie down with a wet cloth folded over his forehead. But the scene was the first indication of a change in Bronevsky. With Rätzel dead, the seething war between the grandfather and his son-in-law burst into the open. Bronevsky, afraid to return to the Russian-controlled inner city and bored with the quiet life in the mansion, prowled the house and gardens with a brooding malaise. Bereft of his nightly companions, the long sleeps that formerly obliterated his mornings, and his afternoon rides in the park, he began to perceive in unfamiliar ways the emptiness of his life. Hour upon vacant hour stretched out ahead of him through the long afternoons and evenings. After an uneasy night, he would awaken in the early morning to a day that yawed before him like a tilting sea. He felt himself drown in the vastness of its space. He would groan, and try to escape back into sleep, but everything mocked his peace: it was spring and the doves cooed in the garden; ribbons of fresh sunlight shone in golden strips below the heavy draperies in his bedroom; the scent of mimosa filtered in through the sitting-room windows and lay upon him like a sated lover. He felt heavy and old and tired. After an hour of pretended sleep his weariness gave way to exhaustion until a kind of sourceless terror finally drove him into getting up and going downstairs. On the grand stairway he remembered the day he realized he was too old to die young. The whole depressing sensation came to him a few days after he was forty—

a number he despised. It *sounded* old. Empty. Hollow. Hollow like a barrel or a drum. It sounded portly. Barrel portly. Drum portly. It echoed with age and decay and mortality. Forty! In the foyer mirror he had suddenly seen his image as he was leaving for an evening in the city. His midsection was no longer slim and his trousers bulged out below his waistcoat, unattractive gaps opening between the buttons at each breath he took. True, not visible to anyone else, but *he* knew about the little stretched openings and they depressed him deeply. In the mirror, he pulled in his stomach and reset his shoulders. He realized with astonishment that the bulge did not entirely vanish. He examined his face closely and saw at once that he looked forty, that if he met himself coming on the street he would think, "There's a fellow that will never see his thirties again. He must be at least forty. Perhaps forty-five." He shuddered and rushed away from the portly figure in the glass. He would exercise more. Watch his eating. Cut back on his wine. He would visit a spa and get his youth back. Yes. That was what he needed, a place that would help him to get back into shape. He deserved that for all the misery he had to endure. He winced as he remembered a veiled reference to his weight. Everyone at the cabaret seemed to have made comments about fat. The comedian had a whole string of absurd jokes about fat people. And it was obvious that they were directed at him. Well, he would show them. A spa. Yes, that was it. He would go to a spa.

In the morning, he had dressed carefully, currying his mustache and adding a little extra scent to his chin and lips. He found Amalia lying languidly in her bed in a sea of pink pillows, her thin face the color of an ivory porcelain saucer. Her nurse was just opening the heavy draperies that kept the sun from the room. "Oh, oh," she cried to the woman as she saw her husband. "Not the sun. Pull the drapes. Bring me my rouge."

Pavel Bronevsky stood at the foot of the bed and smiled at his wife. "Rouge? Nonsense. You look lovely. A maiden awakening from a deep sleep." He came slowly around to the side of the bed, where he sat gingerly on the edge of the coverlet and picked up her small hand, kissing each fingertip.

"Leave us. Leave us," cried Amalia to the nurse. The woman hesitated until Bronevsky leveled his gaze at her over the top of his wife's fingers without raising his lowered head at all. "My dearest, dearest Pavel. How I've missed your visits. Father says I must rest. The doctor says I must rest. Rätzel bullies me into eating things I don't want. The children are so . . . so . . . too much. Too much. If only *we*, you and I, just you and I could be alone forever and ever. How perfect life would be—the two of us alone together the way we were at the beginning. How tiresome everything is without you. I see you so rarely now." She began to weep. "Everyone tells me that I'm not to be excited. I know they're keeping us apart. I know Father means well when he fibs to me about your being gone. He's afraid I'll have another child and not live through it. Why does love have to end in pain and suffering? Why can't one just order children when it's convenient? Oh, my dearest, dearest, I love you." She wept noisily, her mouth pulled down, her nose dripping. Bronevsky patted her mouth and nose with his handkerchief and kissed her forehead. Even through the cloth, her breath came to him foul as a swamp.

"My beloved," he whispered into her hair. "My beloved. I, too, am told that I must not see you. My heart breaks as I stand outside the door denied my sweet love. I yearn for death to take me. . . ."

"No, no. Don't say that. I beg of you. I could not live a minute if I thought you were gone."

"My beloved. . . . My sweet angel. You cannot know my torment. I must do something to keep my mind occupied, my heart from breaking. Perhaps I should offer my services to some good merchant who needs—"

"No, no. I must know that you are near. I must feel that you are outside the door."

Bronevsky sighed deeply. "Ah, but the pain of waiting, waiting, waiting. I must occupy my time doing something useful. If only I could drive this restlessness out of my longing limbs. You cannot imagine the pain of my dreams. Sometimes I wish I were a simple cossack soldier away from all this . . . this luxury, this ease."

Three days later his father-in-law gave him a large sum of money for a new horse and the trappings that went with keeping her. The idea of visiting a spa vanished in the presence of his great joy over the exquisite mare, which he named Rodina. For a few days he was quite happy, but after a time all seemed stale and sour to him again and his misery returned.

And so the years passed, each of them a further betrayal. If he saw his children, their smooth clear skin reminded him of the blotches on his own cheeks, the sacs under his eyes, the slack rubbery feel of his neck. On some mornings, his relentless anxiety drove him to search out his father-in-law. "It's your fault," he would say almost softly to the old man, who had finally begun to read his newspaper seriously. "You are the one who murdered my life. You." He continued in a mild way, speaking quietly without heat, without rancor. "You. You are the killer." He loathed the vague smile on Enerde's face, the ironic eyes that held him in contempt. "You destroyed my life. Do you hear, old man, you destroyed my life." His voice would begin to rise a little as the minutes wore on, and invariably a faint twitch began to pull under his left eye.

"What life?" Enerde would sneer. "Before I bought you, you had no life. A piece of debris floating in the gutter. Nothing more." From such words or similar ones violent explosions were inevitable. Bronevsky's shrieks could be heard well into the upper halls. "Malicious monster. From the beginning you were jealous that Amalia preferred my company to yours. You hated my youth, my virility. *You* never made a son! You were dried up even then. Don't think I don't know the history. The nasty little secrets!"

"Liar. Fop. Fortune hunter!"

"So. I'm a fop, am I? What do you think you are? Let me describe your fine qualities. Oh, yes, permit me to list them, you vengeful, vicious, vindictive old fart. Stingy! Yes, stingy. Mean. Closefisted. Selfish. That's what you are. Begrudging me my poor horse; my one pleasure. Oh, don't think I don't know how you resented paying for her upkeep. My poor Rodina. Sweet beast that she was." Bronevsky would weep a bit for the lost animal, and then suddenly return to his list as some random thought broke into his self-pity. "And ungrateful! Yes, that's the worst. The ingratitude."

"Gratitude? Gratitude? For what? For stealing my daughter?"

"Ha. You were enriched sixfold. And you know it. And as for stealing,

[116]

you're the thief: stealing my children! But I'll get the best. Just wait. You can't outlast me. You're already a bag of bad guts. I see it in your face. . . . Death is whispering in your ear all day, hanging onto your coat-tails, lying in your bed at night, snickering no doubt at the way you're begging to keep going. Well, you won't last, you know. What is it now, seventy-seven? Well, let's see who lasts longer."

Unable to answer some of Bronevsky's taunts, Enerde would suddenly accuse Bronevsky of vague crimes. "You sent the German hoodlum here! Rätzel's death was all your doing! We were safe until your big mouth betrayed us. You! You are the real killer! Tartar!"

Bronevsky, proud of his title, would fairly scream in outrage at this insult and strike out in new areas of attack.

In the heat of these battles the children often escaped to the old sum-merhouse where Rätzel was buried, there to sit on the remaining benches and talk quietly among themselves, sometimes arguing petulantly over minor disagreements, but never allowing these to develop into full-fisted fights. The decaying roofless old shelter became much more of a shrine to them than their mother's elaborate monument with its circle of three adult-sized hand-holding female angels had ever been.

If the children were unable to leave the house, they listened grimly and waited for the shouting to end. But it never ended for long. Their father seemed to revel in these violent encounters. Usually he entered into them drunk, and this made him more imaginative or at least less careful. Bro-nevsky's worst taunts involved Amalia. When Enerde subtly implied one day that each of her pregnancies was the result of a rape, Bronevsky quickly retorted that that was true but that there was no way he could protect himself from an insatiable wife.

Any slur on his daughter drove Enerde into a murderous rage, forcing his heart into furious drumbeats, making him physically ill. Only the ab-solute conviction that the Russian was trying to push him into a heart attack gave him the will to collect himself, to calm his heaving chest, breathe slowly and lie down until the danger passed. But outside of whatever room Enerde took refuge, Bronevsky continued to hurl his insults against the locked door, even pounding on it with his fists until he, too, tired of the futile rage and impotent fury, stomped off to drink himself into total oblivion until the next battle.

Enerde considered hiring assassins to kill the Russian on the rare nights that Bronevsky found the courage to leave the mansion for a surreptitious foray into the city. His lawyers advised against it. He plotted to have thieves do the job during a carefully staged robbery in the house, then abandoned the plan as being too dangerous to the children. Most deliciously, he savored murdering his mortal enemy himself. Watching Bronevsky eat, Enerde pondered poisons. Seeing him freshly shaved brought visions of razors, knives, axes. Every glimpse of his son-in-law fed new fire to the black flame in Enerde's heart. One night he awakened from a harrowing dream in which he had bludgeoned the man into a bloody heap, only to have the corpse rise up and laugh at him. He clutched his convulsing chest and in groaning supplication begged a long-neglected God to grant him a few more weeks.

For the children, the changed relationship between the two men became a fixed point of reference: they called it "the beginning of the war." That it coincided with the first bleak year of peace in Europe when the scarcity of food and fuel left everyone, except the conquerors, hungry and cold, was an irony not lost on them. In time they came to look back upon the years between the arrival of the Germans in 1938 and the fall of Vienna in 1945 with astonishment. Boris alone argued that as children there was no reason they should have been more aware of the tragic times. But Alexander was not mollified. "Grandfather deprived us of the war," he muttered.

It did not take them long to catch up on a little recent history. In the first two years after the war, they frequently rose at five, left the house stealthily after dressing in the dark, and returned home by nine to have breakfast with their grandfather. If Miss Schneider missed them at all, she assumed they were in the playroom where the ghostly snake and her young deprived the governess of forcing the children into early-morning lessons.

What lured the children out of their beds in the predawn hours was the ruins—both new and old—the bombed-out buildings of Vienna that looked like a roofless house of cards. The decaying near-Gothic, mock-Renaissance stone monstrosities crowned and crusted with naked Olympians meant to bolster a dying empire's cynical morale in the previous century took on the appearance of a long-dead Greek city. Dressed in old ski clothes, double-trousered and sweater-layered, mittened and muffled, they single-filed through the hidden arbor gate and glided or sauntered or sometimes ran down the snow-sided corridors carved out beside the invisible roads to the nearest ruins to explore the blasted and ravaged husks of houses and factories, shops and churches. They crawled into old cellars, bomb shelters, substreet utility tunnels, culverts, long-lost burial chambers, sewerage corridors and unfinished excavations, in a fury of curiosity and avidity of interest that no book had ever engendered in them. They crept past sleeping refugees and homeless squatters who lay bundled in rooms whose bomb-exploded windows and long-burned doors gaped like missing teeth.

They dodged the international patrols in the inner city who raced their flag-snapping jeeps down the same wool-white caves of carved snow open only to the sunless, silver dawn, the roar of the engines shuddering miniature avalanches onto the snow-padded sidewalks. "Bastards," Alexander spat after them.

During the second summer after the war, when they had stopped expecting it, a body—or at least its seated skeleton, the nose of a rat sniffing out of one of its eyepits—stared back at them from the wall of a cavern beneath a building where underground water had recently washed away the outer layer of rubble. After the first recoiling shock, the children trained their flashlight back on the figure. Enough of the bones were still intact and connected so that the form seemed to greet them happily with its gargantuan grin and its slight forward-leaning attitude, one hand resting on the earth-clotted knee (the most classic paternal position when addressing youngsters). The rat clambered out of the back of the skull and ran along a beam which rested on the skeleton's shoulder. "If we really had a snake," said Günther, "we could nab that little beast and bring it home for an Aesculapian snack."

He scraped away a bit of the dirt holding the body in its position, reminding Ursula of the previous winter when she had picked up a knobby-ended stick with which to dig out a piece of stained glass in one of the tunnels. "Tibia. About two-thirds of it. Adult, I believe," Günther had said, motioning at the tool, and she had lowered the bone slowly to the sour-smelling ground.

The presence of the resting remains of a total skeleton threw the children into an act of forced casualness, a forgivable cover for the first thrill of fear and revulsion which rippled through them. Melchior alone was horrified.

"Let's take him home," said Günther. "We can examine him better there." He directed the flashlight into one of the eye cavities.

Melchior gasped. "No. No. We have to report him."

"What for? He didn't do anything," said Günther, "just sitting here. Resting—minding his own business. Perfectly innocent."

"We don't actually know that," drawled Paul. "He might be a murderer. A cool, calculating killer. Wandered down here thinking he was safe, and the beam got him. God's own justice: 'Immediate, efficient, and permanent.' "

"That's not funny, not even as a joke." Melchior, deeply offended, would not look at the skeleton. "God doesn't work that way."

"The beam got him, all right," said Boris. "Look here, the back of his head's cracked." He loosened the skull. "If we all carry some of it, we can reconstruct him. All we have to do is clean him up and wire him back together. We can set him up in the playroom."

"I think he belongs in the closet," said Günther to Paul as though the others were not present.

"Much too crowded."

"We could take Grandmother out and make room for him."

"No. She belongs there. She wouldn't be happy anywhere else. She's too comfortable there. People don't like to move once they get used to a place. Now, take this fellow here. He has to be *seated* wherever he goes."

"There's that old chair in the alcove that no one ever uses," offered Ursula.

"You're all obscene." Melchior backed away from the others. "I won't have anything to do with this. He should have a proper burial."

Ursula shook her head. "But, Melchior, he won't get one if we tell someone he's here. He'll just be dumped like the other people who couldn't be identified. At home we could have a special place for him."

Alexander turned to Melchior. "Anyway, we can't tell anyone about him. We're not supposed to be in these old tunnels. The police would ask us how we found him."

"Then let's let someone else find him," argued Melchior lamely.

Ursula turned away from her brothers and gazed at the skeleton. "But they might not for a long time. For months, or years. We can't leave him here. Anyway, we already *have* found him. Now he's ours."

It was a specious argument, since the children had found many curious objects, none of which they ever carried home. Familiar with a hundred openings into the nether regions of the city where water dripped steadily and the ground under them shifted deceptively, they found shards and glass, old doorknobs and twisted hinges, stone and iron relics from an older time.

In a bombed bath where fat Romans sat sweating to cure their rheumatism twenty centuries before, Ursula and Alexander unearthed a piece of dirt-crusted mosaic which turned out to be part of a human face from which a single blue eye stared back at them in sensuous thick-lidded surprise. And once in a weed-choked cemetery they found an angel holding its own head in its leaf-cushioned stone lap, its raised handless arms stretching upward beseeching the view or voice of heaven. For a half-hour they searched the tall grass for the hands, which each knew they intended to place into that same lap. They would no more have taken something belonging to the city than they would have robbed their mother's tomb.

They sneaked the skeleton into the house and up to the playroom (an inadequate and ambiguous name for the top floor by then) before anyone was up. Cleaned and wired together, the bones sat like a spectator in a large wing chair in an alcove, its idiot's grin facing a permanently drape-drawn lead-paned window opening to a balcony which no one ever used. The children dressed the form in a patched and tattered jacket and trousers. "Just for decorum," Günther said, "in case we have visitors."

They referred to it as Adolphus.

12

Ursula was the first of the children to come face to face with one of her father's "friends" who, as far as the children could make out, had first begun to visit the mansion five or six months after the end of the war. This initial encounter took place around midnight in February. Ursula, a born prowler who hated sleep, left the library with a copy of *Gulliver's Travels* shortly after eleven. Everyone else was already long in bed and, as far as she knew, asleep. She loved the silence in the house at that time of night and instead of going to her room, wandered, candle in hand, the length of the various corridors and galleries, pausing at intervals to peer at the brooding portraits of ancestors whose gaze followed her with suspicious and disapproving eyes. The house was cold. It was always cold since the war, although several rooms were kept relatively warm with hearth fires and it was in these that the family spent most of the winter evenings. The rest of the time when fires were not possible or the rooms did not have hearths, the children bundled into warm clothing and ignored the cold. Ursula, who preferred any weather to heat, always astonished her brothers when she padded barefoot on the cold floors without any apparent discomfort. She did not know that she needed less sleep than her brothers; she only knew that she did not sleep as long as they did and thought it was simply because she hated to go to sleep, hated the lost hours. She had once expressed this. Boris told her that her hatred of sleep was clearly related to her inability to accept death and decay and that analysis would probably help her become normal. The twins, however, assured her that the need for sleep was probably a metabolic matter although sleep was not yet much understood by scientists. "As for hating death," Günther said, "that's a sign of good health. Anybody that's fond of it is clearly in trouble."

"I'm not talking about being *fond* of it," said Boris, with exasperated inflections punctuating his statements. "Of course that's not normal. Nor even of being fascinated by it, which quite probably *is* normal. But Ursula has a virulent hatred of it which borders on the pathological. She takes it *personally*, which is absurd. After all, it's a part of life."

"Well, then, it's a part I don't like."

The subject of death or at least its acceptance was another old argument among the children. Alexander said that as long as one had to die, he should die in battle with a sword in his hand. Boris' view that it was an inevitable process that should be accepted as early in life as possible was well-known to everyone. The twins agreed that it was a natural process (unless people were murdered or they committed suicide), but they refused to concede that it should be accepted, saying only that considering the alternative, one should do everything to maintain life. Melchior said that every death was the will of God and that God's will was not an appropriate subject for discussion.

Ursula caught Günther's warning look as she was about to tell Melchior what she thought of God and bit her lower lip. Once before she had told Melchior that if God arranged everything in life, He should have thought things out better. "The arrangements are terrible. Why should people get sick? Why die?"

Melchior had refused to answer.

Wandering into her mother's rooms in the middle of this February night, she held the candle up to the crucifix tied to the headboard of her mother's bed. "I think I could understand it if there was a really good reason. But I can't see a good reason. Günther says it's the law of nature: people die to make room for new people. All right. All right. But why do they have to be sick to do it? Why do they have to hurt? Why not just have them get to be one hundred years old and then die, without being sick, without hurting? Isn't that a good idea?" The room was immensely silent. She sat on a chair beside the bed and watched the large gold crucifix. It had hung there all through her mother's illness, and Ursula remembered how she had once been told by one of the nurses that the crucifix hanging on the bed would help her mother get well, help heal her, help take away the pain because Christ had died in pain for mankind and He would absorb her mother's pain Himself through the crucifix. But in the end her mother did not get well and during the last weeks of her life she screamed with pain every day. How can there be a purpose for such things? No, it made no sense. Christ's dying made no sense. The crucifix hanging on the bed made no sense.

She picked up the candle and left the room. At that precise moment, the door to her father's sitting room opened and a woman wearing a fur coat backed into the foyer on tiptoe, closing the door with great care. She was holding a small flashlight and as she turned away from the door she gave a gasp at seeing Ursula and dropped the light. For another ten seconds they stared at each other without moving. In the soft glow of the candle, the woman seemed beautiful, with a flush on her full face as someone just rising from a hot bath. But then Ursula saw that it was rouge that made the generous color which covered both cheeks and lips. Thick pale hair raged around her face in disarray. She wore a tight purple dress, the fur coat falling to the sides of her eggplant breasts. Even fully dressed she looked like a Rubens nude.

Without looking away from Ursula the woman crouched to the floor and scooped up her flashlight, rising swiftly. In her eyes there was an expression hinting at humor, as though in a moment she might break into rich laughter. But she did not laugh; she brushed past the silent girl without a word and slipped with the same stealth out of the foyer into the corridor. What she left behind was a scent, a smell that was more spice than perfume, a smell of some plant that Ursula could not place, or perhaps the pollen of some flower, pungent, heady, a little sour. Still, it was not an unpleasant smell, and the next morning she told the twins about the incident. "I followed her as far as the stairs. But I didn't let her see me. I didn't need the candle to follow her light. She went out the door in the solarium so I could see her from the landing balcony. She didn't hurry exactly, but she didn't go slowly, either."

"And you never saw her before?"

"No."

"She came from Father's rooms?"

"Yes."

"You didn't see him?"

"No. I think he was asleep. From the way she walked—so quietly—I think she was trying not to wake him."

"Was she carrying anything?"

"The flashlight."

"Anything else?"

Ursula had decided not to mention the canvas bag the woman was carrying, a bag rather like a backpack, only she had it hanging from her shoulder by one of its straps, its folding flap useless because the opening bulged high with food: wax-sealed cheeses, packages of margarine, tinned meat, and wine. Even in the dim candlelight Ursula recognized some of the exposed labels, particularly the wine bottles, which carried on their necks the Enerde crest hanging from elegant chains. "She carried a sack of food," said Ursula.

The twins both nodded. "From her description it's a new one altogether," said Paul.

Günther nodded.

"You've seen her before?" asked Ursula.

"Not that one, but others. And we never ran into them as closely as you did. We saw Father unlock the gate one night about a month ago, so we waited in the old gatekeeper's quarters. But the woman who came the following week and the one that came last week were not the same. We thought for a time they might bump into each other, coming and going as they do, but there is a sort of pattern to it. It's a regular parade."

"And Father gives them food?" asked Ursula.

"Yes," said Günther.

"Why don't they come during the day when it's not so cold?"

The twins looked at her without immediately answering. "It would upset Grandfather," said Günther finally.

Thinking on this answer for a moment, Ursula heard the truth in Günther's careful answer. "You mean Grandfather wouldn't let them visit?"

"Yes, that's what I mean," said Günther. "It's just as well that he doesn't know. The fights are bad enough as things are. Waldi knows, of course, because of the missing wine and food, but he seems to have made a kind of unspoken agreement with Father. He only lets him give away a certain amount. You see, one of the problems is that Grandfather doesn't give Father any more money, at least not nearly as much as he used to give him." Günther did not add, "so this is how he pays them now," but somewhere in her mind Ursula heard the unspoken words.

All that spring and summer and into autumn, Ursula was aware of the night women who came and went past her door on the way to her father's rooms. She found herself listening for them, listening for the creaking of an errant floorboard, for hasty muffled shoeless footsteps (once even a dropped shoe), the swishing of skirts, whispers, laughter; and then one October night an explosion of shouting and screaming that awakened everyone except Alexander, whose dreams were already filled with his own private little wars that allowed no intrusion.

Ursula, running from her room toward the head of the stairs, bumped into the twins leaning against the balustrade. Paul caught her before she reached the first step. "Wait, wait. It's being taken care of."

"What? What is it?"

Günther heaved a deep sigh. "It's some trouble with one of the . . . one of Father's friends."

"What kind of trouble?"

"She awakened Grandfather."

They all looked down toward the stairs as a scream and the crash of something hurled against the wall followed by a woman's voice shrieking a string of colorful oaths and impossible curses zigzagged on the darkened ground floor like blasts of lightning. Ursula heard her grandfather shouting: "Whore! Harlot! How dare . . . ?" Something intervened. A moment later lights came on in the main foyer, but no one seemed to be in the suddenly bright space. The woman's voice continued, but the shrieks no longer formed words; the cries had turned to hisses and sputtering. Ursula heard a sound in the hall behind her and turned to see Melchior and Boris rushing toward them, Melchior's face terrified behind the candle he held out in front of him like an Olympic runner. The flame quickly went out and after a few moments the five children stood completely motionless at the head of the stairs, peering down upon the still-empty foyer. From the direction of their grandfather's large ground-floor suite, the woman's voice went on in a furious lathery growl, more like thick wet breathing than actual shrieks, as though she were drowning. A moment later Berghoch and Graz entered

[123]

the foyer dragging the woman between them, the toes of her shoes making neat parallel black streaks on the marble floor. Ursula recognized at once the head of wild pale hair and the purple dress. The children watched the two men drag the woman past the row of neo-Greek pillars to the front door. When she threw her head back in an effort to halt the two men or at least slow them down, Ursula saw that she was actually foaming at the mouth, only the foam was reddish and it ran down her chin. The front door opened and closed again quickly and a moment later Ursula clearly heard a car's tires hiss on the wet cobbled driveway. After another few moments, the two men returned, Berghoch wiping his hands on his handkerchief. They walked in the direction of Enerde's rooms, and without warning, the lights below suddenly went out and the children were left alone in the dark. Ursula heard Melchior's soft crying get louder. She reached for his shoulders and realized at once that the twins were already leading him away to one of the rooms, back to the light. It was her room that was nearest and it was there that they waited until Melchior finally stopped crying.

"It's too much," said Boris. "Father can't carry on this way without creating a scandal."

"Don't be ridiculous. He's *been* a scandal for years," said Günther, both exhaustion and fury edging his voice. "If he were just more discreet about what he does! But that's just it. He's purposely careless. He probably wanted Grandfather to find out about the women coming to the house at night. He's trying to force Grandfather to give him more money. So many of their fights are about money: it seems to be the only thing that relates them now. Yes, I'm sure he wants Grandfather to know about the parade. That way he thinks Grandfather will go back to paying him so he can live his life as he did before . . . away from the house . . . so the women won't come here." Günther sighed. "No, Boris, don't worry about Father creating a scandal: he *is* the scandal, and he knows Grandfather can't stand it. Grandfather is much more concerned about what other people think than Father is, and Father knows it. So he has an advantage." They talked on for another hour, turning the problem of their father's indiscretions over as they might turn over the body of an unidentifiable dead animal in the garden with a prodding stick.

It was during that previous summer that Ursula first realized that even people who did not live in the house talked about her family in a strangely scurrilous way, always making some oblique reference to her father, some mild-appearing jest charged with malice. An old seamstress, a squat woman with fat hands and a balding head whom Ursula remembered from early childhood, came to the house to deliver some shirts one afternoon. Ursula, returning from the summerhouse where she frequently went to read, was startled by the woman, who suddenly spoke to her from a bench under a chestnut tree near the back gate. She was holding up the bottom of her apron, which bulged with chestnuts. "Why, it's little Ursula—but not little at all! How tall you've gotten. Who would have thought six months could make such a difference. Why, you've got your breasts. Well, well, well, the satyr's little nymph is growing up."

The woman's laugh sent Ursula hurrying to the library, where she discovered that Miss Schneider's definition and description of satyrs (given during an earlier lesson on Greek mythology not covered by the university student the year before) left out one of the horny little fellow's most important attributes: he was apparently more than a charming, furry forest imp who frightened shepherds and shepherdesses lost in the woods.

Ursula sought Günther's wide range of knowledge on such matters and told him what the seamstress had said. "And she laughed, but her eyes didn't laugh. They spit at me. I looked up 'satyr.' It means more than Schnabel told us. It means—"

"I know what it means. What do you want to know?"

"What does she think that Father does that made her use that word?"

Günther told her, his explanation short, direct, and accurate (not as to the nature of satyrs but as to what the seamstress thought).

"You mean, she thinks that Father forced Mother to . . . that he raped . . . ?"

"Yes. It's an absurd idea. An old rumor because there are so many of us. But like others, the seamstress is extremely stupid. I'm surprised she even knew the word 'satyr.' What that woman thinks has nothing to do with him. Nothing to do with us. Pay no attention to her. And the next time she gets familiar with you, kick the bitch in the shins."

But Ursula's anger over the woman's remark refused to diminish after Günther's explanation. She returned to the library and again opened the mythology book with the richly detailed picture of two satyrs—half-human, half-goat creatures—cavorting with naked nymphs whose expressions of frenzied delight denied their dainty gestures at escape attempts. The women's crotches were coyly concealed with garlands of snapdragons, buttercups, and labiates. The satyrs' huge human scrota and penises dangled obscenely to the beasts' curly-haired knees. Ursula slammed the book shut and wished she had kicked the seamstress.

The morning after the shrieking woman was dragged out of the house, Ursula stood spellbound (and barefoot as usual) outside the gaping linen room and heard the two maids discuss her father in low, charged voices. The open door was a symptom of a crisis in the house: the Enerde establishment was a house of closed doors—only confusion left a door ajar. The midnight commotion had thrown everything off center, and all over the house the unspoken rules and habitual patterns of work were momentarily forgotten.

In the morning the grandfather spent several hours with two lawyers in his closed study, and Bronevsky locked himself in his rooms. Miss Schneider, enraged and weepy in turns, excused the children after a half-hour of English grammar and took to her bed claiming a blinding headache. Ursula and her brothers did not talk about the night's events any further. The boys drifted off to the grounds and other areas of the house, all of them sullen and silent. Ursula, in search of her drawing tablet, came across the open linen-room door and listened.

"It was only a matter of time before one of these hussies started some trouble."

"Imagine awakening the old man and demanding money!"

"Terrible. It's all the Russian's fault. Having women coming here in the night! Here in this great proud house. They say when he goes into the city, he has as many as three women sometimes in a single night. Of course, it's a disease . . . that kind of craving. And he wants them to do things with him that no decent woman even knows about."

The voice lowered and an explosive gasp came from the other maid. "And they do it?"

"Who's to know? There's some that will do anything nowadays. It was the war. It turned people into animals. It's the children I think about."

"You think they know?"

"Oh, their knowing about him is not what matters. If they don't now, they'll know soon enough. It's the disease you should ask about. It's hereditary, you know. It runs in the blood like a fire. Things like that always do. Carried down from father to child for generations, always getting worse. And it ends in madness!"

"No!"

"Yes. The parts down there go crazy and it affects the brain. It's a dreadful disease. Unspeakable."

After a long sigh: "Do you think the girl has it too?"

"I'm sure of it. She's no different from the boys when it comes to that. Women get it in the blood too, and in a woman it's even worse, more vulgar—if that's possible. It's like a permanent, burning itch down there. Oh, yes, all those children are tainted with it. Look at the way they're colored. That's always a sure sign . . . those unnatural, sharp colors. Like something in the wild. There's nothing soft about them. Nothing gentle. They're almost frightening with those unsmiling faces like they were listening to something crawling inside their flesh."

"You must be wrong. I've never heard of anything like that. I know some people do it more than others, but I can't imagine going crazy because of it. And the children *are* a bit gloomy some of the time, but I can't see them diseased in this terrible way. They can be really quite nice children."

"You wait . . . and watch. Those childen have the craving. I just know it!"

"But they're only children."

"The boys are almost grown and the girl's already menstruating—much earlier than is normal, I might add. That's another sure sign that something's not quite right with that brood. You'll see. Just give it time to come out. I can already see it in their faces." The maid spoke then in a loud dark whisper. "It's the Russian blood. It's from the old times of the barbarians!" She ended in a tone of high triumph, although her final statement was a roared whisper: "They ate *raw* flesh!"

"No!"

"Yes!"

Ursula crept away and again sought Günther. She found him in the playroom looking through a microscope and told him what the woman had said.

Günther sat back on his high stool, his hands still on the instrument. "Ursula, that stupid woman is ridiculous. I told you all about procreation, how it's done. What happens. I gave you a very good book on it, which I know you read. There's no such thing as the parts going crazy. People go crazy in the head, not in the crotch. Now, stop listening to ignorant people. They know nothing about science and they get everything all wrong from other ignorant people."

Ursula found her drawing tablet in the library, but she did not open it. She pulled down her grandfather's elaborate anatomy books, an exquisite boxed collection of skeletal drawings with colored cellophane overlays which added mounds of muscles to the standing bones, then red rivers of arteries and veins and miles of nerves, and finally a whole market of vegetable- and sausage-shaped organs all neatly tucked with gravity-defying order inside the human trunk. There were certainly no gutty pieces hanging down to the knees. She had copied the drawings a dozen times until she could do them from memory, her brothers sputtering into laughter at her representations of the external male organs. The anatomy chart showed a flaccid penis, but Ursula gave her drawings of it slightly more rigidity, saying that it looked more natural that way, since none of theirs was ever that asleep.

Miss Schneider had discovered one of the drawings one evening as she was sifting through a wastebasket in the classroom. She rushed it to the grandfather and handed it to him with shaking hands. Enerde examined it carefully. "Quite excellent, isn't it?"

"It's . . . it's not right," gasped the woman. She wanted to say "obscene."

"Nonsense. It's very well done. Ursula has a true gift."

"But she's only a child!"

"What does that have to do with it?"

Miss Schneider blinked rapidly and wrung her hands. "I only mean that she's a girl . . . that . . . that a girl ought to have more . . . more girllike interests . . . things that girls are ordinarily interested in."

"Nonsense. Ursula is quite an extraordinary girl. She is interested in everything."

"Permit me to say, sir, that that is precisely the problem. She should be given a little directing. The boys, as you know, all seem to be well-channeled into given areas of interest. It's time we begin to think as to where Ursula is headed. There is no directing her. She reads everything. I've tried to channel her toward the more womanly interests in her reading. And as for drawing, I've tried again and again to encourage her into . . . into some sort of delicacy in that direction. She does flowers quite well, you know, and china painting is a fine feminine art and quite the rage at the moment. . . ."

Enerde stopped her with a raise of his hand. "Miss Schneider, we all appreciate your efforts, but I suggest you leave Ursula's drawing to her. As for her reading, it's precisely her universal interests that make her interesting. I want you to continue the fine job you're doing seeing that all of the children are accomplished in the English language. Just keep up the good work. In time we'll find others to help you; until then, keep the children to some kind of schedule and stress English. It is going to be essential for them to have command of English." He picked up his newspaper, adjusted his gold-rimmed pince-nez, and commenced to read, leaving Miss Schneider holding Ursula's drawing of the human male trunk with its partially erected penis.

[127]

Infuriated at this rebuff but still sufficiently terrified of the grandfather, the governess decided to take the drawing to the father. It was a curious decision and she only thought about its ambiguity later when it was much too late. Bronevsky, whose latest quarrel some hours earlier had been with Berghoch over the whereabouts of the wine-cellar key (in Berghoch's pocket), was drunk on sherry, which he disliked but which was all he could find not under lock. Thus when Miss Schneider showed up at his sitting-room door with a drawing of "a rising cock," as he thought of the picture, he was in a black and vicious humor. He invited her into his rooms after he took the drawing from her hand, speaking with such excessive politeness the governess was at once all befuddled. "Dear, dear lady, how very kind to you to visit a sick man. I *am* very sick, you know. Oh, nothing contagious, but something very serious here." He thumped the heart area of his chest. "The doctors don't give me much time, and no hope at all. How very kind of you to visit, but I know you bring a problem. Yes, yes. Of course, I'm always here to help. Please do sit down. Over here on the sofa. Yes, that's fine. Now, you say there's a problem with this drawing." He held it up. "Hmmm . . . a problem, hmmm."

"The children," she began, "they're not getting the kind of discipline, that is . . . directional discipline that they need. Their grandfather lets them read anything. It's a most unhealthy situation. And now I've discovered the girl is drawing these gross pictures. . . ."

"Really. One of my children drew this? How remarkable. How extraordinary! Yet, perhaps not. No, perhaps not at all. There was great talent in my side of the family—painters, poets, musicians. A regular army of artists." He studied the drawing again. "Yes, even I have hidden gifts. But the opportunity to make use of them was thwarted. Dark forces worked against me." His eyes filled with tears.

Miss Schneider, too, began to blink back tears. "Poor man. Poor, dear, wonderful man. If I could only be of help to you. If there were only some way I might serve . . ."

"There is, dear lady, there is."

"You have only to ask. How can I serve you?" She placed her fingers gingerly on the back of his hand resting on his thigh.

He quickly took the hand in his and brought the fingers to his lips. "How kind, dear lady. Your generous offer is accepted with humble gratitude."

"Yes, yes. Say it. What can I do?"

"I need the key, my dear. And that vicious Berghoch won't give it to me. I'm sure it's on him. I wonder if you could get it for me. . . ."

"The key?" Miss Schneider almost withdrew her hand. "What key?"

"Why, to the wine cellar. All the brandy's been locked up. They're depriving me of my share. It's most distressing."

Miss Schneider's tears dried up quickly. "Well, I can ask. . . ."

"Oh, no, that won't do. I've tried that. You must use your . . . wiles. You must use your . . . hmmm . . . yes, your wiles."

"I'm . . . not sure. He's a very disagreeable person. Very coarse."

Bronevsky dropped her hand and rose to pace back and forth. "Well, don't offer something if you don't mean it."

"Oh, but I do mean it."

"Then do it."

Miss Schneider felt a dismal silence build up in the room as he paced in slippered feet on the carpet in front of her. "Well?" he asked, stopping close to her so that his hips were even with her face.

She blushed deeply. "I . . . I don't know if I can."

"Of course you do. Come now, why did you bring me this picture if you didn't think you could?" He snatched Ursula's drawing off the table and held it in front of her face, its positioning ironically strategic.

Miss Schneider fled from the room with Bronevsky's laughter following her the length of the hall.

The battles between Bronevsky and Enerde increased after the woman in the purple dress was dragged screaming from the house. Usually these shouting matches began soon after lunch, when Bronevsky was beginning to sober from his all-night drinking bouts, and they continued sporadically through the afternoon, ending around dinnertime, when he was fairly drunk again. Enerde had finally given in to letting his son-in-law drink as much as he wished in the hope that the man would drink himself to death or have an accident while he was drunk. The children escaped listening to these harangues whenever they could by retreating to the playroom or the classroom, areas both removed architecturally from the sounds on the main floor, which was essentially the battleground. Enerde no longer visited the other floors after his daughter died. His large suite of rooms on the main floor opened to a hedge-enclosed garden thought of in the eighteenth century as a "secret garden" and in which he and Ursula spent much secret time, he napping in a large awninged wicker sofa while she drew—everything from the veined leaves of the shrubbery to the various birds that fed at the feeders or splashed in the stone fountains.

By the time the occupation entered its third year, the children still raced into the chilly dawns to visit the city at least three or four times a month. In all this time no new teachers were hired. Miss Schneider held classes every day, the hours carefully segmented into given units of study, which the children rather cheerlessly adhered to in the classroom, although they spent a greater number of hours reading on their own. And this the instructress knew and endured with a cold, formidable silence like a deeply insulted woman repeatedly betrayed by a faithless husband. Alone in her room she despaired of the situation and placed all hope on the knowledge that the old man was going to die soon and Bronevsky would suddenly need her to reach his children, from whom he was estranged. She would soon convince him of the necessity for stricter control of the children's reading and a purge of the house of its filthy and corrupting books. What rankled her more than anything else was Ursula's "impure mind." The girl was incapable of being discriminating: she read everything. Showing her that Virgil and Dante could teach one all that was needed for a well-ordered moral life was a waste of time: the girl told her that Homer was much more exciting than Virgil and Boccaccio much funnier than Dante. It was clear that the girl was influenced by her brothers and should have been separated from them long ago. Her reading was bound to leave her low-minded and unprincipled. This was all being made abundantly clear by her warped and

[129]

wicked drawings, which could be found everywhere in the house. (Alexander in a fit of pique over some scolding had left a caricature of the instructress where she would conveniently find it.) As for the boys, only Melchior was not clearly doomed to lead a dissolute, profligate life; yet even he had become withdrawn and no longer liked her, although she had no idea why. Bad sibling influence, most likely. He was, after all, quite malleable. The twins were incapable of the loftier ideas of the past, sunk as they were in their science, narrowing their interests to dissecting and that godless man Darwin. Alexander was nothing but a little fascist who called Plato a reactionary. And Boris, for whom she had once held out some hope, was ensnared by that shameful Jew, Freud. She shuddered at the memory of Boris saying quite clearly one day that the mouth was an oral sexual organ, "according to Freud." The incident had made her physically ill. And now that they were all older, the problems were bound to get worse. Ursula had "developed" too early and was in real danger: after all, even brothers are males. The children were alone on the fourth floor much of the time and only heaven (and the snakes) knew what went on up there. She knew that the childen laughed at her, that the only thing they took seriously from her was the English-language lessons. The rest of the time they studied all manner of subjects over which she had no control, since half the books from the library were up in the playroom with the snakes.

And then everything changed. In the heat of one of the vicious fights between Bronevsky and his father-in-law, Enerde suffered a heart attack. The old man suddenly clutched his chest and slumped to the floor at the entrance to the octagonal drawing room. It was late afternoon. Ursula and Alexander, listening from the main stairway landing, heard their grandfather's hideous gasping and raced down the stairs. Bronevsky was swaying drunkenly over Enerde's heaving form. "Die, you old bastard! That's right, choke and die!"

Both children collided with their father, pushing him to one side. Together they lifted the unconscious grandfather onto a sofa. Ursula, mad with fear, was already pleading with him not to die. Later she was to remember the shock she felt at how light he was, how bony the wide shoulders, how thin the long neck that pulled back his great bearded head. But at the time, she could only hear his gasps and her own scream to Alexander, "Get Günther! Run! Get Günther! Get Paul!"

She never knew how many seconds passed while she clung to her grandfather's chest and spoke to it furiously, actually spoke coherent words— commands—directly to his heart: "Beat! Don't stop. Beat! Beat! Beat!" She was still talking in a febrile whisper when all her brothers ran into the room, and Günther, dropping to his knees, laid his head over the old man's chest. "It's beating. Get the brandy and a blanket."

None of them even glanced at their father, who sat slouched in a chair ten feet away and watched with bitter, sardonic eyes the man who he believed had robbed him of his life.

While her grandfather was convalescing, Ursula sat beside his bed all day, refilling his water glass, covering his shoulders when the bed robe slipped off, reading to him, drawing pictures for him, her eyes anxious behind the smile she wore for him. The doctor assured the children that with care and rest their grandfather would survive the attack, but he warned them that there were to be no more battles. The old man was not to be upset in any way: tranquillity meant survival; any furor could bring death. They agreed among themselves that one of them would always stay with him, spelling each other so that he would never be alone. But within days it became clear that Ursula would not leave him while he was awake. She told her brothers simply that taking care of him was her job; they had other jobs and they could stay with him at night while he slept. They knew better than to argue with her. Paul told Miss Schneider that Ursula would return to the daily lessons when their grandfather was well again.

"We'll see about that," fumed the governess, heading for the door.

"Grandfather says," Günther began slowly, "that anyone who interrupts Ursula while she is reading to him will be hung by his—or her—heels naked from the front gate." None of the boys laughed. None of them even looked up from his book. "I think she is reading *Werther* to him, and you know how Grandfather feels about Goethe's romantic period. It's silly, of course, but it's tranquil enough, and Ursula has a pleasant reading voice."

During the six weeks Ursula spent with her grandfather, she occasionally ran into the governess on the stairs and the woman would ask her how the "dear man" was feeling. The lightness of the governess's voice and the flicker of anticipation in her eyes was not lost on the thirteen-year-old Ursula, who knew that Miss Schneider always took their father's side in the quarrels. By then all the children knew of Miss Schneider's passion for their father, and their contempt for her had developed, quite unknown to themselves, into a subtle hatred for the fawning woman. Her unpleasant manner of cooing flatteries to him in those rare and confusing times when he entered the classroom and watched the children with sullen bewilderment was a hideous embarrassment to them now. Bronevsky was aging badly. His collapsing cheek muscles pulled his mouth down into an expression of perpetual discontent and a nest of wrinkles circled his green, bloodshot eyes. The mustache was dyed.

Unfairly, the children identified Miss Schneider with the "parade." Bronevsky, who had been aware of the governess's mad desire for him for years, was only amused. He was too much the snob to seduce her. Occasionally he borrowed small sums of money from her, which he never repaid. Miss Schneider felt honored in giving him what she could, although she knew his interests lay in women he met in the inner city, women who were more than willing to comfort him in exchange for food and wine from the Enerde cellars, one of the few remaining intact after the war.

A week after the heart attack, Ursula, walking barefoot past the library late at night, heard the governess say, "Be patient; he may yet die any hour. And if not this time, the next. One heart attack usually means another."

Ursula glided past the half-open door without a sound, but glancing in, she saw her father hunched over the table staring into a glass in his hand, a bottle directly in front of him. He was weeping. "None of them loves me, has ever loved me. He has stolen that from me, too."

"Oh, don't think on that, dear sir. He's old; he can't last much longer. When he dies, they will turn to you. I know them. You'll see."

Ursula ran silently back to her grandfather's room, her heart jumping. "Is he all right?" she whispered.

Boris was seated beside the sleeping man, reading. "Of course he's all right. Go to bed."

"He's going to die."

"He's not going to die. The doctor said he's coming along just fine. You heard him."

"One day he's going to die." She stood at the foot of the great canopied bed and watched the old man's beloved face.

"*Of course,* one day he's going to die. One day *everybody's* going to die. Death is the *sine qua non* for the continuity of life."

"It's a stupid system," snarled Ursula, still whispering.

"It's an excellent system. You're being emotional. You know, you're very immature, Ursula," he said loftily, closing his book. "I thought you had outgrown this death business. I think you should be analyzed. Freud would say that your inability to see the logic of death is a sign of infantilism. That's a very bad problem. You have to see that death is inevitable."

"I can see it all right; I just don't like it."

"That's where you're being emotional. If you really saw it, there would be no question of liking it or not liking it."

Ursula wanted to pummel her brother with the book he held so lovingly with both hands. She knew it was one of Freud's. "Boris, I'm not going to argue with you here and wake up Grandfather, but I think you're crazy." She turned to leave.

When Ursula passed the library again, Miss Schneider was gone, although her father still sat at the table, his rounded shoulders hugging the bottle in front of him. She remembered his mole shadow on the high foyer wall on the night she heard him on the stairs outside her room years ago. It seemed to her that he always lived in the dark now. The maids said that he frequently slept all day with the drapes drawn. Sometimes they heard him walking about, talking loudly as though arguing with someone, although they knew he was alone.

Miss Schneider saw her chance to separate Ursula from her brothers after the grandfather was recovered from his heart attack. "You are behind now in some of your lessons," she said to Ursula at the entrance to the classroom. The governess stood with her back to the closed door. "I've moved your things to another room where you will be able to concentrate better and catch up."

"Then I'll be behind for today. I'll always be six weeks behind if we do it this way." Ursula already knew from Alexander each day what they had covered in the lessons during her absence. "I've translated the English stories and completed the French notebook and all the math problems."

"And the Latin?"

Ursula made a face. "I'll do it tonight." Latin bored her.

"You'll do it now. Come along." The woman strode past Ursula to a small storage room at the end of another hall. "You'll be able to concentrate much better here."

The room was badly lit with a single uncovered overhead bulb and one narrow window that faced the gardens. "It's too cold in here," said Ursula, eyeing the depressing clutter of stacked cartons and broken furniture leaning against the walls on all sides.

"It's no colder than the rest of the house."

Ursula knew that was true, and she could not think of any good reason she could have to object to being separated from her brothers. It was clear to her, however, that the governess had no reasonable motive either.

"You'll study here."

"No," said Ursula steadily, "I want to stay with them."

"You can't stay with them. Not anymore. It's time you realized that you are a girl and it's not healthy to be surrounded by so many boys."

"That's silly. I'm not surrounded." For a moment it came to Ursula that Miss Schneider's face looked like a pair of pliers. "What do you mean by surrounded?"

"You are the only girl among a great many boys, and that certainly makes you surrounded. Also, it's time you knew that boys are quite different from girls . . ."

"I already know that."

Miss Schneider looked at Ursula as though the girl had said something crude. "I do not want to hear anything nasty like that from you again."

"I didn't *say* anything nasty."

"Don't interrupt. What I am trying to tell you is that boys can take care of themselves. Always remember that men have strengths we women know nothing about."

"How do you know they have them if you don't know anything about them?"

The governess opened her mouth and snapped it shut again. She placed a copy of *The Aeneid* on a small table in the one vacant corner of the room. "You will simply have to take my word for it. Now, then, translate Book Ten, first into German and then into English. Do not forget that haste makes waste, but that does not mean you can dawdle." She turned to leave in a manner clearly suggesting that the situation was not negotiable.

"I don't like this room."

The woman stopped in the doorway and looked at Ursula over her shoulder. "Learn to like it."

"I won't stay."

"You will stay. If you do not stay, I shall go to your grandfather"—she paused and added slowly—"and start a scene, a very bad scene that will upset him; whatever happens will be *your* fault."

Ursula inhaled sharply. The governess was not exactly smiling, but the spread of her mouth at the final word showed her teeth tightly clenched as if she had just bitten off a portion of some delicious food.

After the door closed, Ursula stood staring at it, stunned into silence, not only at the woman's vicious plan but also at the absolute conviction that she would do as she threatened if given provocation. It was Ursula's first experience with blackmail.

She sat down in front of *The Aeneid* and considered the problem: if she went to her grandfather first and protested being separated from her brothers, he might get upset anyway, no matter how carefully she told him. On the other hand, even if it didn't upset him then, Miss Schneider could still

[133]

start a scene if she were forced to abandon the new arrangements. But if nobody did anything, then Grandfather was safe. Still, if Schnabel could think up such a terrible thing as trying to make him have a heart attack, Grandfather should know about it. But knowing about it might upset him, too. He could get very angry and . . . No. There was nothing to be done.

Staring at the closed book in front of her, Ursula carefully circled the situation again, coming back to something she had hurried past: Miss Schneider could upset him anytime she wanted to . . . she could start a scene about anything. She *wanted* him to die. She said so that night in the library: "One heart attack usually means another." And she said it in a voice not only confident, but reassuring as well, as though she could somehow guarantee the event, *make it happen*. Ursula's hatred for Agnes Schneider began to take on a new shape and a density it did not have before; it ballooned inside her chest as if she were breathing in steam. She felt her skin get tight and hot. "Damn ugly bitch," she whispered, pounding her fists on Virgil. She threw the book on the floor and pushed open the window, the cold air hitting her face, forcing back the hot, bubbling nausea already high in her throat.

After a while, when the bad taste in her mouth began to sink away, she sat down again, taking a new look at the situation. As long as Miss Schneider was in the classroom she could not be somewhere else upsetting anybody. And after lessons, before the garden work, there was tea, when she and her brothers joined their grandfather for an hour and everything was right and wonderful and safe. Between tea and dinner, her grandfather stayed alone in his study. No one would dare disturb him then. After dinner he usually retired early. Looking back over the pattern of a typical day, Ursula saw that keeping Schnabel away from her grandfather was absolutely essential. And it could be done. Still, Miss Schneider sometimes left the classroom and was gone for a half-hour—more than enough time to start something. She envisioned the governess leaving the classroom and hurrying to their grandfather's sitting room where he was reading the newspaper. Now she was knocking on the door; now she was standing in front of him as he looked over the top of his pince-nez, the newspaper resting in his lap. He speaks in a stunned voice. *"What's that? What? The children did what?"* He rises, the newspaper sliding to the floor. He clutches his chest with both arms and begins to gasp air in great rasping gulps.

Ursula bounded out of the chair, tore open the door, and raced down the hall. The old man's sitting room was adjacent to the huge master bedroom on the main floor. She pulled open the door without knocking and stood breathless in front of the old man, who looked at her quizzically over his glasses. "Oh, Grandfather . . . I thought . ... I thought you were sick again." She dropped to her knees beside his chair and began to cry.

"Ursula, Ursula," he said softly, stroking her bowed head. "I'm quite all right. I feel exceptionally well today. You must not worry about me."

"Oh, Grandfather, let me stay with you. I can study here. I don't need Miss Schneider to tell me what to do. Let me read to you. I'll do all the lessons at night. Please let me stay with you." She looked up into his face. "I'll read Goethe to you, and Schiller and Shakespeare, everybody you like. Just let me stay."

"Dear, dear child. You must stop this concern. I feel excellent. I am completely well." He brushed away her tears with his handkerchief. "I intend to live to a hundred—at least."

Ursula sat back on her heels and noticed only then that he was not reading the newspaper; her drawing tablet lay in his lap. It was open to some drawings she had hidden between a number of blank pages. She held her breath and glanced at her grandfather's face. He was smiling.

"I think we have a laughing bear in the house." He chuckled. "Who, one might ask, is this supposed to be?" He tapped his forefinger on the open tablet.

Ursula got up slowly and sat on the arm of his chair and leaned against the old man's shoulder, rubbing her cheek on his downturned head. The face of a white-bearded man with a lion's mane stared back at them from the sketchpad, his fierce eyes radiating beams of light which made all objects transparent. The caricature was clearly the grandfather, his high forehead and cheek blades greatly exaggerated. "I should have known that relaxed fish would have some companions someday." He turned the page: Paul and Günther were drawn in a curiously Siamese-twin form, their slightly overlapping faces attached by a common ear. Both mouths were touched with humor, the expressions just short of smiles, a drop of glistening liquid hanging on the edge of each lower lip. One boy leaned rakishly on a microscope, the other similarly on a telescope. On the following page stood a goateed Boris, white-smocked, his arms folded across his chest and a padlock attached to a metal band firmly sealing his upper cranium. The figure hung suspended from several strings held by a puppeteer, clearly and cruelly Freud. Enerde laughed and turned the page, staring a long moment at a running Melchior whose terrified glance over his own shoulder looked into ill-defined quaking shadows following him. Enerde made no comment. On the next page, Alexander, half-human, half-armored-tank, rolled in circles on an abandoned battlefield. "He may grow out of that," said the old man.

There were five pages of Agnes Schneider. On the first, she rode a broomstick, her witch face studded with warts, the toes of her high-top shoes curled into half-circles. On the two subsequent pages she appeared more human, but not less ugly as she peeked into a keyhole in one, and in the other, leaned her ear (much magnified) against a closed door. In the last two drawings, her warted nose, lengthened by many meters, crawled into various cabinets and drawers while the rest of the figure remained stationary, holding to its breast a massive ornately lettered Dante volume as the eyes rolled heavenward.

"You must not be unkind to Miss Schneider. She has not had a very happy life. Certainly not an easy one. You may find her difficult at times, but I'm sure she has your best interests at heart." He patted her arm and chuckled. "And I advise you to keep these drawings where no one can find them. Perhaps I can keep them for you." Ursula knew he kept a large leather folder filled with her drawings. She nodded.

He carefully removed the pages and leafed through a few blank sheets. "They'll be safe with me." He handed her the tablet. "It's a fine gift, Ursula, and deserves serious training. Soon. In the meantime do not neglect anything else."

"I won't, Grandfather."

Ursula returned to the storage room and picked Virgil off the floor. She stayed with the epic for nearly an hour, yawning through the absurd battle scene until half-asleep she wrote "Aeneas is a dope" in her harshly vertical handwriting into her workbook. She shaded in the loops and wrote "Virgil is a dope" neatly below the first sentence. After a few moments, she added "Werther is a dope." And then "Oliver Twist is a dope." "Tom Sawyer is a dope." She paused, feeling a little giddy over the ease with which dopes appeared on the landscape of literature. "Achilles is a dope"; "Agamemnon is a dope"; "Jason is a dope"; "Creon is a dope." She paused again, giggled, and roared on, "Raskolnikov is a dope"; "Candide is a dope; Julien Sorel is a dope; Rousseau is a dope; Freud is a dope; Boris is a dope; Miss Schneider is a dope." The governess's name brought Ursula back to the woman's nasty smile of two hours before, and the elation vanished. She pushed aside the Latin work and picked up her volume of English and American verse given to her by her grandfather for her thirteenth birthday. Lovingly she turned through the pages, pausing at lines she had once underlined: *This is the forest primeval, the murmuring pines and the hemlock* . . . Why was the language so much more beautiful than German? It was stronger than French and a hundred times more elegant than Russian. *The forest primeval, murmuring.* She loved the lush taste of it as it slid off her tongue like warm honey . . . *primeval* . . . *druids of old with voices sad and prophetic* . . . The words rolled and swirled inside her mouth, and long after she finished speaking them aloud, their sound persisted inside her head like a deliciously lingering taste, leaving her sated with wonder. She was clearly in love with the English language and knew it.

Ursula remained separated from her brothers for a week, during which time she stocked the storage room with her favorite books from the library, hiding them from Miss Schneider in one of the deep cabinets built into the wall. She completed her assigned work quickly and spent the rest of the time reading. She discovered after the first day that she liked being alone, that there was a pleasantness to solitude. The very silence, without the shifting about of her brothers and their occasional bantering or the heavy-footed lurching of the governess and her nagging about what was good for them, gave her a sense of calm. She worried less about her grandfather's health and even got on better with Miss Schneider, although she did not forget for a minute the woman's threat.

When the twins questioned her about the change, she told them that she was doing some extra reading and needed a temporary break from Schnabel hanging over her. She know from Günther's expression that he suspected there was more to the story, but she evaded his questions and decided to bide her time. Alexander was miffed for a few days over her apparent desire to study alone. "We agreed to stay together, remember? I don't like it when you're not there. That old witch picks on me when you're not around."

"Do your work and she'll leave you alone."

"It's not the same."

"Don't worry. I'll be back."

One afternoon as Ursula returned a book to its hiding place, she began absently to rummage through the cabinets and drawers in the room, not actually searching for anything in particular. Two closets were full of nose-tickling, moth–crystal–scented bedding; the third held a stack of boxes filled with business files. Behind these she came upon a trunk secured with an old–fashioned single–bolt lock. She picked it easily with a nail she wiggled loose from the closet door. The smell of mold, as pungent as a living tomato plant, escaped from the chest. Under a layer of old newspapers she found two large books both with identical red leather covers without any printing on them except her grandfather's ornate initials engraved on one corner. The first one she picked up fell open at its center to a double–page painting of five partially naked people connected to each other in various unusual ways. The three women and two men were Oriental, their sex organs so huge they dominated the picture, while the voluminous clothing they wore seemed to swirl about the individuals, clinging to a shoulder here, a leg there, in textures and designs that gave a sense of violent motion to the whole scene, whereas the people's faces with their closed eyes and tiny half–smiling mouths curiously contradicted their joyously curled toes. The scenes on the following two pages were similar, with the women holding the male organs in their hands or to their mouths and the men's tongues or fingers half–submerged in the women's vulvas. A page of narrative with the heading "The Twentieth Century" followed. Ursula discovered that she held Volume II. She closed it and opened the other book at the beginning, finding the title *Erotic Art Through the Ages* above a Greek urn around which several figures were connected without interruption.

For two hours she examined the pictures of five thousand years of love making, from the stilted, ancient Egyptian one–dimensional figures engaged in suggestive coupling, to twentieth–century surrealism in which the bodiless vulvas and penises came together in a clash of colors and paint so thick it looked as if it had been licked onto the canvas with the human tongue.

Ursula carefully returned the books to the chest but did not lock it. She replaced the files, closed the closet door, leaning some cartons back against it, and left the room.

In the summerhouse she sat for a long time beside Rätzel's grave. That people made love for other reasons than procreation was no secret to her, and that it did not always result in a baby, she knew too. Books spoke of desire, passion, lust, and these feelings apparently had nothing to do with procreation, since the same writers used such expressions as "they hoped for" and "longed for" or "prayed for a child." And if men did it with men, and women with women, where no babies were possible, what was passion? What was lust? How did desire come about?

She knew her brothers masturbated, knew exactly what they did, Günther once explaining to her that the act was natural and all men did it, and that it had nothing to do with desire. In fact, her brothers joked about it and had special code words and expressions for it that were marvelously misunderstood by Miss Schneider. The twins' favorite was "feeding the snake"; Günther had shown Ursula semen under his microscope. She thought the wiggly things rather looked like snakes, but Günther told her they resembled tadpoles much more. Boris said that a little daydreaming never hurt anyone (the governess agreed with this, "on the condition that something constructive comes of it"); Alexander, who sometimes lacked imagination, simply said his palm itched; Melchior prayed for forgiveness and strength.

[137]

Günther hadn't said that women did it, yet Grandfather's red books had women doing all kinds of things to themselves as well as to each other. But what made them want to? The question rose up again, there in the cold, decaying summerhouse, above the grave of her old friend: What is desire?

13

Ursula, who had been successfully taught by Günther that everything worth knowing could be learned from books, attacked the library with fresh zeal in her search for the what and why of desire. On the night of her discovery of the erotic art books, she went first to the dictionary, which defined the term desire with synonyms: want, wish, longing, craving—which did not tell her anything new, not that she really expected *that* book to divulge the mystery, but still sometimes it gave clues. Standing in the center of the library long after everyone had gone to bed, she considered where to begin. Her grandfather's fancy red books, hidden in the storage room, began with classical times. Why not? She located the ledger the old man had once hired a dozen scholars to prepare for him, which listed the great themes and ideas of the world and what the most famous thinkers and writers had said on the subject.

Desire was mired in subsections and cross-references, giving the works of the authors and the pages on which the subject was discussed. *Desire as Natural Appetite*—see Plato, Aristotle, Plotinus, Augustine, Aquinas, Dante, Hobbes, Spinoza, Pascal, Descartes, Kant, Hegel, Goethe, Darwin, Freud. Each author's name had the work involved written below it with a location reference. *Desire as Conscious and Judgmental*. The same group followed. *Desire as Subject to Control*. Again the same writers were listed, with another dozen added to them, and several books of the Bible. Below this a further note suggested a review of related subjects: See also: *Being. Matter. Change. Sense. Will. God. Love.*

Ursula turned to Love first and discovered that Love had many more references than did Desire. In fact, it seemed that everybody wrote about Love. Again the subject was broken down, but the very first category sounded promising: *The Nature of Love*. The first reference was Plato's *Symposium*. After an hour of reading the Dialogue, she realized it was putting her to sleep. She turned to the second reference, Aristotle's *Ethics,* only to realize that he was as vague about the nature of Love as Plato and took as long to get to it. Augustine and Aquinas were involved with Love that she knew at once had nothing to do with her grandfather's red books. Virgil and Dante's discussion in Purgatory told her for the fifth time that there were *at least* two kinds of love. Hobbes concluded that Love "is motion toward an object" and "is, therefore, good." Hate was the obverse of this. Spinoza held that love overcame hatred and thus increased joy. Locke said the mind was born blank, a *tabula rasa* upon which the world described itself through the experience of the senses, which, when reflected upon by his thinking apparatus, gave him his ideas about everything. Kant had her yawning within minutes, so she let him slide and went on to Hegel, whom she couldn't find. Darwin and James were also missing and she knew all of Freud's works were in the playroom. The clock in the foyer chimed three as she left the library. At first she decided to take a quick look at Freud before she went to sleep, since the red books had quoted him (as a spokesman?) for the twentieth century. But sleep was too strong and she went instead to her bed. The following night when everyone had retired she again left her room in search of information on this elusive subject which everyone found so difficult to define. She decided to begin with Freud in the playroom.

The old house with its long dark halls and high ceilings seemed to sigh as she mounted the stairs. Walking along the narrow fourth-floor landing, she heard the house moan like a living thing. She stopped and looked down: below her the balustrade of the employee floor jutted out like a bridge of a ship, the single frail wall light turning the urn-shaped newel posts into gnomes hunching in a shadowy row. Again the moan, mingled with a kind of laughter that was not really laughter at all but some softened echo of it, rippled along the walls and touched Ursula's skin. She shivered at the sound and knew it was not the house. The door to the playroom was partially open. She slipped inside and stood still, leaning against the wall. To her right, Adolphus sat in the alcove. At the far end of the room, beyond the familiar tables and chairs, the hand-carved chests full of abandoned playthings, and the huge platform that held the electric train with its miniature tree-lined villages and rolling baize hills crisscrossed with trellises and crowned with churches, a single candle cast its light on two figures lying on a gymnast's mat on the raised portion of the floor meant to be a small stage. Ursula moved closer, half the length of the enormous room, until her hand touched the edge of the train table. She stopped. Twenty feet beyond her, the candle rested in a holder on a chair near the mat on which Paul and Günther lay naked, their bodies entwined, their hands moving over each other's skin in sweeping caresses, profoundly tender. Slowly Günther lay back on the mat, still, except for his pulsating chest and the faintly stirring penis, fully expanded and resting on his belly. Paul rose on his elbow, leaned over his brother's face, and kissed his eyes. Günther's head arched back to meet Paul's mouth: the kiss was silent, long-sustained, until Paul lifted away from it, his tongue moving over Günther's chin, throat, and on to the nipple. He bent over the quivering body, licking and kissing as he moved to the navel, his hand reaching between and beneath the spread legs, his mouth taking the quivering penis fully, deeply, as Günther, dove-moaning, clawed at the mat with curled fingers, his hips arching above his brother's hidden hand.

Ursula, unable to stop watching, was to think of that scene years later as the orgy of the eye (having read somewhere of the "lust of the eye"). *Her* eye, of course, and most certainly *her* orgy, since it was not until both boys had tasted each other in turn and lay in sated sleep beneath an ancient eiderdown, presumably in each other's arms, that she crept away to her own room to ponder at least one of the ways of loving. Of course, she already knew the *ways:* the red books covered all that well enough. Her loving brothers only deepened the why of things. They were wondrously sure of what they were doing; no hesitant fumbling or shy exploration that she had read about in books whenever a man and woman made love together cast the aura of new lovers over them. They had obviously been doing it for years. Thinking all this over, Ursula realized that she felt no surprise, but everything was suddenly changed, the way the onset of her menses two years before had changed everything: abruptly—so it seemed to her— the world was less clear. And now here was this new side to her brothers' lives, this secret side, this thing that was strange and different and thrived wildly and feverishly in the dark of night. But hadn't she *always* (this sense of infinity—going backward—only now considered for the first time, was later to become a fact in her life) known that her two oldest brothers lived somehow inside of each other's lives? Not only were they by far the closest of any of her siblings, but they seemed at times to anticipate each other's actions without talking; and when they were younger they had had a lan- guage all their own, a communication that had the quality of a code running through it made up of random parts of sentences sounding unrelated and usually undecipherable to others. Ursula had soon gotten used to it, as they all had, and until now she gave it no more thought than she did their habit of frequently reading the same book at the same time, lying on the library floor in winter or under one of the shade trees in summer, Günther turning the pages.

She got up and walked about the room, seeing again their amber bodies undulating in the candle's greedy glow, their black body hair in their armpits and groins as mysterious as dark islands on a swelling sea. She sensed a beauty in their embrace that she had not felt toward any of the pictures in the erotic art books. Nothing had been as exquisite as her brothers' long drinking kiss.

On that long night Ursula did not sleep at all. When the first lavender light touched her windowpanes, she felt uneasy, cranky, and exhausted. In a few hours Schnabel would be badgering her over some error in the Virgil translations, when it was all unimportant anyway. All the books she read contradicted themselves or each other. It was curious to her that she had until now accepted these confusions with perfect equanimity, deciding sim- ply that people had different opinions about things at different times. But the memory of her brothers' caresses left nothing simple anymore. Love was some sort of paradox. She had read novels in which men and women felt the first stirrings of love, hungered for each other, and then made love in couched euphemisms: *he possessed her; she relinquished herself; they surren- dered to their demanding desires.* In the Bible, Adam *knew* Eve and they were driven out of Paradise. Dryden said that love was a malady without a cure; Chaucer said it was blind; Shakespeare called it a devil, a madness, a slave, a disease.

[140]

Yet the Bible also said that Love was the fulfilling of the Law, that it was stronger than death, that it was God. And Shakespeare's other face said that it was heavenly, miraculous, brave, eternal. Even Virgil had his say: *Omnia vincit amor.* And supposedly everyone loved a lover, believed that love bettered what was best, and agreed that it knew no limits. People killed because of it and were willing to die for it.

Pale light gave her room a slate patina. And now here was this new thing about love to add to the confusion in the books she had read. Here was this love she had never read about in novels. This fact that fit nowhere. She felt angry at herself, an anger infused with regret for having spied on her brothers. "I'm worse than Schnabel," she muttered. She knew she was facing one of her gray days. No sleep always made her mean, and now this bad feeling of her betrayal of two people she loved would hurt inside of her all day. And there was no one to talk to, no one to tell her that her behavior was not as serious as she made it out to be; and even if there were someone who would say that, it would not be true.

Since their grandfather's heart attack, the Bronevsky children were sullen and untalkative in the mornings: breakfast had become an affair of silence. Although the doctors pronounced him "cured," Enerde looked like a ghost. The children were acutely aware of his quivering hands and the bone color of his skin stretched tightly over his cheeks and temples where a blue vein beat like the jabbing light of a train signal. His beard was thin. His forced joviality saddened and depressed them. When he made small jokes and laughed thinly, Ursula wanted to cry. But on the morning after her sleepless night, Ursula, watching her two oldest brothers surreptitiously (not that they were behaving any differently than usual), felt a dangerous exhilaration that defied her exhaustion. Frequently in the last year or two, she noticed that she sometimes acted from some deeper level of consciousness, that there came from somewhere within her sudden solutions to problems that eluded her when she thought them over consciously. And the problem that needed solving was Miss Schneider's threat. For a week now she had not considered any course of action, but as she watched her two brothers with lowered eyes, one of those proddings from that hidden place inside her urged her to act. She decided abruptly that she was not going to be separated from her brothers again.

She waited until Miss Schneider came to stand in the doorway as she had every morning for as long as Ursula could remember; then she spoke. "Grandfather, Miss Schneider arranged for me to work by myself for a week until I caught up. And she was right. I finished everything, so if you need me, I'll be back upstairs with everyone else, starting today." She stood up and gave Miss Schneider a warm smile. Ursula realized later that whatever was in that smile was unusual enough to get her brothers' total attention: they all stared at her in bemused astonishment. Alexander laughed.

"Eh . . . well, that was wise," said the old man. He patted her hand. "Yes, yes, study hard. That's important."

"But if you need me, Grandfather, you'll call for me, won't you?"

"Yes, yes. I'll call."

The boys stood up also and after bowing faintly to the old man and waiting for Ursula to kiss him, they all left the room. Miss Schneider walked

[141]

ahead of them up the stairs, her shoulders working like a spastic's. In the classroom she turned on Ursula. "*I* make those decisions, not you."

Ursula took her usual place at the table and without taking her eyes from the governess's livid face spoke to her brothers. "Last week, Miss Schneider said that if I did not study alone in the storage room, she would make sure Grandfather had another heart attack."

Melchior gasped, "No!"

Boris and Alexander, already seated, looked from Ursula to the governess, their mouths open and speechless.

Miss Schneider started for the door but found her way barred by Günther, who pulled it closed behind him and remained standing in front of it, his hand still holding the knob.

"Let me pass at once!" said the governess.

Günther leaned against the closed door. "How did she intend to make Grandfather have another attack?" His voice was soft, mild, terrifying.

"She said she would create a scene and get him upset and excited."

Paul, standing behind his chair, addressed Ursula. "Why didn't you tell us this last week?"

"I was afraid she would do it."

"I'm surprised at you, Ursula; you know better than to give in to extortion. Couldn't you see that she could use that threat to make you do anything she wanted, as long as Grandfather lives?"

Ursula nodded.

Miss Schneider, who was shaking with terror, tried feebly to push Günther aside. He didn't budge. "I shall scream," she said, the intended authority in her voice hopelessly lost in the shrill last word.

"Do you feel like screaming?" Günther's smile shocked Ursula. He looked exactly like their father used to look, years ago when he was young. "If you wish to scream, you must do so," he said quietly. "This is a good room for it, wonderfully situated at the end of the wing, insulated on three sides by an extra thickness of brick, the windows heavily draped, the door made of oak, and the room raised no less than a meter above the other rooms on this floor. If anyone wanted to scream, this is certainly the best room for it. You know, of course, that our illustrious great-great-great-grandfather had it especially *built* as a classroom . . . about the time of the American Revolution, as you have so often reminded us." He smiled again, the same cold expression in his eyes denying the benevolence of his lips.

Miss Schneider was whimpering. Ursula knew that the woman was afraid of the boys, had been afraid of them for years, but she also knew that none of them would ever physically harm the governess. But Miss Schneider did not know this. She gathered up what courage she had and tried a new defense. "You're a wicked girl to make up such stories!"

Paul, his hands resting on the back of his chair, did not look at Miss Schneider as he spoke. "Ursula has not yet learned how to lie, but if she stays around you long enough, she will probably learn how to do it badly. It's an art all by itself, and you don't even know that."

Miss Schneider fled to her desk in a far corner of the room and cowered behind it. Ursula knew it was the wrong move. All the governess had to do was admit that she had made the threat and that there was nothing they could do about it. Furthermore, she could tell all of them that she did not care whether they liked it or not, since they could not possibly take such a story to their grandfather. But a show of fear was fatal; it only made her brothers more contemptuous of her. Paul spoke again without turning toward her desk. "We have known for a long time that as a teacher you are no longer of any use to us, and have not been for many years. If it weren't for the library and the other tutors, none of us would know much of anything. Except for English and some French and Latin, we owe you very little." He smiled at Ursula. "And we thank you for those, Miss Schneider. But as we see it, we'd be better off arranging our own lessons. Ursula is perfect proof of it. She's worked alone for the last seven weeks without your help. She doesn't need you to tell her to read a book. And that's the heart of it all—to read everything. Every teacher that ever entered this house, except for you, harped on that. You, as I recall, would have preferred to burn most of those books. In fact, you did burn Ursula's English copy of *Gulliver's Travels,* a gift from another teacher, I believe. And Darwin is missing from the library, as are some of the French poets. Stop me if I'm wrong."

By this time Miss Schneider had recovered her senses and was seated bolt upright in her chair. "Am I being discharged? Do you intend that I be thrown out into the street? You have no right to make such decisions."

" 'No' to the questions. But we are making a decision. From now on you can do whatever amuses you, and as long as any member of the family lives in this house, you have a home. But you will stay away from our grandfather and you will not enter this room again."

"How dare you!" Miss Schneider rose, stretching tall, the knuckles of her fists balanced on the desk.

Paul turned then and Ursula could not see his face. "I dare—we all dare—because your threat is tantamount to a threat of murder."

The governess snorted. "He's old. He's going to die anyway—and soon."

A heavy stillness fell upon the room. It was as though they were holding a memorial silence for someone already dead. Ursula saw that Melchior and Alexander had tears in their eyes. Boris, chewing his bottom lip, was looking down at the closed book in his hand. Günther and Paul were turned away from her. It was Günther who finally spoke. "We know that, Miss Schneider. We all know that very well."

"What makes you think that I will take orders from any of you? I can report this disobedience to your grandfather . . . or even . . . your father."

"He will be drunk," said Paul. "And even if you should find him sober, he won't care. And if he should, he won't know what to do about it. As for going to Grandfather, please know in advance that today we intend to contact his lawyers and tell them of your intention to injure Grandfather. That is not a threat, Miss Schneider; that is information that you should have so that you can act accordingly."

The governess sat down slowly. "I'll be dismissed. I have no place to go. I've given my whole life to you." She began to weep. " 'How sharper than a serpent's tooth . . .' "

"We are not ungrateful to you, Miss Schneider, for what you *have* done for us," said Paul. "But we are years too old for you. For reasons unclear to us, our grandfather does not wish us to study outside this house, at least—as he recently put it—not yet. In his own good time, he will send us to proper schools. As for us, we are all perfectly content to stay here with him. He is the only real parent we have, and for the years of love and time he has given us, we are willing to pay him back in kind."

"I shall be sent away," she wailed.

"No," said Günther. "That, too, would upset Grandfather. On the surface, things will remain the same."

Agnes Schneider placed her hands over her eyes. "None of you ever liked me."

Ursula, embarrassed at the woman's weeping, knew that not even pity could yield to the truth of Miss Schneider's judgment on them. There was nothing that could be said. None of them ever liked her. It was one of those nasty little truths that people usually tried to laugh away or hide under glib protestations, both false and foolish. But none of the children spoke. And after a moment more of snuffling, Miss Schneider pulled herself out of her chair as though she were vaguely crippled and limped toward the door. Günther opened it for her.

"Are you really going to tell the lawyer?" Ursula asked Paul after he closed the door.

"Yes. But perhaps not today."

"You thought everything out so quickly."

"No, not quickly. We've been trying to think of a way to get rid of her for years. You brought the answer in with you."

"We could have been kinder," said Melchior.

"No. That wasn't possible. Kindness at such a time only makes things unclear. Things are now clear."

The children spent the day rearranging the room. Günther brought his microscope down to the classroom. Boris cleared a section of shelf for Freud. Alexander brought up all of their grandfather's American Civil War books from the library. Paul hung his star charts on the wall. Melchior was content with the way things were, since his Latin books already lined the top of Miss Schneider's vacated desk. Ursula brought two of her drawing tablets and the easel the gardener had made for her into the room. After that she returned once more to the storage room and took out the two red books. She locked the chest and returned everything to its former setting. In the classroom she placed the books in the middle of the round oak table without saying anything. Günther moved toward them first, reaching out from behind his microscope to open one to read the title page. He turned several pages. "Paul," he said softly. Three minutes later, as she tilted back in her chair, Ursula watched her five brothers hovering over the books, none of them speaking, Günther slowly turning the pages.

It was Paul who finally spoke after the last page was turned and Boris and Günther and Alexander reopened the first volume. "You surprising girl." He laughed. "Come on, how long have you had them?"

"Only two days. They were locked in a chest under some blankets in the storage room."

Melchior, surprising the others by having looked at every page, now sat back in his chair, a sour expression on his face. "I don't want to think about them," he said.

"Then don't. No one's forcing you to," replied Günther.

Boris, who was studying the last part of Volume II, turned away from the book. "Melchior, I think you should know that the largest collection of erotic art in the world is owned by the Vatican. I believe the King of England has the second-largest collection, and the American Library of Congress the third. After that, various imperial families of Europe follow. Czar Alexander also had an immense collection. One can only speculate on its disposition. It is my understanding that Farouk of Egypt has the oldest. And, naturally, there are many famous private collections that—"

"The Vatican! I don't believe it."

"You can investigate it for yourself. Of course, if you won't believe the encyclopedia, there's no point in bothering, is there?"

Ursula rolled her eyes. Boris, the eternal expert!

Günther held one of the volumes up. "Boris, is this what Freud means by every sexual act involving four individuals?"

Ursula heard the mock innocence in Günther's voice at once. The page her brother held up showed four people attached to form a sort of circle.

"No, not at all. Freud's statement about four individuals involves the concept of fantasizing. The illustration you have there would consequently involve eight individuals."

"And if those eight were also here with these four . . . ?"

"Well then, ah, let me think, that means there would theoretically be twenty-four individuals involved."

"Don't you mean twenty-eight?"

"Twenty-eight?"

"Well, if each act between two people involved four individuals, then each act between four involves eight, and between eight, sixteen more. . . . Well, add those together: four and eight and sixteen is twenty-eight. Isn't it?" Günther's eyebrows disappeared under the swath of black hair on his forehead. "Isn't it?"

Boris frowned and began to put down numbers on a pad. "Yes, that's twenty-eight, but I believe there must be some error in your computation." He added and divided and multiplied furiously.

Ursula choked back her laughter as Paul and Günther gave her dark comical looks.

Boris mumbled that he'd have to go someplace quieter to think the problem out. "I'm sure you're in error, though it eludes me at the moment, but I'll locate it."

Günther nodded sympathetically. "Yes, do that." He turned to Melchior, who was reading Milton with painful intensity. "The reason the Vatican has its collection is that the bishops or cardinals, or whoever decides policy, have to know what they don't want people to see . . . or read. How could they list those things if they didn't know about them? Don't be upset by the Vatican's collection. Think of how human it makes those people. Wouldn't you rather know that *they knew* what people did with each other?" But Melchior was not consoled. He left the room without answering.

Günther shook his head. "He's going to be a sad priest if he lets the Church's dark side disappoint him."

"He'll be all right," said Paul, "once he learns to rationalize censorship. What a gratifying business that must be. Not only does the censor get to

[145]

deprive people of something beautiful or witty or possibly even salacious, but he also gets to enjoy himself with impunity."

Alexander suddenly ran out of the room.

"What's the matter with him?" asked Ursula.

Günther grinned. "He's gone to feed the snake. That's what those pictures make people want to do." He rose, dropping the book back on the table.

"Do they make you want to do it too?"

"Some of them."

She turned to Paul, who had also risen. He nodded. "Some of them."

Ursula saw that her brothers' eyes glittered with excitement. Their whole bodies seemed charged with a restless power, a nervous energy that twitched their fingers, quivered in the muscles in their necks and shoulders. She looked pointedly at their swollen groins, and both boys laughed. Before they left the room, Günther patted her cheek. "It's just possible that you may become a very interesting woman someday." Ursula wondered how she could become that just because she was interested in their excitement.

After they were gone, she watched Boris at the far side of the room still scribbling on the pad. Finally he looked up. "Your error, Günther, lies in . . . Where is everyone?"

"I'm here."

"Obviously. Where did Günther and Paul go?"

"I don't know."

Boris returned to the red books on the table and began leafing through the second volume. "I wish there were more text to some of these pictures."

"Don't they speak for themselves?"

"Well, yes, on the surface of things, but there are always hidden meanings."

"Boris . . . many of those pictures show men making love with men and women with women . . ."

"Of course. You knew about homosexuality before you saw these."

"But not much. In fact, I don't know anything about it. Why does it happen? Why do people do it?"

"Well, Freud says that homosexuality comes from the deepest realm of the psyche, a region most people are totally unaware of, where the most secret longings and desires originate."

"But why? Why those longings rather than the other kind?"

"Freud says that everyone, at some moment in his life, makes the choice of homosexuality or heterosexuality—unconsciously, of course."

"That doesn't answer anything. Why one over the other?"

"Well, ah, he says that homosexuality comes from an unconscious tendency to be a homosexual."

"That doesn't *say* anything."

"Of course it does. There are factors and conditions, forces, internal and external stimuli that create the tendency."

"Like what?"

"They're all very complicated and enigmatic."

"Give me one example. Give me one factor or force."

"You can't isolate them. They're all interactive."

"All right. Give me a bunch of them."

"They don't come in bunches," he snorted. "What a dumb way to put it. Don't try to simplify everything. I told you, Freud says they're enigmatic."

"You mean he doesn't know?"

"I didn't say that."

"But that's what you mean."

"No. You just don't understand."

"If I understood, I wouldn't ask. I want to know."

"Why do you want to know about this all of a sudden?"

Ursula glanced toward the books but remained silent, feeling her brother's eyes avidly staring at her. "Why, Ursula?"

She picked up a pencil and began drawing on the tablet under her elbows. "I want to understand it." She drew the wings of a seabird soaring bodiless over an invisible ocean.

"Is there a particular reason you want to know?"

"I just want to know." She looked up from the blades of feathers. In Boris' face she saw an expression both angry and apprehensive, and she knew at once that he knew that Günther and Paul were lovers. And now he was afraid that *she* knew. For a moment she believed she could read his thinking: he didn't trust her; he believed she would say something someday and then everybody would know. At the same time, he obviously wasn't sure that she knew, which kept him from telling her that she must never say anything. She had to decide on what to tell him.

"I want to know why you're so curious about this." He hesitated as though making some decision himself. "It's important, Ursula."

She shaded in the wingtips and added a slender body to the bird. "I've been reading Plato, and he says that this kind of love, if it is true and lasting, is superior to that which men and women have for each other, although that kind is divine, too, but in a different way."

Boris leaned back in his chair. "Are you sure he's talking about the physical part of it—between men, I mean?"

"He's a little vague about that, but he doesn't condemn it, at least not as far as I've read."

"Then you know that ordinarily people do condemn it."

"Yes. Alexander makes nasty jokes about it and I know that Melchior thinks it's a sin against God."

"What do you think?"

The question surprised her: Boris rarely cared what she thought. "I know so little about it. In the novels I've read, it's always men and women loving each other. Yet, in other books—not novels—the writers talk about all kinds of love, and they all agree that love is the best of all things in the universe, even when they don't say what kind they mean. It seems to me that the different kinds of love are not what matters. They all say that love makes people better, and if that's true, then any kind of love is all right. How could it be a sin against God? Why should anybody condemn it?"

Ursula wanted to answer Boris' question without telling him what she knew, and so talked on rapidly, all the while watching for any shifting expression in his face. "Anyway, all those writers must be right; hating someone always makes me feel bad. Even when I hate Schnabel, I usually

[147]

end up feeling mean toward myself. Do you remember what Rätzel used to say?" Boris shook his head. "Love is the cup that is never empty."

Boris suddenly leaned across the table and clapped his hand over hers. "You know, don't you?"

She looked down at his hand and as the seconds passed, realized that any protestation of surprised ignorance as to what he was referring was fast disappearing. Yet neither did she want to admit the truth. "Ursula, don't say anything if you don't want to, but know that in Austria sex between two men is punishable by many years of prison. It's against the law in most countries."

"That's stupid. What does the law have to do with it?"

Boris shrugged. "It's just the way things are." His eyes darkened. "So you see, we have to keep things to ourselves." He pulled his hand away. "I've known for certain for about a year, but I *feel* that I've always known."

Ursula knew the feeling well, but she said nothing. She returned to her drawing, adding more seabirds, hoping that the discussion had ended. For reasons unclear to her, she was sorry that Boris knew about Günther and Paul and wished he would change the subject. At least he was not being his usual pompous self, but she knew that that could change quickly. The birds rose and soared under her nervously moving hand.

Boris pushed back from the table and crossed his legs. "There are other theories, you know," he continued, his voice no longer low and urgent. "Now, Krafft-Ebing—of course he was not anywhere near the stature of Freud—established a clinical profile in his publication of 1886 that Hartwich, one of his disciples, elaborated on in this century, but which others . . . in particular Albert Moll and Carpenter, and, I believe, Ellis . . . yes, Ellis, I'm sure . . . refuted or at least modified."

Ursula listened to him a moment longer, and then with a deeply relaxed feeling that everything was back to normal, soared with her birds over a dead-calm sea.

Without Miss Schneider hovering over them and nagging them about staying too long with one subject, the children wasted less time, particularly since they spent no more energy in resenting the woman and dreaming up new ways of irritating her. Alexander alone did not know what to do with his time. Within days, the others realized he was going to be a problem. For a time he looked through Günther's microscope, but lost interest quickly when Günther tried to explain each slide to him. He gazed with bewilderment at Paul's star charts. "What are they good for?"

Paul, immersed in a new problem, looked up from his work. "Alexander, I can't answer that for you because my answer won't make any sense to you."

"Yes it will."

Paul, as patient as his twin, glanced at the row of charts. "All right. They tell what is happening in the past."

"Where?"

"Everywhere in the universe."

Alexander moved along the wall frowning at the sky maps dotted with his brother's fine printing. "They all look the same to me."

"Yes, they probably do. Why don't you go read something?"

"What shall I read?"

"Read whatever you want to, whatever interests you." Paul returned to the series of numbers in front of him, his black hair falling back over his forehead.

Alexander drifted away from the wall and sighed heavily. He looked over Boris' shoulder at the copious notes piling up beside an open book his brother was reading. "Why are you copying everything?"

"I am not copying *everything*. I'm paraphrasing, and don't look over my shoulder. It's annoying." Boris moved closer to the table and leaned further over his notes.

Melchior, who had taken over Miss Schneider's desk, offered Alexander one of the Latin texts. "No thanks. I'm never going to read that junk again." He wandered to Ursula's temporarily abandoned easel in front of the window and looked at the unfinished drawing of the section of the garden where Hermes reclined peacefully. "Why don't you finish it?" he asked Ursula, who was firmly wedged into the window seat, a book balanced against her knees, her bare feet flat against the opposing frame.

"Alexander, I can only draw for so long, then I have to do something else. Anyway, I'm reading a wonderful book by an American; it's funny and sad and terrifying and beautiful all at the same time. You'd love it."

"English is too hard," he grumbled.

"But it's worth it. Look, I'll read it to you. It takes place before the Civil War. It's about a boy who goes down this great river on a raft with a slave. They're trying to escape from slavery, but they're going the wrong way and they're in constant danger of getting caught, and all the while strange and wonderful things happen to them."

"No, I'll find something else to do."

"I'll translate it for you as I go along. If you don't understand any part, stop me and I'll explain it."

"No. It's too stuffy in here."

"We can go read in the dining room, or upstairs if you like."

"No, it's too boring."

"It's *not* boring. It's a wonderful story." Ursula, always quick to anger at any attack on her beloved language, softened when she saw Alexander's brooding eyes stare out of the window at the fog-bound trees.

"I don't mean your book. Everything is boring." He slumped into a chair.

"Why don't you read the Civil War books?"

"I don't feel like it right now. I think I'll go into the city."

"What for?"

He shrugged. "Does it have to be *for* something? We haven't done anything since Grandfather got sick. I want to get out."

Ursula saw that Paul and Günther had stopped working and were listening. "No," said Paul. "No more trips to the city for a while. We have to work. You too, Alexander, you have to decide what to do and then do it without anyone telling you to. That's the hardest part—making yourself get started."

"But I don't know what I want to do. All of you know what you want. I'm left out."

Ursula knew that this was not true; they were all well aware of Alexander's ambitions. Boris looked up from his notes. "Your aggressive tendencies, Alexander, clearly identifiable by your desire to enter the military arena, are a sign of the kind of emotional immaturity which—"

"Which might be cured if he could punch you in the mouth," said Günther, leveling an angry gaze at Boris, who returned to his notes with the lofty air of someone above insult.

"Even if you were old enough to join the army," began Paul, "and there was an army that would take you, you would still have to have an education to be an officer."

"They train you for that," mumbled Alexander.

"Only if you can pass certain examinations."

Alexander said he didn't know what to study and thought he ought to learn how to shoot a gun.

"Officers don't shoot," said Günther. "They order others to do that."

"I can't imagine Rommel not shooting a gun," said Alexander defiantly. He always spoke of Rommel as though the general were alive and well and heading somewhere in a command car.

"I can't imagine him even holding a gun, let alone shooting it," said Paul. "Maybe you should think about what you want to do in the army. From the way things are going, even people in the military are all going to be specialists."

"I want to fly airplanes."

All of them turned to look at Alexander, even Melchior, who usually stayed out of such discussions. "You don't have to join the army to fly airplanes. You could just become a pilot."

Melchior's "just" unfortunately diminished his fine idea and Ursula shook her head in exasperation at the loss. "Being a pilot sounds even better than joining the army," she said too quickly. "You wouldn't have to *kill* anybody."

There was a merciless silence. Ursula bit her lip as she looked from one brother to the next. Paul and Günther were fidgeting with their work. Boris pretended to read. Melchior stared at Alexander with horror while the younger boy fixed his eyes on his opening and closing fist resting on the arm of his chair.

"Th-that's not why I want to join the army," he stammered. "The army does . . . other things, too."

None of them asked him to list any additional pursuits that the army might be involved in. Ursula, hating herself for having brought about the curious crisis, knew that at any other time, with any other subject, the twins would have pressured Alexander to name the "other," to list, to give examples, to quote sources, to face facts. The truth was, they *were* facing a fact and all of them knew it: whatever appeal and allure war had, Alexander was deeply infected by it.

Paul finally spoke for all of them. "No one's blaming you for wanting to join the army. If that's what you want to do with your life, you have to do it. You wouldn't try to stop me from studying the stars even if you can't see any value in it, would you?" Alexander shook his head. "So there you are. We can figure out what books you should read and what you should work at so that you can belong to an army someday. I'm not sure where you're going to find one at the moment, but you're not ready anyway, so work to get ready. From the looks of things, the Americans and the Russians are going to be at each other's throats before long. There's trouble between them now over the future of Berlin, and if there is going to be more war, Germany will be America's ally and so will Austria. *Then* there will be an army for you to join."

"You shouldn't encourage him," said Melchior sadly.

"Why not? It's not a dishonorable profession. Doesn't he have as much right to be a soldier as you do a priest?"

The question remained unanswered. In the following days, Paul and Günther made up a list of books from the grandfather's library ledger for Alexander's course of study. They urged him to read the histories of flight from Icarus onward, although Alexander felt that Daedalus' warning to his son was a joke of some kind. "No," said Paul. "It's not a joke, but neither does it have anything to do with flight; however, read it anyway: it has a lot to do with you."

They presented him with mountains of mathematical problems pertaining to navigation and aerodynamics. Paul gave him glossaries on climates and clouds and charts on their classifications, with diagrams and pictures showing their birth and death.

Within a week Alexander was able to work two hours at a time without annoying the others and they all breathed private sighs of relief. One afternoon when Alexander was out of the room, Paul turned to Melchior. "Don't worry; he's not going to kill anybody. He has to study *something* and it might as well be aeronautics. The future of commercial flying is fantastic. Look at the Americans and British airlifting supplies into West Berlin; a city of two and a half million people, almost a million more than Vienna, is being kept alive only by what airplanes can bring to it. No, he's safe. He'll go into some commercial field of flight when he's old enough and sufficiently trained. No one's going to start a war as long as the Americans have those atom bombs to throw around."

Ursula felt better after hearing this, and except for some odd recurring dreams in which she found herself in a doorless, windowless room, she felt happy. Her grandfather seemed to get stronger as the days passed; she could read any book she wanted to, and lately her brothers were more willing to pose for her, with only Boris complaining that it was a nuisance to have someone watching him while he worked. But, in fact, she knew he was flattered, particularly when she sketched an unusually complimentary view of him looking as wise and aloof as a show dog. Paul studied the picture on her easel for some moments. "Who's that? Rudolph Valentino?"

Günther, standing beside his twin, said, "No. No. Don't tell me; let me guess. It's . . . it's Greta Garbo."

Boris snatched the picture from the easel. "I'll keep it for you, Ursula, before these cretins damage it. With one of them looking at the stars and the other at cells, what would *they* know of art?" He left the room with the drawing.

But Ursula's grand project was translating Twain's *Huckleberry Finn* into German, and she spent whole days doing nothing else. "It's already been done," said Boris, his tone tinged with warning.

"Not by me it hasn't," answered Ursula.

Between the nineteenth-century American slang and Huckleberry's rogu-ish grammar, the work gave her deep trouble, but it was the Negro dialect that made her beat her fists on her desk in exasperation and rage in her room late at night. Her English dictionary was of no help at all in dealing with *"Laws bless you, chile, I us right down sho you's dead agin."* She finally developed her own dialect dictionary, listing the repeated words in a formal order and through their reappearance in context divined, sensed, or reasoned out the meaning of the slaves' strange language.

When she needed a rest from Twain's meandering tale, she read English novels. She was fascinated by Swift's pure, clean prose, dry as parchment. The Bröntes' romantic melodramas, however, made her gloomy for days, and she thought Dickens' coincidences too handy, his sentimentality too silly, and his characters more like cartoon figures until with sudden rec-ognition she saw that the author must have invented Miss Schneider's pliered face.

For several weeks after the governess's banishment from the classroom, Ursula did not see her at all except occasionally at dinner, when their grandfather was present. At these times no one said much, and Ursula avoided looking at the woman. When she did finally pass the governess in the upper hall, there occurred one of those grotesque little dances in which two people trying to pass each other move from side to side in the same direction, giving the whole scene the aura of a tango. "For God's sake, let me by," Miss Schneider finally said in a voice so charged with misery that Ursula quickly turned aside and leaned against the wall as the woman rushed past her. Ursula was not used to feeling sorry for people, but upon hearing Miss Schneider's anguished words, she remained standing for some time in the hall leading to the servants' stairway, feeling all the past anger for the woman melt away and something quite alien take its place—a com-mingling of regret and sorrow, burgeoning inside her chest like some lush growth around her heart. She did not know it was compassion. There was as yet no center inside Ursula from which she could look out at the world with an interior perspective all her own. She still saw only through her eyes, viewing the world either up too close, where everything was too ugly, or too far away, where nothing was clear. No self had formed within her yet which enabled her to sense the near and note the far while focusing on the middle distance where there is a logic to the unexplainable, a human meaning to events, and where the heart can see things that blind the eye.

The next day, after a bad night in the exitless room, and without any plan in mind, Ursula visited the governess. Miss Schneider stared blinkingly at Ursula for a full five seconds before she spoke. "What do you want?"

Ursula was not sure. She shook her head, wishing she had an answer.

"Well, whatever it is you want, I have nothing left to give," said Miss Schneider without any heat at all.

"I don't really want anything. I—"

"Oh, yes you do. If you didn't want something you wouldn't be here. You're all the same. You use people until they are worn out and then you discard them. Because of you, I no longer have a position. You have ef-fectively destroyed my life."

"But you said you would hurt Grandfather!"

"Can you really imagine that I would do that?" Miss Schneider's small eyes overflowed with tears.

"But how could I *know* you didn't mean it?"

"Have I ever done anything to hurt that dear man?"

No, Ursula could not say she had, and in the presence of those tears, she was unable to tell the governess of the conversation she had overheard months before about one heart attack usually being followed by another. Anyway, that was hardly a threat to hurt her grandfather.

"Have I ever done *you* any harm?" Miss Schneider seemed to shrink as she wept openly, and she spoke in an unfamiliar tone. Ursula looked past her into the room, realizing that she had never seen the inside of it. It was a large square room, but cluttered with furniture.

"If you're so interested in my room, why don't you come in and look at it?" Miss Schneider's tears were drying on her face and the old iron had returned to her voice. Ursula started to back away, but the governess grasped her wrist with surprising force and pulled her into the room. "Yes, this is how I live, in squalor in the middle of a mansion. The bathroom, if you don't know, is down the hall, and I have to share it with those sloppy, vulgar maids who steal my soap and leave their filth on my towels. Look around, little princess, and see what life is like without money."

Ursula did. But since she had no particular interest in furniture, she could see nothing wrong with it. Perhaps the wallpaper was a bit faded, but beyond that it seemed comfortable with its large bed, heavy desk, bookshelf, deep-cushioned chairs and settee. "What's wrong with it?" she asked.

"No, you wouldn't know, would you? You're too insensitive. All of you. You don't see anything wrong, do you?"

Ursula shook her head as she stood facing two portraits in oval frames hanging on the wall near the bed. "My parents," said Miss Schneider, following Ursula's gaze. "Servants all their lives so that I could have a better life." She turned back to Ursula. "Do you think I have a better life?"

Ursula did not answer.

"Do you know why I am allowed to eat with the family at dinner?" The woman's eyes steamed with hatred. "So that you and your brothers can practice your English and French. Since you were born, everyone who ever came to this house, came here for your use. Your room is appointed with valuable antiques, exquisite linen, even an original painting by a true artist. You have a bath all to yourself. For centuries your family and families like yours have wallowed in luxury—served to you by the rest of the world. And you take everything for granted. Never give a thought to those who have nothing. For years I have lived here in the servants' wing. I did not mind so much that this furniture is graceless and vulgar, but to spend thirteen years living with the domestics—that is unforgivable. Especially since there are suites on the second floor that are unoccupied. And now you and your vicious brothers have cast me out, dismissed me like a common servant. Well, let me tell you something: you may never be poor, but I pray to God you will suffer. Now, get out!"

Ursula bolted from the room, the woman's words pounding in her head like blows. Until the scene in the garden involving her father and the governess, Ursula had seen Miss Schneider only as a teacher. She had never thought of the woman as having had parents or a childhood or possessions. She certainly never considered her social standing. In some curious way the teacher had dropped into the world fully grown, fully educated, without family or friends or the remotest echo of a past or a private life.

Walking in the garden, Ursula looked up at the governess's darkened window. Since early childhood it was always understood by the children that they were never to enter an employee's room. "Of course, Rätzel is different," said their grandfather, "he is family."

Why had she gone to Agnes Schneider's room? When the twins first banned the woman from the classroom, Ursula had felt exalted and victorious. She had single-handedly vanquished their enemy. But now, after hearing the governess talk about her own parents and her loathing of having to live in the servants' quarters, that golden victory turned gray and her exaltation withered like a dying flower.

On the last evening of that year, as the family sat down to a rather jovial dinner, all of them a little giddy with the champagne served at holiday times, Enerde turned to Ursula at his right and said, "My dear, I wonder if you . . ." He stopped talking, tilted his head sideways as though listening to something quite fascinating, and died.

14

When the doctor arrived, he glanced briefly at Enerde lying in his massive four-poster to which the children had carried him, and said, "He doesn't need a physician."

"We know," said Günther. "It's our sister we are worried about. She won't let go of his hand."

Frichter peered over his eyeglasses at Ursula seated on the bed looking down on her grandfather's face. Even as she watched, the flesh seemed to recede from his nose so that only a blade of bone rose above the flattening plane of his cheeks. His mouth fell open.

The doctor, now famous for his lack of sentimentality, was still a quick little man with a smooth childlike face which masked the soul of a misanthrope. Before any of the boys could stop him, he walked briskly to the bed and pulled the dead hand out of Ursula's grasp. For a moment Ursula groped for the hand like someone searching in blindness for an urgently needed object dropped in the dark. Then she whirled around and swung both fists into the doctor's midsection. He gave a little bark as he staggered backward and fell. Before Alexander and Boris pinned her to the carpet, she wiped the nightstand clean of the old man's medicines with a single sweep of her arm and kicked out two panes in the French door leading to the terrace. Alexander, who was covering her chest with his body, held her wrists to the floor and whispered furiously into her crying face, "Now stop. It won't help." He was crying himself. "Come on, it doesn't do any good to get mad."

Ursula writhed wildly under his grip. "Let me up."

The doctor, helped to his feet by the twins, looked down at the thrashing girl with a certain detached interest, as though he were observing a laboratory experiment. "I could give her a sedative."

"You can go to hell, too," said Ursula so calmly that both boys relaxed their grip and she shoved them violently away. She returned to the bed and stood looking down at the old man's flat body. She swore quietly, her voice soft and dead with sorrow.

The doctor picked up his satchel. "Maybe you should tell her she's a girl."

"She knows," said Günther, "but it hasn't made any difference. Anyway, *she's* comfortable with her language." The boys stood away from the bed as if embarrassed by the corpse lying on it, or embarrassed by death itself, its unseemly inexplicability.

Frichter waited a moment longer, still watching her with the same appraising detachment. "With that chest on her she ought to be *feeling* the difference by now."

Ursula looked up quickly. They were all staring at her, except Alexander, who lowered his head in angry-bull fashion, abruptly brushed past the doctor, and strode out of the room. His departure broke up the musing contemplative attention toward her, and the discussion went on to arrangements for the funeral.

When the bells of midnight summoning the new year boomed over the snow-shrouded city, Ursula was again seated beside the old man's bed, Günther and Paul trying to convince her that people no longer sat up all night with the corpse. The bombinating bells briefly silenced them.

"Appropriate somehow," said Paul when the echoes died away.

"No. He should not have died," said Ursula.

"I meant the bells. As though they were sounding for him."

"I know what you meant. I hate those damn bells. I shall hate New Year's Eve forever."

"That's a long time," said Günther.

Boris entered the room and stopped at the foot of the bed. "The trouble with you, Ursula, is you've never learned to accept change." Boris' voice was charged with exasperation. "Death is a part of it. It's a reliable fact."

"No. I hate it. I shall always hate it. I shall never accept it. It's a reliable fact that I shall never, never accept it."

They fell into silence when a timid tapping at the door was followed by Miss Schneider edging into the room. She stood blinking at them, her mouth quivering. "I'm so sorry," she said. "Is there anything I can do?" She did not look at the bed.

"No. Thank you. Nothing," said Paul.

When the woman was gone, Günther pressed Ursula's hand. "Fine control."

"Don't worry, I won't say anything to that old hypocrite. I know she's not sorry. She's been waiting for this." She looked at the sunken face on the pillow. "What do you think he was going to say to me?"

Günther glanced apprehensively at his twin, then changed his expression as he turned to Ursula. "Don't think about that."

"But maybe he felt the heart attack coming, and he was going to say something important to me."

Günther shrugged. "I doubt it. He probably wanted you to pass the salt."

"He didn't eat salt. He never put salt on anything. You know that."

"All right, the sugar, the sauce, the . . . the bread."

"No, he never did that either. He never had to ask for anything. Things were always served to him first. We always saw to that."

"Ursula, you mustn't make something of his last words."

"But he had something definite in mind. I know he did. If only I knew the next word, the verb. He said, '. . . I wonder if you . . .' See? If I knew the next word, I'd have a hint at least."

"Be realistic, Ursula," said Paul kindly. "You know he was always telling you something about the garden, like the lilacs were blooming, or the chestnuts were opening, or how pretty you are. Maybe he was going to tell how the champagne made you look even prettier. It was probably something quite ordinary. You had a lot of private jokes together about your drawing. Remember all those things. Remember him that way, not this way. It's only in our memories that the dead continue to live."

Ursula let it go. Her brothers were only trying to make her feel better. She tried to remember what her grandfather had been talking about before that last unfinished sentence. They had all been laughing at some joke. No, they had just sat down. All that laughing came before, when they were still standing, toasting each other. What were the toasts? Happiness. Good health. Long life. How absurd. Everything was absurd in the presence of Death. You wished someone a long life and all the while Death stood in the room, just waiting. Like the soldier who killed Rätzel. Death was a bastard.

Ursula looked away from her grandfather when the door opened again. There was no knock this time. Her father stood in the doorway. She felt her jaw get rigid. He was very drunk.

"Aren't any of you going to bed?"

Paul shook his head. "No. We are going to stay with him tonight. An old tradition. We have decided to observe it."

"Humph." The sound was a mixture of snort and laughter. He turned and blundered away, leaving the door open. A few minutes later Alexander came in and sat on the sofa. "Melchior's coming," he said.

When he arrived, Melchior knelt beside the bed, his hands steepled in front of his face. In a sweet, clear voice he spoke the Lord's Prayer, giving Ursula the only religious ceremony she was going to hear for her grandfather. At his funeral three days later, attended by several hundred people, most of them old, she did not listen to the priest. She was hallucinating: the roof of the church was swaying, and under it the people, the black-shawled women and bowed men, cowered and waited for it to fall. She saw that they were all going to die and not one of them even thought of running out of the church and saving himself. Someone sang in a quivering voice, a ridiculous song about God waiting at the entrance to heaven to lead the beloved sinner to redemption. The song said that they could all rejoice at death since it gave them something to look forward to, even as this man who was finally united with his Maker. People were weeping, their shoulders shuddering in their attempt to do it quietly. Ursula knew her grandfather would have disliked the singing and crying. At the cemetery, old, lame people hobbled up to her and her brothers and smiled nervously and said inane things about how their grandfather was better off where he was. Ursula looked down into the grave that she had seen in a dream years before. "Down there?" she asked the next mourner who made a similar comment, a big-bellied man in a black overcoat that reeked of cigar smoke. "I don't think so. He loved sunlight and the smell of lilacs and the taste of champagne. He's not going to like it down there one bit." The man pinched up his mouth, glanced at the open grave, and walked quickly away from her. Günther, standing next to her, gave her a narrow glance from under lowered eyebrows and then unexpectedly smiled.

"You're right, of course," he said.

For two nights after the funeral, Ursula tossed through a few hours of shallow sleep, waking before dawn each day as though someone had called her name. On the second night she crept to each of her brothers' rooms, only to find them sleeping soundly. She wandered about the cold house, finally returning to the old man's rooms. The bed was made, the rugs cleaned, and the floor polished; the room looked as though it had not been inhabited for months. Paul and Günther had ordered all the man's mementos and pictures to be put away; and this now gave it the impersonal quality of a rarely used guest suite.

She sat in the old man's great chair by the cold fireplace. "Where are you right now, Grandfather? I think you are near me. Please be near me. I feel all alone. Are you with Mother?" Ursula tried to remember her mother's face; more and more in the last year, the features eluded her. Alone in the middle of the night, with the darkened house settled in silence, she resolved never to forget her grandfather's face, never to let him drift away into that shadowy region, to become gray and transparent as old mirror glass, and finally to fade entirely so that nothing of him remained in her. It was the only way she knew to hit back at death, to face it down, even deny it. So Günther was right after all: in her memory her grandfather was safe.

On the third day after the funeral, Pavel Stephanovitch Bronevsky rang for Miss Schneider and told the excited woman to summon the children to the library. He was profoundly sober.

"The children?"

"Yes, my children," he said in his appealingly soft, still-foreign German.

"Is there anything I can do for you?" The woman blushed deeply and trembled as she spoke.

"Yes. You can find my children in this accursed house and see that they are brought before me. We have business matters that must be settled. One of the old man's attorneys is coming and I have a few things to say to him." He turned away from her and faced the life-size standing portrait of his dead father-in-law hanging over the mantel. When he heard the door close behind the governess, he spoke to the painting. "Now, you bastard, I am in command here. Your voice is finished. Your mouth is stuffed with worms, although I expect they'll get as sick of you as I have been these miserable years." He would have laughed except for Enerde's eyes, which, it seemed to Bronevsky, gazed back at him with raw irony, even changing as the moments bore on, deepening into mockery and scorn. Bronevsky shivered under the gaze and turned away. Years of bitterness, while he waited for the old man to die, had given a touch of cruelty to his face, a frog expression about the mouth, something green in the shadows under his cheekbones. He saw it himself in the mornings when he faced his shaving mirror and tried to smile, to shove his mouth back up to its former charming shape. But the fickle flesh only puffed up the pouches under his eyes. He pulled the skin of his lower face back toward his ears. He looked better. But when he let go, the mouth sagged again and he blamed his father-in-law for that, too. "If you had been fair to me, I would still be young," he said to his own reflection, as though he were having a quiet conversation with Enerde. "You could have let me into the business, let me run some of the money." He spoke on in this way rationally and calmly until unbearable anger rose in him and his words turned to a furious mindless monologue. "You cheated me . . . cold-blooded . . . out of everything . . . my life . . . lost to your smug, vicious indifference. I had a right to something. Cold-blooded thief. You destroyed my life. Killer!" He spoke to the portrait in this same rambling way, his mouth filling with foam when his anger reached its sputtering climax and dissipated into a wild breathing and clenching and unclenching of his hands as tears ran off his face.

Alexander found Ursula on a bench in the summerhouse. Patches of blue snow lay under the barren trees and winter-dead shrubbery. "Father wants to see us. The lawyer is coming to finish up everything."

Ursula dug into a decaying trellis wall with a stick. "I miss him, Alexy. I miss him all the time. I don't know what to do without him."

Alexander sat down beside her. "I know, but it doesn't do any good to think on it. Don't grieve anymore. He was old."

Ursula turned on her brother with instantaneous anger, raising the stick threateningly. "He was *not* old."

Alexander grabbed her wrist. "He *was* old. He was more than eighty years old! He was *ancient*. It was just time for him to die. Now stop." He wrenched the stick from her hand and threw it down. They struggled furiously for a few minutes, Alexander finally wrapping his arms around her tightly. "Now stop. You have to stop now. You can't stay mad all the time over it. You have to stop!"

"He was not *old!*"

"All right. All right. He was not old!"

Ursula's struggles ended as quickly as they had begun, although Alexander still held her. She had been awake since dawn and now experienced an ill-defined sensation that she had already lived the day, that it was coming on toward night. Granite clouds caved the sky over the garden, yet it was only ten in the morning. Time seemed to float slowly above her, leaving her isolated in the center of her sorrow, where there was no sleep, only some mocking parody of it in which she dreamed she was awake and that her grandfather was calling her to go for a walk. When she awakened at the call, all was dark and silent and empty.

When the children entered the library, the lawyer, who had just arrived, was standing behind a massive table, his hands resting on the still-locked briefcase in front of him, ignoring Bronevsky, who stood at one end of the table talking fast. "Of course, my father-in-law told me some time ago that your office would call when . . . when the time came. There are matters that should be considered. The old man and I discussed them frequently so it's not as though I didn't expect your call yesterday." No one spoke and Bronevsky was forced to continue in this humiliating way, knowing the children knew he was lying and that the lawyer probably knew it too. "Naturally, there are a few minor things that still need to be cleared up, so perhaps it's good that you called as soon as you did." He smiled broadly, his hands gesturing nervously first toward the lawyer and then the children, who still stood near the door. "Well, well, let's all sit down. Yes, why not. We might as well be comfortable. No reason to stand when we can sit." He sat down, still gesturing toward the children to come further into the room, his smile anxious, timorous, despairing.

To Ursula, the scene was bizarrely unreal. The lawyer obviously had no intention of sitting. He drummed his fingers on the briefcase. His mouth looked as dry as paper, his skin the color of birchbark. In his black suit, he looked to Ursula like a corpse. He had come often to visit her grandfather, but she had never paid any attention to him. Rätzel once said that lawyers generally presented their clients with impossible choices and hopeless alternatives to them. Her brothers, embarrassed by their father's rapid, fidgety chatter, made no motion to pull chairs closer to the two men, whose distrust and dislike of each other filled the room like another presence. Ursula sat on her grandfather's footstool, precluding anyone's sitting in the old man's chair.

The lawyer unlocked the briefcase.

"No, no, I insist everyone sit first," said Bronevsky, rising. The boys took various chairs about the room, Paul and Günther sitting on a large leather sofa, their eyes on the lawyer. "Yes, that's better. Now, we'll see what's what." He sat down again and turned to the still-standing lawyer, who was removing papers from the case. "I understand," said Bronevsky, "that the Yugoslav property is to be returned to us."

The lawyer did not look up from the document in his hand. "The Yugoslav property is lost. It was lost when the war was lost." The man spoke in a crisp hard voice that Ursula immediately disliked.

"Of course. Yes. Yes. I knew that. But there were rumors about compensation. Reliable rumors. Only a few weeks ago there was speculation in the newspapers, informed speculation in my opinion, that some property would be returned or at least that compensation was forthcoming. I saved the article. I can show it to you."

"Rumors and speculation are not my business."

"Naturally not. I see that. But perhaps in the future, if something comes of it—I mean, if the government could retrieve, for its most valued citizens, that is, some compensation . . . Well, perhaps not in Yugoslavia, but certainly the Danube Basin property. *There* is the real value. What was Yugoslavia anyway but a retreat? It brought in no capital. But the Danube property, now that's a different matter. Melchior frequently spoke of it."

All the children's heads shot up as their father used their grandfather's

Christian name. Even the lawyer caught the reaction and cleared his throat. "The Danube Basin property was sold two years ago. What do you think you have been living on?" The lawyer finally looked up, his spectacles catching the light in such a way that his eyes were hidden behind opaque glass disks.

Bronevsky pulled back. "Sold?" He recovered himself quickly. "Yes, I believe now he did mention it. He was not entirely clear toward the end. He was not himself. His illness, you know."

"When these documents were drawn up," said the lawyer carefully, "he was quite himself. These signatures were witnessed by no fewer than four persons. One was his physician, who declared that Mr. Enerde was clear-headed and in total control of all his faculties. The dates go back over three years."

"Oh, well, yes, *then* he was still very clear."

"You do remember that?"

"Yes, yes, of course. Very clear."

"Good." The lawyer paused. "Let me also remind you that you were present at the time some of these documents were signed."

"I was?" Bronevsky frowned, blinked rapidly, and nodded his head in short jerks. "Yes, yes, of course I was."

The lawyer smiled faintly. "You remember, then, signing some particular documents pertaining to the children's education?"

"Yes, yes, of course. The children's education. Very important. Surely the children's education comes first. We discussed it frequently."

"You still approve of the plans, then?"

"Yes, yes. Once I make up my mind, it's made up for good. I'd like to think the children inherited this trait. A very good trait to help develop character. One of the problems today is the deterioration of character. It's something—"

"It's something we might consider at another time. At the moment we have more important matters at hand."

"To be sure. Please carry on."

The lawyer's smile made Ursula dislike him even more. He had white gums. She imagined that he could safely eat sand or that perhaps he did not have to eat at all. She watched his thin mouth. No, it could not munch an apple or suck out the inside of a wet fig or kiss anyone. It was definitely a sand-eating mouth. If she were to draw him, there would be no mouth to draw, just a paper-thin line. The man began to read in a monotone, stressing nothing, pausing at nothing. As he completed each page, he turned it over slowly and lowered it to the table, continuing without interruption to the next. Ursula saw that every piece was stamped and crimped with large round red seals.

"Wait, wait," said Bronevsky. "What was that last part about the Bavarian estate?" He lit a cigarette with shaking hands.

"I shall finish reading these documents first, and then if you have questions, I shall answer them."

After two more interruptions, exclamations of "What's that? What's that?" from Bronevsky, which brought not even as much as a hesitation from the lawyer, the last page filtered facedown to the table.

"But what does it all mean?" asked Bronevsky, eyeing the stack of pages now back again in the lawyer's hands.

"It means that everything has been sold except this house and its contents, which will be put to auction." The lawyer turned to the children. "Do you understand?" Paul and Günther nodded simultaneously for all of them.

"Everything?" asked Bronevsky, the heels of his hands pressed to his temples, his elbows extended in front of him. "All the foreign properties . . . the alpine house, the Italian villa . . . the . . . the . . .?"

"Everything foreign *and* domestic here in Europe, except, of course, the Swiss holdings, which, because of their form, are quite safe and shall remain as they are. The several real properties in that country shall also remain untouched. However, all that was left in Austria, the mills and factories, all the forests, all the German and Italian properties, the various houses—all are gone. The properties in America and Canada are still intact, and our representatives in those areas have that under control."

"But where is the money?"

"In trust." The lawyer pulled another set of papers out of his briefcase. In a slower voice, he read the old man's will: the funds from the sale of all the holdings were being held in invested trust for the children in the Enerde banks in Switzerland. Each of them could draw fifty thousand dollars a year until the youngest of them, Ursula, reached her twentieth birthday. At that time all the holdings would be turned over to them. They would not be able to realize an advance on that amount, but if they did not draw the full amount in any year they could receive it the following year or at whatever later time they requested it. The lawyer paused and studied the children a moment before he went on. "There are conditions for these bounties," he said, looking back at the papers in his hand. "It was your grandfather's wish that all of you attend university, but not in Austria or in Germany. You will have to leave the country."

"Certainly not!" shouted Bronevsky. "No! I won't have it. This he cannot do! They are my children. I won't permit it." He crossed his arms and leaned back in his chair. "The topic is closed. I am in charge here and I'll hear no more of this business. No more!"

The lawyer waited patiently for Bronevsky to finish. "Mr. Enerde's wish is in the form of a stipulation in his will; only by going to school in a country of his choosing can your children realize their inheritance now. You, yourself, signed certain documents wherein it is agreed by you that the children may leave Austria." The lawyer motioned for silence with a raised hand as Bronevsky was about to speak. "One moment; before you say anything else, let me present you with copies of these papers."

"I signed nothing. Nothing!"

"But I assure you, sir, you did, and in front of witnesses whose signatures are next to your own." The lawyer took additional sheets from his case and placed them in the center of the table. "Your copies of everything, signed by you. Now, then, to continue."

Ursula watched her father lean over the table and pick up the documents. He scanned them myopically, bringing the pages close to his face. "But I'm their father; I have a say in these things." The brief authority in his voice of moments before was liquefying into a whimper.

[161]

"Quite. Which is exactly what you did in those documents. You need have no fear that they will not be supervised while away at school: our non-Austrian representative is seeing to all those matters. He will be their guardian while they are abroad. Everything in that area is being taken care of at this very moment. Now, if we could go on with the remainder of this will, you'll find that all the questions presently in your mind will be answered."

The lawyer was reading again, his tone taking on an intimacy that made Ursula still more uncomfortable. The house and its contents were to be sold at private auction after the children selected for themselves those items they wished to take with them or otherwise dispose of. Part of the proceeds from the sales were to be used to pay legal fees and all other current debts. These matters were to be seen to by Enerde's law firm. Of what remained, a fourth was to be bequeathed to Agnes Schneider, a fourth each to Berghoch and Graz, and the last fourth divided between the two maids.

There was a stunning silence until Bronevsky shattered it. "What about me?" His shrill cry went straight to Ursula's spine.

"Certain provisions have been made for you by codicil." The lawyer stopped. Ursula thought some color had risen on his cheeks.

"Well?" Bronevsky waited, his spread hands braced—fingers down— against the table.

"A sum has been set aside to cover the cost of your burial when the time comes. In the family crypt, of course. Mr. Enerde believed his daughter would have wished you to be taken care of in that respect."

"Go on. What else? What else?"

The attorney did not even hesitate. "There is nothing else."

Bronevsky rose unsteadily, his chair teetering behind him. "This is monstrous!"

"You are not obliged to use the crypt, but by the same token, you may not sell it. Mr. Enerde thought you would find some solace in knowing that you would lie beside your wife."

Ursula watched in dazed shock as her father stalked back and forth in front of the table, striking his fist into his open palm. "The beast," he shouted. "I'll sue. I'll break that will."

"Not likely," said the lawyer, returning some papers to the briefcase. "You signed several documents over the past two years. In one of them you agree never to contest Mr. Enerde's will. You may have forgotten signing them, but I was present each time and I explained every document to you with the greatest care, and—"

"I was drunk, for God's sake. How could I know what I was signing?"

"A physician was present when you swore in front of four witnesses that you were sober. The good doctor concurred with your opinion. We took great precaution at the time to ask you if you understood the matters."

Bronevsky laughed, tears running on his face. "Oh, I'm sure you did. You would take great precaution while questioning the dead."

"Additionally, you were paid quite large sums each time you signed . . ."

"My God." Bronevsky fell back into his chair and covered his face with his hands. He wept noisily.

Ursula turned in anguish to her brothers. "Do something," she whispered. But their faces were filled with the same helpless dismay that she felt in her heart. Melchior was crying. None of them knew what to do for this stranger who was their father. He had never touched them, avoided talking to them, assumed no responsibility for them; so that now in paralytic embarrassment, they were unable to help him.

The door opened violently and Miss Schneider, who Ursula realized at once had been listening behind it, strode into the room and literally pulled the weeping man to his feet. "It will be all right; you can have my share," she said in a voice women generally reserve for hurt children. The governess led him out of the room without ever looking at Ursula or her brothers or even the lawyer, who was cleaning his glasses with profound concentration.

Silence followed the closing of the door, interrupted a few moments later by the lawyer, who, after adjusting his spectacles several times on his nose, reopened his briefcase. "Your grandfather left letters for each of you, and some general instructions that he wished you to follow. I'll cover these before we get to the letters." He finally sat down and picked up a single sheet of paper. "First, there is the matter of Mr. Rätzel; he is to be disinterred and reburied beside your grandfather in the family crypt. There are funds available for this and my office shall see to the matter, since there are certain legalities involved. It goes without saying that your grandfather wished all of you to be present at this ceremony for his old friend."

The lawyer paused and seemed to read from the sheet as the children waited, but he was, in fact, not reading: with his face lowered, Ursula saw that his eyes, the color of gravel, were watching them over the top of his glasses. "The second matter has a certain delicacy to it. It involves your father. There is a remote possibility that somewhere in this city there is a person who is another blood son to him." Ursula heard Melchior gasp, but no sound came from the others. "This does not involve a prior marriage. If there is such a person, he is related only to your father and some woman not known to you."

"Isn't he our half-brother?" Günther spoke softly but Ursula recognized a tightness in his voice that stretched out like a sail in the wind.

"Your grandfather does not wish you to consider him—if indeed he exists—in that relationship. He felt it necessary that you be informed of the possibility of this person in case someone should come forward at this time and make a claim on his behalf against the estate. Your grandfather paid a considerable sum to a woman who made this claim years ago to keep her from becoming a nuisance to him. Additionally—"

"Who is he? How old is he?" Ursula turned to Günther.

"Those questions are not relevant. This person is not related to Mr. Enerde or to your mother and, therefore, has no claim here."

"Do you want us to ask our father?" Günther's voice was suddenly loose and easy, his question as casual as a request for the time of day.

Ursula returned her attention to the lawyer. He had his thin nether lip pulled high over his upper one. With a smack he released his mouth. "It would grieve . . . that is, if he were living, it would grieve your grandfather."

"He is not living," continued Günther. "How old?"

The lawyer exhaled sharply. "If the rumor is true, seventeen or eighteen."

"His name."

"Unknown to us. The woman's sister or aunt . . . some relative, came here last year or the year before and demanded money. She claimed it was for the boy. She called him Vanya. We do not know what family name he uses, if indeed he exists. We do not consider it important."

Ursula remembered the screaming woman in the purple dress whom Graz and Berghoch forcibly turned out of the house. Now her upturned face shone like a beacon in the dark area of her mind where she stored such things as she might put away books she had read but did not wish to read again and yet was unable to give away. She occasionally thought about them, however, without much concern. But now a small new worry like a worm crept into her heart. *Vanya.* Somewhere she had yet another brother! Someone Melchior's age. The lawyer was talking again, still using the curious plural that annoyed Ursula to the point of distraction; who exactly was the "we" this stone-eyed man kept referring to?

"Additionally, we expect all of you to continue to keep this matter quiet. The reputation of the family must be maintained. Now, the third matter involves the use of your inheritance. Until you are of age, you may collect it on the condition that you are in school. After that you need only request it, and it shall be given to you. We believe we have secured the funds in such a way that the trusts cannot be broken. Your yearly allotment is only some of the interest from investments, therefore the principal—remaining intact—will assure income for your progeny for generations. Your grandfather, in his wisdom, left the mechanics of investment to people who are experienced in such matters. That is not to say that any of you should not make investments of your own should you be prudent enough to save funds for it until the entire holdings are placed under your own protection."

"What about our father?" Paul was standing by then. Ursula became aware of his restlessness during the lawyer's long speech and twice heard him whisper something to Günther.

"Your father? What about him?" The lawyer leaned slightly forward. "Which one are you?"

"Paul."

"My brother is asking how our father will live," Günther said bluntly.

"That is not our problem," answered the lawyer, annoyance in his words.

"But it is *our* problem," said Günther.

"It is *not* your problem. You have no problems. Your grandfather has seen to it that you are very well taken care of. He has taken every precaution to make certain that you have all the advantages due the children of a vastly wealthy man, and—"

"Our father is not a wealthy man; he has nothing."

"I was referring to your grandfather."

"I am referring to our father."

"Your father, young man, can go to work. He has never contributed anything to this family."

"He contributed us."

The lawyer took off his glases and glared at Günther. "That's hardly a . . ." He stopped in time.

Günther's smile made Ursula laugh, but she quickly checked herself.

[164]

"Mr. Brückner," continued Günther, "if our father has never worked, what could he possibly do now?"

"I'm sure that's not our concern. For twenty years he has lived in the folds of luxury; it is high time he learned that we do not owe him the cost of his bread, let alone his vices."

"We, too, have lived in the same luxury; is the continuation of it owed us?"

"Yes. You are the inheritors of immense wealth accrued over many generations. Your grandfather wished that to continue. Your father came to this family as a pauper. In fact, he entered it fraudulently, claiming an important position and substantial wealth. He had neither. Your grandfather paid for his upkeep all these years, denying him nothing. He was given a substantial annual allowance to do with as he wished. He squandered it. He was paid additional sums in the last two years, again, very substantial. Did he save any of that? No, he did not! And since you are now feeling sorry for him, let me tell you all that he relinquished—signed away—his guardianship over you without a second thought. In my opinion, he would have signed away your very lives for the amounts your grandfather paid him." The satisfaction in the lawyer's voice created an appalling silence. Apparently realizing that he need not have added the last opinion, Brückner tried for appeasement. "Your grandfather wanted the best for you. You should think on that. It would make him very sad to know that you do not trust his judgment. His love for you is clearly evident in all that he has given you. As for your father . . . well, the man is simply not responsible. Some weakness of character. Inbreeding, possibly. True, he came from an aristocratic family which was once of some importance in Russia, but all that has been swept away. I do not wish to be unduly hard on the man, but—"

Günther laughed. "Your charity would freeze hell."

The lawyer was angered again. "He made your mother extremely unhappy, and he was quite possibly responsible for her—"

"No! No more. Spare us your speculations. Our mother died of an organic disease." Günther turned to Melchior. "Quit crying. Mother died of complications from diabetes, no matter what this ass says."

"She refused to be helped. All your grandfather's pleading went unheeded."

"Who are *you* to say that *that* was our father's fault?"

"She knew of the bastard child—days after it was born."

"So, it's a fact and not a rumor. And if it's true, she must have come to terms with that, since she had four more children of her own after that."

"Quite probably against her will!" spat Brückner.

Günther quit then. Ursula, looking with horror first at the lawyer and then at her brother, saw at once that Günther had given up. She rose unsteadily, odd lights flashing at the perimeter of her vision, and lurched toward the table behind which the lawyer's smug face loomed like a large stone. By the time her brothers pulled her off the man, blood poured from his nose and a large swelling was forming on his upper lip. Alexander and Boris held her against the wall as Melchior helped the lawyer to his feet. Distantly, between her brothers' shoulders, she saw the man hold his handkerchief to his face as he stuffed his papers into the briefcase with his free hand. She could hear herself still screaming at him but the words sounded mushy and wet as the lights danced at the sides of her face. It was Günther who finally led her out of the room, half-dragging her down the hall to the bathroom. Only then did she realize that she was vomiting.

At a dinner gathering one evening a few weeks after the grandfather's death, Dr. Frichter, who had seen the children through their childhood illnesses, said he would rather have doctored tigers. He turned back a shirt cuff and showed his guests a scar on his right forearm where years before one of the children bit him. He claimed he could not remember which one. "They are as alike as a pack of jungle cats. They all had measles at the same time and ran the highest fevers I ever saw. Jabbered a lot of nonsense and saw things that weren't there. It was a fright! If you can imagine six violent children tearing their nightclothes to shreds, running naked to the roof to wallow in the snow! We had a time of it. I suspect there is a good deal of madness in that family."

"From the father, do you think?" asked one of the guests, eagerly wishing confirmation.

The doctor hesitated, sipped wine, pondered both its taste and his answer. "I wouldn't lay it all off to the Russian. There's some dark blood in the Enerde clan. The old man's late marriage—to a mere child. And at that, one already living in his own house, under his protection, so to speak. Something smells."

There was a glitter of knowing glances.

"You mean," asked someone new to the old rumors, ". . . a serving girl?"

"No, no. She was a relative. A niece by marriage. The records show no blood connection. But who's to know what happens under the blanket? I've often thought there was a physical resemblance between Enerde and his young wife. That bronze eye and blond hair. Not all that common, but they both had it."

"And their children were normal?"

"Normal? What's normal in this life? Anyway, there was just the one. Enerde's wife died in childbed, and the daughter born to him ultimately married Bronevsky." He paused, the hesitation of memory halting his face. "As pretty as a lily." Again he hesitated, returning to an earlier tone. "I inherited her medical record. She was frail from the beginning. Not physically, but in some way not easily explained."

"Is it true that her husband's philandering killed her?"

"That's nonsense! It's amazing to me the rubbish people will believe. She had pancreatitis. Ignored it for years. Developed diabetes in stages. Refused to take insulin injections. In the end peripheral vascular disease of the legs followed. A horrible death. She screamed for days. There was very little we could do by then."

"Why?"

"Why what?"

"Why did she refuse?"

"Who knows with that family? Why did those six children try to learn to vomit at will?"

"Is that possible?" Two guests asked the question simultaneously. A sauternes and fruit were being served by then, but interest in the course lagged as the diners waited for the doctor's answer. He held back. "You mean they stuck their fingers down their throats?" The lady who asked made a sour face and shivered.

"No, no, my dear. I don't mean that at all. I mean they sat quietly, each with his own—and her own—vomit bowl in front of him and willed themselves to eject the contents of the stomach."

"But is that possible?"

"Well, I don't know that it *isn't*. The process is coordinated by the brain: the abdominal wall and the diaphragm contract together and squeeze the stomach, which lies between them. At the same time, the pyloric sphincter closes, the cardiac sphincter at the esophagus opens, and up it all comes."

"I have never heard of anything so disgusting!" said the same lady, holding her dinner napkin in front of her mouth with steepled hands.

"Did you actually see them do this, Doctor?"

The question came from another member of the medical world (a specialist in skin disorders and, therefore, not to be taken very seriously); still, the tone of skepticism from the young man irritated the Enerde physician. However, he smiled congenially and continued to pare an apple. "Not personally. Their governess reported it to me. The woman was quite distraught over the matter, particularly since she claimed that three of the children had finally been successful in their efforts."

One of the women further down the table laughed. "Well, we've all heard about her. Certainly no one takes what *she* says seriously."

"Why not? She's known them all their lives. She's vanquished every tutor brought into that house. Few have lasted longer than six months. She may be a little soft in the noodle where Bronevsky is concerned, but I'd not quickly disbelieve anything she said about those children. No, no. I'd give that some thought, some serious thought. She's a woman of considerable learning—and intelligence. Those children don't know it, but they owe her a great deal."

"But the woman's pathetic. Those little red eyes and tight mouth. She seems to have a perpetual cold. And she's sixty if she's a day."

"No, dear lady, she's not much past forty-five, if at all. It's disappointment that gives her that haggard look. And that may soon disappear." The doctor waited, enjoying the dramatic moment as the faces all turned toward him in expectation. "The house is being sold and the children are going abroad to school."

There were exclamations of surprise, and when those died down, someone asked, "Only Enerde's half-dozen?"

There was a roar of laughter. The oblique reference to a rumor that Bronevsky had fathered an illegitimate child opened the conversation to everyone and a chatter of voices, all telling anecdotes about the Enerde family's reduction and ruin, ended the dinner party on a note of satisfaction and camaraderie.

Only the doctor refrained from this hilarity, his eyes fixed upon a point in space directly ahead of him at which he stared and stared like a man suddenly privileged to an astonishingly clear glimpse into the future.

15

Ursula was surprised that her brothers were not furious with her for pummeling Brückner. Günther bandaged her right hand, which she had cut on the lawyer's teeth. "Where did you learn to box like that? It's a fairly accepted fact that women usually slap; they don't use their fists."

"I couldn't hurt him with a slap."

"Hmm. Good point." He examined her hand closely. "You have a bad cut on one knuckle; it should probably be stitched. It's a good thing he didn't have his glasses on. You *really* would have hurt him then—and yourself, too. But, of course, you wouldn't hit a man with glasses on, would you?" He laughed. "Not much you wouldn't."

They did not discuss the lawyer's speculation on their parents' sex life. What they did discuss when they all met in the dining room, after Ursula's injury was taken care of, was their father's upkeep. "As I see it," began Günther, "the only thing we can do is send him money from wherever we go. Schnabel will take care of him until we get settled, and as soon as we draw money from the trust we'll send him whatever he needs. Does everyone agree to that?" Everyone did. "As I understand Grandfather's will, we don't have to say what we do with our money. The only requirements that he made at all are that we stay together for at least three years and that we all go to school until we are twenty-one. I do not foresee any difficulty with any of that." Neither did the others. "And when we finish school, we can always come back."

"True," said Paul, "and we can worry about coming back when the time for it comes. The thing to do now is get together with Father and tell him that we'll take care of him. I'm sure Schnabel will agree to our plan." Paul looked around the tapestried walls of the dining room. "It's too bad that the house has to be sold; if it weren't for that, they could just stay here."

Ursula turned to her grandfather's empty chair. "I don't understand why he wanted the house sold. It's been in the family for almost two hundred years." Even as she spoke, a dark suspicion that her grandfather wanted all of them permanently separated from their father crossed her mind.

"Couldn't we take him with us?" It was Melchior who raised the question that had already come to all of them.

"Everything is being handled by the lawyers," said Paul. "We probably won't be able to do anything."

"You can count on that," said Günther. "We won't see any of our inheritance until we're out of the country. Not only did Grandfather not want Father in the same *city* we are in, he didn't even want him in the same *country*." He paused, anxiety passing across his face like a shadow. "If Ursula hadn't punched that lawyer for us, we'd know what is in those letters Grandfather left for us." Ursula had forgotten all about the letters and groaned. "It's all right, Little Bear, the lawyer who is coming this afternoon will bring them with him."

The second lawyer showed up three hours after Brückner rushed out the front door, hatless, his handkerchief still squashed against his face and one coat lapel hanging by a thread. The new one was younger and taller than Brückner, with a roughly handsome face, dark blond hair, and deeply beautiful cobalt-blue eyes. "I'm sorry my uncle couldn't come; he has a broken nose. The firm decided I could come out, if I didn't have to take on more than two of you at a time." None of the children looked away from the lawyer's face. He upended his briefcase on the dining-room table. (The maids were still cleaning the library carpet and furniture of Ursula's breakfast and Brückner's blood.)

"All this stuff pertains to you, so we might as well sort it out without any ceremony." He piled the case's contents into two separate stacks. "I could really use something to drink," he said, slinging the empty briefcase under the table.

"What would you like?" asked Günther.

"I don't suppose you have any Scotch?"

"I don't even know what it is."

"The Americans drink it. Our office does a lot of work with them and occasionally I run into a bottle of it. I'll just have vodka."

Alexander left to tell Berghoch what the man wanted, and for a minute or more there was silence in the room. Ursula noticed the hair on the lawyer's wrists was pale and thick, somewhat lighter than his head hair, which he had a habit of running his fingers through as though gauging its length. She saw that it was, in fact, longer than other men's hair, and it was this and his corduroy jacket (rather than the traditional three-piece black wool suit) that gave him a remotely disheveled and nonlawyer look. He moved with easy grace, his body both relaxed and quietly waiting.

Alexander returned and a moment later Berghoch showed up with a tray holding a bottle of vodka and a single glass, which he placed in front of the lawyer. The man smiled at it and thanked Berghoch. But even after the cook was out of the room, the lawyer did not touch the bottle. "My name is Conrad. You may call me that if it's comfortable for you. The rest of it is Brandt if you prefer to be formal. Conrad Brückner is my mother's brother."

None of the children said anything. Ursula knew from long experience that strangers in the house were to be carefully examined before one gave one's feelings away. It had driven some tutors to leave within a week of their arrival.

"All right." The attorney shrugged. "Then let's get down to business."

He tilted back in his chair. "As you probably guessed, your grandfather is sending you to Switzerland. Your European holdings are consolidated there, the schools are good, and we have an office in Zurich. My uncle tells me you have houses in that city *and* in Geneva, not to mention the hotels you own that—"

"Switzerland!" said Boris. "But I want to go to the Sorbonne . . . or at least Oxford."

"Sorry," said Brandt.

Ursula's mind raced to the house where Luba and Wolsky disappeared in the middle of the night. "Do shut up, Boris," she said quietly in English. She saw the lawyer turn aside and smile, placing his hand flatly on one of the stacks of papers. "Additionally, he wants you to attend university in Zurich. It's all being arranged."

"Does he want us to emigrate to that country?" asked Paul.

"He doesn't say so. After three years at the university, you may live where you wish. With your resources you could probably buy yourselves a small country." There was no envy or resentment in his voice and Ursula saw that his eyes were laughing. Twice he glanced toward her, an expression of bafflement and sudden lost calm sweeping across his face.

"I think I shall go to America," said Alexander, "and join the army and be a fighter pilot."

"You will probably be right on target for the next war," said Brandt with the same easy nonchalance he had handled everything else, very like someone making arrangements for a picnic. "The auction will take place just prior to your departure. We'll be in touch. Are there any questions?"

It was Günther who asked the question, his tone quiet, reasonable, and without any emotion whatsoever. "Is there any possibility that our father could go with us?"

"None at all," answered Brandt in the same soft tone. There was a moment of silence. "If there's nothing else, I'll leave these with you." He picked up the stack of sealed letters and placed them in the center of the table. "No one in the office knows what is in those, not even my uncle. Our legal staff is extremely curious about them and our investment people hope there is advice on future Austrian investments, and everyone would like me to glean any information I can out of you. Since I know that's impossible, I'll just say good-bye." He reached under the table and picked up the briefcase.

Without looking at the letters, each of the children shook the hand he held out to them. When he came to Ursula, he looked down at her bandaged fingers and for an instant frowned in confusion. Then he nodded faintly, smiled, and brought the inside of her wrist to his mouth. She did not actually hear the kiss, but she clearly felt the warm open lips on her pulse for longer than two heartbeats. When she met his eyes she saw again that suggestion of both humor and amazement, as though he might in the next moment laugh softly within himself. He turned abruptly and left them.

When they heard the front door close behind him, the children raced back to the dining-room table and snatched up their letters. Ursula held hers in both hands without opening it as she watched her brothers pull up the ribbons that broke the seals.

Boris spoke first. "He's giving me a choice: I'm not obliged to leave the country." He looked with astonishment at the others. "He says that if there is any reason I would feel compelled to stay, I should exercise my will."

Paul sighed. "Mine says pretty much the same thing."

"Mine, too," said Melchior.

The boys compared their letters: they all had the option to stay if some compelling reason demanded it. They turned to Ursula. Slowly she pulled up the ribbon, the wax flaking off and fluttering to the floor. When she read the first three words, tears came to her eyes.

Most beloved child:

It would be cruel of me to insist that you leave the nation of your birth. If you came to feel in your heart that your place is here, you must make your own decision. The sale of the Degas hanging in your room will give you sufficient funds to live well until you are of age, when you will come into your inheritance in any case—should you elect to stay in Austria now. It is, however, my deepest wish that you will leave the country with your brothers. I know that you are a brave girl and that you will not be afraid to leave your homeland. When you marry, be wise: choose a man of honor and courage and compassion. At that time an additional inheritance will be given you. But do not marry too soon. You have many gifts that must not be abandoned and that need time to develop and mature.

Know always that you have been a great joy in my life.

Your loving grandfather,
Melchior

Ursula handed her letter to Günther, who gave her his in return. In the cool, high-ceilinged dining room where an aging, doomed emperor once belched pleasantly and told mild jokes after a banquet of exotic foods, the children silently read each other's messages from their dead grandfather. On the walls the darkly colored tapestries of a lost era lent a heavy gloom to the stillness, the elaborate panels portraying scenes of aristocrats in their various pursuits of leisurely pleasures.

"Why did he do this?" said Alexander, looking angrily at the letters now lying randomly back on the table.

Günther shrugged. "He wanted us to have the choice."

"I don't want a choice," grumbled Alexander. "I want all of us to leave. He was right the first time: Austria is finished. Those damn Russians will never leave, so why make us choose?"

Paul picked up one of the letters. "He's not *making* us choose; he's *letting* us choose."

Alexander failed to see the distinction. "Choosing just makes things unclear. It's easier if we don't have to choose."

Ursula, listening to her brother complain, heard the statement clearly and marveled briefly at its truth, but passed it up without thinking further about it. After all, what compelling thing could make them stay? If Grand-

[171]

father wanted them to leave Austria, then that's what they should do. Hadn't he always known what was right for them? Still, she saw Günther and Paul give each other an anxious glance.

In each of the letters, there was a reference to some valuable object that, like Ursula's Degas, if sold, would bring enough to sustain each grandchild until his majority: Paul could sell the eighteenth-century Graff clock in the library; it was the only one of its kind in the world. Günther was given a magnificently ornamented Roman physician's surgical case with over half the instruments intact. "It is yours, dear boy, to keep if you wish, although a medical school's museum in Berlin would probably kill to get it." A sixteenth-century Bible, which once belonged to the Empress Elizabeth, was now Melchior's: "The National Museum wants it. Don't give it to them if you can see a way to keep it." "All of the Freud works with the Doctor's full-page notes on 'late-night considerations' covering the fly leaves . . . , are yours, Boris. I never agreed with what he thought—too farfetched—but that is my prejudice and need not be yours," said Boris' letter. "The university might give you a very nice price for all that unpublished noodleology. Let Brückner handle the sale. He's the best shark they have in that firm when it comes to getting a big bite." Alexander was given the hunting-gun collection. "Don't be sentimental about them. The very old sporting air rifles are much desired by collectors and should bring a good price. As you well know, there are three of them. The rest are fine weapons, and gun clubs will take them happily, but it's the Mauser with all the fancy engraving that will keep you until you are twenty-one. It was especially designed for Franz Josef and has his personal signature on the stock. See Brückner about it." In all the letters the grandfather requested the children to stay together as long as possible, always to help each other, to be kind to one another, and to remember that he had loved them above all else. In the boys' letters there was a command to each of them to take care of his sister.

"I can take care of myself," said Ursula, gathering the letters into a neat stack on the table.

"Oh, we all *know* that," said Günther, grinning. "Grandfather just wants us to patch you up after your fights."

Alexander was still dissatisfied with the idea of a choice. "I want to go; there's nothing that can make me stay here."

"Quit complaining," said Günther. "We're all going. It's clear that Grandfather wanted us to leave Austria and that is exactly what we are going to do." He looked around the table at each of them. "Melchior, what's the matter? Speak, if you want to be heard."

"Why can't Father come with us?"

"Because you have to have a permit to leave the country, and those lawyers are going to make sure he never gets one. They have probably already made sure that he can't ever leave Austria. That firm is powerful and has influence in the government, which is exactly why we are going to be able to leave. You watch, there will be no long delays, no confusion, no difficulties for us at all. As long as they have anything to do with us, they are going to get paid. I'm sure Grandfather saw to that."

Melchior stared morosely at the pile of letters. "I think what Grandfather

[172]

did to Father was unfair. He could have divided things up differently. And . . . and leaving him money only for his burial was . . . wicked."

Ursula, refusing to believe that her grandfather might have done anything wrong, wanted to object; but as she faced Melchior's sad eyes, she could not bring herself to speak. It was Paul who smoothed over the moment. "Yes, it probably was, but he may have had special reasons. And, look, Melchior, we can make it right by helping Father."

"Nothing will ever make it right. Some things are always wrong, and just covering them over won't ever change that."

"Well, then, we shall do as much as we can, at least make things easier for . . ."

Ursula turned as Paul stopped talking and followed the direction of his glance. The heavy double doors to the dining room were open a fraction of an inch. "You need not stand outside, Miss Schneider, you are welcome to come in," said Günther.

The doors drew apart and the governess, all in black, stood in an attitude of humble shyness under the archway. Ursula wondered why she had changed into a black dress; she had shown no signs of mourning their grandfather before; even at the funeral she wore a blue dress and coat. "I've come in behalf of your father," she began in a subdued voice. "We have talked it over and have decided that we can make a home together. But this depends somewhat on your generosity. Since the will allows you to dispose of the furniture in the house as you wish, it is my hope that you will allow us a few pieces for a flat which I hope to find in some quiet place where your father can repair his broken health."

Günther picked the letters off the table, folded them in half, and slipped them into his jacket pocket. "Of course, Miss Schneider, you must take whatever you need. We shall decide in the next few days what we wish to take with us. I doubt that we shall be taking any furniture. Grandfather suggested that we keep certain educational items and these we shall take. The sooner you locate the flat, the better, since we do not know when these auctions are to take place."

"Yes, I'll start looking tomorrow, but it may take some time before I find something acceptable. It must be of quality; he should not be reduced to squalor." Her eyes gleamed hotly.

"Of course," said Günther. "Find the best. We shall meet the expense gladly." There was a satisfying pause as everything seemed to be moving toward the solutions the children had planned. But then, a shriek, the sound of a man under torture, tore into the room as Miss Schneider lurched in fright against the doorway. Behind her, his tear-streaming face twisted with despair, stood the children's father, pulling at his hair with both fists. "Please, I beg you not to leave me," he cried in the voice of a condemned man.

The children stared at the weeping man in helpless bewilderment until Günther, finally finding his voice, rose quickly. "We *have* to go, but we'll send you money as soon as we can."

"That's not the same. I'll be alone. Alone!"

Miss Schneider began to weep. "Oh, please, dear sir, don't say that. Remember our plans. You'll not be alone. I'll care for you. I expect nothing in return. You can have a good life. You can . . ."

[173]

Bronevsky rushed to the table past Miss Schneider as though she did not exist at all, pushing aside the grandfather's great chair. "Do you *all* have to go? Couldn't one of you stay with me? I'll die if you all go." He snuffled loudly and moaned.

By now the boys had risen, but all stood frozen, save Melchior, who walked toward his father, his hand raised in a calming gesture. "I'll stay with you, Father," he said evenly, his eyes dry.

Bronevsky blinked. "You? You? Why should you stay?" He turned from Melchior's extended hand, and stared wildly back at the others, his eyes falling on Ursula. "You. You stay. Yes, that's it. You stay. And we will have a wonderful life together."

To Ursula's horror, he half-fell across the table in reaching for her hand, which she drew back as she shrank away from him, shaking her head rapidly, not aware of the action or even of her own whispering, "No, no, no."

"I beg you, on my life, stay with me. Don't leave me alone. I'll die. Die!"

The twins moved to Ursula's side. "She has to go with us," said Günther in a tone at once both gentle and authoritative.

Miss Schneider, somewhat recovered, tried to pull Bronevsky off the table. "Let her go. What use is she to us? We'll make our own life. We don't need any of them."

Bronevsky pushed the governess away. "I need them. I need her. She will keep me young. She kept the old man alive for years. He knew it; that's why he always had her near him. Well, now it's my turn. She'll keep me young . . . alive. I have a right to that. She's my daughter, my flesh, my blood. Look how much she looks like me . . ."

"We all look like you," said Günther angrily, "except Melchior." There was an ugly silence. "No, you can't have her. Grandfather insisted that she come with us, and that's—"

"Liar. He gave you all a choice!"

None of the children looked toward the bundle of letters sticking out of Günther's pocket, but they all knew that their father and Miss Schneider had been listening at the door the whole time they discussed the letters.

"So . . . I have you, don't I?" said Bronevsky. "You can each make your own choice to leave. Let her choose." He turned again to Ursula. "Stay with me. Stay with your old father."

Miss Schneider, no longer crying, rushed back to the table and stood between Ursula and her father. "No! She must go with them. They need their education; you said so yourself. For God's sake let them go, let them take their—"

"Noooo," screamed Bronevsky, his arms flailing at the governess. "Get out. Get out of this room. I want to be alone with my children." He shrieked obscenities at the woman in Russian and French.

Günther pulled Miss Schneider away from the waving arms. She seemed on the verge of collapse, although Bronevsky had not physically touched her. As the man continued to scream, Günther led the woman to the door. Ursula saw her back-looking face, white and tortured, as her brother pulled the door closed. The room stilled. Bronevsky was finally left alone with his children.

Günther returned to the table. "Sit down, Father." He pulled a chair out for the man. "Sit down and we shall talk about this quietly, sensibly." Bronevsky fell into the chair, his eyes still on Ursula, a muscle twitching rapidly on his lower-left eyelid.

"You'll stay with me, won't you, my little one?" He smiled at her. His expression, trying for warmth and gentleness, became ludicrous like that of a crying clown. "We'll have a fine life, just you and I. Switzerland is not for us. It's too . . . bourgeois, full of cows and peasants and geraniums. So provincial. Smug shopkeepers and American tourists. What do we want with a place like that? What do those people know of living? Of delicacy? Of charm?" He reached toward her across the table as though he expected her to extend her hand, but Ursula pushed her chair still further from the table. Unable to speak, she looked to Günther.

"She is not staying." Günther and Paul spoke simultaneously.

"Let her choose," said Bronevsky, softly now. "Choose, my little cub, choose your father, who loves you. Choose your father and save his life."

Ursula stared at him without speaking. The twitch began to take up the whole left side of his face. He looked terrible; his mouth sagged and his eyes, red with weeping, bore into her. "I can't choose," she whispered. "Grandfather wants me to go."

"He's dead. He doesn't want anything now. Can you deny me my life? I have never asked anything of you. I ask only this: stay with me. You owe me that."

It was Paul who spoke, fury rippling through his words. "She owes you nothing. She is going with us."

"Let her choose." Bronevsky leaned further across the table. "Give me just a few years—three . . . two . . . one. Give me just one year, and then you can join them."

Ursula looked frantically at her brothers. They remained silent. She heard her grandfather's letter: "If you come to feel in your heart that your place is here, you must make your own decision." What was in her heart? Why didn't her heart speak up and tell her what to do? "You can have my painting," she whispered. "The Degas in my room."

Bronevsky shook his head slowly.

"You can have my inheritance. When I get to Zurich, I'll send you everything they give me."

Still Bronevsky shook his head. "It's not the same. I'll not take your inheritance. Just give me one year. One little year of happiness is all I ask."

"Just one year . . . ?" Ursula felt a bad pain begin at the back of her head, as though something were being shoved against her skull. Her shoulders and neck tightened into pain; her jaw became rigid. Her face hurt; her teeth hurt.

At her side, Günther placed his hand on her left shoulder. "You don't have to stay, Ursula. Don't give in to this. One year will become two, then three, then five. You will *never* leave him once you decide to stay for a year. No, you must come with us."

Bronevsky half-rose. "You have no right to try to make up her mind for her. She must choose for herself. She knows her responsibilities."

"Her first responsibility is to herself," said Paul at Ursula's right.

"Choose, dear girl. Choose and do the right thing by your father. I always loved you most. Perhaps you didn't know that. But it's true, and I'm not ashamed to say it."

Suddenly the room flew into wild motion. Alexander, with a roar, hurled himself toward his father. "You never cared anything for any of us. She's not staying here. Melchior wants to stay. Let him keep you company."

Bronevsky laughed and shoved Alexander away from him. "Ursula, just one year, I promise you. After that I'll even make all the arrangements myself so that you can leave. Just say that you'll give me a year. One year." He smiled at her again, his eyes watering with new tears.

Ursula's mind finally began to lose its shock: a year was not so long, and she could help him get settled and comfortable. She would sell the Degas and . . . She stopped planning as she looked at Melchior standing behind her father, his face pale with sorrow. Why didn't her father want Melchior to stay with him? Boris, further down the table, looked pained and embarrassed. She caught his eye and saw him shake his head faintly. Alexander, biting his mouth, shook with rage. "No," he whispered. "No, Ursula, no!"

"One year," said Bronevsky, his eyes never leaving Ursula's face.

She stared into the ice-green glacier of his irises, into the black centers around which a deeper emerald star radiated. The twins had the identical eyes, the identical depth which gave their faces a mysterious quality, a certain kind of darkness one sees in very deep still water.

"Please, Günther," she said, looking at her brother, "tell me what to do."

"You know what to do. None of us has the right to make up your mind for you, he's right on that point. But *you* know what to do."

Ursula looked back at her father, and in that moment there came to her one of those decisions—instantaneous, sourceless, and without warning. "I'm going with my brothers." She heard herself say the words and marveled at the calm in her own voice. In fact, she hardly knew that it *was* her own voice, that she was going to speak at all. She had no idea how she came to her decision. She heard the twins exhale. Had they been holding their breath? She saw Alexander smile, his eyes still flashing. Boris sat down and cleared his throat.

Melchior turned back to his father, his face immensely sad. "If you change your mind about wanting *me* to stay, I'll stay."

Bronevsky's twitch pushed his left eye into a slit. "No. You go with your brothers. I don't need a priest—not yet—and particularly one that looks like you . . . one with *his* face." He spoke without looking at his son. "Ursula, perhaps you should not make up your mind so quickly. Give yourself a little time. In a few days we can talk again. There are many things you should know that could help you in your decision." His voice was soft, no longer pleading, no longer desperate.

"She has made her decision," said Alexander.

"I think not," said Bronevsky. He did not look at Alexander either. "I shall tell you one thing now, my Ursula: the doctors give me no more than a year. My health is gone. I am already a dead man. There is no cure."

"What exactly is the nature of your illness?" Günther's hand tightened on Ursula's shoulder, although his voice, too, was calm, without heat.

"I'd rather not say. There's no use in your having to share the pain. It is enough for Ursula to know that I cannot live more than a year. I don't mind that. We all owe God a death, as the saying goes." He rose unsteadily. "No, I don't mind that at all. But think on it, girl. When your grandfather was sick, you never left his side. Can you do less for me? Can you let me die alone, without friends, without loved ones, without even enough to eat? Give yourself a few hours to think about it." He turned then and walked slowly to the doors, which seemed suddenly too heavy for him to open. He stood facing the panels, his shoulders fallen forward, his hands fumbling at the ornate knobs.

Ursula saw that the back of his head was going bald; a patch of thin hair grew from a perfectly round circle where the scalp was darkened by dye that he used each week now and that turned his once lustrous hair a dull black. Ursula felt a great sadness for his lost hair, for the pathetic ring of almost bald skin that looked like it was covered with coal dust. Melchior, nearest the door, pulled the knobs back for him and Bronevsky shuffled away without another word. "He should have been an actor," said Boris after a moment.

"But perhaps he is ill. He doesn't look well," said Melchior.

"He's straight out of Dostoevski," laughed Günther without mirth. "And he will try everything now, but mostly, Ursula, he will work on pity. It's his best act. He is no more ill than I am." He looked around at his brothers. "She is not to be alone with him, not for a minute. Do you understand, Ursula? You are not to talk to him without one of us always with you."

Ursula stared at the closed door. "But what if he is sick—even dying? Schnabel said she wanted to find a place where he could repair his broken health."

"Only a stupid ploy on her part. She made up that illness, so she could get as much from the house as possible. Well, she can have whatever she wants. She is going to be a hostile ally in this mess: she needs us for the present, but she wants us to leave, and particularly, she wants you to leave. She knows that if you stay, she's out." Günther sat down and took Ursula's hand. "You made the correct decision. Don't go back on it. Can you see yourself living alone with him?"

"But Schnabel will be there."

"No. That's just it. Schnabel won't be there. Do you think that if he can get you to stay, he will keep that old hag around? He'll throw her out the moment he has you to himself and the rest of us are gone. He can't keep his social standing with her. You can open doors for him that Agnes Schneider can't even get near. And he can't open them by himself. People in this town would howl him into the street."

"But Melchior could do as much as I."

Günther hesitated. "Not exactly. It's hard to explain, Ursula. Of course, any of us could keep his present standing for him, but you . . . being a girl, beautiful, brilliant . . . you add the excitement he wants, needs. You can't stay. He'll use you . . . in ways I don't even want to think about. And he's a drunk . . . unpredictable. No. You cannot stay with him!"

[177]

"But what if he *is* dying?"

Günther grasped her by her shoulders and shook her. "Stop that. He is not dying."

Ursula felt an enormous exhaustion. She believed that if Günther released her she would drop to the floor. Inside her chest, a small cold spot began to spread rapidly. She heard her brothers talking around her, all of them telling her to stay fast to her decision, their faces close, anxious, alarmed. In a daze, she heard them only distantly, saw their faces become one, swimming in front of her. "Oh, Grandfather," she cried, "why did you give me a choice?"

For a week Ursula was ill, unable to keep food down. Twice Frichter came, but he could find nothing wrong with her. "She has no fever, complains of no pain. She's strong and healthy. It's something else. What have all of you been up to? What's been going on around here?"

"She's still mourning Grandfather," said Paul.

Frichter eyed the twins suspiciously. "Hummm," he said, refilling his brandy glass. The second time the doctor came, he wanted to talk to Miss Schneider.

"Out," said Günther, "taking care of some personal business."

"Tell her to ring me when she comes in."

The twins nodded politely, but they told the governess nothing. Her usual fawning and sycophantic behavior toward the doctor's profession brought them close to gagging. And Frichter, whom all the kids thoroughly disliked, accepted the attention with the unselfconscious complacency of an old-time courtier. He had learned early in life how to live off the nobility so that he became known as "a society doctor," a term tainted with both envy and contempt. For a number of years Ursula thought he lived at the mansion, so often was he at the dining table or comfortably moving through the house heading for tea in the solarium or her grandfather's billiard room, where he helped himself to the best brandy in the bar as he played the game. During the week of her curious illness, Ursula refused to talk to the doctor at all when he questioned her about symptoms. When he tried to examine her, merely reaching out to take her pulse, she pulled away from him. "No one will ever accuse you of being like your mother," laughed Frichter. "But one could think of a number of ways to subdue you." He smiled and ducked out of the room just as the hurtling lamp crashed against the door.

The twins brought Ursula her drawing tablets and sat for her, made jokes about their fees for modeling, and criticized her work severely, hoping to anger her. It didn't work; she shoved the sketches aside and turned her face to the wall. At night they locked her into her room. Bronevsky ate dinner now with the boys every day. He was talkative, pleasant, and drunk. He asked after Ursula in such a solicitous way that after a few days her enraged brothers ate in the kitchen.

It was Miss Schneider who finally got Ursula out of bed. One morning the woman came to visit the ailing girl, made a few pleasant comments, then told her that she had found a perfect flat and would be very busy for a few days. Ursula, watching the woman, thought that the governess had gained weight and saw that she had waved her hair around her face. On her way out, the woman stopped in front of the Degas. "Why don't I just take this now. There's a perfect spot for it in the sitting room of the flat. It will go marvelously well with your mother's blue silk settee." She reached for the painting.

From the time she was ten, Ursula had begun to sleep naked, and when the governess entered that morning the girl drew the sheets over her bare shoulders. But the moment the woman touched the frame, Ursula sprang out of her bed, snarling. "Not unless you want your arms broken." Miss Schneider staggered back as Ursula stood between her and the painting, her feet firmly planted on the carpet, somewhat apart.

Miss Schneider gasped. "But you're not wearing any clothes!"

Ursula started to laugh, then stopped abruptly. "Get out of my room; go live in your flat and . . . and take *him* with you."

Miss Schneider recovered quickly and smiled. "That's exactly what I intend to do. I'm going to take him away from you." She turned and left, closing the door softly behind her.

Ursula dressed hurriedly, locked her room, and went in search of her brothers, finding them in the library filling out stacks of forms. On the table in front of the remaining vacant chair was one stack with her name on the sheets, every space neatly filled. Only her signature was required. The boys stopped writing and watched her in silence as she read the forms, the documents that were to take her out of the country. As she sat down the twins both held their pens out to her. When she signed everything, she breathed deeply and told them about Miss Schneider and the Degas.

"We'll see that she gets a bonus for getting your lazy rump out of bed," said Günther, filling his pen from the inkwell.

"I was ready to get up today anyway. It all became clear to me last night, Melchior, when you brought me that glass of milk. I never saw you look so sad. You looked more than ever like Grandfather. You offered to stay with Father. Without any consideration for yourself, you offered to stay and take care of Father. And I know you would have sold the empress's Bible, which probably means more to you than all the other things mean to any of us. I don't care about the Degas; I've walked past it for years without even glancing at it, but you always loved that Bible. Grandfather used to let you hold it when we pushed you around. I could never understand why it made you stop crying. To me it's only an old overwritten book. I'd rather read *Lear* or *Hamlet*. I'm not sure I'll ever understand the things you like, but I know you were ready to give everything up for Father. And he turned you away. Without even thinking about what you were offering, he turned you away. If he only wanted one of us around so that he wouldn't be alone, what difference would it make which one of us it was?" Across the table from her, Melchior's large brown eyes gazed back into hers. "You were right," she continued. "Grandfather should not have left him money just for his funeral. It was a terrible thing to do."

For a time none of them spoke. The clock chimed nine. Paul laid down his pen and crossed his elbows on the table. "You want one of us to tell him, Ursula?"

"No. I told him a week ago I was going with you. I'm not going to say it again. And you don't have to lock my door at night anymore. I'll lock it on the inside."

In the weeks that followed, the children quietly selected the things they planned to take with them. They each made a list, compared them, and discovered without much surprise that the lists overlapped dozens of times. All of them agreed on the library ledgers made up by the hired scholars. Each had listed the family photograph albums, several collections of books, their grandfather's portrait, and one of their mother painted a few months before she was married. They hired a storage concern to pack all of the old man's personal effects, the remaining ancestral portraits, all the paintings, some sculptures, a set of Rosenthal Imperial Cobalt china for twenty-four, several sets of silver and crystal, and a half-dozen large clocks. Berghoch, with a wary eye, watched the packers like a suspicious customs officer.

The children selected what clothes still fit them, leaving the rest to the nephews and nieces of the two maids. They carefully packed the individual items mentioned in their grandfather's letters to them. Only Alexander's guns gave them a problem. He wanted to take them *all* with him. Günther phoned the law firm and made inquiries. No guns across the border. Alexander raged, cursed, wept. They finally had the law firm sell all but the emperor's personal hunting gun, which they dismantled, placing the parts in different cases. They slipped the erotic art books into a trunk carrying Ursula's sketches, workbooks, and the family photo albums.

Their father stayed pleasantly drunk, seemingly oblivious of the children's activities. On several occasions he announced to them that he had business to attend to in the city and would not be in for lunch. They watched him leave, his motions studied with sustained control, the marks of that variety of alcoholic who can still function while deeply drunk. At other times he spoke of his own university days fondly, voicing the hope that the boys would do well in school and come back men of stature and respect. He did not mention Ursula. Several times the twins urged her to remind him that she was going away, too. But she refused, saying that he understood her the first time.

Miss Schneider was all helpfulness and pleasantry. "Oh, you'll forget all about us," she gushed with mock dismay. "You'll be too busy with new friends and social evenings to give us a second thought. You'll dance all night while we fade into old age and wither away."

Ursula knew the governess was as resourceful as a spider, having seen her vanquish all the other tutors who ever came to the house, but even she was astonished at the amount of furniture the woman had carted off to her flat. They denied her nothing. When she shyly asked for a valuable silver tea set and its carved ebony serving cart, Günther nodded pleasantly and said, "By all means, take it. Use it in good health."

The maids, too, asked for linen and china and were not refused. What they wanted but were afraid to ask for, they stole. "Let them steal what they want," said Günther. "Better them than strangers." The gardener wanted only the tools, and the children were glad to give them to him. The cook wanted the carving set and some of the wines.

On a cold April morning Rätzel was reburied beside his friend, as the children stood in a tight little knot unable to keep from weeping. The following night, they spirited the gardener up to the playroom. "We found a body," wrote Günther on a pad, "a skeleton. Someone who was killed in the war. He needs a new home." They took the sheet off Adolphus and waited for Graz to go into shock. But he did nothing of the sort. "I remember when you brought him in," he said. "I used to follow you on some of your little trips. Your grandfather was afraid you'd get yourselves arrested, but we soon knew better."

Ursula gasped. "He knew?"

The gardener smiled at their astonished faces and nodded his head. Two hours later, under the light of a cold moon, they lowered Adolphus, wrapped in his sheet, into Rätzel's old grave.

The auction was to be held at the end of May, but as the time drew close, it was clear that the children's father was going to be a much greater problem about selling the house than he led them to believe. As yet, Miss Schneider had not been able to get him to visit the flat, although she said it was "exactly like the house" and that he would want for nothing. For some weeks he had been wandering about the house at night, complaining loudly that certain possessions of his were missing and that he intended to get to the bottom of things.

Two days before the scheduled auction, a whole army of efficient clerks came to the house and tagged and numbered everything that wasn't nailed down and a few things that were. A grim-faced Berghoch stood guard in front of the storage room which held the children's trunks and packed crates. Only Bronevsky's rooms remained untouched. Walking through the house with Alexander late the same afternoon, Ursula went into a spasm of shivering, her teeth chattering.

"Are you cold?"

She shook her head. "It's the house. It's dying around us. Those little white tags dangling off everything. They look like bone flaking off. It's horrible. Alexander, I have terrible nightmares. Last night I dreamed I was walking through a great human skeleton, ribs as tall as this house curling above me."

"Don't think about it. Think of how wonderful it will be in a new place."

The following day, Brückner arrived. "Just to make certain that everything is in order," he said, walking through the lower rooms, examining a tag fluttering from a chair, another taped to a piano, one dangling from a tapestry in the dining room. Miss Schneider offered him coffee. Yes, he might; he had a few extra minutes to spare. "Also, dear lady, I wanted to make sure that Mr. Bronevsky will not be here tomorrow. At our last conversation, you said he would be moved out by now."

Miss Schneider excused herself for a moment and hurried to the kitchen, where the children were writing notes to the gardener. "The lawyer's here." She motioned to Berghoch to bring coffee, and spoke anxiously to the children. "I don't know what to tell him. He thinks your father has already moved."

"Where is Father?" asked Günther.

"I haven't seen him today. I knocked at his door, but received no answer. He may be sleeping late."

"No, he's up," said Boris. "I saw him from my window early this morning. He was walking in the garden."

Miss Schneider frowned deeply. "Walking in the garden? He never walks in the garden anymore. What in the world was he doing walking in the garden? Why didn't you tell someone? Take in the coffee. Mr. Brückner may have some last-minute instructions for you. I'll check the garden." She hurried out toward the back of the house.

Günther turned to Ursula. "Don't break anything of Brückner's. He billed us for his new nose." Paul handed her the loaded coffee tray. Günther nodded. "Good thinking. Now, just pour and we'll get rid of him as soon as possible."

In the dining room, the lawyer was examining one of the tapestries, running the pads of his fingers over the pattern. "That should fetch a hefty price. Wouldn't mind having that myself."

"You're welcome to it," said Günther.

"No, no. Not ethical. Couldn't even think of taking it."

"Of course you could," said Ursula sweetly, pouring his coffee. "We would love for you to have it." Ursula saw Günther give her a beetled look.

"Well, perhaps . . . No! What am I thinking? Of course I can't take it. The idea! Let's get on to business. There are only a few matters left to consider: minor ones to be sure, but still they must be seen to. Now, everything sold at auction must be picked up by Saturday, which leaves us without beds for two days."

"Actually," said Boris, "it leaves *us* without beds."

Brückner almost smiled. "Very droll, but the fact remains, you'll have no place to sleep for two days."

"Why won't they have anyplace to sleep?" Bronevsky, murderously sober, strolled in from the hall, clutching a handful of white tickets, the strings dangling between his fingers like a clutch of boiled spaghetti. He threw them on the table. "What are these doing on the furniture?"

"Sir!" shouted Brückner. "You have removed the auction tickets." He picked one up. "All coded, of course. Oh, this is deplorable."

"What auction?"

"You know very well what auction."

"I don't recall any auction."

The children, still standing, gave each other sidelong looks as Brückner rushed on. "Everything in this house will be sold by tomorrow night."

"No. That's not possible. The accumulations that two centuries of old money could collect are in this house, and you have the gall to stand there and tell me that it is all going to be swept away in a few hours. You, sir, are mad!"

Brückner rubbed his forehead, leaving a red blotch on his thin pale skin. He looked angrily at the twins. "How long has this act been going on?" Both boys gestured emptily with their hands.

Bronevsky faced the children also. "You mean you know about this? This . . . this auction?"

"Yes, Father," said Melchior. "There is going to be an auction. Everything is going to be sold."

Bronevsky breathed fast. "What will Ursula and I use for furniture? How will we live? We need our furniture. You can't be so cruel as to hurt your poor little sister in this way. No, no, I won't permit her to suffer. She must have the best. My dear sweet child. My only daughter. We must have all

[182]

of it. Everything. No beds? Absurd. What nonsense." He pulled a chair up to Ursula's. "Now, my lovely girl, we have plans to make. We shall travel. Imagine the two of us in Paris, Monaco, Rome, Madrid." He smiled sweetly, taking her hand, brushing it across his mustache, kissing her fingers, her palm.

Ursula pulled her hand away. "No! No! I'm not going with you."

"But you love to travel. I have the itinerary all made out. We will be the toast of all Europe. You'll see. Everyone will talk of it."

Ursula saw her brothers' horrified faces through the haze of her own anger. "No," she said, not very loud. "No, Father. I am going away to school with my brothers."

He still smiled, still gazed at her, his eyes softening, vague. He rose slowly. "Yes . . . well . . . yes, I see." He backed out of the room as Ursula rose to go toward him, but Günther suddenly held her arm.

"I want to explain . . ." she said miserably. "I want him to understand . . ." She saw Günther shake his head. A few moments later they heard their father on the stairs and briefly on the upper gallery.

Through his tears Bronevsky saw the white tags hanging from the rearing marble horses guarding the entry to the octagonal room. "An auction! Everything to be bought and destroyed by peasants," he said aloud to one of the house's many mirrors as he reached the upper gallery. "I am fifty-one years old. Who would have thought I could become fifty-one years old? I should have done it before I was forty!" he whispered to the face he no longer recognized. "No. Before then. In Paris. Or even before that. I should have returned to Russia and fought and died. I should never have come to Vienna. I should have gone home." He saw that the bulge below his waistcoat was larger than ever. "Gone home! Yes, I should have done something noble, honorable, courageous. I would have been a great officer . . . without an ounce of fat. Without a bulge. I would have fought like a wolf. To the end. I could have been great. Even if it meant death. At least it would have been a great death." The face in the glass twitched back at him with a vulgar wink. "I can't bear you anymore. I can't bear your stupid bulge. It isn't mine. It's not what I am. You think it's what I am. But you're wrong. I am . . . I am . . . I am young and my dear Rodina waits for me." He ran to his suite; his body felt as light as a young boy's. "I will ride her into the forest where the snow is deep and still and pure." He was himself astride his beloved mare riding toward the white birch trees. All was calm. He took the revolver from its case. It was the only speck of color. He was all in white—the winter uniform of the cossacks. Rodina pranced deeper among the sleeping trees. Her hooves made no sound in the deep snow. He held the reins with great joy as he looked up at the white sky. "This is what I am," he said. "This! This is what I am."

Miss Schneider entered the dining room wringing her hands. "I can't find him anywhere. Boris, are you sure it was he?"

"He went upstairs, Miss Schneider," said Melchior, "but I thought I heard him come back down just a few minutes ago."

[183]

"He did? Just now? How did he seem to you?" She looked from face to face.

It was the lawyer who answered. "He seemed remarkably calm when he was in here."

"Oh, you have no idea how glad I am to hear that. It's been such a trial. Perhaps now he can get some peace. He's so frequently indisposed."

"He was sober," said Günther.

"He . . . wasn't indisposed?"

"He was sober," repeated Günther.

Miss Schneider looked toward the open door, squinting past it into the dim hall. Ursula thought the woman was going to leave; in fact, it seemed to her that as Miss Schneider leaned forward, some part of her which was not body at all was already out of the room, already walking past the great stairs and glancing into various rooms, already hesitantly calling his name.

"I expect you to have him out of here by tomorrow," said Brückner to the preoccupied woman.

"Yes, yes. I understand all that, but just now, I better see if . . . that is, I think . . . This is most unusual. You'll have to excuse me; I must see if he's all right."

"He's sober, so he's all right. But I must have your guarantee that he will be out of the house before the auction."

Miss Schneider still seemed to be out of the room as she peered into the hall. "Yes. Yes. Whatever you say. Only just now I have to see to something else."

"Woman, sit down!" Brückner's near-shout jolted Miss Schneider out of her trance.

"You needn't shout, Mr. Brückner."

"Apparently I do have to shout to get anyone's attention. Now, these tags have to be replaced today. I'll send one of the clerks over with the list. Match the number of the tag with the item on the list and tie the tag back onto the correct item. Is that clear?"

"Yes." Miss Schneider was fidgeting with a button on her blouse.

"Very well. Then be sure to send the list back. No, better yet, have the clerk wait and carry the list back." He hesitated. "Yes, that's best. It shouldn't take more than a few hours."

"Good, we'll do that then straightaway," said the governess.

"Do what?" asked Brückner.

"Whatever you said."

"Miss Schneider, you don't seem to hear me."

A single shot filled the house with echoes, quivering the crystals on the chandelier. Miss Schneider began to scream, "No, no, no," as she rushed toward the gaping door and into the foyer.

The children found their father seated at their grandfather's fine leather-inlaid desk, his head resting low on the wing of the chair where the force of the bullet shoved him, bits of his right frontal lobe spattered against a lamp's white-tagged parchment shade, one eye dangling from a purple stalk on his right cheek, the bridge of his nose sunken into a rosette of blood bubbles.

16

In later years, when memory of certain events merged with distorted dreams of the same events, Ursula was to confuse her dying mother's screams with those of Agnes Schneider as the woman knelt before the slouching corpse of Pavel Bronevsky and held his bloody hand to her chest. (The pistol had fallen under the desk, where Paul retrieved it, lest the grief-maddened governess use it on herself.) When the boys tried to help her up, she struck at them with her free hand and screamed "Murderers!" Ursula, as tall as Miss Schneider and physically stronger, finally pulled her away from the dead man and dragged her, still shrieking, out into the gallery, where the white-tagged, gold-leafed picture frames, empty now of their ancestral portraits, still hung on the walls. Here Ursula propped the governess on a low red velvet empire bench from which the woman slid to the floor, lying prone, her curses reduced to moans, a large glob of saliva running from her open mouth as she twisted her head from side to side on the veined marble squares. Ursula, squatting on her heels, reached into the woman's dress pocket and pulled out a handkerchief. She began to wipe the governess's mouth in a clumsy patting motion, but Miss Schneider snatched the cloth away from her, which led the girl to believe fleetingly that the woman was more conscious of her own actions than she let on. She stopped rolling her head and focused her eyes on Ursula's in a steady stream of hatred. "You— you alone killed him," she said in a voice abruptly composed and cold. "You let him believe you were going to stay with him. You did it to torment me and to kill him. You killed him. You! You!"

Ursula straightened up and backed away, bumping into Brückner, who grasped her arm to keep her steady. "Nonsense," he said casually. "Get off the floor and get someone to clean up the mess." He motioned with his head toward the library. "This auction is going to be held tomorrow exactly as planned." Ursula saw that he held the pistol by the barrel in his left hand. Miss Schneider rose slowly and began to weep again. "And stop that wailing. Now, the police will be here in a few minutes to take away the body. I'll take care of all the questions. You see that the help keeps everything orderly. I expect at least a semblance of decorum be maintained even under these circumstances. I consider what this man did to be in extremely bad taste." Miss Schneider gulped back her sobs. "Move, woman. We don't have all day. I've already had to cancel half my afternoon appointments." Through this speech, Brückner kept a firm grip on Ursula's arm.

Miss Schneider took a step toward the lawyer. "You! You are as guilty as she. You are his killer too. You monster! You let him believe, hope, dream. You have no right to live. God should strike you dead . . . dead, dead! And her too. All of you are his murderers!"

"Get out of my sight," snarled Brückner. "You're disgusting." He turned away from the woman and guided Ursula back to the dining room. But Ursula, looking over her shoulders, saw the governess's plier face open and close, open and close, her mouth working furiously, without sound, without even breath.

In the dining room, Brückner pushed Ursula gently into a chair. "What I have to say I want to say to you alone, before your brothers come in." He sat down in a chair facing her. "Listen to me, and understand me clearly. You are in no way responsible for this. Neither are your brothers. This man chose to die! What he did was cowardly, and you are never to think of his act in any other way."

Ursula looked at Brückner's nose. It didn't look broken, but then slowly the ridge of it began to cave in and one of his eyes popped out of its sockets and hung on his cheek by a glistening blue string. She shook her head and the dangling eye vanished. He was talking again, his nose perfectly attached. "Cowardly!" She heard footsteps in the gallery and looked away from Brückner's stern face. Moments later her brothers came in. None of them was crying. It seemed to Ursula that their faces were very large and open, like faded tulips just before the petals fall. Ursula watched them walk to chairs and sit down, their movements benumbed, sluggish, absent of feeling or purpose, yet oddly stiff. Someone took her hand and stroked it. She knew without looking that it was Günther.

"Did you cover him?" asked the lawyer. "Good."

Someone must have nodded, thought Ursula, since there was no audible answer.

"For months," began the lawyer, "he's been coming to our offices to tell us that your sister was not leaving, that she had elected to stay with him. Of course, we knew this was not true. He tried to hire someone to break the will, but the legal business here is a pretty closed club and we got wind of it before he was back on the street. We told the other firm to stall him. They did."

"How?" asked Melchior.

"The way all fools can be stalled—with hope."

There was a deadly silence. Ursula felt Günther tighten his hold on her hand.

"Could he have broken the will?" asked Paul.

"No. But he could have petitioned for a hearing on guardianship, which would have delayed everything, and which possibly, quite possibly, he might have won." No one said anything and it seemed to Ursula that a long time passed before the lawyer spoke again. "I'll make arrangements to move you to a hotel tonight. Better to get out of this house now. This kind of auction can be quite disturbing and with the trip ahead of you, you're already facing enough stress. I'll phone for a car after the police leave." On the lawyer's last word, they all heard the two-tone siren closing in on the house like fire.

A long time later, when Ursula tried to reconstruct those first few hours after she saw her father's mutilated face, she could only build an airy structure of events dangerously dominated by empty spaces held in place by a few concrete components: Paul picking up the gun which she next saw in Brückner's hand; Miss Schneider rolling on the floor accusing her of murder, then running up the stairs like a cripple because she had only one shoe on; Brückner's dry mouth saying that she, Ursula, was not guilty but that her father possibly had a right to keep his daughter with him; she, in her room, not even knowing that it was for the last time, curled up small in a deep chair by the window while people came and went—Alexander, Günther and Paul, one of the maids, and finally the gardener, who picked up her traveling case and motioned her to follow him. She could not remember whether anyone spoke to her. In the foyer, Günther took her hand and they walked out onto the terrace. Somewhere behind her someone was weeping steadily, monotonously. And then, unaccountably, she smelled her mother's soap, the large lavender oval bars that came wrapped in tissue paper, four to a box stored in the same closet which held her mother's ivory-colored lace-edged bed linen and where as a small child she used to hide playfully from Alexander, the scent covering her like a warm blanket.

She stopped walking and turned to Günther. "It's Mother . . ."

He nodded and pulled her on. "The lilacs."

A long car stood in the driveway and when it began to move, she was in it with her brothers. A moment before the car reached the main gate, Ursula looked out of the window just in time to see a naked man reclining peacefully under an arbor of chestnut trees, his upper body leaning back on one elbow, his other hand hanging over a raised knee. She had an impulse to wave, and for a moment her mind even saw her hand rise in a final salute, but then she saw that that could not have happened because Paul was holding her left hand and Günther her right one, so she started to turn her head toward the naked man as the car passed him, but someone whispered, "Don't look back." And through those words, which seemed to hang in front of her like a printed sign, she caught a glimpse of the white marble man. It was Hermes, the messenger of the gods. She imagined him rising, stretching and expanding until he was taller than the house which he walked into, crushing every wall and roof and then stomping with his bare stone feet upon the debris until it was only dust puffing up between his toes. She shuddered and Günther quickly put his arm around her.

Brückner met them at the hotel, where they had a suite of rooms connected by a little hall. Ursula wondered what the lawyer had done with the gun he was carrying around by the barrel and if Miss Schneider had found her other shoe. It was under the red velvet bench in the gallery if anyone wanted to know.

"Your possessions have been taken to the depot, so there's no concern there. They'll go on ahead of you. The best thing for you to do now is get some rest." He hesitated a moment, then seemed to release a large breath. "There is one more matter, of course." He walked around the sitting room, pausing once to look out the window. "Do you want to attend the funeral?"

At that question Ursula lurched out of her daze, realizing that her mind had not really been working at all. She sat up straight in her chair, arching her back. "Yes."

Brückner turned to her, an expression bordering on alarm on his usually imperturbable face. "You don't have to, you know."

"Yes, we do."

Her brothers were all staring at her; Günther, the closest, frowned hard at her. "You want to?"

"We have to. I remember very little about mother: the pearls she wore on my fourth-birthday dinner. There were three long strands held together at the back of her neck by a sparkling clasp, and she was always touching them, her hand would sort of drift up to them, feel them a bit, and then drift away again. And I remember the scent of her soap, and why I never again went in the front door of the house after she died, because that was where the lilac bushes grew. All the other times that I remember were the sick times, which all run together into the last night when she was dead and someone lifted me up to kiss her. The day before her funeral I heard Grandfather arguing with someone. The other person—I don't remember who he was—insisted that we children shouldn't be made to go to the funeral, but Grandfather said that we had to see it to the end, had to live it to its finish so that we could be through with it and not have to carry that death around with us all the time."

Paul started to speak but stopped.

"What?" said Ursula, looking into his tear-shining eyes.

"You may have forgotten this, Ursula, but you had terrible nightmares about that funeral."

"I haven't forgotten. I had them for about a month. It took me a long time to figure out why I had them and why they ended. After Mother died, Grandfather stopped doing what he did before. He stopped going for walks; he stopped having tea with us; he stopped reading. Remember? After a while, he even stopped eating. I used to go looking for him and I always found him in the same place: he went into that little space off his study, that sort of alcove concealed by a heavy black curtain. And there he would lie in the dark all day. I used to sit in his big chair for hours and wait for him to come out. At night before I went to sleep I thought of him in that dark little space in the wall. I began to believe that he was trying to die. And it scared me. I believed that one day I would open the curtain and he would be dead. Then, when he tore down all the wreaths and all the black cloths on Mother's pictures and he didn't lie in that horrible little hole anymore, my nightmares stopped."

Brückner sat down and reached for his briefcase leaning against his chair. "What about the rest of you?"

Ursula did not look at her brothers. She heard Günther clear his throat. "We shall all go," he said.

"And," added Ursula, "we want him fixed up."

Brückner's briefcase slid off his knees. Alexander picked it up and handed it back to him as the lawyer leaned toward Ursula with the expression of a man unused to listening to the opinions of others. He opened and shut the clasp on his case. "Just what do you mean by fixed up?"

Ursula searched Günther's face, then Paul's. In each, she saw total acquiescence. Melchior and Alexander nodded slowly. Boris crossed his knees and looked as though he had just rendered a diagnosis.

[188]

"We mean," said Ursula slowly, "that we want him repaired, that we want his face put back together again. I know that it can be done. I read it in a book: they do it with putty and . . . things; and the eye . . ."

"The eye can be returned to its socket," finished Günther.

Brückner clapped his hand to his forehead. "I don't believe what I'm hearing! This is sheer stupidity! And, I might add, an immense waste of money."

"It's his money," said Ursula.

Brückner opened his mouth, but snapped it shut again, his teeth making a loud click. He rose, his birchbark face set so that his jawbone was clearly visible beneath the stretched skin. "I may assume from this . . . this absurdity that you wish to have an open-coffin service."

"Yes," said Ursula. "He should be dressed in evening clothes, and wearing his cape . . . and his white gloves. Miss Schneider knows where all those things are."

"Miss Schneider seems to have disappeared."

"Disappeared?" It was Melchior who asked, while the others looked on in puzzlement.

"No one saw her after I ordered her to clean up the library. The other women searched the house, but they could not find her."

"Perhaps she went to her flat," said Boris.

"No," said Ursula. "She's still in the house. Look in Father's rooms. She'll be there."

The lawyer shrugged. "Well, it's no great matter. The gardener can bring the necessary clothes to the mortician. The woman will show up sooner or later to collect her bequest."

"Sooner," said Ursula. "She will be at the funeral. She is not finished with us yet." She saw the lawyer watch her with curiosity.

In the following three days, the children stayed in the hotel, except for the early-morning hours before the city awakened to its daily travail of getting on with the business of living: the trams groaning and creaking on their tracks, delivery trucks lumbering on ancient cobbles, and everywhere the haggling and bickering and humorless joking of shopkeepers and housewives. The Bronevsky children did not run down the old streets as they did during the two years they spent searching for the city's heart. They walked long distances now without hurrying, without speaking. Ursula felt a profound melancholy that she sensed also in her brothers. They did not discuss their father's final act, although Ursula knew that they thought of it as constantly as she did and were watching her anxiously for some kind of bad reaction. What had Brückner said? "This man chose to die." Chose to die! Her mother too had let life slip away indifferently, carelessly. They must have gone mad. How else could one give up the world, never to feel again, never to know again? How could someone give all that up willingly? It was beyond sense, beyond imagination.

At times they all stopped to gaze over some ruin, already softened by time and the weather so that the city had a quality of antiquity to it, a sense of Rome, of Greece, of loss. Ursula could not seem to see enough of the old avenues and abrupt squares, cobblestoned and empty except for the pigeons and gulls that strutted and picked over the damp spots. She knew

[189]

that she was trying to memorize the city for the days when she would need to bring it back to her, when she would need to hold it in her mind the way she might hold in her hands a crystal globe containing the city in miniature, even in its wounded state with the soft wash of dawn-colored houses and shops and churches all perfectly held in time, unchanging, permanent, and dear. What did it matter that its people were flawed with Olympian pride as Boris so often said, or baggaged down with ostentatious good manners, or repressed with counterfeit modesty? What were those flaws, anyway, except the weapons which one used to stay alive? Anything was fair against death. She always came back to her father's bizarre act. Perhaps if she had loved him, if all of them had loved him . . . ? She knew her brothers were haunted by the same question.

On the third morning, near the cathedral, they came upon two jeeps with dented fenders full of soldiers involved in a trilingual argument. Usually the children would have darted down an alley or side street to avoid being questioned, but this was their last day in Vienna and they were armed with passports. At eleven they were to bury their father. At three they were to leave the city of their birth and the great mansion that had sheltered them all their lives. These overwhelming concerns inured them to little dangers.

The children stopped near the jeeps and watched as an American and a Russian driver, neither of whom understood the other's language, leaned over his windshield and bombarded the other with foreign insults. When Alexander laughed, a soldier in the American bunch nudged another next to him and gestured with a hitchhiker's thumb toward the boys and Ursula.

One of the Russians spoke to them angrily in rough German. "Why you out late?"

Günther answered him in Russian. "We are not out late; we are out early."

The Russian grinned a mouth full of large teeth at the children. "Ah, you see, comrades, I told you it would happen. Already the people are becoming Russian." He waved both arms in an expansive, encompassing gesture, as though the six children were the entire population of the city. "There, you see, already they speak our tongue. And not too badly, either. Say something else, pretty boy."

Ursula heard Alexander curse under his breath. "I'd like to punch that pig's fat snoot."

"Shut up," whispered Günther. "We don't need any trouble with them."

Ursula felt Alexander shake beside her. She wrapped her hand around his clenched fist hanging like an anchor at his side, smiled sweetly at the men in the second jeep, and asked in English, "How is your airlift going in Berlin?"

Günther groaned. "Good God! Be quiet," he whispered harshly.

A Britisher in the American jeep roared with laughter and one of the Americans jumped out of the vehicle and looked the children over, up and down, across, a cigarette pinched between his teeth. "It's coming along just fine, sweetheart." He spoke without removing the cigarette from his mouth and continued to gaze at them in an estimating, speculative way, a smile forming behind the little puffs of smoke.

"He looks as if he's thinking of packaging us," whispered Ursula to Alexander. "Maybe we should leave."

The second American jumped out of the jeep. "What did the commie say to them?" he said, looking back at the man in British uniform.

"Oh, he's convinced that the Austrians are becoming Russian because the lad answered him in Russian."

"Yeah? He *would* come to that conclusion, wouldn't he?"

"It's a possibility."

"Like hell it is."

One of the Russians got out and came up to the two Americans. "What about the jeep?"

"Go stick it up your ass," said the American driver without any heat.

"What? What? Stick?"

A second Russian with a flat Mongolian face got out of the jeep and came up to the first: he wanted to know what the American had said. The first Russian shrugged and raised his hands emptily, flapping them down again.

"He said to take your jeep and stick it up your ass," said Alexander joyfully in Russian.

Ursula felt herself jerked suddenly backward, losing Alexander's fist. Someone held her firmly by one wrist and was pulling her away from the four uniformed men, who were no longer standing apart, but who now seemed to form a loose struggling knot. She saw the remaining four men in the two jeeps jump out of their vehicles and run into the tangle of flailing arms and legs and bouncing heads. Then she screamed, "Alexander," wrenched her wrist free, and flew back toward the fight, where she saw Alexander's blue sweater appear, disappear, and reappear among the large blocks of drab uniforms. But Paul caught her, and this time he encircled her waist and lifted her completely off her kicking feet, carrying her back to a doorway, where Melchior and Boris firmly held onto her wrists. Over her shoulder she could see Günther running around the circle of men as though he were looking for an entrance to a tower. He collided with Paul, who ran in the same circle from the opposite direction. Suddenly one of the drab uniform shapes broke free, holding a struggling Alexander up by his armpits and depositing him next to the twins.

Above all the other shouting, Ursula clearly heard the man say in American English, "Get the hell out of here! All of you!" She saw Günther and Paul grab Alexander, whose mouth was bleeding, and drag him cursing and spitting away from the eight soldiers, who seemed to be thoroughly enjoying themselves.

After running down a side street and turning a second corner, the children stopped. Günther stood in front of Alexander and examined his younger brother's cut lip. "It's nothing," he said, "you were lucky." Then he slapped him hard across the face. Alexander held his arms rigid against his sides as Günther slapped him twice more before he moved on to Ursula. "His stupidity I can understand; he doesn't have your brains." He raised his hand. Ursula tightened her face and closed her eyes. But the blow never came; when she opened her eyes after a few seconds, she saw Günther scowling deeply, the hand opened to strike only moments before now closed and pulling at his chin.

"Finish it," said Paul, "if you think you have to."

Günther continued to scowl at Ursula. "I don't know what she's guilty of." He thought a moment longer. "Don't smile at soldiers," he said angrily as he turned away and started walking again.

Ursula and Alexander fell in behind the others. "I punched that fat slob right in the belly," whispered Alexander. "He made a big 'oof' so I know I got him good."

"What a difference there is in the smell of those people," said Ursula. "The Americans smell like cigarettes and chewing gum and shaving soap. Even their sweat smells good. The Russians smell like wet foxes."

Back at the hotel they had breakfast in uneasy, angry silence. Brückner was to pick them up in the limousine at ten and take them to the mortuary. He had spent three days trying to talk them out of attending the funeral. The boys had listened politely, thanked him, and said it had to be done. Ursula would not listen to him at all.

When the lawyer arrived he looked agitated and told them that they could still change their minds. The boys shook their heads as Ursula pulled on a pair of her mother's silk-lined gloves and pretended not to listen. She had carefully sorted through her mother's wardrobe and kept everything that fit, giving the rest away to the two maids. She did not know at the time that the suits and dresses she elected to keep were originally designed for her mother and made of the richest fabrics. She had no particular knowledge of styles and even less interest in them. Three years were to pass before she would discover what had happened to her mother's jewels, that vast collection of diamond and emerald rings and necklaces, earrings, brooches, and bracelets—an accumulation of over two hundred years of gifts placed lovingly, even if anxiously, into the delicate hands of the dangerously fragile Enerde brides and rare daughters. Ursula knew that her mother had worn other jewels, but her memory of them was unclear save for the diamond-clasped three strands of purest pearls, recalled only because of Amalia's unconscious habit of floating her hand over them. Years later, Ursula was to realize that that gesture had its origin in the slow prayer roll of the rosary.

There was to be no religious ceremony for the children's father. Brückner had turned the whole matter of Bronevsky's burial over to a mortician, who listened with increasing rapture as the lawyer read him the specific instructions for the funeral: the body was to be surgically and cosmetically reconstructed, clothed in evening attire, and placed into a bronze casket identical to the one that contained his wife. These were the children's wishes. Brückner added some of his own: a layman with knowledge of the appropriate language was to be hired to say the necessary words at the service. There was to be no music. And finally, in accordance with Enerde's will, the body was to be interred in the family plot, where there was a space waiting for it beside his wife.

The mortician was delighted: it was a good order, an expensive order like in the old days when people had money for such things and did them up properly. Poor funerals depressed him; they gave death a bad name. Everybody always felt better when there was a big splash. He hoped there would be many mourners. Word-of-mouth publicity was the best kind, no doubt about it.

He called a physician acquaintance of his to whom he owed a favor for having thrown some business his way. Would he like an easy, cushy, extremely well-paying job doing a little surgery with no chance of the patient dying? The doctor would.

Next he called his brother-in-law, a real dope who at forty was still only a clerk in a shoe store and who was always in debt up to his nostrils. But he had a deep, passionate voice and he bragged that many people told him he should have been an actor. Well, here was his chance. "You better come over and pick up the stuff so you can rehearse it. The guy has a Russian name. Better to get it right rather than offend the family if the pronunciation isn't just so." The aspiring actor wanted to know if he would get paid. "Of course you'll get paid; about ten times what you're worth."

When the children arrived at the mortuary, the director led them at once to the largest room in the establishment, where their father's body lay deeply bedded in the plush satin lining of the costly casket. Ten rows of chairs, fifteen to a row, with more being added as the children entered the room, astonished Ursula. It was the children's understanding that the whole thing would be quiet and private, with only themselves and the servants in attendance. Melchior had invited Brückner, but the man only gave a curt nod; and none of them knew if that meant he would be at the service or if he was only acknowledging the invitation, and none of them cared.

The physician's needlework and the mortician's clay and putty had brought back Broncvsky's good looks. A puttied eyelid with a strip of thick theatrical lashes neatly concealed the crushed right eyeball, itself more or less reshaped with a hypo of fluid. The doctor, working from a twenty-year-old photograph of the children's father, and tantalized at the idea of performing a little plastic surgery, pulled the fallen cheeks back to their youthful heights, sewing the slack skin in under the sideburns. Magically the pouches disappeared, and with a little tucking and stitching and wiring, the graceful line of the jaw, an elegant feature all of the children had inherited, returned. He cut out the oyster sacks under the skin below the eyes, rolled the excess folds upward, and glued the lids shut. The happy doctor considered the repair of the gaping hole on the right temple his best work. He borrowed the corpse's patella, skin and all, sawed the bone into the proper shape until it matched the left temple perfectly, and with a few smears of putty covering the stitches, and the graying hair freshly darkened with shoe polish and combed to cover the upper portion, the forehead had the smooth contour of a boy of twelve. The physician constructed a new nose out of clay and glued it over the debris of the shattered one, using a flesh-toned putty to give the feature its final former delicate molding and a satin-smooth finish. The mortician applied the final makeup: the powder, a touch of cinnamon rouge to suggest a tan, and more shoe polishing of the winged eyebrows and the combed mustache, which he curled out to delicate points.

When they were finished, the night before the funeral, the doctor and the mortician, gazing at the formally dressed corpse lying regally in its padded satin coffin, were immensely pleased with themselves. "By God," said the doctor, "he was a handsome devil."

"It's the noble blood. It shows every time. You never get this delicacy in ordinary people. I'm glad we took our time and brought him back to his true self." The mortician pulled out his pocket watch and studied it. "He'll hold up for about twelve to fifteen hours, more or less, in this weather. Well, that's all he needs. It's just after midnight now and the service is at eleven tomorrow. There's going to be only a short eulogy, so the guests can spend the rest of the hour enjoying themselves looking at him. At noon we'll seal him up and take him to Central and put him beside his wife, where, as far as anyone knows, he'll look like that forever. You know, that's the satisfying thing in this business: knowing that people go away from here really believing that the body is always going to look exactly the way they last saw it."

When the mortician directed the children to the coffin, he preceded them by a few feet and then stepped aside to watch their expressions and listen to their comments. They disappointed him: their faces disguised all emotion and they never uttered a word. Unable to accept their silence, he attempted to drag compliments from them. "Now, doesn't he look absolutely marvelous?" He paused, waiting, believing that good manners alone would compel them to praise the work. If not praise in their own words, then at least agree with his. "You know, the job was extremely difficult, but I think we pulled it off splendidly, don't you?" Silence. "It took us all day yesterday, and far into last night. Some of us didn't get a wink of sleep." More silence. The man backed away, believing that it was grief that kept the children from appreciating the obvious quality of the work done on the corpse. Well, others, not so stricken, would quickly recognize the excellent finished product, and they were bound to make the comments he loved to hear: "Oh my, how beautiful he looks." "And such a peaceful expression." "Why, he seems only to be sleeping. In a moment he'll sit up and laugh with us again." Such statements always brought a tear of joy to his eyes and a lyrical lift to his heart.

The only way Ursula knew that the man in the coffin was really her father was the fact that except for his mustache he looked exactly like the twins. And for her this was the real shock, even when a split second after recognizing a father turned triplet she saw again the shattered face from the library and she thought: No, I shall not keep that bloody mess in my heart or memory or will or whatever space those horrors insist upon invading and clinging to. I shall not. Only this. I shall remember only this, even though it is bizarre and outrageous—him looking eighteen and wearing rouge. If that's the choice, it will have to be this.

She believed then, standing in front of the overpriced coffin, that because she had decreed it, she would never again see the hanging eyeball, or the monstrous mole-shaped shadow outside her room, or the weeping drunk fumbling across a table trying to pat her hand as he begged her not to deny him. She believed absolutely, in the same way that some people believe legal contracts are by nature moral because of their legality, that she had made a pact with herself which was forever inviolate. What she failed to remember then was the uncontrollable, irrational nature of dreams, those harbingers of news—sometimes already old and almost always too late—coming from the netherworld of the subconscious as close and as distant as hell. Instead, she looked upon the corpse with the belief that she was finishing something forever, that (as her grandfather had once argued) she was seeing a thing to its end so that she would not have to carry this death with her for the rest of her life.

She was glad to see that his hands were gloved as she had requested and that a white ascot concealed his neck, which had begun to get scrawny in the last two or three years. He lay on his black cape with small equal portions of it drawn up around the edge of his shoulders, the garment rolled back an inch to reveal its luxuriant white satin lining.

Only when Ursula turned away from the casket did she realize that the boys had left it and were already seated in the first of the many rows of chairs. She sat between Günther and Paul, none of them speaking, all of them waiting for what they believed would be a short, simple, uncomplicated service because they knew that Brückner, who arranged it, wanted it out of the way and done with as quickly as possible.

Graz was the first of the servants to arrive. He walked to the casket, took a quick glance, and walked away again, to sit in the back of the room in the last row. The two middle-aged maids, wearing their church hats, came together, both weeping quietly as they gazed into the casket, one of them whispering, "To die so young. What a world!" They, too, retreated to the last row of seats. The cook walked past the body without looking at it and went straight out the side door. When Frichter showed up, he studied the corpse for a full five minutes, his hands behind his fat square back. Ursula thought she heard him whistling faintly to himself. Finally he turned, nodded to the children, and sat in the row directly behind them.

An interminable fifteen minutes passed, during which Ursula could hear above the occasional snuffling of the two maids a door somewhere open and close with that attempt at secrecy that in an almost tomb-silent room might as well have passed for cannon fire. But no one entered the room at these times: someone was apparently only taking a quick look.

A few minutes before the hour, the unmistakable footsteps of the governess sounded on the hardwood floor in the foyer. Ursula took a deep breath, simultaneously hearing her brothers do the same. None of them turned to look at her as she entered, but to their surprise, she did not go directly to the casket. She walked instead, rather hurriedly Ursula thought, to the front row on the opposite side of the aisle from the children. Out of the corner of her eye, Ursula could see the woman dressed in black from head to foot, a heavy widow's veil covering her face. A moment later the hired shoe-clerk actor came up the aisle and stood behind a narrow lectern placed upstage and a little to the side of the coffin. He was of that breed of man whose high point in life was his years of military service. When that was over, his life was over. He now passed through the daily monotony of existence, placing shoes on the feet of grumpy customers who complained about the fit, the fabric, and the prices as he stared without interest at their knees. He loved his own voice because people complimented him on it, and secretly he dreamed of being on the stage.

He began in a tone that Moses might have envied: "Death is cruel." He paused meaningfully. "Death is unjust. Death has no respect. Before us lies an adoring husband and a loving father who has been cut down in the prime of his life by this villain of villains."

Ursula felt her brothers shift in their chairs. She heard a door open and turned around just in time to see Brückner, who had apparently also been seated in the back, charge out of the room.

"How can we comfort this sorrowing widow?" asked the shoe clerk in a tone demanding suggestions from the mourners. There was a long pause, but before he could answer his own question—not getting one from the audience—the mortician came scurrying up the aisle violently shaking his head and waving a sheet of paper clutched in his hand. The clerk looked indignant, then alarmed. There was some sibilant whispering between the two brothers-in-law. Ursula caught only part of it. ". . . wrong form." "It's . . . you gave me." The whispering became louder. "Idiot. The widow is already dead." There was an urgent exchange of papers, and the mortician hurried away, while the actor, flustered and no longer securely in control of his material—not having seen it before, let alone having rehearsed it— was left with the indelicate problem of having to get rid of a widow. Death was indeed cruel. He scanned the new form and gulped hugely, his eyebrows jumping. The Bronevsky children were by now all attention. The beginning of the first sonorous speech had awakened them out of their mindless reverie—a state they allowed themselves to drift into for the sake of absorbing time during periods of extreme and tense ennui. But the eulogizer delivering his praise from a wrong set of facts brought them up sharp. Ursula, who had been counting the external stitches in her mother's gray leather gloves, nudged Günther with her elbow. He inclined his head toward her without taking his eyes from the speaker. "Strictly a bonus," he whispered.

In the new eulogy, death was no longer the villain: "Gathered here as we are, we all know the heartbreak of losing one divinely beloved, and what it means to long to be reunited with that one lost to us. Let us not grieve then for this man, whose soul is even now joyously embracing that one who went on ahead of him and who has been waiting for him. Let us think only that they are together for eternity. And let *us,* too, rejoice in that reunion, giving . . . giving Death his due for bringing . . . bringing . . ."

Apparently the correct form did not have the dead couple's names filled in the blanks, and the clerk no longer had the wrong form, which did. He looked down at the man in the coffin frantically. Ursula wondered if he expected any help from that quarter. She heard Alexander successfully choke back his snicker. Boris cleared his throat.

". . . this man and this woman together again in a world where there is no sorrow, no despair, no grief, no pain. Where . . ." Again the blanks stopped him. ". . . where this husband and this wife can savor their love divinely." He went on for another eternal three minutes describing the qualities of the other world and what did and didn't go on "over there" and how the deceased couple would now know the "harmony of eternity." Not being burdened with imagination, he continued to substitute "man and woman" and "husband and wife" whenever the nameless blanks leapt out at him. He was sweating profusely when he came to the end of his speech.

The Bronevsky children, relieved of their tension by the shoe clerk's comic delivery, relaxed in their chairs. The mortician, grim and green about the mouth, motioned impatiently to the mourners to rise and come forward to view the body before the closing of the casket. His acerbic expression was not caused by his brother-in-law's stupid mistake (for which, in fact, he himself was to blame). *That* was nothing; people forgot those things before the speech was over. What rankled his soul was the number of mourners: barely over a dozen. A dozen mourners! And he had gone through the expense and time and trouble (not to mention the crushed anticipation) of putting out two hundred and twenty-five chairs.

The two maids passed beside the coffin, both with handkerchiefs pressed to their mouths and weeping rivers. Graz, nervously sliding the brim of an old fedora through his fingers, passed the body without looking at it again. Frichter remained seated; apparently one trip was enough.

When Ursula and her brothers were later to reconstruct the next ten minutes, none of them could agree upon the exact sequence of events, minute by minute, except for the first ten seconds: they all saw Miss Schneider remove her veiled hat and place it on a vacant chair, rise, sway for a moment, and begin to walk toward the coffin. After that, no two versions were alike. Ursula swore that the woman brought the pistol out of her coat pocket. Günther said it came from her purse. Paul thought he saw it first flash through a scarf she was carrying *over* her purse. Boris was positive that she had it squeezed between her elbow and waist. Alexander said she had it in her hand hanging straight down beside her before she even began walking toward the casket. Melchior didn't see it at all until it was pointed at him. Actually, at that time it was pointed at all of the children.

Ursula said later that the first words the governess uttered, as she stood in front of the casket pointing the twin to their father's brace of elegant dueling pistols at them, were: "Now it's my turn." Günther and Paul said the words were "Now it's your turn." Boris said that according to Freud she would have said, "Now we return." Alexander insisted that the woman said, "Don't ever return." Melchior, greatly distressed, remembered only that he had begun to pray for her soul.

Miss Schneider began her final slide into insanity when she pointed the gun at the Bronevsky children and announced that it was finally Bronevsky's turn. "Suffer!" she commanded them. "You must suffer. You can't just kill and then get on a train and ride away. I order you to suffer!"

Ursula started to rise, but Günther quickly brought his arm across the front of her chest. "That's right," the governess went on. "Try to protect her. But don't think it will do any good. She's the worst of all of you, the little bitch. She *deserves* to have her eyes blown out. How would you like to have your eyes blown out?" She looked directly into Ursula's face. "Answer me, little bitch, how would you like that?"

"Not much," said Ursula quietly.

The governess began to laugh. "How would you like to have your brains splattered all over the lampshade?"

"Not at all," said Ursula even more quietly.

Miss Schneider moved a step closer to the children. Ursula was flanked on her left by Günther, Alexander, and Melchior; to her right sat Paul and Boris. She saw someone move into her peripheral vision at the end of the first row of chairs. It was Brückner. "If you come any closer, swine," said the governess, darting a glance at the lawyer, "I'll shoot her right through

[197]

the eyes." Brückner stopped. "All of you are going to die. I promise him that as I stand before him now. You will watch each other die. I must give him that!" Miss Schneider, now holding the weapon in both hands, took another step toward Ursula, and in that moment, Günther half-rose and with a wild swing of his leg kicked the gun out of the woman's hands. Ursula watched it sail up into the air, high over the woman's screaming upturned face as she grabbed at the empty space above her, turn a full somersault, and fall straight as a dropped stone into the coffin.

Before the governess could even turn, Günther and Paul each grabbed one of her arms. Ursula saw Alexander leap to the casket. A moment later the gardener and the lawyer ran simultaneously into the churning circle, where the governess, cursing and shrieking, writhing and thrusting and shoving her body against the boys holding her, was dragging herself toward the casket. Günther said later that her strength was unbelievable: she actually pulled them along with her to the edge of the bronze box, where all the wild motion stopped with the suddenness of a projector being halted on a single frame of film. A few feet on the other side of the casket, Alexander, holding the pistol in his hand, was removing the clip. Ursula still sat in the same chair, her gloved hands, one over the other, in her lap. She heard Brückner say to the mortician, who was standing near the lectern by then, "Call for an ambulance." The man, apparently too stunned to think, did not move at once. He was watching the governess, whose face and chest were bent over the corpse. She was moaning softly. Paul and Günther let go of her arms. She brought her hands up to her face and with a wail of grief plunged them into the coffin, lifting the corpse's head up to hers.

At the exact moment that the mortician screamed, "Nooo," Miss Schneider, her lips fed with the intensity of fourteen years of repressed passion— suddenly released in her madness—began to kiss violently the beautiful closed eyes and nose and mouth of the man she had loved above all things, all those waiting years.

The mortician, of course, reached the coffin too late, and the others, not thinking about the glue and putty and other fragile substances used to reconstruct Bronevsky's face, dangerously unstable by that late hour, looked on in horror as the eyelid lifted away and the nose squashed flat under those hungry kisses.

The skin on the forehead curled back to reveal a kneebone. In the confusion and grotesqueness of the scene the boys froze, as the woman, uncomprehending the disintegration before her eyes, held the monstrous face with its one death-frozen winking eye, first a few inches from her own, then further until it was almost at arm's length. She began to make a guttural sound like a dog growling, at the same time dropping the thing back into its satin box.

Three of the men—lawyer, gardener, mortician—reached for her as she began to fall.

"Get your sister and brothers out of here," said Brückner harshly to a dazed Günther. "Take the limousine back to the hotel and stay in your rooms until I get there."

From where she sat a few feet away, paralyzed as though the now vanished gun would hold her forever to the spot, Ursula saw that Miss Schneider was still standing, being held up by the men, but her eyes had gone perfectly blank. Her normally colorless lips and her nose were smeared with some black substance that looked to Ursula like grease; and stuck low onto one cheek, there hung what appeared to be an eyelid with a perfect fan of thick black lashes.

17

Not until the children were on the train and the city lay behind them did Ursula remember the other people at the funeral. For an hour she had gazed mindlessly at the green world as it fled past the pane, the thick foliage occasionally split and fragmented by bridge railings and rock walls, and once two rare white cranes, brazenly indifferent, standing in a marsh near the tracks. The train sped into several tunnels of the purest black, blasting out at the other end into an explosion of sunlight and the flashing chartreuse leaves of silver-trunked birches. Abruptly a platform fronting a yellow building where some people sat waiting for the local shot into view, and as she saw those seated forms staring at the speeding special with a kind of spine-arching astonishment, the strangers at the funeral flew into her mind like menacing apparitions in a fragmented dream, sudden, violent, terrifying. She turned quickly to look back at the station, expecting to recognize the people, even thinking that in the next second one of them would raise his arm and make a fist at her; but the track curved and blocked out the platform. She settled back and tried to bring the faceless mourners into focus, but they eluded her. Her brothers must know who they were. She glanced around the compartment: across from her at the opposite window seat slept Alexander, his head nestled against the wing of the plush velour headrest. Next to him, Melchior, with a vacuous expression on his pale, drawn face, gazed straight ahead. Beside him, Boris was reading, his legs crossed in his usual prim way. Beside Ursula, his shoulder touching hers, Günther, too, watched the forests and fields fly past them; and beyond him, Paul, his hands laced behind his head, appeared to be contemplating the luggage rack, tightly packed with their suitcases.

Ursula turned to Günther. "Who were those other people at the funeral?"

"What other people?" His voice was listless with exhaustion.

"The other people in the back of the room."

"There were no other people."

"Yes. Two of them."

"The maids?"

"No, no. Sitting on the other side of the aisle from the maids. I saw them just as we went out the door."

"I don't remember seeing any people in the back of the room . . . except the maids."

Ursula thought a moment. "You had your arm around my shoulder; then just before we reached the door, Brückner came up behind us and said to give him the gun. Alexander still had it; he was right in front of us and he didn't want to give it to Brückner, but you took it away from Alexander. We stopped just near the door. I remember you took your arm away and pulled Alexander around and took the gun away from him. I thought he was going to cry so I turned away and that's when I saw two people seated in the middle of the last row. I only saw them for a second or two because by then you had your arm around me again and we went through the doorway together, walking fast to the outside to get into the car."

"What did they look like?"

Ursula thought back again into those last few seconds in the mortuary. "I don't remember. They were just two people I had never seen before."

"Men? Women?"

"A man and woman . . . I think. Maybe two women."

"What were their ages? About."

Ursula shook her head. "I don't know."

"Can you give me any kind of range?"

"Not old."

"That's a pretty broad range. What were they doing?"

"Nothing, just sitting there."

"Did you make eye contact with either one?"

"No. It all went too fast with Brückner pushing us out the door. They were just shapes sitting there."

Günther smiled. "Yes, I remember the shove he gave us out the door. He must have made a great many promises to Grandfather." He hesitated. "Don't take offense, Little Bear, but I don't think there was anyone else there. Is it possible that you could have imagined—no, not imagined, but confused—those people with some you saw at another time, at another funeral perhaps?"

Ursula thought out her answer carefully. "Possible? Yes, it's possible, but I believe I saw them today . . . in that room. I wish I had remembered them earlier so I could have asked Graz or Brückner. Frichter might have known them, but I didn't see him again."

"You know," began Günther, "there are people who are crazy about funerals; they go to them whenever they can, sometimes two a day. I'm not sure if they are morbid by nature or if they are bored and find that death brings drama to their lives—a little more life, you might say. Or maybe they just want to take their minds off their own troubles. I don't know."

"They sound sick to me."

"Don't be so quick to condemn; perfectly normal people go to the theater and the opera to watch tragedies, and they love the death scenes. They get to cry without being hurt or embarrassed."

"Well, if there were two strangers there this morning who came for the show, they certainly got their money's worth." Ursula realized that she was already doubting that she saw them, or at least that she saw them then, those two faceless strangers that she knew she saw somewhere and about whom she felt at the time there was something distantly and uncomfortably familiar. As always, she tried to piece the day's events together. She remembered everything clearly up to the moment Miss Schneider held the gun and came walking toward her. She even remembered thinking that it was the same ornate gun that had killed her father and wondered why Brückner had given it to the governess. This did not turn out to be the case; the weapons were merely identical. She heard Miss Schneider talk to her, but she could not remember answering the woman, although everyone said she did. Even Brückner, when he met them back at the hotel, watched her with a funny look on his face, finally telling her that she had held up very well under pressure.

Melchior asked the lawyer if Miss Schneider would be cared for.

"Rest easy," Brückner assured them. "The house was sold on the day of the auction and it brought a good deal more than we anticipated. Miss Schneider will want for nothing. By the way, the house was bought by a business concern. The people also wanted all of the furnishings so it may become some sort of place for guests of the concern."

Alexander wanted to know who bought it, but Brückner told him that the sale was confidential and he was not at liberty to tell them anything further. "However," he went on, "the price is excellent. All current expenses will be paid in full and a large amount left over for the other bequests in your grandfather's will. Agnes Schneider, of course, will have to be institutionalized for the rest of her life. She has been taken to a local hospital temporarily, but we plan to have her moved to an excellent facility in the country, where she will receive the best of care. Frichter believes she is quite mad now. Extremely dangerous to herself. I have located the flat she leased. I've ordered the furniture that she removed be returned to the house. I'm sure the buyers will want all of it, and I'll see that the money paid for it is put aside in trust for her continued care."

Brückner paced back and forth in front of the children in the suite's sitting room. Ursula knew that he wanted to tell them something further—carefully. She had become aware of his habit of long silences just before he had something difficult to tell them. It was interesting to her to watch him think: his face would begin to tighten up and then sort of spread out as if a sponge were being squeezed and released inside him. He did this a few times and then stared out of the window with his hands clutched behind his back. She knew that when he turned around he would be ready to speak. He was. "Ten years ago I tried to convince your grandfather not to let you attend your mother's funeral. Yes, Ursula, I was the one you heard arguing with your grandfather." He gave her a faint nod. "For the last three days I have tried to convince you not to attend this one. I was wrong the first time. And if that madwoman had not shown up today, I would have been wrong again. Your father is now buried; I went with the hearse to the cemetery and watched him being put into the ground—next to your mother. It is closed. Finished. You have seen it to its end." He looked at each of their faces, then seemed to talk to himself. "I do not know why, but for the last three days I have felt an uneasy foreboding about this funeral. I felt to the marrow of my bones that something was going to go wrong. We had not been able to find the Schneider woman before the services and frankly I had a bad feeling that she might try to do some damage. That premonition was certainly accurate. I tell you this now because it is over and because I do not want you to leave your homeland thinking that I was indifferent to your wishes—your needs, if you will. Also, there is something else: I believe now that it was not my place to make any allusions to your parents' intimate lives. I hope you will forget my tactlessness. It was un-thinking of me."

Ursula saw for the first time that he was a sad man, that behind the tight mouth and gravel-gray eyes there was someone else quite different who perhaps would like to sink his teeth into the flesh of a plum and drink champagne and perhaps even kiss someone. He looked at his watch. "We must be going within the next few minutes. Your train, I am sure, will leave on time." He turned to Paul and Günther. "I expect you two to keep this family together. Maintain discipline. Behave yourselves. Be discreet. And do not forget that you are descended on both sides from the nobility, but remember, too, that it is not blood alone that makes a man or woman noble." He paused in front of Melchior and smiled rather wistfully. "Don't give *all* your money away." Boris was already clearing his throat and trying to look sage when Brückner reached him. "You're too young to be the caretaker of so many airs. Be careful they aren't mistaken for mere flatu-lence." Boris reddened and swallowed hard. Alexander looked into the lawyer's face defiantly, but Brückner only smiled. "It's much easier to make a war than keep the peace. Don't take the easy way out." Alexander's expression never changed, and the lawyer shrugged and moved on to Ur-sula. "As for you, you worry me most. You are a violent girl. There are other ways of settling disputes. Learn to control your anger. Direct it. Channel it. It is not always necessary to use your fists. And it is not exactly gracious." Ursula flushed deeply; in his eyes she saw a faint glow of warmth, something tender, soft, and concerned.

He moved away from her. "Well, that's all. No, there's one more thing: I expect to hear from you. I expect answers to my letters." He glanced at his watch. "Now, it is time to go. Call if there are any emergencies. I don't expect any, but there is always the unexpected."

At the station, Graz and Berghoch and Brückner saw them off. The gardener was crying, the tears running off his face as he kissed each of the boys. He held Ursula close to him and stroked her hair with his large thick-nailed hands. "Most perfect flower . . . most prized." He kissed her cheeks, her forehead, and abruptly let her go, walking away into the crowd of people rushing along the iron-dark platform between the lines of trains. Ursula watched him disappear. Dear Graz, she thought, suddenly weeping; how little I looked at you, how rarely I thought of you, and now you cry when I go away, and who knows if we will ever see one another again. She wanted to run after him and write him one more note—perhaps to thank him for something, for everything. But in the next moment he vanished into the crush of the crowd. Berghoch, by her side, took her arm and led her to a luggage wagon out of the stream of people. "If you can't find a good cook, write to me and I'll come." Ursula nodded. She saw that he, too, was weeping, blinking furiously to keep the tears back. He took the cigarette from his mouth and flipped it away. "Well, I don't like good-byes, so it's until we meet again. When you come back, I'll cook all your favorites for you." He kissed her hand but did not let go of it immediately. "A very intelligent hand," he said, kissing it again. Then he led her back through the crowd to the train. "She will come back," he said, and let her go, and like Graz, he, too, walked quickly away and was swallowed by the crowd.

She stepped quickly near her brothers, where Brückner embraced each of the boys. He stopped in front of Ursula. Again she saw the softness come to his eyes, a curious dilation of his pupils, as though he were opening something inside of himself into which she alone could enter. "In your mother's clothes," he said, taking a handkerchief from his breast pocket and drying her face, "you look quite grown up. Much more than fifteen."

"I don't want to go," she mumbled, unable to stop weeping.

"Of course you do. With your mind . . . you're going to love the university. Now, get on the train." He paused. "There is one more thing." With Brückner there was always one more thing. "Your grandfather made me a gift of one of your tablets a few weeks before he died. It's the one that is all birds. I rather fancy birds. I have a few in my home. Those tablets were his most prized possessions. He gave me one in gratitude for work I did regarding some foreign investments. I love particularly that row of wet ravens huddling on a fence. Now go."

Ursula was still crying. He gave her the handkerchief. She looked at it and mumbled, "I'm sorry I broke your nose."

He laughed. "No you're not. You think I had it coming. Don't give up convictions for sentimental reasons or any other reasons unless you discover you are really wrong."

Ursula looked back into his eyes and saw there were tears in them. She offered him his handkerchief but he shook his head. "Keep it." He leaned toward her and kissed her mouth. "Salty, of course," he said gently, pushing her toward the doorway to the train. "But it will sweeten." He smiled again. "By the way, Conrad says to say good-bye and wish you well. Hurry now; your brothers are already in the compartment, and Alexander is glaring at me. If he sees you crying, he'll consider it my fault and will come out to fight me."

Ursula turned and saw Alexander glowering from the train. She mouthed a word at him and watched him turn reluctantly away. Brückner shook his head in admiration. "I wish I had that much control over him. I might be able to keep him from killing himself someday. . . ." He grasped Ursula's hands. "I didn't mean that . . . not in that way. Alexander will not kill himself. But he wants to fight someone—anyone, apparently—and that could prove to be dangerous." He stopped talking and held her hands together in his. "Now, listen," he began hurriedly, looking hard into her glistening, frightened eyes. "I tried to tell you this a few days ago, but perhaps I didn't say enough. He killed himself because he could not take hold of his own life. He wanted your grandfather to take care of him, just as he wanted you to take care of him. He knew you would never throw

[203]

him out. With you, he saw thirty more years of fancy living ahead of him. You did the right thing. If you feel guilty about his death, you won't be in control of your own life; he will be controlling it from the grave. Only a bully wants to control the lives of others. That's what most suicides are— bullies, people who say if I can't have such and such, I'll kill it. They think to kill the world by killing themselves." He glanced around at the crowd. "Come." In the passageway, he stopped in front of the children's com- partment, where one of them had already pulled down the shade. "Never mind about my nose. I understand what happened to you. I think at heart you have a good sense of the rightness of things." He brushed her hair off her forehead with a soft motion. "One more thing: you showed great courage today looking into that gun barrel. I was amazed. Your grandfather was right when he said we finally have a real Enerde woman."

"But I was afraid."

"I know you were afraid; we were all afraid. But you did and said exactly the right things. You may not know this, but courage is shown when we know what to fear—when we act correctly about our fear. The ancients knew what they were talking about. It's courage that makes the other virtues possible. Don't start fearing ghosts. Don't let that death haunt you. Feeling guilt is a waste of energy when you are innocent." He kissed her forehead. "Go now." He opened the door to the compartment, and nodding once at the boys' upturned faces, walked quickly out of the train.

Searching the crowd from the window, Ursula saw Brückner standing a short distance away. He did not wave, and she, too, only stared back at him without any gesture. The train moved a few feet, gasped, jerked, stopped, moved again and stopped, then moved steadily along the platform. Ursula watched the dark suit and felt hat until someone on the platform walked into her line of vision, absorbing the single figure her eyes sought.

By the time the train neared Linz, Ursula realized that her brothers were deeply depressed. She listened to them argue sullenly, aimlessly, about nothing and finally fall into silence. Each small town through which they passed was familiar and dear, for this was their old route to the Bavarian house where the carousel of all white horses had stood near a little lake in a green park planted by their great-grandfather.

A thin persistent rain began falling through the early evening. Ursula thought of it as following the train. It added to the dreariness of the ruined towns, the bombed-out factories; and most particularly the run-down farms which filled the darkening landscape. The small fields and clusters of houses looked mildewed under the gray rain. In a cemetery a black flower of umbrellas hovered around a lowering coffin. Everywhere, the people wore old, somber-colored clothing which gave them the appearance of mine workers coming out of the earth. It seemed to Ursula that the day had been stretching itself out until she could no longer remember how it began. The fight between the Russians and the Americans over the jeep seemed to her to have happened a week ago. There were hours that blanked out entirely; and events that she thought she remembered as having occurred in a certain way, her brothers remembered quite differently. It was this latter confusion that finally made her decide that she had been mistaken about the two

[204]

additional mourners: they were probably at her grandfather's funeral and not her father's.

Staring out of the train at the mists creeping among the wet trees in the failing light, Ursula felt a tightening sorrow for her father wrap itself around her heart like a squeezing fist. She had never known him. She had never even tried to know him. Yet, no one had stopped her. No one would have even tried to stop her. Not until he begged her to stay with him did she ever actually talk to him. For over fifteen years she lived in the same house with him, and not once in all that time did she have a single conversation with him. He was right: he had never asked her for anything, and she had never offered anything. In the end, she had denied him the single request he made of her.

The train moved slowly at Linz, passing a long platform lined with watching people. Ursula looked into their faces, which seemed to be only inches from hers. No one smiled. They looked mean, sinister. They clutched string-wrapped packages and shabby suitcases and stared back at her sullenly. A few people held nothing—their idle hands, hanging from frayed sleeves, twitched restlessly, as menacing as snakes. At the end of the platform, as the train picked up speed, a man screamed something at her, and Ursula lurched back and pushed her face against the wing of the chair. With her eyes closed, she became increasingly aware of the heartbeat of the train. It seemed to her that it pounded against her own chest like two hearts feeding on each other. She began to harbor the irrational notion that when the train stopped her heart would stop. That's stupid, she thought with total calm; perhaps I, too, am mad. She tried to pull away from the beat of the train and listen to her brothers, who were arguing again, but the pounding sounded through their words.

". . . because he wanted us to return someday," said Boris. "After all, selling the house didn't mean he wanted us not to be Austrians. He simply wanted us to go away to school."

"He didn't have to sell the house for that," said Günther. "And it wasn't a matter of money. That's what's so incomprehensible. We've had houses stand empty all over Central Europe, just waiting for us to stay in them a month out of the year or some years not at all. And even if we were away to school, the house wouldn't have been em . . ." Günther stopped.

Ursula, staring at Günther, saw the answer in his eyes. "That's why he did it, isn't it?" she said harshly. "So that Father couldn't live in it! So that he'd be poor and have no place to go. Brückner pretended it was the money. That was all a lie. The house didn't have to be sold. He did it for spite, and—"

"Stop, Ursula. Stop!" said Paul, biting his lower lip.

"No. It's so *obvious*. We were too stupid to see it. And that isn't all. That's why he gave us a choice!"

The boys all stared at her then, Günther shaking his head rapidly. "No, Ursula, don't. No more."

"Yes. That's why he gave us a choice to stay in Vienna. He knew we would turn Father down. Grandfather knew we would do what *he* wanted us to. And Father would be turned down and *know* it. It was one more way he could . . . he could *kill* Father. Don't you see it?" She was weeping, pulling at her face with half-closed fists. "And we helped. *I* helped." She sobbed out the nasty truth.

"No, Ursula, Father didn't know we had a choice until after he listened in on us in the dining room that day," said Günther, pulling her hands from her face.

"Don't be stupid, Günther. You know he would have found out anyway. I don't believe Brückner didn't know what was in those letters, and he would have let Father know somehow!" She lowered her head. "Oh, Grandfather, how could you do it?" She cried. The train beat against her chest. "Everything's lost! Everyone's dead! We're alone!" She wept into the terrifying emptiness.

"The rest of you go to the dining car. We'll be along in a few minutes," said Günther.

Ursula, hearing Günther's instructions, tried to stop crying, but the tears came from her unreasonably, from a terrifying depth through which she seemed to pass slowly, not actually falling, yet moving steadily downward through tears which came out of the graves in her soul, her mother's, her grandfather's, Rätzel's, her father's. They welled over her until she believed she was drowning. She gasped for breath, fighting to open her mouth wide, rolling her head back, searching around her, gulping for air that would not taste of ashes and wet cement. But there was no other air. She saw the ashes pour over her, fill the space she breathed, fill her mouth, fall through the softening cement through which she herself steadily descended, down, down, down. Miss Schneider stood on the rim of the squirming pit shooting her gun down into Ursula's face. She felt the bullets enter her eyes and explode in hideous slow motion. She screamed and fell quickly through a dark opening. When she opened her eyes, Paul and Günther were holding her down, one of them pressing a glass to her mouth. "Drink." She gulped the liquid quickly. "Easy, easy." It burned her throat without heat. She turned away from the glass.

Someone spoke from the open doorway. "Is she okay?"

"Yes. Thank you. She's fine now. Thank you very much." Paul was speaking. The person in the doorway said something else and vanished.

Ursula sat up and pushed the glass away with her palm as the twins anxiously searched her face. Günther pressed a handkerchief to her mouth. "Ursula?"

She shook her head and pushed her brothers away, weeping again quietly, without urgency. Günther stroked her hair as Paul buttoned her jacket and straightened the collar of her blouse. "You can't go through the rest of your life worrying about Grandfather's motives," said Günther quietly. "He believed Father was a bad influence. Maybe he was right. Maybe he was wrong. It doesn't matter anymore. We have to make our own lives now, no matter what happened in the past."

Ursula said nothing, but in that moment she decided that someday she would ask Brückner about the private letters.

During dinner, Günther suddenly asked if any of them remembered any strangers at the funeral. Alexander, who had already drunk three glasses of wine, said he thought Miss Schneider was fairly strange.

"There will be no more jokes about Miss Schneider," said Günther so

[206]

pointedly that the words sounded like absolute law passed in the highest of courts. Ursula looked up from her food which she had been worrying around the plate and caught Günther's eye, knowing at once that the mad-woman was no longer a matter of laughter. It would be the same as making jokes about a cripple. No one commented, and the rest of the dinner was a dismal affair, one of those ritual meals customary after a funeral. They drank three bottles of wine and left the food uneaten.

The rain continued steadily as the train sped toward Salzburg. Ursula, churning in uneasy sleep, awakened at the slightest change in the beat and sound of the engine. Once at the very moment that she turned toward the window, a locomotive roaring from the opposite direction shot its cyclo-pean beam into her eyes and shrieked its warning siren. Involuntarily she screamed back and curled into a tight knot, shaking horribly, her heart bouncing in her chest. Günther quickly put his arm around her. "It's all right. It's only another train."

Paul woke up. "Where are we?"

"Salzburg," said Günther.

As the locomotive stopped, Ursula peered through a thin crack at the edge of the blind and saw that the people stared at the train with resentment, the bitterness around their mouths as palpable as the taste of vinegar. "What's wrong with them?"she asked.

Günther sighed. "Nothing that wasn't wrong last year."

"Those people out there look like they want to kill someone."

Günther reached past her and lifted a corner of the curtain. "The Russians and the other allies again haven't been able to agree on what Austria can control in her own right again. The Americans have restored the airfields in their zone to the Austrian government, but only for agricultural purposes. What the people really want is the allies to relinquish all control of Austrian mail and telegraph administration, all transportation facilities, and to end the fight over the Carinthian frontier. And those are only the small things. They want normal foreign trade restored. But most of all they want the Russians out of the country. And at the present there seems to be no hope for that. They could stay here for years."

Within an hour after the train left Salzburg, a gaunt middle-aged man entered their compartment and asked to see their travel documents. Word-lessly Günther handed him the packet of six passports and special traveling permits. The man sucked on a pipe and looked into each face with mem-orizing care. Ursula, watching his eyes, was drawing him in her mind. He returned the papers and left.

"You know," said Ursula after twenty minutes of failed sketching, "those people used to wear uniforms, at least some kind of distinguishing hat."

Günther uncrossed his knees and pulled up the curtain. All was dark. "They still do." He got up and walked to the door. "At least *real* agents and conductors on trains do."

Alexander woke up and yawned. "Where are we?" Melchior still slept, but Boris was reading.

"Headed for Innsbruck," said Paul softly. He was watching his twin. "You think he's not with the railway?"

Günther shrugged. "Ursula's right. Up to now, everyone associated with the railroad had on a uniform." He pulled open the door. The gaunt man stood in the passageway outside the compartment, his elbows propped against the window ledge, the cold pipe clamped between his teeth.

"Sir, is there something about us that interests you in particular?" said Günther. Ursula heard her grandfather's quiet authority in her brother's voice.

The man examined the inside of his pipe as though he expected something to crawl out of it. He sniffed it. "Only seeing to it that you're comfortable." He spoke in an easy, affable way and returned the pipe to his mouth. Ursula had the curious notion that it was a prop of some kind. "I am a detective. For the line," he continued, producing a badge as quickly as a magician pulls a sunflower from his sleeve and makes it vanish again. "We've had a little trouble . . . refugees . . . rebels . . . riffraff. All manner of people trying to sabotage the trains."

"Why?" asked Günther.

"To embarrass the government. The Communists want control. They'll do anything to disrupt the order of things. That's what gets them into power. Internal trouble. If they can cause internal confusion and dissension, they weaken the country and then they get in. There are railway strikes in Germany. We'd like to avoid those." He nodded to them and walked away.

None of the children spoke until the door was again closed, although the detective's presence seemed to linger a moment longer. Günther raised the door shade into the passageway.

"What was that badge he flashed around?" asked Ursula.

"He told you. He's a detective for the railroad," said Boris.

"He put it away so fast I couldn't read it. Could you?"

"I didn't have to. He wouldn't show us a counterfeit badge since he knew we could always ask to see it again if we wanted to."

"But we didn't. And he knew we wouldn't ask. The badge may as well have been a tourist card. I don't think he is with the railroad at all."

Melchior tsked reprovingly. "What a suspicious girl you are; give people the benefit of believing them when they tell you something. Anyway, why should he lie?"

"I don't know. I just don't believe him."

Günther turned out the light.

"I want to read!" said Boris heatedly.

"Be quiet. Let's see if he comes back."

Two American soldiers walked by, their military caps pushed jauntily back. And ten minutes later the detective strolled past, fussing with his pipe and not even turning his face toward the Bronevsky compartment.

"Are you satisfied now?" asked Boris.

"No," said Günther, standing flat against the door. "He has stopped near the vestibule. I can see his pipe. He is not leaving the car."

"What does that prove?" Boris' question was charged with exasperation.

"Maybe nothing," said Günther.

"And maybe he's a spy," said Alexander.

"Of course he is, and he's after you," said Boris. "He's going to find out all your little secrets and report you to the Allied Command." He laughed. "Why are you all so suspicious, or are you acting on Ursula's *intuition*?"

[208]

"Hers *and* mine," said Günther. "Now be quiet. Let's see what he does."

But the detective did nothing except relight his pipe several times and lean against the window ledge.

"If he's a detective, why doesn't he move through the train?" Günther's question remained unanswered. "There are other cars full of people traveling."

"Well, *I'm* going to move through the train," said Boris, rising. "I do not intend to sit here in the dark." He left, whistling.

A minute later the door reopened. "Please turn on the light." It was the detective, with his hand on Boris' shoulder. The man pulled the door closed behind him and lowered the shade. "I'm sorry but you're all going to have to stay in this car. No wandering around the train."

Günther rose. "Who are you? What do you want of us?"

"Nothing at all, dear boy, except to make sure that you are safe." He took out the badge again, slowly this time, allowing them time to read it.

"The police? What do the police want with us? Our traveling papers are in order. We're permitted to leave the country. Everything is documented." Günther took out the travel packet again.

The man held up his hand as though to wave the papers away. "I don't need to see those again. I know they're in order."

"I demand an explanation," said Boris.

"Yes, of course," said the man. "Please sit and I'll explain." He cleared his throat. "It has been decided that for security reasons, you should be escorted to your destination. Nothing to be alarmed about, just a precaution."

"Who decided that?" asked Paul.

"I don't have all the details, the precise information. But it was decided in Vienna."

"But you didn't get on the train until it reached Salzburg," said Ursula.

The man smiled at her, his head tilted slightly. "I would like to know how you came to that conclusion."

"We went to the dining car before we reached Salzburg, and no one stopped us from leaving the car. And in Salzburg Alexander even got off the train for a few minutes."

"Your quite right. I got on at Salzburg."

Günther gave Ursula a little nudge with his elbow. "Then . . ." he began, "someone called and told you we needed protection?"

"Yes. A firm in Vienna."

"Against what?"

"These are unsettled times. The people in Vienna feel that added precautions are advisable."

"He's talking in circles," whispered Ursula to Günther as Boris complained to the man about the restriction in a petulant, offended way.

"I know," Günther whispered back. The train was slowing. "We're coming into Innsbruck," he said to the policeman. "Is it possible for one of us to get off and make a phone call?"

"I'm afraid not. We've been asked to keep you on board. Safer that way."

Ursula knew the whole business made no sense. If Brückner wanted them escorted, he would have sent someone along with them from Vienna. No, there was something definitely wrong, something just beyond her comprehension, just beyond the curtained window. She reached for the window sash but the policeman in two sudden strides across the compartment covered her hand with his.

"No, miss. Do not touch the curtain, please."

She pulled her hand away. "Who's out there?" Again they all waited for the inspector to answer, their faces watching him with rising suspicion. He shrugged with such casual indifference that Ursula felt at once that he was going to lie.

"Who can say? Riffraff. Hoodlums."

"What do such people have to do with us?" said Boris with insulted indignation.

The inspector seemed not to hear this. "When the train stops, you will all remain in the compartment with the curtains drawn. I shall be in the passageway outside, or at least very nearby."

"Just what or who is threatening our safety? Who cares where we go? No one knows us." Günther's impatience immediately infected the others.

Ursula, listening to her brothers all protest at the same time, remained silent. The whole business was curiously lacking in sense. For reasons unknown to them, a plain-clothes policeman boarded the train at Salzburg for the sole purpose of watching *them*. Why wasn't everyone on the train in some kind of danger? He said a firm in Vienna had requested these measures. The only firm that they knew who had that kind of clout was Brückner's tribe. Why would Brückner have them escorted out of Austria? The policeman seemed to be in a reverie, although the boys were still firing questions at him, none of which he answered. It was just possible, thought Ursula, that it didn't make sense to him either, that he did *not* know the details, the precise information. She saw that he was not difficult to sketch now. The pretended easy, relaxed manner was gone. He had abandoned the pipe. His face had a weary, watchful expression. At Innsbruck, they all fell silent until the man left the compartment, again telling them that he would remain in the passageway outside while the train was in the station. They were not to open their door.

"He's not going to tell us anything," said Günther. "When we get to Zurich we can phone Brückner."

"I deeply resent being chaperoned," said Boris. "And to Switzerland of all places. Under the protection of a nanny!"

Melchior, awake since the policeman entered the compartment, frowned deeply. "Maybe something terrible has happened." The train began to move again.

"Like *what?*" asked Boris.

Melchior shook his head. "I don't know."

"Boris," said Ursula, "we have a guard outside our door. Don't you think that's odd?"

"Not at all. Grandfather always had private bodyguards."

"He's not a private bodyguard. He is a policeman who has been directed to conduct us safely to Zurich," said Günther. "And that *is* odd, because policemen don't do work like that." The train picked up speed as the children argued.

"Perhaps he does it in his spare time," said Boris.

"You think he's on *vacation?*"

"He could be. I certainly know how to find out." He jumped up and opened the door before the others could stop him.

But the plainclothesman was not in the passageway; a uniformed policeman stood leaning against the window this time, a cigarette between his lips. Günther quickly pushed Boris aside. "Officer, the other man who was here said that there were railway strikes all over the country, that in fact we might be delayed at the frontier . . ."

"Yeah? I didn't know that." He spoke through a mouth full of smoke.

"Then you're not here because of the strikes?"

"Nah. I'm here to see nobody leaves the car. The killing at the station in the capital has got everybody up. They thought the killer could be on the train. But they haven't found anybody, and believe me, they searched good."

"Yes," said Günther. "That was a terrible thing." All the children rose and came to stand near the door. "Do they have any idea who did the killings?"

"Only one guy died," said the officer, raising the window slightly. "Christ, it's cold out there." He flipped the cigarette into the darkness.

"Well, you know the Alps at night. Are there any suspects?"

"Nah. All the reports are crazy. Some say it was a man. Some say it was a woman dressed like a man. Who knows? The world's gone haywire since the war. Imagine a *woman* carving up some guy's liver in broad daylight at a railway station and then getting away. Nah, it had to be a guy."

A door from the vestibule opened and the plainclothesman walked quickly to the compartment door, carrying a cup of coffee. "I told you not to talk to anyone."

"No damage. Just some kids, Inspector."

"Get back to your post!"

The man shrugged and left.

"All right, Inspector," said Günther softly. "Who died in the railway station in Vienna?"

The inspector edged into the compartment, his face both grave and angry. "I told you not to open your door."

"Who, Inspector? Who died?"

The man winced and contemplated the cup in his hand. Something's happening, thought Ursula. I can feel something happening. Don't answer too quickly. Give me a stranger's name. She felt a sharp light like a stab inside her head. Around her the boys leaned toward the Inspector. "At the next stop, I intend to make a phone call," said Günther.

The inspector shook his head.

"Yes," said Günther, "Mr. Brückner will tell us if *you* won't."

"He can't," said the man, looking at them with his weary eyes. "He's dead."

18

"It's Schneider!" said Ursula. "You can argue all you want; nothing will change that." She turned her face away from her brothers and watched the black night as the train fled through the Alps. Through tears, she thought of Brückner. Poor Brückner. Dead. He loved Grandfather. He hated Father. He enjoyed reading the will that left Father nothing but his own grave. Who but Agnes Schneider would kill Brückner?

"Ursula, how could it be Miss Schneider?" argued Günther. "She's totally mad. You saw her; she looked like someone dead. Her eyes were completely empty. How could she dress up in men's clothing, get to the train station, and then actually *find* Brückner and stab him? Where did she get the men's clothing and the knife? How did she get to the station? *And* get away. She is an insane person! What happened on that train platform took thought, planning, resourcefulness. Schneider is mad. She couldn't think up a plan like that, let alone execute it."

"We've been over all that," said Ursula. "We don't know she couldn't do it. We don't know enough about craziness to say what she could do or couldn't do. Schneider was always resourceful. Maybe Frichter was wrong. Maybe she wasn't as crazy as he thought."

"She was locked up, for God's sake," said Alexander. "They took her to a nuthouse. The inspector said it was some kind of street fight that Brückner got involved in. Except that he was an innocent bystander. . . ."

"Do you believe that? Do all of you really believe that?" Ursula looked into each of her brothers' faces. "You knew Brückner! He probably wouldn't stop to watch a parade, let alone a street fight. If he was an innocent bystander, it was only because *we* were already on the train and she couldn't get to us. So she got him."

"But, Ursula," said Günther, "you saw her at the funeral. She was catatonic! How could she?"

"I don't know. I don't know how she did it, but I know in my *blood* she did it."

"Dressed as a man?"

"Please, Günther. She did it. Believe it. I know she did it." Ursula saw her brothers' bewildered faces staring at her with disbelieving amazement. She returned her attention to the black Alps speeding past the window, away from the train platform where she saw on the sharp edge of her imagination Brückner lying dead in a blanket of his own blood, his liver actually protruding from his body, the knife—a butcher knife, because she had seen one used this way once before—lying beside him.

Ursula was wrong about the murder weapon. Brückner was killed with a surgical instrument but they did not know this until the next day when they reached Conrad Brandt by phone.

"How did you find out?" asked the young lawyer.

Günther told him about the uniformed policeman's story. "That, together with the inspector your office put on the train in Salzburg, gave us a pretty good idea that whatever happened had to do with us. Did you really believe the killer was on the train?"

"It was a possibility. There were witnesses. One said that a man of that general description jumped on the moving train just as it left the station."

"Man? Are they sure it was a man?" All the children leaned toward the phone.

The long silence on the other end made Günther think he had lost the connection. "Mr. Brandt? Are you there?"

"Yes."

"Are they sure it was a man?"

"The killer had on men's clothing. And he had to have powerful strength to use a surgical instrument that way." His voice was low and hesitant and tense.

"A surgical instrument? Your uncle was killed with a surgical instrument?" Before the lawyer could answer, Günther spoke again. "Where is Miss Schneider?"

Again Brandt hesitated for several moments. "We don't know," he said finally. "The doctor had her taken to an emergency hospital, and while he was making the necessary arrangements for her temporary confinement until she could be permanently placed, someone left her alone in a room. They thought she was totally incapacitated. She was on a stretcher and appeared to be unconscious. It's an old story. When the nurse returned to the room, the woman was gone. They are looking for her, of course."

"Didn't Frichter contact your office and say that she was missing, that she had gotten away?"

"Yes. But my uncle didn't get the message. And none of us knew what took place at the mortuary until the doctor told us later. My uncle didn't call in during the day. And he never returned from the train station."

Ursula, her ear close to the phone, pulled away from it. "He was at the cemetery burying Father; then he came to the hotel and went with us to the station. That's why he never got the message."

"That was not our fault," said Alexander petulantly.

"Don't be such a dope, Alexander. It's nobody's fault—except the people at the hospital who left her alone." She turned to Günther. "Ask him if anybody thought to ask if any surgical knives are missing from the hospital." Günther did. The hospital people were asked and were unsure, but they thought it was possible. Ursula got up from the table and walked to French doors opening to a stone balcony. Below it, a vast lawn stretched to a glacier-green lake. "Now she's out there somewhere—loose."

Günther handed the phone to Paul and rose. "Ursula, she can't get out of the country. She has no resources . . ."

"She managed to get some men's clothing and a surgical knife."

"You insist that it was she; it's not necessarily—"

[213]

"Gunther!" Ursula opened the doors and stepped onto the balcony. Günther followed.

"Listen, Ursula, they'll get her. Don't be afraid."

"I'm not afraid! I'm angry! Brückner wanted the best for us. We trusted him. He became a real friend. We're really alone now."

"We'll make new friends."

Ursula glanced back into the room at the other four boys seated at the table. Paul had hung up the phone. Her brothers looked morose and surly, as though they had been fighting. "We've never had friends. I think sometimes that Grandfather didn't want us to."

"Why wouldn't he?"

She faced him. "You know why." Günther's eyes were liquid green and his sullen expression reminded her of their father. "Because no one was ever good enough for us." She saw him wince. "It's true, isn't it?" He said nothing. "I have never known a girl my own age. I remember once when we were skiing and Alexander brought a boy and girl he met on the slopes back to the house we were staying in at Innsbruck. Grandfather found out they were some shopkeeper's children and he very gently got them to leave. Very gently, but very definitely. Afterward he told Alexander that they were not the kind of people who came through *our* front door. I think I was about seven, but I always remembered it. At home there was no problem because the world was locked out at the gate, and all our little trips to the zoos and other places were carefully supervised. We never had a tutor or teacher who had children. Alexander once said that Grandfather deprived us of the war. But he did more than that: he deprived us of the world. We've read everything, but we know nothing about other people."

Günther's eyes darkened. "It doesn't have to be that way anymore, Little Bear."

"But it will," she said. "We'll go to the university but our lives will still be surrounded by lawyers and bankers and bodyguards."

Paul joined them. "Brandt says for us not to worry. His office is taking care of everything. He said he'll come for a visit in a month or so."

Ursula laughed mirthlessly and turned away.

"Did I say something funny?"

"Unfortunately, no," said Günther.

By the time Conrad Brandt showed up in November the Bronevsky children were well into their first year at the university. The twins immersed themselves in science and fencing. Every night at dinner, Boris, with the fluency of a politician, held forth on the vast importance of psychoanalysis. No one listened to him. When he found free time he challenged his siblings to chess matches, which he habitually lost, even to Alexander. Ursula hated the game but always beat him. "You think too far ahead, in terms of some future grand strategy, while you ignore the present details," said Ursula one night after the third lost game. Outraged, he claimed that it was impossible to "cogitate incontiguously." She shrugged and returned to translating Twain into Russian.

For some weeks, no one knew what Alexander was studying, his stories changing daily. The twins finally discovered he was taking no classes and

[214]

forced him into various history courses that Günther said "couldn't do him any harm."

Melchior, in the school of theology, was immensely unhappy. "It has no meaning for me," he said sadly. "I wish I could go somewhere else."

"Where?" Ursula wanted to know.

He shook his head and left the table. They all knew he was going to his room to pray.

Ursula took an oil-painting class and discovered that it was not her medium. She went back to watercolors and ink. Her foreign-literature classes kept her reading away the long hours of the night when sleep would not come.

The servants were discreet, distant, and secretive. Ursula was convinced they were all bodyguards and spies hired by the law firm in Zurich. "I'll bet they send in weekly reports of everything we do and every place we go." She was particularly suspicious of the uniformed driver, whose sharp face darkened by his visored cap filled a dozen pages of her drawing tablet. "He pretends to be a mute when he thinks we aren't around," she said to the twins one day. "I saw him use sign language with the man at the kiosk near the park."

"Maybe the kiosk man is deaf," said Paul.

"No. I already checked that. I had a long silly conversation with him and looked for all the signs. He both hears and speaks."

When Brandt arrived in November, he looked even more disheveled than Ursula remembered. His sea-dark eyes held an anxious, turbulent look. He again needed a haircut. "No problems in school or with the entrance examinations?"

"How could we have problems," said Ursula, "when Grandfather donated a library wing to this university and established dozens of laboratories and scholarships in schools all over this country?"

"Yes, that could hold problems at bay." For a moment the smile she remembered returned to his eyes, but it vanished quickly, replaced by the air of distraction. He gave them some fiscal reports and additional information on their trusts. Ursula had the notion that these dry matters interested him no more than they did her and her brothers.

"Miss Schneider?" asked Günther when Brandt asked them if they had any questions.

"Vanished."

"Vanished?" asked the twins simultaneously.

"Completely. The police followed hundreds of leads, rumors, alleged sightings."

"Did anyone think to look in our house?" asked Ursula.

"Not until we received a tip that she had been seen there. It turned out not to be true. The best bet is that she is somewhere in the Russian zone, but our police have no jurisdiction there."

"And the murder of your uncle?" asked Alexander. "Was anyone ever arrested?"

"Dozens. And all were released." Ursula watched the lawyer's eyes cloud with vagueness. At first she thought it was grief and then realized he was preparing to tell them something difficult.

"What is it?" she asked.

He looked at her sharply, released his pent breath, and folded his hands on the table in front of him. "There *is* something I have to tell you. There's been an accident."

"What kind of accident?" The boys all leaned forward at Günther's slow question. Ursula sat perfectly still, watching Brandt's eyes. He did not look at any of them, but instead seemed to examine the inside of his laced hands.

"The two women, the maids who received a bequest from your grandfather, ingested some poisonous mushrooms. They apparently failed to recognize some bad ones, and—"

"No," said Ursula quietly.

"What?" The lawyer jerked back in his chair as though he'd been hit.

"Those two never made that mistake," she said. "After every warm rain they used to hunt mushrooms in their spare time. They had an absolute passion for them. We used to make jokes about it."

Brandt turned to the twins. "Is that your opinion, too?"

"I'm afraid Ursula's right," said Paul. "Berghoch, who was not always delicate about people, said the two maids were better than a pair of truffling hogs. He frequently prepared their mushrooms for them. They had secret places where they hunted them. It sounds absurd, but hunting mushrooms was the great pleasure in their lives. Did they get very ill?"

"They got very dead."

Melchior rose and stumbled away from the table, Brandt half-rising. "Is he all right?"

"Yes," said Günther. "Please, Mr. Brandt, we have to ask you something."

"Come on, all of you, no more formality: call me Conrad. Now, you're implying something. What do you have to ask?"

"Were autopsies done?"

"Of course. They found signs of the poison in the stomachs. I don't know a damn thing about mushrooms, but the examiners said the variety is called *Amanita* something-or-other."

"*Amanita!*" said Günther. "That's not believable. All of us recognize that group immediately. It's one of the most common lethal mushroom there is. Berghoch taught us to recognize those years ago. The maids would never have made that mistake."

"Quite right," said Boris over his roofed fingers, "unless, of course, they were not in their right minds."

"I don't get you," said Brandt.

"If they were temporarily unbalanced, they might make such a mistake."

Ursula glared at him. "I don't get you either. What do you mean, unbalanced?"

"If they were inebriated, they might make such a mistake."

"Excuse me, but were they drinkers?" asked Brandt.

"No," said Ursula. "Anyway, let's say they *were* drinking at that time, wouldn't that be in the autopsy report too?"

Brandt nodded. "Yes. And there was no mention of alcohol."

"She hated them," said Ursula.

"Who?"

"Miss Schneider. She hated them because she had to live on the servants' floor with them and use the same bath. And they sometimes stole her soap. And like everybody else, they laughed at her. She was everybody's joke because she was in love with our father." In the consuming silence that followed, Ursula thought of the two old maids in their black uniforms. She had caricatured them as spiders, as frogs, as clucking hens. On her kinder days she had painted still lifes of their tumbling piles of subtle-colored mushrooms, and they had cried with delight when she gave them the pictures. And now they were dead of an impossible cause.

"You are saying that these women could not have made this mistake?"

"It doesn't seem possible to us," said Günther.

"It doesn't seem possible that Miss Schneider could have had anything to do with their deaths, either," said the lawyer. "They moved to Potzleindorf into a small cottage of their own and lived very well off their bequests. It seems to me that hunting mushrooms in a totally new area might make a difference in their recognizing—"

"It's not the locality," interrupted Boris. "It's the fungi themselves. They would have been cognizant of their error the moment they began to prepare them."

"All right, but how could the governess have found them? And let's say she had. The two women knew what took place at the funeral. Would they have let her into their house?"

Ursula visualized Miss Schneider knocking at a cottage door. One of the old women—Gertle probably—answers. "Why, it's Agnes Schneider! Ola dear, look here, it's Agnes Schneider." It is dark outside. The wind is sharp. Miss Schneider shivers. "May I come in?"

Ursula erased the picture. "When did this accident happen?" she asked.

"Ten days ago."

"Yes, they would have let her in." For two weeks there were warm rains all over Central Europe. Perfect mushrooming time. Then abruptly the weather turned cold. It was snowing ten days ago. There was no sharp wind. Agnes Schneider, dressed only in thin clothes and carrying a worn handbag, is standing in the snow, her fingers blue, icicles hanging from her wet nose. Gertle and Ola let her in. She tells them that she has been living in some war ruins. She only wants to warm up a little and then she will leave. They are amazed and sympathetic—and wildly curious. They protest, clucking away simultaneously at how sorry they are to hear of her misfortune. She must come sit by the stove, dry her clothes, have a glass of hot tea, stay for dinner. In the morning, they will put their heads together and think of something. They enjoy showing her their charming wee cottage, remembering how the governess mistreated them, said they were low class and stupid. *Now* who was stupid? They laugh and tell anecdotes about the old days while they are preparing dinner. Agnes Schneider offers to help. She will set the table, make the salad, stir the mushrooms. When Gerle and Ola are turned away, Agnes takes a small sack of sliced *Amanita verna* out of her dress pocket and slips the contents into the pan. During dinner they tell more stories. Agnes includes a few of her own. No, she doesn't want any mushrooms; they give her gas. But thank you. Later they make a bed for her on the sofa. Then Ola says she is tired and will go to bed. Gertle yawns and becomes silent. Agnes waits.

"Also," said Brandt, "you should know that we no longer believe she had anything to do with my uncle's death. At first we thought there was a remote possibility. But you must consider all the facts. Whoever killed him robbed him of his briefcase. It only came to us later that he had it with him. Why would Agnes Schneider steal his case? We think my uncle was killed by someone who believed he was carrying valuables."

"Was he?" asked Paul.

"No."

"Then why him?" asked Günther. "Why not some other man?"

"Why not him? He was well-dressed. He looked affluent. A chauffeur drove him around. And for that matter, other men have been attacked. There are quite a few robberies now. There is discontent in the land, particularly in the big cities. Displaced persons. Returning prisoners of war. Defeated soldiers. People brutalized by the war. People without hope."

Günther changed the subject. "What about the knife? Did they ever trace it to that hospital?"

"We never had the weapon. The autopsy determined it was a surgical instrument. The killer took it with him."

A whole new picture appeared to Ursula. Brückner was watching the train. Someone walked in front of him. He moved to one side. The figure moved with him. The lawyer moved again. Ursula heard him say: "Sir, make up your mind!" Then she saw the knife come out of a coat pocket. It entered Brückner's body at the opening below the vest. Only a shirt to cut through there.

She shook her head and everything jumped about. "Did he die at once?"

"No, not immediately. In fact, there was something curious about that. Witnesses said he could not speak, his throat had apparently filled with blood. But he raised his hand and with one finger pointed to the ceiling above him."

"To the *ceiling?*" asked Ursula.

"To the temporary protective ceiling over the platform. We still don't know what it means. He may have been doing something entirely different or attempting to. The description is secondhand. We just don't know." He turned to Ursula alone then. "I know you think Miss Schneider killed my uncle, but from all the statements we've taken from bystanders, none of them have come up with her description. The differences in the descriptions are laughable: the killer was tall; he was short. He was thin; he was fat. He was young; he was middle-aged. He was a man dressed as a woman; he was a woman dressed as a man. There seems to be one general agreement, and that is the color of his overcoat . . . ."

"Gray," said Ursula softly.

Brandt drew in his breath. "How did you know?"

Ursula smiled at her brothers' shocked expression. "One of the two strangers at the funeral was wearing a gray overcoat."

"What strangers?"

"In the very last row at the back of the room at my father's funeral sat two strangers. One of them was wearing a gray overcoat."

"You're sure?"

"Yes. Colors are important to me. And upon reflection I must have thought it odd, since it was warm."

[218]

"Do you recall anything else about them?"

"No."

"Were they men or women?"

"I don't know. I even began to believe these last months that I had not seen them. At least not there. But I did see them there."

"Well, that's a lead. We'll check with the mortuary. They may remember them." He changed the subject again, asking about their classes: were they enjoying them? They all gave dutifully positive responses. The lawyer appeared to listen, but Ursula had the impression he wasn't particularly interested in their uninteresting answers. The twins asked him to stay the night, since his train was not leaving until the next day.

At dinner Boris spoke more enthusiastically about his successes at the university, but the others remained silent. Melchior, who claimed an upset stomach, had a glass of milk in his room. Brandt asked if the servant staff was satisfactory. In fact, the servants—three women and two men—all Swiss, moved about the house like well-designed, well-oiled robots. He asked the children about their other activities. They played tennis, sailed, swam, went horseback riding, were becoming proficient at fencing, heard a weekly concert. In the winter they would go skiing and skating. Ursula felt that he was not satisfied with the answers. He seemed to expect different ones. Apparently Günther had the same feeling. "Is there anything particular you'd like to know?" he finally asked Brandt during a long lull in the awkward conversation.

"Well, not particular exactly. I'm merely trying to determine if you're content. For example: are you making any friends?"

The moment he said it, Ursula knew this was what he'd wanted to ask all along. She waited, knowing that only Boris had made friends. He spoke up at once. "Oh, quite," he began in a remotely British drawl. "In my field I've met some excellent chaps. They've asked me to join a fraternal organization—an intellectual one, of course. Nothing frivolous, you understand. We meet to discuss the vast importance of psychoanalysis and exchange any knowledge of new developments in the field. We hope to bring out an important paper of our own one day. *And*, I hope, in the not-too-distant future. How's that for excitement?"

Brandt managed a smile. "Oh, yes, very exciting."

Ursula caught his eye and saw him redden. He was saved by Alexander's contribution. "I'm going to join a shooting club. There's one at the university, but there's a much better one at Winterthur and a great one near Baden. They don't just have target practice; they go out on real hunts, wild boar and deer and that kind of thing."

"Be careful," was the best Brandt could manage, and again he raised his eyes to Ursula, who tried for a bored expression, not quite sure what her face said to the man.

They had fruit and port on the terrace overlooking the lake. "Beautiful surroundings," said Brandt. "I understand the house has been in the family for over a hundred years."

"The new bathrooms for only about thirty," said Günther. "Grandfather had them made larger with fireplaces in them. He used to say that bathing by firewarmth and firelight was one of the ultimate pleasures in life."

Brandt seemed to have no response to this. Ursula rescued him. "Grand-father was right, of course, as you can find out for yourself tonight."

"Yes, thank you."

In the pale glow of the terrace light she saw that his face was softly handsome, the rough edges lost in the night. A servant brought coffee and while the man filled cups and brought the tray with sugar and cream and brandy around, everyone remained silent. It was one of the absolute rules of the house of Enerde that no one ever continued a conversation in the presence of servants, even if the talk was no more than an impersonal remark on the weather.

They retired at ten. Ursula, who took the same room on the second floor that she had had as a child, the same room in which Luba's tears fell on her half-sleeping face in the middle of an unforgettable night, lay awake for two hours listening to the night sounds. The twins on the floor above were closing their shutters. In a half-hour they would be making love. Next to them was Boris' room. Across from him was the room assigned to the lawyer. She wondered if he was in the tub, a fire snapping gaily in the hearth, the ancient iridescent Chinese-ginger-bowl collection on the shelves turning dull from the steam. In the tub he leaned back, probably his hands hanging over the sides. Perhaps his feet were crossed or his knees were raised. Tiny beads of perspiration formed on his forehead; his eyes were closed; he sighed with pleasure; his chest hair rose softly under the water; his belly was smooth as stone; in his groin the organ pulsated to the warmth, rising and weaving gently like a sea creature undulating upward on the sea floor. Deep in the center of her own body something stirred for a mere few seconds.

She shook away the image and got up. In the room next to hers, she heard Alexander mumble angrily in his sleep. She pulled on a dress and left her room, stopping at Alexander's door to see if he was covered. The light in his room was on as always. He was moaning. It was a familiar sound to her, as familiar as the position of his sleep, curled up like a snail, his thumb in his mouth. She brought the eiderdown over his shoulder and left him with a feeling of sadness.

The house had two front entrances: one facing the large rose garden and circular drive leading to the wrought-iron gate at the street; the other, more elaborate with its neo-Roman arches, faced two acres of lawn—patterned with formal flowerbeds, begonias, asters, and marigolds—that stretched to the lake. A boathouse held a sailboat and a dinghy, a changing room and a bath. On one perimeter corner sat the gardener's cottage, resembling a comical alpine hat. On the other a white pavilion with a domed roof created a sympathetic balance. The low lawn lights on the path to the lake cast a glow across the stones, distorting Ursula's shadow into a giantess as she passed across their apex. Night-blooming jasmine dominated the thin dark-ness. At the pavilion on the water's edge she sat on one of the curved benches and thought of her father's funeral. If she could hypnotize herself back to the moment she saw the two strangers, she might remember some-thing beyond the gray coat. She had long ago decided the people wore hats. She would have remembered hair. And they must have been ordinary hats or they would have left some kind of impression. The person in the gray coat did not entirely prove Agnes Schneider's innocence of Brückner's murder. There was more than one gray coat in the world.

A deep sadness crept into her heart. Pavel Bronevsky was loved by only one person, and that person was loved by no one at all. Whatever love was, it was beyond comprehension. It defied physical descriptions, and beggared abstract ones. All her reading had brought her no closer to understanding why it happened as it did, why someone loved one person rather than a different one. Why didn't Miss Schneider fall in love with Father's valet? Or Graz? Or Berghoch? Or one of the tutors? It was all strange and without reason.

The pale pavilion lamps cast a somber light on the lake water and surrounding flowerbeds. Suddenly, into this night-scented glow walked Conrad Brandt. He stopped at the top step of the pavilion. "I happened to glance out my window and saw you walking toward the lake. Are you all right? Is something wrong?"

She shook her head, feeling a curious tightening in her throat. "I don't sleep very much," she said. "This is a good place to think things out."

"Do you have something to think out?"

"Doesn't everybody?"

"I thought perhaps you meant some particular problem." He sat on the bench next to her. "I hope you're not worrying about the deaths in Vienna. I believe the two women simply made a fatal error. Even experts can make bad judgments. Perhaps their eyesight was no longer good or they were tired."

"Yes, perhaps," said Ursula, seeing that he deeply wanted her to believe that the whole business was only a tragic mistake. And, of course, that *was* one of the possibilities.

Brandt twice started to speak and each time pulled back.

"Is there something else?"

"Yes. I sense some disturbance here."

"Disturbance?"

"Some unspoken problem."

Ursula nodded. "Yes. No wonder you can feel it; it's always close to the surface. You should know that Melchior is very unhappy. He finds university life unendurable. He wants to leave."

"Where does he want to go?"

"Into the Church."

"He wants to become a priest?"

"I'm not sure about that. I can't see him as a priest. A hermit perhaps, dressed in sackcloth, wandering in the desert."

"Are you serious?"

"Yes."

"That would certainly upset your grandfather, were he living."

"No. It wouldn't. That's just it. He knew exactly what Melchior wanted, as we all did. He simply failed to consider it in his will, or perhaps he wanted Melchoir to wait with his decision. In either case, the conclusion will be the same: Melchior will leave. I don't know when. He doesn't care about his inheritance. He would rather give it all away."

[221]

"He must not leave." There was a touch of steel in Brandt's voice that made Ursula search his face.

"Why is it so important that he stay?"

After a long hesitation Brandt spoke slowly. "I'm sure your grandfather did not want any of his wealth to go to the Church. He has established various foundations and many charities, as you know; but not one of them benefits a religious order. He made this very clear in his later life and ultimately in his will."

"Can't Melchior do what he wants with his own wealth? Can't he give it away?"

"No. At least not for a while."

"Then he will give himself."

In the blurred light, Ursula was unsure of Brandt's expression, but he seemed for a moment to hold his breath. A night wind rippled the water on the lake as silence between them deepened. Brandt got up and walked across the pavilion to look out over the water. "My uncle loved you," he said.

"I loved him, too," said Ursula.

"I'm not sure you understand. He loved you as a man loves a woman."

Ursula, unable to speak, put her hand over her mouth to keep back any other sound as the tears filled her eyes.

"He saw himself as an absolute fool because he was in love with a girl who was thirty years younger than he. I don't know why I had to tell you this. It just seemed to be the right time for it." He turned to face her. "Why are you crying?"

She shook her head. The image that came to her was not Conrad Brückner's, but Agnes Schneider's—Agnes Schneider telling her she would suffer.

19

Ursula could not answer Conrad Brandt's question. She herself did not know why the news that Brückner had loved her should bring such instant and uncontrollable tears. She had felt his loss as a friend deeply, but this new knowledge of his feelings intensified and compounded her grief.

Brandt quickly put his arm around her. "I'm sorry I told you. If I had known it would make you feel this way . . ." He stroked her hair. "I didn't mean to hurt you." He turned her toward him, folding both arms around her. But after a few moments he began quite slowly to draw his chest away from hers. In a vaguely awkward way, she was to recall only later, he removed his coat and drew it around her shoulders. "You could get chilled. It might be a good idea to go in now."

He arose, and in the first instant of his standing, she thought he was going to leave her there, so quickly did he walk away to the steps of the pavilion. But in the second instant she saw the mysterious rounded rise in the crotch she was always quick to notice in her brothers, and about which they made endless jokes: the committee meeting, the fleur-de-lis in bloom.

They returned to the house in silence, he following her on the night-scented path. In the kitchen she asked him if he would like coffee or tea before he went up. "No," he said. "Whiskey if you have some."

She went to the dining-room cupboard and returned with a bottle of Scotch. "I remember that you didn't drink the vodka that day you came to see us, and you asked for this. Will it still do?"

He took the bottle and read the label. "It's only the best Scotch in the world."

"Günther said we should always keep it on hand for you."

He took the glass she held out to him, and for a moment, with glass in one hand and bottle in the other, he seemed to want to say something. His face worked itself into twists and frowns, but after a moment he shook his head, mumbled a vague thank-you, and hurried from the room. Ursula heard him climb both flights of stairs two steps at a time.

When she returned to her room, she stood in front of the long mirror and pulled off her dress to look at her own naked body, which she had taken for granted for years. He must have felt the nipples through her dress and his shirt. Perhaps he even knew that she wore nothing underneath. She touched her breasts and the nipples hardened. Slowly she caressed the long line of her waist, traced the outward surge of her hips, drew back inward to the lush wine-red triangle, molded her open hands over the rich thighs. She stood up tall. Her body. What was her body to her? It was pleasing to look at, pleasing to touch. She untied the black ribbon on the nape of her neck and the wine-dark hair fell free over her shoulders and back. What was her body, that a man had come near her, touched her and wanted her in the way she had read about and that she had seen in pictures? And another man had loved her and died without telling her. Why didn't she know that he had loved her? Why didn't her body tell her? Perhaps there was something wrong with her. In all the books the women always knew. Sometimes they knew that men loved them even before the men knew it.

When sleep finally came to her, she dreamed not of the two Conrads, but of her father. They were riding horses side by side somewhere in the country. He was jolly, laughing and telling her to speed up. She tried, using her crop, but the horse did not go any faster. His mane became glazed with white paint. His head reared back and it took on the hardness of plaster and paint, the eyes and open mouth became exaggerated with bright blues and reds. She could not remember a blue-eyed horse. When she looked at her father's mount, she saw that his animal was impaled with a bright metal pole. Like her own mount, his animal rose and fell in an up-and-down sliding motion on the pole. Yet this carousel was composed of only two horses, no music, and none of the usual machinery needed to run it. They were alone on two painted plaster horses riding across a meadow covered with red poppies. "If the flowers were yellow," he said to her, "we could get off and rest, but these are death." She looked down at the ground and saw the flowers turn into blood, and all the while the carousel horse slid up and down and raced across the meadow. When she started to cry out, it was Günther's hand that reached from the other mount for the reins to her horse. The plaster animals merged together as Günther comforted her, holding her tightly in his arms as he stroked her hair.

In the morning, Brandt drank three cups of coffee but ate nothing. He looked morose and angry. "I hope you'll call me before any of you seriously think of making any changes in your living arrangements. There are other men in our firm who see to the Enerde holdings, but it's my job to supervise your living . . . ah, conditions for the three years your grandfather expected you to stay here."

"Supervision!" Boris drew himself up in high dudgeon. "I, for one, do not need supervision."

"All right, I've used the wrong word. It's my job to see that you stay enrolled at the university and that you continue to live together. After that you're on your own. I'd appreciate it if you didn't give me any problems in those two areas." He glanced around at the boys, but Ursula saw that he carefully avoided looking at her. "If you get any ideas about doing other than what your grandfather wished, let me know. Maybe I can help. Maybe we can adjust your wishes in keeping with his. I don't want you to lose anything he left you, but at the same time I don't want you to be miserable either." This time he looked directly at Melchior. But Melchior turned his eyes down to the food on his plate.

It was Alexander who broke the heavy silence with a complete non sequitur. "Did you fight in the war?"

Brandt's face held the expression of a man who had just been personally insulted by a total stranger. "Yes. What of it?"

"Did you kill a lot of people?"

Brandt laughed, his face softening. "Yes," he said. "Most of the Russian armies in Stalingrad until our general surrendered to them."

Ursula, furious at Alexander's questions, kicked his shin under the table. But it was Günther who spoke to him. "Your comments have no place at this table, Alexy." In Russian he added, "Keep your mouth shut, you stupid little shit."

Brandt laughed again. "It's all right," he said in Russian. "Let him ask what he wants. Actually, Alexander, I don't know if I killed anyone. I was not a very good shot. I was drafted seven days after I received my certificate to practice law. After five years with Paulus' Sixth Army, I was a guest of the Russian government until the end of the war. Borrowing some Russian rags and having learned the local language, three of us escaped during the celebrating at the end of hostilities. We walked a thousand miles. There were so many displaced persons, nobody really cared about three more. My uncle was happy to see me and a little surprised. He thought I was dead. We two are the last of our family. *Were.* Now there is just me."

When it was time for him to go, they all went to the circular driveway to see him off. While the taxi waited, he again asked them not to make any changes without calling him. Ursula stood back under the arch to the front door. He nodded to her before he got into the car, but once inside, he turned and looked at her again, his eyes hard, penetrating, and disturbed.

[224]

The look went straight to Ursula's spine like a needle. He raised his hand in a final salute and turned away.

On the train back to Vienna, Conrad Brandt cursed himself for having told Ursula about his uncle's feelings for her. Why had he done that? It had hurt her. Had he wanted to hurt her? He listened for answers but heard only more questions. Hadn't he wanted to tell her something quite different? Hadn't he stayed the extra day just to be near her? Hadn't his heart leapt madly when he saw her walking to the lake? Hadn't he gone down to the pavilion to be close to her? Yes. Yes. Yes! He groaned at the knowledge of what had happened to him. What could possibly come of it? When did it begin? Three years after he walked home from Russia, he discovered that his middle-aged uncle with whom he lived in a large, comfortable, well-staffed house in Grinzing was buying red ties and ordering younger-looking suits all the way from Rome. One Saturday morning, he hardly recognized the man across the breakfast table from him. "Look, Uncle, I'm not going to ask you who she is, but that alpine-blue turtleneck you've got on would go better with a pair of white sailing pants and canvas shoes. I don't think it quite makes it with that black double-breasted." He didn't comment on the pomade on his uncle's hair.

"I see nothing wrong with trying to look one's best," said his uncle, washing down a handful of vitamins with his apple juice.

At the office Brandt quickly glanced at his uncle's calendar: he was spending the morning at the Enerde mansion.

For two weeks he needled the older man gently. "What have they got over there, a new teacher? A sleek-tongued, brown-eyed lady from Paris? A shy tweedy blond from Norwich? A stunning Swede with plump arms? Come on, Uncle, who's driving you crazy?"

His uncle refused to comment. And then that fall when the grandfather was still alive, he saw the Enerde tribe—as Brandt thought of them— traveling to Salzburg by train. He and his uncle were headed south to the lake country for a few days' holiday. At the depot his uncle suddenly slipped behind one of the pillars on the platform as they came upon the Enerdes waiting for their train. Two of the boys were in a heated argument; another sat on a trunk close to the wall; the twin boys and the girl made a triangle somewhat apart from the others. Brandt stood mesmerized at the great beauty in the twin children's faces. And then the girl, dressed in a long-waisted black cossack suit with a stand-up fur collar, a garment right out of the thirties and something the Duchess of Windsor might have fought for, turned and looked straight into his face, her oddly Tartar-cast eyes so brilliantly green against the purest, clearest whites, he felt himself momentarily hypnotized. The train's strident whistle made her twist away, bringing one gloved hand up to her ear, the other reached for the shoulder of one of the twins. *Oh, happy shoulder!* he thought, and realized in that moment the extent of his uncle's obsession. "One could drown in those eyes," he said later to the older man, who only nodded miserably.

When he finally met her and kissed the pulse of her bandaged hand, he truly believed he felt only lust. He had purposely delayed this trip to Zurich to give himself time to get over whatever it was he felt for her. Instead, he now knew what was in his heart, and it astonished him. He had gotten drunk to erase the memory of her breast against his chest, to obliterate the knowledge that under her dress she was naked. When he finally slept, she came to him in dreams, her greenfire eyes laughing at him, her pale naked body darting just beyond his reach as he ran after her in a garden of strange, unidentifiable fruit and lush vines that swayed and shivered against him, their very leaves emitting a golden glittering laughter. In the morning, he had addressed himself quite calmly in the shaving mirror. "You idiot, how could you let this happen?"

The holidays came, and with no classes to attend, the children became first morose, then depressed. Melchior, who had been going to Mass each Sunday, was the only one who observed Christmas, but fell to nagging and finally weeping when the others failed to show any interest. The cook, a needle-nosed French lady, bought and trimmed a tree which fell over twice because she had not anchored it properly. She accused Alexander of kicking it, but he denied this heatedly and said he only kicked the broken ornaments out of the way, since they were scattered on the carpet near the entry hall to the drawing room. None of them bought any gifts, so that the tree took on the forlorn look Christmas trees always degenerated to in January. Günther ordered it to be thrown out a few days after Christmas. Although they had talked about going skiing, none of them made any plans, and New Year's Eve came upon them swiftly, with Ursula refusing to come out of her room. Alexander wheedled, coaxed, cajoled through the locked door. "Come on, Ursula, please come out. There's just us. We've got some terrific champagne."

"You can have mine. Go away."

Melchior tried. "Ursula, please unlock your door. Grandfather doesn't want you to act like this."

"How do you know?"

He gave up quickly and let the twins try. Günther knocked. "I'll leave a glass of champagne out here on this table."

"I don't want it. I'm not going to celebrate his death."

"How interesting to see you wrong occasionally. We're celebrating his life."

Ursula opened the door and went downstairs with them. They consumed three bottles of champagne somewhat too rapidly, toasting their grandfather, Rätzel, and Brückner before Alexander, a little drunk after the sixth glass, became surly and offered to punch Boris in the mouth for suggesting they raise their glasses to Freud. Ursula, already sullen and peevish, urged Alexander on. "Yes, do, Alexy. You owe it to him." When she was cheerful, alcohol made her more so, but when she was ill-tempered even a small amount turned her mean. Ursula smiled sweetly. "Really, you do. Only last week at the booksellers' fair I heard him say to some stout girl with adorable little kohl-circled eyes that he had a younger brother whom he was secretly analyzing for signs of infantilism. And by the way, Alexander, did you know that you are an easy subject, that you respond perfectly, with marvelous naiveté, to any charged question, without any awareness that you are under—"

[226]

"Ursula! Shut up!" Günther spoke through closed teeth.

"No, I don't think so. I like this discussion. Hit him, Alexy. What right does some pig-eyed future hausfrau have to the knowledge that you are easy to make a fool of? Think of how all her chirping little friends will twit and twitter when they meet this dunce of a brother."

Günther rose quickly, and brushing past Paul's restraining arm, stepped between Alexander's upraised fists and Boris' retreating figure and knocked-over chair. "I'm going to kill him," said Alexander, crying.

"No." Günther might have been denying a child's request to go out and play. He pushed the swaying Alexander sharply back toward the couch and faced Ursula. "I wasn't going to do this anymore." Then he slapped her, twice, hard. She raised her hand, not for protection as it appeared, but raised it to hit back. Günther caught her wrist and hit her again with his free right hand, harder than before. The sting from this final blow brought tears to her eyes and a copper taste into her mouth. She felt herself whispering a word through numbed lips. For perhaps ten seconds the room circled around her through a thin sheet of water. Melchior seemed to be resting his bent head between his hands. Boris was struggling helplessly, comically, with an upside-down chair. Alexander with closed eyes lay prone on the couch where his brother had pushed him. Paul alone seemed to be watching the punishment. She shook her head and focused on Günther's face, seeing at once the filled eyes, the sharp twist of his mouth as he bit his lip. Slowly he lowered her raised wrist and released it, but he did not take his eyes from hers and for those few seconds she was held by their centers, lured by a still deeper space, black with a black star center bereft of color into which she moved now easily, smoothly, without groping, without will, even without wonder. She was to think of it later as an opening in time and not as some entry into space. But at the moment of its occurrence, she failed to think at all as she rubbed the dark red indentations his hand had left on her wrist. Günther was still standing completely motionless in the center of the room when she turned away from him without speaking and left quickly.

She lay on her bed in the dark for some hours, believing she was thinking of nothing, and not until she heard the faint bombinating of bells did she remember the bells of Vienna booming over the city only a year ago on the night her grandfather died. Only a year! A year ago on this night he had died and left her alone in the world. How stupid it was to leave the city of her life. She had read of people cast adrift at sea, and that is what she was—out of reach of land, of the only land that was home. The university appalled her with its Calvinistic view of the world. Its rigid rules of organization, lectures, examinations. She loathed the coffee shops where the students discussed politics in professorial tones, all of them sounding like Boris. The fairs and holidays with their smell of new sausages and old cheese left her gagging. In the restaurants everything swam in cream: veal, liver, vegetables. And everyone was fat and full of laughter and good cheer. She wanted to weep at their stupid laughter and discovered she was already crying. She longed for her grandfather, for the deep places in the Vienna garden where they had been alone together. But most of all, above and beyond all the past sorrows, she wished she could stop the present one by

[227]

taking back the word she had spoken when Günther hit her and which she knew he heard or saw formed on her lips. What had made her say it? Rage certainly. But more than that: some terrible thing inside her had brought forth the word and now it would always lie between them, an enemy of their love. A spreading dark spot where only light had lived. She wept at the loss, the terrible irretrievable loss of love. She was responsible for its death. She had killed it cruelly, without thinking, as someone slaps absently the mosquito buzzing near one's ear or sees landed and feeding on one's ankle. All that she had mourned before—the death of her mother and Rätzel and her grandfather, the loss of Luba and Wolsky—were sorrows that came upon her without her fault. But the loss of Günther's love was all her fault. Why had she told of seeing Boris and the girl in the bookfair? What did it matter that Boris was analyzing Alexander if, in fact, he was? Now she had killed the love she held most dear by revealing a knowledge that she swore to herself long ago she would never reveal. Now Günther knew that she knew. She covered her streaming eyes at the memory of Günther's expression. "Oh, please, please, go away," she whispered to the clouded, hurt face that would not change, that remained with her as clear as a photograph imprinted on the inner side of her eyes. "Make him not have heard it." But he had heard it and she knew it. And what of Paul? Did he see the word too, the grotesque word that coarsened, vulgarized, demeaned his love for his brother? She imagined them clasped together far back in their childhood, their babyhood, back in their mother's womb. She had never thought of this love as anything but perfectly right, no matter what the world said, and now she had given it the world's name, a stupid ugly name that turned everything to mud.

Sometime after midnight, she heard the stairs creak with the weight of hesitating footsteps. They stopped before her door. She could see the raised hand curled to knock. But there was no knock. She rose and crept to the door and leaned her ear against it. Then even before she opened the door, before she heard him whisper her name, she knew it was Günther. When the whisper came, as soft as leaves murmuring, she opened the door and stood before him naked. Behind her the room was dark save for the windows where the glow from pale stars made a square of space less black to the night-accustomed eye. Behind Günther a dim light shone from a wall sconce. He entered the room and closed the door cautiously. In the darkness, the silence was explosive, but when Günther spoke, his voice was soft, unhurried, easy, and without tension. "Forgive me." He reached his hand out and touched her bruised face.

She pulled his hand down to her breast and held it there under her own. "Günther, love me." She felt his breath close to hers and quickly covered his mouth with her lips. "Love me. I'm sick of reading about it in books. Show me everything. Tell me everything."

"How do you know I could love a woman when you know the other thing with me and Paul?"

"I've seen it. You think I couldn't see it? I've seen you swell down there when you were around girls. You're one of those people who can love both. I know it." She reached down and covered his rising penis with her cupped hand. "Love me. Please love me. Forgive me for the dirty word."

"Already forgotten." He moaned softly as she rubbed him through his clothes.

"Please, Günther. Do this for me. I want to know it. I don't want it from a stranger. Please love me. I want it from you."

"Ursula, as lovers we could be fatal for each other."

"No. I don't believe that."

"Believe it."

"No. Love me."

He turned on the light switch beside the door and walked to her bed. "I can love you without danger of conception, but once awakened you will not be the same girl, and I do not know what direction you will take. All love is a risk."

"I don't care. I'll take the risk."

"My God, Ursula, don't ask this of me!"

"Günther, you're erect. You want me." She unbuckled his belt and undid the buttons, plunging her hand into the opening. His gasp thrilled her.

"Ursula, Ursula. We could go on for fifty years without this. . . ."

"No." She pulled up his shirt and brought her breast against his chest, swaying her body against the exposed penis.

"Stop," he said. He began to undress, pulling off his clothes in front of her unhurriedly in a calm, preoccupied way that made her think he was estimating something as she had seen him work problems in a notebook. He kissed her then, a long soft kiss. Slowly he turned and drew her onto the bed and knelt on the floor beside her, spreading her knees as he brought his face between her thighs. At the touch of his tongue all memory left her. Nothing she had heard or read of love or even seen of it in her grandfather's scarlet cloth books remained, and only later was she to think how impoverished, colorless, and without power her imagination had been.

But that was much later. Within minutes after Günther's mouth touched her, her body roared with energy, immense, violent, shocking energy, beyond her control. She was stunned at the outward pulsation of her flesh, as though her very skin were throbbing with growth. She felt on the edge of pain. In another moment it would be past endurance. But then her skin released her and for several seconds she was hurtling uncontrolled in a million directions, passing the pale stars. And then the power was gone and she was falling from a great height, but slowly, peacefully, without fear, without alarm. She found her body waiting; her hands were clutching Günther's shoulder and she was weeping. Through a haze she saw Günther rise from the floor and sit back on the edge of a chair, where he quickly brought himself to ejaculation, the spume forming a ghostly lace arch as he gave a long haunting moan.

In the following months Günther came to Ursula several nights each week to make their rapturous, ardent, biologically sterile love. At first they discussed in great seriousness the unacceptability of actual penetration as they might talk urgently of a dangerous door that led to a world of unknown but certain peril. Then, abruptly, they stopped talking about the dangers. It was almost as if they had somehow resolved the issue, as if it had been forever settled between them, when, in fact, the problem had only deepened to a level at which they were no longer able to bring it up. Ursula desired her brother with a maddening passion and knew it. She longed to have him enter her. Instead he taught her the fine art of bringing him to slow excruciating crises with her hands and ultimately her mouth. She was enormously eager to learn. Together they pored over the double-volumed illustrations of erotic love, sometimes laughing themselves limp at the blasé expressions of some of the participants. But usually the pictures excited them, particularly ones in which the couples were clearly connected genitally where the lips had visually taken the penis like a tongue into the vaginal mouth. Occasionally after they made love, Ursula fell into long bouts of depression. Her moods swung to polar opposites: one day she was intensely joyful, worked hard and long and drew good, funny pictures. But the next day, she read all evening after classes and refused to eat or even talk to her brothers. On these days Günther always went to her bed. "Ursula, you can't keep up this violent change of moods. What *is* the matter?"

She would hold him tightly to her, his penis pressed against her flat belly or clutched between her legs. "You know. what it is. You know. You know." He answered her with caresses.

Frequently now she began to cry when he made love to her. One night, as he lay half-asleep against her tense body, she opened the lips and placed the cap of his penis between them and pushed against him. He awakened fully, quickly moving away from her. "We can't," he said, grasping her by the shoulders and holding her at arm's length as she stretched her hips toward him. "Now stop."

"No. I want it. I want you inside of me." She grasped his erect penis in trembling hands. "Please, Günther. Don't you see? We're . . . unfinished the way we are. We have to complete it. Every cell in my body waits for this completion."

"No. We can't. My God, what if . . . ? No. We can't! We can't even continue this. You know exactly what it will lead to. You keep treating this as if it were innocent fun, like tennis or horseback riding."

"It is."

"No! Ursula, you well know it is not only the possibility of impregnation that stops us."

"I don't know that at all," she said stubbornly. "What difference does it make to the world? You and Paul have been lovers for years. Is anybody hurt? Outraged? I don't believe that God cares. As long as I don't fall pregnant, what harm is there?" She leaned toward him, kissing his shoulder, his neck. "There's no harm," she whispered. "Please love me . . . completely." She brushed her lips over his mouth, nose, his eyelids, edging her body closer. They were facing each other, touching from forehead to foot. She stopped talking, holding her breath as she felt his indecision as clearly as physical heat, a fire burning against her body. Yes, she urged silently. Yes. Yes. Yes.

But instead of covering her as she believed he finally would, he spoke in a calm, quiet voice. "I believe at heart you have a good sense of the rightness of things."

For a blind moment the statement came echoing across a great distance. And then she began to hit him. But he had apparently expected this, too, and quickly overcame her, pinning her wrists to the bed as they fought silently until she was reduced to helpless, hopeless weeping. He comforted her then as he did when they were children. For a time longer they lay quietly in each other's arms and it was this hour that was to haunt her again and again like a whispering ghost. Following her through time, a spirit specter, itself a fragment of time but a fragment that would not lie down and die. In silence, their dangerous game ended, both knowing in that hour that it was ending.

For days afterward she would awaken at night to find herself groping in the dark for something lost in a dream. Exhausted, she would plunge her face into the pillow that once tasted of her brother's rich hair. In time, the cries within her silenced and she returned to her drawing and spent more hours at her studies. Curiously, it was Paul who brought her back into her old routine. Of all her brothers he was the most courteous, the most considerate of others' feelings. Her love for Paul was soft and pliable but as tenacious as morning light. She had long known that her sweep of moods, especially into gloom, was similar to his. Over the years it was Paul alone who seemed to understand her dark days beginning around the time of her mother's last illness, when the hours yawned out ahead of her like a pit full of her dying mother's muted cries. And he was the only one of her brothers who also experienced frequent insomnia. They reacted similarly to physical pain, shrinking inside themselves at the onset of migraine headaches from which they both suffered. Günther's urging them to enter the pain and examine it, to find its width and breadth, its sound and color, only drew blanks as they braced themselves against it, Ursula grumbling, "Width? Color? My skull feels like it's shrinking and the roots of my teeth are making knots and you want me to know what color that is? Please, Günther, go play with your microscope, go create some new germs, but close the door softly on your way out." Paul would add something of his own, after which they would lock themselves in a dark room and silently wait out the pain.

One day soon after Ursula's last night with Günther, she looked up from the blank drawing tablet in her lap to see Paul watching her from the steps of the pavilion where she used to capture the sailboats and lakebirds on her creamy paper. He joined her on the bench and gently released a strand of her hair caught in the turtle neck of the sweater she was wearing. It was Günther's sweater. "Ursula, what I know of love is that it is terrible, agonizing, possibly even fatal, which is probably fine, since I don't believe I could live without it. I have loved him for as long as I can remember and I don't have to visit the Vatican or Venice to know that the lover is nearer divinity than the beloved. That is not to say that he does not love me, but only that apparently it is true that in all—at least almost all—love relationships one partner loves more profoundly, or perhaps only more desperately, than the other. His versatility, of course, makes everything more complex. I have known forever that he was different from me in that respect. That he can love us both is not pain for me. In one sense you are as much mine as his—being our sister; in another, you have certain fascinations for me because sometimes your face has his expression and your voice his muted music." He took her hand and stroked it. "Even these longish bones are like his and mine. Don't cry. This is not sad. Fatal, perhaps, but not sad.

[231]

And I am not of that orchard variety that resorts to rouge and kohl-circled eyes. Nor do the coy horrors from Bosch's nasty garden of delights frighten me. Very simply: I love my brother. It has been said that one can choose to love. I recall no such choice. However, had we been older and the idea for this passion come to me for consideration, I would not have hesitated for a millionth of a second. You remember the joke about the war: 'The situation is hopeless but not unendurable.' Please stop crying; it's so unlike you. He had to end it, you know, as he and I must one day. You are both meant for families. Of that I'm certain."

"And what of you?"

"I don't know. I cannot imagine loving anyone but him. Yet I know the time will come when I will lose him. He knows my fears. But the others must also be considered."

"Boris?"

"He knows, as you well know, and would like to 'cure' me."

"And Melchior?"

"Opened the wrong door—actually we forgot to lock it—one magnificent snowy afternoon two years ago when your lover and mine was showing me something quite new in the way of slow delight. Poor Melchior. He was horrified. Not because it was against man's law but because God objected. He rushed off to that little church with the suntanned Christ. Do you remember it?" Ursula nodded. "He wanted a cure too. A cure of souls. Mine and Günther's. He begged us both to give up our bodies for Christ. He urged purges. He did not know then nor does he now that my twin is not identical in that one respect."

"And Alexander?"

"Too self-centered to notice. When one day he does, he will pretend he doesn't. If that fails, he will fight to his last breath to keep it secret. Of all of us, he is the most provincial. He's joined a hunting club. I'm sure some vulgar social club is next."

They fell silent as three swans drifted past the pavilion. "Please know that it has not been easy for Günther either," said Paul. "He knows that you are hurt. You have to realize also that you have become richly beautiful. Even you must know that by now. As a little girl you were extraordinary, skin like ice. Now everything is fire. And you have a scent . . . some exquisite plant . . . I don't know. Perhaps it's just a freshness, a spring morning. It's lovely."

"It was my fault that it began. I forced him into it."

He smiled at her, brushing her hair away from her downturned face. "So did I," he said softly.

Every Sunday during that first year away from Vienna the children walked with Melchior to the nearest Catholic church, which they watched him enter with bemused detachment and from which they watched him come an hour later, their expressions still both engrossed and remote, as though they were not quite aware that the building their brother entered *was* a church, but only a place where he had to keep an appointment at a given time while they sat outside and waited on a nearby park bench when the weather was pleasant or in a coffeehouse when snow fell or the cold spring rains beat down on the park. They had stopped badgering him about his penitent posture—head hanging, hands held behind. "You don't have to carry us on your back, you know!" Ursula said to him angrily on one of their first trips to the church. And yet it was she who some months later due to a migraine miasma did not join her brothers on their Sunday sojourn and said afterward, "Damn, I missed church!" as though she had actually entered the building all those Sundays and heard the priest as she idly summed up some aesthetic evaluation of the stations of the cross, comparing them to those seen in several dozen visited cathedrals and mountainside chapels from Rome to the Black Sea, every one of them as familiar and alien to her as her mother's sickroom.

One particular May morning Melchior did not come out at the expected time and when the others entered after a half-hour of courteous waiting they found him lying prostrate in front of the tearstained Virgin weeping quietly while a priest hovered over him in black-robed dismay. "It's all right; he's ours," said Günther as the twins raised their brother from the stone floor and led him from the church. Two Sundays later when he did not appear as the others waited in the garden, Paul went to fetch him and discovered that he was gone. He apparently took nothing except the clothes he wore, not even the treasured Bible once held as a futile shield by an about-to-be-murdered bishop and later in shallow piousness by a lovely but equally doomed empress. There was a sealed letter propped up against the pillow on his carefully made bed. It was addressed to Ursula.

Paul, in a premonition of peril, slipped the letter into his pocket without telling the others of its existence. He returned to his waiting siblings. "He's not there and his bed's made." Günther and Ursula, seeing Paul's expression, returned quickly to the house. Behind them, Boris speculated out loud that Melchior probably no longer needed an escort to take him to church.

Once inside their brother's room Paul gave Ursula the letter. "He's gone for good; I'm sure of it."

Ursula turned the sealed envelope over several times and in a curious certainty that she was to remember later, divined its message. "It's going to say that I'm headed for hell. Well, too bad! I *don't* believe in hell." The three of them read the letter together:

My Sister,
   I know that you are freeing yourself of sin. I beg you to keep your relationship with our brother a thing of the past. God will forgive you for that if you will stay resolved and strong. I shall pray for you.

M.

Paul shook his head. "This letter does not exist. Destroy it. I'll phone Brandt."

Ursula, whose temple began to churn her blood black even before she finished reading Melchior's words, tore the letter to bits and flushed it down the toilet. "That simpering, egotistical prig," she hissed furiously. "How dare he! The conceit of his virtue is absolutely revolting. And what about *your* soul?" She stared through angry tears at Günther, seated at the foot of Melchior's bed.

"Lost, I'm afraid. I think he gave up on Paul and me years ago."

"And what gives him the right to spy on us?"

"Ursula, stop. He didn't have to spy; his room is directly above yours."

"Ahhh." Ursula beat her forehead with her fists.

"Stop." Günther took the meanly closed hands and held them in his.

Ursula laughed angrily. "He thinks I made a moral choice."

"You did," said Günther.

Conrad Brandt showed up the next morning. "I would have come yesterday if there had been a plane. Have you heard from him?" They all shook their heads as they watched Brandt drink deeply from his coffee cup. "I can't sleep on a train. May I have some more?" He held his cup toward Ursula, seated on the sofa with Paul. She filled his cup and placed the tray with its silver coffee service on a low table in front of the lawyer. "He spoke to none of you about any plans to leave?"

"No," said Günther. "We would all have discussed it had he confided in any of us."

"I rather suspect he's gone off to be a choirboy somewhere," said Boris, crossing his knees and dipping his elegantly shod foot. Ursula glanced toward Boris, but Günther spoke for her. "Shut up, Boris, and try not to be such an arrogant ass."

"Well, I think it's damned inconsiderate of him to leave without a word to anyone. He could have at least left a note."

Alexander broke the sudden stillness. "Saying what? 'I am running away from home to become a choirboy'?" Only Alexander laughed.

"I take it there was no word of any kind?" Brandt spoke directly to the twins.

"That's correct," Günther said.

"Then it's time that I tell you that we must put all of our knowledge together and try to reason out where he's gone." Brandt looked harried and tired.

"I don't understand what you're so concerned about," said Boris, taking a cigarette out of a gold case. "He'll be back. He'll get homesick and show up—sufficiently contrite, I assume—needing nothing more than a bath. What can happen to him in Switzerland?"

"He won't be back," said Ursula.

Brandt turned his bloodshot eyes toward her. "You sound very certain. How can you be so sure?"

"Grandfather made a mistake; he should not have insisted that Melchoir attend university. Grandfather knew what Melchior wanted. We all knew."

"That's true," said Günther. "He's lived an eremitic life since he was about four or five; and believe me, living it with the rest of us—the five of us—was bloody difficult for him. I think he's gone into a church somewhere. I mean permanently."

"To become a priest?" asked Brandt.

"No," said Ursula. "I don't think so. Not a priest. He doesn't think that way. Confessions and all that."

"You once said he would probably become a hermit."

"Yes, a hermit. I can see him as a hermit in a cave somewhere, or wandering in some wilderness."

"How about a monk?" Brandt asked.

"Possibly." She thought about Melchior's years of denial of life. "Yes, a monk."

"But he never said anything about this to you?" Ursula shook her head. "Do all of you think that's a reasonable conclusion—that he has probably gone to some retreat? Perhaps to a monastery?"

The twins nodded. Alexander and Boris agreed.

"Is there a chance he will call you when he gets settled somewhere?"

Ursula wasn't sure, but Günther believed Melchior would call them. "He is not really inconsiderate. He knows we will worry. I think we'll hear from him." Paul and Alexander agreed. Boris shrugged and lit his cigarette.

"If the general feeling is that he will contact you, I'll stay in Zurich for a few days." He rose. "I'll have to make some calls."

"Did you bring luggage?" asked Günther as they all rose.

"I thought I'd stay at a hotel."

"Why? We have a half-dozen empty rooms here. Take whichever suits you."

Brandt seemed to think about this as he looked out of the window at the lake. "If you're sure . . ."

"Of course we're sure," said Paul.

After the lawyer left the room to use the telephone the children speculated over his hesitation at staying with them. "We probably bore him," said Alexander. "I'll bet he likes nightclubs and casinos."

"No," said Günther, "he just doesn't want to appear presumptuous."

"He doesn't want to tell us what he knows," said Ursula. The boys stared at her. "Look how odd he is, all jumpy and funny. He hasn't said one word about Schneider . . . or the extra people at the funeral, or what the police have done about finding Brückner's killer. Wouldn't you mention those things to us?"

"He's worried about Melchior," said Paul. "He just hasn't gotten around to those things."

"No, he hasn't, and he's not going to unless we force it, and even then he's probably going to be evasive and put us off with—"

"Ursula . . ." Günther smiled at her and made a faint motion toward the door.

Conrad Brandt walked heavily back into the room. "She's right. I was hoping not to have to tell you anything at all." He put his hand out to Boris. "Let me have one of your fancy cigarettes. I'm out." He remained standing. "Let's start with my uncle's killer. The police are no closer today than they were a year ago. However, I privately sought out each of the witnesses and created a sort of picture of the man—or woman—in the gray coat. They told me the same mismatched stories they told the police. But when I asked two of them why they thought the person was a woman dressed as a man, they said he—or she—wore makeup, rouge, powder—"

"Not Agnes Schneider," said Alexander.

"Right, not Agnes Schneider," said Boris.

"Now, then, the extra people at the funeral. The director said he counted only thirteen. He expressed his great disappointment at so small a showing, et cetera, et cetera. There were the six of you, the maids, Graz, Berghoch, Frichter, Miss Schneider, and my uncle. That's thirteen. But it didn't come to me for a long time that I might have the wrong thirteen. So three weeks ago, at a funeral I had to arrange, I took a casual count of the people present. It was a small funeral; there were only seven. After it was over, I asked the director how many mourners there were. He had counted only six. You see, since I arranged it, he did not count me, just as a year ago, he did not count my uncle. That still left me with one too many if Ursula saw two extra people in the back of the room. I returned once more to ask about the count, and only in passing did the director happen to mention that he never counted anyone who did not stay for the service. Who left?"

"Berghoch left," said Boris. "I remember he walked out the side door without ever looking at Father."

"But we are still left with thirteen people. Ursula, you *saw* those strangers at that funeral. They were not an apparition."

"There are two more things I have to tell you. Believe me, I'd rather be evasive and put you off. First, Graz was killed in a construction accident. It was his funeral I arranged three weeks ago. I'm sorry."

The children crowded around the lawyer. "How . . . ?" asked Günther.

Ursula, waiting for the answer, saw the lawyer give her a quick pain-filled glance. "After you left, he moved to Salzburg. He didn't *have* to work. Your grandfather's bequest left him very well off. But Frichter and Berghoch both told me at the funeral that Graz couldn't stand the inactivity. In time he took a job in a park there. Some building was going on next door. He couldn't hear the truck or the crane or the falling platform. He was crushed under a ton of bricks. It was thoroughly investigated. The report ended by saying that his deafness killed him."

Ursula slumped to the sofa and put her hands over her face. "Graz. Gentle Graz." She felt Günther's arm cover her shoulder.

"What else?" asked Paul.

"A week ago, Frichter called me in great excitement. He frequently takes flowers to your family's plot. I've verified this with the caretakers. A week ago he claims he saw a woman lying on your father's grave. When he came near, she sprang up and ran away, screaming obscenities at him. She was wildly dressed, with hair all roaring around her head. He ran after her, but lost her among the hedgerows. He was sure the woman was Agnes Schnei-der."

20

"They searched everywhere, the grounds, the maintenance buildings, even the locked crypts. It was not the first time we heard reports that a woman acting strangely wandered through that area of the cemetery, and even around those graves, but this time the report came from someone who actually knew her."

"Did he talk to her at all?" asked Günther.

"Apparently not. She screamed curses at him and shrieked that she'd get him too."

"Get him *too?*" asked Alexander. "Doesn't that mean that she's got someone else already?"

"Not necessarily. It could mean that she was merely adding him to the list of people she intends to harm."

"Do the descriptions that the other reports give fit Agnes Schneider?" asked Ursula.

Brandt paused before he answered. "More or less. Why do you ask that?"

"It's sort of like the list of the thirteen. They could be different women."

"Yes, they could, but I'd say that the other descriptions fit her rather more than less."

Ursula's mind saw Agnes Schneider lying on her beloved's grave. She was whispering her adoration into the grass and moss growing over it. Around her prone body, the three heavy-thighed angels lifted their graceful garlands and danced. Ursula turned away from the scene with disgust. It wouldn't be so bad if her mother weren't buried beside him.

Through the long day of waiting for answers from Brandt's calls, Ursula tried to read, but after a page or two, her imagination would drift away to Melchior. For months he had had to listen to her and Günther in her bed. She saw him cringe, cover his ears, weep silently, and then pray a steady, monotonous repetition of prayers for her soul. The whole idea of Melchior's knowledge and beseeching both enraged and humilated her. She knew from his unhappiness with the university that he did not leave because of what he heard come from her bedroom; yet the certainty that she had added to his misery left her with a feeling of meanness toward herself. She went in search of the twins and found Brandt asleep beside the telephone, his head fallen forward on one arm on the desk, while the other hand actually touched the telephone. She tiptoed away.

Walking past the music solarium, she heard Boris' voice. "I still say it was a rash, foolish, unfair act. He had no right to leave." Ursula entered. The twins were seated in opposing easy chairs as Boris walked about the room in a brilliant red blazer, his hands in the pockets of his white flannel trousers. He looked like the Swiss flag. Alexander, seated on an ottoman, was flipping through a magazine. Boris went on. "What is religion anyway but a neat little bundle of charming superstitions."

"Not so little," said Günther.

"Not so neat," said Ursula.

"He could at least have waited until he had a decent education."

The twins and Ursula remained conspicuously silent, whereas Alexander, after obviously waiting for one of them to speak, shrugged and said, "What for?"

"Education needs no justification," said Boris with sweeping grandeur.

"That's bullshit," rejoined Alexander. "Why go if you're not going to use it for something?"

"Because the whole idea of being well-educated has nothing to do with the use of that education," said Boris loftily.

"That doesn't even make sense. You never make sense, do you know that?" said Alexander, dropping the magazine.

Ursula could see a fight coming. Günther stopped it before it started. "Don't do it, Alexy!"

"What?"

"Whatever stupidity you're thinking of doing."

Alexander picked up the magazine again and rolled it up. "He should have talked it over with us first. We should have had that chance."

Ursula knew what those words meant: they would have liked to have another chance with Melchior, a chance to be kinder, to sympathize with his piety even if they could not understand it.

They all froze when they heard the telephone ring. It rang only once. Minutes later, a rumpled Brandt burst into the room. "They found him," he said desperately. "And lost him again."

The Bronevskys, standing around the lawyer by then, all began to talk at once. "Let me explain. When he left here he went over to the monastery at Einsiedeln. But he stayed only one day, then asked them to send him somewhere else. And they did."

"Where?" asked Ursula.

"Somewhere in Italy. To another monastery in northern Italy."

Alexander laughed nervously. "If they know where they sent him, then he's not lost."

"He's *walking*," said Brandt with a shudder of exasperation. "Walking, for God's sake."

"Probably," said Ursula.

Brandt gave her a quick glance and laughed briefly. He was obviously relieved. "I don't understand, however, why he left one monastery to go to another."

"Because the one he left is rich."

"Ursula's right," said Günther. "We've been there with our grandfather and mother. It's a huge baroque Benedictine monastery. It's a pilgrimage center. The Church in Rome declared it as a place of miracles. It was founded around Charlemagne's time, but the present buildings are from the eighteenth century. Melchior would be comfortable living around the tenth century but not the eighteenth, with all that fancy architecture. Even the famous dark Madonna is adorned with jewels. But where did they send him?"

Brandt took a scrap of paper from his pocket. "Monte Tre Croci."

Ursula ran for the atlas in the library, already scanning the page of northern Italy as she hurried back to the solarium. On the table they all hunched over the map and searched the Alps for Monte Tre Croci. "Here it is," said Günther. "Northwest of Verbania on Lago Maggiore, very near the frontier. We were near there one summer in the mountains above Cannobio. Remember?"

"I remember the wind," said Alexander.

Ursula, too, remembered the wind: not a howl, but a perpetual shriek like something coming from an animal with a crushed paw. They all sat back and looked at the open map as though it were a dangerous incomprehensible weapon.

"What's the matter with the place?" asked Brandt, eyeing the map with suspicion when he saw the others draw away from it.

"It's in the Alps," said Paul, "but not on one of the main passes between Switzerland and Italy. It's on a sort of ledge some kilometers away from the road, if it's the place I remember. It was a hermitage turned monastery, a remote, primitive place, built around the twelfth century by men who felt the monasteries were becoming too worldly. There are storms up there . . . terrifying thunder, screaming winds. Even in the rather good hotel we were in further down in one of the valleys, we were without electricity for three days during a storm."

"I assume you were supplied candles."

"Better than that . . . Grandfather always made sure we carried a suitcase full of our own when we traveled anywhere, because Melchior was afraid of the dark."

Brandt looked back at the map, his face just awakening to what the Bronevsky siblings already knew. "They won't give him candles?"

The twins both shook their heads. "They will expect him to use them for religious rites, studies, work, but not to keep away the dark so he can sleep," said Günther.

There was nothing to do but wait. The people at the Einsiedeln monastery notified Monte Tre Croci to send word as soon as Melchior arrived. Brandt was flabbergasted and angered that Tre Croci had no telephone. Word would be taken by one of the brothers sent on muleback to the nearest town and there sent on by phone or wire. Meanwhile the police in Switzerland and northern Italy were searching the roads and highways for a young man dressed in the brown robes of a monk, robes he had begged for from the Einsiedeln brothers, giving in exchange the suit of clothing and shoes he was wearing.

Ursula tried to read, wondering if the Swiss monks had given Melchior reliable sandals. She and the twins had estimated the walking distance to Tre Croci to be over three hundred kilometers. "If he stays on the roads," said Ursula.

Brandt, watching them, abruptly stood up. "Do you think he might not? Might not stay on the roads?"

"I wouldn't," said Ursula.

"Why not?" Brandt turned to the twins when Ursula did not answer him. "Am I to assume that neither of you would either?"

"No, we would not stay on the roads," answered Günther. "Please understand: we would know that someone would come looking for us. And Melchior has *that* reason plus another one more basic to his nature. A road is a convenience, a luxury, an indulgence. He wants to give up comforts. He is not using the roads."

Brandt, his expression deeply troubled, smoked furiously. "What way will he go, then?"

"It's due south," said Paul. "He'll cut straight down across the country."

"But that's absurd. It's ridiculous and dangerous!"

"In Switzerland?" asked Ursula. "What way dangerous?"

Brandt jabbed out his cigarette and paced in front of the window facing the lake. "He's obviously an innocent." He lit another cigarette.

Ursula had the odd notion that the lawyer was trying to tell them something in code. "Does that make him more in danger than anyone else?"

"There are always those who take advantage of innocent young people."

Ursula searched for the clues to the code. "But he's dressed as a monk, and people respect that. And this country is not known for being dangerous. In fact, it has a reputation for being safe. And the country people are generous; they'll give him something to eat and a place to sleep. I don't understand the dangers you're talking about. What kind of advantage?" Ursula saw that Brandt was carefully turned away from her and the twins before he spoke.

"You—all of you—represent enormous wealth. Unscrupulous individuals wouldn't hesitate to use criminal means to get some of that wealth."

"But no one knows who he is," she said. "To the world, he is only a poor hermit making his way to some remote monastery. And I'm sure he's not carrying any money. He never carries any. He doesn't even wear a watch. What could anyone steal from him? The worst thing that can happen to him is frostbite and maybe getting stung by nettles." Ursula meant to reassure the attorney with this light view of the dangers facing Melchior, but when Brandt turned away from the window she was stunned at the anxiety in his eyes.

"You must understand. He's my responsibility. I have to know where he is. It's important that I know where he is. I've got to make some more calls." He started for the door.

"Before you go, I'd like to know something," said Ursula. He stopped in front of her. "How did you find out Melchior went to Einsiedeln?"

"I contacted our people here in Zurich and had them call every monastery in the area, every Catholic church, every retreat."

"What did you tell them? I mean, what did your people tell them?"

Brandt reddened. "I had them lie. I told them to say that Melchior was a runaway and that his parents were prostrate with worry and grief."

Ursula nodded, but she felt the lawyer's anxiety and restlessness rush against her like a hot wind. Considering all the circumstances, Melchior was not in the kind of danger that should turn Brandt into a man frenzied with apprehension. She said nothing to the twins, and later while she listened to them playing the pianos, she even forgot the lawyer's worry for a little while as an old fond scene came back to her. She was seated in a chair next to her grandfather in the music room of the Vienna house. The twins, leaning forward over the two keyboards of the immense pianos, were mirror-imaged in the dark reflecting glass of the room's vast windows, so that kaleidoscopically four twins' hands raced over the keys and filled the air with Mozart as the family listened in breathless awe. The vision dissolved when the twins of the present scene stopped playing as Brandt came to tell them that there was no news, that the police had covered every road Melchior might have taken. Ursula thought he looked frantic.

Throughout the evening, four calls came for Boris: one of his clubs was meeting the next afternoon; one of his friends wanted to borrow a book and would come by later; if the weather was good on Saturday would he have time for an early tennis game; had he read the new article on paranoiac disorders in *The Analyst Journal*. During each of these calls, Brandt left the phone desk and paced the floor outside the room as Boris chatted leisurely with his friends. One call was for Alexander. Ursula, seeing the lawyer stalk back and forth, opened the door to tell Boris to get off the wire.

"It's Alexander this time, but even he has been on it for over five minutes. And he is talking to a girl, so I may never get that phone back." He looked at her with desperate eyes, their deep blue star centers glittering with impatience. Ursula hurried into the room. "Get off the phone, Alexander."

"But I'm talking to a *very* good friend."

"Unless you're talking to Melchior, get off the phone. I'm counting to ten; then I'll take it away from you."

Alexander made a frog face, but said good-bye after whispering something to the person at the other end.

Brandt returned to the desk to take up his vigil again. He gave Ursula a halfhearted smile. "Frankly, I would have liked to see you take it away from him."

She ignored the remark. "I know you're worried about Melchior, but why are you worried . . . so *much?* It's the end of May. The weather is warm. He's dressed as a monk; if he needs anything, I'm sure people will give it to him. And he's not stupid. You'll see; he will find his way to the monastery."

Brandt picked up a pen and appeared to examine its design. Once he looked up at her but quickly trained his eyes on the object in his hand. "*You* would," he said. "You'd make it. But he seems so fragile to me, so unlike the rest of you."

Again she moved around his words. "Is there something you're not telling us? Is there something else, something . . . dangerous, that makes you so anxious about Melchior?"

Brandt answered her immediately. "No, of course not."

She knew he was lying. "Because if there is, we should know it, no matter how bad it is." She spoke softly, waiting for him to look up. When he did, his eyes held a reserve, a certain formal expression, distant, remote, impersonal. She almost laughed. "Is that the look you use in court when you want to hold something back?"

"Do you believe I'm holding something back?"

[241]

"Yes."

He shook his head. "No. If I had something I could tell you, I would."

Ursula searched his face for a blush, a quiver, a faltering, anything that would tell her the truth. But his expression remained as steadfast as stone, and perhaps it was this rigid composure that totally convinced her that he was lying. She left the room quickly, although she heard him rise behind her, and in a whisper so soft she was not sure she actually heard it, he said her name. She was to convince herself later that she only imagined it.

During dinner none of them spoke. Boris and Alexander were furious because Günther would no longer let them use the telephone; and they both left the table before the dessert arrived. After dinner, Ursula, the twins, and Brandt drank coffee on the terrace. A large sailboat, its rigging outlined with streamers of lights, floated by, laughter rippling in its wake.

"Melchior impressed me as being shy," said Brandt after a long silence. "Whom would he ask for help?"

"Country people, farm people," said Günther.

"Would he ask someone to drive him to this place if he got fed up with walking?"

"He won't get fed up," said Ursula. "He may be afraid of the dark and he doesn't like games and sports the way the rest of us do, but he is quite strong in other ways."

"Is he trusting?"

"Trusting? What do you mean?" asked Paul.

"Is he easily fooled? I mean, would he be taken in by anyone offering him help without expecting to get anything in return . . . or would he be suspicious?"

There it was again, thought Ursula, that extra concern, that veiled apprehension that made no sense in the presence of the facts.

"Melchior, suspicious?" said Günther. "No. You don't understand Melchior. He probably won't need any help. He'll be too busy giving it."

"Would he give his real name, if asked?"

"Certainly. He never learned how to lie."

At Günther's answer, Brandt got up and commenced to pace. Ursula watched the same tight anxiety she had seen earlier gather in his face like a shadow, his eyes darkening under his brows, his mouth turning hard and grim. He lit a cigarette and paced. A servant brought brandy, and for a few minutes as the man refilled the coffee cups and put out glasses for the liquor, none of them spoke. The twins each took a brandy glass, but Brandt ignored his.

When they were alone again, Ursula offered him a glass from the tray, but he shook his head. "No, I have to stay awake."

"Would his name mean anything to anyone?" asked Ursula.

"Your grandfather is a famous man in this country."

"But Melchior does not have the same surname, and he would never identify himself as an Enerde grandson."

"Ursula, the world is full of unscrupulous people who make it their business to discover exactly that kind of thing."

"But the monks at Einsiedeln did not know who he was and still don't and the people at Tre Croci do not know who he is, and he is not using the roads, so who in the world could do him harm?"

Brandt stopped walking. "There were people in Vienna who knew who you were. And the two women who died, and Berghoch, and Frichter, even Graz, any of them could have unwittingly mentioned to someone that you were coming here. It was not something we could keep secret." He began to walk again. "Your grandfather should have sent you to an American university. He even considered it. But my uncle talked him out of it. He wanted you nearby where he could . . . watch over you."

"Is someone watching over us?" asked Ursula. The twins, too, seemed to lean toward Brandt for his answer.

The lawyer gave a short mirthless laugh. "Yes, I am. Or at least I thought I was, except that I've lost one of you." He picked up the brandy glass, but then put it back down without drinking.

"Omitting Miss Schneider for the moment, what people in Vienna would want to harm us? And how could they?" asked Ursula.

"Anyone with a criminal intent. They could kidnap one of you. I had hoped not to have to say this."

Ursula realized at once that this was exactly what he wanted to say. She had given the lawyer a way out by asking questions that called for general answers. Angry at herself, she got up and bade the three men good night, touching both twins' shoulders as she passed between their chairs. At the French doors she paused. "You'll let us know at once if you get any word?"

"Of course," said Brandt. "I wish you a good night's sleep."

"Thank you," she said, trying for a cynical smile. "But with all those criminals out there, do you think I should lock my windows?"

Günther glanced over his shoulder at her and gave her a droll smile. Paul laughed. But Conrad Brandt, she saw, had the grace to appear embarrassed.

Ursula read for several hours, letting the book fall against her chest each time she heard one of her brothers enter his room. The house seemed to resound with the closing of doors. She heard the twins' shutters lock into place long after midnight. She returned to her book, but drifted away from it again as she imagined Conrad Brandt asleep at the phone desk, his head resting on his arm, his hand on the phone.

At two, she got up, pulled her bedspread around her body, and opened the doors to her balcony. The lake was a black abyss at the edge of the lawn. The gardener's cottage was also black, but in the pavilion, a small red light gleamed briefly, then paled, gleamed again and paled again. She knew at once what it was. Conrad Brandt was not asleep at the desk with his hand on the phone. He was in the pavilion, smoking, his attention not on the lake, but on the house. She stepped out on the balcony and looked over the ledge at the floors below and the one above. All the windows were dark. Hers alone had light pouring from it, and as she stood watching the cigarette wink its feverish light at her, she knew she was silhouetted in her own light and that he was watching her. She stepped back into the room and turned out the lamp. But then she returned to the balcony in her single garment to watch the man light a new cigarette from the old one. At the thought of the cigarette in his mouth, she let the coverlet slip from her shoulders and fall to the floor of the balcony. Naked, in the spring night, she watched the red light glow and pale repeatedly, receiving from his waxing and waning breath a perverse pleasure that stirred the flesh of her thighs and hardened the nipples of her breasts.

[243]

For the next two days she watched his worrying intensify. He ate little and apparently slept only an hour during the day while the twins kept vigil by the telephone. Even Boris asked him if he were feeling ill, so haggard did his face become. He answered that he felt splendid, then snarled at Boris to stay off the "damn phone," although a baffled Boris had not used it since Günther forbade him to do so. Brandt no longer touched any alcohol, not even wine at dinner. Every few hours he checked with the monastery at Einsiedeln or the police or the office in Zurich. He smoked incessantly.

By Wednesday morning, the fifth day after Melchior's flight, he found Ursula curled up in a chair alone in the library. "Why don't you trust me?" he asked in a raspy, angry voice, his face drawn and pale.

She evaded the question. "You need rest, and you're smoking too much. Your voice sounds bad. Does your throat hurt?"

He moved closer to her chair and looked down on her from his high rage. "I don't need a bunch of kids to tell me how to take care of myself."

"Oh? Have my sweet, sympathetic brothers been giving you free medical advice, too?" For a moment Ursula had the impression that he was swaying. She started to rise. "Conrad?" But he turned and stalked from the room.

On the afternoon of that same day a priest from Einsiedeln phoned to say that Melchior had reached Monte Tre Croci. The abbot at the Italian monastery was sending a letter to clear up some details. Conrad Brandt's elation infected all of them. He had several Scotches and talked fast about the good-natured Swiss, their sobermindedness and generosity. He laughed at Boris' bad puns and commended Alexander's plans to take flying lessons. He asked the twins to play some Chopin for him, and he lavishly admired a row of Ursula's watercolors hanging on the first-landing wall. By dinnertime he was quite drunk and the twins put him to bed.

Ursula and the twins found Brandt packed and ready to leave early the next morning. "I'm going to borrow your car and drive for a couple of days," he said.

"You're going to Italy?" said Ursula. The twins showed surprise at her question.

"Who said I was going to Italy? I didn't tell anyone I was going to Italy, did I?"

"Are you going to try to bring Melchior back?"

He turned to the twins. "Does she ever answer a question?"

"Try different questions," said Paul.

"I didn't hear you answer *hers,*" said Günther.

He nodded. "Yes, I'm going to Italy. If I think Melchior is safe there, I shall make no effort to bring him back."

"Safe!" said Ursula. "I wish I understood your obsession with safety."

He started to answer her, but checked himself.

"You were going to say . . . ?"

"Nothing," he said, shaking his head.

Ursula stormed away in a rage, leaving the twins to see Brandt off.

Günther found her later in the pavilion. "You're an ill-tempered girl today. What is it?"

"Don't you see that he is lying to us?"

"No, I don't. I can't recall anything he said that could be termed a lie."

"It's not what he said; it's what he didn't say. He knows something, and he's not telling us."

"About what?"

"I don't know. I only feel it."

"Not good enough, Ursula, to label him a liar."

The driver returned alone three days later, saying only that Mr. Brandt had returned to Vienna and that he would call them in a few days. They were not to worry: Melchior was in a safe place.

Melchior's departure left a void in their lives that none of them could quite understand. His religious fervor had always annoyed and embarrassed them; but now that it was gone, they felt its absence as one feels the absence of faint background music so intimate as to be sensed only by its loss. The distant, barely audible sea had ceased to throb.

Ursula wrote to him weekly but received no answer. "Maybe letters are against the rules," said Alexander.

It was the abbot at Monte Tre Croci who finally answered one of her letters: Melchior was in good health and well-suited to life at the monastery. His piety and hard work were an inspiration to many. The twins read the letter. "What kind of work do you suppose he does?" asked Günther of no one in particular.

"Everything that no one else will do," said Ursula.

"I hope they have him translating Latin and Greek," said Paul. "He has a real talent for that."

"He's cleaning latrines and weeding turnip patches," said Ursula, trying to read between the abbot's few uninformative lines.

All summer the Broncvskys spent the long days sailing on the lake, riding in the nearby hills, learning how to drive a car. Boris' friends began to come by the house. Several times during the summer nights Ursula passed the alcove off the sitting room and discovered Boris and one of his "female colleagues" embracing on the sofa. But usually they came in the afternoon and their constant chatter on psychosexual dysfunctions drove Ursula to her room or the pavilion to read. The twins fled to the pianos. Alexander put on his finest slacks and sweaters and went visiting. Ursula knew he had a girl somewhere, but since he never volunteered any information, she asked for none. Brandt phoned once a week and in a formal tone inquired after their health, desires, and needs. He was formally answered by the twins or Ursula. Their health was sound, their desires satisfied, and their needs fulfilled. Occasionally when Ursula spoke to him, Brandt would linger on the line, saying nothing. She would ask him if there was any other news and he would say no. She always ended up hanging up first. The summer passed uneventfully and without problems. As the year waned they were again deeply immersed in their studies.

Late one night, after the first snowfall, as Ursula wandered back to her room from the library, she heard a distinct hiccuping sobbing, punctuated by several ohs of pain coming from the bath opposite her room. The door was open only a crack but enough to let Ursula peek into the well-lighted room. With a gasp, she shoved the door open. Before her seated on the toilet was a naked girl, blond and pretty, forcing a bottle brush into her vagina. "Great God, what are you doing?" she whispered harshly. The girl's thighs were bloody to her knees and with each jab of the long-handled brush she cried her little "oh-oh-ohs" of pain. Ursula locked the door and stood in front of the girl. "Stop that. Stop that at once."

"I can't," wailed the girl. "I have to get them all out. Oh, oh, oh." She shoved the brush in and out. Ursula reached down and grasped the plunging hands, holding them still. "Get what out?"

"The babies, the little things that turn into babies. Alexander put them into me." She sobbed hopelessly, her hands falling away to the side of the toilet. Very carefully Ursula pulled the blood-soaked brush from the girl's vagina.

"That's not the way to do it. It wouldn't even work that way. All you need is a little soapy water in a douche bag. You can even do it without a bag just by lying in the tub and pouring some soaped water in as you pull up your stomach muscles after exhaling all your breath. For God's sake, you've torn yourself to shreds. Who told you to use a brush like this?" The girl shook her head and continued to cry. "Don't you know *anything* about your own body? What do you think semen is? Didn't you look at it?"

"I didn't know he was going to put his thing in there."

"Where did you think he was going to put it? Into your navel?"

"I didn't know. I didn't know what he was doing. I only felt it on my . . . my place down there. Then the stuff was all slimy afterward."

"Of course it's slimy. It's supposed to be slimy. But you don't get it out of you with a bottle brush. Don't you know where the semen goes that Alexander so generously parts with? There are hundreds of books on it with very good pictures. Now, stop crying and clean yourself up."

But the girl didn't move. "Does this mean I'm pregnant?"

"I don't know. Have you had all your menstrual months?" She nodded. "All right, then, when was your last one?"

"Three weeks ago."

"Good. And how long have you been making love with Alexander?"

"Tonight was . . . the first time."

"Why, that bloody fraud. He's been looking so smug lately, I assumed he'd been at it for months."

"No." She blushed hotly. "I only let him look."

"So how did it get from looking to this?"

"I think it was the champagne. After three glasses I felt so funny, everything he said seemed to be all right. So he asked if he could slip off my underpants and take another look. I couldn't see any harm in it, so I let him. But then he took his thing out and rubbed it against me down there. He said it would be all right and that it was safe as long as he just rubbed, but then something happened. I don't know when exactly, but he stopped rubbing and pushed it in and kept pushing and pushing and pushing, even when I begged him not to. And then he sort of cried out and when he got off me I was all sticky and slimy. He said I better wash up. He said he was awfully sorry but he just couldn't stop."

"And where is this adorable brother of mine now?"

"He fell asleep on the sofa downstairs."

"Never mind him for the moment," she said, turning on the water in the tub. "Get in." The girl climbed clumsily into the tub. "You have to find out about your body. Get some books with good pictures and then get yourself fitted with an anticonception device. Once you see how your insides are organized, you'll see how the device works. It's a little rubber cap that fits over the cervix and keeps the sperm from traveling to the egg."

Ursula paused and flushed the toilet's bloody contents. She handed the girl a soft washcloth. "Why don't you take a course in anatomy?"

"I don't like science and anyway my mother says a girl should study things that will help her be a good mother and wife."

"Your mother should have taken a course in anatomy."

The tub was filling as Ursula sat on the laundry hamper contemplating the crying girl. What a poor dope, her insides all shredded. That wasn't going to heal in a day!

"At least now we'll finally be engaged," said the girl, drying her eyes with the back of her hand.

Ursula took a deep breath. "Did you make such an agreement with him: three glasses of champagne and a speedy seduction equals instant engagement for marriage?"

"Well, no, not the way *you* put it, but that's the way it works. I mean, once a boy does that to you, he's supposed to marry you. And I know Alexander wouldn't go back on his word. He's much too honorable."

"Did he give you some word?"

"No, not exactly."

Ursula wondered if she should tell the girl the truth: Alexander had no intention of marrying anyone for at least ten years. His sights were on flying fighter planes, and in his views, a wife was a detriment to a budding military career. Additionally, Alexander was barely eighteen, and as he often put it, the world was full of girls just waiting to find him. In the meantime, he was eagerly watching the Korean war, hoping it would not be over before he could offer himself to the United Nations and qualify for an elegant little wound and a glorious big medal.

Ursula considered waking Alexander up and punching him in the mouth. But perhaps letting the girl tell him that they were now engaged was a far better cure. "You should tell Alexander about your wedding plans as soon as possible. He will want to meet your parents so the banns can be posted."

"Thank you for being so nice. I've seen you at the university but you always seemed in a hurry, and you never talk to anyone. Alexander says you're antisocial. But I think you're nice to help me like this." She paused at her washing and looked shyly at Ursula through reddened eyes. "Would you stand up with me at my wedding?"

Ursula felt her heart do a curious bulging, as though it were actually enlarging. She slammed the toilet seat down and sat on it. "Listen," she said, facing the naked girl. "You're doing a very stupid thing assuming Alexander is going to . . . " She wanted to say "marry you," but it sounded grossly cruel. Instead she said, "get married right away. In my family men do not marry young. My grandfather was forty-six when he got married; my father was over thirty. It's a sort of custom with us."

"But that doesn't matter. People marry when they fall in love. Maybe they had to fall in love first."

[247]

"Is Alexander in love?"

"Yes, Oh, yes, yes, yes."

"Did he say so?"

"Yes." Her eyes glowed, then dimmed. "You don't *want* to stand up with me, do you?" She started to cry again. "Why don't you like me?"

Ursula felt clammy with a cold rage rising in her chest. "I don't even know your name."

"It's Lisle, but everyone calls me Shatzie. You can call me Shatzie, if you like."

"Listen, Lisle. Don't make any plans for a while. How old are you?"

"I'll be eighteen soon. My mother got married before she was eighteen, and so did my grandmother. I'd like to do that too."

Ursula pulled the chained plug out of the tub. "Let that bloody water out, and start over fresh and then . . . then go home. Forget Alexander. He's a dope."

The girl started crying again, louder this time. She pulled herself up clumsily out of the water. Reddish scum covered her hips and thighs. Flecks of red foam stuck to her soft belly and white breasts. She looked like a faded paper flower blown into the gutter. Ursula wound a towel around the dripping figure. She wanted to say something else to her—something to make her stop crying, stop thinking about marriage to Alexander, something to make her smarter. But she left the bathroom without speaking. Pity was like tasting nausea on an empty stomach: there was simply nothing one could throw up.

Ursula said nothing to Alexander about her encounter with the girl, but she noticed in the following weeks that he refused to take phone calls and that he was frequently quarrelsome and belligerent. He began to spend some of his weekends at the hunting lodge near Winterthur, commenting that there was no company like the company of men, particularly brothers-in-arms. He was apparently a big hit at the club. He allowed the emperor's gun to be on display for a whole day in the trophy room during a special club event.

Lisle called Ursula every day and begged her to talk to Alexander for her. "Please, Ursula, he won't talk to me and he goes the other way when he sees me." The conversations always ended with the girl crying and Ursula swearing.

And then abruptly three days passed without the girl calling. At dinner that Saturday night, Alexander, again his buoyant self, announced that he was going out for the evening.

"Oh, I forgot to mention to you," said Ursula. "Lisle asked you to be sure to call her."

Alexander jerked his head around. "When?"

"Whenever you have time."

"No, I mean when did she call?"

"Every day for three weeks."

Alexander shifted uneasily, but he recovered quickly. "Today?"

"No, not today or yesterday or the day before. Tell me, was anyone else injured?"

"What do you mean, injured?" asked Alexander.

"Does she have an older brother who is looking for you with a dueling pistol? No, of course not. I forgot; she mentioned she was an only child. As I recall, she wished she had a brother. So what did she do? Just try to hit you? You could easily hold her off with a pugilist's traditional raised-arm defense, hence the bruise on your handsome wrist." Alexander dropped his right hand into his lap. "That girl is truly unbelievable: she did not even use her fingernails." Ursula paused. "Damn, I forgot that, too: she hasn't any fingernails. I remember now she was nibbling on them in the bathtub." She smiled faintly at Alexander. "So she simply pummeled you with her futile fists. What in the world did you tell her?"

By this time the twins and Boris were staring at Alexander, who had reddened fiercely. "You hit a girl?" asked Boris.

"Of course not," blurted Alexander. "*She* hit me."

"Why?" asked Paul, his head tilted in disbelief.

"Because she insisted that I marry her!"

"Couldn't you have let her down gently?" asked Ursula. "I mean, couldn't you have looked sad, even cried a little and said you weren't good enough for her sweetness, that you were a brute, that you'd only ruin her life, et cetera, et cetera, et cetera? Something out of literature would have done the job, too; she has very romantic notions: you had to return to Austria to save Vienna from the Russians and you would surely die there, and where would she be then, poor lovely lost girl, her life over. Something like that. Something out of Flaubert or even Tolstoy. You certainly remember poor Natasha falling for that handsome, already married ape. By the way, just what did you tell her?"

"That's nobody's business but mine."

"Unless, of course, she's pregnant. Then it will become her parents' business and I suppose various others'." Ursula already knew that Lisle was not pregnant. "And since she's such a good girl, she would have to tell her parents that you raped her."

Alexander's chair fell back as he lurched up. "I never raped her."

"Oh, *I* believe you. Do you think her father will?" asked Ursula.

Günther spread his hands flat on the table in front of him. "Could it look like rape?"

"What do you mean, could it look like rape?" Alexander's exasperation carried an edge of fear in it. He straightened his chair and sat again.

Günther, looking down at some point between his spread hands, spoke softly. "You know exactly what I mean."

"No, I did not rape her, and she's not pregnant."

"That's not an answer to my question. Could whatever you did have the *appearance* of rape?"

Alexander shook his head. "No, of course not; she was perfectly willing."

"Alexander," said Ursula, "if she *says* it was rape, it will have more than its appearance. She is an ignorant girl, and she might say anything. A lot depends on what you told her when she spoke of marriage."

"I didn't tell her anything."

"Then what did you do?"

"I laughed."

Ursula looked around the table at each of her brothers: they were all

[249]

looking down at the silver or the dishes or perhaps at nothing. "I don't think you can do that more than a few times, Alexander, before someone gets very upset."

Alexander jumped up. "And I don't think that what I do is anybody's business at this table." He rushed out of the dining room mumbling under his breath. For a week, the others refused to talk to him. Then one night a week later during a long silence at dinner, he said quietly, "I know I shouldn't have laughed when that girl said I had to marry her."

"Then tell her you're sorry, and explain to her why you can't marry," said Günther.

Alexander nodded. "I guess I'll do that."

"Soon," said Ursula.

"Yes," said Alexander.

The day after this quiet exchange, Alexander in a sober mood made his last trip to Winterthur. Sometime in the afternoon, during the last Saturday in November, he and a friend were walking along a rocky stream when another hunter farther up the mountain mistook the movement in the shrubbery to be that of a deer. He felled Alexander with a single shot through the heart.

21

Ursula and the twins returned to the house at six that Saturday carrying ice skates. They were bright-cheeked from the cold and a little giddy from laughing over the odd attire of a pair of skaters on the park ice pavilion. "But a homburg!" said Ursula. "And a three-piece suit—meant for a cabinet meeting at least."

"Don't forget his lady friend," said Günther, "with her glass-eyed little fur skins and carrying her alligator handbag as she waltzed with him."

"I thought they were rather charming. So staid, so solemn, so Swiss," said Paul. "Ah, the car's here. Alexy's home early. Good." He pushed open the door.

The priest stood in the middle of the foyer under a crystal chandelier. It cast a particularly cruel glare: too many bulbs, too bright, so that the man's face had a touch of brutishness to it—a loose-hanging jaw, a low forehead jutting over eyes lost in shadow. A uniformed policeman stood off a little to his right.

Ursula clutched Günther's arm as a ripple of terror ran through her body. "What?" she whispered.

The priest was already talking, already holding his arms out to them as if to embrace all three. "Be strong. It is the Lord's will," he intoned too quickly for Ursula and the twins to prepare themselves for the policeman's words.

"It's your brother. There's been a tragic accident."

"Melchior!" whispered Ursula.

"A shooting," the policeman was saying. "Completely accidental. They shoot at anything that moves—those people! There should be better training . . ."

"The Lord has called him to his bosom," intoned the priest.

Ursula heard Paul make a choking sound deep in his throat. Günther placed his hand over her fingers clutching his arm. She looked from priest to policeman and back again. "A shooting?" she whispered. "Impossible. . . ."

"Which . . . brother?" said Günther, his attention hard on the policeman.

The man raised a sheet of paper he had been holding down at his side. "Bronevsky, Alexander."

"No," said Ursula. She could feel Paul take her other hand. "No. You're wrong. He took the car today, and it's in the driveway. He's home."

"An officer drove it back. I'm sorry."

"No," she said again. "No." Both twins leaned closer to her, so that for a few moments she could not move at all.

"Someone will have to identify . . ." The officer was still scanning the paper.

Ursula broke away from her brothers and snatched the sheet from the man's hands. She read quickly. ". . . through the chest area by another member of the club who at this time remains unnamed and unknown. All members' guns have been confiscated until the autopsy has been performed and ballistics has determined which weapon fired the fatal shot. The investigation is to commence at once. Notification of the family urgent. Body taken to Central Morgue for examination." Ursula felt Günther's breath close to her. Paul was holding the corner of the sheet of paper, which was shaking in her hand. "It has to be a mistake," she said, already knowing it was not.

"Rely on the Lord to help you through this time of sorrow. Take comfort in the knowledge that your brother is with Him, that He called that child to come to Him, and . . ."

Ursula whirled around, the sheet of paper still clutched in her hand. Shaking violently, she tried to speak to the priest but the words stuck in her throat as she tried to scream at the man, who had backed off a few paces. The twins quickly took Ursula's arms and pulled her away into the library. Before closing the door, Günther motioned to the officer. "Give us a few minutes, please."

Once they were alone, Günther spoke softly. "Listen, it's going to be Alexander. Paul and I have to go identify him."

"I'm going with you."

"No, Ursula, please."

Ursula looked into Günther's stricken eyes. "We have to do it together. I can't stay here alone."

"Stay with the priest. He means well."

"I'd strangle him."

"Let her come," said Paul.

Günther bowed his head, his shoulders jerking with a sudden spasm. "All right. We go together."

They rode with the policeman, leaving the priest standing in the foyer looking vaguely hurt because they had refused his offer to go with them.

Alexander was dressed in the gray-green uniform of his hunting club. In death, his face had lost the brooding quality they all shared. The flattening of his features pulled back his sullen full lower lip, giving him a near-smiling expression that made Ursula shrink with anguish as the body was wheeled before them. She turned her face against Paul's shoulder and moaned. Around her the voices, dust-dry, choked the air in the room. "Yes, it's our brother. I want . . ." said Günther. "I want to see the wound." Paul pulled Ursula away from the table, and together they sat on a bench near the granite-gray wall.

"It's not customary," said the officer.

Ursula, watching, saw Günther pull away the cloth that covered Alexander's body and bend over the chest, his head turning first one way and then the other, as though he were examining a piece of artwork in a glass case. Neither the two morgue attendants nor the policeman tried to stop him. "How is it they do not know who fired the gun?"

"When we find the bullet we'll know," said the officer. He glanced at Ursula and lowered his voice. "From the other wound it's clear it went straight through him and out the back. They are searching for it now at the site."

"Don't the others know who fired it?"

"All the guns were fired this afternoon. They always fire them at set targets before they go out on a hunt. It's a special rite they have, checking out their firearms."

"But they must know who fired at that particular time."

"No one's come forth."

"Witnesses?"

"No one's come forth."

Günther pulled the cloth back over Alexander's chest, and with a motion Ursula was to see again and again in her long sleepless nights, he stroked his dead brother's face.

When Ursula and the twins returned home, they found the priest in the sitting room with a distraught Boris. "It's a mistake, isn't it? How could they make such a stupid mistake? This man keeps trying to comfort me and he doesn't even know me. He says . . . he says . . ." Boris stopped talking and stared dumbly at his sister's and brothers' faces. "It's a mistake! Tell me it's a mistake!" None of them answered him. He turned away slowly and fell into a chair. Ursula knelt beside him, patting his hand in an aimless, distracted way as he wept openly.

"Courage, my boy," said the priest, rising from the sofa, his black garment ending at his highly polished shoes.

"Please leave us," said Ursula, looking up from the floor.

"But you need the comfort of your faith now. It will give you strength." He looked to the twins.

"Please," said Paul. "Leave us."

The priest clasped his hands and glided noiselessly out of the room.

"Melchior," said Ursula. "We must get in touch with Melchior."

"Not to mention Conrad Brandt," said Günther.

The only way they knew to reach Melchior was by mail. Brandt would have better connections. But when Günther reached Brandt and told him that Alexander had been killed in a hunting accident, none of them could understand the lawyer's reaction. Günther quickly held the phone at arm's length for all of them to hear. Ursula could hear him ten feet away. "Don't leave the house! Don't let anyone in! Stay away from the windows!" There was a sudden silence; then a calmer Brandt spoke. "What I mean is that until I get there, don't do anything."

"We want to reach Melchior. You were able to get word to that monastery before. Please tell us how you—"

"No. Don't do anything. I'll get a plane tonight. The Americans will give me a ride. I have some friends there." Again he paused. By now all of them were standing around the phone. "Günther, give me your word none of you will leave the house for any reason. And you'll have no one in."

Günther agreed. After hanging up, Günther, frowning deeply, sat looking at the phone. "He never asked where Alexy was shot, or even by whom."

"What does it matter?" said Boris. "An accident is an accident. We can only imagine how the poor man who fired the shot must feel."

Ursula saw the twins give each other one of their secret looks: a barely perceptible rise of energy in the eyes and then a casual comment. "Yes," said Paul. "What a thing to have to live with."

For years Ursula had known this language, knowing that the throwaway comment came for the sake of harmony or secrecy or safety.

"We shall have to take him back to Vienna," said Boris. "He must be buried with Father and Mother and Grandfather." He lit a cigarette and offered his case to the twins, who shook their heads without speaking. "I think we should consider a crypt. I know Great-Grandfather believed in returning everyone to the earth, but that's so barbaric. An above-ground crypt with vaults, that's the thing. We could have everyone moved. Of course, it wouldn't be necessary to go back more than a hundred years, but I think . . ."

Ursula got up, giving the twins a look of anguished despair. "Excuse me," she said, knocking over a footstool as she stumbled from the room.

Günther followed her. "Ursula."

"I felt so badly for him, and now I wish he would just shut up. How can he adjust so quickly, so easily? He wants to develop a new family necropolis and move the dead into a more fashionable neighborhood. I swear, Günther, sometimes he drives me crazy."

"Come on," said Günther. In the library, he took brandy and glasses from a cupboard and poured them each a drink.

"What's the matter with Conrad?" she asked. "What did he mean, 'Stay away from the windows'? I don't understand his thinking. He believes we are in some kind of danger."

"Overreaction, I expect." Günther leaned his head on the back of the chair and closed his eyes.

Paul joined them. "Boris is drawing up plans for the crypt. At least it will keep him occupied."

"He's disgusting," said Ursula. "He deals with death by making a better home for the dead." She took a long swallow of the brandy and shrank inward with the warmth of the liquor, trying to erase Alexander's near-smiling expression.

Brandt arrived just after midnight. The twins rose to meet him, but Ursula watched from the sofa as he stood in the doorway to the library, his face wild with both anxiety and relief. "Mr. Brandt," she asked quietly, "why did you think we would be dead?"

"Dead? No. No. I had no such idea! I'm just glad to see that all of you haven't fallen apart from this terrible tragedy."

Paul rang the bell and ordered coffee. "Boris is asleep on the sofa in the sitting room. He's all right. But we must get word to Melchior."

Brandt nodded. "Tomorrow."

"And will you tell us tomorrow why we couldn't leave the house or have anyone in or go near the windows?" asked Ursula.

Brandt managed a faint embarrassed smile. "I didn't understand the facts. My first thought was that you were all in danger. Some bloody fool with a gun . . . it sounded insane. If Alexander could be shot, any of you could be shot. I didn't think. Please understand, I became a little unhinged."

Günther gave her a glance as if to say: See, overreaction. Ursula said nothing, but gave Günther a look of her own that she knew he would understand.

"I called the local police here while I was waiting for my American friends to find me a flight over. There seems to be a good deal of confusion about what happened. Apparently there were several people shooting at the time. It's surprising there aren't more such accidents, although those clubs usually have some stiff rules about the given areas they can track into. Still, the mountains are rugged and one can easily get dislocated or lost."

"Did they identify the shell?" asked Ursula.

"They haven't found it. It was already sundown when it happened, and the dark comes early. And now it's snowing. . . ."

Ursula got up and pulled open the heavy drapes on the tall library windows. The snow was falling straight down without a whisper of a wind to give it the faintest slant. It fell in large lacy flakes, covering the balconies and outer stairs, haloing the round external lamps, obliterating the lawns and walks, deepening the blackness of the lake. Ursula left the window and opened the door to the outside. She stepped out quickly, closing the door behind her. Near the edge of the balcony, she turned and looked back into the room. The twins were still seated but Brandt was already up and running. He raced toward her, leaving the door behind him open. When she felt his hands grasp her wrists, she wrenched them free and stepped back. "Liar," she whispered, tears of rage filling her eyes. His face close to hers was blurred but still she saw the pain run across it like a knife blade. He did not speak at all, but this time he held onto her, picking her up and carrying her back into the room. "She's barefoot," he said flatly, releasing her slowly, his face still close to hers, his eyes still locked to hers.

[254]

Ursula shook the snow from her hair. "I'm tired," she said, turning away from the lawyer. She could feel the twins watching her as she picked up a book from the table and left the library.

At the top of the stairs she passed her own room and entered Alexander's. She lay on his bed in the dark and began to weep. "Did you really think you could make us safe, Grandfather?"

Sometime during the night Günther found her. "I thought you'd come here." He lay beside her and cradled her head in his arm. "What happened tonight out there in the snow?"

"Conrad wasn't concerned about my being barefoot. He was afraid of someone with a gun."

"So it *was* a test?"

"Yes."

"What else happened?"

"I don't know."

"Did he say anything to you?"

"No. What happens tomorrow?"

"He does not want us to return to Vienna. He thinks we should bury Alexander here; or *he* should take him home and have it done there, quietly."

"You think Alexy's death was an accident, don't you?"

"Yes. Why would a member of the club shoot him?"

"Why hasn't someone come forth?"

"Fear. Guilt. Shame. Or there is the possibility that whoever fired at that moment did not know that he hit Alexander. There were more than twenty men, all of them supposedly behind the line of fire stretching across several wooded ravines and mountains."

"Was Alexander behind the line of fire?"

"That's still being investigated. If he rushed on ahead so he could bag a deer . . . Actually that sounds like something he might do."

"Yes, it also sounds like something someone besides you could figure out he might do. I mean: it's no secret that Alexander is impulsive." What she had said brought her to tears again. "Was, was, was!" she whispered.

"Ursula, it will take time to come to terms with this."

"I hate that expression: everything is a matter of coming to terms. Everything is a compromise."

"With death it's the best you can opt for."

In the morning, they all met for breakfast, Conrad Brandt looking as if he had not slept for a week. They all waited for him to tell them what to do on this day. He drank coffee and smoked, but did not eat. It was still snowing. "Is it necessary for Melchior to leave the monastery now? I mean, will he want to leave that place for his brother's funeral?"

"I should think *so!*" said Boris.

"Perhaps not," said Ursula, ignoring Boris' urgent statement. "He's never answered any of our letters. I heard from the abbot once—a few very general comments saying that Melchior had adjusted to his new life. Don't you want him to come?" Ursula watched Brandt's hand holding the cigarette. It quivered ever so slightly. She quickly sought his eyes, thinking: he will lie now. But she saw instantly that he was not on guard.

"No, I don't want him to come." His voice was angry and he did not look at her.

Ursula knew her direct question had forced him into the truth. There was no doubt left in her mind that Brandt was convinced they were all in danger. He had tried to conceal his fears from them, and he would continue to try, but he would be more subtle after this. He would always be on guard now. What really amazed Ursula was that the twins did not feel Brandt's fears. If she could find out what Brandt knew, what secret thing he kept to himself . . . As it was, she had nothing to go on except feelings—anxiety, suspicion, uncertainty. And she could not go to Günther and Paul with feelings alone.

She watched Brandt surreptitiously and remembered the night in the pavilion. And then there was last night. At the moment he picked her up in the snow she was remotely astonished that she had trapped him so easily, but as his grasp of her grew fiercely intense, his arms holding her tightly against his chest, she knew it was neither her bare feet nor the phantom assassin that caused him to pick her up. She could feel his hand clutch her thigh, his arm encircling her shoulders and touch her breast. She could feel him hold his breath as he carried her. If she could get closer to him! If she could seem to want to be near him, she might discover what strange secret he was keeping from them. In moments of intimacy, people revealed their innermost secrets. She and Günther had talked their feelings out to each other, revealing hidden thoughts that she had never spoken of to anyone. That was the one thing she was sure of in an intimate relationship: intimacy extended beyond the physical touching. There was a different touching that had nothing to do with the body. Yes, she had to reach Conrad Brandt in another way. Anger only made him cautious. Suspicion made him guarded. She listened to him carefully as he continued telling them what would happen in the days ahead.

"The autopsy will take some time. Perhaps two or three days. Then they will release him to us. We can have a service here in Zurich; and if you all agree, I shall take him home."

Boris brought up his plans for a new family crypt. Ursula, catching Günther's glance, shrugged faintly. Günther nodded. "Let him," said their signals. "What difference does it make?" Brandt asked them if they wished this done. The twins and Ursula nodded. "It must be something quite magnificent," Boris said with uncommon enthusiasm. "I suggest we go back to Great-Great-Great-Grandfather Augustus and his princess. She was a Wittelsbach, you know. *His* grandfather fought the Turks. Did you know that?"

"Yes," said Brandt. "My uncle told me."

"And there should be some special figures carved. Perhaps something from mythology. We'll put our heads together and send you our plans for that part of it. But I think the ground for the crypt should be bought at once and the structure built immediately. It must be enormous and mag-nificent." Boris' eyes were glittering with his idea. "Of course, the family arms should be carved over the entrance."

"Yes," said Brandt. "It will be done as you wish."

Ursula, feeling a rise of nausea in her throat, looked away from her uneaten breakfast. It was Paul who rescued them. "Boris, why don't you complete the drawings you started last night? Conrad can take them with him and give them to the architects."

After Boris rushed off to make new plans, the others went to the library. "There are a few things I have to clear up," began Brandt. "I'd rather the police didn't have to ask you these questions, but they will. I thought we might go over them now." He was pacing again. "Did Alexander have any enemies?"

"We didn't know any of the people at his club. They meet in a lodge over near Winterthur," said Günther.

"I didn't mean just at the club; I meant anywhere?"

"There was a girl . . ." said Ursula, feeling uncomfortable about bringing up Lisle.

"A girl?"

"You better tell him the whole thing," said Günther.

Ursula made the story brief. Alexander had seduced Lisle and then refused to marry her. She had been upset and angry but apparently was not pregnant. Alexander then stopped seeing her or talking to her on the phone. About ten days ago she stopped calling. None of them had seen or heard from her since. Ursula was fascinated by Brandt's expression as he wrote this information down in a notebook. She could only describe the look as his "lawyer's face," so totally absent was it of surprise or judgment or even of interest. He said he would have that "area" investigated himself and they need not mention it to the police. At noon he left them for several hours after promising to get in touch with Melchior. Ursula stayed with the twins in the solarium for the rest of the day listening to them play Mozart.

Brandt returned early in the evening. "Melchior will call tonight," he said. "The abbot has agreed to tell him about Alexander." He detailed for them his information of the investigation. The search for the bullet that killed Alexander was called off because of the weather. All the men had been questioned. They were stunned and heartsick over the accident. Alexander was much loved; he was a remarkable young man of sterling character and generous to a fault. Everyone liked him. And on top of that, he was an excellent shot. They sent their heartfelt condolences to the family and would like to attend the services.

Ursula listened to all this with mounting disgust and rage. Yes, yes. Fine. Thank you. But who shot him? The friendly hunters are home having dinner while someone is placing Alexander's heart on a scale. She began walking around the room as Brandt talked.

"So far the autopsy shows that Alexander died instantly; he was not in pain. He did not suffer. . . ."

"No, that's left for us," she said, stopping in front of the seated lawyer. "Let's go back to the heartsick hunters in their charming green caps and big Swiss bellies. Are you saying that none of them knows who fired the shot?"

Brandt shook his head. "None of them knows." He was seated with one ankle over his knee, his hands hanging loosely off the chair arms. He looked immensely tired and for a fleeting second Ursula had the impulse to comfort him. Günther dispelled the feeling. "Ursula, the investigation has only begun. When they find the bullet—"

"If they find it. What if they don't, so that it's not traceable to any of the guns they have?"

"Then any one of them could have fired—"

"Or none of them. You must have thought of that."

Brandt spoke immediately. "No, I hadn't thought of that."

"Of course you thought it. That's what you thought from the very beginning." She saw the twins and Boris on the periphery of her vision lean forward.

The lawyer breathed deeply. "It's always a good idea to consider all the possibilities. It came from my consideration that one of the club members might be an impostor. But that the shot came from another quarter entirely . . . well, if I entertained that thought at all, I certainly disabused myself of it." He lit a cigarette.

Ursula laughed harshly. He had on his lawyer's face. "I'm sorry, but you must be speaking a foreign language that I don't understand. I'll do my best to follow you. I entertain—charming concept—the thought that Alexander was not shot by any of the club members."

"Do you have a candidate?"

"Do you?"

"I'm afraid not. But I'll certainly listen to any suggestions. Agnes Schneider, perhaps? Remarkable woman! She would have had to know a good deal about guns to know enough to use a steel-jacketed bullet of that size that could go all the way through the body and get lost in the forest or the stream beyond. And what a shot! The gun was fired from two to three hundred meters late in the day when shadows already nestled in the valleys."

Their eyes locked, and Ursula believed that beyond the anger she saw in his, she also saw a pleading, a faint sign to her to stop this conversation. The fire in the hearth crackled noisily and she turned away from him as though that were her signal to quit. But she knew the way was open to him. The plea was faint, but only because he was working desperately at concealing it. She had to get to him when he was alone.

The call from Melchior came after dinner. He sounded surprisingly calm, his deepest concern being for *their* sorrow and loss. He readily agreed to Brandt taking Alexander's body back to Vienna. When they asked him if he wanted to come to Zurich for a service for his brother, he told them his abbot had already arranged a special Mass for Alexander at Tre Croci. Ursula thought his voice had a deeper, richer resonance. "He sounds good," said Paul. "Less fragile somehow." They all agreed and this was a curious conciliation for them that Ursula thought about but could not understand. "Perhaps he's overcome his fear of the dark."

"And of closed spaces and crowds and thunder," said Günther.

"And maybe of us," she added.

Günther smiled at her. "Quite possibly."

Ursula went to her room at midnight, leaving Brandt and the twins still talking in the library. Boris was usually in bed by eleven. Sometime before one, she heard the twins' footsteps on the stairs going to the third floor. She listened for Brandt to come up the same stairs. But there was no sound. Snow fell steadily on her balcony as she waited. As the clock chimed one, she took a book from her desk and went down to the library. The door was open and the only lights came from the flames in the hearth and the snow-paled external lamps on the terrace. He was seated in a deep chair in front of the fire. She turned on one of the lamps and walked to a case to shelve her book. When she turned she gave a small gasp. "Oh, you frightened me. I didn't know there was anyone here." He rose. "Please, don't get up; I'm only returning a book."

"Ursula . . ."

She turned out the lamp and pretended to leave, but hesitantly paused when he spoke her name. "Yes?"

"Can't we at least be friends?"

Again hesitantly, she joined him in front of the fire. "I thought we were."

"You don't trust me."

She saw that he would not sit until she did. She picked the ottoman in front of his chair. When he sat down again, she marveled at the ease with which the setting had come together. "It's all so strange," she began. "I don't know what to make of it. I want so much to understand what's happening. It's so meaningless for Alexander to get killed in a stupid accident." She put her hands over her face, allowing herself a few small sobs.

In seconds she felt his arms hover over her, barely touching her bowed shoulders. She sobbed again softly and his hands fully rested on her, pulling her to him. "Dear girl. Don't grieve anymore."

She slipped to the floor and rested her face against his knee, counting on the firelight to cast the right glow. "We're so in the dark," she said. "First, your dear uncle, and then the two poor old women, and then Graz, and now Alexander. Accident upon accident, and all of us bewildered and confused and unable to make anything of it. How can you be surprised that I am suspicious? I can't believe in that many coincidences."

He was stroking her hair, but he remained silent. She looked up at him, tears glistening in her eyes, her moistened lips barely parted. In the next moment he was kneeling beside her, holding her hard against his chest, his mouth kissing her eyes, her cheeks, moving to her waiting lips. The kiss was long and tender, sustained by a constant renewal of intensity and energy that seemed to rise from his entire body and culminate at her mouth. She answered his kiss both shyly and aggressively, playing first one and then the other so that he would sense her uncertainty. When she felt his body tremble she drew away, modestly lowering her head. But he drew her chin up and smiled at her, his face beautiful in the firelight. "*Now* is the moment you shouldn't trust me. You must know how abysmally I love you."

She sought his eyes. "Enough to tell me what horrible little secrets you're keeping from us?"

He pulled away from her. "Ahhh . . . another trick! Brandt, you idiot!" He raised his arm as if to strike her, but let it fall leadenly to his side. "I thought it was real." He laughed bitterly. "I thought you were grieving and vulnerable. I believed that sweet mouth was making an honest reply to my kiss." He rose to his feet and stalked from the room.

On her knees by the hearth, Ursula felt the fire caress her skin with sensual warmth. She drew her arms tightly around her and rocked with bowed head. For the first time in her life she felt true, implacable shame.

22

For five days Conrad Brandt worked with the police and several private investigators of his own in an attempt to determine exactly who shot Alexander. The shell was not found, although the police cleared the snow from the area and dug up the soggy earth where it should have been. There was a strong opinion that it was washed into the creek and carried downstream or even that it entered the creek after it passed through Alexander's heart. Brandt's private investigators checked into the background of every member of the hunting club—all wealthy solid Swiss businessmen who had no motives to kill an extraordinarily rich young foreigner who had already donated enough money to the club for the additional construction of a game room to their beloved old lodge. As many of the members told Brandt, Alexander made them feel young again. Some wept as they reminisced over the young man's charm. The investigators quietly checked into Lisle's life and family. She was an only child of stern parents of whom she was terrified. They had probably never heard of Alexander. Armed with a list of names, they checked out everyone Alexander had known among the students. They investigated his professors. Nothing unusual showed up on the profiles they drew of all these individuals. Brandt sat at the phone desk and considered each innocent name. He had to make the children believe it was an accident, a stupid, pointless, meaningless accident. He wished he could believe it himself. He had not had a gun in his hands since Stalingrad and the loss of this boy's life made him revile in low, seething, uncontrollable curses all guns and gun clubs. The club had created the setting, the opportunity.

In five days he saw Ursula only three times. The first time he almost ran into her on the stairs at three in the morning. She was barefoot and wearing a sweater and skirt, her splendid legs pale as cream flashing mysteriously in the muted wall lamps. She was carrying a sketchpad and averted her face as she hurried silently past him. He wondered if she ever slept. The second time he did not know immediately that it was she. It was the first brilliant blue morning after three days of snow when from his bedroom window he saw a figure standing at the edge of the lake, apparently gazing across the water. The person wore all white—jacket, pants, and boots. He thought he was seeing one of the twins until she pulled down the jacket hood and the magnificent burgundy hair spilled over her shoulders. The third time she was all in black standing between the twins, her face veiled, her hands gloved, as she appeared to listen to a priest intone the last words for Alexander, who looked rather dapper in his satin-lined bronze coffin. In mourning, she was hauntingly beautiful. His desire for her at that moment made him shrink inside himself and loathe what he termed his consistently base nature. He saw himself remove the black clothes that gave her slim body a vaguely fragile appearance, the veiled hat, the high-collared suit, the boots. But of course he knew she was not fragile. He had felt the full breasts and supple naked body that first night in the pavilion when he realized with shock that had she been anyone else, he would have taken her at once on that very spot. After that first contact, he could never undress her in his mind and find her wearing undergarments. He thought of her as merely covering herself for the sake of propriety with the simplest single garment like a woman emerging for a few hours from Paradise into a world where other women wore layers and layers of underclothing that encased their bodies in iron and hard rubber. She alone could be naked for him, and this he knew doomed him. After his previous visit to Zurich he had given up the women he knew in Vienna. Without even thinking about his reasons, he simply put them away from him by no longer accepting the dinner and party and weekend invitations that once filled his idle hours. At first he made excuses, but then he gave that up, too. He filled his evenings and weekends with work. In his lonely nights he dreamed his desperate dreams of the girl in the pavilion in another country. Yet she seemed to loathe him instinctively. He thought of his poor uncle whose middle-aged passion for her had doomed *him,* too, and the only thing she ever gave him was a broken nose. Well, at least she was more subtle now: she no longer used her fists to get what she wanted. He shivered at the memory of the kiss, of her tongue hesitantly exploring the inner side of his lips. Where in God's earth had she learned that! And he had been taken in by it, accepted it at the time as though it were the most natural way in the world for a near-seventeen-year-old girl to react to a world-weary thirty-three-year-old man's kiss.

Looking at her now, dry-eyed, her full lips paler than ever behind the black veil, he felt the hopelessness of his love for her sweep over him like the rush of hot dust he had felt on the battlefields in endless Russia when he was convinced he was going to die in the war. It was clear to him that in some way his dead uncle's law firm and the Enerde family were somehow bizarrely locked on the same side of a vendetta whose opposition was totally unknown. What, he wondered, would Ursula make of the fact that the two remaining lawyers who had personally worked with her grandfather in settling the plans for the future of his grandchildren's immense wealth had both died in the past year? Krammer was killed in a hit-and-run accident as he crossed the street near the firm's office building. Glöck, a cheerful man and an expert mountain climber, lost his footing and his rope and dropped a thousand feet to his death from a mountain he had scaled a dozen times. Accident upon accident plagued the lawyers, the servants, and now the children themselves, of the Enerde family. Only he no longer believed in accidents. What did Uncle Conrad have in his briefcase that made the thief ignore his wallet? And then there was a conversation, so mild and seemingly unimportant, between himself and his uncle that he had actually forgotten it until long after his uncle's death, until the day he came upon a tablet of her drawings that his uncle loved. "We must sit down, my dear nephew, and talk about that family someday soon. There are a few matters that are not in our files at the office, and you should know about them, just in case I should get too senile or indolent to continue with the law." They had both laughed. "She's a remarkable girl. Look at these egrets. The mean fire in their eyes. She was her grandfather's favorite, you know. When she marries, she will inherit her mother's jewels in the bank in Zurich. But that's not relevant at the moment. There is a file I keep here at home that you should be apprised of. Refer to it only if something extraordinary should happen."

"Extraordinary?" he had asked.

"Yes. If, for example, something should happen to one of the children."

"Like what?"

"God knows." His uncle had returned his attention to the book of birds. "I held her as an infant. The grandfather used to carry her everywhere, from room to room, with a distracted nurse or two running after him. When she was about seven or eight, it became quite obvious that she would be a great beauty, the strange hair, the extraordinary color of her eyes. . . . At twelve she was already a woman, tall with magnificent legs. I used to watch her as she skated with her brothers. The grace, the limber body. It was enough to make a strong man lose all conscience. And then, of course, there was that intelligence. I could have loved her for that alone. You should see her caricatures. Immensely humorous, but also done with wit and a knowing that strikes to the bone."

Something extraordinary had happened: Uncle Conrad had been murdered, his briefcase stolen, and the file he spoke of was nowhere to be found. Had his uncle put the file in his briefcase on that day because the children were leaving and he had intended to tell them something that was in that file and then changed his mind? If the thief had been an ordinary thief, wouldn't he have thrown away the case when he saw it held only legal papers? Wouldn't he have slung it into the gutter between two cars in sheer exasperation and fury at finding no money in it? But the case had never been found, although the firm had the railway station and streets around it searched and had offered a reward more than ten times the briefcase's surface value. Ah, Uncle, he thought, I need a sign, a clue. I see killers everywhere. He turned to look at the church full of people: the four children, the hunting club in full force, the servants, some student friends. Is there a killer among you? Someone my uncle feared? He no longer believed in bodyguards although he would keep them in place for the time being, especially since the children were not aware of them and they might yet report something important one day that would warn him. Of what? Of whom? God: if you're granting any desperate wishes these days, tell me what was in that file. He felt foolish thinking such a thought and yet if there was a God who listened to desperate men, let Him hear this one: keep them from harm! His eyes turned to Ursula standing in the family mourner's alcove, her hands clutching the twins' hands on each side of her. And if You happen to be doing any small favors, God, do me a selfish one: make her think better of me. For the merest moment Brandt held Ursula's glance, but she quickly lowered her eyes.

By nightfall, Alexander's coffin was on a train that in another hour would be headed for Vienna. Conrad Brandt returned to the house by the lake only to discover that Ursula refused to see anyone. "She's taking it very badly," said Boris. "We'll tell her you came to say good-bye." Brandt delayed his departure as long as possible in the wild hope that she might come down from her room and he could see her one more time. But the time slipped by and he found himself repeating various instructions to the boys to be careful and to take care of each other. He told them for the third time that they were not to be distressed when they received documents from other members of the law firm informing them that Alexander's wealth would be distributed among the remaining five children. When he saw the looks of identical revulsion pass across the twins' faces, he gave up and left.

On the train he stayed in the car with Alexander's coffin and considered his own future. Nothing like traveling with the dead to make one take stock of one's options, he thought. He could give up the firm and emigrate. The United States? Why not? The Americans weren't nearly as outraged at the Austrians as they were the Germans, although they should have been. Australia? It had the advantage of being even further away from her than America. What would he do in Australia? What would he do anywhere? It was not a matter of having to work. He worked because he didn't know how not to. His uncle left him everything—the firm, the office building, a fine house in Grinzing, a summer place in the lake country, some excellent stock investments that were getting better all the time. By everyone's standards, even his own, he was wealthy; not the way the Bronevskys were wealthy, but then there were perhaps only a dozen families in the world that were rich in the way they were. He could buy a boat and sail it around the world. And probably die of boredom. He could join some scientific expedition headed for a three-year trip up the Amazon. And do what? If the colors of the jungle didn't keep her constantly in his mind, the knowledge that there were no phones to keep him apprised of her safety would. Her safety! That's where it all fell apart. He couldn't go anywhere. He couldn't do anything except stay where he was and try to keep her safe. Yet how could he protect her? How could he protect any of them when he had already failed? He leaned his forehead against Alexy's coffin and wept.

At the frontier, he got off and met the children's driver in the waiting room. They walked out of the station and strolled on a nearby street as they talked. "Let me know at once. Anything, anything you consider unusual. Anybody hanging around their house. Any car that keeps showing up on the street. And watch the lake for any boat that has snoopers on it, people that come too close, people with binoculars. I don't mean the once-in-a while sailboat. I mean anything that turns into a pattern. Take nothing for granted. Double-check any tradespeople. Now, the most difficult problem is going to involve their friends. I've given you the names and pictures of those we know and which we've checked out. They're okay."

"Sir, if we had some idea of what we're looking for . . . a man . . . a woman . . . ?"

"Hoffner, I wish to God I knew." Brandt looked away to the train. "It's almost time to go. Listen, check daily with the others, but remember, be discreet. Those kids have to live some kind of normal life. They can't know they're being watched all the time." He lit a cigarette, his hands shaking. "Uh, one more thing: the girl, she's bound to start seeing . . . new friends."

"You mean men?"

"Yes, I mean men."

"She's the most secret of all of them. A strange number, that one. Prowls the house at all hours of the night. Sails alone at six, seven in the morning, although the twins forbid it. No friends so far, boys or girls. A real loner. If she's with anybody, she's with the twins."

"I've noticed. Well, stay with it, I've got to go."

When Ursula did not come down for dinner, Günther took her a tray. "Conrad wasted an hour waiting for you to come down."

"It was his hour."

"Unkind."

She shrugged and opened the doors to the balcony, ignoring the tray he placed on her desk. It was snowing again.

"I couldn't tell," said Günther, "whether he was a man waiting to make an apology or waiting to have one made to him. Would you know by any chance?"

"No."

"Is there any reason you refused to see him?"

"No."

"Is there any reason he paced around our sitting room for almost an hour repeating himself like an absentminded scholar, and stopping every few minutes with his head all atilt so that it was obvious even to Boris that he was listening for your footsteps?"

"I have no way of knowing the answer to that. Why didn't you ask him?"

"He seemed a bit on the fragile side. And with taking Alexy home for us still ahead of him, I didn't want to add to the possibility of breakage in case it was a difficult answer."

"A lawyer break? You must have forgotten Rätzel's view of that profession. 'To lawyers all truth is clay.' "

"You believed Brückner a friend, and you know damn well this man is too." He sat down abruptly. "Ah, Günther the dope!" He snapped his fingers. "The balcony scene where Romeo picks up a barefoot Juliet! Ursula, turn around and look at me."

"What?"

"Did you sleep with him?"

"No."

"Did you think about it?"

"I think about it with every man I see, students, professors; even strangers on the street aren't safe."

He rose. "I suppose I could whip you. . . ."

"Only if you make it fun."

"It won't be fun, Ursula."

"Then don't try it."

They stood in the center of the room in arm's reach of each other. "When did we become enemies?" he asked softly.

[264]

She began to cry. "Oh, Günther. I did a stupid thing."

"How stupid?"

"I pretended I wanted him."

"And . . . ?"

"I was only trying to find out what he knew that he wasn't telling us."

"Let's go back one step—to your pretending. How exactly did you . . . ah . . . manage that?"

"I got him to kiss me. Believe me, it was easy."

"I believe you. Then what?"

"He liked it."

"Did he? Amazing!"

"And he believed it. I mean he believed in it. Only I asked him too soon what he knew that he wasn't telling us. He got mad and left."

"Left where?"

"The library."

"Ah, the middle of the night; a fire in the hearth; you *know* he's there; you go in search of . . . ah, let's see: *The Augustan Age of English Poetry*, Volume Two."

"I offended him."

"Yes, you did. You also played a very dangerous game. By the way, how was it?"

She shook her bowed head, "I don't know. I guess I liked it."

"You guess? How many guesses do you get?"

"All right. I liked it, but I'm not sure I liked it because of *him*. He could have been anyone."

"Ursula, you are not just anyone to *him*. That is quite obvious now. He is a good man; do not offend him again."

Long after he kissed her good night, long after he was gone from the room, she lay thinking of him and the thing that she did not tell him. Yes, she had enjoyed Brandt's kiss, enjoyed it because she imagined with every nerve in her body that it was Günther who was kissing her.

The Christmas holidays came and went with a major disappointment that deeply depressed the Bronevskys: they had hoped to visit Melchior at Monte Tre Croci, but the abbot put them off. The condition of that order had never entirely given up the old desert hermitage rules of total renunciation. Thus, for a time, young monks had to live a reclusive, solitary life of silence and denial in order to purify their souls of the original corruption of the Fall. And Melchior had already entered his state of rigorous abandonment of all human contact. Ursula imagined him sitting cross-legged in a cave with only a burlap bag over his shoulders. It was an old cliché that she had always thought patently ridiculous. The abbot, however, dispelled the image in an answer to Günther's letter asking if Melchior was still at Tre Croci. He was, and it was clear that God had touched him with a special grace, for he found no hardship too harsh, no isolation too lonely, no work too heavy.

Conrad Brandt called several times a week, and since Ursula loathed the telephone she rarely heard his voice or even knew that he had called. On the three occasions that she did speak to him, she found him distant and abrupt, the conversations marked more by the uncomfortable silences than the words they actually spoke to each other.

Toward the end of spring, a visiting university physicist offered Paul the opportunity to attend a special three-month symposium with a prestigious Swedish scientific organization in Stockholm. In the first bright celebration of the event, Ursula, Günther, and Boris encouraged him to go.

"It's internationally famous," said Boris. "You can't dream of turning it down. What an opportunity. One can't even buy an invitation like that."

But Ursula knew that Paul would do more than *dream* of turning it down; he *would* turn it down.

"I suppose you will have to call Conrad," continued Boris. "He is such a worrier, but don't let him talk you out of it. Anyway, you're not really leaving the university here; you'll still be enrolled. And you'll be back by fall. I wish someone had extended such an honor to me. Of course, there are great plans here to create a vast center for psychological studies. And I shall be here for that, in its inception, at the laying of the cornerstone, so to speak. And mark my word, I'll gather some honors of my own when the time is ripe."

Boris was the only one pleased with Paul's invitation, and he continued to babble on about it for several days, while Ursula watched a silent drama take place between the twins. She knew they did not talk about Paul's leaving, yet inside their decorous and careful silence, she knew their arguments. She could hear Günther in her own imagination. "You have to go. It's not just the honor, it's the work you want. All your life has been reaching for this moment. These people recognize the genius you have to offer to the field. In fifty or seventy-five years, man will be traveling in space as casually as we travel to the mountains. You will be a part of that. You've earned this! You want it! Go!"

She could see Paul slowly shake his head, and she remembered what he had said to her once in the middle of another sorrow. "What I know of love is that it is terrible, agonizing, possibly even fatal. Very simply: I love my brother. Yet I know the time will come when I will lose him." She imagined Paul thinking: *But not this way. Not through a choice of mine.*

Then abruptly Paul seemed to relax. Late one afternoon, Ursula came home to find him in fencing kit. He was whistling cheerfully, examining a foil.

"I thought one needed a partner for this game to make it really sporty," she said, eyeing his easiness. He had clearly put the problem away from him, as though he had torn off a restraining garment and cast it down.

"When my other half comes in, you may come watch me pin him to the wall." He struck a pose.

"So you have refused it."

"It was nothing."

Ursula heard the door open behind her. Watching Paul's face, she did not have to turn to know Günther had entered the room.

"Did you mail it?" asked Günther.

Paul placed the foil on a side table. "I'll deliver it myself in the morning."

"I don't think you should do that," said Günther.

"Yes, I should. I don't know why I even hesitated. Do you suppose listening to Boris can cause infection? Perhaps we should quarantine him."

"Tear it up."

"No."

"You're going."

"No."

"And so am I." Günther took a large envelope from his jacket pocket. "Tickets to Stockholm."

23

"Are you going to be all right?" Günther asked Ursula later.

"If you mean can I endure boring Boris alone for a whole summer, yes, I'll be all right."

"Actually, I didn't mean that. I feel that I've sacrificed you to this trip. You'll be alone."

"You had no choice."

"Not true. That's exactly what I did have—that choice: you or him."

"He would never have left you, Günther."

"I know. That's what decided me. I couldn't let him throw away that opportunity. But it meant sacrificing you."

She shrugged. "Do you remember how easy everything was at home? Things were so clear."

"They only seemed clear. Grandfather always rounded off the sharp edges. And we were isolated, removed from the world—the *real* world, as people say. We did not have to hide anything. Inside our walled garden we did as we pleased—for the most part. And on holidays we journeyed only to other guarded walls. Even on our secret trips into the city we never talked to anyone. It was always under our control. Even the disorders in our lives were orderly, neatly compartmentalized: Father generally stayed drunk in his rooms, Rätzel refereed the tutors' quarrels, and Schneider arranged our education hour by hour while somewhere in the real world, war roared on for five appalling years before it touched us. That's why things seemed easy, clear. Everything was in its place. Now we're outside the wall . . . except for Melchior, who has found a new one, much higher and stronger. But the rest of us . . . the rest of us are outside. And we have to choose how to order our lives. We have to put things in their proper places ourselves, and if we make mistakes there are no bells to bring us to prayer or sound the alarm."

"What do you want me to promise you?"

"To begin with, don't go sailing alone anymore."

[267]

"That's *not* what you want to talk about, Günther."

He was standing then, looking out on the lake. "It's a good place to begin."

"Fine, you have my word. What else?"

"It's not easy for me to leave you here alone, Ursula. You must know that I'm already worrying about you." His eyes were grave, dark, troubled, as he faced her. "I want you to have friends, not be alone this much; and yet I'm afraid of those friends."

"If that's what you're worried about, you can rest easy. I don't know how to make friends. There must be some knack to it that I never mastered. And I don't mind being alone."

"You don't mind because Paul and I are always near, and you know that you can stop being alone anytime you want to."

"If it will comfort you, I'll get chummy with Boris' buddies."

"How chummy?"

"Günther, have you looked them over lately, listened to their endless prattle on multiple-personality disorders? Apparently that's the latest quirk. Do you really think I could get too chummy with any of them?"

He smiled then. "Remember it's only for the summer."

"I'll remember." He met her eyes, but she turned away and there was left between them some unfinished issue, some unspoken words that one of them should have uttered. It did not matter which one. *All dangerous games forbidden.* Perhaps he could not say them because he knew that with his past mistakes regarding her, he had no right to say them as a command. And she did not say them because in her mind they were not necessary, although she knew that this was what he wanted promised.

The twins left on the morning of the last day of the term. "Hoffner won't suspect anything that way," said Günther. Ursula and the twins had long ago reasoned that their driver was a guard who answered to Conrad Brandt. Their grandfather's drivers had all been bodyguards for the children. It was an easy connection. Then, too, Conrad spent entirely too much time with the man.

"You'll have to send our luggage on to us. I'll phone you the address when we get there. The bags are locked in our closets at the moment. We'll be in Stockholm in about five days, take the train to the coast through France, and then go by ship. You know, of course, that Conrad will come tearing over here. And he'll be livid and probably wildly offended that we didn't tell him first. Be nice to him." Günther made a mock-sinister face. "But not too nice."

"I'll hold his . . . hand," said Ursula, smiling sweetly.

The three of them were light and easy with each other because the parting was hard. Ursula thought later that their jokes had a touch of desperation to them. "When do you intend to tell Boris?" asked Paul.

"In about a month," she had answered, "when he notices that there are fewer people at the table." They nodded. "How long do I have to lie to Conrad?"

Günther considered this a bit. "That depends on how close he brings your feet to the fire. The full five days if you can stand the pain." She nodded.

Finally it was time. The twins kissed her good-bye. "Go," she said. "I may faint if we keep this up."

"I'm counting on you not to." Günther's voice was almost a whisper. He walked quickly away to his twin waiting at the door. Not until they were out of the house and she could no longer hear their footsteps did Ursula feel the tears on her own face and with them the first sinking sensation of despair.

"No," she said fiercely, brushing away the tears. "Not yet!" She went about her usual routine for the day, but at dinnertime Boris called her on the intercom.

"Do you know what time it is?"

"Yes, and I'm not coming down for dinner either." She waited for the last word to sink in.

"Doesn't anybody want anything? It looks awfully good."

"No. Nobody wants anything."

"Well, I'll tell the cook. Frankly I'm starved."

Ursula peeled an orange and ate it as she watched the boat lights on the lake. Later, with the map of Europe spread out in front of her, she followed the twins' train to Amsterdam. In the morning they would get on a ship headed into the North Sea. In the morning she would go to the kitchen at five, make a pot of tea, and pour it into three cups, which she would then pour down the drain, leaving the used cups on the dining-room table with three rumpled napkins and a plate holding a few bread crumbs. Leaving the butter pot and the honey bowl out would add a bit. During the night, she made her brothers' beds look slept in and brought their packed suitcases down from the third floor and placed them back on the racks in the storage room below the stairs which held everyone's luggage when not in use, and all the sports equipment: skis, skates, tennis rackets, foils, guns, even their beloved old worn soccer ball.

About the time Günther and Paul were getting on the ship in the Netherlands, she was leaving the house with her sketchpad and headed for the university library reading room, where she found a deep comfortable chair in which she fell asleep almost immediately. When she woke up in the afternoon, she went to the zoo and sketched all the big cats.

At seven, she took a cab home. Hoffner met her at the gate. "Very glad to see you, miss. You could have called; I'd have come to pick you up."

"Didn't want to be a nuisance. How do you like my cats?" She opened a page and showed him a tiger. "Do you know how much meat he eats in one day?"

"Not my line, miss. Have you seen the two young gentlemen?"

"They said they were going sailing."

"When was this, miss?"

"Today."

"Thank you, miss."

Boris jumped up when she came into the sitting room. "Where is everybody?"

"You're here," she said.

"Where are Günther and Paul?"

"Sailing, I believe."

"No, they're not, the boat's in."

"I could have sworn they said they were going sailing today."

When Ursula sat down to dinner with Boris at eight, the twins had been gone thirty-seven hours. She told the cook not to wait for them. "They probably went to the films."

"Not very proper of them not to let a body know," said the woman with sharp irritation.

"Most inconsiderate," commiserated Boris.

"Deplorable," said Ursula. She retired to her room immediately after dinner.

She was awakened at dawn by someone coming down the third-floor stairs. When she peeked out of her room, she saw Hoffner standing hesitantly on the landing to the first floor. He seemed to be looking at her watercolors. When he walked on, she pulled on a robe and followed him. Outside the phone room she listened to him talking. "No, sir, they've not come in. I can't say for sure. The girl said they told her they were going sailing." There was a long silence before Hoffner spoke again. "Personally? Two days ago. There's evidence they've been here since, but no one's actually seen them except the girl." He paused again. "Yes, sir. In the morning. I'll have talked to the others again by then, sir." He hung up, and Ursula ran silently back to her room.

At eight, the twins would be gone forty-nine hours, but Brandt wouldn't know that. If he waited another day before he came to Zurich, she would have to put him off only two more days. But Conrad Brandt did not wait another day; he arrived at eight that morning.

She was momentarily astonished at seeing him drinking coffee with Boris in the dining room. He rose when she entered. "Please, no formalities. How pleasant to see you again. My brothers say I behaved like a cad when you were here the last time. Sorry." She smiled and took her breakfast from the sideboard, knowing that he was watching her. "Are you here on business?" She looked at him over the rim of her cup.

"I don't want to alarm you, but Paul and Günther did not come home last night."

"Did not come home? You mean they're not here?"

"No."

He watched her with such intensity that she knew this moment would make or break her lie. She looked to Boris. "For God's sake, where are they?" She raised her voice a notch to match her level of hysteria.

Brandt's expression softened. "I'm sorry, I thought perhaps you knew where they might have gone."

"They'll phone. I'm sure they will. They wouldn't let us worry." She kept the urgency in her voice. If he thought she was not worried, he'd know in a second she was lying.

"But I am worrying," said Brandt. "Have they ever been gone all night before?"

Ursula shook her head and looked to Boris. "Have they?" She pushed her breakfast plate away.

"Well, not that I know of. I've heard them come in late, but not this late."

[270]

"Did they tell you they were going sailing yesterday?"

"Yes," said Ursula.

"But the boat's not been out," said Boris. "I know. I saw it there yesterday morning and again in the afternoon. I even considered going out, but it's not fun without a good stiff breeze."

"How can you think about things like that when they're missing?" said Ursula.

"They're not actually missing," said Boris. "I'm sure they're all right. You two worry too much. After all, it's the end of the term; they're probably celebrating somewhere with friends."

"Do they have many friends?" asked Brandt. He looked at Ursula, but Boris answered.

"Well, they've never brought anyone here, but that doesn't mean they don't have any."

"Boris, when exactly did you see them last?" asked Brandt.

"Ah. Good question. Let's see . . . today's Friday. I did not see them yesterday. Now, ah . . . on Wednesday, I saw them at dinner. No . . . wait. I did not see them at dinner. In fact, I had dinner alone that night. Ursula, you must have seen them. You said they didn't want any dinner. They were here yesterday morning. I recall their breakfast dishes hadn't been cleared when I came down." He pondered, making a humming sound. "I have to say, Tuesday dinner. I recall they went directly up."

"And you?" said Brandt, facing Ursula.

She frowned. "I really can't remember exactly, I mean the exact hour."

"I'll settle for the exact day."

"Yesterday," she said, looking him straight in the eyes.

"Morning or afternoon?"

"Morning."

"And what did they say?"

"About what?"

"About where they were going."

"They said they were going sailing."

"What did *you* do yesterday?"

"I went to the zoological gardens."

Brandt got up and wandered around the room, pausing at a tapestry of Leda and the Swan. He ran his hand along the side of his head. "Will you both be here for dinner?"

They both answered that they would.

"I have some things that need my attention. Let's just assume they're going to call. I'll see you both at dinner then?"

Ursula nodded.

"By all means," said Boris.

From the second landing Ursula saw Brandt talk to Hoffner, who was motioning toward the street and back to the coach house over which he lived in some rooms with the houseman. Moments later they drove away. All day she imagined the twins at sea, the two of them reclining side by side on deck chairs, reading. Strangers glanced at them, then stared.

When she came down for dinner, Brandt was having a drink with Boris in the sitting room. His face looked dazed. "No calls at all?"

"No," said Boris. "It's damned inconsiderate of them. Frankly, I intend to speak to them about this. People should behave decently."

Brandt gave Ursula a faint nod. When dinner was announced, he said, "I'm sorry, I can't eat. You two, please go ahead. I'll just sit in the library." He walked slowly, exhaustion rounding his shoulders.

Ursula sat opposite Boris for a few minutes as her brother talked and ate. "You know, it's not like Günther and Paul to be inconsiderate."

He continued to eat as Ursula thought of the man in the library. If *she* hadn't known where the twins were, she would be wild with worry. She got up. "Boris, go ahead with your dinner. I'm really not hungry. I'll see you in a little while."

Moments later she entered the library softly and found him seated before the cold hearth, his shoulders hunched over like someone in mourning. Her need to comfort him was a physical craving, like a terrible hunger. She walked to his chair and touched his shoulder lightly, but he only shook his bowed head. She took a deep breath. "They're all right, Conrad. They're safe."

His head shot up and his hand grabbed her wrist, pulling her to her knees. "All right, you little witch, where are they?"

"You tricked me!"

"You bet I did. I was counting on there being a heart inside all that ice. Now, I want straight answers. Where are they?"

"That's none of your business." She turned her hand to get out of his grip.

"You want it broken?" He twisted her arm behind her back and pulled up sharply.

Ursula gasped and arched her shoulders into the pain, bringing her head up sharply against his chest. Stars shot away from her eyes. Abruptly the pain was gone, and for a blinding moment she did not even know that his mouth was crushed against hers in a hard, ungiving, angry kiss. Instinctively she leaned into it, rose to it, sought it. But reason brought her back and she broke away, whispering, "Bastard!" and neatly ducked his swinging open hand.

He fell back in his chair, pushing the heels of his hands against his forehead. "Christ!"

Ursula got up from the floor and sat in the chair several feet away, facing his. "You can stop worrying; they're safe."

He stared at her with burning eyes. "Really? Do you know that my uncle's killer followed you to Zurich sometime last year and murdered Alexander? Wherever Paul and Günther are now, the killer may be in the next house, or the next room or—"

"You know who it is, and you haven't done anything?" She realized she was close to screaming.

"No, I don't know who it is."

"Then how do you know that?"

"It's an assumption I have to make because of other things that have happened. You must tell me where your brothers are."

"What things?"

"Please, Ursula. Who knows where they are?"

"I'm the only one."

"Are you sure?"

"Yes."

"When did they leave?"

"Early Wednesday morning." She glanced at her watch. "They have been gone sixty-one hours and thirty-seven minutes."

"So the unmade beds . . . the teacups . . . all that was to lead someone into thinking they were still here."

"We had to fool Hoffner."

Brandt smiled faintly. "Where did they go?"

Ursula took a deep breath. "If you tell me what you know, I'll tell you where they are."

Brandt ran his hand through his hair, tilting his head downward. He gave a brief sardonic laugh. "Now, that's an interesting form of blackmail. I should have seen it coming. All right, who starts first?"

"You do."

He laughed again, the same bitter sound as before. "All right. The first year after you left Vienna, two of the lawyers in my office who worked out the terms of your grandfather's will died in somewhat unusual accidents. In January of this year, Dr. Frichter was in an automobile crash. The mechanic says the car's brakes failed. Fortunately, the doctor survived, but he was hospitalized for several weeks and is now permanently confined to a wheelchair. In March, the last man in our office who worked on that will burned to death in his alpine house while on holiday. Now, where are your brothers?"

"Stockholm."

"Stockholm? What the hell are they doing in Stockholm?"

"Paul received an invitation to attend a three-month physicists' symposium with that famous scientific group that's working on the future of space exploration. He wouldn't go alone, so Günther went with him."

"How did they travel?"

"By train to the Netherlands and then by ship."

"Whom did the invitation come from?"

"A physicist who belongs to the Stockholm organization. He was a visiting lecturer here this year. I have his name upstairs."

Brandt looked at his watch. "It's too late to get to him tonight. I'll have to work that out in the morning. How did they get their luggage past Hoffner?"

"They didn't. I intend to ship it as soon as they phone me the address."

"You don't have their address?"

"No. They are still at sea. They should arrive in Stockholm Sunday morning."

"What is the name of the ship?"

"I don't know."

"Well, there can't be so many. I can get that."

"Are you going to spoil it for them?"

He lit a cigarette. "For God's sake, Ursula, don't you know that I want the best for all of you? I'm not trying to spoil anything. I'm only going to make sure they're safe. They won't even know about it. If everything is

[273]

legitimate, which from the sound of things it probably is, Paul can attend his symposium, and the two of them will be back here in the fall. That group in Stockholm is internationally known. They don't invite just anyone, and they protect their people. The biggest thefts in the world today involve the stealing of scientists. So it's the trip *to* Stockholm that worries me. I'm assuming nobody knew the hour of their departure or their route."

"No one did. We knew Hoffner would get wind of it if anyone knew, and he would call you. We kept everything secret."

"Don't you ever include Boris in anything?"

"No; he has a big mouth, and all his friends hang around the house listening to him expound on 'psychotic episodes' and 'diagnostic criteria.' We let him think Paul turned down the invitation." She paused. "If the killer followed us to Zurich, he had to return to Vienna to try to kill Dr. Frichter and to kill that lawyer."

"Yes. Assuming it's the same person."

"Why? Why your uncle, why Alexander?"

"I don't know. There are so many missing factors. The Schneider woman was never found. The two extra people at the funeral are still a total mystery. I have nothing to take to the police: everything was an accident. Finding hard evidence is like picking up water in a sieve.

"In the morning, I'll find out what ship your brothers are on and see if everything is all right. I'll be damned if I'm going to sit up with that telephone until Sunday."

Silence fell over them like sudden darkness, his eyes continuing to watch her in a wide and wondrous gaze, his mouth concealed by his hand-turned-fist to hold the cigarette that sent blue smoke past his face. Finally he spoke. "I'm sorry I hurt you."

"It's not important. It doesn't matter." She knew she owed him an apology, too, but in a curious way was unable to word it. Was it to be for the vulgar name she had called him? Or keeping her brothers' where-abouts a secret while he worried? Or lying to him? Or was it to be for accepting his kiss—violent as it was—and then pulling away from it in anger?

He put out the cigarette with what she thought was excessive care, and rose. She saw him concentrate, like a man faced with a grim, implacable, totally unacceptable, mad purpose. He moved slowly toward her until he stood in front of her chair. With unsteady knees she rose so that she had to touch his thighs and groin with her breasts, so close was he to her chair. She heard his breathing waver, then his arms took her, and this time the kiss was long and soft and loving. She felt his body against her as she leaned into the swelling groin. She rose on tiptoe and moved her thighs outward. "Yes," she said into his mouth. "Yes, yes, yes." He was nodding, laughing lowly in his throat, and looking, looking past her at the sofa on the far side of the room.

"And I'll take my coffee and brandy in the library. Bring it straightaway."

Ursula froze as she heard Boris in the gallery. Brandt cursed under his breath. They broke away from each other, Ursula moving to the hearth to worry the logs with a poker. She did not dare turn as Boris burst into the room.

[274]

"Aha! So here's where you two have been hiding. Well, let me tell you, you missed a splendid meal. I'm having coffee and brandy. Anyone going to join me? I say, Ursula, look at the mess you're making. Conrad, could you light her fire for her?"

Ursula turned quickly to catch Brandt's expression, putting her hand over her mouth to suppress her urgent laughter. But he was facing the far wall where the empty sofa with its casually tossed pillows seemed to float dreamily.

He knelt beside her on one knee and fumbled for matches in his coat pocket. Ursula leaned toward him as the flame caught the paper and kindling in bright colors, and released her pent-up breath slowly into his left ear, her moistened lips touching his skin. "Yes," she whispered. He turned to her, his eyes clouded, his mouth slightly open and breathing shallowly, but he said nothing.

A maid brought in a serving cart. Boris played host with great aplomb, telling them the history of the several liquors and brandies on the trays. During one of Boris' pauses, Brandt told him about the twins' Stockholm trip.

"I'm not surprised; I told him he should go. I'm glad he took my advice," said Boris. "Now, take this bottle here . . ." Ursula, long since seated again on the chair by the fire, turned Boris off, yawned, and said she thought she would go to bed. She glanced at Conrad, who was staring into his brandy glass as though something were swimming in it. He did not look up as she left the room.

Ursula bathed and got into bed, intensely conscious of her nakedness. She had thought of this hour since the night in the pavilion when he had comforted her. No, before that. The very first time he came to the house and kissed her pulse, the dark centers of his expressive midnight-blue eyes opening for her alone, she had felt an odd tightening in her chest; and when he spoke, his warm low voice caressed her skin. Slowly his habits—running his hand through his hair, speaking quietly and gently, bringing secret laughter into his eyes—had all become dear to her. She was sure he would come to her bed. He would wait an appropriate amount of time; then he would yawn, stretch, say he was tired, and pretend to go to his usual guest room on the third floor. Only he would come to her room instead. Hours passed. She heard Boris on the stairs, heard his door close. After another half-hour she put on a robe and went in search of Conrad. But he was nowhere in the house. She went to the coach house, only to find the car gone. Back in the kitchen she rang Hoffner's quarters. The driver answered in a sleepy voice. No, he didn't know where Mr. Brandt had gone. He left two hours ago. Could he be of any help? Ursula said that there was a long-distance call for the lawyer and would Hoffner give him that message as soon as he saw him. She wandered about the house slowly, trying to calm down, but a black rage took hold of her heart as tears, bitter and unceasing, ran on her face.

Brandt did not return the next day, or the next. On Sunday, Günther called to tell her that he and Paul were in beautiful Stockholm. He gave her the address for their luggage and asked her if she had any trouble with

Brandt. She said she did not. He asked her if everything was all right. She said, "Yes," and started to cry.

"Ursula, what is it?"

"I miss you."

"I know," he said.

For days Ursula moped, snarling at Boris for no reason and for every reason. Early in the mornings, she went sailing alone, her mood black and brooding: to hell with the rules. At night, she prowled around the house like an angry cat. Boris became offended when she no longer ate at the scheduled mealtimes. "The cook has complained to me about your nocturnal habits. Apparently you won't have dinner with me, but you think nothing of eating at midnight and leaving things out and . . ." Ursula walked out on his lecture.

She was mad with loneliness. She came to understand what being alone before the twins left had really amounted to: she was like the rich man pretending to be poor until it became inconvenient, at which time he quickly rejoined his wealth. She was like the child pretending to be lost until he got hungry, at which time he went home to dinner. It was not company she craved, it was the twins' company. She had taken it for granted forever, their humor, their care, their love. Worst of all, she did not know what to make of Conrad Brandt's silent departure, his cruel rejection of her. The car was returned two days later. When he reestablished his triweekly calls from Vienna, Boris answered the phone, and as far as she knew, Brandt did not ask to speak to her. "By the way, old girl, Conrad sends his best," Boris said to her on several occasions.

After a few weeks she began to notice Boris' odd new language. "What are you talking, British? What's with all this 'how jolly' and 'I say,' and 'old chap,' and 'old girl,' and 'smashing'?"

"Well, if you'd act like a normal person, I'd introduce you to my friends. Some of them are here from England, which should interest you, considering your fondness for that language. And they're terribly nice chaps."

Usually she would have mimicked his "terribly nice chaps," but even ragging Boris held no more humor for her.

Toward the middle of summer she returned one night from a concert to discover the house filled with young people. The servants carried trays of champagne and hors d'oeuvres throughout the large rooms festively decorated with a great many bouquets of flowers. She stopped one of the maids. "What is all this?"

The girl smiled uncertainly. "Why, it's Master Boris' birthday party."

"It's not his birthday." When she saw the girl look about anxiously, Ursula spoke quickly. "It's all right; he's just celebrating it a little early." She took a canapé from the girl's tray. "Very nice," she said. "Please don't let me keep you from your work."

She found Boris holding court on the terrace, his impeccably clad form gracefully leaning against the stone balustrade. He was gesturing with his champagne glass. "The way I see it, the day will come when analysis will be a routine part of everyone's life. People will have annual sessions in the same way one sees his dentist or has a physical checkup with his private physician. It's absurd to think the mind doesn't need the same kind of care."

Ursula motioned to him from the French doors, smiling broadly. He waved gaily, excused himself, and left the circle of talking people. "Happy birthday," she said to him in Russian.

"Now, don't give me away, Ursula. I wanted to have a party and that seemed like a legitimate reason."

"Why did you need a reason?"

"It just . . . somehow . . . makes everything more . . . more centered."

"On you?"

"Well, yes, rather."

"Presents?"

"I told them very specifically not to bring any."

"They very specifically disobeyed you. There is a mountain of them in the gallery."

"I know. Isn't it marvelous?"

"You're a pig, Boris. Have I mentioned that to you recently?"

"Just don't give me away," he said, his eyes pleading with her. He was wearing an admiral-blue, gold-crested blazer with white slacks.

"Is that the house of Romanov you're representing?"

"Please, Ursula . . ."

"Actually, you look more like you're in someone's navy." She made a faint sign with her head. "Two cruisers coming alongside."

"What . . . ?"

Two young men joined them. "I say, Boris, who's the *lovely* lady, and why is she all in black?" said one of them, smiling at Ursula.

"My sister, Ursula." Boris gave the two men's names, which she forgot instantly. They both kissed her hand and made faint bows.

"I didn't even know you had a sister, old chap," said the second man. "Where in the world have you been keeping her? She's positively smashing."

Boris smiled. "Yes, I'm just about to take her around." He put his hand on Ursula's elbow and moved her quickly away. "Ursula, if you'll go change into some other color, I'll introduce you to someone *really* nice."

"I'm not going to change my clothes and I don't want to meet anyone *really* nice. Now, if you don't mind . . ."

"Here he is. Now, say something pleasant," he whispered to her. "John, I want you to meet my sister. Ursula . . . Lord John Skye."

In the first fleeting second upon meeting him, Ursula received the remote impression that she had seen him before somewhere. He neither bowed nor kissed her hand, but seemed to linger in time, as though holding back the moment, almost as though he were physically grasping it to him, like a man holding a live bird in his hands. He appeared to be several years older than Boris, although his blond hair was cut like an English schoolboy's. She detected a certain weariness in his slate-gray eyes, a remote touch of fatigue, a downward pull to his mouth that gave age and gravity to his face. Alexander used to put on a similar world-weary, disgruntled, life-is-so-boring expression that used to drive Ursula, who refused to be bored, crazy. But when the man spoke, the clipped British accent negated all languor, all ennui; and Ursula decided that the features so curiously sugges-

[277]

tive of an abiding boredom resulted from a genetic misalliance. "Thank you, Boris. It is my very great pleasure to meet you, Miss Bronevsky."

Ursula shook his extended hand. "Have we met before?" she asked.

"No. I would have remembered."

"Oh, good," said Boris. "I can see that you two are going to get on brilliantly. Find some champagne and enjoy yourselves. Don't forget the Queensberry Rules. I can't referee; I have to play host." He sailed away from them and was quickly absorbed by another group of brightly dressed young men and women.

"I do wish your brother wouldn't make so much of titles."

"The family gave up one in my father's generation, and Boris has felt cheated ever since. But if you're serious, tell him not to use yours when he introduces you."

"I have. He doesn't mind very well."

"Lord Skye. Hmm, there must be a pun in there somewhere."

"Don't search on my account. Everyone just calls me Skye."

"I don't suppose you happen to be from the Isle of?"

He laughed a deep warm laughter that matched the richness of his speaking voice. "No. Better. The Isle of Man. My family prefers the insular reclusiveness and . . . well, the other benefits."

"The lower taxes?"

His lips turned upward into a stunning smile. "Quite right. Boris tells me you're a genius at caricature." A maid held a tray of filled champagne glasses out to them. John Skye took the tray from her hands. "Yes, thank you." He nodded to Ursula to follow him.

She looked at the confused maid. "Just get another one; and the next time, don't give it up so easily to the first pretty face."

She walked with Skye to the end of the gallery, where he stopped at a door. "Where does this go?"

"I wouldn't dream of spoiling your surprise."

"Ah! A wardrobe?" He raised his eyebrows at her in a comical way.

She made a shrugging gesture with her shoulders and raised her hands emptily.

"A loo? A vault?"

This time she raised her eyebrows.

"A secret passageway to the end of the rainbow?"

"Or the end of the world," she said.

"Here, hold this." He handed her the tray, paused, and carefully reached for the knob. "Wait. Some magic words." He ran his hand through his pale hair, pushing it off his forehead, and with that gesture Ursula realized that he reminded her of Conrad Brandt. So that's where she had seen him before.

He closed his eyes, mumbled something, and pushed open the door. Before them stood the two closed grand pianos on their raised daises, and placed gracefully around them stood the velvet chairs and sofas where for a hundred years the family and guests had listened to visiting composers and musicians in the hush of wealth and privilege. Skye whistled softly. "Who plays?"

"My oldest brothers." She handed him the tray of champagne. "Do enjoy yourself." She turned quickly and walked out of the room, closing the door. She left the house by a garden exit, and from the pavilion watched the party go on for another two hours. There were still a few slurred voices and some tired laughter coming from the sitting room when Ursula came in and went to her bed. She slept without dreaming.

In the morning the house was back in perfect order. No evidence of the party remained except the vases of flowers. Boris was breakfasting on the covered terrace. "Would you mind telling me what you said to John Skye last night?"

Outside, a summer rain fell steadily over the city. "I didn't say anything to him. I showed him the music room. He seemed to be interested in it."

"Well, let me tell you, he left a very short time after I introduced you to him. And he seemed upset, truly upset. Now, I consider him a very important friend."

"Actually, I thought he was a terribly nice chap."

"You did?"

"Oh, quite."

"I can't imagine what upset him. He seemed genuinely distressed. By the way, there's a package for you in the foyer." Ursula immediately thought of the twins, who had been writing her several times a week all summer and frequently sent her funny gifts. The previous week a whole stack of small colorful magazines called "comic books," published in America, came in the mail with Günther's cover letter. "They are either a new art form or a new literary form or both. Hard to determine on first viewing."

But the package in the foyer was not from the twins. It was from John Skye and it held seventeen pure white Madagascar orchids. Ursula rang for the housekeeper. "Do something with these. Whatever you wish. I don't want them." The woman gasped at the box of rare flowers, and was still admiring them with the kitchen staff a few minutes later when Ursula, raincoated and hooded, her sketchpads and pencils in a protective case, left the house and took a taxi to the zoo. If John Skye came to the house, he was not going to find her at home.

The zoo, however, turned out to be disappointing. In the rain, the ape grotto was so obviously phony with its manmade backdrops that she wondered if the huddled, grunting gorillas weren't only actors in costume. Across a fouled moat, a brown bear stared at her balefully like a ruined fighter. The lions looked ill.

She finally entered a small restaurant and ordered coffee. Moments later, John Skye slid into the chair across the table from hers. She had to work at not showing surprise. "So Boris told you where I spend my time."

"Don't blame Boris. I've been following you all day, ever since you left your house."

She put on her sweetest smile. "You have no idea how flattered I am."

"I wish that were true."

"And thank you so much for the flowers, but please don't send any more."

He shook his head. "I don't understand. What happened last night?"

"Nothing happened last night."

"You didn't have to run away. I don't attack young girls."

[279]

"I didn't run away. It was not my party. I did not wish to be a part of it."

"I had the impression that you didn't mind my company."

Ursula saw a trap up ahead: if she said he had a *false* impression, he would ask her why she did mind his company, and this she could not answer. As it turned out, he asked the question anyway, since she did not speak. "If I was correct, then we can start again. If not, I have to wonder why: why do you dislike me?"

Ursula thought carefully. "I don't dislike you; I don't even know you. Why should I—on a few moments' meeting—have any feelings about you at all?" She had to smile inwardly at herself: compared to her pitched battles with Conrad Brandt, this peculiar relationship smacked of the mid-nineteenth century.

"Perhaps we could start again then."

They fell silent as the waitress brought Ursula's coffee. Skye shook his head at the woman's request for his order.

"I don't think we should," said Ursula. "There were whole bunches of girls at that party last night; why not start with one of them?"

"Bunches. Yes. As common as weeds."

She watched a shadow of anger cross his face. "I'm sorry," she said, "but I can't start—as you put it—something with anyone just now." Ursula knew his next question and watched it rise on his face.

"Is there someone else?"

"No," she said.

"Then I don't understand."

"I don't understand either." It was a better answer, she thought, than simply telling him she did not want him or going into a long dissertation on why he shouldn't expect her to.

"We can keep it light. Just be friends."

"No, we can't. That's not what you want." She got up to leave.

"I'm not going to give up trying."

She didn't answer, but paid quickly for the coffee she did not drink and walked back out into the rain. In the taxi on the way home, she reconsidered John Skye and his extraordinary face that came back to her with such ease. Why had she turned him down so absolutely? Because somewhere on the outer edge of all her thinking was Conrad Brandt. He was on her mind in the last moment before sleep and still there on the first moment of awakening. His physical rejection of her on the last night she saw him was like a permanent, throbbing bruise on her body. Vaguely she had divined what had happened: once he'd had time to think about what he was about to do, he had decided it was wrong. She found no consolation in this answer and it did not lessen the pain of her disappointment and rejection. Ah, men, she thought. One minute they're as loose as goats and the next they're as moral as gods. Where did he go when he left the house that night? She knew she was jealous of those hours.

The next evening she came down to dinner and discovered they had a guest. "I'm sure you remember Skye," Boris said to her with a stern warning look.

"Vaguely," she said.

[280]

"Don't pay any attention to her," said Boris. "She has a wicked sense of humor, and I have to confess that for a well-bred, well-brought-up young woman, she behaves very badly sometimes."

"I find her to be charming company," said Skye, his manner so easy and relaxed it unnerved Ursula a little. After dinner the two men played chess and Skye won three fast games.

Annoyed, Boris went off to mix himself a drink. "Don't congratulate yourself, he's a terrible chess player. Even my brother Alexander used to beat him."

"Alexander?"

"He died last year in a hunting accident." Ursula looked away, tears rising to her eyes.

"I had no idea."

Boris returned and Ursula left for her room.

The following night John Skye was there for dinner again. "Are you a houseguest or just a bad habit my brother has formed?"

"The latter, I'm afraid, although I'd prefer to be the former."

"Ursula, what an insulting thing to say. Apologize at once!" said Boris.

"Are you insulted, Lord Skye?"

"Not in the least."

"Should I apologize?"

"I should be deeply offended if you did."

Boris snorted with exasperation. "You two are ganging up on me. I can tell."

Thus, after a week, Skye became a regular dinner guest, sitting on the terrace with Ursula and Boris for cocktails before dinner or having brandy with them in the library after dinner. He always brought something: flowers, a superb wine, rare cognac. On warm nights they sat in the pavilion and watched the lighted boats and drank coffee. Ursula began to get used to seeing his long handsome sweatered back as he stood with pocketed hands, gazing out over the black lake. On weekends they sailed. As they were mooring the boat one day, the sunlight caught his blond hair, turning it lighter than ever, and when he looked up at her, the gray slate of his eyes had turned to teal. She felt an agonizing urge to touch him, but she quelled it quickly and returned to the house without speaking to him. It was a tactical error, and she knew it. At dinner, he stood behind her chair before Boris came down and in a graceful movement she could watch in the mirror on the opposite wall, he bent over her, raised the mass of hair from her shoulders, and put his mouth on the side of her neck, moving his open lips over her skin, his teeth opening and closing in a gentle kneading motion. She did nothing to stop him as the nerves in her breasts and groin hardened her nipples and began the melting sensation between her thighs. When Boris joined them he ate steadily and talked about his day, while Ursula and Skye ate hardly at all, remained silent, and carefully did not look at each other.

Later in the night, she thought: if he just didn't smell so good. His scent was an exquisite mixture of ancient and familiar unnameable spices that brought water to her mouth and actually made her want to taste his skin. And he knew.

Impulsively she called Günther. "Is something wrong?" he asked her.

[281]

"No, I just wanted to hear your voice."

"You sound . . . odd."

"I'm fine," she lied. "Just fine."

Later, she remembered the maids in the Vienna house talking about the dark madness in the Bronevsky flesh. If not a madness, then certainly some blind, unrelenting, remorseless force that brought her to these fierce planes of desire for him, when she had so singularly, weeks ago, decided that she did not want him. It was with this peculiar insanity, she believed, that she had seduced Günther and forced herself on Conrad. Ah, yes, she thought, when she finally got to her bed and lay awake in the deep darkness, she was certainly Count Pavel Bronevsky's daughter.

Then she began to dream about him. In her sleep he became her lover. The nerves of desire convulsed in her thighs, pounded the muscle of her heart. She raged at her own weakness when in conscious moments she caught herself dreamily thinking of him: of his unsmiling face watching her across the table, of his manner lately of appearing to listen to some distant voice when she passed him. The more she denied him to herself, the more she desired him. "No! No! No!" she would say aloud fiercely. "He is an arrogant, insolent, cynical wanton . . ." Then she would laugh at herself. "Much like me, in fact."

The question she could not answer came to her every night. Why not? Why not take him? Why not have him at least once—and then order him away? What amazed her was her own ruthless, unreasonable rejection of him.

Then abruptly her dreams became violent and terrified her. She began to think she was mad. Skye was in all of them, and in all of them the pattern was the same—love and death—the commingling of the voluptuous and the macabre. In one moment she was locked in a sexual embrace with him; in the next she had just killed him with one of her father's dueling pistols. She watched herself enter and pass through all the phases of lovemaking she had enjoyed with Günther, except that in her dreams, at the end of each tender climactic moment she murdered her lover. She moved from gun to knife with ease; and in one particularly bizarre episode she held a grenade against his chest. It exploded in wonderfully graphic slow motion, leaving her unscratched but him blown to bits.

In the last days of summer, when the breeze was already deceptively cold and carried the smell of snow from the distant moutain peaks, she fell into a profound melancholy. For two days she did not come down for dinner. Boris asked her if she were ill. She said no. He and Skye continued to have dinner together. On the third night, Boris phoned to say he would be dining with friends in the city. "Get Ursula to eat something," he said to Skye. "Find out what's wrong with her."

When Ursula came in late in the day from an afternoon of sketching trees in the park, she found Skye seated in her favorite reading chair in her room. She watched his silhouette rise, darken the faintly glowing window, and move toward her. Shadows throbbed and pulsated in the room like living things half-hidden in forests. He was whispering her name. When his hand touched her face she could feel his breath, fresh as spring water. Then she picked up the scent, curiously familiar and dear, as old as her life and much loved. A male scent. Savory. Spicy. Desirable. His mouth covered hers and everything in her stirred—glands, flesh, memory. In a single motion with both hands she tore open his shirt, sending the buttons flying. Something in her cells said "Don't think! Don't think!" She was undressing both him and herself, pulling away the garments in destructive fury until they were both naked and she could hear only her own breathing and his gasps. She held the penis in both hands. Kissed it. He was whispering something, but she shook her head. "Now! Now! Now!" she said. And his whispering stopped. They were on the floor, she striding his spread thighs; when he entered her, his crisis came after hers. When he stopped quivering she took him to her bed and pulled him down on top of her. "Again," she said.

He started to laugh and seemed unable to stop until she felt his tears on her face. "In a few minutes," he murmured. He was good to his word. But this time the loving was gentle and sweet and long. He moved his mouth over her body, kissing softly as she had once seen Günther and Paul do, even as Günther and she had done. And when he finally reentered her, his motions were an ecstatic rhythm that brought her to the longest moment of energetic rapture she had yet known.

Afterward in the silence, he asked in a quiet voice: "But whom were you loving?"

She did not answer him, thinking: Who indeed? Günther? John Skye? Conrad Brandt? What man was she really lying beside in the dark? She, who believed love needed light, had not let this lover lighten the room.

"Do you know who you are with in the dark? If not me, who?"

She heard in his voice the grim tightening of a jealous heart. "It doesn't matter."

"It matters!" He turned on the light. "Dammit, it matters! I want it to be me!"

"You expect too much."

"Who is he?"

"You fool. Does it have to be anyone? I like it. That's all."

He sat up, breathing hard, his eyes narrowing. "Yes, it has to be someone. It has to be me!"

She sat on the edge of the bed. "Why does it have to be just you? I thought you'd know all about Freud's four people."

"That has nothing to do with this. I want you to know that I'm the one who's inside of you."

"It doesn't matter who it is."

This time he hit her, slapping her hard across the face. "It *has* to matter! It has to be me! Oh, my God, I'm sorry." He embraced her quickly with intense strength, kissing her face. "Forgive me. Please, I beg of you, forgive me."

Ursula laughed. "Imbecile."

"You don't understand. I'm in love with you." He seemed to be in a daze. "How could there be anyone else? You were a virgin."

"Technically," she said dryly.

"I'm not sure I know what that means." He spoke with fresh anger.

She sighed. "Oh, Skye. Don't count on very much from me. Take what you can get. You can't have it all. I took you because I was depressed.

Everything seemed dead to me. . . . This is a denial of death. It's the only thing I could think of doing at the moment. I had to. I was ready to set the house on fire."

"You still don't understand. I am in *love* with you. I want *all* of your love, not just this." He got up and collected his torn clothing, Ursula lying on her stomach naked on the bed watching him with amusement. "I *will* have it all," he said. He gazed at her lying with her head at the foot of the bed, her feet on the pillows, her chin cupped in her hands, propped on her elbows, the brilliant hair fanned on her back. He sat down beside her and with great tenderness stroked her back, buttocks, thighs. "A true thoroughbred." He spoke softly. "I'm flying home in the morning to England but I'll be back and then . . . then, I'll have it all."

That was on Thursday. When Skye did not show up for dinner the next night, Boris wondered aloud if they should phone him.

Ursula advised against it. "He's gone to England. Left this morning. Said to give you his best and say good-bye. Said he'd be back."

"Damned odd of him," said Boris.

"Yes," mused Ursula.

Boris did not come down for dinner on Saturday night. Ursula finally went up to get him, but he was not in his room. She told the cook to leave something out for him.

The next morning he did not show up for breakfast. Again Ursula went to his room. His bed had not been slept in. She called Hoffner and asked if Boris had taken the car. He had not. "Is something wrong, miss?"

"I don't know. Boris did not come home last night."

A few minutes later, Hoffner came to the house and looked into Boris' room himself. All his clothing was there, his shoes, his shaving kit.

On the terrace, Ursula waited. Should she call Brandt now or wait a few more hours? Hoffner came to see her. "Did he say anything about where he might be going?"

She shook her head and gazed at the lake. There was something peculiar about the lake but she couldn't quite zero in on it. Suddenly she grasped Hoffner's arm. "Isn't that our sailboat out on the water?"

The man shaded his eyes. "Yes. Anchored."

"But it's always moored when it's not in use." She began running down the stone stairs even before she knew she was running. Hoffner ran behind her.

"I'll get the small boat out, miss. Don't do a thing."

Ursula ignored him. At the edge of the lake she tore off her shoes and dived into the soft green water. Twenty meters out, the sailboat bobbed above its anchor. Gasping for breath, her heart beating itself to pulp in her chest, Ursula climbed the hooked ladder. The boat was empty except for Boris' shoes and socks. About this time Hoffner reached the sailboat with the skiff. Together they carefully went over every object in the boat. "I don't understand what it's doing out here." A terrible fear began to pound in her head. With Hoffner beside her, she looked over the stern of the boat. Eighteen inches under the water something bright was undulating gracefully. Ursula began to scream. Looking up at them with open eyes, his head nodding gently, was Boris.

24

Still screaming, Ursula flailed her arms savagely into the water to reach her brother, but Hoffner pulled her back. "No, miss, we shouldn't touch anything until the police—"

"Get him up!" she screamed. "Get him up!"

He pushed her away from the stern. "No, miss. There's no point."

"Nooo!" she shrieked as she pulled away from him, and would have dived into the lake had he not grasped her around the waist and held her tight.

"He's been dead a long time, miss. Come, let's get back into the little boat and row back to the shore and we'll let the police bring him in. They'll want to know what's happened here. They'll want to see it exactly as we found it."

Ursula stared at Hoffner's sharp face under his chauffeur's hat. "He's dead?" she whispered. "He's dead? But he is such a good swimmer."

"Yes, miss. Now, please, into the boat. Here, let me wrap my coat around you. Shouldn't get a chill. Now, there's a good girl. No, hold the coat. That's right. Good girl."

Ursula was to remember later how Hoffner continued to talk to her, softly, unceasingly, the way one talks to a sick pet. In the house, they went straight to the kithen. Hoffner whispered to the housekeeper. "Warm some whiskey. Get her into some dry clothes. I'll call Brandt." But Ursula left them and walked back through the gallery, the sitting room, and onto the terrace. It was an unmercifully beautiful day, scented with autumn flowers, chrysanthemums, carnations, a few last pale roses. She stared at the lake, at the white-sailed boat bobbing dreamily on the glacier-green water. She started down the stone stairs, but a hand took her by the wrist and gently urged her away from the stairs. "Time to get dry, miss. Time to get dry." Hoffner led her back into the sitting room, where one of the maids stood holding a robe open. "There, that's right, put your arm in there. That's a good girl. Now, let's dry this hair a bit." Hoffner clumsily ran a towel over Ursula's hair. "There, that's better." He took her by the wrist again and they walked to the phone room, where he pulled another chair to the desk. "Here, now you sit here. That's a good girl. Now, I'm going to make some calls, and I want you to sit right here beside me, miss. Yes, that's right."

Moments later, Ursula heard the man's voice change. He spoke faster, sharper. "It's Master Boris, sir. Drowned. Not yet, sir. Right here beside me. Yes, sir. Right here within my reach. No, I don't think she should, sir. There seems to be a good deal of . . . ah . . . disturbance. Yes, I'll do that and I'll call you back in a few minutes." He rang off and a moment later began to speak again. "Yes, there's been an accident. A drowning." He continued to talk a little longer, almost turning his back to Ursula, although every few moments he would glance back at her and once he reached out and straightened the collar on her robe in an absentminded way as he might straighten a picture on the wall. A few minutes later he made another call. "It's me again, sir. Yes, they're on their way." He seemed to listen for a long time. "Well, she noticed the boat wasn't moored, swam out to it before I could stop her. Actually we saw him at the same time just under the surface. Naturally, I had to keep her from . . . Well, I'm sure you know. Yes, sir. Still here beside me. Yes, I'll see the women take care of her until you can get here. . . . What? . . . Yes, if you think that's best, sir, I'll keep her with me until you come." He paused for the last time. "I'd say bundle up, sir. It's on the cold side." Ursula watched him hang up the telephone. "Now, the police are going to come in a few minutes, miss, and they'll take care of everything. I want you to stay in the library. We'll light up a few logs and get you dried."

The housekeeper entered with a tray. "We should take her upstairs and change her clothes. Put her to bed, would be the best."

"No, I promised him I wouldn't let her out of my sight. We'll take her to the library. Have someone start a fire and bring in some blankets. Put that in there." He motioned to the tray. "All right, miss, we'll go to the library and wait for the police."

Ursula rose when he took her wrist again. Everything seemed very sharp and clear, as though a bright light were being cast on it. The housekeeper had a broad nose with a small growth on one nostril, and she was crying. Hoffner's hand that held her wrist was heavily veined and had large knuckles. She wondered where his cap was. His brown eyes were close together and his nose must have been broken once or twice, since it slanted off at a slight angle. Actually, it was a rather interesting face and would caricature out in four or five lines.

In the library, Hoffner told her to sit near the fire in the chair with the blankets. He gave her a glass. "Now, drink that," he said. "No, wait, I'll just taste it first. See if it's warmed proper." He took the glass back and drank from it. After a moment he returned it to her. "Just right. Now, you drink that and we'll just sit here and warm up by the fire." He sat in the chair beside hers. At one point he got up and pulled the draperies closed. Ursula held the glass but did not drink from it.

Presently two men joined them and Hoffner rose to talk to them at the far end of the room. It seemed to Ursula they were whispering part of the time, their voices coming in and out of her range of hearing as though two entirely separate conversations were going on. "Enerde, yes. The same. The banking family. Only the children's name is Bronevsky. Enerde was the grandfather. There were six, but if you'll recall, one was killed in a hunting mishap last year."

The men recalled. "How long did you say this one's been missing?" asked one of the men.

"Since last night. He didn't show up for dinner at eight."

"Is there anyone else in the house besides the girl?"

"Only the help."

"And you're the chauffeur?" Ursula heard some paper rustling. "I see," said the officer. "And these names? The same capacity?"

"Yes."

"How old was the young man?"

"Twenty, I believe."

"Experienced with the craft?"

"Exceptionally so."

"Swimmer?"

"Excellent."

"We don't know anything yet. They've brought him up. Probably died sometime yesterday afternoon by the look of him." There was some whispering and then a period of silence and finally footsteps and the closing of a door. Hoffner returned to Ursula's chair and looked into her face.

"I want to see him," she said.

"Oh, I don't think you should, miss. Let Mr. Brandt take care of that. He'll be here soon."

"Where is my brother?"

"They're taking him away now, miss. There's nothing to be done for him. You best wait here until Mr. Brandt comes."

Ursula slipped out of her robe and walked to the door, but Hoffner got to it first. "Please, miss, come back to the fire and get yourself dry."

For several seconds Ursula waited for him to let her pass. "Hoffner, don't stop me from doing what I have to do." He nodded and let her pass, falling in behind her.

The ambulance was backing down a utility driveway toward the gardener's cottage as Ursula reached the terrace. She walked rapidly toward the lake and the cluster of men standing in the pavilion. She had the lurid sensation that she was in a dream, one of those particularly bizarre dreams in which one is suddenly unaccountably naked. She saw one of the men turn and then motion to the others grouped in a circle around Boris' body. He was lying on a canvas sheet on the pavilion floor. Ursula knelt beside him and pushed the wet hair off his forehead. "Oh, Boris. Boris. You should not have died now," she whispered. He was fully dressed except for his shoes and socks. Ursula sat back on her heels and looked up at the circle of men. "How did he die?"

The men shifted uneasily, no one answering. She repeated the question. "We're fairly certain he drowned," said one of them.

"Drowned with all his clothes on?"

"Well, the anchor seems to be mucked up in the lake growth along the shore. We think he went down to check the problem and for some queer reason got his foot caught in the anchor line. He may have panicked."

"My brother Boris jump in the water with his clothes on? Are you mad? He was the most . . . most correct person who ever lived. He would have changed into a swimsuit. There are suits on the boat."

Ursula recognized the man who squatted down beside her as a police investigator she had seen at the house the year before, when Alexander was killed.

[287]

"You can see here where the line tangled around his ankle and . . ." Ursula looked at Boris' bare white foot and the marks the man pointed to.

"No. It doesn't fit. None of it fits. Why would he anchor the boat twenty meters from the shore? Why wouldn't he bring it in?"

"Well, we'll know more after the autopsy. We'll clear everything up then."

Ursula shivered. "As you did with Alexander?"

There was again the motion of uneasy men, men shifting their positions, looking away, fidgeting with pads and pencils, watches, cuticles.

"He could have fallen overboard, miss," said the inspector.

"No. Not Boris. Any of the rest of us, but not Boris." She picked up his hand and held it in hers.

"Please, miss, let's go back to the house." Hoffner spoke softly, touching her on the shoulder.

"His watch is missing," she said.

"His watch?" asked the inspector. He motioned to the other men and at once two of them hurried to the boat mooring. Moments later the police launch inched up to the still-anchored sailboat. "We'll be checking out everything, miss. We'll be sending divers down. We'll get to the truth." He placed his hand gently under her elbow. "You should go in now. We have to take him away."

Ursula looked past Hoffner and the inspector at the waiting ambulance with its blue light blinking on and off. In a little while, Boris will be lying on a table. Someone will cut him open and take out his heart and place it on a scale. She moaned. The inspector took Boris' hand away from her, as Hoffner brought her slowly to her feet.

Ursula was in the library with Hoffner (who still refused to let her out of his sight) when Conrad Brandt arrived. The lawyer came running into the room, his eyes wild. He stopped in front of Ursula wrapped in a blanket, sitting in front of the window facing the lake. He made a slight motion of his head to Hoffner, who left the room at once. Brandt reached out and touched her shoulder. She looked at him with dry eyes. "Are you going to tell me it was an accident?"

He shook his head. "No. It was made to look like an accident."

"Who is killing us? Why? *Why* are they killing us?" She looked up at him with large vacant eyes, her voice soft, dreamy, absent of anger.

Brandt shook his head. "Ursula, you should get some rest."

"You know I was not close to Boris. I always thought he was rather silly. I didn't treat him very well. And now it's too late. He looked up at me from under the water. He was nodding like this." She began to nod in a slow mechanical way.

Brandt pulled Ursula out of her chair. She was deadweight in his arms. "Listen to me, Ursula, we are not going to wait for anyone else to die. And I'm going to need you. You're going to have to get some rest, and then the four of us are going to sit down and work out some answers. It dawned on me, during this summer, that I have questioned dozens of people who knew your grandfather, but I never questioned the people who knew him best, who saw him every day and who were closest to him. Ursula, I never questioned you."

"Me?"

"You and your brothers. Now, Günther and Paul are going to be here in a little while, and we are going to sit down and go back over your lives, search everyone's memory for any clue that will turn up something for us to go on."

"If we knew anything, don't you think we would have told you?"

"Unless you thought it had no significance. . . ."

She shook her head and turned her face away from him. "There isn't anything."

"Yes, there is. I just don't know what it is . . . yet." He picked her up in his arms and carried her out of the room. In the gallery sat a man with a medical case. Brandt motioned him to follow, as he carried Ursula to her room. "Give her something to knock her out for a few hours. I want her rested and thinking straight when she wakes up."

Ursula looked up from her pillow as the doctor pushed up the sleeve of her dress. She saw him hold the hypodermic up to the light. Beyond him Conrad Brandt stood watching. Tears filled her eyes as she saw his anxious face. "I'm sorry, Conrad." The doctor plunged the needle into her arm and stepped away.

Brandt leaned over Ursula, his eyes anxious, perplexed. "Why? Why are you sorry?" But Ursula drifted away, all the sorrow and regret and grief dissolving in the vast, soft indifference of drugged unconsciousness.

When she awakened, Günther was seated on the side of the bed. He leaned over her and kissed her. She embraced him and the terrible tears of guilt and remorse and loss she had not been able to weep before came from her hot and heavy with wrenching sobs. Günther made no attempt to stop her. He merely held her close to him until the convulsion slowly ceased.

It was after midnight when the twins and Ursula met with Brandt at the study table in the library. "The first thing I have to tell you is that the police believe Boris dived into the water to retrieve his watch and not to untangle the anchor as they first thought. Divers found the watch at the bottom of the lake. The clasp was broken. They believe that when Boris saw or felt the watch fall from his wrist, he hurriedly anchored the boat, tore off his shoes and socks, and dived in after it. He stayed down too long searching for it, and when he finally started back up, the line tangled around his foot and he panicked."

He looked at each of them individually. Ursula, who was looking absently at the cover of her sketchpad on the table, felt his eyes on her but did not look up.

The lawyer continued. "Does that sound like Boris?" None of them answered. "Was that watch that important to him?"

"It was a Patek Philippe. The most expensive watch made. He was inordinately proud of it," said Günther.

"Yes. But would he have gone down after it? With his money he could easily have bought another."

Ursula, waiting for Günther's answer, realized that Boris *would* have gone in after it. He *was* ridiculously proud of that silly watch, showing it off every chance he got, making sure his cuff didn't cover it.

"It's possible," said Günther.

"Not good enough. Almost anything's possible. How likely is it? In a range of say a hundred percent, what percentage would you give his diving into the water to retrieve it?"

Again they were all silent. Ursula saw Boris gesture casually with his left hand on the night of the party, the filled champagne glass sparkling. She felt tears fill her eyes and quickly opened the sketchpad to a blank page. From a ceramic bowl she picked a lead pencil.

"Eighty to ninety percent," said Günther finally.

"Do the two of you agree with that?"

Again Ursula felt Brandt's eyes on her. She nodded. Paul also agreed.

"Then it *could* have been an accident."

Ursula finally looked up at Brandt. The faintest smile touched his mouth. "I don't believe it," she said.

"No. I don't either," said the lawyer. "For the anchor line to tangle around his foot, the line had to be slack. I pointed this out to the police. They seemed to think that if Boris had just thrown it out it would have still been slack. But I went over and picked up the weather reports. It was a breezy day when he took the boat out. The line would have straightened out almost at once. The inspector suggested that possibly Boris got caught in the line before he even went in search of the watch, but that leaves the whole down-too-long-searching-for-the-watch theory out. Anyway, Hoffner tells me Boris was an expert with the boat. Didn't you go out several times a week?"

Ursula nodded as she saw Skye leaning over the tiller to brush a strand of hair from her face. She drew his eyes warm with laughter and light.

"Was he injured in any other way?" asked Paul.

"Not that we know of yet. If you're asking about obvious injuries—a knock on the head or something like that—no. Anything else will show up . . . later.

"Meanwhile, I think we should discuss some other matters. This seems to be as good a time as any. At least it will give you something else to think about." He took a glass from a tray on the table and poured Scotch into it, asking in a casual motion with the bottle if the others wanted any. No one did. "It came to me in the last few weeks, as I mentioned to Ursula, that over the last year I have questioned a large number of people, mostly your grandfather's former employees and some business associates, without finding out anything. And yet I never asked any of you about people who might have hated your grandfather enough to get at you. Please understand that the rich always have enemies; it comes with the privileged state. But this kind of enmity is usually abstract and distant. It comes from envy. It *can* be malicious, but very few people commit murder because of it.

"I don't think there is any point in reconsidering Agnes Schneider. Anyway, from what I gather, she hated his grandchildren more than she hated him, and she already made her effort and failed. And I cannot fathom anyone helping her. Her madness additionally makes her an unlikely suspect. Now then, in your recollection was there ever a servant who would have had cause to do your grandfather harm?"

Ursula continued to draw as she listened to Brandt and the twins discuss half-forgotten servants who had been dismissed or who had left with rancor. They remembered people she was too young to have taken notice of. She sketched Skye's eyebrows and shaded in his nose.

"There was a driver," said Paul, "who belonged to the Nazi party. Grandfather physically kicked him out of the house."

"I found him already. He died in the war."

Ursula drew Skye's elegant mouth and the fine strong line of his chin.

"Let me give you some names, and you tell me who they are or if they mean anything to you at all." He began to read from a list. Ursula took a deep breath and caught Günther's glance as Luba's and Wolsky's names entered the room like ghosts. She returned to the drawing as Paul and Günther filled in the information on the names. She drew his heavy mop of English hair that had reminded her of Brandt.

"Magda Himmel," said Conrad. Both boys shook their heads. "She was not a governess, an instructor?" The twins shook their heads again. Brandt read several more names. "Some of these people are dead, but I thought they might bring back something else, some association."

Ursula drew in the outline of Skye's head, shading an ear, adding the line of his neck and an open shirt. He was remarkably easy to draw. She looked away from the sketch when Brandt rose and began his habit of pacing. "The motive can only be revenge, since all of your wealth goes to various worthy causes: universities, scientific organizations, charitable institutions, should all of you . . ."

"Die," said Ursula.

"Yes." He stopped at the table and poured more Scotch into his glass before he began to pace again. "You probably know already that Boris' share of the fortune will now be divided among the four of you."

Ursula heard Boris talk about his future. "I'll gather some honors of my own." She covered her eyes with the heels of her hands. "Revenge doesn't make sense either," she said. "Why kill your uncle and the other lawyers and the servants?"

"Yes. Why indeed?" Brandt stopped behind her chair and looked down at the drawing. "Is that Alexander or Melchior?"

Ursula began to rise slowly, odd colors entering the periphery of her vision, her breath stopping in her throat, her heart falling absolutely silent. She twisted away from the drawing, cupped her hands over her mouth, and screamed into them, the sound muted and harsh. The room began to spin as Brandt caught her, his glass falling to the carpet. She screamed again, the same hoarse cry into her hands. Brandt was still holding her, but she wrenched free and started to run toward the French doors to the terrace. Günther, immediately near her at the first scream, brought her down with a flying tackle, inches before she would have gone through the glass. He pinned her to the floor as she twisted her head from side to side, dry cries coming from her mouth.

"My God!" said Brandt. "What the hell happened?" He was shaking.

Paul picked up the drawing and held it up at an angle. "It isn't either one of them."

"Well, who the hell is he?"

Paul looked down at Ursula and Günther. "I don't know. We'll have to ask Ursula. I think she knows."

Günther brought Ursula to her feet. "No matter what happens, don't be afraid," he said gently as he patted her mouth with his handkerchief. She looked into his eyes and began to weep silently. "It's all right. We're all here." He brought her back to her chair and placed the drawing in front of her. "Does he look like that?"

She nodded, unable to speak.

"You didn't see it?" asked Paul.

She shook her head.

"Not even a flicker in your brain? Not even a single second of confusion, of uncertainty? Not a dim suspicion, brushed away, a . . . a remote nudge from one of the senses telling you to *look* again?"

Ursula looked at the drawing, then at Paul helplessly, and shook her head to his questions. "You never drew him?" Again she shook her head. "When did he show up?"

Ursula shuddered. "Boris' b-b-birthday party."

Both twins spoke at once.

"*Birthday* party?"

She nodded. "He w-wanted to give a party, and he . . . he th-thought he should have a reason."

"Will somebody, for God's sake, explain to me what's going on?" said Brandt from the opposite side of the table.

Günther took the tablet, turned it around, and threw it down in front of the lawyer. "There's your killer."

"Who is he?"

"What's his name, Ursula?" asked Günther.

She laughed bitterly through her tears and reached for Brandt's list of names, moving her fingers down the page until she stopped at Magda Himmel. "His name is Vanya . . . No, Ivan—Ivan Himmel."

"What does he go by?" asked Günther.

"John Skye."

Brandt sat down in front of the drawing. "I don't get it."

"Do you remember your uncle pointing at the ceiling before he died, or at the roof?" said Ursula.

"Yes."

"He wasn't pointing at the ceiling; he was pointing at the sky. You know English—our word 'himmel' is 'sky' in theirs."

"I still don't get it. Who is he?"

"He's our half-brother," said Paul.

"He's our father's *bastard!*" cried Ursula.

Günther shushed her softly. "Don't make it worse."

She turned to him and saw in his eyes the question she knew she would soon have to answer. "Günther . . ." Again he hushed her.

"How did he get here?" asked Brandt.

Ursula shook her head. "He was Boris' friend."

"Where is he now?" asked Brandt.

"He returned to England. He lives in England."

Brandt rose and rang the bell. He returned to the table and sat opposite Ursula. "Tell me everything you can about him. Where exactly does he live in England?"

"The Isle of Man. That's all I know."

Brandt seemed to contemplate this a moment. "Familiar for some reason, but I don't know why. It will come to me. What day did you first see him?"

Ursula thought back and gave the date. She saw that Brandt had on his lawyer's face and was writing her answers on a notebook.

"How old is he?"

"About Melchior's age," said Günther. "Twenty-one. Give or take a few months. How did you get Magda Himmel's name?"

"Canceled checks. I had the old files opened when I couldn't get any leads. Your grandfather's personal account: he paid money to a great number of people. Whenever the reason for the payment wasn't specified in the records or was for other reasons unclear, I took the recipient's name. Magda Himmel showed up for years."

"How is it you didn't know about her? Your uncle did," said Paul.

"Yes, he must have. He wrote the checks. He did not keep that particular file at the office. He kept it at home. We always planned to discuss it, and then, it was suddenly too late. He was killed. I believe he had it in the briefcase that was stolen from him. I think it was his intention to show it to you, but for some reason he changed his mind. When did this man leave for England?"

Ursula bit her lip. "Three days ago."

Brandt looked at her hard. "Three days ago? How was he traveling? Car? Train?"

"By airplane."

"Well, that's easily checked. Where did he live here in Zurich?"

"I don't know."

At this point Hoffner came in. "You wanted me, sir?"

Brandt tilted back his chair. "Yes, Hoffner. Come look at this picture."

Hoffner looked down at the drawing. "Yes, Master Boris' friend."

"Is he on the list I gave you?"

"Oh, yes, sir."

"He is?"

"He is one of the young titled gentlemen, sir. Remember? You checked all those yourself."

"Do we have a picture of him?"

"Yes, sir. One of those English school group pictures."

"Bring me the picture and anything else you have on him."

Ursula and the twins were now seated opposite Brandt, watching him with sharp attention. "I'm sorry," said the lawyer finally, "that you have to know that I checked up on all your friends, had you followed, investigated all your professors. That place in Stockholm where you two are staying . . . one of the security guards is our man. You know about Hoffner. I tried to keep it all natural, normal. Two of the servants here are our people. Please don't be upset."

"We're not upset, Conrad," said Günther. "We've always known it. We lived the same way at home. Grandfather had guards everywhere for years. Even our trips into the city when we sneaked out of the house were carefully watched, only we didn't know it at the time."

Hoffner returned with a leather case, opened it to a given page, and placed it in front of Brandt. "I don't know how the hell this can be right. We cleared him. *I* cleared him. He is the son of Lord John Skye. He does live on the Isle of Man. He is twenty-one years of age. Here's his school record, and here is a picture of him." He turned the book toward Ursula. "Is that he?"

Among a group of young boys, standing in three rows in front of a soccer ball, stood an unsmiling John Skye, looking off to the side as though he were watching something in the distance, and there very clearly, if one were looking for it, was the Bronevsky profile. Ursula nodded. "Yes, it's a small picture and five or six years old, but I know that's John."

At the saying of Skye's Christian name, Brandt's head shot up and he looked at her for a long steady moment. "What else can you tell me about him?"

She glanced up at Hoffner. "He came here often. Boris seemed to enjoy his company very much, said he was important to him."

"Did they ever go sailing together?"

"All three of us did."

"Was he good at it?"

"Yes."

"Did he talk about his family?"

"Not very much."

"Hoffner, you want to add anything?"

"Well, sir, he was an extremely polite young man. Well-bred I would say. Spent many evenings here. He was generous. Always brought something, as I recall. The ladies, I remember, were much taken by the orchids."

"Orchids? He brought the women orchids?"

Ursula heard Günther shift in his chair. Paul cleared his throat.

"Oh, no, sir. He brought them for the young lady here, but she gave them to the women."

"You gave them away?" asked Brandt, turning to Ursula.

"There was a whole carton full of them . . . a lot of them," said Ursula.

Brandt nodded. "Is there anything else, Hoffner?"

"Like what, sir?"

"Anything that struck you as unusual?"

"Not really, sir. He seemed like a fine, well-groomed young man. Likable, pleasant, not given to airs."

"Thank you, Hoffner."

Brandt again leaned back in his chair. "How does your illegitimate half-brother end up becoming the only child of Lord John Skye, a wealthy English widower who from the looks of things denied his son very little? From this record, he's been here at university for a year. Why didn't he show up here at the house before? He's not on the gun-club roster—that I know. If he's the killer, he had to have a lot of help. It doesn't quite come together. Ahh, Christ, what I wouldn't give for my uncle's lost records. Well, let's give it up for tonight. I've sent word to the abbot at Monte Tre Croci. He will probably call me tomorrow." He stood up and rubbed the back of his neck with one hand as he picked up Ursula's drawing pad with the other. "I think I'll just take this up with me, if nobody minds. I recommend you three get some sleep. I don't think tomorrow will be a very good day for any of us." He looked directly at Ursula. "Are you going to be all right?"

She nodded. "We'll take care of her," said Paul. They waited until they heard the lawyer's footsteps on the stairs. "Ursula, what is he really like? Is he as Hoffner says?"

"Yes. I know it's hard to believe, but he is. I can't imagine him killing anyone. If he were terrible and unkind . . . but he wasn't. He seemed really to like Boris." Ursula continued to face Paul, but to her other side she could feel Günther waiting. If she could avoid him until the next day, she would be strong enough to lie to him. "I'm very tired."

"Yes," said Günther, "It's been a long day. Let's go up."

At her room she kissed them both and slipped away softly, locking the door behind her. She washed her face with cold water and ran a brush through her hair, feeling immensely relieved to be away from the twins. When she emerged from the bathroom, Günther was seated in the chair beside her bed. She caught her breath and glanced at the locked door.

"The balcony," he said.

"Günther, I'm very tired."

"I know you are. My better half says I should not question you tonight, since you would have no resistance—which is why I am here. He graciously submits that we abandoned you by going to Stockholm, something else I did not need to be told. But I believe we had an agreement, you and I. How long have you been lovers?"

Only her desk light shone in the room, leaving the far side where her brother sat dusky with shadows. "You may not believe this, but we were not lovers, are not lovers."

"You are right. I don't believe it. A whole box full of orchids for the young lady? How could you resist such attention?"

"I did resist it." She turned away from him.

"No. Look at me." He turned on the lamp beside her bed. "Tell me again you are not lovers."

"We are not lovers." She sat at the foot of the bed.

"Look at me." She faced him squarely as he got up and stood over her. "Say it again."

"We are not lovers. We are not lovers." She started to cry. "We are *not* lovers."

"Ah, perhaps I'm asking the wrong question. Do you love him?"

"No," she said sharply. "Günther. I swear to you I rejected him."

"But he never gave up?"

"No."

"Do you also swear to me that you never made love with him?" The hesitation gave her away instantly, and for a few seconds she thought he was going to hit her with his clenched fists, but then he loosened his hand and pulled her to a standing position. "If you were not in love with him—why?"

Their faces were inches apart. "Only once, Günther. One night. I swear it. I was in such despair. He was convenient."

"When?"

She covered her face with her hands, but he pulled them away. "Three days ago."

"And he left for England immediately after that?"

"The next morning."

[295]

"I suppose if he hadn't left, he would have become convenient again."

"I don't know. It wasn't just that. There was something else about him . . ."

"I know—he was polite! Pleasant! Likable! Well-bred!" He released her and turned to leave.

She was crying again. "He smelled like you!" she said to his retreating figure.

The statement stopped Günther at the door. He returned to the bed and sat beside her, putting his arm around her, rocking her gently as he had done when they were both children.

Conrad Brandt was also awake, sitting in his darkened room smoking, remembering what Ursula had said before the narcotic closed her eyes and took her away: "I'm sorry, Conrad." And then tonight as she looked at the English boys' school picture: ". . . that's John." Coming from her in that moment, the softly spoken name had stunned him. This man with the soft name had sent her orchids, had gone sailing with her, spent many evenings with her. And then there was that reaction when she saw who he was. If Günther hadn't caught her, she would have gone through the glass doors. He shuddered as his imagination finished what she had intended. He saw the glass explode in the fury of her lunge, saw her lacerated and bleeding body lying on the stone terrace, the rain beating down on her ruined face, her cut throat. He groaned. Why did she want to hurt herself? What was John Skye to her? What was this fine, well-groomed, likable, generous young man to her before she knew he was her half-brother? Would he spend many evenings just visiting Boris?

Brandt raged at himself for the mistakes he had made. He who had never touched a woman in anger, who did not believe that sex was men and women fighting each other, had actually raised his hand against her. He looked back upon the night he twisted her arm with shuddering remorse and astonishment. He had done everything wrong. The whole mad scenario from the time he tricked her into feeling sorry for him so that she would reveal the twins' whereabouts until the moment he left the house without even talking to her had been a series of idiotic blunders. He had actually twisted her arm! But in light of what he did next, twisting her arm was mild and forgivable. Even as he stood up, his brain screaming at him to stop, his body strode mindlessly toward her: he intended to take her by force. But to his immense and unfathomable joy, she rose, brushed her breasts against him the length of his body, accepted his mad embrace with her strong arms, answered his kiss with pliant consenting lips and wide open eyes. And then the whispered words *yes, yes, yes,* that brought him to the very edge of tears and later entered and dominated every sad, insane, glorious, impossible daydream he could concoct.

And then Boris entered the room, and the stunning girl became both kitten and lioness, secretly letting him know that she would be waiting for him when the clown act was over.

And then he threw the miracle away. All his logic, his reasoning, what he termed his nobler nature, lectured him into the cruelest act of all: he abandoned her, left her stalking at the entrance to her cave, waiting for the promised lover who never showed up. And everything was predicated on

[296]

his being a thinking, moral man: she was a young girl ostensibly under his care and protection and he had no right to be anything more to her. Take her to bed? Have you lost your mind? Your *reason*—that *sine qua non* of the moral process? Going to her might have been a violation of his responsibility, but not going to her was cruel beyond forgiveness. The horror of that cruelty came out of hiding at every chance it got and leered at him with taunting ugliness: fool, fool, fool!

And the girl—the fatal girl that he loved—had drawn into her pride and slammed shut the cave's gate And yet, there were some strange sounds that reached him from within. "I'm sorry, Conrad." And still more strange and which he believed came from the heart: ". . . that's John." No, he refused to think it. If madness didn't lie that way, then certainly murder did. If he once began imagining her in every man's bed, he would become a babbling lunatic. He had to keep all his wits intact. The world was closing in around all of them, but now at least figures became discernible; individual forms broke away from the massive wall against which he had relentlessly, uselessly beat his will for two years since his beloved uncle lay bleeding to death on the platform between two receding trains. He had long since reasoned that they had searched the wrong train.

25

Ursula got up early feeling brittle with exhaustion, convinced that if she as much as fell to her knees, all her bones would shatter. She had slept badly, waking hourly out of dream fragments that raced her heart and convulsed her body with shivering, although she could not remember the splinters of events that caused her terror. Wrapped in a blanket, she stood at the balcony doors and watched a hard rain beat against the dark stone. Was Skye her brothers' killer? Did he purposely miss his airplane and return to the house secretly and wait for Boris, kill him, and tie the line around his foot? Where did he hide? There were a dozen rooms in the house that no one entered for weeks at a time. In all their houses, there were always some rooms that everyone loved and lived in daily; but there were others that were as forgotten as tombs that one visited only on rare occasions. Did Skye perhaps not leave the house at all, but instead stay in one of those rooms after he left her on the night they made love? Did he wait until she left the house and Boris was alone? Did he pretend he'd just arrived as Boris was going to the lake? She could hear Boris' silly British. "I say, old chap, you've come at an awfully good time. The breeze is positively ripping. Let's take her out for a fly. Too bad old Ursula's gone out drawing." She saw them in the boat, saw Skye drop anchor, saw him push Boris overboard and go in after him, holding him underwater until he stopped struggling, then rip off the watch and let it drop to the bottom, then swim away further along the shore, then go to his rooms, pack, and fly home to England. And the year before, had he followed Alexander for days, known when he would be hunting, waited in the misty forest, and shot him through the heart? She groaned. Had she made love to her half-brother, her brothers' murderer? She wanted to crawl into bed and never get up again. She thought about this prospect with comfort. She could die there and all the horrors would be over. "Not quite," said a voice she had not heard in a long time. "*If* he is the murderer he will then kill Melchior and Paul and Günther and when all of you are interred in Boris' magnificent new tomb, he will stand outside of it and roar with laughter. *If* he is the murderer." The voice came from someone who had a sense of the rightness of things. She got up quickly, showered, and dressed in warm clothes. She could not afford to catch cold or get chilled: there were things to do. There was Conrad Brandt to face. He would want to know more about John Skye. His puzzled expression and then that look of outrage as she and the twins discussed their half-brother floated back to her. What were his suspicions regarding her and John Skye? How much had her reaction given away? How stupidly she had behaved when the drawing revealed the long-lost Vanya. Right out of some Russian novel, Günther used to say. Well, *calm* from here on. And then there was another problem sure to develop into a fight. She and the twins had already decided to take Boris to Vienna themselves. And Conrad Brandt was definitely going to object. Conrad wouldn't win this one.

Downstairs she found Brandt with the phone in one hand and a cup of coffee in the other. "I'll call you back." He hung up and put down the cup. He was his usual remotely disheveled self: his coat needed pressing, and he had not shaved. "Before your brothers come down and we begin this impossible day, there is something I have to say to you. I made a bad mistake this summer when I was here. I know now I should not have left without seeing you. The fact is, I even knew it then. I'm sorry."

"Why did you go?"

"I don't know. Some sense that I shouldn't . . . ah . . . that I shouldn't . . . that, ah . . . I . . ." He rubbed his forehead as he struggled miserably into speechlessness.

"I'd like to ask you something," she said after the silence became too long.

He nodded. "Please go ahead."

"I've always been curious where you went that night."

He took a deep breath and colored visibly. "Where I went?"

"How interesting to see a lawyer actually blush. Why don't you lie if that will make it easier?"

"No." He shook his head. "The truth is easier. I went to a brothel."

"I don't believe you."

"I did. I hadn't been to one since I was sixteen. If it's of any interest to you, the woman asked me afterward who Ursula was. I was just a little drunk on Boris' brandy." He drank some coffee, then said in a manner so casual it bordered on the bizarre, "What did you do?"

"I went to sleep. It had been an exhausting day as I recall."

He nodded and quickly looked down at some papers on the desk, picking up one and reading from it before he spoke. "Did you ever see John Skye before the birthday party?"

"No."

"I've been making calls for the last two hours trying to pick up information on him. Nothing's come back so far. It's too early for one thing; the various registry offices aren't open yet. And for another, I can't find anybody who has anything but good to say about him. The servants all think he's a fine young man of sterling character. What did you think of him?"

Ursula had been waiting for one of Brandt's fixed, unblinking stares. "I never thought about him one way or the other," she said with complete and callous composure.

"Didn't he have dinner here every night for the last six weeks?"

"I don't know, since *I* didn't have dinner here every night for the last six weeks."

"Ah. But you did go sailing alone with him a time or two."

"A time or two."

"And he never talked about himself?"

"Not to me."

"I find that a little hard to believe."

"Do you?"

Suddenly the guard dropped as though he had physically disarmed himself, taken a hidden weapon and placed it on the desk between them. "Don't fight me, Ursula."

"Then don't force me to."

"You have the advantage; you know how I feel."

She turned away from his anguished eyes with a certain confusion and odd anger.

Into this charged silence walked the twins, both of them stopping abruptly, both looking from Ursula to Brandt and back again. "Is this a private war or can anyone join?" asked Günther, raising his eyebrows.

Ursula turned her attention to a sixteenth-century map on the wall.

"Just going over some information I've gathered on John Skye. To begin with, I can't profile him out as a killer. We'll see what comes up in the next few hours. We have to make sure he is who you think he is. The birth registry in Vienna will help. The university records here in the city should give us something. Of course, his family in England will have to be handled somewhat delicately. Also, we need to know where his real mother is. She stopped receiving your grandfather's checks at the end of the war. Our offices will get on those matters first thing." He spoke directly to Ursula. "You're the only one who saw him almost every day; did he have a visible birthmark?"

"Not that I noticed. Also, the servants saw him almost every day, as did Hoffner. In fact, I thought they were rather chummy."

"Yes. Hoffner said John Skye always had a pleasant greeting for him." Brandt got up. "If there's nothing else at the moment, I'll go shave." He ran his hand roughly across his cheeks and chin. It was a gesture so won-

[299]

derfully masculine that Ursula caught herself enjoying it, and turned away from it.

After Brandt left, Günther sat on the edge of the desk and asked again one of the lawyer's questions. "Did he have a visible birthmark?" He raised his hand in a gesture of silence. "I know: you didn't notice. Did he have a not-so-visible birthmark that you might have noticed?"

"I don't know. I didn't turn on the light."

"Now, that's revealing. For a girl who enjoys looking at naked men as much as you . . ."

"At that moment I wasn't interested in what he looked like. Please, Günther. Stop."

"Yes," said Paul. "You agreed last night to forget it. Now let her forget it."

"Just one thing and I'll drop it," said Günther. "Now that you know who he is, was there anything that he said or did that makes you believe now that he, himself, was capable of killing Alexander and Boris?"

Ursula closed her eyes and bowed her head as she saw again the shudder of pain that crossed Skye's face when she told him about Alexander's death. "No," she said.

"No flashes of cruelty, of cynicism, of suppressed rage?"

She shook her head. "No." She did not want to tell Günther that Skye was tender and loving.

"The perfect gentleman?"

She nodded. "Yes."

"He sounds just a little too flawless for me," said Günther angrily.

"I don't know," said Paul. "He sounds rather like us."

"You know, Paul," said Ursula, "that's the very best description of him anyone could give." She turned to Günther. "He even has your appalling sense of humor."

He ignored her statement. "Is this a case of our not *wanting* him to be the killer?"

"For God's sake, Günther, I don't want him to be the killer, do you?" She did not give him a chance to answer. "Are we going to behave like Father and Grandfather? Haven't we learned anything? He's our half-brother! And I'll tell you something: we're fast running out of brothers. I would love to have discovered him now, if only the circumstances were different. Do you think I would have pushed him into bed if I had known who he was?" She could feel the beginnings of a migraine behind her left eye.

"What bothers me is why you didn't recognize him."

"His coloring, I suppose. It's very different from ours. His hair is dark blond, an ironic touch of Melchior, who is, however, a clearer blond. He has gray eyes, an odd mercury gray, changeable with streaks sometimes teal in color, sometimes darker silver." She ignored Günther's scowl and flaring nostrils, but acknowledged Paul's warning glance. "Then, too, he is British, very proper British. And he is taller than any of you. Almost as tall as Conrad, and a little broader in a way that's hard to describe. He has yours, and Father's splendid back—long, graceful. . . ."

"Is this the woman or the artist speaking?" growled Günther. "Enough. I don't want to hear how magnificent he is. If he is Vanya, he had to know who you are. . . ."

[300]

"So did you and I, Günther!" The pain spread down into her cheekbone.
"Not the same!"
"Yes, it is. I was the one who wasn't the gentleman."
"It's not the same, Ursula."
She gave an angry laugh and spoke to Paul. "Tell him it's the same. He's never going to believe it from me."
"What's the same?" Brandt stood in the doorway.
Paul made an offhand gesture as if to wave the subject into casual oblivion. "Just making some family comparisons. We still have to prove John Skye is our brother."
"I wish you'd all stop treating me as though I were an idiot. I'd like to believe that you aren't keeping anything important from me. My uncle warned me that you were a very secretive trio."
"Conrad," said Paul, "believe me, it was not important."
"Well, *you* I can believe. Those two I'm not so sure about." He shrugged. "All right, let's make some decisions. First, I'll take Boris back to Vienna, and—"
"No," said Ursula, "not this time."
"She's right," said Paul. "We're all going home."
Günther nodded. "And when you get hold of the abbot, tell him Melchior has to come too. Better yet, I'll talk to him."
Brandt took his notes off the desk. "I'm against any of you returning to Vienna now. There could be some danger for you. This may be what someone is waiting for."
"Somewhere, someday, Conrad, we have to face our enemy," said Günther. "You can't tuck us away in some pleasant little country in a sunny cage guarded by a private army forever. The enemy found us long ago and he got past your guard. He may even have exchanged pleasantries with one of your men. All our lives, someone else has taken care of our problems, smoothed out the wrinkles, trimmed off the rough edges. We believe that our old servants, as well as the people in your office who have died, all died because of us. We can't let anything else happen. There is still Berghoch and Dr. Frichter. . . ."
Brandt turned abruptly away from them, rolling up the papers in his hand. "He's dead," he said with his back to them.
"I thought he survived the accident," said Ursula.
"The doctor, yes. Though I understand he is much too ill to leave his home now. But the other man . . ."
"Berghoch?" said Ursula. "Berghoch is dead?"
"Yes." Brandt turned and faced them, attempting his lawyer's expression. It was a little off-center, as though it might leave him any minute and be replaced by a rush of tears. "He dealt in the black market, as you know. Nothing critical, cigarettes mostly. I think he did it for a little excitement. He obviously didn't need the money. He used to bring me an occasional bottle of Scotch. My American friends were already supplying me, but I didn't tell him that. He was so pleased to be able to do it. Someone entered his house, robbed and killed him, probably someone who was also in the black-market business. I think they thought he had money hidden there. The place was thoroughly torn apart."
Ursula heard Paul ask "when" at the same time Günther asked "how"

[301]

Berghoch was killed. "Bludgeoned," said Brandt in a flat voice. "I'd grown fond of him." After a moment of sad silence, he went on. "It happened a month ago. I had intended to tell you when I saw you, but then this happened, and I felt I ought to wait a little longer. Let some time pass. I'm sorry to have to tell you now."

Ursula walked to a window overlooking a drenched, spent garden. It would soon be winter again. The earth would die. In her remembered dreams since Alexander died, death had begun to follow her in its various disguises: sometimes it ambled after her in the comical rattling, grinning skeleton of Adolphus; occasionally she heard it flop around behind her in the shape of decaying flesh held together only by a bloated, bile-colored human skin, boneless, supported only by the worms crawling inside of it, feeding on it, but usually she encountered it at a given moment when she glanced over her shoulder and saw in the permanent twilight her father's face with its dangling eyeball and putty-pulped nose, with its displaced theatrical eyelash on Miss Schneider, who entered the same improbable dream, materializing out of absolutely nothing and vanishing into the same nothingness as she herself was unaccountably thrust into the mad governess's position, struggling horribly, futilely to keep the obscene thing from forcing its slippery, insistent kiss upon her mouth.

Ursula leaned her forehead against the cold glass and listened as Waldi cut her hair. *Our kind does not die so easily. In fact, I have decided against it. Ursula and Berghoch refuse to go.* She placed her open hands against the glass. "Oh, Waldi," she whispered, the tears running down her face. "Oh, Waldi, you promised me you'd never die."

She felt arms encircle her, turn her slowly, stroke her hair with loving tenderness. "Günther, Waldi promised he would not die. Do you remember?" But it was not Günther who held her. Conrad Brandt's arms were fully around her, yet there was no pressure to them. He was barely touching her. When she looked up into his face, he seemed to be waiting to breathe, a mixture of hopeless desire and raging despair warring in his eyes.

Ursula brushed the tears from her cheeks with her open hands and stepped back and to the side. As Brandt lowered his arms, she caught sight of Paul's hand against Günther's chest in the faint, delicate motion of keeping his twin from taking the lawyer's place. The curious tableau etched itself in her mind in one of those moments which is never to be forgotten and yet whose meaning is too multifaceted to be understood at the time. It was she herself who broke the spell. "I'm sorry for crying. At least now there is no one left who has to die for us."

When Brandt again faced them, he was calm. "It will be a long day. We should have some breakfast."

Three hours later the calls began coming in. Brandt's firm in Vienna was on the line first: the birth registry showed a boy child born to one Magda Himmel at a given date in 1932. There was no mention of the child's father. "Vanya is one month younger than Melchior," said Paul as Brandt wrote the information on a pad for them to read.

"Yes, if there's more. Of course, I want it!" said the lawyer with growing irritation, clamping the phone to his ear. He wrote: *The woman, Magda Himmel, died nine days later of a uterine infection.* After writing this on the pad, Brandt slowly lowered the phone as he sat upright to read his own words. The twins and Ursula, crowding around him at the time, pulled away from the notation. None of them spoke. Brandt quickly returned to the phone. "What else do you have? . . . What do you mean, 'nothing'? What happened to the child?" He listened, tapping the pencil on the desk. "All right, follow that up, as well as the records of all foundling homes. The checks were endorsed by a Magda Himmel as late as April of 1945. Find out how they were delivered. And relatives, find the woman's relatives. I *know* it's going to take a little time. So start now. Call me immediately if you come up with anything."

An hour later the abbot from Monte Tre Croci called. He spoke to Günther and agreed with him at once that Melchior should come home for a few days to be with his sister and brothers.

In the early afternoon the police inspector arrived. He told them that the examination of the body verified death by drowning and that there were no marks on the body that could suggest foul play. The abrasions above the right ankle were caused by the towline. Looking pointedly at Ursula, the man said he was deeply grieved over the family's tragic loss. "There is one question I would like to ask for the record. Did he have any enemies?"

"Only the person who murdered him," said Ursula.

The inspector gave Brandt and the twins a pained look and said he had to be going. Brandt walked with him to the front door and Ursula knew they were making arrangements to have the body taken somewhere.

During the afternoon as rain fell steadily and they waited for the phone to ring, Ursula asked Brandt if the people who broke into Berghoch's house and killed him had been caught.

"No," said Brandt. "And they didn't break in. He apparently knew them and opened the door to them, which is what makes the police believe the murderer or murderers were involved with him in the black-market business."

"He didn't work that way," said Ursula. "He would never let anyone into his house who was in that business."

"Of course not," said Günther. "He worked with black-market people all during the war. We all knew it. But he would buy what he wanted through some merchant in a legitimate shop who was in the business himself; he would never do it directly off the street or out of some truck or some warehouse. And the idea that someone should come to our home was a total anathema to him."

"The police are right," said Ursula. "He knew his killer, but it was no one in the black market."

"Did you see his body, Conrad?" asked Paul.

Brandt got up to pace as Ursula and the twins watched him. "Yes. I identified him. Our office, of course, services his trust. There was something a little amusing about that. In all his documents, he gave our firm as the next of kin. In fact, he rather treated me like a son. We had dinner together occasionally and most of the time he talked about your family. Nothing very private, you understand. But your precocity interested him rather deeply. You had a good teacher in him."

"How was he . . . I mean *where* was he actually hit?" asked Günther.

"On the back of the head. Someone hit him with a piece of iron."

"Not Ewald Berghoch," said Paul.

"What?"

"What we mean," said Günther, "is that the person who killed him was very well known to him."

"How can you be so sure?"

"He was a fighter; he would never let anyone he didn't know get behind him."

"And he was very strong," added Ursula. "Grandfather's guards found him years ago living in one of our forests. He had come back from the war—the First World War—and he had no place to go, so he lived in the forest with some men who had been soldiers with him in the army. Grandfather put them all to work. Waldi was a sort of famous cook." She smiled faintly at the old jokes. "He convinced Grandfather that he made rat stews when he was in the war. Once we asked him if he really made stews out of rats and he said that actually he made them out of snakes but that the other soldiers would have been disgusted if he told them the truth. He said he would pour the snake stew over a pile of maggots that he told the soldiers was rice. He said they enjoyed the dish tremendously and no one ever complained or got sick."

Brandt stopped walking. "So he was like all the others. I thought Berghoch's case was different because he actually was murdered. The others all could have been accidents, but not Berghoch. And now what you tell me forces me to conclude that the appearance of his death was as contrived as all the others. That leaves only the good doctor, who is convinced his automobile brakes were tampered with. He told me at the time that he believed someone was trying to kill him. He's hired bodyguards, but considering everything that's happened, that won't save him. I'm amazed at the size of this thing."

The Vienna firm called back twice in the evening; once to say that there was no record of a Magda Himmel listed with any of the guilds or unions, and that the families in Vienna named Himmel knew of no women related to them who died in 1932. In fact, there was no woman of that name in any of the families and no one could remember any in this century. The second piece of information involved the child, or more specifically did not involve the child: no orphanage or charitable organization had received a child at that time or of that name at any time. Conrad turned back to Ursula and the twins. "Where would your father have met her?"

Günther finally spoke after all three of them hung back, less out of embarrassment than ignorance. "Actually, we knew very little about his life outside the house. And to be brutally frank, we didn't care. We didn't care about his life at home either. Grandfather was our parent, and Rätzel, and Graz, and Berghoch, and a couple of the teachers that we came to love. Mother was a total mystery, and Father an endless embarrassment. We saw your uncle oftener than we saw our father."

"But you must have had some notion of where he went when he went out."

"Cabarets," said Ursula. "When he dressed in his beautiful evening clothes, he went to cabarets. Grandfather use to say very casually to Rätzel that

[304]

Father's whorehouse bills were a luxury he—Grandfather—didn't mind paying."

"He said that in front of you as children?" Brandt blinked with amazement.

"I think Grandfather wanted us to hear it; but I don't think the places Father went were brothels." Ursula gave Brandt a dropped-lidded look that had the lawyer biting his lip. "I think they were cabarets where he met ladies that he then took to hotels. Two or three afternoons a week he went out to ride his horse. The servants used to say that he was rumored to be the best rider in Vienna."

"Forgive me for asking this, but was he . . . selective? I mean . . ."

"We know what you mean," said Günther. "He must have been at first. He chose Mother."

"Ah . . . yes."

"There were a great many stories," continued Günther. "We heard them mostly from the servants—how Father courted Mother and wouldn't give up until Grandfather allowed them to marry. He was very much against the marriage. He always claimed that Father used some kind of trickery to make Mother want him." It was deep night by then and the rain fell intermittently, peevishly, with little sighs of wind that brushed leaves against glass.

"Did they go out much?"

"Go out?" asked Paul.

"To parties, dinners, social functions?"

The twins looked at each other. "How odd," said Günther, "that we never thought of that, but in our memory, they never went out."

"They never went out even before we were born. They never went out at all, anywhere, at any time," said Ursula. "The maids used to talk about Mother being shy and not being able to meet people. They said that her idea of heaven was to be alone on the estate with Father forever. Apparently Father's idea of heaven took in a lot more territory. She never left the estate with him after they were married. They never traveled together and they went to no social functions. She sometimes traveled with Grandfather when he took us somewhere. I remember that she went with us to Rome. But Father was not with us."

"That's right," said Paul. "I had forgotten that. She had an audience!"

Ursula nodded. "Yes. I remember there were two nurses with us on that trip and they were all excited about something. They spoke about God hearing her now and making her well. It was a long time before I figured it out, and by then she was dead and Grandfather was furious at the Church and the pope and God for not curing Mother; so we never went to church again."

Brandt shook his head. "So they never went anywhere together?"

"No," said Ursula, reaching into his eyes. "And you're thinking 'Poor man! Poor man!' "

"No . . . I . . . ah . . ." Brandt's expression pleaded with the twins to help him out.

"Well, you should! You should be thinking that. He was cheated! Father was cheated of his wife and he was cheated of his children." Tears of rage

[305]

rose in her eyes. "Between your firm and our grandfather, he never had a chance."

"Ursula, don't," said Günther. "It's all over."

"No. That's just it! It isn't all over. If Father and Mother had lived an ordinary life, there wouldn't be any Vanya. As it was, Father became a joke. The servants used to say that men locked up their wives when Father went prowling. 'The Russian wolf was stalking the ewes!' "

"Their wives?" asked Brandt.

"Yes," said Günther. "It was a sort of dreary jest that Father was looking for a wife, anybody's wife. He apparently did not seek out single women. I'm not sure that was still true by the time of the Parade."

"The Parade?"

Paul explained that they had called the many women in and out late at night the Parade, as Brandt drew interlocking squares in the margin of his legal pad. Ursula leaned across the desk to see him write "Count Pavel Stephanovitch Bronevsky" and after the name several exclamation marks standing like a row of astonished ghosts. "They came to the house right up to the end," finished Paul.

Brandt was filling in the loops and circles of her father's name when Ursula asked the question. "Who bought our house?"

"An import-export firm. A foreign firm. Yes, a *foreign* firm!" He stood up, knocking over his chair. "A British firm! That contract! I saw it only once. Just once!" His face turned wild with excitement. "And there is only one thing I remember about it. I don't even remember the name of the company. The 'Something-something Limited!' but I remember its home-office address. Not all of it, just the one odd name: 'The Isle of Man.' "

26

In the morning Conrad met Ursula and the twins for breakfast, all three of them morosely silent as he detailed his plans to them. "I'm expecting a call from England today. So far we know that there is a connection between the two families—yours and Lord John Skye's. His firm bought the Enerde mansion. Why? His son, or at least the person he claims as a son, was fathered by a man who lived in that mansion."

"Adopted?" asked Günther.

"My first thought, and certainly a distinct possibility. We'll have to wait for the call from England. For some reason, Lord Skye was in Vienna at the same time that Magda Himmel had a baby and died. He took the child with him to England and raised him as his own. Perhaps he and his lady couldn't have any."

"Are you saying that his name Vanya Himmel was a mere coincidence? That's just a little too much Dickens for me," said Ursula.

"You're right, of course. I can't answer that, any more than I can answer the question of the woman who called herself Magda Himmel all those years your grandfather was paying her to keep quiet about a baby she didn't have. What I find the most confusing is why the Englishman bought the mansion. There is always the outside chance that he bought it simply because he knew about it; it's a famous home. If he adopted a foundling, he may not even have known who the child's father was, and buying the estate merely involved an extraordinary coincidence."

"Do you believe that?" asked Ursula.

"No," said Brandt.

For a half-hour he presented Ursula and the twins with various theories: Lord Skye knew who the father was and bought the mansion for his son because he appreciated the irony of it. The three rolled their eyes at each other and Günther commented that, as far as irony went, this variety of it was fairly expensive. Brandt tried again: "When Lord Skye was in Vienna in 1932 he was a guest in the house, some elaborate party perhaps, at which he heard that one of the maids was in a delicate condition. He adopted her child when it was born, and because of that . . . ah, because of that . . ." He didn't finish. The expressions on the Bronevsky children's faces silenced his speech but made him smile. "I'm trying to consider all the possibilities, and the three of you look at me as though I've lost my mind. How about a little help? *You* suggest something."

They couldn't. They looked at him glumly. "Know, however," said Günther, "that there have been no parties in that house since the day our parents were married."

Brandt squinted at the twins through his cigarette smoke. "I find that . . . sad. Didn't you kids have parties?"

"Not in that house," said Ursula. "In this one, the one in Italy, the one in Salzburg, and in Bavaria. In fact, everywhere except Vienna, everywhere that our father didn't go; and he *never* traveled with us."

Brandt, watching her face, wondered how many years it had taken these children to learn those strange blank expressions. With their hauntingly beautiful features, he hated to see them turn on their mannequin masks, bereft of all animation, all warmth, all tenderness.

When the call from England came, Brandt listened to his man in London for a full minute before he spoke. "Hang on," he said. He placed the phone on the desk and looked for a long moment at Ursula and the twins. They weren't going to like it. "John Skye is the legitimate son of Lord John and Lady Madeline Skye. The records are quite clear on this matter."

"They are also quite forged," said Ursula. "He is our brother."

"How can you be so *sure?*"

Ursula looked away, frowning faintly, a look of pain running across her features as she lowered her eyes. For a moment Brandt had the impression she was going to cry.

"You can take her word for it," said Günther slowly, an anger rising in his voice that was not lost on Brandt. "If Ursula says he is our brother, then he is our brother."

Ursula raised her face with fresh defiance. "Your records, the ones you yourself compiled in checking out John, say that Lord Skye was a widower. Ask your man in England when Lady Skye died."

Something close to fear touched Brandt as he picked up the phone and asked the question. The answer came immediately: "Nineteen-thirty-two."

"Where? Ask him *where* she died?"

Again the answer came at once. "Vienna."

"Oh, God," said Ursula. "We had it backwards."

Brandt told his agent he would call him back in twenty minutes. "I don't get it," he said to her. "What did we have backwards?"

"Don't you see it?"

"No," said Brandt. He turned to the twins, who were both frowning at their sister.

"We had it reversed. His name was not changed to John Skye. He was always John Skye—except for the hospital records. It was she who went through a name change."

"Who?" asked Brandt, leaning across the desk. "Who went through a name change?"

"Lady Madeline is Magda Himmel. In English Magda is a short form of Madeline, which is derived from Magdalene. Remember, Günther . . . Paul . . . one of those other English teachers we had was crazy about Keats. *The Eve of St. Agnes* was her favorite poem; the girl in it who ran away with her lover was named Madeline. . . ."

Günther nodded his head. "All right, I remember it. Now what?"

"Somehow Lady Madeline met Father . . . and had his baby."

"All right, fine," said Brandt. "Why did she change her name? She was already married, had been for seven years. She could have passed the kid off as her husband's." Brandt saw Ursula give him a murderous look.

"It's possible he didn't want it . . . if he knew it wasn't his," said Günther. "And when she died, he had a change of heart."

The murderous look moved off and covered Günther. "And maybe she didn't *want* to," said Ursula. "Maybe she was in love with Father and she wanted to have Count Pavel Bronevsky's baby! You men! Pass the kid off as someone else's! It wasn't his so he didn't want it! Can't you *ever* look at the other side?"

"Okay. Okay," murmured Brandt. "So she enters a hospital under a phony name and has this baby which she may or may not want to keep. Only, she dies."

"Yes. She dies." Ursula relaxed. "And maybe now the child is the only thing the husband has left of her. I don't know what unhappy drama took place there over twenty years ago that made her use a false name, but I know that that's what she did. And he took the baby back to England as his son. If you still don't believe it, Conrad, ask your man in London where John was born. It's all going to come together."

"Not quite!" said Brandt. "Who was the woman your grandfather paid off all those years?"

Ursula shrugged. "Does it make any difference now? Didn't you say Grandfather stopped paying her when the war ended? Maybe she was a nurse at the hospital and saw an opportunity."

"It makes a lot of difference. She may be the missing clue we need most.

[308]

But for the moment let's get back to young Lord Skye. Let's assume we now know that he is your half-brother. Why have the servants and my lawyers been killed? Why Alexander and Boris?" Brandt took a deep breath. "Let's assume, *just* for the sake of the argument, that John Skye befriended you and Boris in order to kill you *both*. Why haven't you—"

"We've thought of that," said Günther. "Two accidents at the same time at the same location—barring poisoned mushrooms—would raise many more questions."

Brandt never took his eyes away from Ursula. "What was the last thing he said to you?"

"Who?"

Brandt seethed. Her question gave her time to think. "John Skye."

"He said 'good-bye.' " She spoke without changing expression.

Brandt ran his hand through his hair. How could a seventeen-year-old girl make him feel so stupid? He called his contact back in London and discovered that Lord John's son was born in Vienna. He told the Bronevskys that after the funeral his office would fully investigate the Skye family. He would pull all the documents on the sale of the Enerde mansion. He would check back into the events of 1932. He would question people who were staffed at the hospital where Lady Madeline died. He would thoroughly investigate Lord Skye's reasons for being in Vienna at the time that his wife gave birth to another man's child. Ursula and the twins seemed to be listening attentively, yet at odd intervals, he received the impression that they were only pretending. There were looks between them that enraged him because he could not read them. There was no rolling of eyes or even lowering of lids; it was a language in which the skin around their eyes did not move at all. He was convinced that a whole conversation passed between them as he kept on with his inane and meaningless speech that they did not even hear.

By noon Brandt had hired a private railway coach to take the family back to Austria the next day. Boris' body would be delivered to the coach in its sealed coffin in the morning. Hoffner would pick up Melchior at the station at four this afternoon. Brandt checked his list to see what he had forgotten. He was alone in the library by then and deeply depressed: the girl hated him, the boys were hostile toward him, particularly Günther, and all of them distrusted him. They were in terrible danger. Of that he was certain, yet they seemed to resent his concern for them. The private coach was going to be guarded by five men, which they thought was unnecessary. He had asked them to stay at his home in Grinzing, but they thanked him politely and told him they preferred to stay at a hotel.

If he had them at his house in Grinzing, he could watch over them himself. Since his uncle's murder he had carried a revolver which at this moment was upstairs in his briefcase, so convinced was he that whoever murdered Boris would try to kill Ursula next.

There were other problems. The guns in the house were gone. When he and Hoffner searched the house while Ursula slept her narcotic sleep, they discovered that the twins' target pistols were gone from the room under the stairs where the sports equipment was stored. Who had armed himself? If it was the twins, then quite possibly they had plans of their own. He wished he could ship them all to America for a month until he sorted things out. But they were of age and could no longer be sent to their rooms because they didn't mind. He got up to pace, wondering how he could keep them confined to their hotel in Vienna. The funeral was no problem. His office had already hired a small army to protect them there. And once they were inside the crypt Boris had designed and ordered built—just in time, he thought angrily, as things turned out, to receive the designer himself—they were totally protected. Unless someone mined the bloody thing. But he believed the killer would not do this; for some unfathomable reason, everyone's death had to appear accidental, and he could not see the murderer changing his method of operation now.

He stopped at the window when he saw the twins and Ursula in the pavilion, where they stood facing the lake, the girl between the two young men. Ursula was gesturing with her open hand. Günther turned profile as he listened, his head tilted a little. Paul put his hands in his pockets and rose on his toes and dropped back on his heels several times, a habit of his that Brandt had noticed before. The two young men were identical and yet he had no difficulty in telling them apart. His uncle told him once that their sister alone had this ability, that even the grandfather could not tell one from the other. It had taken Brandt some time to think out the subtle difference that had allowed him the ability Ursula had.

As he stood observing them, he deeply felt his love for them, these three strangely beautiful people with their sensuous faces and gracefully athletic bodies. An only child himself, orphaned at five by the flu epidemic after the Great War, he wanted the men as his brothers and the girl as his wife. But at that moment he would have settled on just being able to eavesdrop on their conversation. He was convinced they were making some plan of their own, some plan that did not include him. And if that was the case, how could he *begin* to protect them? They were as familiar with Vienna as he was, and if they thought they were being followed, they could easily lose their trackers. He would simply have to stay with them every minute, even if it meant checking into the same hotel with them.

Still, he watched them with a curious joy, the way one might watch magnificent animals in the wild, three gold-eyed leopards, relaxed and easy and totally fearless, with an air of secrecy and mystery about them that he knew was forever beyond him. As he contemplated the three young people, they did something that brought Conrad Brandt's face suddenly close to the glass: Ursula and Günther kissed each other. It was not an overlong kiss, but their leaning into it clearly let him know that it was not sisterly-brotherly, either. And then, as Ursula looked down at the water, the twins kissed each other over her lowered head. That part he had already sensed, but not the other, not Ursula and Günther, although he should have, he thought, isolated all during their childhood from kids their own age, and always *taught* not to make friends. Still, probably just fun and games. Günther, he reasoned, was too levelheaded for anything more serious with his sister.

He stood back a little from the window when he saw them walking to the house, marveling at their athletic grace. These were the children of suicides. How could those two weak and careless parents hold and bequeath the genes that produced such Olympian proportions of splendor and brilliance? The three stopped just short of the stone terrace. They did not speak, but he saw their expressions change, and when they moved again Conrad knew they would enter the room with all their feelings hidden and their plans as solidly determined and concealed from him as if they had encased them in stone. But what good could their plans do them when somewhere loose in the world walked a murderer who had already killed ten times? Who stalked the darker jungle behind them, weapons poised, waiting for the three to move into the open, into the light, where they could be killed with ease?

Brandt decided he would cautiously work on the twins, sound them out on any particular ideas they might have regarding their brother's funeral service. Would they like to inspect the crypt first, make some decisions regarding the reburial of their grandfather and their parents? No one had been moved into it yet. He reasoned that if he kept them busy he could keep his eye on them; or, if they gave him certain hours when they could not be with him, he would know at least the times that they intended to do something on their own. But when he made the suggestion on working out a plan to people the crypt, Günther pleasantly put him off. "We thought you and Melchior should do that. My twin and my sister loathe graveyards. And I am of the same mind. None of us is sentimental about the dead, and we have no interest in where or how you house them. I suppose for the sake of sanitation and seemliness they should be put out of sight. Melchior has no end of talents in this area. He will have many good suggestions regarding protocol, and you, of course, have all the organizational ability." There was no hint of malice or sarcasm in his statement and yet Conrad felt that Günther had just slammed a door in his face. He decided that he always had time to bring the matter up again later, especially if he could make Melchior an ally.

To Brandt's surprise and immense satisfaction, Melchior became exactly that, although Conrad did not know this immediately. He left the twins and Ursula alone with their brother when Melchior first arrived, dressed in his black formless robe that clearly surprised the other three. "Don't you wear different clothes when you're away from the monastery?" asked Ursula as they all entered the library.

A thinner Melchior smiled gently at his sister. "I have no different clothes."

"I have a black blazer and slacks I'd happily part with," said Günther.

Brandt did not hear the young monk's answer as he excused himself and left. He mixed himself a drink and wandered along the gallery to the conservatory where he had once listened to the twins playing the pianos as he watched Ursula listening, tears running unchecked on her face. He was already in love with her then, but could only sit by motionless and entranced as he sensed the strange bond that existed between the twin boys and their sister. Now as he sat thinking of the four in the library, he wondered how they were dealing with their new loss and if they would tell Melchior about John Skye. They no longer mentioned their old governess or the many accidents that had befallen the people who once rounded their world. He did not believe for a second that they would not contact John Skye. Yet how would they bring a meeting about? At the moment he was in England, probably riding to hounds from Ursula's description of him. In any case, the funeral must be first on their minds so there was a little time before he had to start worrying about what they were up to.

Three hours later when they all met for dinner, Ursula said with a certain shy reserve, "Conrad, Melchior thinks we *should* stay with you in Grinzing if your kind offer is still open. He prefers to stay at that small church parish house bordering your neighboring district, near the Beethoven monument." She looked at him as though waiting for his agreement or approval.

Brandt couldn't believe his good luck, and for a moment sought the twins' faces, only to find the same expression of waiting acceptance on theirs. He laughed with relief. "Of course! Of course the offer is still open. I'd be more than delighted." For the briefest fraction of a second the side of him that was lawyer felt a tiny hesitation in his brain. It was no more than a twinge in his inner ear, a sensation dealing with balance or distance perception: as though he had put down a wineglass and almost grazed his dinner plate with it. But only almost. He dismissed the feeling at once.

Ursula smiled at him a soft, demure smile, and Günther said in a voice both kind and sincere, "Very decent of you to put us up."

"Not at all. Not at all." He became a little gregarious and toned it down quickly when he realized that all four of them remained silent and sad as the servants took away their uneaten dinners and brought coffee and brandy and fruit. They lingered with him at the table as he covered the details of the trip to Vienna. ". . . and then, after the service, you might give me some idea of how you'd like the crypt . . . ah . . . filled. Boris was going to do that. I think he'd want the rest of you to take over that responsibility now. I know it's not a job you want, but I need help from all of you on this."

Melchior nodded. Ursula and the twins did not look at each other. She was peeling an orange as the boys in identical fashion caressed the stems of their brandy glasses. "Yes," said Paul finally. "I think he would have wanted us to do that."

"And then, you might want to stay an extra day or two before you return to university. I'll leave the order in for the coach. Is there anything special that any of you need? I have to call my home tonight anyway. If there's anything, anything at all, I'll have my staff take care of it." Apparently there was nothing. He wished she needed something that only he could get for her. He felt foolish thinking such thoughts. My God, he was suffering from a hero syndrome—he wanted to save her from some terrible danger: from being shot, from drowning, from falling in front of a train. He wanted to save her brothers, not just for their own sake, but for hers. He took a deep breath and let the fantasies slip away. He would be lucky if he could have a quiet funeral and get them back on their private coach and out of the country as soon as possible without any problems.

The train trip back to Vienna had the quality of a dream. With the help of the Zurich office staff and the railroad personnel the Bronevskys and their dead brother were boarded in secrecy before dawn, two hours before the train left Zurich, thus the darkness and the silence with which everyone moved lent an air of unreality to the departure. Brandt, sharply aware of all sounds and forms in the dark, thought of footsteps he had heard following him in dreams. Every form he did not immediately recognize was a man with a gun moving in to kill his beloved, every darker shadow was a knifer, a gleaming blade winking from under his coat. Brandt walked hurriedly immediately behind the four Bronevskys, his gun in his overcoat pocket. Hoffner walked in front of them, well armed and ready to kill, as Brandt had instructed him.

When they entered the luxurious coach, Brandt at once pulled the draperies closed so that the table lamps and wall sconces cast the only light in the car, a peach tone both gentle and somber. Once they were on their way, Brandt tried to read but found himself drifting away from the page and watching Ursula and the twins. Melchior had left the car's sitting room early in the trip to sleep in one of the berths in back. Ursula, in a dark rich fur, discarded coat and high-heeled shoes and curled her legs up on the sofa beside Paul. Her creamy calves and high-arched feet stirred Brandt's desire. She wore a seafoam-green knit dress that gave such a clear definition of her breasts he could have wept with both joy and despair. He undressed her at once and saw himself cup each breast, moving his mouth from one nipple to the other with an agony of ecstasy. He loathed himself for desiring her at these moments when far more critical considerations should have demanded his attention. At one point when Günther left his chair to sit beside her, Brandt saw him stroke the silk-stockinged ankle in such a proprietary fashion that he turned his face forcibly away only to discover he was facing a mirror which reflected the brother and sister in its oval glass. He smoked, drummed his fingers, paced. He tried to sleep, but after a few minutes returned to the salon knowing that he didn't want to give up a single minute of being in the same room with her.

They arrived in Vienna in the early evening. Boris' body was taken directly to the church where Melchior planned to stay. All was arranged for the funeral, and interment was to take place the next afternoon.

When Brandt arrived with Ursula and the twins at his home in Grinzing, his whole staff was there to meet them. To Conrad's delight his instructions had all been followed: the house was ablaze with flowers and the dark mahogany woods of the wall paneling and stairs shone like polished copper under the crystal chandeliers. They had a light supper of cold pheasant, white wine, cheese, and fruit. Brandt tried not to appear too happy; after all, the reason for their journey was sad and it would be crass of him to be cheerful. Still, when he, with a maid in attendance, had shown Ursula to the best bedroom in the house, she had said with a wan smile, "How very lovely your house is, and this room in particular. We do thank you for your kind generosity," his heart had filled with aching joy.

They all retired early. Brandt sat at the alcove desk in his bedroom and tried to read some of his mail sent over from his office, but his mind refused to see or hear or think of the law. It thought and saw and heard only the girl in the next room. Several times, as he commanded his feet to stop at once, he tiptoed to the connecting door and placed his greedy ear against it. There was no sound from her. She was sleeping. He paced and despaired.

And then, a few minutes after midnight as he lay thrashing in his bed, he heard the soft knock on the door between the two rooms. At first he could not quite believe that she would actually knock on his door. But then he quickly reasoned that she probably wanted another pillow or an extra coverlet, or perhaps the fire had gone out in the hearth. He put on his bathrobe and his most composed expression, took a deep breath, and opened the door.

Dressed in a white flowing gown, she stood in a soft halo of light holding two filled champagne glasses. "Every night for almost as long as I can remember, Grandfather used to have a glass of champagne with us before we went to sleep. He claimed it created pleasant dreams. Günther thinks it might be more beneficial for the carotid artery. I always thought it was just a lovely custom that we should carry on. There is so much sadness in the world."

He stepped back to let her enter as he took the glass she handed him. She sat on the side of his bed and raised her glass. "To Uncle Conrad."

Oh, marvelous girl, he thought, to drink to his beloved uncle. "To Uncle Conrad," he said, and they drained their glasses.

She stood up, took his glass, and placed them both on the nightstand. Then she turned back to him and slowly unfastened a single ribbon at her throat. The gown fell away. She stood naked before him. Dumbly and as if in a dream, he tore off his own robe and walked into her open arms, moving at once to the bed. He wanted to laugh, cry, shout with joy, but all sound stuck in his throat. He entered her immediately, discovering that she was warmly wet, obviously aroused. He tried to look into her eyes, but her face became blurred. He thought he was moving his body on hers and then vaguely realized he wasn't. He wasn't moving anything, and his eyes were beginning to go blind. He blinked and for a split second her face was absolutely clear to him, her mirroring green eyes open, serene, lovely. Her mouth was the sweetest faint smile. He had never seen such loveliness. And it was this thought that entered his failing brain before it vanished into oblivion.

27

Conrad Brandt opened one eye painfully and squinted at the rain beating on his bedroom windows as drums pounded a steady rhythm inside his head. He flinched, groaned, and rolled over. On the table near him stood two champagne glasses. The whole scene from the night before sprang into his brain like a gigantic zigzag of lightning on a black night revealing everything in lurid detail: her body waiting for his, her lovely face on the pillow, her mouth opening slightly as she raised her head to meet his kiss

at the exact moment that he entered her. He groaned, cringing at his stupidity. In the next moment he bounded out of bed, only to find the room
roaring at him as it tilted at an absurdly grotesque angle. Slowly, as he
steadied himself against the bed, the walls, floor, and ceiling settled into
place like a just-abandoned rocking horse running out of momentum. Scooping
his robe off the floor, he swore at himself with the blackest rage he had
ever known. If it weren't for the terrible danger she was in, he could
luxuriate in the thought of beating her. God knows she had it coming! He
pounded the heel of his hand against his forehead, only to feel the drums
pick up their tempo. What a bloody damn fool I am. I should have been
on guard! I know her! I even knew the three of them were up to something!
Of course they would try it before the funeral. They were not sentimental
about the dead. They had to have the advantage of surprise just in case
anyone was waiting for them at the funeral—and they knew it.

He went to her room, not that he expected her to be there, but there
was an outside chance she had left him a note telling him not to worry.
She hadn't. The green knit dress she had worn on the train was draped over
the arm of a chair. He picked it up and plunged his face into it, her scent
pulling a helpless, involuntary groan from him.

Back in his room, he dressed hurriedly, trying to formulate some idea
of what they were up to. Whatever they put into his champagne had knocked
him out for five hours. As he reached for his coat in a closet off the foyer,
he caught sight of his face in a mirror. He regarded it with contempt and
fury and tried to remember if she had actually said the words that kept
coming back to him: "Bye-bye, Conrad." He finally decided she had said
them while she was still under him, while he was trying to bring her face
into focus. And he actually did for a half-second see her clearly. Oh, the
smile, the lovely, faint, angelic smile on her lips when she said the words.

Well, what would he have said? Probably, "Sweet dreams, sweetheart,"
à la American cinema tough guy. Oh, he was tough all right. He had
survived Stalingrad and two and a half years of Russian imprisonment, only
to come home to be driven mad by a seventeen-year-old girl with eyes the
color of wet emeralds.

He walked half the length of his driveway in the heavy rain before he
realized his car was not there. And she was adding insult to the worst kind
of injury: those damn kids had even taken his car. He raced back to the
house and phoned one of his lawyers to bring over his car at once: "Don't
ask me any goddamn questions; just get your ass out of bed and bring me
your car immediately."

A half-hour later he was running up the stone steps of the church where
they had left Melchior the night before. Racing in through the ancient
swinging doors, he stopped himself by slamming into the font. At the altar,
Melchior knelt in prayer. Of course they wouldn't take him with them.
They carefully hid him in the little-known church where he wouldn't get
in their way and probably would be safe. They must be thinking that if the
murderer could get to Boris, he could get to Melchior as well. And they
were right. No, Melchior had not suggested they stay in Grinzing. They
put the idea into his head. He could hear Ursula: "Conrad has invited us
to stay at his house. What do you think?"

"I think that's a very fine thing for him to offer."

"Good, we'll do it then, and there's that lovely old church in Heiligenstadt; perhaps you'd like to stay there. It's where we are having the Mass for Boris. The father is most kind about making all the arrangements. Perhaps he needs someone from the family to help him with details."

"Yes, of course, a good idea."

Brandt saw the twins nodding gravely and look at Ursula and talk to her with their eyes.

He left the church quietly but began running again outside, skidding on the wet cobblestones as he raced to the car. If she wasn't already dead, he swore he'd strangle her the moment he found her. If she was dead he'd kill her murderer and then shoot himself. He patted the gun in his coat pocket and wished he'd taken some target practice recently. All this nonsense ran through his head as he drove madly to the Enerde mansion.

Ursula and the twins had made their plans in Zurich, agreeing that no one else was going to die because of them. "You know he's got to be on the killer's list," said Ursula. "I don't understand why they didn't get to him already. As Brückner's nephew, the murderers have to believe Conrad is as dangerous to them as Brückner was."

"Right. They can't assume Conrad did not know what was in his uncle's briefcase," reasoned Günther.

"So," said Paul, "we *have* to go back. To the police, everything looks like a series of unfortunate accidents. *They* won't do anything, and the idea of living with a staff of bodyguards invades my sense of privacy."

"Well, Conrad's going to be our biggest problem. There's no point in telling him he's in danger. If he's ever considered it, he's also already dismissed it," said Günther. "And he's not going to let us out of his sight. He'll have people following us everywhere we go. I'm afraid we'll have to put him out of commission. And we have to do it during the first night in town. He's already suspicious, but he thinks we won't do anything before the funeral. So it's straightaway." They were standing in the pavilion looking over the smooth water where their brother had so recently been murdered. "Ursula, I'll give you something to put in his drink. Do you think you could be convincing?"

"Do you think I could?" She leaned against him and kissed him on the mouth, grazing his teeth and open lips with her tongue.

"Watch it, girl," he said. "Be careful with him; I think if he ever really got mad, he could be dangerous."

"I'll take care of him *and* I'll be careful."

Günther gazed at her through slit eyes. "No details, please, or I'll have to challenge him. And we know he's a bad shot."

Their forced humor kept them to their purpose. They agreed with all of Conrad's plans, at times pretending to be slightly disagreeable or arguing with him just enough to keep his suspicions at bay. "Five guards for one railroad car? Expecting Apaches on the plains of the Danube valley, are you?" asked Paul. Conrad gave him a baleful look and went on with his plans. Once in Vienna, the act was easier: they were tired from the journey and the funeral the next day was going to be an ordeal. Perhaps they should retire early. Brandt quickly agreed.

When Ursula met Günther and Paul after her brief encounter with Conrad, the twins were already in their host's car. "What kept you?" asked Günther. "Wasn't it fast-acting enough?"

"A few minutes *too* fast. Let's go."

"I won't ask what that means," said Günther.

"Very thoughtful of you."

They drove in silence the rest of the way; and it was not until the pale gate lights came into view that Günther slowed down. The rain had not yet begun. Fast clouds ran before a three-quarter moon. In its light, the great gaudy mansion rose against the moving sky like a black mountain, all cliffs and steep slopes. "God," said Ursula. "I'd forgotten how ugly it was. Something Poe might have dreamed up in one of his worst nightmares."

"Aptly put," said Paul. "It should have ravens circling it—or bats."

Günther drove past the gate and coasted to a stop under some plane trees at the end of a cul-de-sac. "I don't suppose it would do any good to ask you again to stay with the car," he said to Ursula.

"No, it would not." Even as she spoke, Ursula realized that she had always known that at the end of the road stood the house in Vienna. She had known it from the beginning, on the day she was led out of it by her brothers. On the train roaring away from it across Europe. At the news of Brückner's death she knew it. During all the long quiet days at the university in Zurich, the days of reading and studying and drawing, the bright summer days sailing on the lake, the brighter winter days skiing on the slopes, through all dreams and love and hope she had known that an unfinished tragedy perpetrated in that great ugly house before she was even born had put a hook into their lives, and until they returned and withdrew it by living out the last scene of somebody else's drama, there was no life for her or her brothers. Alexander and Boris had already been sacrificed to it, and with them the other innocent dead.

They entered the estate through the old rose-arbor gate which they had used for three years in their ramblings about the city. At the summerhouse they paused over the bones of Adolphus and studied the mansion. "Someone's in Grandfather's rooms, and he's either still awake or he sleeps with the lights on," whispered Ursula.

"One way to find out," said Günther. "The French doors to that suite open onto the secret garden. Do you think you can still find your way into it from the outside?"

"Yes," said Ursula.

"The hedge may have closed up," said Paul.

"No. It was too shady there. That's why the opening was possible at all. Doesn't look like they've cut down any trees. It will open."

They passed through the hedge with relative ease, moving along the low inner shrubbery to the fountain and then to the stone table and benches where Ursula used to draw her grandfather and his beloved songbirds that fed on various feeders in the garden.

They glided the last few feet to the marble terrace before which two stone nudes of human scale stood twenty feet apart holding garlands in their open arms as if motioning someone in the house to come out to the garden. Ursula felt the damp living moss growing on one of the pedestals as she leaned against it.

"I always rather liked this one's ass," whispered Günther as he reached up to pat the round buttocks of the stone nymph. He dropped quickly back to a squatting position, pulling Ursula down with him. All three raised their heads slowly over the box hedge flanking the two nudes. In the great red-walled room with its baroque-gilded mirrors and rare Gobelin tapestries sat a man staring into the fire, a cigarette held loosely in his hand. His hair and beard were a white-gray and cropped close to his scalp and chin. His face was long with a high forehead, and it seemed to Ursula, who saw him in three-quarter profile, that his eyelids were hooded almost to closing. He had a fine gaunt nose clearly outlined by the flickering firelight.

"Who?" whispered Paul.

Both Ursula and Günther shook their heads in the dark. Then at the pressure of Günther's hand, the three moved simultaneously past the first nude to the second. "I was hoping there would be someone in the other chair," whispered Günther. "Look at the picture hanging over the mantel in the exact place where Mother's used to be. Any guesses on who she is?"

The young woman in the life-size standing portrait had short blond wavy hair and a sweet innocent smile one rarely sees on adults. She was perhaps nineteen and wearing a softly draped petal-skirted dress of the mid-twenties. She held a small bunch of spring flowers in one hand; the other rested lightly on the back of an unoccupied damask chair.

"She's faintly familiar," said Ursula. "It's an interesting painting. She looks as though she's asking someone to sit down." A door closed. The seated man did not turn. Moments later a tall young man walked into the Bronevskys' line of vision. Ursula gasped and clutched Günther's arm.

"That him?"

"Yes." She shivered. "He's supposed to be in England riding to hounds or some such drivel."

"Don't believe everything a man tells you."

"He's one of us all right," said Paul. "Look at the way he turns his head. That's Father. That slow poising of the head as though he's listening to something going on in another room or outside. The white-wolf-on-the-Steppe look. I used to love those old Russian stories."

They watched as Skye sat in the chair opposite the older man, leaned forward, his elbows on his knees, his bowed head in his hands.

"That boy has troubles," said Günther.

The older man apparently spoke. Skye looked up briefly, gave a helpless shrug, and returned to his posture of despondency. The other man put out his cigarette and rose, turning his back to the fire and looking down on the young man. He talked earnestly, occasionally gesturing with his hands.

"All right," said Günther. "We have to face them sometime. Now?"

"Yes," said Ursula. "Now."

"Now," said Paul.

Ursula and the twins crossed the terrace and Günther pushed open the two doors. "Please, sir. Don't ring the bell." Günther spoke softly, the pistol in his hand directed at Skye, whose astonishment brought him out of his chair. The older man pulled his hand away from the tasseled cord without touching it. "You," said Günther, motioning to Skye with the weapon. "Sit down."

After the first shock the two men facing the twins showed no further surprise, and neither of them showed any fear. The older man took out a cigarette case and lit a fresh cigarette. For a moment he hesitated and Ursula realized that his natural inclination was to offer everyone else a cigarette, too. He put the case back into his pocket. "Is this the girl, John?"

"Yes, Father."

"And I take it . . . these are two of the brothers?"

"I've never met them, sir, but I think so."

"You can put your weapons away, gentlemen. My son and I are unarmed. Would you like something to drink?"

"No, thanks," said Günther. "And we'll just keep these handy." He made a slight motion with the pistol.

"As you wish. However, I'm going to have some brandy." He walked to a tray resting on a large black-lacquered secretary where Ursula used to draw while her grandfather read the newspaper in front of the fire. "You're sure?" He gestured with the decanter. Both twins shook their heads. "John?" Skye also turned him down. "Well, we have an interesting situation here. I suppose I should ask why three young people all in black—looking a little like commandos, I might add—have trespassed on my property, broken into my home, and are holding me and my son at gunpoint. But I won't."

Ursula turned to Skye, whose eyes had never left her. He rose and started toward her, his expression anxious, questioning.

"If you come near me, one of my brothers will probably shoot you."

"I think the young lady may be right, John. Why don't you just stay where you are and we'll get this sorted out."

"Boris is dead," said Ursula to Skye, who closed his eyes at her words, twisted away from her, and fell back into his chair, his face a white mask of suffering.

"Now, John, I'll do the talking here. Why don't you three sit down wherever you like and I'll tell you a story." He turned his big chair so that it was parallel to his son's.

Ursula looked to Günther, who motioned her to a tapestried chaise longue opposite the father and son. Paul sat beside her. Günther lifted a straight-backed chair away from the wall and brought it close to the chaise.

"Yes. That's better." He looked at them through blue smoke. "I take it you are the children of Count Pavel Bronevsky."

"That's right," said Günther.

"And I am John Skye and this distraught young man here is my son." He drank from the glass, a long swallow, making a slight face after it, ridging his forehead and raising the hooded eyelids. "I draw your attention," he began softly, "to the painting." He motioned with his head at the picture over the mantel. "She is lovely, isn't she? Not *your* brilliant fire, my dear"— he smiled faintly at Ursula—"but a much calmer girl, a much milder girl, not at all precocious as I understand you to be. Not bold, not a bit of the wild in her. But a guileless, gentle, modest, shy girl. That picture was

[319]

painted a few weeks before she was married. You would not have believed her exquisite refinement, her sweetness, her innocence.

"They were very happy in their marriage. The man considered himself the luckiest in the world. They lived a life of propriety and gentleness. Nothing vulgar touched them, nothing coarse, crude, or unseemly."

Ursula looked at the portrait as the man spoke. The girl's pale fingers had a boneless quality to them, Madonna hands as Ursula thought of them, meant for prayers and mourning, perhaps a little dismayed wringing. She glanced at her own clearly defined, well-boned hands lying impatiently in her lap, and returned her attention to the man.

"Their only sorrow was that after a number of blissful years, they were still childless. They traveled extensively, filling in their lives with beautiful objects for their home. They came here to the city of dreams. She adored this city, the flowers, the parks, the music. For some curious reason, she believed that they would conceive a child here."

Ursula felt Skye watching her. When she glanced at him, his eyes glistened. She wondered how often he had heard the old man's story. He was clearly not listening to it now. Lord Skye returned to the tray and again poured from the decanter.

"I think this is going to get worse before it gets better," whispered Paul.

"Is that possible?" whispered Ursula.

"Just listen," said Günther, giving them a black look.

Lord Skye returned to his stage and continued. "One autumn afternoon— it was one of those lovely rainy days, mild and sweet before winter—they met a man at a gallery. They had come to bid on a painting. It is possible that the man they met came to get out of the rain. He introduced himself, presenting a card. He was quite proper and made an altogether acceptable impression. It never occurred to the husband that the man had only pursuit on his mind. But pursue her he did, discovering the hours when the husband was gone." He paused to light another cigarette. Taking a deep breath, he stopped directly before Ursula and the twins. "The husband, unaware, returned on business matters to England for a few weeks. She wanted to stay in the city of dreams for the opera season. And while she was here alone, he came and took her—by force!"

Günther and Paul simultaneously reached for Ursula's hands, holding her to the chaise. "Liar," she growled. "Liar. Liar. Liar." The room filled with her voice.

The old man smiled. "Not a delicate thought, is it?"

"He may have been all the rotten things you think he was," said Ursula, tears of rage in her eyes. *"But rape was not his style."*

"But it was! We have proof of that!"

"What proof? Did she say it . . . that he raped her?"

"Yes! Not to the husband, but to someone else."

"Bring that someone else. Let him stand before us and say it."

"In time, my dear, in time."

"Now."

"No, there is more."

"I'll bet there is," said Günther. "Enough to justify ten murders?"

"Father, please . . ."

Skye's voice made Ursula stare at him. "Is that what he's told you all these years? That Count Bronevsky *raped* your mother?"

"Young woman, please hear me out."

Günther turned to Ursula. "Let him finish."

"Thank you, young man. When she discovered she was carrying his child, she ran away. The shame for her was unendurable. I searched for her. I thought she had returned to England. I searched everywhere . . . in the wrong country. Then I was contacted—"

"By whom?" asked Paul.

Lord Skye held up his hand for silence. "My name was on her lips when she died."

"Your contact told you this?" asked Günther.

"Yes. But, please, there is one more thing."

"Something still worse, no doubt."

"Yes." He looked at the painting, and Ursula saw for the first time the mirroring tears in his eyes. "She had no resources of her own. She contacted the great Enerdes." He looked back at Ursula and the twins, a hideous smile on his face. "My *wife* came here, begging. . . ."

"And she was turned down," said Günther in a flat voice.

"Yes!"

Ursula, whose composure was returning, looked up at the picture again. "Was it snowing?"

"What?"

"And was she in rags and barefoot, the baby in her arms?"

"How dare you jest!" The old man clenched his fists and moved toward Ursula menacingly. The twins rose at once.

"I dare, Sir John, because it's all a lie." She leaned back and contemplated the old man. "Why don't you send him somewhere?" She motioned to Skye. "And we'll tell you what really happened." Ursula felt the twins' eyes on her, but she continued to gaze at the old man.

"No. Whatever you have to say, I want him to hear."

She shrugged. "Remember, Sir John, that you made that decision."

"I'll remember."

"My father, sir, had one extraordinary ability. It may not say much for him, but that's no matter here. He had the capacity or the knack or whatever it takes to make women fall passionately in love with him. I know of only two—now three—instances firsthand. But this ability of his is legend in this city. We had a governess. I believe now that she must be dead." Again she felt the twins stare at her. "Anyway, she fell in love with my father. She would have happily given up her life for him, been his slave, killed for him. When he died, she went quite mad.

"And then there is the case of my mother. I never knew her very well, but there is one thing of which I was absolutely sure. I could not have formulated it at the time of her death. I was much too young, but I did come to understand it in the years since."

"And that was?" asked Sir John.

"That no matter what my father did, through all his escapades, his . . . his liaisons with other ladies, my mother never stopped loving him. I know nothing about marriage except what I've read in books. I was not allowed to see my parents' marriage even in the simplest sense of seeing them live together. My grandfather took that away from us. But I know that my mother loved my father until her very last breath. And if there is a hell, she will find it and love him even there."

"Bold girl!"

"Yes, Lord Skye. I am none of the divine things Lady Madeline was. I'm not sure I have a month's loyalty in me, let alone a lifetime. But who knows if I . . . if there is someone, and we are brave enough and worthy of it . . ."

"It?"

"Of love. Of love, then . . . who knows? Who knows?" Ursula saw Skye lean forward, but she carefully avoided his eyes.

"And the *third* lady in your experience?"

"Do you really want me to go on?"

"By all means. I am surprised you have such a romantic bent. I was told that you are very direct and not at all sentimental."

"I don't know what I am." She felt Günther's hand on her shoulder.

"Please, go on. I'm interested in your theory of the third lady."

"I never met her, as you well know. And before I can talk about her—since I am in the dark and must guess at things—I must remind you, as I'm sure you already know, that when two people love, one is always more possessed than the other." Paul sat down again beside her. She smiled at him and took his hand.

"And this pertains to the third lady?"

"No, sir, it pertains to you."

"To me? To me?" His nostrils flared; his voice sharpened. "What has it to do with me?"

"I don't know whether she ran away or whether you sent her away, but I know one thing: Lady Madeline was in love with my father."

"How dare you!" He was shaking, his voice only a harsh whisper.

"Because it's true."

"It is *not* true. She may have been momentarily infatuated with him, but she loved me. *Me!*"

"Then she would not have had to change her name and hide to have his child. Did you really leave her alone and go to England on business without her? Let her go *alone* to the opera?"

Lord Skye returned again to the decanter. He held it for a long time without pouring. The silence in the room pushed at the walls and ceiling. Skye rose and stood under his mother's portrait. "Father?"

"It isn't what you think, John," said the old man, turning quickly.

"What do I think, Father?"

"That I abandoned her. I didn't abandon her. I swear to you. Never. Not for a moment. I left for a few days after she told me about him, only to clear up my thinking. When I returned, she was gone. I searched. God knows I searched. I didn't know she had changed her name. And then the doctor contacted me. My name . . ." His voice broke. "My name was on her lips when she died."

Ursula clutched Paul's hand tighter. "The doctor!" she whispered. She saw a silver knife scoop up a little mountain of caviar, saw it heaped on a finger of toast, saw it enter Frichter's wide-open mouth. Another followed before the first was chewed. From her high window she saw him walk in the garden after lunch, saw him stand on the edge of the fish pond, take out his penis and urinate into the water.

"But, Father, all our plans!"

"They don't change. They still denied her. She might have lived had they helped her. One of the richest families in Europe denied her."

"No, Sir John," said Günther. "That did not happen either. My grandfather paid a certain Magda Himmel for years. He made a large settlement on her at the end of the war. I always assumed it was for her child's education."

"Impossible!"

"We have the canceled checks, the signatures."

"But she lived only nine days."

"*We* know that now. But Grandfather did not. He always paid all of Father's debts. Anyone coming to him for help, was helped."

Lord Skye clutched the decanter to his heaving chest. "I don't believe you." He seemed to stagger. Günther placed the pistol on the table behind him and rushed to the old man.

"Sir, let me help you."

Ursula and Paul stood up quickly, Paul pocketing his gun. Skye walked slowly toward the old man. "Father, what have we done? I love this girl. I mean to make her mine."

"No," screamed the old man. "Not *that* family. They killed her. The doctor told me everything. These are lies they bring. They killed my Madeline. He didn't even want her. They didn't want the child. The doctor told me how they refused to take the child." He rushed away from Günther's helping hands, ran to the table and picked up the pistol. "No," he screamed again. "Never." He fired at Ursula. The first shot broke an alabaster vase on the mantel. The second would have hit her had Skye not stepped in front of her and taken the bullet in his stomach. The third hit him in almost the same spot before Günther knocked the gun out of the old man's hand and it slid across the floor and hit the wall.

Too terrified to scream or move during the shooting, Ursula now found herself holding up Skye. As he fell, he carried her to the floor with him. Here, with his head against her breast, he tried to speak. Ursula, seeing the blood bubble up through the shredded clothing, put her hand over it. "Oh, stop! Stop! Don't! Don't!" she cried at the insistent blood that covered her fingers and rose up her wrist. She heard Skye whisper and brought her face down to his, looking into the black centers of his eyes that opened inwardly deeper and deeper like an infinity of mirrors in which she saw herself endlessly reflected. He tried to speak, but no sound came from him. He arched his back to raise his head, bringing his lips to hers. She leaned down to meet him, the kiss a mere touching as she watched the light leave his eyes.

It was Günther's hand that brought down Skye's eyelids, as Paul, also kneeling beside his weeping sister, took her hand from the dead man's wound.

Lord John Skye had fallen to his knees, where he remained, looking into his dead boy's face. "My son. Oh, my son! He *is* my son, you know." He spoke softly, as though he feared he might awaken him.

Günther nodded. "Yes, we know."

"She wanted me to have him, you know. The doctor told me everything, how she said my name, told me to come get my son. So you see, he is my son."

"Yes, sir. What about your plans, sir?"

"My plans? I have no plans. Do I have some plans?"

"Yes, sir. Your son mentioned them. Think, sir. The plans. What are the plans? We should do something about them. Your son thinks we should do something about them."

"I can't remember. John, what were our plans? John?"

"The doctor," said Günther. "Remember the doctor?"

Lord Skye looked over his shoulder furtively, then back at Günther. "You know, I never liked that fellow. No culture. Crude. Vulgar. Never associate with a vulgar man," he whispered. "It demeans the spirit."

"Yes, sir. I'll remember. Did the plans include the doctor in some way? How is it going to work? How will we get rid of them?"

"Ah, yes. Now I remember. Get rid of them. All of them. Wipe their name off the face of the earth. It's a proper justice." He held his hand over his heart and smiled faintly at Günther. "It is, you know. It fits the crime."

"Yes, sir. It does. But how do we do it? How, sir?"

"I don't have the details. He takes care of all that. A vulgar man, but good at that kind of thing, good with details." He began to cough.

"Yes, sir." Günther held the old man up as he gasped for air.

He wiped his mouth with his hand, moving it slower and slower until it dragged down over his neck and chest. He smiled at Günther again. "Send my son in to me when he wakes up. Yes. Send him in. My son." He leaned against Günther with a deep sigh.

"He's dead," said Günther, holding his fingertips to the old man's neck.

Ursula still held Skye's head against her breast, her bloodied hand on his chest. She looked at the twins and back at Skye's face. "It's over," said Paul. "Come."

"We can't leave him here," she whispered, pushing the thick hair away from his forehead and kissing the smooth brow.

"We'll come back for him. We can't do anything for him now," said Paul, lifting Skye's head slowly to the floor. "Come. On your feet." He pulled her up. "Walk. Come on."

Ursula, still looking at Skye's dead face as she backed away from him, heard some commotion behind her. A door was open into the hall and at the terrace where they had entered stood a man with a gun. Only then did she see that it was raining.

"I suppose, Doctor," said Günther, "we should have known it was you. You're the only one that didn't die."

"You've ruined everything. Look at this carnage," said Frichter with exasperation.

"The old man had a heart attack. He shot his son."

"That's not his son."

"Oh, yes, he was. Believe it, Doctor, he was his son. My father obviously

[324]

saw to his beginning; he looks like a Bronevsky . . . but he was the son of that man lying beside him."

Ursula looked more closely at the man at the terrace door. "Günther, that's one of the people I saw at Father's funeral."

"How careless of you, Frichter. Did you place him at the funeral so he would recognize us all when you sent him out to kill us? Why didn't you just give him our pictures? You must have collected plenty over the years."

"Not of Brückner," said the doctor petulantly.

"Ah. Of course. Your first victim. But perhaps not. What did you do with Agnes Schneider?"

"She was hopeless. When she walked out of that clinic, I thought I could use her, but she was finished. Seeing Bronevsky come unglued before her eyes really did it. I found her back here. She was completely useless to me. She . . . ah . . . died quietly."

Günther nodded. "In an asylum, where you, as her doctor, visited her frequently. What did you tell them she had? A bad heart? I assume you signed the death certificate."

"All irrelevant."

"What was in Brückner's briefcase that you needed so desperately?"

"His hospital name and where he was born and, of course, his mother's name," said Frichter, nodding with his head at the dead Skye.

"I thought you knew all that."

"I did. But as you must know by now, I could not have anyone else know it. I needed to get all those records. They did not know she was dead. And then there were signatures that I needed for the manufacture of certain documents and the destruction of others."

"For a codicil."

"Yes. If all of you were out of the way, this young man would have inherited the entire fortune. He would have been the last heir."

"So the lawyers had to be out of the way also. They would have denied the possibility of a codicil and the whole thing would have gone to grants and charities—if we were out of the way and there were no other heirs. So you created an heir."

"And you killed him or let him get killed by coming here. Sit down, all of you. Over there in those three chairs. Not too close together." He motioned to the man at the French doors. "Get that gun on the floor over there. That's going to be very useful."

Ursula sat between the twins. "Could . . . I . . . please cover them?" She looked down at Skye and his father.

"Don't move. Throw something over that mess. There, that wall hanging will do." Frichter walked back and forth in front of them. "You know you ruined it for me; I should kill you now."

"But then it wouldn't look like an accident, would it?" said Günther. "And there would be much more thorough investigations." Günther paused. "Why did Lord John buy the house?"

"Heh, heh. One of the touches I like best. I destroyed the documents on the sale of the house. After you're all gone, I'll bring out the gift papers. Your dear grandfather left the house to Lord John's son. Just a little more insurance to let the world know Enerde acknowledged the seventh child.

[325]

Lord John appreciated that touch, I might add, just in case you have any sentimental thoughts on the old fellow."

Günther nodded. "By the way, assuming all of us were accidentally killed and Skye inherited the entire fortune through the long-lost codicil that you forged with Grandfather's name, what was in it for you?"

"Plenty."

"Ah, the codicil mentioned you?"

"Certainly not."

"A private arrangement with Lord Skye?"

"He was very grateful for all I had done for his poor wife. A man with that kind of conscience is always grateful. I told him his wife completely forgave him. He was much comforted by that."

"I'm sure he was. He must have been a very generous man."

"Not like your grandfather."

"Grandfather not generous? That's ridiculous. He was always giving. Noblesse oblige. He was a great believer in it."

"Don't tell me about it. I was totally repulsed when I heard the content of that disgusting will. A man of Enerde's stature giving pieces of one of the most elegant fortunes in Europe to servants. Like Tolstoy—giving his holdings to his serfs. That's positively communistic. No. No. Couldn't have that. Your grandfather was a great disappointment to me."

"Especially since he left you nothing," said Paul. "How many generations of your family doctored ours?"

"Four!" said Frichter with sudden violence. "You can see how unfair he was. Giving to those two old fungus-gathering hags, and a deaf gardener with dirt under his fingernails, and a cheap little crook like Berghoch. Imagine such slime getting a piece of that fortune each month. And . . . and nothing to me."

"I go back to my question: how much were you supposed to get out of it?" said Günther.

Frichter gave a little giggle. "The dowry."

"What dowry?" asked Ursula. "What are you talking about?"

"Why, my dear child, you do remember there was to be a dowry given when you married. It's in the will."

"No, I don't remember."

"It was not specified, but I've always known what it was. Enerde brides have carried the dowry with them down through the centuries, and always their adoring spouses added to them. Not to mention adoring fathers."

"I still don't know what you're talking about," said Ursula. She looked down at the tapestry covering Skye and his father, her heart shrinking inside her. She reached out to touch it.

"No," whispered Paul, taking her hand. "Later."

"You've never thought of it?" said Frichter with an astonished laugh. Ursula shook her head. "Didn't you ever wonder what happened to your mother's jewels?"

Again Ursula shook her head.

Frichter's eyes glittered. A twitch pulled at the corner of his mouth; his words came out sputtering. "They're in the vaults in Switzerland! A massive collection! Perhaps the greatest private collection in the world! The empress's famous pearls. The Turk's emeralds, not *bought,* by the way, but paid by a prince for the return of his son captured in battle. The great star sapphires of a French king, sold to clothe an army. And . . . and . . . the diamonds! The diamonds! You will not believe the diamonds. One necklace alone could buy a kingdom—and did. Ah . . . and Prince Eugene's star rubies. He had a passion for red. It should have been purple. Heh, heh . . . if you get my meaning. Ah, must not forget the jade. The Imperial Jade. Very funny story. Won in a card game. Never mind the story. Perhaps not so funny. The Brazil aquamarines bought to match an eye. Must not forget the amethysts, from the same country . . . and also from the New World . . . the ah . . . ah . . . I forget the name. But jewels of every kind, every size, from everywhere. Ah, the Czech garnets, the Orange River solitaires—twenty, thirty, forty carats. And from Burma, the rubies . . . the blood of the pigeon. From Australia—the flashing fiery opals. And Ceylon! Ceylon! Everything from Ceylon: an island of jewels. . . ." He was slobbering, spittle running down his chin. His eyes turned huge, moist.

"Wouldn't they have had to go to a girl?" asked Günther blandly.

"And they would have. The old man there was going to have the boy marry soon, and the jewels would have been collected from the vaults. But I would have been the bride to receive them. It makes me blush to think of it. Heh, heh."

"Now that everything is lost, we might as well say good-bye and go home," said Günther. "It will be morning soon. Conrad will wonder what became of us. By the way, you let Conrad live."

"Yes, I still needed him. I had to have someone know about my automobile accident. I should say, my nonaccident. It's quite remarkable how quickly he believed everything. And he was frightfully upset. Such a considerate young man. I spent a few weeks in the hospital. Blood pressure, gout, arthritis. All the infirmities of my age. He came to visit, wanted to know all the details. Took him into my confidence. Told him I thought the brakes were tampered with. His day was coming soon." He stood with his back to the fire and rubbed his rump. "He's no problem, but you three are."

"Don't you know when you're finished?" said Günther. "What's the point in killing us now? You will gain nothing. Not a pearl of the great dowry."

"Oh, but you're wrong. In a little while I shall arrange the final accident, and you three will be no more. And that will leave only Melchior. Melchior, who does not want a single schilling of the fortune. Melchior, who will welcome an old and trusted friend of the family to help him give it all away. I've saved him just for such an eventuality—insurance, so to speak, in case the English did not work out. The boy there was not keen on the plan from the beginning, and then when he met you"—he nodded his head at Ursula—"well, he tried to talk his father out of it. Very sticky these last few days. What did you do to him, my dear? You should have seen the old lord rage when the boy told him we should stop this . . . 'this insanity.' Yes, that's what he called it: 'this insanity.' Twenty years of careful planning all squashed because a boy falls in love with a girl. Ridiculous. So you see

I had to keep Melchior alive for insurance. I could always have gotten rid of him at that absurd hermitage where he plods about barefoot, digging potatoes and riding his donkey up and down the steep mountain paths. And you'll recall, he was always fond of me."

"Yes," said Ursula, her sorrow turning to rage. "The rest of us hated you."

"True. And I could never understand why. I was nice to all of you."

"Because you were always so greedy," she said. "A vulgar, greedy *little* man with sauce on your chin and egg on your tie. I used to watch you pee into the fishpond. You are the kind of rotten thing that would pee into the last fresh water on earth."

"Ursula, there's no point to this," said Günther.

"There's no point in waiting for an accident, either. I refuse to watch us all die by blueprint. Why don't you shoot me now, Frichter?" She walked up to him, standing a head taller than he. "Well, *little* man?" She was shaking with rage.

Frichter laughed. "You always were the most outrageous of them all. Do you remember when you bit me? I thought I'd have to have rabies shots."

"Instead *I* had to have them," said Ursula, and walked to the man who was holding the gun. "What do you get out of all this?" The man did not answer, but continued to watch her with tired, flat, disinterested eyes.

"He's incorruptible, my dear, so you can quit trying to corrupt him. When you reach his level, there's nothing left to corrupt."

"Speaking of corruption, who was the second Magda Himmel?" asked Günther.

Frichter giggled. "Now you've gone and embarrassed me."

Ursula stopped in front of the doctor again and looked into the mean, merry eyes. "*You* were." She heard Günther laugh and Paul draw in his breath sharply.

"It was such a fortuitous opportunity. Too good to throw away."

Ursula nodded. "And did the original Magda have Lord Skye's name on her lips when she died?"

"Not exactly. In fact, she cursed him. But then, I always knew who she was. Your father asked me to look after her during her pregnancy."

"One small cheer for Father," said Paul.

"You're welcome to give him a big one. He gave me money for her care. Of course, he wanted nothing more to do with her; it was the pursuit that he enjoyed, and the child did not interest him at all."

"Father gave away money? Remarkable," said Paul.

"He was really quite generous in his own way. I thought rather highly of him." The doctor rambled on about his early experiences with the Enerde family as Ursula sat again between her brothers.

She took Paul's hand and looked into his face. "Why are we waiting?" whispered her eyes. She could see the bulge the gun made in his pocket.

He looked past her at his twin, ignoring her question.

"Doctor," said Günther, "you must have quite a staff to have made this operation so successful."

"Indeed not. Too many cooks and all that, don't you know. Besides Frederich, there are only myself and one other man."

"The one just outside in the hall?"

Ursula's head shot toward the door. It was open a few inches. She could see the glint of the concealed man's belt or buttons or perhaps it was his gun.

"Ho, ho," laughed Frichter. "You always were a sharp one. That's Sepp, a fine swimmer and an excellent marksman. Did you know Alexander took lessons from him? Nicely ironic, I thought. Now, I have to go get my medical case and put a few things together if you're all going to have an accident. We'll start at first light, Frederich here will keep you company until I return. Sepp will get the car ready in a little while. A tragic joyride. A little too much to drink. You kids still like champagne the way you used to? Of course you do. Half a dozen bottles should do it. This town will believe anything about the great Enerdes." He smiled at them. "Such a handsome trio. What sensual mouths! Do you ever play any interesting games together?" He laughed hugely. "Ah, Frederich, if they give you any trouble, shoot them."

"It won't be an accident," said Günther.

"We'll place the gun in someone else's hand and rearrange the props." He looked pointedly at the tapestry covering the bodies.

Conrad Brandt remembered an old story of Berghoch's—the cook never tired of telling the lawyer about the Enerde children's escapades. "Those kids used to get up before dawn and sneak off the place through an old gate on the south side and explore every part of the city. At first it worried the grandfather, but we all soon realized they could take care of themselves. You know, one time they brought back a skeleton!"

Brandt skirted the mansion and came upon his own car parked in a cul-de-sac. He found the gate quickly, although he did not know of the secret latch so had to climb over the thorny roses, their long canes ripping his clothes and tearing his skin. He cursed steadily as the rain ran into the collar of his coat and squished in his shoes. Near the kitchen garden he ducked behind a chestnut tree as a man came out of the house carrying a carton with both arms. Brandt followed him to the carriage garage, where the man placed the carton under an awning and backed a car out beside it, leaving the motor running. Brandt, only a few feet away behind the open door to the building, watched the man take a bottle of champagne out of the carton, open it, take a long swig, and pour the rest of it over the seats of the car. He dropped the empty bottle on the back seat. He repeated the performance. When he reached for the third bottle, Conrad handed it to him with his left hand while with his right he smashed a fourth bottle against the side of the man's head. Sepp went down without a sound, blood gushing from his nose and mouth. Conrad pulled the body into a utility closet in the garage and bolted the door.

He entered the dimly lit house through the kitchen, dashing from door to wall, from one room to the next, flattening himself into the shadows and waiting a few seconds after each move, his ears straining for any sound. In the vast foyer he considered the grand staircase. Should he go up or continue searching the lower floor? Hard footsteps determined his move. From a darkened alcove which he shared with a larger-than-life marble Diana of astonishing proportions, he saw Dr. Frichter descend the stairs carrying what appeared to be a medical bag. He wondered where the doctor's wheelchair was at that moment. He removed his shoes, leaving them behind the hunting maiden's stag, and followed Frichter in his wet socks.

Brandt knew of the grandfather's ground-floor chambers. His uncle had casually mentioned the famous red morning room with its rare carpets, famous tapestries, shimmering chandeliers, and secret garden. "The girl almost grew up in those rooms," he said once to his nephew. "She was always there when I arrived. I used to worry that the old man could read my mind."

But Brandt did not know the layout of the quarters, so that when Frichter abruptly disappeared Conrad had to choose one of three doors in an anteroom through which the door passed. He stopped to listen at each door, unaware that the rooms were soundproof. Each ornate door seemed to beckon to him. He put his hand on one, only to have his eyes drawn to another. He finally opened one with immense care, only to have it click loudly as it swung away from him. There was no one in it. He recognized the great four-poster bed his uncle had told him about, carved for a king of France.

He held his gun in one hand as he pushed open the second door. It was a library, empty at the moment of any readers. At least now he knew the right door. Again he turned the ornate lever, the mechanism making a resounding click as it fell open. He saw Ursula and the twins, standing together, look toward him, their expressions showing no shock. The doctor was holding a hypodermic needle up to the light, squeezing the plunger lightly. "Sepp, bring the car around to the front," he said. "This will take only a moment."

Paul pulled the gun from his pocket. "Behind you, Conrad," he said in an even voice. Conrad ducked behind the door as Frederich's first bullet grazed his arm. Frederich, in a wavering of uncertainty, turned his weapon toward the Bronevskys, where Paul, in a wild motion, pushed Ursula to the floor and stepped in front of his brother, firing at the doctor at the exact moment that Frederich's second bullet entered his chest. Conrad dropped Frederich with everything in his gun before the man could shoot again. The doctor still held the hypodermic in his hand as he sat on the floor, his head leaning against Lord Skye's chair, blood pouring from his left eye, his mouth wide open as if to eat the world.

Ursula and Günther knelt on the floor with Paul between them, both of them holding him in their arms. He was still conscious. "Poor Skye," he whispered. He frowned, then smiled, looking up into their agonized faces. "I love . . . I love . . ." He did not finish.

For days Conrad watched Ursula and Günther at the hospital sitting silently beside their still-unconscious brother, who the doctors said could not live. They sent for specialists from Switzerland and England, men who came and agreed with the local physicians that Paul would die.

Although the waiting brother and sister still lived at Conrad's house, he rarely saw them there. Usually he found them in Paul's room, one on each side of the bed, each holding their unconscious brother's hand as though to send their heartbeats into him. Conrad despaired at the fear in their faces.

He begged them to come home, to eat, to rest. "At least spell each other," he whispered at them from the foot of the bed. "Take turns staying with him." Gently they refused.

When the doctors or nurses worked on Paul, Günther and Ursula waited in the room next to his that they had taken for themselves. Conrad appealed to the doctors to convince the brother and sister to go home. "It won't do any good; I've tried," said one of the surgeons who had operated on Paul. "Anyway, I don't know that they aren't doing any good. They've already given him their blood; who knows what else they are giving him. That boy should have died of his wounds before this—damaged liver, punctured lung, internal hemorrhaging. It was a real mess in there."

Alone in his house at night, Conrad paced and fretted away the hours. A hundred times he walked into the bedroom in which Ursula had spent only half a night. The maid had lit the fire, turned down the bed, and draped the white silk gown across the foot of it. And thus it remained untouched as he despaired. What would become of those two if Paul died? The three were so intimately allied in his mind that the thought of the death of one of them sent terrible imaginings churning through him. They could become recluses; they could go mad; they could kill themselves. He shuddered and rushed to phone the hospital. There was no change.

He tried to work, but found his mind drifting back to the mansion to the moment when he had picked up a large tapestry on the floor and found the bodies of Skye and Lord John under it. Skye was clearly a Bronevsky; the shape of his head and hands, the wing sweep of the eyebrows, the clearly delineated mouth all marked him as the count's son.

Later, in a suite on the second floor, Conrad found his uncle's briefcase. He took it away quietly to examine in private, after the ambulances and the police and the funerals, after Lord John and his son's bodies were returned to England, after the theories and the facts and the fictions were agreed upon by the authorities.

On the thirteenth day, as Conrad entered Paul's room he found both Ursula and Günther asleep in their chairs, exhaustion covering their faces like white masks. He turned to leave, but his whispered name made him whirl around. Paul's eyes were open. "How long have these two been here?"

Conrad stopped at the foot of the bed and blinked back tears. "Apparently, long enough."

"Do you think I should wake them?"

"Yes, but not just yet." They were still both whispering. "Wait until I'm gone." He left at once, knowing that the three of them should be allowed to give full vent to their emotional release, and that they would not do this with an outsider present.

Two hours later Ursula and Günther arrived home in a cab. "He's going to make it," said Günther, his eyes glistening. "We've just come from the parish house. We left Melchior to thank God for us. Could I have a drink?" He turned, and leading a subdued Ursula by the arm, followed Brandt into the sitting room. "Listen, Little Bear, I know we agreed to take on only one thing at a time, but please allow a little hiatus between those things."

She nodded. "I'm so tired."

"A drink will help you sleep," said Günther.

Conrad, who had expected Ursula to be elated and joyous, was disappointed at her melancholy state. He suggested champagne to Günther.

"No, thank you, not yet. When Paul comes home. Brandy for us now."

When Conrad handed Ursula her glass, she did not return his smile, but looked away quickly. He could see tears mirrored in her eyes. He remembered that she had not wept at Skye's and Boris' funerals, and this had worried him, but then he decided that she was saving her energy for Paul. And now she is grieving for them, he thought. Yet, that answer did not quite satisfy him. Günther was effusive with relief. He spoke rapidly and wondrously of his brother's wounds. "He's already made medical history." As the brandy took hold of him, he rose and walked about the room, stopping to pause at a window facing a fountain in the garden. "How excessive we Bronevskys are . . . and redundant . . . to make the same point twice."

Ursula's terrible moan coincided instantaneously with Günther's mad rush to her side. "Forgive me," he whispered harshly as he drew the shaking girl up and led her out of the room.

Conrad, with confusion and fear gripping his heart, hurried after them. "What is it? Please, for God's sake, what is it?" He fell back as he caught Günther's look and the faint shake of his head. He watched him take Ursula to her room.

An hour later he returned to the sitting room, his face grave. Conrad rose. "What upset her?"

"My stupidity. I wasn't thinking. I shouldn't have said it, at least not so she could hear it."

"You mean about something being . . . redundant?"

"Yes."

"What *did* you mean?"

Günther hesitated and rubbed his forehead, briefly closing his eyes. "Haven't you wondered about Skye's death?"

"One of the doctor's men shot him."

"No. His father shot him."

"Why? That's insane."

Günther spoke evenly. "I didn't want to tell you this, but you have to know it. He was aiming at Ursula. Skye stepped in front of a bullet meant for her, just as Paul took one meant for me. You see . . . he loved her."

"And she?" Conrad waited on the edge of the world.

"No. When he told her, she turned him away. She told him she could not love him. There was nothing between them in Zurich." He looked straight into Conrad's eyes as he spoke; then he picked up his abandoned glass and replenished it from the decanter. "I'm sorry we drugged you." Brandt was glad that Günther was not looking at him at that moment, so deeply did he blush. "Ursula was sure you were next on the killer's list— as we discovered from Frichter you were. We couldn't take the risk of having you come with us. We couldn't have anyone else dying for us. Particularly you. I don't think Ursula could have borne that. In time, she will stop grieving for him. Please understand what she is feeling. The others

[332]

who died because of us, never knew it. He was different. He was our brother, and he knew what he was doing and she knows that. And he was also more . . . specific."

"Specific? Ah, yes. I see. For her alone, not for all of you. He did it for her alone."

Günther nodded. "She will come out of it."

Conrad held Günther's word in his hands like a gift: *Particularly you. I don't think Ursula could have borne that.* The words astonished him. His heart pounded furiously, yet he was afraid to believe the words, for in the weeks that followed he saw no change in Ursula.

Paul came home from the hospital in November and for days Conrad watched the three of them, sometimes sitting close together without touching or talking, watching the snow fall. He believed they were mourning, and privately he mourned with them. At other times they seemed in good spirits and made plans for the future. They would travel for a while, visit London, Paris, New York, San Francisco. "And the Sierras. I understand the skiing is wonderful in the Sierras," said Günther. "And, Ursula, remember Grandfather's picture books of rare birds? I think they all live in the Americas. And there's the coastline . . . wild and magnificent. We'll sit on the beach under a white umbrella and watch the seabirds while you paint."

Conrad was both glad and unhappy at hearing these plans, glad because they were recovering, unhappy because now they would leave. He visualized them boarding steamships and trains with a retinue of discreet servants. He saw them driving elegant motorcars to fashionable resorts. They would write him funny letters for a while and then a few postcards and then nothing. He would read about them in foreign newspapers, see their pictures in fashionable magazines, the twins impeccably dressed, Ursula a stunning international beauty.

Yet, Conrad noticed that Günther made most of the plans while the other two smiled and nodded, but sometimes they looked away to the rain beating on the windows or toward the dark granite horizon above the city before snowfall. At these moments Conrad felt a persistent unreasonable uneasiness and longed for spring.

Ursula was polite and considerate to him, but there was a reserve, a distance in her manner that made him despair. At night he heard her pacing in her room. Several times as he listened at the door that separated them, he thought he heard her muffled sobs. With agony he pulled away his hand that already encircled the knob.

One lovely morning when it was still winter, he saw her standing in the garden looking at the ground. He followed her gaze and saw the touch of blue; the first crocus was breaking through the brittle snow. Abruptly she knelt before it and smashed it back into the mud with her fists, harsh cries coming from her throat. He ran into the bright sun and pulled her to her feet. "You can't go on like this," he cried at her twisted, agonized face. She collapsed in his arms, hot tears against his neck. He carried her to her room and turned her over to a maid, who only shook her head.

Early one evening, Melchior came to tell them he was returning to Monte Tre Croci in the morning. "I hope you're not going to walk," said Brandt.

Melchior smiled. "No." He picked up a colorful travel brochure from the table and put it down again.

"We are making some travel plans ourselves," said Günther.

Melchior nodded and turned to Paul. "And you are fully recovered?"

"Yes," said Paul, looking intensely into his brother's face. "Can you stay for a while?"

Melchior shook his head slowly. "No," he said softly. "You'll have to work it out yourself."

Conrad suddenly sensed a charged atmosphere in the room. He quickly looked to Ursula. She rose from her chair as Melchior turned to meet her. "You're not afraid of the dark anymore, are you?" she said.

"No. But you are," he whispered, touching her face with a gentle hand.

Conrad, watching the four of them from outside the circle in which they stood, felt a wonder at the silent language passing among them. Something had happened. Something was wrong. Then abruptly the young priest was shaking his hand. "I'll see myself out. Thank you."

Moments late Conrad heard the front door close. He looked back at the twins and Ursula when Günther spoke. "When did he come to see you?"

"I sent for him the day before I left the hospital."

"Why does he make us his business?"

"He doesn't. He refused to help then as he did tonight. He knows we have to work it out alone."

"There's nothing to work out. Nothing!"

"Ah, Günther . . ."

"You've come to some false conclusion. We stay together. All of us."

"No," said Paul. "That was Grandfather's way, and Great-Grandfather's, and all those who came before him. Build a wall, crown it with shards of glass, bolt the gate, shut the world out, live in the shelter of arrogance and pride and vanity. That's why they always intermarried."

Günther sank into a chair. "He convinced you, didn't he? With his gibberish . . . his holy canting."

"He didn't even try. He knew when I sent for him that I'd already made up my mind. He knew I only wanted reassurance. He refused to give it. He was right. Last summer you gave everything up to come with me to Sweden because I couldn't bear to be without you. Are you going to do that the rest of your life?"

Conrad watched from the shadows as Paul towered over his twin. He saw Ursula, her hand over her mouth, lean against the wing of Günther's chair, her eyes on Paul, who spoke again. "We come from careless people, my brother. Like them, we have satisfied the smallest hunger with a feast. Help me end it."

Günther shook his bowed head. "I can't."

"I can," said Paul. "I've contacted the people in Sweden. They want me to come back. I'm going, Günther."

Günther's head shot up. "You could wait a year."

"Under a white umbrella on a Pacific coast watching seabirds? No, I think not. For God's sake, learn from Grandfather's terrible mistake with Father." Ursula leaned over the back of the chair and placed her hands on Günther's shoulder. He reached up to hold them. Paul smiled. "You'll have to resolve that yourselves, too." As Paul left the room, he paused briefly in front of Brandt. "You're a patient man, Conrad," he said softly. "Wait a little longer."

Three days later Paul was gone, and Conrad was left alone with Günther and Ursula. His life became curiously raw. He was unable to sleep. All food was tasteless. He hurt everywhere: his shoulders felt like hammered iron, his head ached constantly. When he stretched, his bones made odd noises. For days he watched Ursula and Günther sitting in his garden. Günther smoking cigarettes ceaselessly; Ursula, her face blank and white, staring at nothing. Paul's words haunted Brandt, but he no longer dared to hope for anything. Ursula became more distant, rarely joining himself and Günther for dinner. She no longer sketched or read. He heard from the maid that she did nothing except sit by the window and stare into space.

One day, in the middle of spring, Conrad found Günther's packed bags in the foyer. He ran to Ursula's room. The brother and sister stood facing each other, Günther speaking sharply. "He was right. We have to solve it now. Here. Today. You know the answer and so do I. We would only go back to where we left off two years ago. Out of comfort, or pity, even love. No more, Ursula. No more. Remember Brückner. The rightness of things. He loves you. And I've known about you for a long time. I knew it in Zurich. I understand. It's right. You know it's right."

Conrad, seeing the pain in Ursula's face, spoke from the doorway. "Don't leave her now, Günther. For God's sake, don't leave her now."

Günther held his sister to his chest. "I have to leave her; she won't get well if I stay. *I* won't get well if I stay.

"I have to work. It's the only salvation for me. It's the only way I can give both of them up. He is better than I, more brave. We were fleshed together like Siamese twins joined at the heart. But he had the courage to cut into the heart." He was weeping. "And she would give up everything to stay with me and comfort me. Such sacrifices cannot even be earned. If I can find any good in me at all, it will have to be in work. Grandfather said that it alone can ennoble an impoverished soul. Well, I don't know about souls; I'm not sure I have one.

"Take care of her. I give her up to you. If I weren't her brother . . . I'd kill to keep her." He laughed through his tears at Brandt's expression. "You thought it was someone else? No. No one else." He brushed Ursula's hair from her face. "I have to go now, Little Bear." He raised her chin and kissed her softly on the lips. "Tell me it's right." She nodded faintly. "Say it."

"Yes. I love him."

Günther stepped back and faced Brandt; for a moment their eyes met with force. Then Günther walked past the stunned lawyer, and for a few minutes Conrad could hear him talk to a servant. Then a door closed.

He looked at Ursula standing in the center of the room. For once she looked frail and frightened; then he walked toward her as she turned to meet him.

JACK LEVINE

JACK LEVINE

Text by FRANK GETLEIN

HARRY N. ABRAMS, INC., *PUBLISHERS*, NEW YORK

Frontispiece
PLATE I. **The Trial** 1953–54
72 × 63″
The Art Institute of Chicago
Gift of Mr. and Mrs. Edwin E. Hokin and Goodman Fund

Library of Congress Catalog Card Number: 66–10297

HARRY N. ABRAMS, INCORPORATED, NEW YORK
Printed and bound in Japan

LIST OF ILLUSTRATIONS

*Color plates are marked with an asterisk**

SINCE THE END OF the Napoleonic Wars it has been normal for the artist in the Western world to hold himself somewhat apart from society. This attitude is in marked contrast to the entire history of Western art from Cimabue and Giotto through Fragonard and David. In all those centuries, on one set of terms or another, the European artist took it for granted that this profession occupied an honorable, useful, and well-understood place within society, considerably below that of the princes whom he served, perhaps, but somewhat above the skilled craftsmen from whom his trade had sprung.

This attitude of detachment, or apartness, is often spoken of as the alienation of the artist, but in truth it is much more various than that term implies; it may range from the all but self-parody of Whistler to the jolly boys' club atmosphere of Sloan and Glackens. The artist keeps himself aloof because he can have a better time on the outside, or because he has seen the cruel punishment society mindlessly inflicts upon its lesser members. The artist comes to hate society, which he regards as linked inextricably to injustice and oppression.

Jack Levine has certainly shared in his profession's apartness from the rest of society. Since an artist's work is the chief witness to his motivation, it is safe to assume that Levine's reasons for holding himself apart center on the social injustice and oppression that continue to mark even the affluent society of the 1960's in America. Michael Harrington's study, *The Other America*, revealed what have been called "pockets of poverty" still existing in the midst of our unprecedented prosperity. Jack Levine knew of such pockets long before Harrington did, for he was born into one of them, in Boston, in 1915. He has painted their inhabitants ever since he began to paint, and he paints them still, despite his own early and sustained success as an artist in an affluent society.

One of the remarkable things about Jack Levine is that he has kept alive the fires of compassion and indignation that feed his art, long after he himself has had any reason to complain of his treatment at the hands of society. As an artist, indeed, Levine never has had reason to complain. Or, at least, he has not had the usual reasons of failure to be understood or appreciated. As he relates in his memories of childhood, he was permitted and encouraged to draw at an age before he could properly read and write. As a young Bostonian, one of his earliest memories was of the Boston Police Strike and of the National Guard patrolling the streets in full battle dress. The boy, dropping in at the store where his sister was employed, sketched the soldiers whose firm action brought Governor Calvin Coolidge to the vice presidency, then to the presidency, of the United States. Levine was four and swears he remembers it. Interestingly, what he remembers is his own act of recording it all in crayon.

Within the family, then, his vocation was understood and accepted at a time when most American families still reacted to a child's serious interest in any of the arts by asking why this should happen to them. The young Levine, as he relates, enrolled himself in class after class, with instructor after instructor, finally finding Harold Zimmerman at a settlement house in Roxbury. From Zimmerman, and at the Museum of Fine Arts in Boston, he began to learn systematically of the whole golden train of painters of the past. Presently, with his classmate Hyman Bloom, he came to the attention of Denman W. Ross, of the Department of Fine Arts at Harvard. Ross, a teacher of wide erudition and great sensitivity, was alert to the actual situation of poor boys in Boston. He gave Levine and Bloom studios and a weekly allowance of $12 each. Levine was fourteen. The Great Depression was beginning. All around him the boy saw the subjects of his art for years to come. But, under the instruction of Ross, he also immersed himself in the past, finding that continuity in art which has been of prime importance to him ever since.

In this he has again set himself apart, this time not only from society at large but also from the inner society of artists of his own time and place. It is probably from this double isolation that Levine draws the lonely strength that fortifies his art.

If the artist since the fall of Napoleon has been isolated from society, he has created a subculture of his own, often known by the name of the district—the Latin Quarter, Bohemia, Greenwich Village, Bloomsbury, Euston Road—where artists in any number settled. These artistic communities evolved into private worlds, closed systems, with their own values, goals, and heroes, unknown to the larger community. From these smaller worlds, too, Levine has been isolated. He has been isolated precisely by that devotion to the art of the past and that unceasing effort to measure himself against the artistic standards of the past that he learned as an adolescent from Zimmerman and Ross.

The artistic community of the last century or more, whether centered on the Impressionists and Cubists in Paris or the action painters and Pop artists of New York, has consistently been characterized by a search for new means of expression, new ways with paint—or without paint—new images and non-images. With a consistency of his own, Jack Levine has no less fervently pursued the mastery of the art of painting as that art was perfected by Titian and Rembrandt, by Daumier and Degas, and, in the twentieth century, by Soutine and Rouault.

He has thus created a paradoxical position for himself that is perhaps unique in the art of his time. He has taken a noble idiom of painting, one fashioned by generations of great artists, all of them at peace, not to say in union, with their societies, and used it for his own strictly modern purposes of incisive social criticism and social compassion. Levine weeps for the poor and cries shame against those individuals and institutions he regards as responsible for social exploitation; and he does so in a language devised, in part at least, by painters accustomed to placing social and economic exploiters just a little below the angels and saints.

At the same time he cultivates the virtues of classical painting as worthwhile in and for themselves. The combination sets him apart from society as a whole and from the artistic community within it.

Since his late teens, in the mid-thirties, Levine has lived through three dominant manners in American art, each of which was widely proclaimed as the only conceivable way for an American to paint. All three, however much their followers have denigrated the others, have had in common a conviction that only with the mode in question did American painting "come of age"; thus lightly are the achievements of artists like Winslow Homer and Thomas Eakins dismissed in the heat of instant art history. As Levine approached maturity, he was informed on every side that American painting had also reached maturity—in the works of Thomas Hart Benton, John Steuart Curry, and Grant Wood, the leading regionalists. It was felt then, as it has been since by a dwindling band of the faithful, that American art should have nothing to do with the art of Europe; indeed, that the Eastern seaboard is somehow un-American. An American painter, to be worthy of the name, ought to have hay in his hair and to paint straight on with none of those fancy glazes. Levine, child of the Boston slums, a first-generation American, utterly enthralled by the handling of paint and subject by Rembrandt and Titian, was unqualified in every imaginable way except one: he did paint American subjects. It is just that his America would never have been recognized by the American Legion of Cedar Rapids.

Even in his military service, Levine managed to maintain his isolation from American art. Before the war he had participated in Federal Art Projects, sponsored by the Work Projects Administration, an agency created under Franklin D. Roosevelt to counteract widespread unemployment. Levine did not join the War Artists unit, which had become the refuge of the old WPA crowd during World War II. Declining the chance to paint portraits of generals, Levine entered

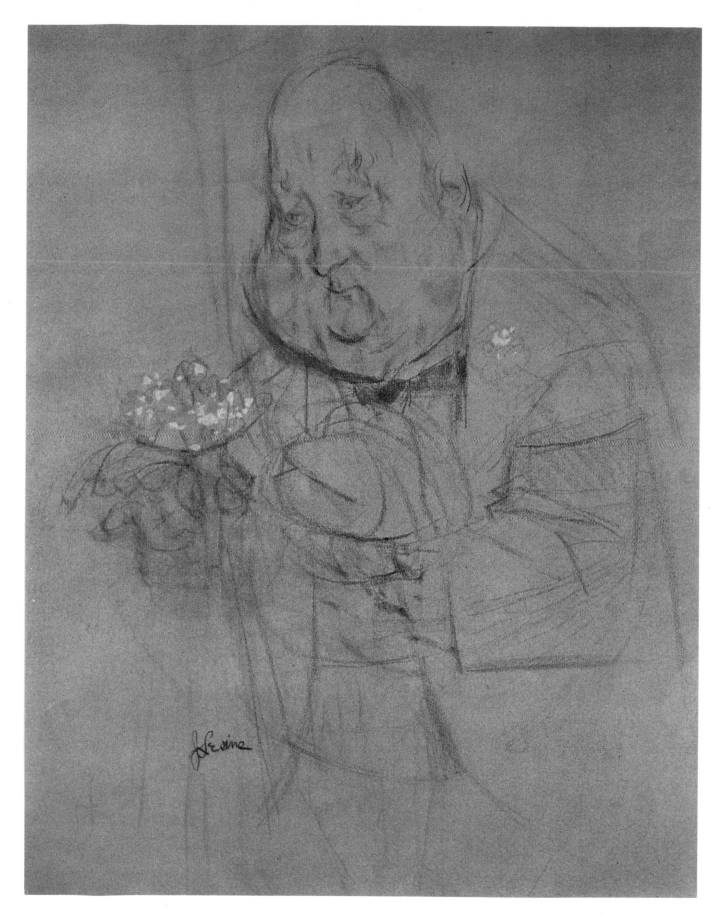

PLATE 2. **The Mourner** 1952
Charcoal and pastel, 23 × 18″
The Downtown Gallery, New York

ordinary military service and sweated out the war on Ascension Island, a bleak and lonely outpost in the Atlantic used as a fueling stop by the Air Force. Never in danger from enemy action, Levine knew intimately the overwhelming threat of military life—sheer boredom and a growing resentment at the perpetuation of bureaucratic idiocy by entrenched mediocrity. The experience was to figure in a few of his paintings after the war.

When the war did end, Levine, who had left the WPA with some recognition as a *Wunderkind*, returned to the United States to find that an entirely new kind of painting, variously called Abstract Expressionism or action painting, was the accepted fashion. Like the American scene of his teens, the new manner was widely felt to be the final coming of age of American painting and the only permissible way for an American to paint.

Levine never actually essayed anything remotely like Abstract Expressionism. He was incapable of letting himself go to that extent, and he was incapable of doing something he did not believe in just because it was the fashion. But for a year or so in the postwar period he did experiment in manner more than he ever did before or has since. This is the period of the pawnshop pictures. All that is necessary in order to realize their fundamentally conservative nature is to conjure up in the mind's eye the look of a Kline or a De Kooning or a Pollock of the same time. For Levine, however, the departure was enormous—there are whole areas in some of his big paintings that have to be explained. But the experiment was not a success, and the artist returned to his steady mastery of more traditional methods. At the same time he consulted chemists about the new mediums coming into use. He concluded that his ancient techniques with oil paint and plenty of time for drying between glazes gave the picture as good a chance for a long life as could be hoped for.

For more than a decade he jeered at what he regarded as the pretensions of Abstract Expressionism, and one morning he awoke to find that all his minority-of-one predictions had come true. The "space cadets," as he called them, were no longer the rage of fashion. They had been displaced by Pop artists, younger men who copied comic strips or fabricated enormous shirts or modeled hamburgers in plaster painted lurid colors. Of their work it was said, among other things, that it exposed the shallowness of urban America and that it penetrated the fraud underlying American institutions. No one mentioned that Levine, for one, had been doing both those things for some time. Once more he found himself an outsider, doing work that always found its own market but was regarded as outside the stream of fashion.

It is this, probably, that has saved him from the familiar fate of the artist of protest who finds himself accepted. In the theater and the novel it is a regular occurrence for an artist to make a reputation as a man of protest, to become universally accepted, and gradually to discover that things are not as bad as they had seemed. This accompaniment of prosperity, a losing of the edge, has been spared Levine. However well his work has sold, he has always been conscious of being divorced from the mainstream of fashionable painting. He has never lacked experts, in museums and in art magazines, to announce in passing that Levine is passé, working in a manner out of the question in the twentieth century.

Is it? The only answer lies in the work, and the work convinces at a glance. With more than a glance, with attention and care, the work persuades overwhelmingly that, whatever anyone imagines the imperatives of art history to be this year, Jack Levine has fashioned for himself an entirely viable and legitimate manner in art, combining, at times disconcertingly, all the felicities of technique ever dreamed of by the old masters with a corrosive, biting observation of current reality that could only be twentieth-century American.

As befits a contemporary American devoted to the old European masters, Levine deliberately sets out to paint what is called a "major picture" quite regularly. Minor works in his production are more often than not related to major

PLATE 3. **First Draft for "Gangster's Funeral"** 1952
Gouache, 20 1/2 × 25"
The Downtown Gallery, New York

ones: full-fledged oil studies for individual characters in his big ensembles, a bit of still life, a group to be placed within or alongside a larger group. The first of these major efforts is *String Quartette* (plate 8), painted from 1934 to 1937, begun when the artist was nineteen.

The picture belongs to the Metropolitan Museum of Art, New York, but even without this distinction it announced at once the arrival of a fully mature artist. It revealed, too, several characteristics that have stayed in Levine's painting ever since.

He has noted that one very special quality he admires in the work of Rembrandt and Titian is their mastery of the group portrait. It is a mastery he has constantly pursued himself, and the pursuit begins, in public view at least, with *String Quartette*. The subject by definition is a group portrait. The members are intimately related to each other, note by note, beat by beat, the relationships changing subtly and steadily, as the music demands. The subject, therefore, can be regarded almost as a laboratory experiment for Levine, an abstract version of the kind of situation he instinctively seeks in the narrative of urban life.

A comparison between life observed and life made into art can be made, thanks to the drawing of the same subject (plate 7) done when Levine was sixteen, and left by Denman Ross to the Fogg Art Museum. The drawing is exquisite of line and beautifully competent in creating three musicians on paper as definite individuals. But the painting of a few years later goes far beyond the faithful transcription of life observed. There is figure composition. There is a complex professional relationship among the players. And there is possibly a personal note as well. At the very center of the picture, the bow hand of the young cellist comes for a second into close union with the fingering hand of his older colleague: for the young musician, as for the young painter, growth can only come out of the achievements of those who have gone before.

Irony is never absent from a painting by Levine and it is present even here, although affectionately so: the music of the spheres, of a more than mortal beauty, can only come out of the time-ravaged flesh and spirit of man.

The irony is considerably less affectionate in a picture (plate 10) also painted in 1937, a major work of Levine's WPA days, *The Feast of Pure Reason*. Levine recalls the WPA with a kind of practical nostalgia which is common to artists associated with the program, but unknown to those who worked in other phases of it. As Levine says in retrospect, "When else could an American artist be assured of his materials, a place to work, and $23 every week?" The picture should reassure people who worry that fifty cents' worth of government interest in the arts will turn our culture into a propaganda machine on the Soviet model. This Boston boy of twenty-two could think of nothing finer to do with the government's money than to attack the government.

The title is from Joyce's *Ulysses*; at one point in the hilarious journey through "night town," Stephen briefly regains consciousness, takes in his surroundings of utter degradation, and murmurs, "This feast of pure reason." Three characters familiar to any urban New Englander or reader of Edwin O'Connor's novel, *The Last Hurrah*, were painted about twenty years before the novel appeared and painted without a shred of the sentimentality of the novel. The crooked American big-city politician may well have his historical justification, but Levine, a member of the downtrodden class supposedly benefited by the crooks, does not accept this point of view. The three are presented almost as evil idols, embodiments of squat, brutal power. Each expresses a variation on the common theme: the tough cop assumes the classic pose of brute strength congratulating itself; the ward heeler's fingers in mid-calculation combine with his flabby face to

PLATE 4. **Tevya and His Horse** 1957
Oil on paper, 24 × 36″
Collection Nancy and Arnold Perl, New York

personify low cunning; the elegant boss is taken one step further into stupefying self-satisfaction. The unholy trinity is framed by a triangle of tawdry sham elegance, the cut-glass decanter, the French frame of a picture on the wall, and the plaster cast of the Winged Victory, symbolizing, no doubt, a victory at the polls and a victory minus a head.

Today Levine deprecates the picture a little: "It depended for its motivation on the bitter assumptions of a boy." All the same, the picture is a very clear statement of what Levine has been up to ever since, the exposure of the unjust ruler to the ridicule of his subjects.

That task is taken up with no distracting hint of caricature in *Welcome Home* (plate 18), the single major painting relating to Levine's military service. That in itself is odd. Most soldiers in a citizen army dream of getting out and exposing the army for the organized idiocy it seems, and Jack Levine was well equipped to do the job. Yet this single work stands by itself in that category of sweet revenge. Moreover, it speedily reveals so great an extension of the artist's progress in the mastery of space composition that the act of vengeance fades in importance compared to the style in which that act is consummated.

The expressionist exaggerations and distortions of *The Feast of Pure Reason* are not so much abandoned as incorporated into a smoother, more subtle, and in a way more realistic presentation. Like the Venetians he admires, Levine separates the surface plane of the picture from the plane of the scene itself; the two are not even parallel, let alone identical. From the resulting tilt of things, a new dynamic movement enters, beautifully managed for maximum but quiet statement. The incline of the festive table and that of the tiled floor meet to form the architectural center of the picture. At just that point of meeting occurs the waiter's extraordinarily deferential pouring of the wine. The waiter himself is a marvel of comic invention: the bowlike bend of the body manages to imply both the unworthiness of the servitor and his simultaneous determination to advance close enough to serve. The completely mechanical nature of this obeisance is revealed in the face.

Ceremonial eating was important in Venetian painting, and it has been a constant subject for Levine. Usually the act of eating clashes in tone with the nature of the ceremony, an effect heightened here by the sketch quality of the dishes, the silver, and the chicken bones. In contrast, the human flesh is felt in its every blood vessel and nerve ending. The most sensitive flesh in the ensemble belongs to another Levine character making her initial appearance, the woman attached to power, bored, bitter, and thinking her own thoughts as power salutes itself.

Years later, in 1959, the soldier's revenge was taken in full. *Welcome Home* was included in an exhibition of twentieth-century American art shown in Moscow, over the belated but sincere protest of President Eisenhower, who found the central figure of the general a "lampoon" rather than art. Typically, Levine said that he had no complaint: "You get denounced by the President of the United States, you've hit the top."

In this painting, Levine has adapted and perfected a kind of "white writing" stemming from Tintoretto and entirely different from that devised by the West Coast artist Mark Tobey. In Tintoretto and in one or two other North Italians there occasionally appears what seems almost a route map for discharged electrical energy. Most often seen in religious subjects, these swift white networks appear as light along the folds of silk or taffeta, or light along the waves of troubled waters; but beyond plausible explanation, these crackling, myriad stems and branches actually express the release of divine energy among men.

PLATE 5.
Jewish Cantors in the Synagogue 1930
Crayon, 17 × 11 1/2"
Fogg Art Museum, Harvard University,
Cambridge, Mass.

In Levine's hands this device often becomes a mockery by exaggeration. It is not in the least necessary to be aware of the Venetian art history involved, for, in and by itself, this crackling of light reflections over a surface achieves precisely the effect desired, of a more than human splendor lavished upon humans who are somehow just a shade less than human.

In *Welcome Home* this shimmering light, appropriately, decorates the waiter's uniform, a Ganymede at a banquet of the gods. In *Reception in Miami* (plate 36), no less appropriately, the light divine is all over the picture, for the subject is the presentation of two American ladies to two authentic if somewhat fading divinities of our time, the Duke of Windsor and his Duchess. Levine rarely uses actual historical figures; more often he creates characters as a dramatist does, characters at once highly individual and the epitome of a type, a profession, a social relationship. Once in a great while, though, he encounters historical personages who are themselves of that essential, archetypal quality, and he employs them. Behind the royalty and his consort towers a copy—reversed for reasons of composition—of the well-known Canova sculpture, *Eros and Psyche*: the affair of love and the soul rendered into eternal ice. In the painting the statue is balanced by the equally monumental figure of the maître d'hôtel, snapping his fingers to signal the ceremonies onward and at the same time giving just a faint suggestion that he is a puppet master pulling invisible strings which control the rest of the dramatis personae. As for them, the gentleman and the two ladies seem like puppets at the end of some string. The Duke and Duchess, in contrast, seem almost carved and painted figures, lavishly decorated and bejeweled, and rolled in upon invisible wheels. Baroque space opens behind the group, emphasizing and compensating for the crowded feeling of the actual ensemble. Like the Canova *Eros*, there are symbols of sex here, devoid of response. The daring décolletage of the woman in the center is utterly without sexual appeal. The nude back of her companion is also singularly nonsexual and is, furthermore, made to follow the swelling, vulgar line of the flunky's belly.

Over all runs and glistens the light. It appears in the background along the glass of the chandelier, among the palms, along a swag of drapery. Present on all the men's clothes, it comes into full, free play upon the gowns of the ladies. It darts about like lightning over the silks and satins, unifying the three spreads of fabric into a single continuum of illumination. Was it for this that the hand now holding a cigarette holder relinquished the scepter of the sceptered isle? It was. Following the play of lightning downward, we come to the center. Equidistant from all three shimmering skirts stands a little lap dog, himself hardly existing except as pure shimmer. Out of this play of light a leg emerges to scratch at an intruding flea, and thus the dog performs a curtsy of his own.

It is a cruel picture.

Once perfected, of course, the "white writing" of Levine, like that of Tintoretto, is subject to use for any purpose the creator can fit it to. *The Tombstone Cutter* (plate 35), painted a year before *Reception in Miami*, balances the cold eye with a warm heart, a balance that Levine strikes in his overall production, never within a single work.

The Tombstone Cutter is resting or reflecting, the hard chisel still in his hand, the work in progress behind him, an elaborately carved yet modest monument on which may be seen the Lion of Judah and the Star of David. The chisel, held precisely and tapped away at, has carved all those elaborations, but the process has also traced its patterns on the face and body of the worker. The face especially is a mass of white lines, explainable readily enough as marble dust, yet really expressing the identity achieved between a patient worker and the work.

Beyond the technical devices of space and sheer beautiful painting, Levine follows the Old Masters in working according to an *istoria*, or, as he calls it, a scenario or story line. The difference, of course, is that while the vast majority of subjects treated by Old Masters were given to the painters by a universally known set of people and events—the Bible or the Greek and Roman myths—Levine finds his own mythic events in the urban and national life around him. He loves painting in the grand style and travels to Europe frequently in order to see more of it than is easily available in this country. But America continues to hold the persons and events, the scenario, which he depends upon to keep him working at top form. "Without the challenge of plot building," he once said, "mental laziness sets in."

What is perhaps Levine's best known painting, *Gangster's Funeral* (plates 62, 64, 77), has such a scenario, and the scenario itself was built, partly in public, even before a stroke was placed on the final canvas. Levine was making a number of public appearances that year, mostly discussing the question of how the artist works. He never had any doubt on that question and described the process in detail, using the work he was planning as the prime example:

"What do people wear at a gangster funeral? If they be wearing street clothes instead of cutaways, it becomes possible to have the fat man show a broad mourning band on his thick little arm....A widow, in deep mourning, clad in rich furs. Better yet, two widows. One very, very shapely. The chief of police comes to pay his last respects—a face at once porcine and acute—under no circumstances off to one side as a watcher...." And again: "...I want the painting as a comedy. It must not be a tragedy. I will show the corpse, but the emphasis could be on the embalming."

And so it is. But it is not only the corpse that is embalmed. The mellow gold light of the mortuary chapel pumps its preserving juices into the whole cast of characters as each of them in his own variant registers the fact of death. Levine registers his own comment by noting that among the crowd there are really only two old-style crooks, the two younger men in the middle. And they appear hopelessly outnumbered by the rotund and the respectable, including the police chief, porcine and acute, behind the second, less official widow. Comedy is maintained, the corpse de-emphasized by the extreme foreshortening of the casket. This zooms us into the picture, past the body to the patrolman on duty, who, like us, is a watcher at a gathering of the mighty.

The picture works out exactly according to the scenario set up in advance by the artist, and Levine takes pride in such fulfillment. "I see no harm," he wrote at about this time, "in putting the conscious mind to work."

At about the same time the artist's conscious mind began to reflect on aspects of the American government. More than aspects—a series of paintings begins, more or less concurrently with the beginning of the Eisenhower administration, which examines the three great branches of the American system of government: legislative, judicial, and executive.

The judicial appears first. *The Trial* (frontispiece, plate 1), preceded and accompanied by a great many related pictures, is one of the most tightly organized of Levine's paintings. Abstractly speaking, it is a perfect example of those systems of triangles that museum docents are forever finding in Renaissance pictures, to the amazement of the young. But the triangles are not only a compositional device. They also symbolize the organization of our system of justice, with the weary judge at the apex, his hands a little triangle of their own. Shakespeare's phrase, "the law's delay," is embodied in passing in every patient, worn face in the scene. Compression is built in by the shortness of the distance from the surface plane of the picture to the stop plane of the back wall; and compression, of course, is the very essence of trial procedure. The weight of the triangle not only bears upon those at the bottom, but drags on the man at the peak; this emerging Levine insight was never more clearly stated.

Election Night (plates 71, 73) continues the political examination. Space is so compressed as to contain a whole cast of minor characters hardly seen at first glance. When we do see them, we notice that they are not simply there; they are providing detailed contrast with the triumphant party downstage center. To the left of the pillar a couple stands in close embrace. To the right may be seen a trio—the bartender, the cop, and a minor celebrant—in earnest conversation. Between them and the center, two professionals, the bellhop and the waiter, attend to each other, if only to avoid collision. The background, in short, is packed with interactive human relationships.

The figures in the triumphant group, in contrast, are in total isolation from one another. The movement of isolation begins with the couple in the lower right ignoring each other. He stares fitfully at the nude back presented to him. The owner of the back drapes a glittering hand on the back of the chair of the man on her left, who does not notice her as he reaches for the tray of the cigarette girl, who ignores him. Dead center are the lady in the funny hat and the victor himself, who vaguely recalls the king of Jordaens' *The King Drinks*, except that here there is no mockery of power by its victims; here, power mocks itself. A toady makes a fervent pitch to the winner, who does not hear a word he says; the toady, too, pauses in mid-plea to cast an appraising, appreciative glance at the exposed charms of the cigarette girl—another appreciation unreturned. To the right of this little play, the bored and refined lady fingers her pearls and casts a glance of her own at the girl, not so simple as passing lust, but more poignant. Meanwhile, she is herself ignoring the woman in the lower right, thus completing the circle, a chain of broken links.

Turning aside from political power and its effects, Levine in *Medicine Show* (plates 80, 89) portrays the basic operation of fraud upon the gullible. The example chosen is the classic one of the hawker of magical cures, here portrayed by a character somewhat reminiscent of Daumier's Robert Macaire. The quality of the sky, the quality of the crowd, with its sailor in the foreground, the red brick Gothic church, and the gas tank, all suggest the artist's native Boston. To the clear and open street scene, the barker brings touches of elegance: the plug hat, the gold fringe, the mortar and pestle, and the dazzling nudity of the two girls. The crowd responds. Placed as they are, the girls almost seem to be one nude body with two heads, honest boredom and aggressive good cheer. Everything about the barker radiates confidence supreme, the hand gestures, the head tilt, the casual brush-step of the foot—everything but the eyes, where may be seen the fundamental uneasiness of the cheat. Microphone and anatomical chart underline that it is the contemporary, electronic medicine show that is a target as much as the old one portrayed. The medicine is "Veleno," the Italian for "poison."

A pair of powerful pictures shifts the focus of Levine's continuing examination of power to another land, Spain, that agony of the liberal conscience. *The Turnkey* (plates 98, 102) and *The Spanish Prison* (plates 138, 139) are companion pieces, different sides of the same coin. The austere bareness of the prison imposes itself on conqueror as well as conquered. The bits of florid costume or gimcrackery are futile efforts to ease the bleakness. In contrast, the prisoner seems more fully human than either the decorated turnkey or the shadowy guard. It is no accident that the face of the bleak dictator resembles strongly that of one of the mourners, a small-time hoodlum if ever there was one, at the *Funeral*. A dry felicity of paint reveals a startling similarity between the texture of the flesh and shirt of the prisoner and the plastered wall against which prisoners are shot.

Inauguration (plate 106) masterfully uses the chill light of January in Washington to mock the colorless image on the television screen through which most Americans witness this august ritual of the Republic. The President resembles Wilson, perhaps, and Truman; the First Lady may be modeled on Mamie Eisenhower or Eleanor Roosevelt; Levine takes his images where he finds them. There is an almost viselike effect produced by the heraldry in front and the electronic apparatus over the heads of the nation's two chief officers. Meanwhile, hovering in space like a Tiepolo angel is the television director, whose elbow suggests that he is really stage manager of the whole proceeding.

The commentary on civic virtue and social justice is brought up to date with two pictures. *Witches' Sabbath* (plates 146, 151) is Levine's ironic salute to the legislative branch of the government, a depiction of the loyalty investigations of the 1950's. The Ku Klux Klan hoods in the background link the scene with the genuine witches' sabbaths of European tradition, and we are not at all surprised to see the goat as a participant, balanced precisely by the veterans' organization men around the table full of "evidence." There is the famous pumpkin and the no-less-famous Woodstock typewriter, here doubling the effect: the reporter using the typewriter also recalls Senator McCarthy's genius for gulling the press with wild stories so close to deadline that they could not be checked properly. The Senator himself is the central figure, attended by a Shriner, by a somewhat appalled representative of conventional legislative propriety, and, close in, by the strange figure of Roy Cohn.

Birmingham '63 (plates 152, 153) speaks entirely for itself. It may indeed be the single painting of social comment in Levine's career in which he felt that no overt comment by arrangement or selection was needed. All he had to do was paint as well as he could. The "message" was built into the subject. The calm dedication of the five Negroes speaks for virtue with a directness rare for the artist. The savage dogs speak for the white community.

Along with these major studies of power and its effects on those who wield it, Levine has always, as he says, "indulged himself" in painting flesh and in painting gorgeous fabrics. Yet even when dealing in pure painterliness, the artist is incapable of relinquishing his habitual irony. The scenes of burlesque, particularly, implacably contrast the promised eroticism of the subject with the inevitable vacancy of the minds above the bodies. With the best will in the world Levine paints a *Fêtes Galantes* (plate 109), and the swooning violins and twinkling sugar daddies are offset by that feminine social boredom he sees and paints so well.

The boredom of sex alamode is occasionally reversed and set moving in the opposite direction: a male boredom with cornucopias of female flesh, and more than boredom, the beginnings of a mild revulsion. The bared bosoms of the burlesque pictures and the all-but-bared bosoms of the night club scenes appear in social situations, as characters—or perhaps props—in social comedies stage-managed by the artist, comedies complete with contrasting characters, men stirred by passing lust, a lust cheated by the boredom expressed, painfully or poignantly, in the faces of the female objects of desire. The whole effect, a constant in Levine's social theater, is not unrelated to the spirit of the ancient, lowlife legend of the whore who smoked, chewed gum, and read the papers while performing her professional duties. The point of the legend is the complete dissociation of sex from the person; the same person could as readily be catching up on the news while tending an assembly line machine which functions automatically and which will signal when her momentary attention is called for. This is very much the effect created by the slight distance almost always evident in Levine's women, and evident without exception when these women are placed in a social setting as decorative accessories to the men of power who constitute the painter's chief concern. The First Lady in the *Inauguration* shares this feminine distance with the wives of ward heelers at their election-night party. Both types share it with the hardworking burlesque dancers whose naked charms are really unrelated to the calculating intelligence, or absence of intelligence, in the faces above the bonanzas of flesh.

PLATE 6.
Study for "Black Freighter" 1958
Oil on paper, 26 × 20"
Collection
Mr. and Mrs. William A. Marsteller,
New York

The male revulsion, on the contrary, is not perceived and rendered in the persons of characters in the social sex dramas that appear as subplots to the drama of power. Rather, it is solicited in the response of the viewer of those "indulgences" of the artist in apparently straight-on, no-nonsense, more or less classical nudes that turn up from time to time in his work. These are never the simple, beautiful painting of beautiful women they usually appear to be at first sight. The flesh tones are superbly rendered; the play of paint, from that of the first sketch on canvas to that of highlights floating in the glaze, easily matches the sensuousness evoked by the subject. Yet prolonged examination invariably reveals a crack in the crystal, a flaw in the flesh. The noble proportions, often enough, are just a shade *too* noble. The light, which is often arranged so as to appear flattering in the extreme, nevertheless "fails" at one area or another of the flesh before us, and we are uncomfortably aware of the seeds of death beneath the ample skin. Minor blemishes are faithfully included in the topography, and somehow become more important than perhaps they really ought to be; certainly such small misfortunes become more important, more central to Levine's vision of feminine loveliness than they usually are in "life." But then, this is not life; this is art. And it is art of a very special kind, an art always shot through with a glittering intelligence that questions and measures all things.

Thus Levine's highly personal use of the classical conventions of beautiful painting extends even to that most classical of subjects, the female nude. Here, as always, the manner of painting is based solidly on what Levine—in common with practically all artists, connoisseurs, collectors, and critics up to a generation or so ago—regards as the perfection of the medium as achieved by Italian, Flemish, Dutch, and Spanish painters of the late Renaissance and the Baroque epochs. The way with paint is that of those great painters, but the point of view is later—or earlier. An indication may be found in a subject Levine has turned to more than once, a subject which also attracted his artist heroes of three and more centuries ago: *Adam and Eve* (plate 115), the first parents of mankind, whose sin deprived us all of easy living in Eden and cast us out into the bleak world of thought and knowledge. In this one instance alone, dealing with a subject used by so many of the ancient painters he admires as an occasion for an act of worship of the nude, Levine turns away from the utter confidence of Venice and toward the nervousness and uneasiness of the Northern European artists. The model is Cranach. The spirit is that of the moment in Genesis when the couple, in the act of sinning, suddenly know that they are naked and become ashamed.

That sequence of cause and effect is simply impossible in most of the masters Levine has learned from; it is even a contradiction in terms. Not so in Cranach and most of his fellow Germans. Not so in the whole tradition of medieval sculpture and illumination. The shame derives not from conventional gestures but from the very structure and disposition of the body itself. There is, for Levine as for medieval artists, a shame in the naked bodies of Adam and Eve that may be felt even on the body's own terms.

Medieval motives are well enough known, or at least there is general agreement on what those motives must have been, for the artistic production seems to reflect so clearly the thoroughly documented attitudes of medieval Christianity toward sex and the human body. It may be taken for granted that Levine's attitudes are different. In the context of all his work, it seems a fair guess that in the female nude, as in the judge, the legislator, the president, the magnate, Levine is mocking power, this time a power far more widely distributed and far more widely given conscious obedience than the usual subjects of his research. The power in question is sex itself. Despite the presence of that commercialized sex we think of as peculiarly American in *Medicine Show* and the burlesque pictures, the subject goes deeper than that. It is sex in its aspect of "human bondage," that power for liberation and fulfillment so often used, on a domestic or personal scale, to create and maintain a tyranny over the mind of man.

Adam and Eve bears its title on the surface of the picture, in a manner often used in the time of Cranach, but the names are spelled out in Hebrew letters. The picture thus relates to a continuing series of pictures, most of them smaller, of Jewish kings, prophets, heroes, and wise men. Most are figures from the Old Testament, but not all, *Maimonides* (plate 117) and *Hillel* (plate 79) being among them. Levine is proud of the quality of his Hebrew lettering in these paintings, and well he might be, for it does not come as readily to his fingers as it would to those of many Jewish boys of his time and place in Boston. At an early point in his studies of the wisdom of the Gentiles in oil paint, the boy Levine decided that he could dispense with the wisdom of his own people. In a remarkable act of adolescent independence, he refused *bar mitzvah*, or confirmation, and the course of Hebrew studies leading to that rite. No doubt he felt that his own coming to maturity would take place in an entirely different language, that of art.

Nevertheless he must have known, or have come to know later, what a shock his boyish independence had to be to any Jewish family. At any rate, he has described the imaginary portraits of Jewish notables as a memorial to his father. A religious father could ask for no more profound testimony that the heritage received from the elders had been successfully passed on to the son.

Levine often addresses himself to an ancient subject, usually from Classical mythology. When he does, the odds are strong that the myth will be modernized in its characters and general manner and will contribute to a sardonic laugh at some aspect of contemporary civilization. This is the final effect of his recent *The Judgment of Paris* (plates 128, 137, 150, 154, 159, 162–169), another favorite theme of many of his favorite painters of the past. The three divine beauties are three separate but related jokes on the theme of female vanity; Paris turns out to be a beatnik (plate 168), a reminder, among other things, that for several years now Levine has lived in Greenwich Village and has observed the "beat" world as it impinges upon the world of domestic harmony and child raising that is his own.

Turning the same approach inside out, Levine also takes an episode from current history and invests it with something of the quality of myth. *1932 (In memory of George Grosz)* (plates 118, 120), the chilling picture of Hitler bowing to Hindenburg as he assumes power, is an outstanding example.

The continuing studies of Jewish figures are something else again. There is no effort to mock the myth or anything else. The time factor is eliminated entirely; these ancients are seen as men like ourselves and speaking to ourselves, which, of course, is the point of the Bible. Saul, as an example, comes across to almost any casual reader of his story as a tragic villain, the first king of the Israelites, a man who took power against the forebodings of Israel as expressed by Samuel, a man demented by power, finally, and the foe of David. Yet David himself saw him differently, as is evident in many details, chiefly in his refusal to kill Saul when he had the chance and in his sincere mourning for him. Levine's portrait presents *King Saul* (plate 54) through the compassionate understanding of *King David* (plate 14).

David, too, one of the most subtle and complex political leaders in all history, is painted with all that subtlety and complexity intact, a brooding intellect in mature age contemplating its own failures. There is an interesting contrast in the two figures of *Hillel* (plate 79) and *King Asa* (plate 69), whose great heads are much alike in shape and coloring. But the aged king sleeps in power, while the aged teacher pursues to the end his task of making truth and goodness known. All of these aspects of the Jewish hero come together in the noble head of *Maimonides* (plate 117). The court physician was close to power but never infected with the fever. There is a constant yet controlled intellectual curiosity in the eyes. There is majesty in the face as a whole, but it is the majesty of wisdom, the majesty that questions rather than commands. In some ways, the face of Maimonides suggests an idealized intellectual portrait of the artist himself.

In the skeptical view of all human pretensions to greatness, in the steady scrutiny of fact and motive, in the readiness to look behind the brocade for the machinery of might, all of which characterize Levine's paintings, it may be that the Jewish wisdom, self-consciously refused in the refusal of *bar mitzvah*, has returned all the same to animate the whole body of the artist's work.

More steadily and more fervently than any devotion to the heroes of the Old Testament has been Levine's conscious devotion to the achievements of his masters, the great painters of the past. His veneration and gratitude are expressed in *Six Masters: A Devotion* (plate 160). The heads here improbably brought together are faithful copies of self-portraits by six of Levine's heroes and teachers: Rembrandt, Titian, Rubens, El Greco, Velasquez, and Goya. All six are remembered in a great deal of Levine's painting, with the emphasis shifting through the years from one to another. In recent years, certainly, it would appear that Titian and Rubens are more strongly influential than the rest.

Yet it must be acknowledged that the spirit of Levine's art is closer to the spirit of Goya than to that of any artist of the past. The Goya of the dark paintings and of the great series of etchings is already the skeptical, questioning artistic intelligence that Levine has become. This is one reason that admirers of Levine's work were long puzzled that he never addressed himself to prints. If his particular attitude toward the world is very rare in oil painting, it is perhaps the dominant attitude evident in the five-hundred-year history of printmaking. But, despite the work of his wife, Ruth Gikow, who was one of the leaders of the American print revival begun during the WPA days, Levine made almost no prints until 1963, when he perfected an earlier study of classical methods of etching.

From the prints of that year two examples may be taken as the artist's memorial to his master, Goya. The subjects are indubitably Spanish, *The General* (plate 155; see also *The Turnkey*, plates 98, 102) and *The Spanish Prisoner* (plate 139). In the latter, General Franco is shown in a cell which combines the peculiarly Spanish mixture of both senses of *cell*, the one in the monastery and the one in the prison. The granular texture of aquatint in both plates memorializes Goya, who used a similar technique in a very similar spirit. In *The Spanish Prisoner*, the soft and velvety blacks create an ironic contrast of light and shadow between the silenced victim and the all but invisible guard. This was the authentic Spain of Goya. It is one extreme of the world of Jack Levine.

"Power tends to corrupt," said Lord Acton; "absolute power corrupts absolutely."

It has been and is the mission of Jack Levine in art to measure the infinite degrees between the tendency to and the absolute corruption of power.

26

PLATE 7. **Quartette** 1931
Pencil on gray paper, 5 3/8 × 11 1/8"
Fogg Art Museum, Harvard University, Cambridge, Mass.
Gift of Dr. Denman W. Ross

THE PLATES

Unless otherwise noted, all works are oil on canvas

Jack Levine

PLATE 8. **String Quartette** 1934–37
Tempera and oil on Masonite, 48×67"
The Metropolitan Museum of Art, New York
Arthur H. Hearn Fund, 1942

PLATE 9. **The Street** 1938
59 1/2 × 83"
The Museum of Modern Art, New York, on extended loan from
the United States WPA Art Program

PLATE 10. **The Feast of Pure Reason** 1937
42 × 48"
The Museum of Modern Art, New York, on extended loan from
the United States WPA Art Program

PLATE II. **Man and Dog** 1939
19 × 12"
Museum of Fine Arts, Boston

PLATE 12. **Neighborhood Physician** 1939
Oil on composition board, 48 × 30″
Walker Art Center, Minneapolis

PLATE 13. **Neighborhood Physician**
(detail of plate 12)

PLATE 14. **King David** 1941
10 × 8″
Collection Mr. and Mrs. James S. Plaut,
Cambridge, Mass.

PLATE 15. **Street Scene, No. 1** 1939
30 × 40"
Museum of Fine Arts, Boston

PLATE 16. **The Syndicate** 1939
36 1/4 × 45″
Collection Joseph H. Hirshhorn, New York

PLATE 17. **The Syndicate**
(detail of plate 16)

PLATE 18. **Welcome Home** 1946

40 × 60"

The Brooklyn Museum. J. B. Woodward Memorial Fund

PLATE 19. **City Lights** 1940
54×36"
Collection Edith and Milton Lowenthal,
New York

PLATE 20. **The Banquet** 1941
25 1/4 × 30″
Collection Mr. and Mrs. Roy R. Neuberger, New York

PLATE 21. **The Card Players** 1941
15 3/8 × 13 1/4"
Private Collection

PLATE 22. **Horse** 1947
Charcoal, 23 × 30"
Collection Edwin H. Miller, Belmont, Mass.

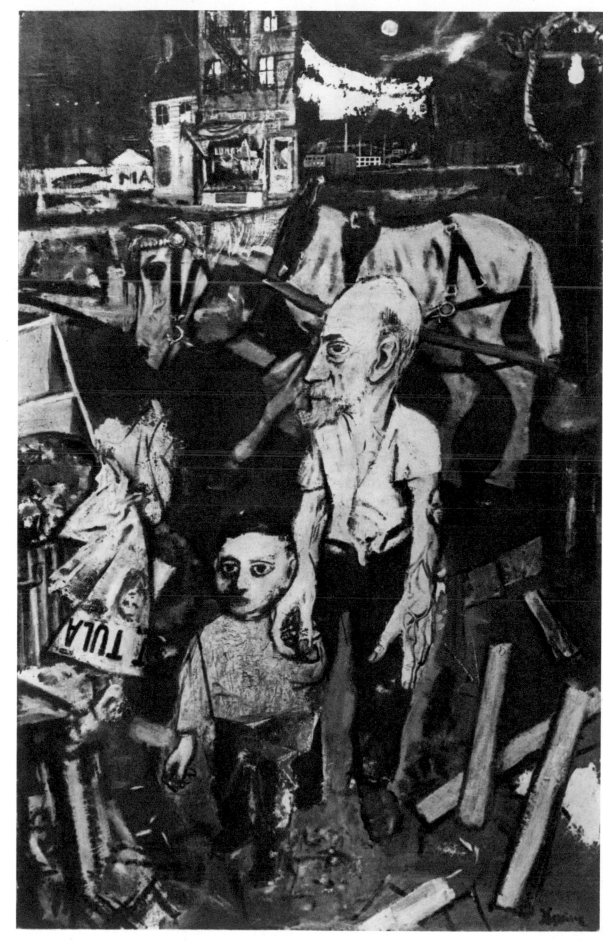

PLATE 23. **The Passing Scene** 1941
Oil on composition board, 48 × 39 3/4"
The Museum of Modern Art, New York
Mrs. Simon Guggenheim Fund

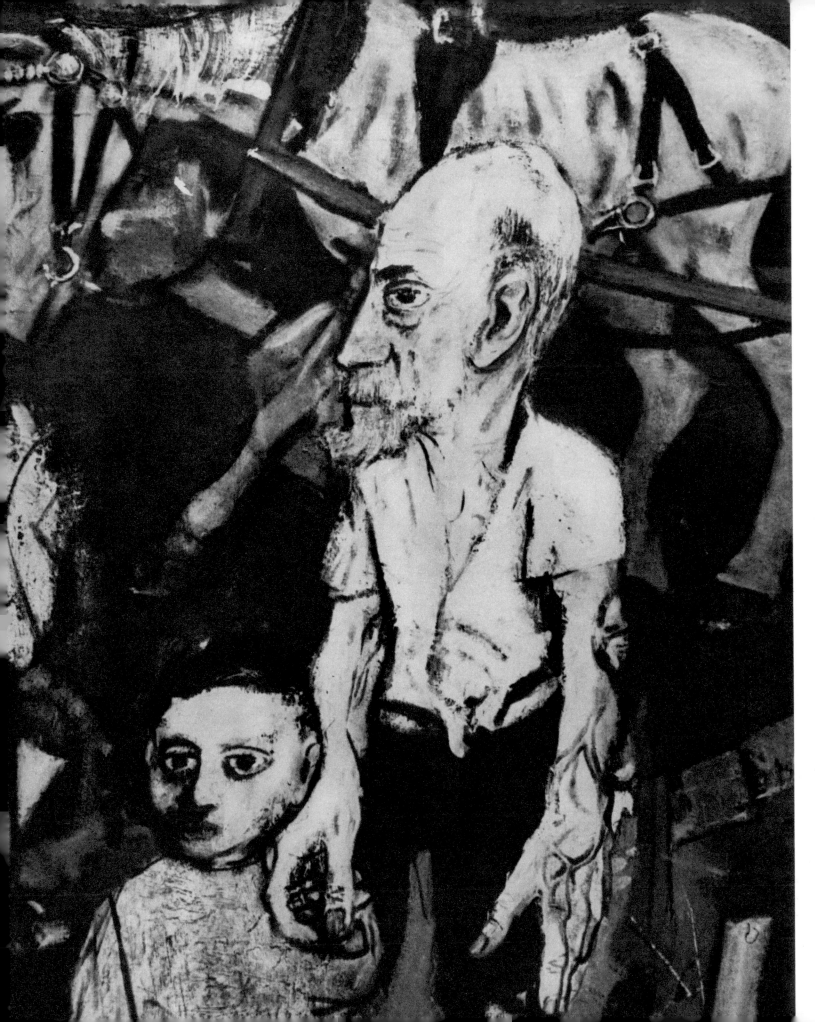

PLATE 24. **The Passing Scene**
(detail of plate 23)

PLATE 25. **The King** 1945
10×7″
Collection Mrs. Milton Lurie Kramer,
New York

PLATE 26. **The Pensionnaire** 1945
36 × 28"
University of Nebraska,
Lincoln, Neb.
F. M. Hall Collection

PLATE 27. **The Last King** 1948
Oil on gesso board, 16 1/2 × 20 1/2″
Collection Argus Chemical Corporation, Brooklyn

PLATE 28. **Gentleman from the South** 1946
22 × 15″
Collection Dr. and Mrs. J. B. Yasinow,
Philadelphia

PLATE 29. **Mars Confounded** 1946
18 × 22"
Collection Mr. and Mrs. John J. Carney, New York

PLATE 30. **The Reluctant Ploughshare** 1946
Gouache, 19 × 22″
Collection IBM Corporation, New York

PLATE 31. **Portrait of Ruth Gikow** 1948
Pencil, 11 × 8 1/4″
Fogg Art Museum, Harvard University,
Cambridge, Mass.
Meta and Paul J. Sachs Collection

PLATE 32. **Warrior's Return** 1946
Oil on panel, 20 × 24″
Collection Ruth Gikow, New York

PLATE 33. **The White Horse** 1946

35 × 40″

Museum of Art, University of Oklahoma, Norman, Okla.

PLATE 34. **The White Horse**
(detail of plate 33)

PLATE 35.
The Tombstone Cutter 1947
36 × 30"
Collection
Mr. and Mrs. Lawrence A. Fleischman,
Detroit

PLATE 36. **Reception in Miami** 1948
50 × 56"
Collection Joseph H. Hirshhorn, New York

PLATE 37. **Magic for the Millions** 1948
50 × 20″
Collection Mrs. Sidney Gerber,
Mercer Island, Wash.

PLATE 38. **Act of Legislature** 1949
35 × 20″
Collection Joseph H. Hirshhorn, New York

PLATE 39. **Study for "Act of Legislature"** 1949
24 × 19"
Collection Dr. and Mrs. Raymond R. Meyers, Buffalo

PLATE 40. **Study for "Gangster's Funeral," Verification of Remains** 1952
Charcoal, 18 1/4 × 23 3/4"
Collection Ida and Moses Soyer, New York

PLATE 41. **Homage to Boston** 1949
20 × 50"
Collection Joseph H. Hirshhorn, New York

PLATE 42. **The Little Warrior** 1949
8 × 10"
Collection Jerome Zipkin, New York

PLATE 43. **Lady with Pink** 1949
24 × 20″
Estate of Harry A. Blutman, M.D.

PLATE 44. **Store Front** 1949

24 × 20″

Sybil and Stephen Stone Foundation, Newton Centre, Mass.

PLATE 45. **Reception in Miami**
(detail of plate 36)

PLATE 46. **Woodstock Pastoral** 1949
25 × 31"
California Palace of the Legion of Honor, San Francisco,
The Mildred Anna Williams Collection

PLATE 47. **The Abundant Life**
(detail of plate 48)

PLATE 48. **The Abundant Life** 1950
30 × 36"
Collection Mr. and Mrs. Joseph Strick, Los Angeles

PLATE 49. **Study for "Medicine Show"** 1954
Pencil, 11 × 13 3/4"
Collection Mr. and Mrs. Philip Sills, New York

PLATE 50. **Euclid Avenue** 1950

36 × 30"

The Wolf Collection, Great Neck, New York

PLATE 51. **Benediction** 1951
29 × 39″
Sybil and Stephen Stone Foundation,
Newton Centre, Mass.

PLATE 52. **Dogma** 1951
10 × 8″
Collection
Mrs. Kathryn E. Hurd,
New York

PLATE 53. **Expulsion from Elysium** 1951
19 1/2 × 27 1/2"
Collection Muriel and David Harris, New York

PLATE 54. **King Saul** 1952
12 × 9″
Collection Dr. and Mrs. Abram Kanof, Brooklyn

PLATE 55. **The Humanist** 1951
35 × 27 1/2"
Collection Mrs. Edith Gregor Halpert,
New York

PLATE 56.
Study for "Pawnshop" 1949
Oil on panel, 10 × 8"
Collection
Mr. and Mrs. John C. Denman
Bellevue, Wash.

PLATE 57. **Pawnshop** 1951
80 × 96"
Collection Dr. and Mrs. Abraham Melamed, Milwaukee

PLATE 58. **Under the El** 1952
36 × 58"
The Phillips Collection, Washington, D.C.

PLATE 59. **The Golden Anatomy Lesson** 1952
42 × 48"
Munson-Williams-Proctor Institute, Utica, N.Y.

PLATE 61. **The Model Repulsed or The Shy Artist** 1952
15 × 20″
Collection Mrs. Joseph Gersten, Brockton, Mass.

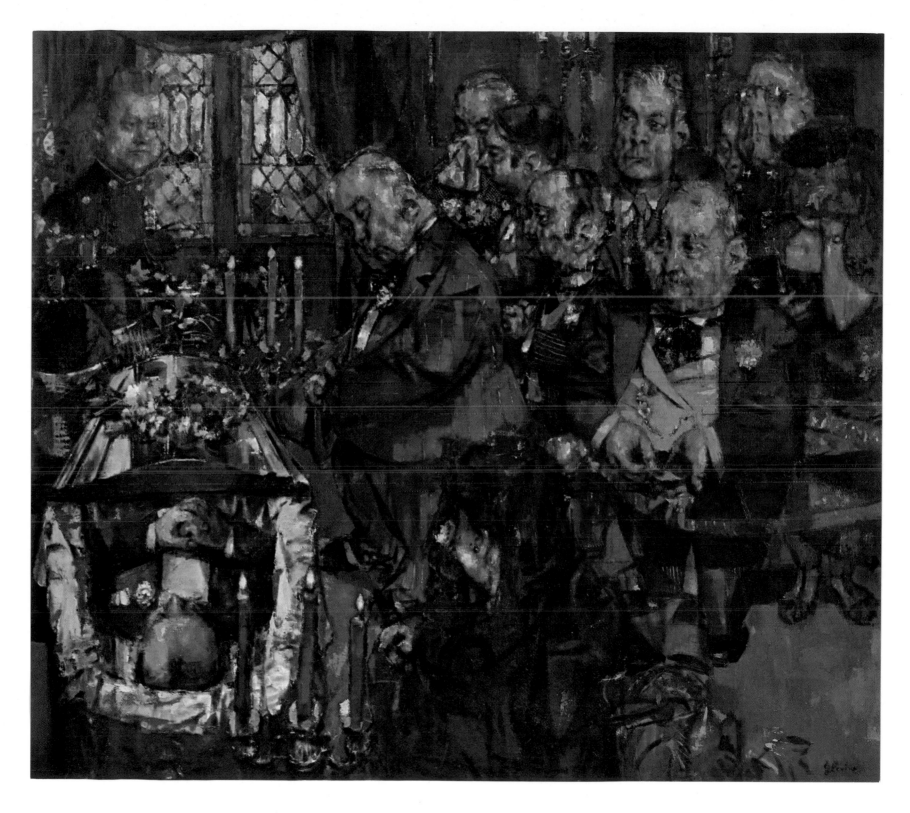

PLATE 62. **Gangster's Funeral** 1952–53
63 × 72"
Whitney Museum of American Art, New York

PLATE 63. **The Sob** 1952
20 × 24"
Collection Mr. and Mrs. Stanley Marcus, Dallas

PLATE 64. **Study for "Gangster's Funeral"** 1953
35 × 40"
The University of Iowa, Iowa City

PLATE 65. **Courtroom Study** 1953
36 × 40"
Collection Nate B. and Frances Spingold, New York

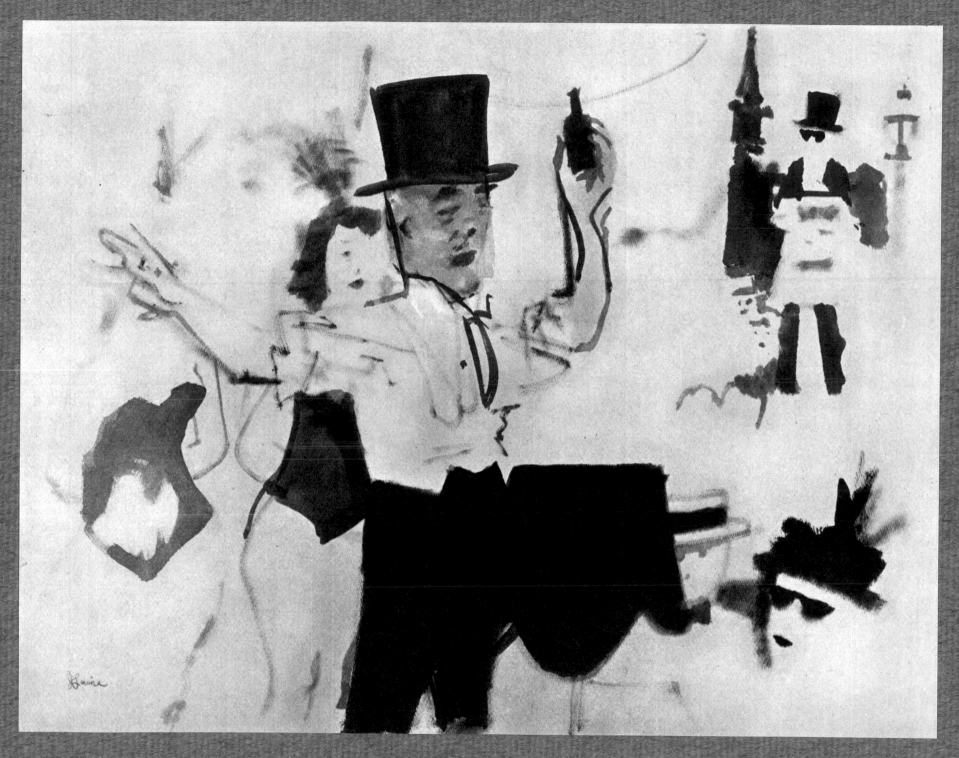

PLATE 66. **Medicine Man** 1958
Oil wash, 20 × 25 1/2"
Collection Mr. and Mrs. Roy R. Neuberger, New York

PLATE 67. **The Judge** 1953
42 × 48″
Collection Lawrence H. Bloedel, Williamstown, Mass.

PLATE 68. **The Judge**
(detail of plate 67)

PLATE 69. **King Asa** 1953
10 × 8″
Fogg Art Museum, Harvard University,
Cambridge, Mass.
Meta and Paul J. Sachs Collection

PLATE 70. **The Offering** 1953
39 × 24″
Collection Mrs. Edith Gregor Halpert, New York

PLATE 71. **Election Night** 1954
63 × 72″
The Museum of Modern Art, New York
Gift of Joseph H. Hirshhorn

PLATE 72. **The Banquet** 1954
30 × 25 1/4"
Collection Mr. and Mrs. Louis Sternberg,
Hewlitt Bay Park, New York

PLATE 73. **Election Night II** 1954–55
20 × 24"
Collection Mr. and Mrs. Morton A. Spring, New York

PLATE 74. **The Bath** 1954
15 × 20″
Collection Herbert and Anne Steinmann, New York

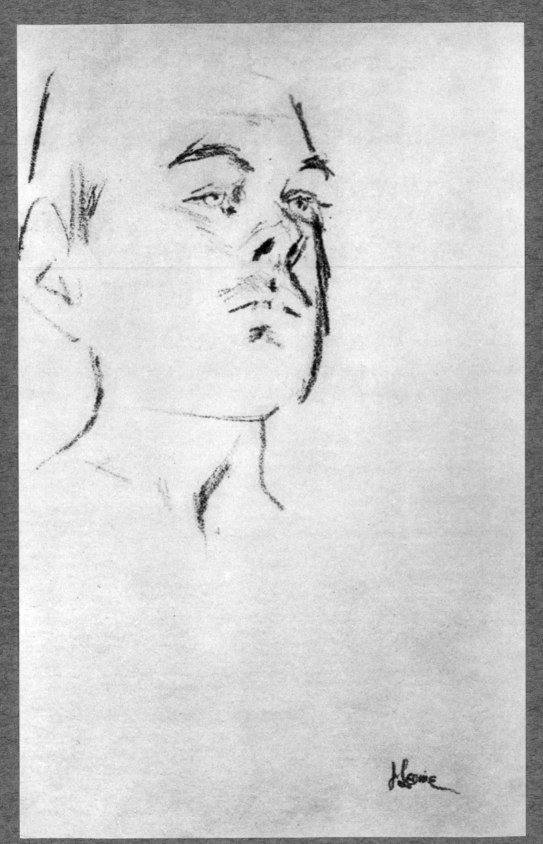

PLATE 75. **Man's Head** c. 1960
Chalk, 20 × 12 1/2"
Collection Mr. and Mrs. Philip Sills, New York

PLATE 76. **Invoices** 1954
21 × 24″
Collection Mr. and Mrs. Irving Levick, Buffalo

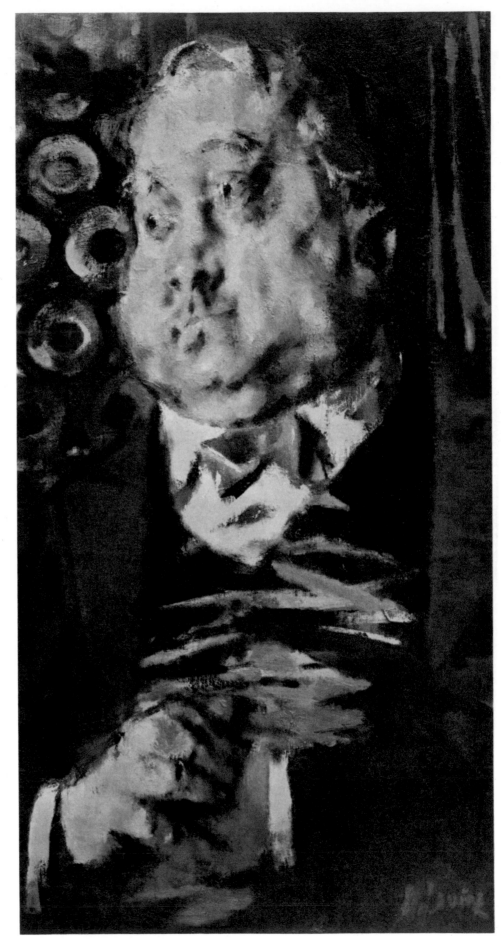

PLATE 77. **Study for "Gangster's Funeral"** 1954–55
28 1/2 × 15"
Collection Mr. and Mrs. Irving Levick, Buffalo

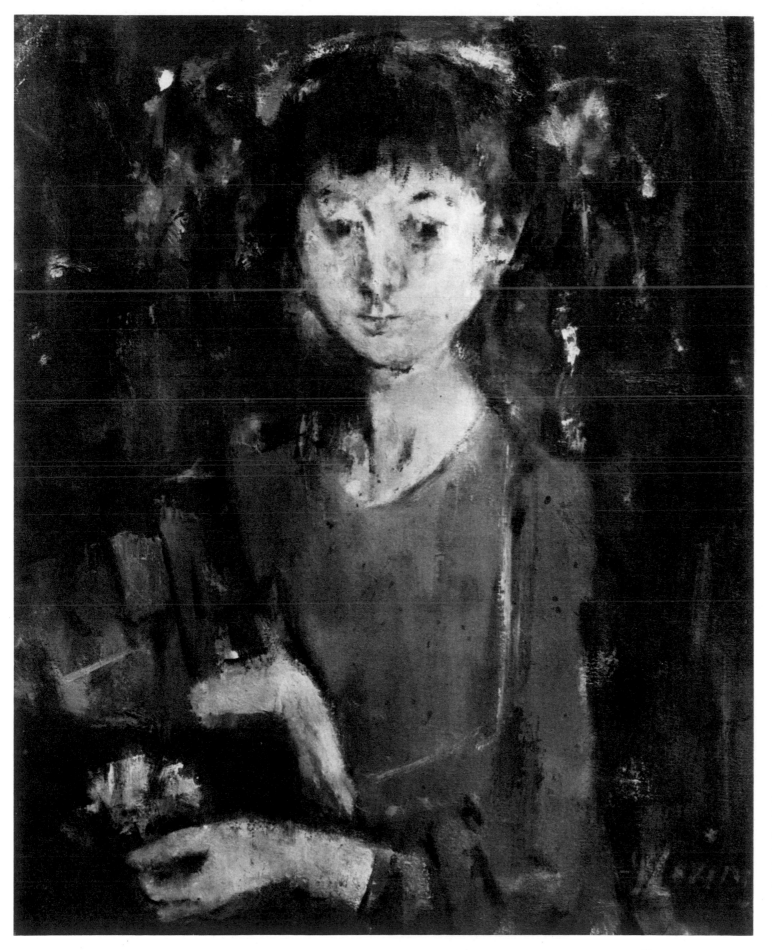

PLATE 78.
Girl in Blue 1955
20 × 16″
Collection
Mr. and Mrs. David Borowitz,
Chicago

PLATE 79. **Hillel** 1955
10 × 8″
Collection Nate B. and Frances Spingold,
New York

PLATE 80. **Medicine Show** 1955–56
72×63″
The Metropolitan Museum
of Art, New York
Gift of Hugo Kastor, 1956

PLATE 81. **Medicine Show I** 1955
42 × 48″
The Pennsylvania Academy of the Fine Arts, Philadelphia

PLATE 82. **Medicine Show I**
(detail of plate 81)

PLATE 83.
Study for "Medicine Show III" 1955
16 × 14"
Collection Maurice Weir, New York

PLATE 84.
Head Study for "Volpone" 1963
Brush and ink, 17 × 11 1/2″
Collection Richard Brown Baker,
New York

PLATE 85. **The Political Arena** 1955
28 × 32"
Collection The Honorable and Mrs. William Benton,
Southport, Conn.

PLATE 86. **Head** 1956
20 × 15"
Collection Willard W. Cummings,
New York

PLATE 87. **Reclining Nude** 1956

15 × 20″

Collection Mrs. Oliver Baker, New York

PLATE 88. **The Scribe** 1956
10 × 8"
Collection Joseph H. Hirshhorn, New York

PLATE 89. **Medicine Show**
(detail of plate 80)

PLATE 90.
**Thirty-Five Minutes from
Times Square** 1956
48×39"
Collection Joseph H. Hirshhorn,
New York

Lady Would-be

PLATE 94. **The Pink Hat** 1957
25 × 18"
Collection Mr. and Mrs. Howard Sloan,
New York

PLATE 95.
Showgirl 1957
16 × 14"
Collection
The Honorable and Mrs. William Benton,
Southport, Conn.

PLATE 96.
Susanna as a Charro 1957–64
60 × 40"
Collection Ruth Gikow, New York

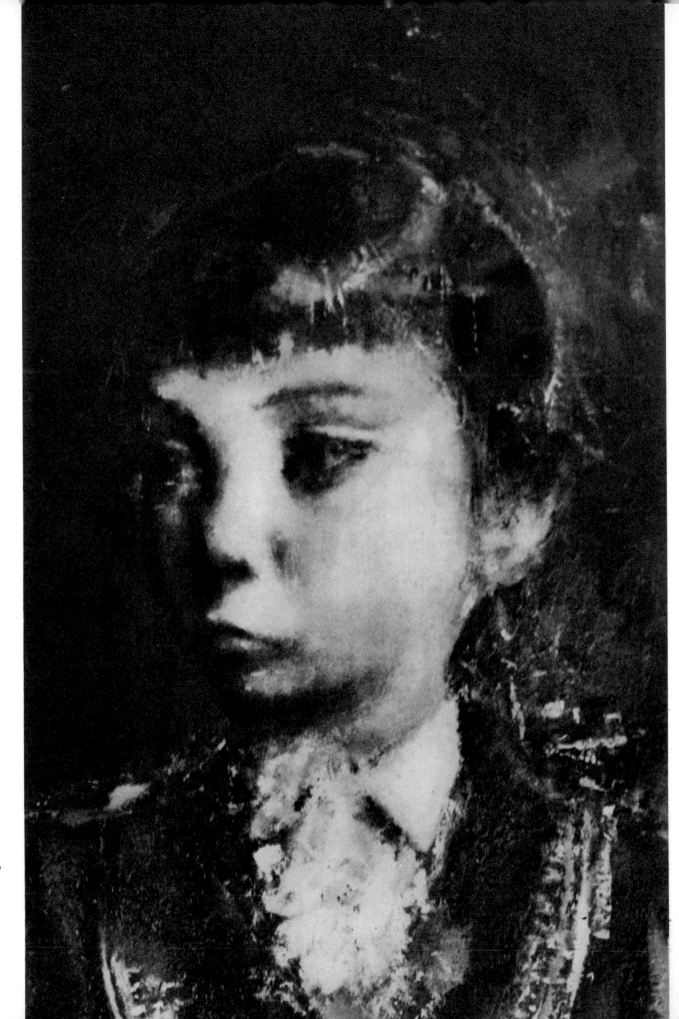

PLATE 97. **Susanna as a Charro**
(detail of plate 96)

PLATE 98. **The Turnkey** 1956
54×60"
The Joseph H. Hirshhorn Foundation, New York

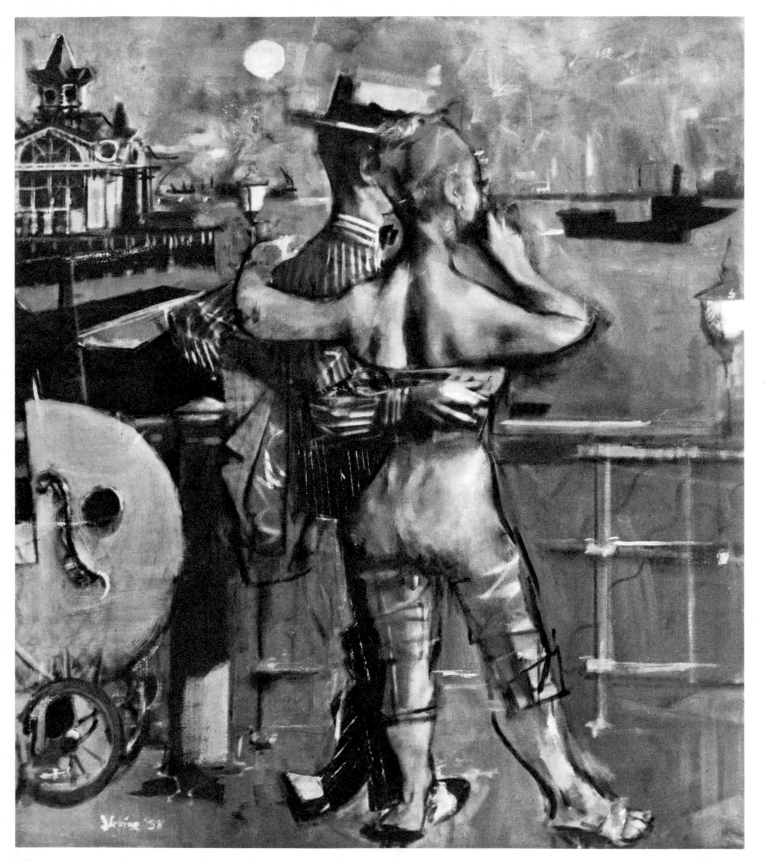

PLATE 99.
The Black Freighter 1958
40 × 35″
Collection
Mr. and Mrs. Roy R. Neuberger,
New York

OPPOSITE:
PLATE 100. **The Black Freighter**
(detail of plate 99)

PLATE 101.
The Girls from Fleugel Street 1958
64×56″
Collection Armand G. Erpf, New York

PLATE 102. **The Turnkey**
(detail of plate 98)

PLATE 103.
Inauguration II 1958
32 × 28″
Collection
Allied Maintenance Corporation,
New York

PLATE 104. **Medicine Show IV** 1958

35 × 40"

Wichita Art Museum, Wichita, Kan. Roland P. Murdock Collection

PLATE 105. **The Senator** 1958
35 × 40″
Collection Armand G. Erpf, New York

PLATE 106. **Inauguration** 1956–58
72 × 80″
The Sara Roby Foundation, New York

PLATE 107. **The Battle of the Naked Men** 1959
49 × 56"
Collection Edgar Kaufmann, Jr., New York

PLATE 108. **Beatnik Girl** 1959
24 × 21″
Collection
Mr. and Mrs. Michael Erlanger,
Redding Center, Conn.

PLATE 109. **Fêtes Galantes** 1959
49 × 56″
Collection Mr. and Mrs. David Pincus, Philadelphia

PLATE 110. **Study for "Volpone"** 1963
Brush and ink, 11 1/2 × 17"
Collection Mr. and Mrs. Philip Sills, New York

PLATE III. **Girl in Orange** 1959
20 × 16"
Collection William S. Zierler, New York

PLATE 112. **Lady with Opera Glasses** 1959
14 × 12″
Collection Mrs. Herbert A. Goldstone, New York

PLATE 113. **"Love, Oh Careless Love"** 1959

56 × 64″

Collection Mr. and Mrs. Charles B. Benenson, Scarsdale, N. Y.

PLATE 114.
"Love, Oh Careless Love"
(detail of plate 113)

PLATE 115. **Adam and Eve** 1959
48 × 42"
The Abrams Family Collection,
New York

PLATE 116. **"Love, Oh Careless Love"**
(detail of plate 113)

PLATE 117. **Maimonides** 1959
10 × 8″
Collection Sidney P. Lipkins, New York

PLATE 118. **1932 (In memory of George Grosz)** 1959
56 × 49″
Collection Mr. and Mrs. Dalton Trumbo,
Los Angeles

PLATE 119. **Man with Pick** 1963
Pencil, 16 1/2 × 11″
Collection Martin Michel, New York

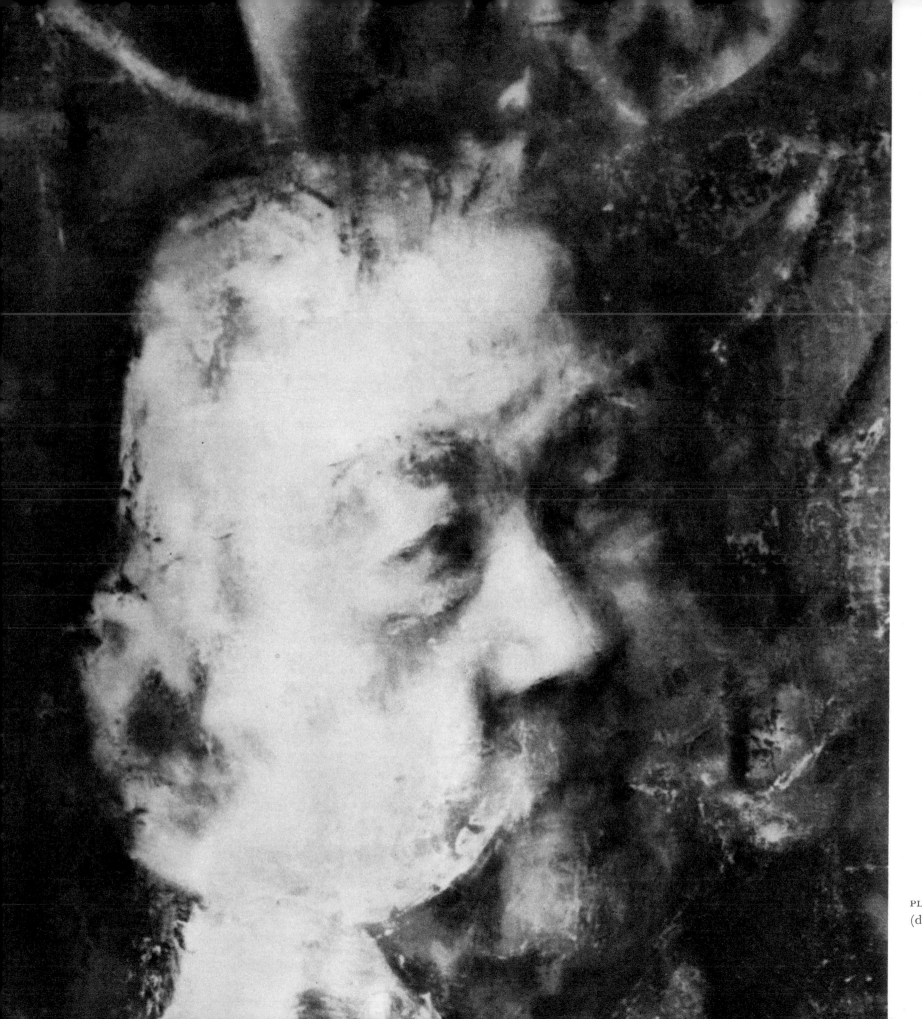

PLATE 120. **1932**
(detail of plate 118)

PLATE 121. **Oak Street** 1959
40×35″
Collection
Mr. and Mrs. Frank J. Winton,
Birmingham, Mich.

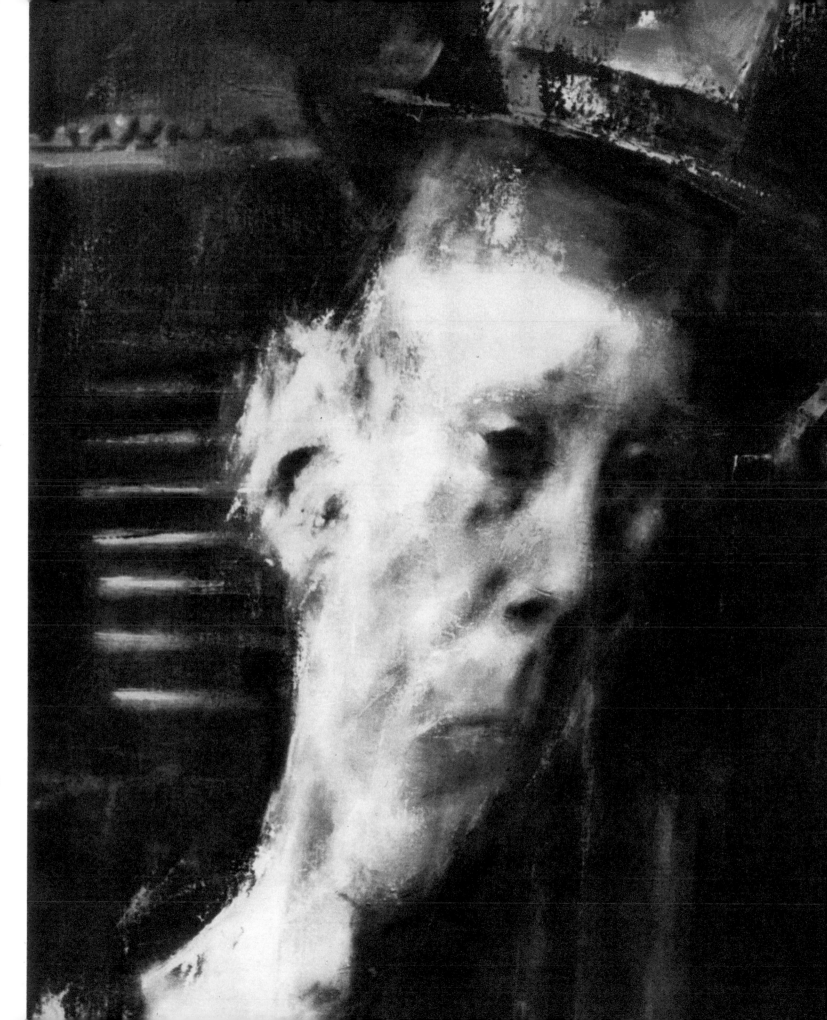

PLATE 122. **Oak Street**
(detail of plate 121)

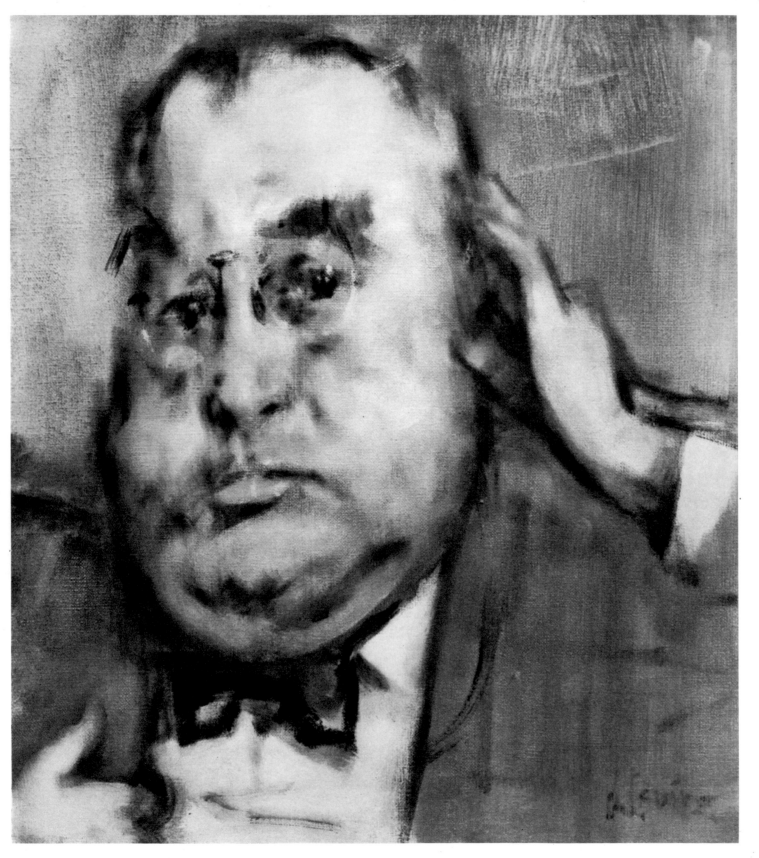

PLATE 123. **The Senator** 1959
15 × 13 1/2"
Collection
Dr. and Mrs. Milton H. Miller,
Madison, Wis.

PLATE 124. **The Princess** 1960
78 × 48″
Collection Armand G. Erpf, New York

PLATE 125.
The Three Graces 1959
24×21"
Collection L. Arnold Weissberger, New York

PLATE 126. **The Three Graces**
(detail of plate 125)

PLATE 127.
The Boy David Playing the Harp 1960
16 × 14"
Collection
Mr. and Mrs. Matthew A. Meyer,
New York

PLATE 128. **Study for "Judgment of Paris"** 1963
Brush and ink, 11 × 15 1/2"
Collection Mr. and Mrs. Philip Sills, New York

PLATE 129. **Café** 1960
42 × 48″
Collection Randolph-Macon Woman's College, Lynchburg, Va.

PLATE 130. **Café Figaro** 1960

21 × 24″

Collection Dr. and Mrs. J. B. Yasinow, Philadelphia

PLATE 131.
Portrait of Joan 1960
32 × 26″
Collection L. Arnold Weissberger,
New York

PLATE 132. **Bedroom Scene** 1961
20 × 16″
Collection Nancy and Arnold Perl, New York

OPPOSITE:
PLATE 133. **The Princess**
(detail of plate 124)

PLATE 134. **Blue Angel** 1961
26 × 32"
Collection Mr. and Mrs. Alvin P. Gutman, Elkins Park, Pa.

PLATE 135. **Cain and Abel** 1961
64 × 48"
The Alan Gallery, New York

PLATE 136.
Teresina 1961
32 × 26"
Collection
Mr. and Mrs. Jacob M. Kaplan,
New York

PLATE 137. **Study for "Judgment of Paris VIII"** 1963
Brush and ink, 11 1/2 × 17"
Collection The Honorable and Mrs. William Benton, Southport, Conn.

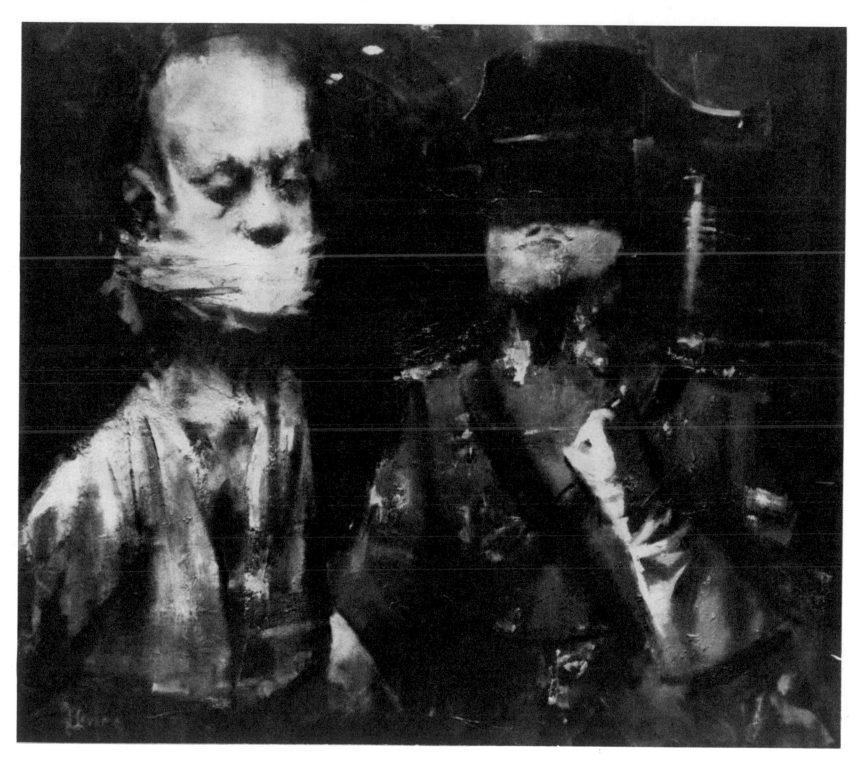

PLATE 138. **The Spanish Prison** 1961
28 × 32"
Collection L. Arnold Weissberger, New York

PLATE 139. **The Spanish Prisoner** 1963
Scraped aquatint, 12 5/8 × 17 1/2″

PLATE 140. **Titian Misremembered** 1961
21 × 24"
Collection L. Arnold Weissberger, New York

PLATE 141. **The Art Lover** 1962
56 × 49"
Art USA, The Johnson Collection,
Racine, Wis.

PLATE 142. **The Last Waltz** 1962
78 × 48″
Collection Joseph H. Hirshhorn, New York

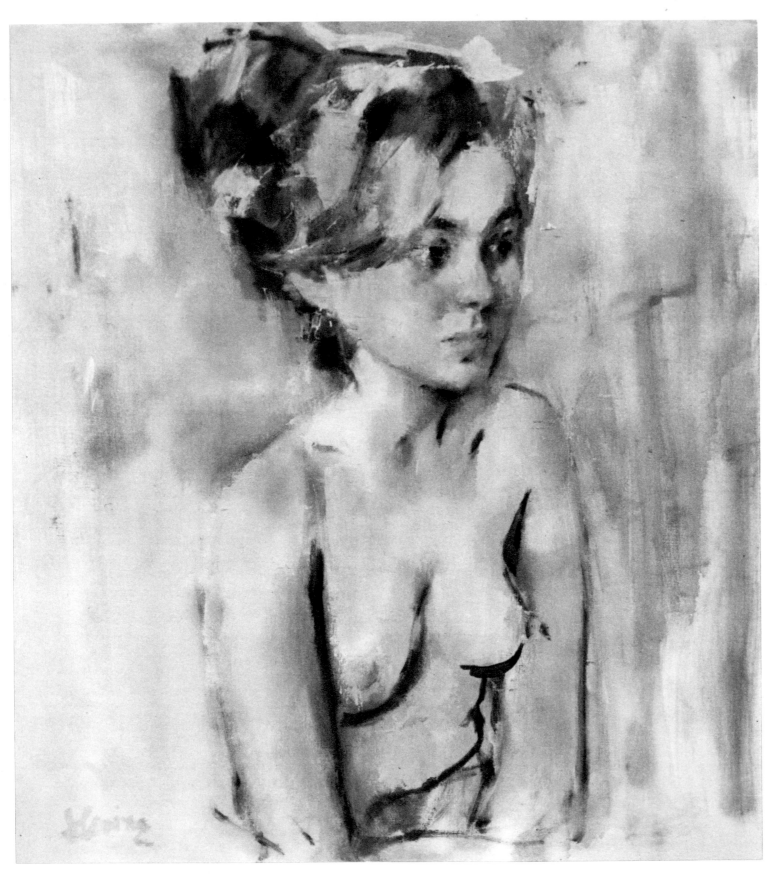

PLATE 143.
Girl with Blond Hair 1962
24 × 21"
Garelick's Galleries, Detroit

PLATE 144. **Flowers** 1962
24 × 21″
Collection Joseph H. Hirshhorn,
New York

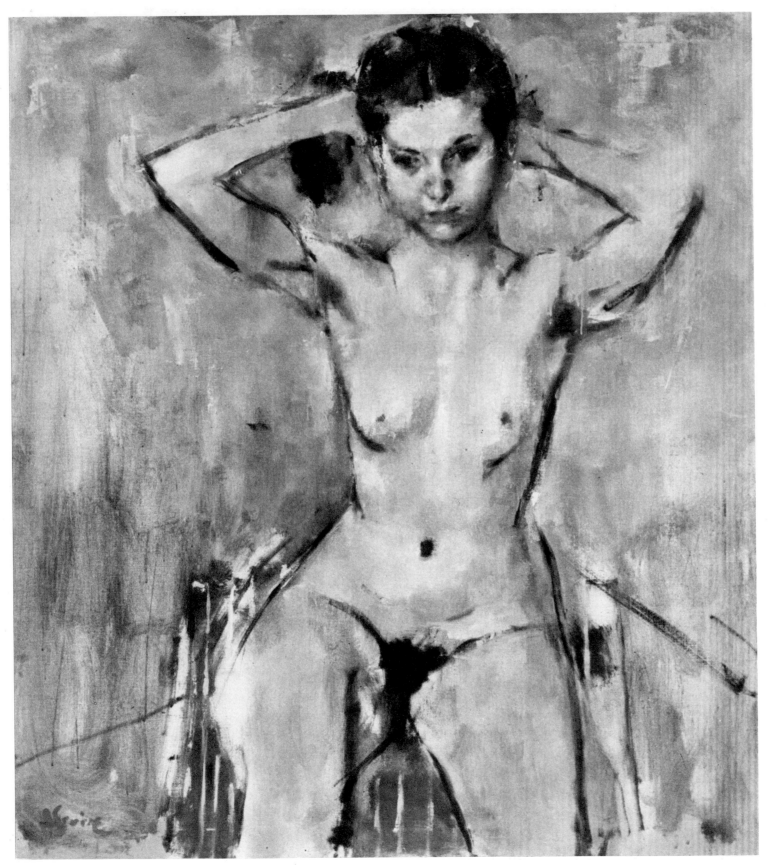

PLATE 145
Girl Fixing Her Hair 1962
40 × 35"
Collection Jerome S. Greene,
Scarsdale, N. Y.

PLATE 146. **Witches' Sabbath** 1963
96 × 84″
Collection
The Honorable and Mrs. William Benton,
Southport, Conn.

PLATE 147. **Girl with Red Hair** 1962
32 × 26"
Collection L. Arnold Weissberger,
New York

PLATE 149. **In Soho** 1962

35 × 40″

Collection Mr. and Mrs. Percy Uris, Palm Beach

PLATE 150. **The Judgment of Paris V** 1964
21 × 24″
Collection The Honorable and Mrs. William Benton, Southport, Conn.

PLATE 151.
Memo for "Witches' Sabbath" 1962
32 × 26"
The Alan Gallery, New York

PLATE 152. **Birmingham '63** 1963

72×78″

Collection Mr. and Mrs. Charles Benton, Evanston, Ill.

FOLLOWING PAGE:

PLATE 153. **Birmingham '63**

(detail of plate 152)

PLATE 154. **Study for "Judgment of Paris VII"** 1963
Brush and ink, 11 1/2 × 17"
Collection The Honorable and Mrs. William Benton, Southport, Conn.

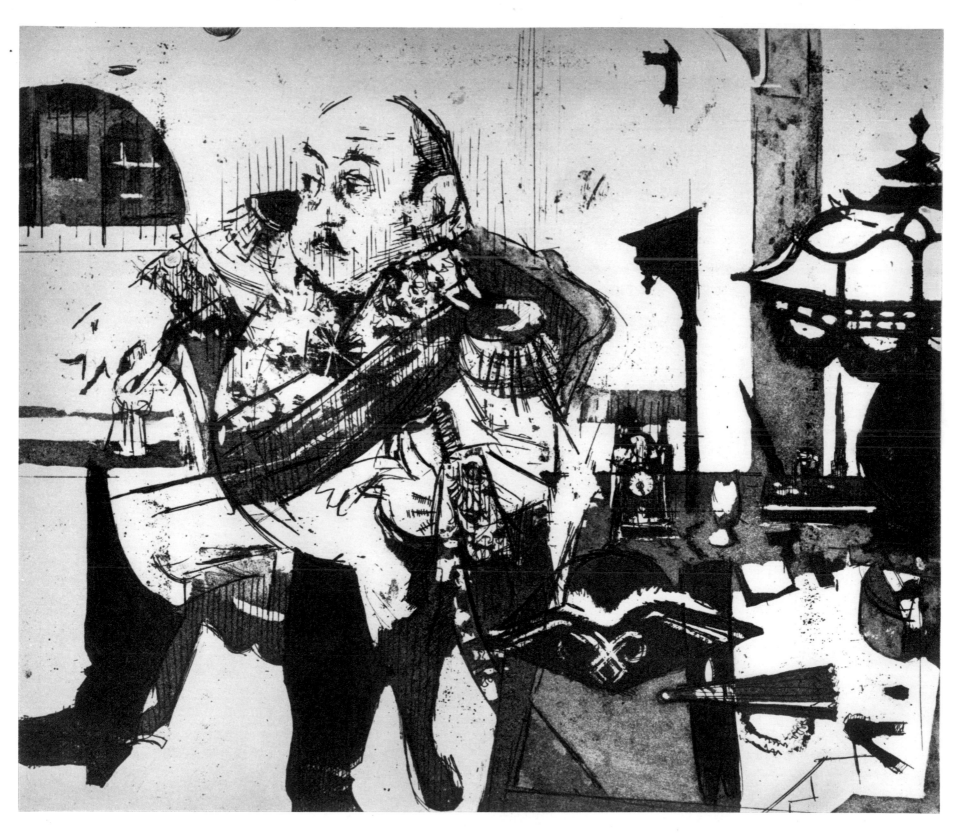

PLATE 155. **The General** 1963
Etching and aquatint, 14 × 17 1/2"

PLATE 156. **Portrait of a Girl** 1963
32 × 26″
Private Collection

PLATE 157. **Lady in the Woods** 1963
26 × 32"
Private Collection

PLATE 158. **Reconstruction** 1963
35 × 40"
Collection Mr. and Mrs. John C. Marin, Jr., New York

PLATE 159. **The Judgment of Paris VI** 1964
21 × 24″
Collection The Honorable and Mrs. William Benton, Southport, Conn.

PLATE 160. **Six Masters: A Devotion** 1963
49 × 56″
Collection Mr. and Mrs. Arthur J. Steel, New York

PLATE 161. **Aileen** 1964
24 × 21″
Collection
Mr. and Mrs. Sidney Frauwirth,
New Bedford, Mass.

PLATE 162. **The Judgment of Paris I** 1964
32 × 26"
Collection Dr. Bernard S. Cohen,
Gloucester, Mass.

PLATE 163. **Study for "Judgment of Paris X"** 1963
Brush and ink, 11 1/2 × 17"
Collection The Honorable and Mrs. William Benton, Southport, Conn.

PLATE 164. **The Judgment of Paris II** 1964

21 × 24"

Collection Mr. and Mrs. Philip Sills, New York

PLATE 165. **The Judgment of Paris III** 1964
26 × 32"
Collection The Honorable and Mrs. William Benton, Southport, Conn.

PLATE 166. **The Judgment of Paris IV** 1964
26 × 32″
Collection The Honorable and Mrs. William Benton, Southport, Conn.

PLATE 167. **The Judgment of Paris V**
(detail, The Artist) 1964
26 × 32"
Collection
The Honorable and Mrs. William Benton,
Southport, Conn.

PLATE 168. **The Judgment of Paris** 1965
54×64″
Collection The Honorable and Mrs. William Benton, Southport, Conn.

OPPOSITE:

PLATE 169. **The Judgment of Paris VI**
(detail of plate 159)